M000265705

THE GOBLIN WARS OMNIBUS

PART ONE:
Siege of Talonrend

PART TWO:
Death of a King

PART THREE:
Rebirth of a God

an epic fantasy adventure by

Stuart Thaman

The Goblin Wars Omnibus

PART ONE
Siege of Talonrend

PART TWO
Death of a King

PART THREE
Rebirth of a God

Copyright © 2013, 2015, 2016 by Stuart Thaman

All rights reserved. No part of this publication may be reproduced, distributed or
transmitted in any form or by any means, including photocopying, recording, or
other electronic or mechanical methods, without the prior written permission of the
publisher, except in the case of brief quotations embodied in critical reviews and
certain other noncommercial uses permitted by copyright law.
For permission requests, write to the publisher, addressed
"Attention: Permissions Coordinator," at the email address below

Nef House Publishing
stuartthaman@gmail.com

Publisher's Note: This is a work of fiction. Names, characters,
places, and incidents are a product of the author's imagination. Locales and public
names are sometimes used for atmospheric purposes. Any resemblance to actual
people, living or dead, or to businesses, companies, events, institutions, or locales is
completely coincidental.

Cover art by Jason Nguyen
Cover design by J Caleb Clark; jcalebdesign.com

Ordering Information:
Quantity sales. Special discounts are available on quantity purchases by corporations,
associations, and others. For details, contact the "Special Sales Department" at the
email address above.

The Goblin Wars Omnibus / Stuart Thaman – 1st ed.
ISBN-13: 978-0692649626 | ISBN-10: 069264962X

For everyone who grew up on fantasy.

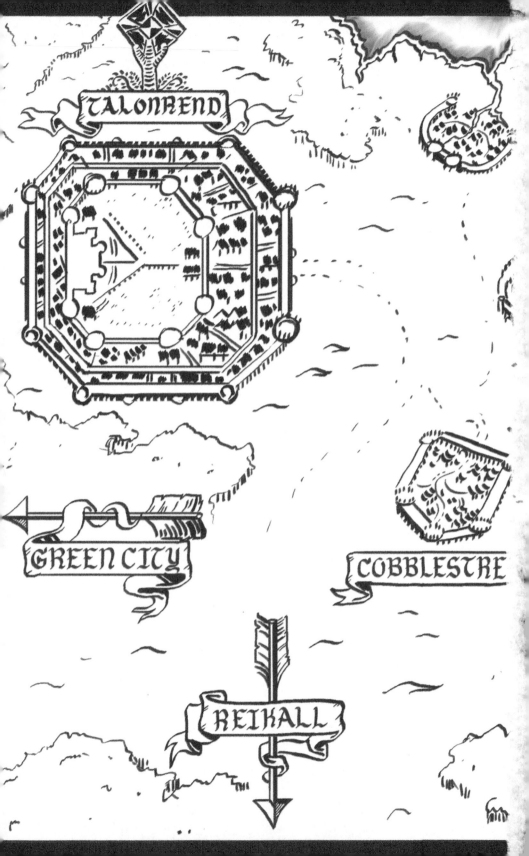

TALONREND

GREEN CITY

COBBLESTRE

REIKALL

THE GOBLIN WARS

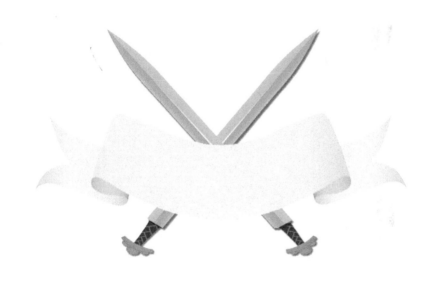

PART ONE

Siege of Talonrend

I N THE SHADOWY depths at the center of Kanebullar Mountain, Lady Scrapple writhed with excitement. She was queen of the goblin race, Mistress of the Mountain, and had worked for centuries to bring her greatest plan to fruition.

Utilizing the hive mind she had magically constructed among her kin, she peered through the eyes of a goblin several miles from her mountain lair. The goblin was nameless, an expendable drone created specifically by Lady Scrapple to serve a singular purpose as one of her many scouts.

The goblin crouched low on a rooftop in the center of a village which the humans called Cobblestreet. It watched, its eyes only moving when Lady Scrapple commanded them. The humans moved about their lives in complete ignorance.

Even if her scout was seen, it would not matter. Surely, the humans would kill any goblin on sight, but the Mistress of the Mountain was not concerned. Hundreds of new goblins were born every week, growing from huge tentacles that spread out through the ground from Lady Scrapple's massive body.

Each goblin began as a tiny bud, an outgrowth of flesh from the queen's own body, and rose up through the bedrock of Kanebullar

Mountain like some sort of grotesque flower. After only a few weeks of gestation, the budding goblin cocoon would split open, revealing a fully formed offspring ready to serve the hive.

Though her mind was vast, Lady Scrapple did not possess the strength or will to directly control every action of every goblin in her mountain. Instead, she created a semblance of free will to occupy their minds, and that imitation of autonomy had led to the development of society within the mountain.

Lady Scrapple turned her attention back to her scout in Cobblestreet. *They don't suspect a thing,* she mused. For nothing but her own amusement, she made the goblin jump down from the rooftop to reveal itself.

Humans shrieked and ran into their buildings out of fear, but not all of them. Only the women and children feared a single goblin enough to run. Several nearby human males rushed at the goblin. One of them had a sword, but the others only balled their fists. She could have commanded her scout to run or to fight back, but Lady Scrapple's concern for a single individual was nonexistent.

In a moment, the humans had knocked her goblin to the ground and slit its throat. Fearfully, they remained on their guard and searched the nearby buildings for other goblins. Lady Scrapple relished their response. The humans considered goblins to be so easy to kill that they would not even alert their city guard. She knew she could send an entire score of goblins to the village without humanity understanding the severity of the actual threat against them.

That disrespect fueled her plan.

When the real war began, humanity would not be ready. They would see goblins moving on the horizon, but they would not prepare their army. They would send soldiers to kill the goblins, but they would never send enough.

Humanity would not be ready.

4

GRAVLOX MADE HIS way slowly through the tight quarters of a dark mineshaft. His goblin eyes were well-adjusted to the lightless bowels of the mountain, but he still had trouble identifying the goblin standing before him.

"Have you found the vein?" the miner asked. Even by goblin standards, his voice was thin and high-pitched. Gravlox recognized him as Blabar, one of the other foremen.

Gravlox rubbed his calloused hands together. "Not yet," he replied. "Perhaps we will find it tomorrow."

"I heard a rumor that might interest you," Blabar continued, lowering his voice despite the two of them being alone.

"Oh?" Gravlox prompted. He had never particularly enjoyed the deception and treachery so loved by his kin, but he understood the value of secrets.

Blabar snickered. "One of the miners in the eastern tunnel found a pool of mercury this morning. You know what that means," he let his voice trail off, allowing Gravlox to make his own conclusion.

"Where there is mercury, there is gold," Gravlox finished. Though the maxim did not always hold true, Gravlox was becoming desperate. The section of tunnels he oversaw had not struck a gold vein in months.

"I know the name of the goblin who found the mercury," Blabar whispered, a sinister smile plastered to his pale face.

Gravlox let out a heavy sigh. "I don't want to hurt anyone," he said. "It shouldn't have to come to that."

Blabar ran a dirty hand through his already greasy, dust-filled hair. "I've also heard he hasn't reported the location of the vein to his foreman. He might be waiting to entertain offers. Let me kill him before he gets the chance."

Gravlox mulled the idea over in his head. In all his years as a foreman, he had never taken another goblin life with his own hands, though he had ordered several assassinations to be carried out. "You know what it means if the miner's death is tied to our coterie?"

"Of course, Gravlox," Blabar reassured him. "We can use a different poison, one that will point to a different mine."

"Misdirection?" Gravlox wondered aloud. "It could work. If we only had the resources to buy him off and take the vein for ourselves," he murmured to himself. "Killing is risky."

"But you have me," Blabar cooed. "And I have never been caught."

Gravlox knew he was right, but the notion didn't bring him any comfort. How easy would it be for Blabar to remove him and take control of the mining operation himself? Perhaps it was that very fear which made him acquiesce.

"So," Gravlox replied with a nod. "Which poison do you have in mind?"

"The north tunnel already has a reputation for using Heart-Stopper, but the ingredients are extremely rare. We could use something more mundane, but the risk would be higher." Blabar knew how Gravlox would respond.

"We will use the Heart-Stopper," he said at once. "We do it perfectly or we don't do it all."

Blabar nodded his head in excitement. "Once we poison him, we can send our own miners into his tunnel to find the mercury for ourselves."

"Of course," Gravlox said. He was filled with trepidation, but didn't see any other choice before him. If he appeared weak to a subordinate, especially one so apt in the art of murder, he would not survive long. On the other hand, if his mine continued to fail, he would be replaced by his own superiors before long.

Blabar handed him a rolled piece of paper which Gravlox quickly deposited in one of his many pockets. "Bring me the ingredients when you can," he said.

Gravlox shook the goblin's hand and departed, ready to begin work on his new task before he could change his mind.

An hour or so later, Gravlox arrived in the cave he called home.

"If only I had magic," he lamented, looking over the ingredients list. The goblin race was not known to frequently possess magic, but powerful shaman were occasionally born who could bend the elements to their will. Such power would make a poisoning like the one Gravlox planned obsolete.

"Yes, this poison will be very hard to acquire," Gravlox said.

Pulling a small clump of cave moss from a jar to eat as he went, Gravlox left his cave and started back toward the center of the mountain.

The center of Kanebullar Mountain contained a system of storehouses and businesses cut into the stone, a vast area full of goblins going about their day. Gravlox ducked into one of the first cave openings, a general store he frequented often.

Behind the counter, a female goblin waved to Gravlox as he entered. "Hi, Grav," she said with a smile.

"Hello, Vorst," Gravlox responded. She was smaller than him, if only by a couple inches, and she possessed a melodious voice full of life which Gravlox found intoxicating.

"How's it going?" she asked, moving from behind the counter to stand next to him.

7

"Pretty well," Gravlox responded, smiling. "I only need a few things," he said, not wanting to give away his intention. He drew the list out of his pocket and slowly unfolded it, treating the object like some revered artifact. "Do you have any spotted lizards?" he asked, looking around the cluttered shop.

"I think so, what do you need them for?" Vorst responded, pointing to a small cage filled with lizards at the back of the cave.

"Oh, just a new recipe I want to try," he lied. He felt bad deceiving his friend, but he couldn't be too careful. "What kind of lizards do you sell?" As much as he tried, he couldn't keep the nervousness from his voice.

"We have the ones with yellow spots and the ones with orange spots. Here, let me get you a bag." Vorst grabbed a burlap sack from behind the counter and moved to the cage, reaching in to grab a few lizards. "What kind of recipe is this for? Most people don't like the taste of lizard."

"I need the ones with orange spots, two of them, please," Gravlox said, trying hard to think of a recipe that might call for lizards. He was never known as a good cook and he didn't know many recipes off the top of his head. "I'm making... a soup. Yes, of course, it's a new recipe that one of the miner's wives taught me today. Soup with bits of ground up lizard, among other things."

"You know that the lizards with the orange spots are poisonous, right?" she questioned. "You can only eat their eyes and heads. Their bellies will make you sick." Gravlox panicked in his mind, thinking that his plot was discovered.

"Yes, well..." The foreman stumbled over his words, trying to avoid Vorst's gaze. "If you prepare them right and heat them high enough, it should boil the toxins out, so the recipe says." It was a pretty convincing lie, Gravlox told himself. Luckily, it seemed to work.

"Oh, that sounds pretty interesting, Grav, you'll have to let me come over and try it when it's done," Vorst said with a warm smile. Gravlox hated it when she called him Grav. It felt so personal. It wasn't that Gravlox didn't want Vorst to think of him that way, he just wasn't used to it.

"Sure thing," he replied casually, picking a few other things off of the shelves in the store and taking them to the counter. He was able to find almost everything for his poison in her shop and also bought himself a leg of mutton to eat that night.

"I should have asked her to come eat dinner at my cave tonight," Gravlox mumbled to himself as he exited the store. He had never found the courage to ask Vorst to do anything with him. He always did all of his shopping in her store, but that was about as far as the relationship went.

Gravlox's cave felt lonely that night. He spread out the ingredients for his poison on the small wooden table in the center of the damp cavern. He had two lizards with orange spots, a bushel of hibiscus leaves, some odd looking cave mushrooms, and little pouch containing a fine brown powder that supposedly came from bats that had been ground between rocks.

He sat on a three-legged stool and looked over the ingredients. "Only one thing left," he whispered over his shaking hands.

He contemplated his decision for a long moment, questioning his bravery and resolve. Gravlox was startled out of his sullen thoughts by a quick knock on the door. Panicking, he looked around the small hovel for something to use to cover the ingredients on his table. Frantically searching for a solution, Gravlox knocked over a jar of mead from a shelf and sent it shattering to the floor.

The door to his cave opened behind the scrambling goblin which set his heart to racing. Gravlox feared that his chest would explode from the adrenaline in his veins.

"Hey Grav!" came the beautiful voice from the doorway. Gravlox slowly stood, turned around, and tried to hide his embarrassment.

"Hey Vorst, what are you doing here?" he sputtered, trying hard to use his body to block the table of poison ingredients. "I mean, it's nice to see you here..." Gravlox managed to say. His eyes intently scanned the floor.

"Is everything alright?" Vorst asked with concern in her voice. "I heard something shatter, what is going on in here?" She peered behind Gravlox to the table and inspected the mess on the floor. "What are you doing, Grav?"

"Oh, nothing," Gravlox said past a growing lump in his throat. "Just getting ready to test out that recipe, you know." Even as he said it, he knew he wasn't very convincing.

"Um, Gravlox, I hate to pry, but who are you planning on killing? I work at a shop that sells reagents for poisons, you know. I can tell a would-be assassin when I see one." She grinned from ear to ear, moving around the stunned goblin to look closer at the table. "I hope it isn't me," she whispered to Gravlox jokingly.

"How do you even know where I live?" the foreman sputtered, confused and taken aback. The cool demeanor with which Vorst spoke about his plan was unnerving.

"I followed you, silly. After you left my shop, I just walked behind you. You were so nervous, you never saw me. I'm curious; tell me who you plan on killing!" Gravlox was so entranced by Vorst's beautiful voice that he barely understood the words she spoke.

Gravlox unrolled the paper Blabar had given him and showed it to her.

Vorst took a moment to go over the list and found all the ingredients except for one already assembled on the table. "This poison is pretty intricate," she said, looking Gravlox in the eyes as she spoke. "Are you sure you know what you are doing?"

Slowly, Gravlox began to nod. "Yes. It needs to be done. If the mine is to survive, we must take things into our own hands. I'm ready." It was as confident as the foreman had ever sounded in his life, and his own words terrified him.

"Well then," Vorst said, putting a hand on the male goblin's shoulder, "let's go get that last ingredient together. What is it..." her finger traced down the list, looking for the final item. "Necrotic dust? I'm not even sure what that means!" The look of surprise on Vorst's face was almost as profound as that of Gravlox.

"I think we have to get that from a necromancer," Gravlox replied, not sure what to say.

"Let's go find ourselves a necromancer and get some dust. We leave in the morning. I'll meet you here." With that, Vorst bounded from the cave and left Gravlox standing in front of his table with a baffled expression plastered to his face.

"What have I done?" he questioned. His plan had been revealed so easily. He trusted Vorst not to sell him out, but where would they find the dust they needed? In all his years, he had never even left Kanebullar Mountain.

Two

*Y*OU WILL NEVER *be king. You will never sit upon your brother's throne. Your fate is not in this kingdom. Your destiny has been written elsewhere. You will never be king.* The dreams were always the same. He shifted and rolled in the oversized bed, always restless, with the voice of his god echoing in his skull. Herod Firesbane had endured the same dream for nearly thirty years, every single night. *You will never be king. You will never sit upon your brother's throne. Your fate is not in this kingdom. Your destiny has been written elsewhere. You will never be king.*

When Herod was born, he was taken to the Oracle of Vrysinoch to have his destiny foretold. Like his older brother before him, Herod had received a favorable prophecy. The wrinkled and decrepit oracle told his parents that Herod would grow to be tall, strong, handsome, intelligent, and brave, just like his brother. The Oracle of Vrysinoch proclaimed that Herod would one day inherit his brother's kingdom. King Lucius Firesbane, Herod's older brother, had been destined to die in combat before producing any heirs, according to the oracle.

As long as Herod could remember, he had haunting dreams of the moment the oracle spoke over him. He was just an infant, barely a month old, but he saw the moment vividly in his mind. His parents, the former king and queen of Talonrend, held him before the oracle, deep within the castle that was their home. Castle Talon, the seat of the monarchy, was built over an extensive system of caves and underground rivers. In the deepest cave, miles beneath the surface, stood the most holy place in the entire kingdom: the Temple of Vrysinoch. Other than the oracle, no one was allowed to enter the temple at any moment. The prophecy of a newborn prince was one of the few exceptions.

The king and queen stood underneath a great marble statue of their god, the winged Vrysinoch, and placed the newborn prince into the stone bowl at the statue's feet. Vrysinoch's likeness stood forty feet tall in the dark cavern, his four angelic wings spread out to encircle the entire temple with their jagged ends forming the doorway. The deity held a sword in one hand with half of the blade buried deep in the stone at the statue's feet. His other hand grasped an emerald the size of a boulder, raising it up toward the ceiling of the cavern as if presenting the sacred relic to the world. The emerald shimmered in the palm of Vrysinoch's hand and bathed the cavern in an eerie green light.

The oracle had spoken his prophecy, much to the delight of the king and queen, but a different prophecy had been spoken directly to Herod. *You will never be king. You will never sit upon your brother's throne. Your fate is not in this kingdom. Your destiny has been written elsewhere. You will never be king.* It was the voice of his god, Vrysinoch, sounding in the mind of the young prince. Herod heard the voice every single night for his entire life, always the same, always calmly telling him that he will never reign.

The restless prince of Talonrend awoke in his bed with beads of sweat staining his pillow. He looked up, gazing from his sheets to the white canopy that hung on the ceiling of his bedchamber. The unrelenting gaze of Vrysinoch met the pained eyes of Herod, causing the prince to turn away. A white tapestry displaying the visage of Talonrend's winged god was a common adornment above almost every bed in the kingdom. The canopies were meant to bring good luck, and the overly zealous priests in every village and hamlet made sure that images of Vrysinoch could be easily seen. The tapestry in the chamber of Prince Herod served only to torment the haunted man.

Herod stood and rubbed the weariness from his eyes. He slid his cold feet into a pair of animal skin slippers and stretched his back. His bedchamber was located right next to the royal reception hall that housed the throne. That was perhaps the worst part of his daily awakening, walking past the empty throne where his brother was supposed to sit and reign. The old king and queen from Herod's dreams were long since buried in the royal mausoleum, enjoying their eternal flight through the heavens on the wings of Vrysinoch.

Herod's brother, Prince Lucius Firesbane, ascended to the throne in his late twenties, ruling the kingdom through an age of unrivaled prosperity. Then, one spring, King Lucius set out to travel with one of the kingdom's many trade caravans, a wagon train of resources and finished goods leaving Talonrend and heading south to do business with the various villages along the Clawflow River. Lucius always believed that a great king must walk among his subjects. The trading caravans were the best way to mingle with the common folk.

That caravan was over a year ago. His trips usually lasted a few months or a season at the most. No word ever came back about the King's whereabouts; no traveler from the south ever said a word about the king passing through. It is as if the king of Talonrend disappeared.

Herod stopped a moment before opening the iron-banded door of his bedchamber. His tabard hung on peg next to the door and a pair of swords dangled in their sheaths underneath the cloth. An array of training weapons, some dulled and some with edges fine enough to shave with, leaned in a wooden rack next to the door. Herod glanced at the two swords hanging on the peg as he pulled the tabard over his head. A fine layer of dust coated the leather belt and the two sheathes. The weapons, a matched pair of enchanted swords crafted by Talonrend's most respected smith, had not moved in years. The training weapons were covered in pits and dents from countless hours of martial practice but the enchanted swords, Maelstrom and Regret by name, had never been drawn. Herod mulled over the idea of strapping the swords onto his waist and setting out to find his lost brother himself. The prince shook his head. The idea was fleeting and fled his mind as soon as he opened the door and walked into the throne room.

"Good morning, sir. Sleep well?" The king's steward was always awake before anyone in the castle and eternally in a good mood. Something about the way in which the young servant conducted himself, being perfectly dressed and composed day after day, bothered Herod. The steward was too clean, too well dressed, and too handsome. It was disconcerting for Herod to see the man every day when he woke up. The prince had always been cautious though, seeing a treasonous spy from another kingdom behind every smiling face.

"Yes, of course. I slept just as well last night as the night before. It's getting to be damned cold in that room though. Tell someone to bring up the winter sheets from storage." Prince Herod tried to wave the eager steward away as he took a seat at the long table beneath his brother's empty throne.

"Yes, I fear that the nights are becoming a bit chilly," the steward replied, standing uncomfortably close to the prince. "Perhaps, if my king would prefer to have a woman warm his bed, or even a wife to give the kingdom an heir—" Herod slammed his fist into the large wooden table and made bowls and platters of food shake from the force.

"This is the last time I am going to tell you this!" Herod screamed, far beyond his breaking point with the annoying steward. "I am not going to marry or produce any sort of legitimate or illegitimate heir to my brother's throne! It is impossible! I am NOT

15

the king!" He accentuated the word 'not' with a slam of his fist, this time into the chest of the unsuspecting steward. "Lucius still reigns in Talonrend. I merely serve as his regent until his return. No progeny of mine will ever rule from that throne."

The kingdom was in disarray without Lucius to lead them. Everyone assumed that he was dead or never planning on returning. The people looked to Herod to lead them. Every time anyone in the castle referred to him as their king or bowed before him, Herod heard the soft words of Vrysinoch echoing through his head—*you will never be king.* With every decree and edict that Prince Herod signed in his brother's name, the winged god reminded him of his fate. *You will never sit upon your brother's throne.* The words tormented him and relentlessly coursed through his brain.

Herod grabbed a small chunk of bread and shoved the rest of his food away. He rose from the table, motioning for the castle's guard commander to join him. Darius, clad in his usual coat of mail with a great helm by his side, stood at once and walked next to the troubled prince. "Did you have another dream from Vrysinoch, my liege?" He asked, falling into step with Herod.

"The same as always, Darius. It never changes." The two of them walked out of the castle and onto the immense wooden drawbridge. Herod stopped next to one of the many banners that bordered the castle walls and leaned against the parapet, gazing out into the morning.

"If my god does not wish for me to rule this kingdom, why is it that my brother has not returned from his journey? Where is Lucius? Why has there been no word of his trip from anyone?" Herod began to tear little bits of bread from his chunk and toss them into the moat below. Feeding the ducks that lived in the moat was always comforting to Herod. Even when he was a little boy, Herod would save some portion of his meal and take it out to the ducks. Something about the way they ate the scraps that he dropped into the moat was serene and calming. The ducks had no idea that Herod was tormented. They didn't understand the dilemma that the

16

kingdom was forced to endure. They simply ate little scraps of food and kept on swimming.

"I have no answer for you, Herod. I have never heard the voice of Vrysinoch. I go to the temple almost every day and pray that Vrysinoch guides my path, but I fear that the words of the priests are as close to god as I can get. Most men in the realm would give their arm to hear the voice of Vrysinoch." The captain of the guard set his helmet down atop the parapet where the morning sun made the polished metal shine. Darius rubbed his fingers on the hilt of his short sword and wondered why Vrysinoch had never spoken to him. The sword, his symbol of office, had a hilt carved into the image of a bird's claw. The sharp talons ended in a small emerald that was the symbol of the kingdom's religion.

"Look out at the city, Darius. All the houses, all the people going about their lives, look at them." Herod spread his arm out wide and soaked in the sight of his brother's kingdom. Castle Talon had been built on the closest thing to a hill in a hundred miles. Its foundation stood only twenty or thirty feet above the rest of the kingdom, but it was enough elevation to give a fantastic view of the city. The most prominent structure, the Tower of Wings, which served as the public temple to Vrysinoch at the heart of the city, was always magnificent in the bright morning sun.

Rising a hundred feet above the ground, the beautiful work of art was a pillar of sculptures more than it was a temple. Priests had constructed the building out of black stone taken from the caves under Castle Talon. Somehow, the cold black stone reflected the bright light of the sun with a searing intensity while at the same time offering a sort of translucent quality to the tower. Anyone looking at the tower would feel blinded by the light reflected from the walls but, at the same moment, they could see all the way through the walls to the other side. Not even the priests could explain the phenomenon without calling it a miracle.

The tower was intricately carved, every single inch of the exterior walls being crafted into wings. The wings wrapped around the whole building, interlocking with one another, to form a perfectly cylindrical tower. The top of the structure resembled the hilt of the guard captain's sword, a talon clutching an emerald.

The most interesting part of the city, at least in Herod's mind, was the wall. It was formally named the Wall of Lucius but the common folk all referred to the massive defensive structure as Terror's Lament. The wall, designed and built at the hand of Lucius, was an amazing work of military genius. It rose sixty feet above the city, a monstrous behemoth of smooth stone. Terror's Lament was so much more than just a tall barrier to guard the city. It was actually constructed of three walls, the outermost and innermost being a full sixty feet in height. The wall in the center was only forty feet high, and, instead of having a flat walkway on the top for archers and other soldiers to be stationed, it tapered into a rounded edge no wider than a few inches.

Any invader would first be tasked with scaling the smooth outer wall, climbing the full sixty feet with either a ladder or ropes. The ascent would be made under the direct fire of archers from the walls and ballistae from the towers that marked the corners of the square city. The inside face of the outermost wall was covered in barbed spikes, set at an angle to catch anyone attempting to jump or rappel down to the ground. The shorter and rounded middle wall had much the same defenses as the exterior wall. It was smooth on the side facing away from the city but held an array of upward reaching spikes on the interior face.

The interior wall, the thickest of the three, was hollow. It contained hundreds of archer slots, ballistae dotting the top of its parapet, and two thick chains attached to either side of each section. The chains were stretched taut from the top of each tower, two on each exterior face of the four sides of the square wall. At the end of each chain dangled a solid iron ball, covered in tiny dimples. The chains could be released from the ball end, causing the heavy metal to sweep like a pendulum down the face of the wall, clearing all invaders attempting to climb into the city. Although those defense mechanisms had never been used, many of the guards had taken bets on how far an unfortunate soldier would be thrown by the massive iron balls as they swung.

Further adding to the city's seemingly impregnable defenses, a maze of sorts was constructed for all of the traffic moving through the wall's gates. Only two gates existed that would take anyone beyond the walls altogether, but several other gates were present between the layers. None of them ever lined up evenly with another gate at a different layer and all were spaced far enough apart to prevent a battering ram from being able to turn and maneuver. The reason for the intricate defenses wasn't because of any sort of impending doom or overt threat to the city, but was merely a result of King Lucius' desire to protect his people at all costs. The resources and labor were available, so the king had the walls constructed.

Lucius always wanted to be remembered by the name King Lucius the Builder, but of late he was only referred to as King Lucius the Missing.

Prince Herod let his gaze fall, settling back on the ducks swimming around the moat. "What are we going to do, Darius? I fear that if I proclaim my brother to be lost and take his throne, Vrysinoch will strike me down before I make it up the steps to the royal seat. That is my dilemma."

The wizened guard captain had been pondering that circumstance for weeks now, ever since Herod confided in him. "I do not know, sir. I would not want to be the one to make your decision. We can probably delay any sort of action until a second year has passed without sign of your brother. I do not know how long the peasants will be satisfied, having a regent ruling over them and collecting their taxes." Darius started to inch his sword out of its scabbard, a nervous tick that betrayed the fear behind his calm eyes.

"It isn't the peasants that I am worried about. How long will it be before word of a leaderless city reaches the ears of those who would do us harm? It isn't another kingdom I fear, Darius. We are on the frontier! There isn't another city large enough to have an army within two hundred miles. But that is exactly what I fear." The prince clenched his fist, crumbling the remaining piece of bread to crumbs in his hand.

"What do you mean, sir? We don't have much contact with the other castles of the realm and I know of none that wish us ill will," the dutiful captain replied.

"The monsters, they are who I fear, the creatures that live in the wilderness." The prince let the ball of bread crumbs fall into the water below and pointed at Kanebullar Mountain, far on the horizon. "There. That is where evil lurks. We are the only castle that the villains of the wilds have ever seen. We are their only enemy, the only beacon that holds the darkness at bay. When my ancestors left the Green City, they followed a prophet for years until they found this spot. People flocked to their cause, blindly pursuing the dreams of a religious zealot. That is why I fear the monsters of the wilds so much. If they come against us in force and breach our walls, no rescue will ever come." He let his hand fall back to his side, brushing the remaining crumbs off of his tabard.

"Let us pray that Vrysinoch will never let an enemy breach our walls. The only creatures of the night who would dare to risk Terror's Lament are the goblins, too stupid to know any better. In the twenty years since the wall's construction, the goblins are the only enemies who have tried to attack our city." Darius put a hand on his prince's shoulder, hoping to comfort him and bring him some sort of peace, however fleeting it may be.

"Yes, I know. Those walls should stand for hundreds of years. No land army could ever climb our walls or knock them down..." Herod envisioned the death that would accompany such an attack and shuddered. "What would happen if the goblins, in league with some necromancer or powerful wizard, were able to summon and control a dragon? Will our walls save us from that? A million goblins? That is an army we could destroy against our gates. A thousand goblins with a single dragon? That is an army that would surely consume our city in a matter of moments." Herod turned to walk back inside the castle, his voice shaking with worry.

"Then perhaps it is time to test the words of Vrysinoch. Sit on the throne and take your brother's place. Claim your birthright. The coronation of a new king in Talonrend would show the wilds that we are not leaderless. They will fear the might with which you rule your lands," Darius told him plainly.

"Crossbows," Herod called back to the drawbridge where Darius stood. "Start training your troops to use longer-ranged crossbows. We need something that can kill a dragon." Herod walked into the castle and let the heavy doors of the keep close behind him.

"I know we need something to stop a dragon, but a crossbow won't do it, my liege," Darius mumbled to the morning air. "I will go to the artificers and the craftsmen and see if they have any better ideas than crossbows." The guard captain made his way down the drawbridge and into the city with his eyes cautiously darting up toward the sky to look for signs of fire.

Still mindlessly playing with the hilt of his jewel encrusted sword, Darius crossed onto the cobblestone street and into the city, heading in the direction of the artificer's guild house. The streets were busy with people going about their everyday business. Merchants of all sorts called out prices for their wares and women stood in the windows of brothels, blatantly showing theirs. Everything was in order.

Lately, tensions were high in the city. The public was starting to grow concerned with the absence of their king and many people blamed Darius. The trade caravan that King Lucius had departed with was escorted by a heavily armed contingent of Darius' soldiers. Many of the common folk suspected that Darius had ordered the assassination of the king on the road in some sort of planned coup. Luckily for Darius, no one in any position of real power believed the rumors.

Darius decided that the time had come for him to step up the search effort for the king's missing caravan. He took a detour on his way to the artificer's guild, stopping by one of the seedier taverns on the city's south side. The bar, aptly named "Terror's Legs" for its position against the great stone wall, was always full of patrons willing to trade some information for a few coins. Even early in the morning on a bright sunny day, the stench of alcohol and vomit assaulted the dignified captain's nostrils as he opened the rickety door to the tavern.

"What are you doing back in here, Darius? I thought I told you to never come back in my tavern again!" Nancy, the old and hobbled barkeep, hated Darius. The guard captain wasn't fond of her either. The last time that Darius had ventured into Terror's Legs, a fight had broken out. Darius didn't often drink, but when he did, he usually got into a brawl or duel with someone. Darius did not take insults to his honor or dignity lightly. Most negative things spoken his way were met with a gauntlet tossed in the offender's face.

"Oh, come now Nancy, you can't still be upset! It was just a little fight, nothing out of the ordinary. This is a bar, after all." The guard captain took a seat at the wooden counter and looked around the room for someone who might give him information. Not too many of the patrons left in the tavern were conscious enough to be of any use.

"Just a little fight?" the haggard wench yelled back at him, "you killed two of my customers! Stabbed them in the alley! If you weren't in charge of the jail, I would have you arrested!" The woman did have a point, Darius silently agreed.

"To be fair," he responded calmly, "they were the ones who said that I couldn't even swing a sword after drinking three pitchers of your spiced ale." He grinned at Nancy, leaning over the bar and motioning for her to do the same so he could whisper to her. "I'm looking for someone. A warrior," Darius whispered to her.

"We get a lot of men in here who claim to be warriors. You're gonna' have to be more specific than that if you want to find anyone useful." Nancy was holding her hand out on the bar as she leaned in close to talk to the captain.

"Maybe this will jog your memory," Darius said as he dropped a coin into her hand. "I need someone to find a king. Someone I can trust. Know anyone?"

Nancy pulled back and bit the coin to make sure it was real before putting it into a pocket on her apron. She put a finger to the edge of her mouth and pondered the question. After a few moments of mindlessly cleaning the bar with a dirty towel, Nancy returned to the captain. "See that man in the back of the bar?" she whispered, motioning with a nod to one of the passed out patrons in the corner. Darius smiled and got up from his stool and talk to the man.

A forceful hand on his arm stopped him before he left his seat. "No, not him," Nancy scolded. "He isn't the warrior you are looking for. He can connect you though. I get it; you don't want to send another search party after the king publicly. The peasants would be in uproar if they thought the government was desperate. Talk to that man in the back. He knows everyone with the skills you are looking for. I think he used to be a pit fighter or something. He can arrange the meeting." Darius dropped another coin onto the bar and rose from his seat, smiling as he made his way to the blacked-out man.

It took a few shakes before the slumped patron managed to open his eyes and look at Darius. "Hey, what do you want?" he groaned. The weary man shielded his eyes from the sun that came in through the open window set into the door.

Darius sat down with a thud in the stool opposite the drunken man and let the armor plates of his gear clang against the wood. The captain drew forth his sword from its scabbard, making the motion slowly, and forced the metal of the weapon to ring as it was drawn. He placed the sword on the gouged wooden table with the point aimed directly for the drunken man's chest. "I am Darius. This sword marks my station within Castle Talon. Do you know of me?" The captain didn't know where to begin soliciting information.

"Hey, am I being arrested?" The man began to rise from his seat, the alcohol in his blood obviously impairing his efforts. A quick shove of Darius' sword had the man sitting down again in a hurry.

"I am captain of the royal guard. No, you are not being arrested, sir. I am here to speak to you about some information." Darius took a small silver coin out from the pouch on his waist and laid it down on the table, tantalizing the drunken man.

Without taking his eyes off the coin, the drunken man seemed to sober up a little and brushed some of the sweat from his brow. "What sort of information are you coming here to find, oh gracious guard captain?" the man slurred. His head swaying back and forth as he spoke.

"I need to find a fighter," Darius said, keeping his voice low and a hand on the hilt of his drawn weapon.

"Should o' been here last night!" the drunk replied, laughing and nearly throwing up on himself as his chortle quickly turned into a cough.

"Not a brawler, not that sort of fighter. I need a champion, someone who can fight out in the wilds. Someone who can fight alone. I was told that you were the one to see. Now, can you help me or am I wasting my time?" Darius pulled his sword back and slid it into its sheath, taking comfort in the familiarity of the cold metal against his hip. He never liked to have his weapon drawn.

"I know of a man," the drunkard responded and reached for the coin. His grimy fingers got halfway across the table before Darius snatched the money up.

"This man," the captain said, skeptical, "are you sure he is a true champion? I need someone resourceful, someone cunning and lithe, but with the strength and prowess of a veteran pit fighter." He let the coin drop back to the table and roll to the drunk.

The stinking man snatched it up in an instant and clutched it tight to his face as he spoke. "Yes, of course. You need a crusader, a real paladin. I know of one, trained by the Tower of Wings, a perfect fighter. He just isn't one for... well, talking. Most people don't get along with him. I can arrange a meeting with you. Just tell me the time and place." The drunken man grinned and stared at his coin with sheer delight.

"I am going to believe you. Against my better judgment, I will trust this man. Tell him to be at the drawbridge to Castle Talon tomorrow at sunrise. Make sure he comes prepared with full arms and armor. He will be tested." Much to the delight of the drunken man, Darius dropped a second coin onto the table and left the tavern without another word.

Darius spent the rest of the day fruitlessly trying to figure out a way to defend the city against a possible aerial assault involving a dragon. The artificer's guild turned him away as soon the captain told them that it was a dragon he feared. In all of the histories of the various kingdoms around the world, a dragon had only ever been seen once. It ravaged the Green City, the home of Talonrend's ancestors, but that was thousands of years ago. Darius accepted the fact that no one in the city would help him build defenses against a dragon and went to tell his prince of the meeting scheduled for the next morning.

"My liege," Darius knocked on the door to Prince Herod's bedchamber. "I might have found someone to go and fetch our beloved king," he said as the door opened. Herod was visibly intrigued by the idea.

"Who is it?" he asked excitedly. "Have you hired another band of mercenaries to go and find Lucius and bring him back to his throne?"

"Not exactly," Darius said as he stepped into the prince's room. "I have a man coming here tomorrow at dawn to prove his worth. He has the reputation of a champion, a true fighter. Self-reliant, resourceful, cunning, strong—he should be what we are looking for to go and fetch your brother."

"What is his name? Is he one of the pit fighters?"

"His name is... well, actually... I never got his name. I haven't met him yet either," Darius confessed. "I am told that he is a paladin, trained by the clergy in the tower. I was also told that he isn't too good with socializing and doesn't get along well with others."

25

That brought a frown to the prince's sullen face.

"You haven't even met this man? You hired some ruffian off the street to go and find the ruler of our kingdom?" Herod was visibly upset and paced the room nervously.

"I haven't hired him yet!" Darius explained, trying to calm the prince. "I want to test him before I pay him. He will be at the drawbridge at dawn. If he is the right person for the job, we will take him to the cave to be blessed." The guard captain left the room with a flourish of his cloak, angered by the prince's lack of trust in his decision.

Thankfully, the acclaimed champion arrived at dawn the next morning. Darius stood right outside the castle doors and watched the man's approach from the end of the drawbridge. The brawny stranger cut an impressive image. He was tall, not freakishly tall, but a full head taller than the guard captain with shoulders as wide as the length of Darius' sword. His head was shaved bald but he sported a long black beard, braided at his chin and hanging down well past his waist. He wore a thick leather belt attached to loose, flowing pants that indicated function over fashion. The belt connected to a harness on his chest that supported the man's minimal armor. Instead of a breastplate or other traditional protection, the man strode toward the drawbridge wearing two leather straps crisscrossing his chest and a sleeve of chainmail covering his left arm and ending in a thick steel gauntlet. A set of large throwing axes hung loosely from the man's side. His right arm, back, and his chest were entirely unprotected.

The hilt of a hand-and-a-half sword could be seen sticking up above the man's muscled shoulders and neck. He walked with the steady pace of a seasoned veteran, slowly making his approach while never taking his eyes off of Darius. "I hope you have come prepared!" the guard captain called out across the bridge before ducking back into the castle.

A bowstring thrummed from the parapet above the castle doors. The warrior's head jerked up with the sound as an arrow flew from the ledge and headed right for the hulking man. He crouched, just slightly, waiting until the last moment to spring out of the way and clear of the shot. The arrow bit deep into the wood of the bridge and vibrated where it was lodged. Stepping up his pace, the warrior saw a second archer drawing back his bowstring but he was easily able to dodge the poorly aimed projectile.

Grimacing, the warrior lowered his head and charged for the castle doors. Two more arrows plunked into the wood behind him but he made it to the entrance unharmed. The heavy doors of Castle Talon swung open easily behind the weight of the man's armored shoulder as he barged through. Much to his surprise, there wasn't an army waiting for him to battle on the other side of the door.

The ferocious warrior straightened and extended to his full height. He strode into the throne room, ready for single combat against his solitary opponent. Prince Herod stood in front of the empty throne, clad in full plate emblazoned with runes and symbols of Vrysinoch. In one hand the Prince held a falchion, the bottom half of the blade cruelly serrated. His other hand held a small dagger with a large crossbar designed for defensive parrying. The prince lifted his falchion up to his great helm, bowed, and began to charge.

The warrior in the doorway growled and set his feet in a defensive posture while he brought one of the throwing axes up from his side. The first whirling axe cleared the charging prince's head, sailing far too high and landing at the foot of the throne. A second axe went soaring in at the prince, its path perfectly in line with the royal seal of Vrysinoch on the front of Herod's breastplate.

Attempting to use the parrying dagger to knock the axe away, Herod dropped his hand and swung, solidly connecting with the deadly projectile. The axe's course diverted, causing it to ricochet harmlessly off of Herod's thick armor. With speed surprising for someone so heavily armored, Herod closed the gap between the two fighters before a third axe could even be readied.

The stranger, attempting to take advantage of the heavily ar-

27

mored prince, turned and pivoted at the last second, flattening his back against the stone of the castle's wall. Herod read the man's foot movements and anticipated the move flawlessly. The prince spread his arms out wide and hit the man squarely in the jaw with the hilt of the falchion as he passed by. Having less mobility, it took Herod a second to fully turn around and look for his prey.

A plated gauntlet connected with the back of Herod's helm in a resounding crash of metal against metal. The ornate great helm, now dented, flew from the prince's head and skittered to a stop against the wooden door. Grunting, Herod swung both of his weapons in wide from the sides and right for the gut of his attacker.

The nimble fighter was able to quickly bring his armored left arm into the path of the falchion and turn the blade away before it could bite into his flesh. His longer arms and larger physique allowed the man to grab the armored wrist of the prince and stop the dagger a full foot short of its mark. Wasting no time, the warrior reared back and delivered a devastating headbutt to the prince's unarmored face that sent him flying against the doors.

Blood oozed from the prince's ruined nose in thick spurts. He tossed the dagger down to the ground and charged in with both hands on the hilt of his falchion. Herod led with a stab that was easily sidestepped by the more agile fighter. Thinking to slice the larger man in half, Herod pulled his hands in and moved the blade in a vicious loop toward his dodging opponent. Metal rang out against metal as the blade of the falchion connected with the armored left arm of the fighter. The well protected arm rolled with the blow and deflected it rather than trying to absorb the hit.

Before Herod could pull his weapon back to strike again, a plated fist crunched into his breastplate, startling him and knocking him back. The man struck out again, kicking Herod's leg and forcing him to shift his weight to his back foot. The next blow came in the form of an armored punch to the wrist of Herod's primary sword hand and sent the falchion flying to the ground. The man dropped low and rushed the prince. He lowered his head at the last moment which allowed the hilt of the sword still strapped to his back to land solidly on the prince's exposed neck.

Herod doubled over in pain. With his back against the castle doors, he had nowhere to run. Fighting out of desperation, Herod attempted to grapple the larger man and wrestle him to the floor. In the blink of an eye, the prince was sprawled out on his back. Herod's face was smeared with blood and the hulking stranger stood over him and laughed.

"Congratulations," came the voice of Darius as he walked out from his hiding spot behind the throne. "Herod, my liege, I do believe that we have found ourselves a champion." The guard captain helped his prince up off his back and returned his weapons to him. Looking at the unknown warrior, he smiled and said, "Well met, good sir. You fought wonderfully, besting your own prince in single combat without even drawing your sword. Might we have the honor of learning your name, brave stranger?"

"Gideon," the stranger said with a gravelly voice.

Herod patted Gideon on the shoulder. "You fought well," he said as he inspected the dent on the back of his great helm.

"Why have you brought me here?" Gideon asked. His voice sounded like the low rumble of a landslide.

"I was told that you are a paladin, trained by the tower in the holy art of war. Is that accurate? I saw no use of holy magic in your duel with the prince." Darius was skeptical of Gideon's training. He had never seen someone so easily best a seasoned warrior without drawing a blade.

"I was trained by the tower, that is correct," was the only response the man offered.

"And what are you now, besides just strong and large?" Herod asked, nursing his bruised neck.

"I left the tower after my training," Gideon explained. "They train men to fight side by side, tower shields and maces forming an impenetrable wall. As far as I am concerned, in order for a warrior to excel to the heights of fighting perfection, he must learn to do combat alone."

"Yes, our legions are trained to fight as a cohesive unit," Darius said, considering the lone nature of the warrior before him. "If you were selected for training at the tower, that must mean Vrysinoch speaks to you. Can you still manipulate the holy powers of Vrysinoch?"

"The winged one speaks to me still, although it seems to be more at his pleasure than mine. When I was training with the other paladins, I could command the holy energies at my will, bending them to strike my foes at any moment. Now, it is only in times of great need that Vrysinoch chooses to aid my cause. I do not consider myself a paladin." Darius moved around the man and inspected his muscled frame for the distinctive tattoo of the paladins.

Just above Gideon's right shoulder blade, partially obscured by the hilt of his sword, was a small mark: a talon clutching an emerald. "Your mark has not faded. Vrysinoch still names you among his elite. You are a paladin, by all accounts. You are just..." Darius paused, searching for the right word. "Unique," he continued, "the most unique paladin I have ever met."

"We need you to go out into the wilderness, alone, and find my brother, the king." Herod liked this warrior, especially because a man with few friends ran little risk of telling the wrong person about his mission.

"So, the rumors are true then," Gideon said, looking past the prince and his guard to the empty throne at the center of the room.

"Yes, well," Darius said, "we aren't exactly sure where the king is. We have no reason to believe that he is dead, but if you find that to be the case, bring back proof."

"You will be paid on your return," Herod was quick to put in, "double if you bring the king back to his castle. We don't want to financially encourage you to kill my dear brother..."

"I will need equipment, provisions, gear for a long journey," Gideon remarked, looking to Darius to arrange supplies for his trip.

"Along those lines, we would like you to come to the royal

temple, the cavern underneath Castle Talon. We are hoping that the high priest in the temple will facilitate your blessing." Darius turned around and led the trio to a door at the back of the throne room that led to the caverns.

"Who knows," Gideon mumbled, "maybe Vrysinoch would enjoy seeing me again." The group made their way down the steep tunnels underneath the castle in silence.

After the long trek, the three arrived at the edge of the room that housed the statue of Vrysinoch. The interlocking wings that created the entranceway into the temple were too low for Gideon to stride through and forced him to duck to enter the cave. The priest was there, standing beneath the statue, waiting for the group.

"We have come to seek the blessing of Vrysinoch," Herod said, making his way to stand next to a bowl at the foot of the winged god.

"Yes, yes," the old and withered priest said, "I knew you would come to me today." When the high priest spoke, the emerald light in the room seemed to shift and dance with every word, settling down as soon as the man stopped talking.

"This one, however," the priest continued, "is already blessed by the winged god. I'm afraid that I am unable to help. No blessing of mine could improve the powers already bestowed upon this man by Vrysinoch himself." That news was shocking to everyone, including Gideon. The three surprised men stood dumbfounded in front of the priest.

"You are the highest priest in the kingdom, the chosen of our lord. Certainly there is something that you can do?" Darius was at a loss for words. He looked from the priest and back to Gideon for some sort of answer.

"Well, there might be something that I can do," the priest said in a mystic tone. "I might be able to convince Vrysinoch to bestow his blessing upon your weapons instead. The usual weapon enchantments that the tower gives to the paladins are for their shields. This one carries no such shield." The old priest pointed a crooked finger up toward the hilt of the hand-and-a-half sword strapped to the warriors muscled back. "Yes," he continued, "if you would just place your sword inside the bowl at the foot of the statue, we can try."

Gideon took a step away from the priest. "I do not think that would be wise," he said with a grating tone.

"And why is that?" Darius inquired with sudden curiosity.

"My sword is already enchanted," the warrior said, "and quite powerfully so." Gideon took another step back from the priest with his hands up in a defensive posture.

"Do you doubt the powers of Vrysinoch, warrior?" the priest asked. His voice dripped with accusation. "That sword looks sturdy enough to bear multiple enchantments, even one as strong as the blessing of a god."

Gideon took another step back and bumped his head into the stone wings of the statue that formed the entry into the cavern. "You don't understand," he said, glaring at the priest. "My sword is honor-bound to my hands. I cannot draw it here." Darius' eyes jumped to the weapon with a hint of recognition.

"What does that mean?" Herod asked the guard captain. The prince's hands moved nervously to the hilts of his own weapons.

"An honor-bound weapon," Darius explained in frightful tones, "is magically entwined with the soul of its owner. It is a powerful enchantment, the properties of which are still largely a mystery. The priests of the tower seldom imbue a weapon with so strong an enchantment. While the power given to an honor-bound warrior and his weapon is certainly significant, so is the cost." Herod leaned closer to the captain, hanging on every word.

"The cost is immense," Gideon interrupted, finishing the explanation. "Every time I draw the weapon from its sheath, it drains part of my soul, feasting upon my life energy. True, it makes the weapon incredibly powerful, but if I do not allow the sword to take the life of another after I have drawn it, I cannot let it leave my hand. In essence, from the moment I draw my sword, it begins to kill me. Unless it kills someone else quickly, I will be consumed by it. My life force is strong enough to resist the sword for an hour, maybe two, but then I will die. The only way to return the sword to its sheath is to sate its hunger for souls."

There was a long pause in the cavern. Gideon stared at the statue of Vrysinoch and everyone else stared at him. "Best not to take it out, then…" Herod said quietly to break the silence.

"If you don't kill, you will die," the priest said, "every single time you bring it forth. Vrysinoch protect you, my son." The wrinkled hands of the priest ushered the group out of the temple, obviously eager to be far away from the sword.

"Does your sword have a name, Gideon?" Darius asked when they reached the drawbridge once more.

Walking out of the castle, his sword on his back and axes by his side, Gideon glanced over his shoulder and nodded.

G RAVLOX AWOKE THE next morning long before the
sun's rays began to warm the mountain. Vorst was waiting for him by the time he collected his gear and opened
the door to his cave. "Hi Grav!" she said, bright and chipper. For a
moment, Gravlox considered the fact that she might be so willing to
follow him into the wild for the sake of murdering him for her own
advancement, but the thought was fleeting and melted away as
soon as Vorst smiled.

"I decided to leave the other poison ingredients here, in my
cave, just in case," Gravlox said as he shut the wooden door behind
him.

"Probably a good idea." Vorst nodded her head in agreement
as she inspected the heavy pack that Gravlox wore on his back.
"What all did you bring? How long do you think this journey is going to take?" The burlap sack on the hunched goblin's shoulders
was bulging.

"Food, mostly," Gravlox responded, hefting the sack in an attempt to impress Vorst with how easily he could lift it.

"Are you really not bringing any weapons?" Vorst asked.

Gravlox stammered, not knowing what to say. "I actually don't own any," was all he could think to say. While fights and killings were commonplace anywhere in the mountain, Gravlox always felt safe in his mine and had never given the need for a weapon serious consideration.

Vorst set her small travelling pack down on the ground and produced two squat short swords, complete with scabbards and belts. She tossed one of the weapons to Gravlox who embarrassingly fumbled it to the ground.

"Here, let me do it," Vorst said, kneeling down and buckling the sword around the waist of her travelling companion. After the awkward moment passed, Vorst patted Gravlox on the shoulder and smiled. The female goblin turned, starting toward the exit of the mountain complex.

Gravlox, being a mining foreman, lived near to where he worked in the heart of the mountain. "Come on," Vorst said, waving to him, "the exit is over this way." Vorst bounded down the dark tunnels, full of excitement and the lust for adventure.

When they reached an area bathed in sunlight from the outside world, Gravlox stopped.

"You have been outside before?" he asked, trying unsuccessfully to hide his surprise. Miners had no need of visiting the outside world and goblins in general rarely left the mountain.

"Of course, silly. Who do you think goes and gathers up all the supplies for the store? I do!" Gravlox stood in a shadow, not wanting to exit the mountain, unsure of his every step.

"Come on," Vorst continued, turning back and grabbing Gravlox by the hand, leading him to the end of the tunnel and the outside world. "You miner goblins never leave the darkness? Doesn't it get boring, being cooped up all the time in the dark?"

Gravlox shook his head. He was at a loss for words, a sensation that he was quickly becoming used to around Vorst.

The bright sunlight at the end of the tunnel stung the miner's eyes, causing him to lift his hand and squint painfully ahead. Gravlox hesitated in the cavern, fearing that the sunlight might burn his skin and reduce him to a pile of ash. "Hurry up, Grav!" Vorst called to him, dancing in the warm sunlight.

Gravlox took a tentative step into the open air, gazing upon the farming terraces that lined the southern side of Kanebullar Mountain. Everywhere he looked, Gravlox saw goblins going about their work in the harsh sunlight, farming the land, tending to livestock, or simply resting. He moved another step out of the tunnel, letting the sun wash over his pale skin and heat his body.

Within a moment, Gravlox was running and skipping, trying to keep up with Vorst as she bounded down the terraces. Farming goblins yelled and cursed at the pair, who trampled more than a few crops as they continued their gallivanting. Nearly halfway down the sculpted mountain face, Vorst stopped, panting heavily. She sat down hard upon a rock, throwing her hands in the air, and let out a contented sigh.

Gravlox was right behind her, collapsing to the ground in his jubilant exhaustion. Both of the goblins were sweating and breathing heavily, staring up into the sky. A long moment passed before either of them spoke.

"How do you like being outside?" Vorst asked, her voice sounding small and far away, as if she was lost in some sort of ethereal daydream.

"Wonderful. The outside is just wonderful," Gravlox replied. "I can't believe that I have never left the tunnels before…" He let his voice trail off, closing his eyes and thoroughly enjoying the warmth and beauty of the outside world. "Everything is just so warm," Gravlox said, barely audible.

"And dry. I can't stand being stuck in the wet caves and tunnels of the mountain. Everything out here is just so fresh and beautiful and dry. I love it here." Vorst was lying down next to Gravlox on the grassy terrace, her head casually brushing up against the edge of the foreman's shoulder.

"Look, up in the sky, there!" Vorst pointed at a small black object fluttering through the milky white clouds.

Following her hand, Gravlox peered into the sky. "What is it?" he asked, a hint of fear in his voice. "Should we get back into the mountain and warn the others?"

Vorst laughed aloud, rolling in the grass. "No, silly," she said between her laughter, "that's an eagle." As if on cue, the great bird of prey loosed a piercing shriek, breaking the sky and shattering the serenity of the moment. The eagle caused many of the goblins to look up into the sky, wondering what they had just heard. Eagles were not uncommon around the mountain, but the way that the bird overhead had cawed, it set everyone's nerves on edge. The eagle sounded like it had screamed, as if out of pain or hatred. There was anger behind the piercing screech of the great winged beast and all the goblins standing in the terraces could feel it.

"Let's get moving along," Vorst said, cautiously standing and keeping her eyes peeled on the sky. "That was peculiar." The two goblins rose up from the grassy terrace and continued down the mountain face, eventually arriving at the edge of the heavily wooded plain that surrounded their home.

"So," Gravlox said, stopping before entering the tree line, "where should we start to look for necrotic dust? Where can we find a necromancer?" He tried to hide his nervousness, but failed miserably.

"I know a place where ghost flowers grow," Vorst replied, skipping past the first few trees and into the forest. "There is a graveyard not too far from here. I think it is only a few days walk from the mountain, near one of the human villages along the riverbank." She drew her sword and used it to point the way.

"Lead on, Vorst!" Gravlox said with a smile, bounding after her once more. He spent the entire day trying to keep up with his spry companion. Vorst led him through the forest in the direction of the riverbank, always a few steps ahead of him. Gravlox tried to stop many times, usually to investigate some plant or animal he had never seen before. Vorst was eager though, relentlessly leading him farther away from the safety of the mountain.

"Shhh," Vorst whispered when she finally came to a stop, motioning for Gravlox to be quiet. The two goblins crept up to an open glen, a grassy area void of the tall trees that made up the rest of the forest. "Look there, Grav, look at those stumps." Vorst was crouched behind a small bush, pointing to four tree stumps in the clearing.

"What about them?" Gravlox asked, not realizing the significance of the stumps. He peered around the bush, trying to get a better look into the glen.

"They were cut down," Vorst explained, making a motion with her hand to resemble a forester with an axe. "Humans do that. They cut the trees down for timber, just like we do."

Gravlox shrank down behind the bush, trying to remain as stealthy as possible. "What do we do? Are there humans nearby? I can't smell them." The frightened goblin drew his short sword, not even sure how to hold it properly. Vorst put a hand on Gravlox's shoulder, keeping him back while she stood up and looked around the edge of the bushes into the clearing.

"No one is here," she said, standing up fully and bounding into the glen with her normal excitement. Gravlox stood up slowly, still tightly clutching the hilt of his weapon. The glen was large, with a small stream running between the tree stumps and back into the woods. "Let's camp here tonight," Vorst said.

"Alright," Gravlox replied, grateful for a break. He sat down on one of the stumps, rubbing his weary feet with one hand while still grasping his sword with the other.

"Grav, check out these tracks. Some animals have been through here, probably to drink from the stream. We should follow their tracks and see if we can find them." Vorst bent low over the tracks, following the large prints closely.

"What are the tracks from?" Gravlox asked, "Humans?" He walked over to the tracks slowly, unsure of himself.

"Those aren't human feet," Vorst said skeptically, pointing to the impressions in the mud. "Humans usually wear cloth on their feet, from what I've heard. These prints look like two big and pointy toes." The two goblins stared at the tracks, having no idea that they were made by a rather large elk.

"Alright, let's go find this animal." Gravlox stood up straight, looking down the path of the tracks, trying to impress Vorst with his bravery. They started to follow the tracks, attempting to remain silent and undetected by the animal they were stalking. It didn't take long before they came upon a cave, its smell indicating that more than one animal lived inside.

"That is where we should camp," Gravlox said, desiring the familiarity of the cave to the open air of the forest.

Out from behind the cave emerged the elk, towering over the goblins, its antlers each the size of a goblin and half. Gravlox shrieked in fear, turning to run from the menacing creature.

Vorst, much calmer in the presence of danger, rolled to her side, coming to a crouch behind a small boulder and taking her short bow from her back. The elk, disturbed and threatened by the terrified shouts of Gravlox, lowered its head and began pawing at the ground with its hoofs.

"Gravlox!" Vorst called out, trying to get the poor goblin's attention. "Run, but not too far from here. Lead the beast in a circle!" A smile broke out on the younger goblin's face as Gravlox took off, the elk pursuing. Steadying her hands, Vorst nocked an arrow. Her breathing slowed to a deep, calm serenity. She pulled the bowstring back, just slightly, testing the tension, feeling the supple wood in her hand. Vorst's body moved with the path of the elk, tracking her shot perfectly.

In a split second, Vorst exploded into action, closing her eyes and loosing three shots into the elk over the course of a single exhale. The massive beast hit the ground hard, sliding from its own momentum, and coming to rest just inches behind Gravlox. Opening her eyes, Vorst returned her bow to her shoulder and stood from her crouched position, calmly striding over to the fallen animal. It took a few moments for Gravlox to even realize that the elk had fallen. He turned around, shock and awe plastered plainly on his face at the sight of Vorst removing her arrows from the body of the slain creature.

"What the... How did you..." Gravlox threw his hands in the air, letting his sword fall to the ground. "Where did you learn to do that?" he muttered under his breath as he approached the dead elk. Vorst stood, her three arrows dripping blood onto the soft ground.

"Don't worry about it, Gravlox, I've got your back. Nice work." She cleaned the arrow heads off on the hide of the animal and replaced them in her quiver.

"How do you know how to shoot like that?" Gravlox was truly stunned. The impressive archer standing before him shrugged like it was nothing, pulling a small knife from her pack and starting to cut into the flesh of the elk.

"You pick up certain skills when you spend a lot of time outside the mountain," she said nonchalantly. Vorst continued to cut the elk, removing the hide in large chunks. Gravlox sat down on the grass beside her, watching her work, admiring her familiarity with the carcass. "Here, try this," she said, holding out a piece of the elk's meat in her bloody hands.

Gravlox took the chunk of meat and brought it to his mouth, biting in. Blood dribbled down his chin as he ate the morsel, savoring the flavor. "If you like that, you should try it cooked. It tastes even better when you roast it over a fire," Vorst explained, wrapping a massive section of meat in the cut pieces of elk hide. She continued to dress the animal, removing the antlers and as much meat as she could carry.

After an hour or so with the dead elk, the two goblins made their way back to the grassy clearing and began to prepare a fire. The sun was low in the sky and the sounds of roasting elk meat filled the air by the time they finished setting their campsite. Vorst had cleaned the hides, setting them down on the grass to use as cushioned mats. Gravlox, not knowing the meaning of night and day as it related to the sun, became frightened with the onset of

40

darkness.

Even though he could see perfectly fine in almost any environment, and the darkness actually aided his vision, he fidgeted nervously with the hilt of his blade. "I've never actually met a human, Vorst. I don't know anything about them. Well, to be honest, I don't know anything about anything out here. I have lived my entire life in the mines beneath the mountain. Do humans hunt at night?"

Vorst laughed aloud, shaking her head and sending hot droplets of grease all over their campsite. "No, silly. Humans are weak. Their bodies tire after even the most meaningless activity. Whenever it gets dark, humans lie down and sleep, like an animal." She demonstrated a human sleeping by lying down and crossing her arms over her bare chest.

"Why do they do that? Couldn't someone just walk up to them and kill them while they sleep?" Gravlox didn't understand the need for sleep, never having felt the need himself.

"They just do it," Vorst explained. "And humans do other strange things, too," she continued, sitting up on the hide.

"They sound primitive," Gravlox mused, wondering how the humans could get anything done. In Kanebullar Mountain, the fluctuating temperatures caused by the sun's rise and fall dictated separations between days.

"You haven't seen a human yet," Vorst said. "They aren't as primitive as you might think."

Gravlox and Vorst waited in the glen for some time, lying down or sitting on the hides, eating roasted elk meat and drinking from the stream. As goblins, they did not need to sleep as humans did, but they still had to rest for a few hours in order for their bodies to recover.

"We should follow the stream," Vorst said a long while later, heading in that direction. "If we walk alongside the stream, we should be able to follow it to the river. From there, I think we can find the graveyard with the ghost flowers. I haven't been there in a long time, but I should remember where it is." Gravlox simply nodded his head, the knuckles of his hand turning white as he clutched the hilt of his sword. He hoped that he would never have to meet a human. He tried in vain to telepathically beg Lady Scrapple to keep him safe from the humans, a goblin prayer of sorts.

It was around midday by the time that the goblin pair arrived at a small ridge with a clear view to the graveyard. "What exactly are we doing here?" Gravlox asked, his eyes darting about the area, searching for humans. The village that buried their dead in the graveyard was just on the other side of the Clawflow. Gravlox and Vorst could see people walking about the streets of the small village, keeping to themselves and never bothering to look across the river at the distant spies.

"Ghost flowers are the closest thing I know to necrotic dust," Vorst explained, pointing at the graves. "I was thinking that if we start pulling up the ghost flowers, maybe some necromancer will come to try and stop us." The way she laid out the plan so casually terrified Gravlox.

"So, you want to anger a necromancer into coming to us? That seems..." Gravlox paused, trying to think of a way to politely explain his apprehension. "Dangerous. Yes, that plan feels very risky. What happens if the necromancer shows up? Do we just ask him for some dust?" Gravlox was shaking his head, wanting more than anything to just return to his mountain lair.

"Look, ghost flowers aren't used for much. The only things that goblins ever need them for is dark magic. I imagine that human necromancers must harvest the flowers regularly for their spells," Vorst said nonchalantly, as though she were just explaining an everyday activity. "As for when one would arrive to check on the flowers, I figured you would just be the hero and kill him," she continued, patting the hilt of Gravlox's sword.

The scared goblin swallowed hard, trying to be brave. "Sounds like a good plan to me," he muttered.

"Where are these ghost flowers, anyway? All I see are normal flowers," Gravlox wondered, inspecting the graves as best he could from the ridge.

"They only appear at night!" Vorst hit him lightly on the shoulder, "don't you know anything?" The female goblin stood, peering across the river to the human settlement. "I wonder what that town is called. Humans always give interesting names to their little villages."

"What should we do while we wait for night?" Gravlox asked tentatively, fearing the answer.

Vorst looked at their surroundings, pondering the question. She walked around the small clearing behind the ridge, out of view of the river and graveyard, and picked up two fairly long sticks. "Here," she said, tossing one to Gravlox, "spar with me. I want to see if you are any good or not." Before she even finished her sentence, Vorst charged, catching the terrified foreman off guard.

Gravlox had just enough time to shrug his heavy pack off of his shoulders and roll out of the way of Vorst's first swing. He could feel the wind from the stick rushing over his head and his eyes grew wide. He knew that the blow would have hurt and maybe even have knocked him out. Gravlox saw only the sky from his back and kicked out wildly, knocking Vorst back and keeping her momentarily at bay.

Using the temporary pause to remove her bow and pack, Vorst began to jump on her feet, loosening her limbs for combat. Thinking to turn the surprise to his favor, Gravlox leapt forward, his arms spread wide, the stick in his right hand. Already light on her feet, Vorst dodged the lunge with ease, striking out at the back of the soaring goblin as he missed his mark. Gravlox hit the ground on his chest, groaning loudly and sending up a cloud of dust.

Vorst took a few steps back, letting Gravlox get to his feet. She charged in again, swinging the stick for Gravlox's head, allowing him to easily duck out of the way.

With a yell that surprised both of them, Gravlox swung his own weapon, a large sweeping motion he hoped would take the younger goblin's legs out from under her. Vorst, instead of jumping over the

43

strike, rolled over the stick as it passed underneath her. She attempted to continue the roll and come up on the side of Gravlox, ready to strike at his exposed flank, but the sharp crack of a stick on her back changed her mind.

Gravlox scored a hit, bringing his branch in close when he saw the roll and hitting Vorst on the back. "Sorry," he breathed, not wanting to hurt his friend.

Vorst, more surprised than hurt by the hit, scrambled away and rose to her feet a few paces from Gravlox. She pulled her arm back and launched the stick at Gravlox, sending it whirling end over end. Much to her delight, Gravlox slapped the missile out of the air and then rushed in, leading with a stab that pushed Vorst back to the outside edge of the clearing.

A quick series of stabs followed the initial thrust, slowly putting Vorst's back to a tree. Gravlox stabbed in low, thinking he had won the duel. With a smile on her face, Vorst stepped down hard on the branch, snapping it in half against the ground. At the same time, she reached her hands up behind her head and grabbed the lowest branches of the tree. Using her upper body, Vorst was able to quickly flip upwards, her foot catching Gravlox in the chin and sending him sprawling to the ground.

Vorst, completely inverted, used her curled legs to fly out from the tree, landing on Gravlox with a cruel headbutt. He dropped his stick, the wind knocked out of his small lungs. Seizing the opportunity, Vorst grabbed the tip of the branch she had broken off of Gravlox's makeshift sword and pressed it tightly to his neck.

"You're dead," she said with a grin before tossing the stick away and standing. "That wasn't too bad though, for your first time."

Gravlox, nursing a bruise that was quickly turning black on his chest, stood up and stretched. "At least I managed to get a hit," he said playfully. "I'm hungry. Can we eat more of that meat?" He moved over to Vorst's pack, opening it and taking out a large chunk of elk. He tossed half of it to Vorst and sat down to consume his portion, blood running freely down his chin.

The two goblins ate in silence and waited for night to fall. Vorst scavenged around for wood appropriate for her to fletch arrows and set to work. Gravlox, wanting to feel useful, attempted to fletch arrows himself, but ended up ruining every piece of wood he touched.

Nightfall found the two goblins sitting on the ridge, a dozen fresh arrows in Vorst's quiver, a frightful expression on Gravlox's face. As the sun disappeared behind the horizon, small red flowers growing on the graves began to glow a soft blue. Wisps of ethereal smoke drifted up from a patch of the flowers, slowly drifting into the night sky.

The blue glow began to grow, consuming the red flowers, shifting in the moonlight and making the shadows of the gravestones dance. "Just wait," Vorst said, mesmerized by the lights. The glowing images surrounding the red flowers expanded, slithering into the air, vines of soft light spreading out to surround the tombstones. Little blue flowers of light began to bloom on the tops of the tombstones, each one opening with a gentle sucking sound, as though the flowers were absorbing the very energy of the air.

"The flowers are beautiful," Gravlox murmured. He was truly awestruck. "We can't go and smash those," he continued, his voice small. "They are too beautiful. Why don't those grow in the caves of Kanebullar Mountain?" The light was dancing off of the two goblins in eerie, shifting patterns.

Footsteps crunched through the underbrush on the other side of the graveyard. Vorst grabbed the back of Gravlox's neck and pulled him back behind the ridge, tucking into a roll to avoid being seen. "Someone is here," is all she said, reaching for her short bow.

"Where?" Gravlox asked, not having heard the footsteps. He looked around frantically, drawing his sword from its sheath at his side. The two goblins crawled on their bellies back up to the top of the ridge, trying to get a better look at their visitor.

"It could be the necromancer we need to find." Vorst sounded excited. Gravlox wished with all of his heart that she was wrong.

Out from the woods on the other side of the graveyard stepped a human wearing a dark robe. The figure moved silently, swiftly approaching the graves. The robe's hood was pulled down low over the human's face, completely masking the person's identity.

Vorst slowly took an arrow out of her quiver and set it against her bowstring. The feathers tied to the shaft brushed her cheek as Vorst pulled on the bowstring, slowly adding tension, never taking her eyes from the cloaked figure.

The human approached one of the graves and produced a small metal lantern from somewhere deep inside the robe. Vorst held her bow steady, the arrow nocked and aimed for the hooded person. The human opened a small door on the front of the lantern, spoke a line of words completely foreign to the goblins, and motioned with a hand for the flowers to enter the lantern. They obeyed. Ghost flowers from the tombstone began to drift slowly into the lantern, tendrils of blue light playfully encircling the human.

Vorst exhaled, her breath hot and heavy. The small goblin closed her eyes as she pulled the bowstring back further, drawing the arrowhead against the wood of the bow's handle. The hooded figure bent slightly, beckoning to the flowers, welcoming them into the lantern where their soft light was extinguished.

The thrum of Vorst's bowstring broke the halcyon serenity of the night air. The arrow flew, passing through the ghastly tendrils of a ghost flower and causing the wisps to scatter into the wind. The robed figure jerked forward and dropped the lantern onto the grass, leaning heavily on the top of the tomb stone. Vorst nocked another arrow, pulling the bowstring back to loose again.

"Wait," Gravlox whispered, "you wounded it already. Shouldn't we just capture the thing?" He put a hand on Vorst's arm, lowering her bow. The female goblin opened her eyes and saw Gravlox staring at her, begging for her to spare the life of the human she had just shot.

"Let's go," she said, slinging the bow over her shoulder and jumping down the ridge to the graveyard. Gravlox followed quickly behind, his sword in hand. The goblin pair descended upon the wounded human quickly, knocking the person to the ground. Gravlox swung his sword, connecting the heavy hilt of the weapon with the soft back of the human's head. The hooded figure slumped to the ground, twitching a few times before lying still.

"Did you kill it?" Vorst asked, hardly believing what she had just seen from the timid foreman. Gravlox simply shook his head and began to lift the human off the ground. The two of them carried the unconscious figure back over the ridge and into the grassy clearing. Vorst worked quickly to remove her arrow and patch the wound, tossing the bloody arrowhead into her pack to reuse later.

Blood stained the human's black robe, but the wound was not deep enough to be fatal.

Four

G IDEON STRODE TO the gates beneath Terror's Lament with his sword strapped to his back. His travelling gear was light, nothing more than some simple traps and snares and his gleaming armor. The four throwing axes on Gideon's hip clanged together with his stride like the high-pitched ring of funeral bells.

Not many enemies were known to Talonrend, so the guard-houses along the walls were never heavily manned. The people trusted their thick walls more than the reach of any guardsman's pike or sword.

Without much to go on, Gideon couldn't be positive which di-rection to take outside the city gates. The king's caravan had origi-nally set out to the south, to visit the smaller villages on the edges of the Clawflow. Having long ago lost his horse in an arena bet, Gide-on was forced to travel on foot, something he hated doing. He had no friends to ask along on the journey, so Gideon simply set out to the south, leaving the city of Talonrend behind him.

The landscape was pleasant although ultimately boring. For miles around the high walls of the city, nothing was visible except for grassy plains in all directions. Kanebullar Mountain stood high on the horizon, surrounded by a thick forest of hills and trees. Mountains stood far to the north, but only after journeying through the plains for days could anyone even make out enough of their shape to know they existed. Most of the plains around the city of Talonrend had been plowed and built into farms to sustain the population, but some areas of the countryside were too stony and lacked the proper topsoil for agriculture.

Gideon stuck to the barren section of the plains, preferring to walk atop the stony cave ceilings that ran under the entire kingdom than to trudge along the road. Travelers and farmers always wanted to speak to people like Gideon, seeing his sword and asking if he was coming from the arena. The gladiator pits were immensely popular in Talonrend. Every stocky farm boy and drunken blacksmith in the entire kingdom eventually made their way to the great pit in the center of the city. In order to save the kingdom's population, some king or other a long time ago set forth an edict that outlawed fighting to the death against other men. The ban on mortal matches was lifted on a fighter after he survived a full year in the arena against non-human opponents. Too many farm boys and blacksmiths never returned to their villages and the country side had suffered.

Gideon had made his life in the pits before being trained as a paladin at the tower. When he was young, he worked in a smith's shop. He was never allowed to work on any of the projects, but the master smith paid him to carry the materials around the shop. Gideon spent his days hauling carts of raw ore, moving rods of metal around the shop, and bringing heavy hammers to and from the smiths at their anvils.

When he turned sixteen, Gideon signed up for his first fight in the pits. A fighting agent had approached him at the smith's shop after noticing the bulging muscles in the young man's back and arms. He recruited Gideon without even testing him, bringing him into the arena with a broadsword to fight against wolves and bulls and other beasts of the wild. Gideon didn't know it at the time, but the arena agent had paid the owner of the blacksmith shop hand-somely to take the boy in and get him ready for combat.

In his first year in the pit, Gideon astounded the crowd. He slew handfuls of wolves with his sword, knocking them out of the air with great sweeps of his weapon and keeping them at bay with his reach. His final trial before entering into mortal combat with other men had been harrowing to say the least. Gideon stood in the center of the arena with the sand beneath his boots and his broadsword in hand. The arena agent had arranged everything, spending an amazing amount of money to coordinate the fight.

The crowd went into a frenzy when the iron gate at the end of the arena lowered. In his usual stoic style, Gideon watched the monster emerge without so much as a flinch. A hundred paces away, standing over nine feet tall, strode a minotaur. The beast was covered in thick, matted hair, with gnarled horns twisting and curving their way to the sky. He wore two heavy chains on his shoulders that crossed over his chest. The minotaur's heavy hooves thundered on the dry floor of the arena and left clouds of dust in its wake.

Gideon's immense opponent was wielding two weapons, both with wicked edges that gleamed in the sun. His right hand grasped a long metal bar, the top of which was edged with five razor blades, each the length of a sword, running vertically parallel to the shaft of the pole. The staff itself was nearly as tall as Gideon, but the minotaur swung it effortlessly, as if it were made of air. In the four meaty fingers of his left hand, the beast held a magnificent scimitar, its hilt encrusted with jewels.

The brawny blacksmith's assistant was armed with a two-handed broadsword and a sleeve of plate armor covering the left side of his body that ended in a heavy gauntlet. The crowd roared to life at the sight of the two opponents facing each other in the sand. Gideon stood at the center of it all, determined to make a name for himself in the pits and earn his glory. He didn't fight for the fame of a gladiator's life and he certainly wasn't trying to impress anyone in particular. He fought simply for himself—he wanted to be the best at everything he did.

With a strange calmness, Gideon stood in the center of the sand that day and waited for the minotaur to come to him. The broadsword was heavy and its wrapped leather handle fit nicely into the palm of his hand. The minotaur snorted, his breath fogging the air before his immense snout. The crowd held its breath for what felt like an eternity as the two opponents stood motionless, scrutinizing each other from a distance.

Finally breaking the tension, the minotaur began to move forward with the five-bladed pole cocked behind his head. Just twenty or thirty paces from the solitary man, the minotaur let loose. The crowd hushed, expecting the warrior to be impaled on the spot. Gideon judged the shot as it left the meaty hand, his eyes never leaving the wicked staff as it sailed over his head and missed the mark by inches. Sand splashed in a great wave as the unorthodox javelin bit into the ground and buried itself far behind Gideon. The minotaur tightened his strong grip on his sword and continued forward. Something about the small size of the jeweled scimitar made it look almost comical in the hands of such a hulking beast.

Gideon, not wanting to underestimate his opponent, rolled out of range of the first swing, ducking and dodging, keeping his own weapon low to prevent the massive hooves from caving in his chest. He knew that it would only take one solid hit from the minotaur to lay him out. After a full minute of avoiding the minotaur's heavy swings, Gideon realized that he could not tire the beast. A minotaur's endurance would last for days, especially when driven by the adrenaline of single combat.

The warrior strode along his path out of Talonrend, not even realizing that his feet were mimicking his own movements of his fight in the pit with the minotaur. He turned and rolled along the rocky ground, dodging the scimitar, ducking under strikes, reliving the entire combat from memory.

Gideon tried to think of a plan while he dodged, tried to come up with some sort of offense that would get him inside the swinging scimitar before his own endurance gave out and he collapsed to the sand. He had never fought a minotaur, never even seen a minotaur before, but he know enough just from the corded muscles of the beast's body that he would not survive a direct test of strength.

A swing came in for Gideon's head, the tip of the curved blade entering his vision from the left. The warrior feigned a dodge, moving his feet to jump back and to his right and outside the weapon's deadly reach. At the last moment, Gideon pivoted into the swing, bringing his own weapon up to block the attack, hoping to surprise the minotaur. The beast slashed across its body, wielding the scimitar in its left hand, and was able to quickly follow the parry with a brutal punch to Gideon's chest.

The warrior staggered backward and tried to catch his breath after the mighty blow. The roar of the crowd around him was deafening. Relentless, the creature pressed his advantage, swinging wildly at the retreating man. Gideon dodged most of the attacks, parried the few that came in too close, and continued to move away from his snarling foe.

Finally, Gideon saw an opportunity. He had retreated far enough to catch a glimpse of the heavy metal javelin protruding from the sand to his right. His first thought was to retrieve it and use the length of the weapon to keep the monster back. No, he thought, the minotaur's reach with the small sword would still best the length of the heavy pole.

The minotaur pressed him again, unleashing a chain of fast attacks that Gideon was forced to parry. The man planted his feet, determined to not let the shaft of the javelin out of his sight. His broadsword came up in a flash, barely catching the scimitar's point on the hilt. Using the exact same maneuver that had scored a hit on himself, Gideon pressed the weapons together and punched out with his left hand, catching the beast in its hairy chest. If the minotaur noticed the blow, he didn't show it.

Hoping to impose a test of brawn, the minotaur leaned in and pressed with all of his might against the smaller warrior, forcing the blade of the scimitar closer and closer to the man's neck. At the last moment, Gideon turned his shoulder hard, dropping the blade of his own sword into the sand and letting the overbalanced minotaur crush through the block. Had Gideon not ducked into the attack, he would have been eviscerated where he stood.

The smaller man had slipped under the large minotaur's arms and managed to get the blade of his sword on the creature's shoulder, slashing a long gash from the top of his arm to the chain at the center of his muscled chest. The infuriated minotaur spun quickly and blasted Gideon's jaw with his hand and narrowly missed with the scimitar that followed, a strike that surely would have decapitated the man. Gideon had timed it all perfectly. Collecting his wits and rubbing his jaw, the warrior managed to escape to the buried javelin as the monster howled in pain, much to the delight of the crowd. Blood oozed from the wound and dripped into the sand.

Gideon dropped his sword at the base of the javelin and used both of his strong arms to tear the weapon free. The arena floor let go of its prize in a whirl of sand that temporarily blinded the minotaur. Not wasting the opportunity, Gideon charged in with the weapon, swinging wildly with the butt of the heavy pole at his hip. The long and slender blades cut a deep wound into the side of the minotaur, causing more blood to spill forth. The beast howled again but did not fall.

Surprisingly, the minotaur reached down and tore the strange spear from Gideon's grip, dropping his own scimitar in the process. Scrambling, Gideon launched himself to the ground and grasped after the hilt of his broadsword. His hand found it, but not in time. The heavy pole smashed down on the back of Gideon's legs, rending his flesh. The clever beast then revealed the true function of the weapon, rotating it in his fierce grip and using the five blades to shave the skin from the back of Gideon's legs.

The pain was dizzying, but Gideon fought on. He knew that he didn't have much time left; the next blow from the pole would likely shred his skull to bloody ribbons. The minotaur lifted the weapon high to the roar of the frenzied crowd, seeking to make the final strike more dramatic.

Gideon took the chance to roll, sending waves of pain from his legs all the way to his eyes. His vision began to fade. Dark spots formed wherever he looked but he had his broadsword grasped firmly in hand. The beast bent over to strike, putting all of his bulk into the attack. The young blacksmith's assistant set the broadsword's hilt against his side in the sand and used the leverage to lift the sharp blade at the last second. The massive minotaur wasn't quick enough to shift his feet and avoid the blade.

The screams of the beast could be heard for miles. It wrenched away, covering the downed Gideon in blood, and howled into the sky. The two handed sword had impaled the mighty creature. Half of the blade protruding from the beast's back, half from the front. Gideon slowly climbed to his knees, his torn legs barely supporting his weight.

Suddenly, a mighty fist crashed into his neck, sending him sprawling back to the sand. The minotaur was laughing with the sword still plunged deep into his bloody chest. Gideon grabbed the ground with his hands and used the strength of his upper body to roll forward into a crouch. Standing upright just a few paces away was the laughing minotaur. It reached down, one hand grabbing the hilt of the sword and the other grasping the blade close to his body. Gideon scrambled on his hands and knees, trying to get away but never taking his eyes from the gruesome sight.

The crowd went quiet, expecting to see the bloody giant rip the sword from his own chest and fight on. Instead, the minotaur used his brute strength to break the forged blade in half. He tossed the bloody hilt to the crowd and began to shake, arching his back and convulsing. The second half of the blade dropped to the sand with a spurt of thick blood.

Gideon managed to get to his feet as he watched the astounding spectacle. With the minotaur's own scimitar in hand, he slowly began to circle the beast. The crowd went wild at the sight of both combatants leaking blood all over the sand, the minotaur unaware of the warrior standing behind him. Gideon raised the scimitar up, thinking to cut the gruesome head from the hairy shoulders of the minotaur, but the beast sensed him at the last moment and turned. The monster couldn't get the javelin in line to spike Gideon but was able to dodge the killing blow, losing only a horn in the process.

Gideon was quick to retrieve the twisted, severed horn from the sand and used it in his left hand as a dagger. The minotaur took the offensive again, attempting to charge Gideon and open his gut with the end of the pole. Blood loss from the sword wound in the minotaur's chest slowed him and caused him to stagger as the thick, dark blood began to fall from the beast's mouth. Mustering his last reserves of energy, Gideon struck out with one quick, low feint with the scimitar to force the beast to lower the pole. A flick of his wrist brought the sharp horn up under the minotaur's chin. A singular, powerful flex of Gideon's arm had the end of the horn protruding from the top of the creature's skull and the minotaur fell to the sand, lifelessly twitching as the crowd screamed for more.

In dramatic fashion, Gideon dropped the jeweled scimitar down on the top of the minotaur's lifeless chest and collapsed to the sand next to the slain beast, exhausted and nearly dead.

It took the warrior three weeks under the care of the Vrysinoch priests at the tower before he was able to stand unassisted. It was at the tower that Gideon was recruited to fight for the city as a paladin. He spent ten years living there, training with the other paladins and becoming a true warrior. Holy paladins of Vrysinoch are trained to use large shields and maces and to fight side by side, using each other for support on the battlefield.

After his decade of rigorous training, Gideon took his weapons and left the tower, never entering it again. Typically, a paladin who has graduated from the tower either receives a commission in the royal army as an officer or is chosen to be one of the king's guards. Not wanting to dedicate his life to the service of one man or even one city, Gideon abandoned his life as a paladin.

He took his tower shield and his enchanted mace to the black-smith where he used to work and sought to have something better crafted. Not being able to pay for his gear, Gideon returned to his old job hauling ore and materials. It took him almost two years to pay for the re-forging of his holy weapons. The shield and mace, along with a decent portion of Gideon's blood, were melted down into a single sword entwined with the warrior's powerful soul.

A screech brought Gideon back to the road in front of him, shattering his peaceful memories. His eyes immediately shot sky-ward, searching for the bird that had screamed. An eagle, the divine beast of Vrysinoch, was a fortuitous portent for the wandering war-rior. Gideon listened, hearing the powerful call of the eagle echoing off of the high city walls behind him. The screech was full of vio-lence and strength, mimicking the blood in Gideon's own veins. His pace quickened to a light jog, adrenaline coursing through the great warrior's body.

"Vrysinoch!" Gideon called to the sky, yelling at a black spot on the horizon he assumed to be the distant eagle. "Grant me your blessing!" he shouted, breaking out in a run. The axes on his side thudded against his powerful thighs with each hulking stride and his sword bounced up and down in the leather scabbard on his back.

Gideon did not know why he had begun running. Something about the way the eagle had cawed ignited a holy passion in the paladin. The divine symbol etched into his back from his training at the tower began to glow and radiate with heat. The warrior kept his pace, jogging for a few miles before finally coming to a rest outside a small hamlet on the edge of the Clawflow. He made his camp out-side the town, not wanting to spend money on a room at an inn or tavern. He waited until the dawn before beginning his search for information concerning the lost king.

The villages along the Clawflow River all belonged to Talon-rend and swore allegiance to Castle Talon, but few citizens from the small towns frequented their capitol city. The river ran from north to south, beginning somewhere in the snowy mountains to the north of Talonrend and continuing through the land for hundreds of miles before splitting into many tributaries. The Clawflow not only served as the lifeblood of the villages, but also created a natural barrier to the wilds. All of the human settlements were located on the western bank of the river; no villagers wanted to brave the untamed wilderness of the great forest in the east. Always dominating the horizon, the massive form of Kanebullar Mountain could be seen from almost anywhere, towering above the shadowy forest.

There was another kingdom far to the south of Talonrend and beyond the reaches of the Clawflow. Reikall was only a few days ride on horseback to the south of the river but the two kingdoms had almost no communication or trade between them. Gideon had a sneaking suspicion that his southerly neighbors were somehow behind the disappearance of King Lucius.

Every five years, dignitaries from Reikall made the trip to Castle Talon to partake in diplomatic discussions. Well, that was the agreement at least. It had been over twenty years since anyone from Reikall had been seen. Geographically, the two cities were not far from each other, but in the minds of the citizens of Talonrend, Reikall was all but forgotten. The two kingdoms had no trade between them and had never been at war. It was whispered, of course, that King Lucius would send the worst criminals of the realm to exile in Reikall, a statement that the rumormongers could never prove true or false.

Like everyone else, Gideon had only heard rumors of the kingdom of Reikall, but even so, a nagging feeling tugged at his gut and caused him to turn his gaze upon the southern horizon.

Gideon welcomed the journey with a sigh of contentment.

Five

D ARIUS WATCHED AN interrogation through the heavy iron bars of the cell. The guard captain held a small silk cloth over his mouth, a futile effort to keep the pervading stench at bay. Under Terror's Lament, buried hundreds of feet below the massive stone walls and tucked away in a cavern that few knew existed, was the dungeon. The man being interrogated was nearly dead, having offered up no pertinent information. Darius was still no closer to finding King Lucius.

"Death is such a flirt," King Lucius' steward mused, grabbing a small piece of iron with a heavily gloved hand. "You never know just how much one man can take before death comes for him. Sometimes it feels like I've been doing this for hours, sometimes they die with the first tiny cut. Interrogation is such an imperfect science, wouldn't you say?"

The tortured man tied to the bloody table in front of the steward didn't respond. He merely whimpered, barely even attempting to struggle. The king's royal steward, Jan by name, although most everyone used his title when addressing him, also served as the dungeon's primary interrogator. The steward lifted the heavy piece of iron out of the fire and pressed it gently to the bound man's eye-

58

lid, laughing quietly as the skin began to crackle and pop.

"One more time, good sir," the steward taunted, lifting the iron from the smoldering face, "where is the king? Everyone knows that you went with him in the caravan, your own family will attest to that." The man's face contorted in horror at the mention of his family.

"Tell me where the king has run off to, and I will end this. One stab of my dagger, deep into your heart, and this all ends. Your daughter won't have to answer any questions, your wife won't have to answer any questions..." Jan was twirling his dagger around in his hand, staring at the ceiling as though he were discussing the weather with an old friend over a casual game of chess. The steward lifted the small strap of hemp from the man's mouth, prompting him to speak.

"I... I already told..." the words came out in between violent sobs that sent blood splattering to the table.

"Yes, yes, the king left the caravan before you arrived at the southern village of Cobblestreet," Jan interrupted. Darius shook his head at the bars, looking away, knowing what was coming next. "It seems that everyone who has wandered back into Talonrend from that caravan has the same sad tale to tell. The only problem is, I don't believe it. I say you killed our dear Lucius. You and your merchant band united and slew the king and his guards and now all spin the same pathetic web of lies." The steward reached under the table to a thick wooden crank and began turning it, lifting the table up to a vertical position. "Your lies will not save you. Not here."

With a flick of his practiced wrist, Jan replaced the rope in the merchant's mouth, looping the ends of the hemp around a hook on the back of the table and completely immobilizing the man. The look of sheer terror on the man's burnt face was enough to make Darius leave the room. This was the third interrogation he had seen in as many hours, having lost the contents of his stomach only minutes into the first.

With the table in position perpendicular to the floor, Jan picked up a heavy axe from the floor, its edge heavily stained with old blood. He held the axe up against the man's pale neck, gently rubbing it back and forth, bringing a thin red line of fresh blood to the blade. The tortured man closed what was left of his eyelids, waiting for the end. Jan started to laugh. His victims never understood. "You only get to die quickly if you give me what I want!" he bellowed, cackling away with evil, sadistic joy.

One perfectly placed blow severed both of the man's ankles, dropping his bloody feet to the floor. Jan's leather boot kicked the feet away, burying them in a pile of filth and other rotting parts. "Now, just to let you know what is happening, although I don't suspect that you have much time left in the first place," Jan picked up a large bucket from a table behind him and placed it under the man's bleeding stumps as he spoke. The steward had to use both hands to lift a heavy bag from the table, pouring its white contents into the bucket, filling it to the top with fine salt. The bloody stumps writhed in pain just an inch above the grains.

"Now, this bucket here is full of salt," Jan explained, wiping the blood and grime from his hands onto a towel. "Right now, that isn't much of a problem for you. I tied the ropes too tightly for you to fall into it." King Lucius' steward bent down and took a pinch of salt from the bucket and sprinkled it into the savage burn on the man's face. "I assure you, you do *not* want to end up in that bucket." The man howled through clenched teeth, fighting against his restraints at the new wave of pain.

Jan walked to the corner of the room to a set of a dozen ropes attached to pulleys in the stone ceiling. After sorting through them for a moment, he grasped one of the ropes and smiled at the man on the table. "Better flex," he said in a melodic voice, yanking down firmly on the rope. In the blink of an eye, the hook at the back of the table released, causing the man to violently jerk downward, no longer supported by the ropes but still unable to escape the table with his arms tied out wide.

Jan hurried out of the small chamber, locking the door behind him. "I'll send the wolves in tomorrow to clean up your mess," he called back over his shoulder as he continued down the hallway past the other cells.

"Do you always have to be so dramatic at the end?" Darius asked, falling into step beside the king's steward. The captain kept his silk cloth over his mouth until the pair exited the dungeon entirely.

"I like the drama of a good interrogation," the man replied, his voice dripping with malice. "Besides, that's what the king pays me to do, to interrogate people and then make them disappear."

"Yes," the captain said solemnly, disgusted by the horror of it all, "judging by the smell in that room, you don't bury the bodies. Ever." Darius was glad to step into the sunlight of the warm afternoon and breathe the fresh air. "We still don't know much about the king. All of the merchants that have wandered back to Talonrend just say that the king left the caravan with some of his guards at some little village along the Clawflow."

Jan stopped at the exit to the tunnel, leaning against the smooth stone of Terror's Lament as he thought. "They said that the king left somewhere around Cobblestreet. That pathetic village is quite a long ways from Castle Talon, one of the southernmost settlements along the river. What could he be looking for? Where is the rest of the caravan?"

Darius fiddled with the hilt of his sword, pondering the situation. After a moment, he simply threw his hands up in the air, defeated. "None of this makes sense," he said, exasperated. "Why have some of the merchants left the caravan, but others have not returned? I truly believe that those men I saw you torture hid nothing. They honestly have no more answers than we do..." Darius' voice trailed off as he shook his head.

"Thank you, good captain of the guard. I take pride in my work. No one hides their secrets from me. No one." Jan took off the heavy leather apron he was wearing and hung it on a wooden peg just inside the iron door to the dungeon. It took him a few moments to produce the proper key from a deep pocket on his royal finery and lock the door. The two men took a few steps away from the wall before turning. Jan spoke a simple arcane command word and the door vanished into the wall so thoroughly that it was as if the portal never existed.

"I will never understand how you do that, Jan." For what seemed like the thousandth time that day, Darius shook his head in disbelief. Jan simply nodded to the captain, folding his hands behind his back and assuming his regal posture before departing for the castle. The guard captain continued out from the wall in the direction of the artificer's guild, hoping to find some answers through less violent means.

The artificer's guild hall was an interesting structure. When Talonrend was first settled hundreds of years ago by the refugees from the Green City, the building was a small palace. The residence had two turrets flanking the ornate wooden door with leering stone gargoyles keeping watch from above. The guild hall ran east to west within the city, each end marked by a formidable round tower molded to the shape of an eagle's grasping talons. No one has ever been quite sure how the artificer's guild came to possess the palace, but it had been their home since before the birth of King Lucius' parents.

Darius approached the guild hall quickly; he never enjoyed his meetings with the arrogant artificers and he wanted the whole affair to be concluded quickly. As was normal with every visit to the strange guild hall, the door opened before Darius was in range to knock.

"Hello again, good captain Darius," the porter said in a mellow voice, beckoning to Darius with one hand as he held the door ajar. "So good it is to see you today. Shall I inform my master of your arrival?"

"Yes, yes, of course," Darius muttered as he strode into the ornately decorated foyer. In the blink of an eye, the master of the artificer's guild stood in the foyer as well, right in front of the startled captain, a tiny wisp of smoke dancing to the ceiling.

"Please," Darius said with a start, "Lady Keturah, your sudden arrivals only serve to frighten me. Perhaps you could..." Darius tried to clear his head and recover from the frightening appearance of the guild master he so despised dealing with. "Knock... or something... before you just show up like that..." Truly at a loss for words, Darius simply took a step back from the imposing woman and produced a small leather sack full of coins from his belt.

"What exactly would you like me to knock upon, guard captain Darius?" Keturah's voice had a melodic quality to it that sounded almost incorporeal, like a beautiful ghost was whispering her words just after she spoke them. "Your head, perhaps?" Keturah lifted a slender, gloved hand into the air, making a knocking motion a foot from Darius' forehead. The guard captain felt the magical hand tapping on his head as surely as he felt the wooden floor beneath his boots.

With a flick of his wrist, Darius tossed the sack of coins to the intoxicatingly beautiful woman. Keturah was dressed in a flowing silk dress the deep color of blood with a black corset laced up her chest. Her long, curly red tresses matched the color of her raiment perfectly, almost blending into the soft fabric itself. Keturah's hair bounced playfully as she reached up and caught the flying coins, allowing Darius to catch a few glimpses of the woman's striking green eyes. She was unerringly attractive, her pale, lithe arms ending in black leather gloves covered in runes.

Keturah snatched the money out of the air and looked at it intensely, weighing the contents in her mind. She smiled, sending a wave a relief through the nervous captain. With a snap of her fingers, the gold vanished. "So, you are serious this time. You brought enough gold to convince me that either you have actually spotted a dragon or this meeting is about something else altogether." Darius lost himself in the thin, ghostly echo of Keturah's words, barely understanding them as the woman spoke.

"I need you to find the king," Darius stammered, never taking his eyes from the lovely mouth of the guild master.

"An interesting proposition. Just where do you think our precious Lucius has run off to?" The woman smiled as she spoke, her thin red lips nearly hypnotizing the enamored captain. "Surely you do not expect to find him here, yes?" Darius didn't miss the subtle glance of Keturah's eyes to an ornate door on the side of the room. Still, the man's increased heart rate betrayed him, turning his face red. "Follow me," Keturah whispered, echoed by her high-pitched ethereal counterpart. She reached out, taking the rough hand of the guard captain in her delicate, gloved grasp.

Keturah led Darius deeper into the guild hall, heading East, through corridors lined with statues and portraits of famous, and sometimes infamous, artificers. Darius was barely able to take the sights in, having never been beyond the foyer of the grand building. Keturah moved quickly, guiding him by the hand through the various twist and turns of the mansion. Finally, they arrived in front of a solid stone wall, the base of the eastern round tower.

With a gentle shove, Keturah pushed the man away from the stone and squared her shoulders to it. "Get behind me," she said, using a tone that brokered no alternative. Darius nervously toyed with the hilt of his short sword, honestly wondering if he was about to die. The woman, and the guild she represented, terrified him. Darius had never been blessed with any powers beyond the martial, divine or arcane. Magic and magic wielders, especially beautiful ones, held a distinct advantage over the anxious man.

Keturah spoke her name to the wall forcefully, projecting her voice much louder than Darius thought possible given her slender frame. Something about her astral echo changed when she spoke to the stones. The ghastly quality hidden underneath the woman's melodious voice grew in volume and speed, pronouncing Keturah's name even before her natural voice did.

The stones of the tower's base shifted ever so slightly, quivering with energy, before erupting into flame. The gout of liquid inferno washed over Keturah, blinding Darius momentarily as he ducked down behind her. Lines of fire continued down the hallway behind the pair, congealing onto the floor in a pool of sublimated flame.

Darius could feel the intense blast of heat licking at the edges of his body. He quickly retracted his arms in to his chest, curling up as tightly as he could against the dizzying onslaught. Much to his disbelief, his skin was not burned. With Keturah in front of him, Darius was able to endure the fire without any serious injury.

As quickly as the geyser had erupted, the hallway calmed. Everything looked just as it had a moment before, without a burn or char to be seen anywhere. Keturah turned and lifted the man from his crouch, brushing his shoulders off and smilingly sweetly. "See, I told you to stay behind me." Her voice had returned to normal; well, as normal as her voice ever was. The woman was unscathed by the maelstrom of fire, looking perhaps even more radiant than before.

The two continued up a dark, unlit staircase winding tightly around itself as it ascended. Keturah took the pitch black steps two at a time, her footfalls placed perfectly on the stone. After several full rotations, they arrived at the top of the tower, its stone walls set with intricate stained glass. There was a bronze telescope on a tripod standing in the center of the room, facing east.

"Based on everything I have already seen in this place, I'm betting that telescope is no ordinary device." Darius took a hesitant step forward, approaching the telescope with a measure of reverence.

"That would be correct," Keturah said, moving swiftly to position herself behind the fine bronze instrument. "Now, where should we begin our search?" The graceful woman swiveled the telescope back and forth, aiming it at the stained glass windows, one after another. Darius then realized that she wasn't looking through the scenes painted on the glass, she was looking into them.

"We have learned that the king left the merchant caravan he was travelling with around the town of Cobblestreet. You might try starting there." Keturah turned the bronze telescope to a window depicting the small village of Cobblestreet and watched for a long moment. Darius watched the woman with anticipation, hoping she would be able to locate the missing king with ease.

"Well," she said, standing up and returning her gaze to the captain, "he is not in Cobblestreet. Most of the merchants are still there, camped outside of the village, milling about and doing nothing. The king's royal banners and his large tent are clearly visible, but peering inside the tent reveals nothing."

"What about my men stationed to guard the king? Is there any sign of the twenty armed soldiers that served as Lucius' escort?" The captain's mind raced with possibilities. He had learned of the king's departure from the caravan already and with the amount of money he had paid the guild master, Darius expected more information.

Keturah leaned over the telescope again, further examining the area surrounding the small riverfront village. "I see a few armed men, nothing the level of a royal escort though." The woman turned the telescope just slightly, aiming it at the very edges of the stained glass window. "There are tracks in the mud from horses, leaving out to the south of the encampment," she said, shaking her head. "I do not have the range to follow them. The windows are only so big."

"Continue to search. I want to know every single thing about the town. There must be other clues around the village." Darius was impatiently pacing the small tower room, his right hand fidgeting with the hilt of his sword.

Keturah continued to scan the telescope over the window, inspecting every street in the muddy village. Darius was quick to notice the sudden quickening in the woman's breathing as the telescope aimed at the far edge of the town, opposite the camp.

"What is it?" he asked in a frantic voice, "have you found something?" Darius moved behind the woman, hoping to look through the scope and see the king, alive and well.

Keturah shook her head, continuing to look through the instrument as she spoke. "This is certainly interesting. It appears as though the little town of Cobblestreet has some uninvited guests." She moved the scope even further to the edge of window, straining her vision to its magical limits.

"I can't quite make out what is happening, but on the other side of the river..." Keturah stopped her scan, rubbing her eyes before returning to the telescope. "Yes, there are two goblins camped out on the fringes of the town in a small clearing. Right next to the Cobblestreet graveyard, it seems this pair of armed goblins is spying on the city. Certainly is unusual behavior for such an unintelligent race." Keturah stood up, letting Darius view the bizarre scene for himself.

The image was cut off at the edge, not showing the entire clearing, but Darius could easily see two small goblins sitting down on the grass. "Why would there only be two of the wretched vermin?" Darius muttered to himself, trying to look beyond the small clearing to see the rest of the area. Something at the edge of his vision caught the guard captain's attentive gaze.

"Did you see the boots at the very edge of the view?" he asked, looking back to Keturah. The expression on her confused face told Darius that she had not.

Keturah shoved the man aside, peering back into the stained glass. "Those aren't goblin boots. As far as I know, goblins don't even wear boots. Those feet belong to a humanoid, either a man or an elf, perhaps a cleric of some sort, judging by the hem of the robe. That is all I can see. The stained glass images don't extend far enough."

"What do we do?" Darius asked, fearing that a goblin raiding party was waiting just beyond their vision.

"We send a scout. That is what we do." Keturah's voice, amplified by the ethereal echo behind it, was commanding. "I trust that you have already sent an expedition to find the dear king? They must be warned."

"Yes," Darius agreed. "Our fastest scouts will be dispatched to warn the town."

"I have someone faster," Keturah said with a sly grin. She cupped her hands in front of her mouth, whispering arcane words of evocation into them. When she revealed her hands again, a large black scorpion sat upon her fingers, clicking its massive claws together. Keturah set the creature down upon the stone of the tower and breathed on its back, a thick cloud of billowing smoke escaping her mouth and enveloping the scorpion.

"Taurnil," Keturah whispered to the swirling wisps with her ghostly, disembodied voice. "Taurnil, arise, my champion, awaken from the abyss." Keturah and Darius both took a step back, giving the scorpion as much room as possible in the small chamber at the top of the guild hall's eastern tower.

The smoke swirled about the black scorpion faster and faster, the insect's body beginning to pop and crack with the magic of transformation. Obsidian flakes of the scorpion's exoskeleton fell to the floor and dissolved as a humanoid shape grew within the smoke. Taurnil stood five and half feet tall, his sinewy flesh pulled taut over thick lengths of corded muscle. His body was completely devoid of hair, his skin the color of pale ash mixed with acrid snow. The room smelled strongly of sulfur, the pungent odor stinging Darius' nostrils.

The demon, or whatever Taurnil truly was, grinned, showing his jagged teeth stained brown and red from years of eating flesh. The beast's face was flat, with a wide nose so stretched over the underlying bone that it appeared as two gaping holes in the center of its head. His eyes were dramatic enough to send Darius running from the room, had Keturah's command over the creature not been so apparent. The monstrous being craned its neck about the room, its eyes showing nothing but the deepest black. The room reflected blurry off of the crystalline eyes, giving a haunting, soulless aura to the foul humanoid.

Keturah moved to the creature's side, placing an arm gently on its boney shoulder in a loving manner. "Taurnil, my dearest champion, go now. Fly to the settlement of Cobblestreet, southeast of this place, along the Clawflow River. Go there, warn the king's soldiers of goblin activity in the region. Then go across the river, near the human graveyard, and kill every goblin you can find." Taurnil smiled devilishly at his last command.

"I do as you command." The creature's voice was more a hiss than recognizable speech. Taurnil bowed his head in obedience to his master. Keturah pushed up a small section of the stone, causing the wall to swing open and revealing a sizeable door in the tower between two of the stained glass windows. "I shall return once I have gorged upon the souls of goblins," the beast hissed, turning for the door.

Taurnil's back shifted and churned, the taut flesh splitting on either side of the demon's distinct vertebrae. Two massive wings unfolded themselves from beneath the flesh, hooked spikes of bone accenting the bottom of each leathery appendage. Taurnil spread the wings wide, filling the small chamber, flexing with raw power. The thin wings were translucent, bulging veins showing clearly throughout. The wings were torn in places, small holes letting the sunlight of the morning shine through them.

"A powerful and winged lich died near Talonrend once," Keturah explained, recognizing the shocked expression on Darius' face. "Of course, I couldn't just let the wings go to waste. Taurnil here was most appreciative." Turning back to her champion, Keturah bade him to leave with a calm wave of her gloved hand.

"I have seen too much for a man my age," Darius muttered to himself. Keturah simply laughed, watching her demonic companion fly out of the tower.

Six

"WHY HASN'T HE woken up yet, Vorst? I thought he would be awake by now..." Gravlox was nervous. Even though the man's chest still rose and fell with steady, rhythmic breathing, Gravlox feared for the man's life.

"It has been a full night. I figured that he would wake up with dawn, most humans do anyway." Vorst sounded inquisitive rather than nervous like her companion. "Go to the river and get some water. Maybe if we splash it on him, he will realize that I didn't kill him. Humans are so stupid."

A few moments later the man was coughing up a runny mixture of river water and blood, frightfully looking about the clearing at his captors. The man was almost six feet tall, greatly dwarfing the goblins that held him hostage. He continued to cough, struggling against the ropes that bound his body.

"Wha—? Goblins!" the man shouted when his eyes fell upon the image of Vorst holding her bow. It was clear from the sneer in the man's voice that his initial surprise was replaced with disgust.

"Yes, goblins," Vorst responded in a halting version of the human tongue. "Just goblins," she said calmly. Vorst lowered her bow slightly and sounded out the word 'necromancer' in the man's direction.

Gravlox nearly fell over dead from shock at hearing Vorst's beautiful voice speak the human language. His mind started to ask her how she came to speak their language, but his mouth would not move. Gravlox sat slack-jawed on the grass, dumbfounded.

"Necromancer?" the man questioned, rising up to a sitting position. If he felt any fear or apprehension toward his captors, he did a fine job of hiding it. "I can assure you," he continued, "I am no necromancer, nor do I have any desire to become such an abomination."

The calm manner with which he conversed with the goblins alerted Vorst to how powerful the man must be. She drew an arrow from her quiver and began to take aim at the man. Gravlox caught the man glancing toward the lantern sitting next to Vorst's pack. Not sure what powers it might possess, Gravlox drew his sword and walked to the magical lantern, ready to smash it if need be.

The man leaned forward in his bindings, staring hard at Vorst. "What are you?" she said, unsure as to just how dangerous her captive was. A smile broke out on the man's face as Vorst finished her question.

Kill him. Without a moment of hesitation, Vorst loosed her arrow, taking the man full in the chest and knocking him to the ground. He sputtered just once before his life ended. *Keep the lantern, toss the body into the river where the current is strong.* Vorst stood, placing her bow over her shoulder, and moved to grab the man by his ankles.

"Help me dump him, Gravlox," she said, dragging the man through the clearing toward the river.

"What is going on? Why did you kill him?" Gravlox remained frozen in place, standing above the lantern with his sword drawn.

"Lady Scrapple commanded it. I am not one to go against her orders." The tone of Vorst's voice indicated that she had disobeyed the Mistress of the Mountain sometime in the past and did not entertain the possibility of ever doing it again.

"She speaks to you? Lady Scrapple speaks to you?" Gravlox was amazed. He had never heard the voice of his mother.

"She does, on occasion. Only when I am in trouble, it seems." Vorst had the corpse almost to the river by the time Gravlox managed to pick up the man's arms and help.

"Why does she protect you?" Gravlox asked after they had tossed the body into the river.

"I assumed she spoke to all goblins," Vorst replied calmly, rubbing her hands against the grass to try to remove the stench of human. Gravlox knew she was lying, but decided it was better to let it go and ask his questions later. If Lady Scrapple talked to all goblins, why had she never spoken to him?

"We should get going," Vorst said as she gathered up their supplies. "I do not like this place. It reeks of humans. Grab the lantern, I know enough about ghost flowers to make a potent enough poison." Her command was final and sucked all the joyful life from her voice.

The two goblins didn't speak as they headed out of the clearing in the direction of Kanebullar Mountain.

They had been on the trail for about an hour before Gravlox finally found the courage to break the silence. "Vorst, you aren't acting like yourself. What is going on?" He didn't know how to phrase the question properly. He really just wanted to know who his companion actually was and how she came to speak the human language.

Vorst sighed. "Grav, I think you need to ask that question to yourself. *You* are more than *you* let on." Vorst stopped on the trail, turning to face Gravlox and look him in the eye. "Lady Scrapple has me watching you."

"Why?" he pleaded more than asked. It was clear from his expression that Gravlox assumed he was about to die. "For plotting to kill a miner?" He put his hands in the air, ready to defend himself.

"No, silly Gravlox, of course not!" Vorst laughed, "You weren't made to be just a foreman, or even the leader of a mine. You were born with certain.... powers." She paused a moment before continuing. "Lady Scrapple made sure of it."

"What sort of powers?" Gravlox asked, looking at his hands, expecting them to suddenly feel stronger and bulge with muscle.

"Alright Gravlox, I don't know if you are ready for this or not, but I will try to show you." Vorst closed her eyes, silently conversing with Lady Scrapple and seeking her approval. She drew her short sword from its scabbard at her side, holding it firmly in her hand. "Close your eyes and imagine the ground right behind you. Picture yourself five feet from me, instead of just two."

Trusting fully in Vorst's judgment, Gravlox did just that. Vorst stabbed out hard with her sword, aiming for Gravlox's vulnerable neck. Faster than Vorst's mind and eyes could even register, Gravlox was standing further away, out of her sword's biting reach.

"Open your eyes, silly," Vorst said in her usual voice, full of life and melody. The gasp that escaped Gravlox's mouth sent birds fluttering from the trees.

Gravlox simply stood on the trail, a dumbfounded expression etched onto his hairless face. "How did you do that?" he finally stammered, barely audible. The frightened goblin touched his body, wondering if he was even real.

"*I* didn't do that, Grav, *you* did!" Vorst jumped about, excited that Gravlox was finally discovering his powers. "You were created by Lady Scrapple to be a shaman, Gravlox. You just never figured it out on your own. Some goblins need a little pushing."

Gravlox let the explanation sink in, wondering how he had lived his entire life without knowing he was a shaman. "What else can I do?" he asked, eager to learn of his abilities.

"I can't help you there. Goblin shaman aren't like human mages or wizards. Goblins don't spend years in a school learning all of their powers, they just kind of come to us when we are ready. You have to discover things for yourself." Vorst started to skip down the path back toward Kanebullar Mountain.

73

"How long have you known?" Gravlox asked, running to catch up to Vorst as his mind raced. "About me, that is," he clarified.

"Lady Scrapple told me a while ago," Vorst called back over her shoulder, vaulting a fallen log that blocked the path. The two goblins sped off through the forest, Gravlox trying hard to keep pace with his lithe companion, eventually arriving at the small creek where they had previously felled the elk.

Gravlox ran with his head down, breathing heavily and not even aware that Vorst had abruptly stopped at the edge of the small clearing. The two goblins rolled into the glen, fully entangled. Gravlox was too absorbed in his thoughts and emotions to have noticed the line of human crossbowmen kneeling on the other side of the grass.

Gravlox did, however, manage to hear the click they made as the bolts fired out from their bows, cutting a horizontal line of death through the afternoon air. Had it not been for his ungraceful tumble into the back of his friend, the two goblins would have surely been cut to ribbons by the volley. Fourteen crossbow bolts sailed above the goblin pair, thudding into the trees and other brush behind them.

The foreman froze, not sure what course of action he should take. Vorst didn't waste a single moment, leaping into action with her usual confidence. The crossbows, taking time to reload, had used up all of their effectiveness in the first volley. Vorst's short bow was much more mobile, ripping the life from three of the men before they even drew their swords.

"Get up!" Vorst called to Gravlox, still lying prone on the grass. The nearest two crossbowmen charged, their gleaming sword points leading the way. Vorst swung her bow, more of an attempt to distract the men than deal any damage. It worked, buying the goblin a split second to draw her own sword and toss her travelling pack to the ground. Gravlox was up by the time the soldiers closed the gap, squaring off against the two. Vorst barely rose to the height of the average man's waist, so she used her shortness to her advantage, ducking in under the sweeping strikes of the soldiers.

Both swords crossed above her head harmlessly as she scored a hit on the back of one knee, rolling out to the other side, near the reloading crossbowmen. Moving purely out of desperation, Gravlox parried the first strike high, knocking the blade away and stepping into the attack, bringing his body right up against the shining armor of the human soldier. The goblin foreman reached within himself, trying to find his inner wellspring of power, the conduit between the realm of magic and his pale fingertips.

Blood showered from the back of the soldier, pieces of his metal chain armor flying all over the grass and bits of gore splattering the man's comrades. Gravlox slowly withdrew his hand from the far side of the man's chest cavity. Blood dripped from his fingers to stain the green grass. A few of the crossbowmen paused, lowering their weapons as they watched the corpse of the man fall. A large hole gaped in the soldier's chest. Gravlox stood behind the torn remnants of the human, staring at the lines of blood on his own arm.

The man fighting against Vorst stopped, staring slack jawed at the scene, allowing her plenty of time to put her sword to deadly work.

Sensing a lull in the combat, the leader of the guard patrol stepped forward, calling for his soldiers to stay their weapons. The leader, designated by the bright white cape he wore, kept his hands in the air before him and made no moves to unsheathe his sword. "Taurnil!" he called out with a smile.

The heavy beating of wings heralded the demon's arrival. Taurnil landed softly on the grass in front of the humans, just an arm's length from the small goblins. The beast's skin was eerily similar in color and texture to that of the goblins, but that is where the similarities ended.

Taurnil opened his mouth, revealing a circular maw of jagged teeth, three elongated tongues dancing about happily. Gravlox could make out the terrified face of one of the crossbowmen through a ragged tear in the monster's huge wing. Bone claws at the bottom of each wing pulsated with energy, hungry for a kill. The ashen-skinned nightmare wore no armor, its long claws serving as its only conventional weapons.

Gravlox and Vorst stood close to each other, both expecting the other to act first. Vorst looked at her wooden bow longingly, the weapon lying just inches behind one of Taurnil's pale feet. Gravlox glanced down at his own weapon, the hilt of his sword clutched tightly in his shaking hand.

Taurnil stretched his muscled arms out wide and clicked his claws violently in the air. The demon rushed in, using one beat of his wings to lift him from the ground. Taurnil's scything talons creased the air, screaming in from the sides, wide enough to decapitate both goblins at once. Gravlox lifted his arm to block the coming death, not wanting to look the demon in the face.

Taurnil's mighty claw struck Gravlox's arm, hitting him with full force. The short goblin felt the pulse of energy within him, the magic racing to his limb, absorbing the entire attack without the claw even breaking his skin. Taurnil used his winged speed to continue over the goblins and landed down behind them.

Gravlox felt the well of magic within him begin to dwindle, having spent almost all of his remaining energy blocking the first attack. Taurnil reared his head back and spat, launching a spray of green bile toward the goblins. Thinking fast, Vorst pushed Gravlox to the side and rolled the opposite direction. The acid began to smolder and melt the ground where it landed.

The pale demon strode in, heading directly for Vorst, thinking his victory nigh with the two opponents split on the battlefield. Vorst lifted her sword in front of her and readied her defense. The great winged beast slashed out at the small goblin, his muscled arm sweeping in above the sword. Vorst jerked her defense skyward at the last moment, hoping to sever the claws from the demon, but only succeed in entangling her blade.

Taurnil was stronger than Vorst could have ever imagined,

wrapping his sinewy fingers around the blade and disarming her with a flick of his powerful wrist. Vorst could only watch in horror as her weapon tumbled to the grass. Her peripheral vision picked up the action of Taurnil's wing, but it was too late. Vorst was disarmed, with no way to block and nowhere to dodge.

The barbed end of Taurnil's right wing came driving up, the demon having pulled his wings in suddenly and arching his back. The bone spear bit deeply into the soft flesh of Vorst's hip, rending it open and spilling forth her blood in a great rush of agony. Vorst howled in pain.

Gravlox was behind the beast, hoping to decapitate the demon while it struck. His short sword came down in a flurry, all of the goblin's strength behind the blow. Just inches from the taut and ashen neck, the left wing of the monster snapped in tight, the top of it coming into perfect line with the descending blade. Gravlox chopped down and cut a deep wound in the top of the leathery wing.

Taurnil pulled back, dislodging his barb from Vorst's side, and curling away. One flap of his wings sent him high into the air, relative to the short goblins, and placed him safely out of their reach. Blood flowed freely from the top of Taurnil's wing but it flowed faster from Vorst's hip.

Vorst tried to roll and retrieve her bow, hoping to shoot the flying demon from the air. She didn't get far, her leg failing beneath her the moment she put weight upon it.

Gravlox watched her crumble to the bloody grass, clutching her wound. The rage welled up inside him, a red wall of seething anger. Gravlox swung his sword about in the grip of his hand, letting his acrimony build. With a fierce, primal growl, Gravlox leveled his blade and charged, intent on skewering the beast where he hovered.

The goblin foreman leaped from the ground, his small but powerful miner's legs catapulting him into range. He stabbed out, a vicious thrust aimed right for the grey chest of his foe. Taurnil curled his wings in tightly about his body, rolling in the air to deflect the blow, gravity pulling him to the ground. Gravlox's sword struck true, slicing a clean path through both wings and pinning them to the beast's chest. Taurnil's roll rent the sword from the goblin's hand, the hilt of the weapon acting as the head of a nail, keeping the monster's arms pinned inside his wings.

Gravlox fell to his back on the bloodstained grass, coming up quickly in a roll. Taurnil began to retreat back to the line of crossbowmen. The line of soldiers had reloaded by then and leveled their bows at the two goblins. Gravlox, his adrenaline-fueled bloodlust all but dissipated, looked upon the line of soldiers and despaired. He could not stand against that volley.

The shaman fell to his knees beside his writhing companion, expecting the end to come swiftly. He bent low over Vorst, attempting to apologize for getting them both killed, but the beautiful goblin female was already gone, her mind having fled to the peaceful sanctuary of the unconscious.

Eight crossbows clicked. The soldiers fired a hail of deadly bolts into the air. Gravlox felt the last remnants of energy deep inside his body fading; the well of power was nearly dry. His hands clutched at the slick ground, the dirt and blood feeling sickeningly warm beneath his pale fingers. With a cry, Gravlox ripped two handfuls of dirt from the ground, throwing them into the path of the iron-tipped bolts as one last act of desperation. The ground beneath the small clumps of earth rolled and a roiling temblor rose up from the goblin's fingertips, racing toward the soldiers. The wall of vibrating grass and soil shot forth, sending a turbid column of dust into the air.

The growing tremor absorbed the bolts, soaking up their added energy. The captain, being the singular standing soldier of the group, was the only human fortunate enough to have the time to escape before the shockwave of earth hit the line. Soldiers flew from their crouched positions with wild abandon, the sheer energy of the wave blowing apart their weapons and bones like twigs in a tornado.

Taurnil and the lone surviving soldier ran for their lives. The wave of earth dissipated far from the fleeing pair, its magic spent. Gravlox collapsed to his back, truly exhausted, the power within him utterly depleted. In the same belabored heartbeat, two score of additional soldiers sprinted into the clearing, weapons at the ready.

They were goblin soldiers though, coming to aid the fallen pair. Their leader, a heroic goblin warchief by the name of Yael, rushed to Vorst, quickly tending to her grievous wound. The goblin soldiers secured the area, making sure that Taurnil and the human had fled and no other men were nearby.

It took nearly two hours to return Vorst to consciousness. Her hip was patched with rugged strips of leather, an herbal poultice filling in the wound and aiding the healing process. Gravlox merely sat next to the wounded goblin, watching the other goblins work to save her life, not speaking a word. Finally, Yael approached the shaken foreman. "Lady Scrapple sent me here with a warband of drones to help you," he explained. When she saw the vision of Vorst killing the man by the river, she knew there would be a fight. Yael sat on the ground next to Gravlox.

"Why does Lady Scrapple only speak to her? Why is it that I have never heard her voice?" Gravlox was staring in the direction of Kanebullar Mountain, his mind reeling with a thousand questions.

Yael let out a long sigh. "Lady Scrapple cannot feel you. You are not connected to her by the magical bonds that unite all of the goblins. The drones, these soldiers I brought with me, they are merely manifestations of Lady Scrapple's will. They do not think, they do not make decisions, they are simply tools, like the crude weapons they wield." Gravlox spent a long moment digesting the profound words.

"What have I done to so offend the Mistress of the Mountain? I never wanted to be cast out from her favor..." Gravlox let his head fall, staring into the dried blood beneath him, sorrow stamped clearly on his face.

Yael shook his head. "You were not cast out by our mother,

never that," he reached a hand out to Gravlox's shoulder, trying to comfort the troubled goblin. "The well of magic that resides inside you is limitless. It is too powerful for even Lady Scrapple to hope to comprehend. Her psionic magic has no hold over you. You, foreman Gravlox, are the first goblin that is truly free. No part of your will is bound to that of our common creator." Yael stood, returning to help the injured Vorst as her mind returned to her corporeal body.

Gravlox gazed into his hands, clenching his fists and trying to call upon the energy within him. The shamanistic power was unresponsive. "Your friend here is a high ranking associate of the Ministry of Assassination," Yael said as he checked the bandage on Vorst's side. "She was assigned to keep tabs on you, reporting your life to Lady Scrapple, and to kill you if the need arose. Clearly, that need has not yet arisen." Yael was gathering his warband together, calling the mindless soldiers to his side.

"What am I to do?" Gravlox asked, still looking at his hands more than anything.

"Lady Scrapple wishes you to head south. A very tentative alliance has been formed between the goblins and a powerful, ancient necromancer. Go to Reikall, that is where you will find him. I cannot guarantee your safety though, for the robed man you captured and killed earlier was the necromancer's son, sent to be a spy among the humans." Yael drew his sword as he spoke, tossing it to the ground at Gravlox's feet. "You may need a new weapon when you get to Reikall. Try to salvage what alliance you can with the necromancer. We need him. Lady Scrapple needs him. All goblins need him. For whatever reason, our mother determined that Vorst's life was worth more than the life of the necromancer's son and possibly the alliance."

Gravlox could hardly believe the words he was hearing. Yael started to march his warband out of the small clearing, leaving the looted remnants of the human squad scattered about the grass and upturned dirt. "I will use these drones to keep the humans busy.

This necromancer with which Lady Scrapple has entangled us captured the human's leader, their beloved King Lucius. We cannot be sure what will become of him, especially now, but war is brewing between our races."

Vorst was sitting up by then, looking at Gravlox, trying to gauge his reaction. "We are the children of fire, the heroes born of the sacred mountain," she said, her voice small and riddled with pain. "Will you rise to the challenge, Grav? Will you travel through the immense forest to the far away kingdom of Reikall with me?"

"*Limitless*," Gravlox muttered, nodding his head.

Seven

IN A DARK cave a hundred feet below the elaborate guild house, Keturah waited impatiently. Her delicate foot tapped, the sole of her slipper rapidly clicking against the wet stone of the chamber. The cave was completely lightless, a black dome devoid of torches at the very depths of the extensive cave system beneath all of Talonrend.

Keturah's footfalls echoed off the walls of the empty cavern, a hollow sound accompanied by the slow dripping of water somewhere in the distance. The woman paced back and forth, her gloved hands running through her long hair. A delicate lace band was wrapped tightly about her head, fully covering the woman's lovely green eyes. The thin white fabric, commonly referred to as moon-lace, illuminated the sight of the wearer so long as the darkness itself was not magically imbued.

The tall guild master used her magically enhanced vision to look about the cavern, trying to discern the slightest ripple in the air that would indicate the arrival of her overdue guest. At the back of the chamber, the stagnant air finally began to shimmer and swirl. Keturah walked quickly to the spot, enacting a minor enchantment to protect herself from the heat of the teleportation.

The air began to split as if invisible hands were pulling it apart like a thick curtain. A tiny scarlet bead of magical energy appeared on the floor and slowly rose toward the ceiling. The orb passed through the air with a crackle, surrounding Keturah with magical heat.

As the portal opened, it offered a stunning view of the other side. The portal connected to the top of a high castle tower, far to the south. The panoramic view of the wasteland beneath the stone tower was breathtaking. Plumes of acrid smoke danced with the charred rain of brimstone and hellfire that covered the kingdom of Reikall. Burnt frames of farmhouses and stables dotted the country-side like lonely tombstones standing guard in an empty cemetery. The smoke billowing up from great fissures in the ground was laced with toxic poison, suffocating what little flora remained in the dead kingdom.

A man walked into view of the portal, dressed in simple cloth-ing with a heavy cloth bandana covering his mouth. With a smile, Keturah reached her hand through the red portal, welcoming the tingling sensation of spatial dislocation that shocked her body. The man on top of the tower touched her own, using it to balance him-self as he took a small step that moved him over a hundred miles in a heartbeat. The portal stayed open, continuing to swirl and shim-mer in the dark air of the cavern, displaying a constant background of fiery carnage.

"Well met, fair sister Keturah," the man said with a grin.

"You're late, brother," was all that Keturah said in response. Her scowl showed clearly how little she tolerated tardiness.

"How fares our intrigue with the crown?" the man asked, try-ing his best to ignore Keturah's frown.

"Darius is a persistent bastard," Keturah sneered with a shake of her head. "I had to show him our goblin associates outside of Cobblestreet. He only sent one man to find the king, some long for-gotten paladin. I have Taurnil out as well, a more capable hero by far."

"You showed him the goblins, the ones who killed my son? I will flay the skin from their bones myself if I ever see those two." He spat as he spoke, wondering how a pair of goblins could have killed his own child; even a fledgling magician should have been able to deal with a pair of goblin scouts. "No matter, I have other sons. Any child of mine who cannot defend himself against two goblins is not worthy to inherit the kingdom I am building. How much did you tell Darius? I always believed our plan to rely on the element of surprise, a unified strike to quickly overwhelm the city."

Keturah wondered in the back of her mind just how much the ties of family meant to her brother. "I haven't spoken to the goblins in some time, but I believe they will understand this latest development. The plan has changed slightly, not in concept but perhaps in timing. If I can instill enough fear in Herod, he will issue a call to arms and send forth the army. With the Vrysinoch Guard deployed to the field against our goblin allies, your own army will meet little resistance inside the city. Darius' tenacity might work in our favor, dear brother."

"I have never liked that little whelp. He goes on and on about honor and valor, things that have no place in the proper scheme of leadership. The king should be the most powerful man in the realm, not just the one lucky enough to have been born a prince."

"Or the most powerful woman, brother," Keturah laughed. "Do not forget our agreement. Reikall is yours, as it already is. Talonrend will bend its weary knees to me. I wish to rule over a kingdom of living subjects, not a scarred land of mindless undead." Keturah let her gaze fall again on the ruin of Reikall visible through the rippling portal. Something about all that fire and sulfur *was* appealing, she thought, picturing Talonrend suffering from equal destruction.

As if reading her thoughts, the tyrant of Reikall smiled. "Yes, the intoxicating aroma of death appeals to everyone, whether they admit it or not. So, if we can get the goblins to assemble an army in the field, we are certain that Darius will send the Vrysinoch Guard to meet it? I like the sound of that plan. You always find ways to please me, sister."

"Yes, well, the only problem remains with Herod. No matter how much Darius begs the king to dispatch the army, Herod will likely wait, evacuating the villages along the Clawflow to the safety of his high walls. The prince will not assume the throne until he sees his brother's bloody corpse. According to the priests, only the rightful king can dispatch the holy army of Vrysinoch. Our prince is so weak that he would never go against the priests lest he lose favor with the city. We can prevent Herod from evacuating the villages by downplaying the goblin presence. With any luck, we can force Herod to move the army out of the city when our own machinations have come to fruition."

"Yes, Herod is a tricky one. He will not produce an heir of his own and he will not sit on that damned seat himself. I have been trying for months to get him or anyone to claim himself as king. Without a king, the army will never leave the city. If he recalls the villagers and does not meet the goblin army head on, our plan may fail. Now that Darius has seen our little friends, he will surely begin to ready the city's own defenses. I do not want to waste a hundred thousand of my soldiers just to get ten of them over the walls." The man's tone was stern, leaving no room for debate on the topic.

"I understand, brother," Keturah said, her eyes still scanning the destruction of Reikall. "We will not move until every piece is precisely in place. Taurnil should have no trouble dispatching the two goblin scouts, which will ease the fears of the villagers. Once they are pacified, I will have the goblin army move from their mountain lair and march north, assembling quickly in the field, a force that will demand the entire attention of Talonrend. With the villagers so vulnerable, Herod will have no choice but to move the Vrysinoch Guard out of the city, whether he has the approval of the priests or not."

"It would certainly be easier if Herod would just accept that fact that he is the king. If that were the case, the priests would demand that he send the army to war, not prevent it." He let out a long sigh, frustrated that the tenacious guard captain was impeding his plan. I trust that you have already instructed Taurnil to kill the paladin that is at this moment heading for my borders?"

"Why certainly, brother," Keturah responded, the ghostly echo behind her voice filling the dark chamber with confident laughter. "That poor paladin is likely lying dead in the field at this very moment."

"Good," the man said with a nod, "I don't want anyone wandering into my kingdom uninvited."

Keturah noticed a fresh spray of blood on her brother's shirt and harrumphed. "You've been recruiting more troops, I take it?" she said, pointing out the small splatter. "You warlocks use such barbaric methods of coercion."

The man smiled, inspecting the blood stain. "How many times have I told you, Keturah? I am no simple warlock. A warlock is but an average wizard who prefers a darker taint on his magic. A powerful necromancer such as myself creates the very essence of undeath. I have an entire kingdom of perfectly obedient undead thralls at my command!" He lifted his hands above his head, sending a narrow bolt of dark grey fire leaping from one open palm to the other. The small ball of energy congealed in his left hand, slowly taking the shape of an eyeless creature about the size of a dog with long, black claws like a jungle cat and festering wounds covering its hide.

Yawning, the beast took life, moving its sightless head about the air, its jagged teeth dripping with black saliva. In one fluid motion, the necromancer broke the beast in half, releasing a wave of magical energy much larger than the one that had created it. With a snap of his finger, Keturah's brother absorbed the energy into his hands, leaving no evidence that the small creature ever existed.

"Power begets power," he said with a grin.

Keturah could only watch then as he stepped back through the portal and left. The cave darkened as the portal closed, leaving her standing in the dark. "Goodbye, Jan," she said as she began the spell that would return her to her chambers in the guild hall above.

LATER THAT DAY, just after nightfall, Darius sat behind his large desk in the center of the barracks that housed the Talonrend city guards. His familiar sword sat on the desk next to a stack of leather bound books, one of which was opened to a list of names. Candles and torches hung on wall sconces around the stone room but Darius was alone.

"I cannot bother the prince with this goblin nonsense until I am sure it is more than just a simple pair of creatures sent to scout," he mused aloud. He had been sitting behind the desk since dawn, looking through ledgers that were filled with the names and ranks of each soldier serving in the guard. Another book, much smaller than the one open before him, held the identities of all the guards that had attended the king on his journey.

"There is too much coincidence here..." he pushed through more pages, running his fingers over the names. "Why would two lone goblins appear outside the city where the king disappeared?" Darius mindlessly flipped his feather pen into the air, trying to play it all out in his head.

A cricket began to chirp somewhere in the room, breaking the man's concentration. "Someone has to be cooperating with either the goblins or whatever kidnapped the king! Goblins do not target royalty and they certainly do not hold hostages for ransom!" he yelled, more to hear himself say it than for any real gain. Darius had been thinking that very thought since the moment Keturah had shown the goblins to him.

It can't be the goblins, they are too dim-witted to formulate complex plans with other races, Darius thought, tossing his weighted pen from

87

one hand to the other as he stared into the flames of the candle on his desk.

The guard captain scanned through the names on the page for what felt like the hundredth time that hour. "Someone has to be on the inside, someone! Kings do not simply vanish and goblins do not simply appear *when* kings vanish." Darius knew every name on the list of guards personally. He had recruited each and every soldier himself. As far as he knew, they were men loyal to the throne to their last breath.

"Maybe it was just a simple coincidence..." Darius said, closing the book with a thud. "Maybe these two goblins got lost or separated from their tribe and wandered near the village." Darius knew in the back of his mind that a mere coincidence was not the case. He regretted not taking more action when the king had first gone missing.

The guard captain had sent a search party out, of course, but no word has been heard from them either. *I should have sent runners to every single village, sent a dozen search parties in every direction. This all could have been avoided.*

He spun his sword around idly on his desk as he thought. *Where would the king have gone? Why would he leave his caravan?* Not paying much attention to his actions, the tip of Darius' short sword bumped into his inkwell, knocking it to the floor where it shattered.

"Ugh..." Darius mumbled as he bent over to collect the broken glass. It wasn't the first time he had knocked over an inkwell.

His hands full of inky, black glass, it took the man a moment to notice that the stones of the floor were stained with some other than his mess. Blood was dripping onto the hard rock just a few feet from where the inkwell had shattered.

"What on earth..." his voice trailed off as his gaze locked on the growing pool of crimson blood. Slowly, his eyes followed the dripping up to the high stone ceiling of the barracks. "Lieutenant!" he barked, hoping that someone would hear him and come to his aid. "Guards!" he shouted, unable to take his eyes from the black pool of shadows on the ceiling. "Anyone!" came the final ring of his panicked voice.

Darius crouched on the floor by his desk, his hands covered in ink and broken glass, and knew that he was about to die. The tight collection of shadows on the ceiling was darker than it should have been, darker than the darkest night Darius had ever seen. His jaw tightened. His stomach tensed.

Slowly, the shadows began to move. Darius stood and reached for his sword, bits of glass biting into his hand as they were crushed against the hilt. He lifted the weapon in front of his chest and set his feet solidly underneath him. Fear rattled his mind and confused his senses.

Two ragged wings stretched forth from the abyssal darkness. Blood dripped from vicious wounds the beast had recently received. Its powerful claws dug into the stone, holding his body firm as it turned its head to glare at the man.

"Taurnil," Darius said, defiantly. He locked stares with the awful creature. His own blood began to run down his arm from the shards of glass tearing open his flesh.

"Darius," the monster hissed back at him. Taurnil's mouth was full of jagged teeth and his three long tongues licked the air with anticipation.

"This is where it ends," Darius said with a slight moment of resolve. "At least now I know what happened to my king. I welcome this reaping, that I may join Lucius in Vrysinoch's paradise." His eyes never left Taurnil's black orbs as the winged demon let go of the ceiling and charged.

The ragged wings beat the air with ferocity, blowing loose sheaves of paper from the desk onto the floor. Darius tried to mount a valiant last defense, but he was quickly overwhelmed. The strong beast held every advantage and Darius' feeble sword was easily slapped from his grip. Black ink splattered the demon's face, only adding to the terror the pale monster evoked.

Three tongues latched onto the captain's forehead and face, oozing vile poison into the man's body. Darius struggled under the powerful grip of the monster, trying to get enough room to stab. His struggle was brief. The poison coursed through his veins, turning his innards to nothing more than smoldering ash. Darius' body shuddered twice and then went limp in Taurnil's arms.

One scything sweep of his massive claw severed the captain's head from his shoulders. The bloody captain hit the stone floor in two pieces with a wet thud, like a thick leather boot being pulled out of mud.

Taurnil took a step back before letting the rest of the body slide from his powerful arms. The beast smiled. He walked to the head, staring at it for a long while before bending down and lifting the bloody lump from the stone. "So this is what an honorable man looks like," Taurnil hissed, inspecting the disembodied head.

He kicked Darius' sword across the room where it clanged against the wall. "I fight without your useless steel, without your cowardly armor, and yet I have never fallen to a human in single combat." Taurnil turned the head over in his hands, inspecting every inch of it. "Perhaps it is not tools your species lacks, but courage."

Taurnil remembered the two goblins that had bested him at Cobblestreet. "That goblin loved its companion and would have gladly sacrificed itself for another," he said to the head, looking again into Darius' dead eyes. With a smirk, Taurnil nudged the bloody corpse with his naked foot.

"No," he hissed through a smile of jagged teeth, "I have never been weak enough to feel such primal emotion. That is not what makes someone strong. True power can only come from the abyss, and I am its chosen avatar, the singular paragon of might in this world and all others." Taurnil lifted off from the stone floor and exited the barracks through a broken window set high in the stone.

The beast met its master in the dark of night behind the artificer's guild hall. Casually, Taurnil tossed the head to the ground at

Keturah's feet like he was throwing a coin to a beggar. "Behold your captain," he hissed.

"Rally around his feet," she responded with a chuckle, "or perhaps just his head."

Eight

YOU WILL NEVER be king. You will never sit upon your brother's throne. Your fate is not in this kingdom. Your destiny has been written elsewhere. You will never be king.

Herod awoke in the middle of the night with cold sweat covering his brow. Vrysinoch would not let him find rest. The castle was quiet. Shadows danced along the walls from the few torches that still burned low. The prince stood and pulled his robe tight about his chest to ward off the cold night air.

He pulled a torch from the wall and started to leave the bedchamber before turning for his sword belt. Herod often went for walks about the castle at night but the hairs standing on the back of his neck told him to go armed. His sweaty hands rubbed the remaining sleep from his eyes and he strapped his sword to his left hip, a matching dagger to his right.

The prince of Talonrend did not know exactly where he was going, but he left his room nonetheless, locking the heavy wooden door behind him. He walked down the short hallway that connected his personal quarters to the throne room and stood in front of the empty chair that had consumed his life.

In the dim, scattered torchlight of the airy castle, the throne's green cushions danced with life. It was an immense chair, carved from the very stone of the castle and much wider than any of the kings who had ever sat upon it. The back displayed a pattern of wings, an interlocking design resembling the tower in the city's center.

"Why do you torment me, Vrysinoch?" Herod asked the empty throne. The prince's fingers slowly traced the great talon that protruded from the arm of the chair, its claws clutching an old white skull. "The priests in the tower tell me that you are a good god, providing for all of my needs, protecting me when I am weak." The emerald placed in the skull's eye socket was cold to the touch.

"Why can I not find peace and rest? Why do you torment me?" Herod drew his sword and pointed it right at the center of the throne. His glare and threatening posture challenged Vrysinoch. "If you weren't made from the very stone of the floor I would throw you in the moat myself." Herod spun his sword around in his hand and slid it back into the scabbard at his hip. The sound of the metal ringing against his leather sheath echoed in the empty chamber.

Herod turned from the throne swiftly, his robe fanning out behind him. He stormed to the door with a great scowl stamped on his royal face. The prince had never left the castle in the dead of night before, at least not without a formal guard and good reason. The heavy wood and iron doors were locked. Herod took a step back, thinking to simply return to his room or perhaps walk about the parapet, but a thought struck him and he turned back to the door.

Reaching inside a deep pocket on his robe he produced the key to his personal chamber. Without thinking about it, he pushed the key into the iron lock on the door and turned it. A subtle clicking sound accompanied the opening of the door. He felt the cool breeze of the night air brush against his cheek and heard footsteps coming from the drawbridge. Herod drew both of his weapons and pushed the door open quietly, standing in the entryway with visible defiance.

A huddled figure hurriedly moved to the castle. Whoever it

was, they hadn't noticed Herod, likely absorbed in their own thoughts. The prince stepped quickly to the side and closed the heavy door behind him, waiting in the shadows of the parapet for the person to approach.

Herod exhaled a long breath, steadying his nerves and calming the rise and fall of his chest. The prince was a seasoned warrior, a veteran of many hunting skirmishes with beasts in the wild. He waited, watching every step of his foe before springing into action. Like a cat leaping upon an unsuspecting field mouse, Herod launched his body into action. The muscular prince quickly overpowered his prey, knocking the man to the ground.

Sentries on the parapet above heard the commotion and began shouting. Herod wrestled the smaller man to his back in moment, the point of his dagger coming to rest right beneath the fool's chin. The prince's sword hovered just over the man's scalp, both weapons poised for an easy kill.

"Jan..." came the exasperated and surprised voice of the prince as he untangled himself from the king's steward. "What in Vrysinoch's name are you doing out here?"

The terrified man picked himself up, dusting his robes off and collecting his thoughts. "My apologies, my liege. I did not mean to frighten you," he said as Herod replaced the weapons in their sheaths.

"And why are you outside at this hour? Why are you awake?" Herod scrutinized the man's appearance trying in vain to find anything out of place.

"Well, sir, I may live in the castle but I do not spend every single moment of my time in it. I was out in the city on personal business." Jan began to walk into the castle, leaving Herod standing in front of the doors with a confused expression on his face.

"I could have killed you," the prince called to the steward.

"Yes, my prince, I am well aware," Jan smiled, showing no signs of fatigue for the late hour. "I am glad you chose not to."

Herod nodded and took a few steps away from the castle doors to stand on the wooden drawbridge. The man stood there, leaning on one of the drawbridge's heavy chains, and stared into the calm water of the moat below. None of the ducks that often floated atop the water could be seen.

Something in the back of Herod's mind told him to be worried. He fumbled through the pocket of his robe and pulled out the metal key to his bedchamber.

"The key to my personal quarters is the same key that opened the front door to the castle..." Herod turned on his heels and moved swiftly to the castle doors, testing the key again. Sure enough, the key turned easily in the lock and the door opened on its heavy hinges.

"I knew I should have never trusted that one..." Herod returned the key to his pocket and took a step back, looking up to the sentries on the parapet above.

"Where can I find a locksmith?" he called to them, barely making out their faces in the dancing torchlight.

"There is an armorsmith that makes doors and chests just right down the road, not far at all, the building with the red roof," the drowsy sentry pointed toward a huge structure that towered over the other buildings in the area.

"Yes, I know the place well," the prince shouted back to the sentry. "Master Brenning, the head smith of that forge, crafted my armor for me. I did not know he made locks." Herod began walking toward the smith's shop, his hand subconsciously fondling the top of the metal key inside his pocket. "If Jan comes back out of the castle before dawn, shoot him down and then come get me." Herod's expression was as solid as a statue. The two sentries on the parapet did not question his order. "I want to know every time that man leaves the castle and when he returns. Someone find Darius for me, go wake him and send him to Master Brenning, I need to speak with him at once." Herod walked from the castle with a quick burst of energy filling his step, his robes fanning out behind him.

Master Brenning's forge, Dragon's Breath Armory, was a colossal business. The burly armorsmith employed a score or more of the city's best weapon and armor crafters. Herod arrived at the door to the business and found it unlocked. Two of the four stone chimneys were billowing thick black smoke into the night air.

The ring of metal against metal and a stinging burst of heat greeted the prince as he entered the busy forge. Even in the dead of night, a few smiths stood at their anvils and forges practicing their art. The fires at each of the stations bathed the room in a soft orange light, shadows growing and dying on every wall as the artisans moved.

None of the smiths took notice of Herod's entry and the prince moved quickly to the staircase at the back of the room. Master Brenning worked on the top floor of Dragon's Breath Armory by himself. Herod passed by the second floor, a space that served as a storage area for raw materials, and arrived in front of a heavy steel door that barred entry into the highest level. The prince knocked on the door sharply and waited a few moments before a small hatch on the metal surface opened.

Master Brenning's bearded face filled the tiny portal like a grizzly bear peering into a pot of honey. With a gruff nod the master smith opened the entire door and stood aside as Herod walked into his chambers. The room was sweltering from the heat of the active forges below but no fire burned within the room save one lonely candle held in the smith's right hand. Master Brenning hadn't bothered to put the candle on a tray; rather, he held it and let the hot wax drip onto his bare hand. If it bothered him in the least, he didn't show it.

"Your captain of guards allows you to wander the streets of Talonrend without armor or escort?" The gruff man was covered in a thick mane of curly black hair that barely revealed his mouth when he spoke.

"Master Brenning," Herod said, clapping the strong smith on the shoulder. "Long ago you taught me that not every protection is visible in the form of a steel breastplate or an armed man at my side." The two men sat down at a small wooden table next to the smith's tiny cot against the far wall of the room. Remnants of the smith's uneaten dinner were still strewn about the surface.

Master Brenning used the lit nub of a candle to light a candelabra on his table before extinguishing the nub in the palm of his hand with a grunt. "Something must be troubling you greatly. Princes do not simply knock on my door in the middle of the night. What's on your mind, Herod?" Master Brenning spoke in a monotone base that sounded vaguely of a wagon wheel rolling over a bed of crushed rocks.

Herod placed the key from his pocket on the table between them and slid it over to the smith. "I need to know who made this key." Master Brenning didn't even bother to pick the thing up before asserting that it was not his work.

"I haven't made keys since I was an apprentice, before you were born, I would bet." Brenning's eyes never left the prince. "What does this key unlock?"

"It is the key to my personal chambers," Herod replied, taking the key back and holding it in front of the candle flames. "It also unlocks the main castle doors, as I learned tonight."

The smith's eyes closed for a moment as he digested the words. "Where is your escort? As the last living heir to the throne, you should be guarded at all times."

Herod's fist slammed into the tabletop. "Lucius will return! He is not dead!" the prince shouted in a brief outburst of rage. "I am not the king... I will never be king..." The prince hung his head, his thoughts fixated on his brother.

"It is the castle steward that holds a copy of this key, is it not?" Master Brenning acted as though the prince's outburst was nothing more than a passing gust of wind.

"King Lucius' steward, not mine. Darius, the guard captain, serves as my personal assistant, not that I have ever found much need for him in that capacity. What business does that conniving little man have in keeping a key to my personal chambers?" Herod tried to recall in his mind if he had ever noticed anything amiss in his chamber.

"You cannot trust that coward. I would suggest that you have your man Darius arrest him at once. It was a clever disguise, changing your lock instead of carrying two keys." Master Brenning took a tankard of warm ale from the table and finished it in one long draught.

"I know, I rarely leave the castle when the door is locked, I have no idea how long he has had access to my room."

"So," the bearded smith said as he wiped the foaming ale from his mouth, "I assume that you came to me for a new lock on your door. I would suggest perhaps a new piece of armor as well. You have enemies here, Herod." The burly man looked around the room nervously. "Especially since the disappearance of your brother. The whole city is on edge, most of them wondering when you will become their king."

Herod sneered, anticipating the voice of Vrysinoch in his head. He knew every word that the winged god would say to him. "I cannot become king. Not until I see my brother's corpse will I even consider it." The prince shook his head. "You make the armor for the tower's paladins, what are the priests saying about our situation? Have you heard any rumors there?"

Master Brenning laughed, a great booming sound that shook the small table. "The priests are always talking, Herod. You should know better than anyone about that. The priests and clerics in the tower don't respect you at all. The people may love you and love for you to be their king, but the holy men would never allow it."

"You tell me nothing that I do not already know." Herod stood, wanting to leave the hot room. "Can you make me a new lock by tomorrow? You said something about new armor as well. If it fits under my tabard, I'll take it." Master Brenning nodded with excitement.

"Hey, rumor at the forge is that you sent one of my assistants to go fetch your brother!" Brenning was up and about, rummaging through his cupboards for more ale, no doubt.

Herod stopped and scratched his head, not sure at first what the old smith was even talking about. "Gideon?" he asked, remembering the warrior's name.

"The very same!" Master Brenning found what he was looking for, a large silver horn filled with frothy dark beer. He took a healthy swig before continuing. "He was one of my best. He helped me build things that most smiths can only dream about. That one is strong, he will find your king if there is anything left of him to be found."

Herod watched in amazement as Master Brenning finished his ale and moved to put on his heavy leather apron, wasting no time getting to work. The prince left the hairy man's chamber and continued out of the building. He was just past the front door when he realized that Darius had not found him yet.

The prince made his way quickly to the barracks where Darius worked. One of the sentries from atop the castle parapet was standing in front of the large wooden door that blocked the entrance to the barracks.

"Prince Herod," the man called out, tipping his helmet as he spoke. "We have not located the guard captain yet. He was not in the barracks and there are no signs of a struggle within. It seems he is simply out and about this night."

Herod shook his head. "Alright," he said, saluting the soldier. "Notify me the moment he appears. I must speak with him."

The guard nodded. "I sent two soldiers out into the town to look for him but it is unlikely that they will find him tonight. He will show up in the morning and I will send him to you personally, sir."

The prince liked this soldier. For some reason, Herod felt like the man could be trusted. That feeling of trust was quickly soured by the growing knot of fear in Herod's stomach. It was unlike Darius to vanish without having told anyone where he could be found or when he would return.

Nine

G RAVLOX AND VORST left Yael and his band of goblins with fresh supplies, heading south toward Reikall. Despite the goblin's best efforts, Vorst still needed time to let her body recover from the battle with Taurnil. The two adventurers made slow progress through the thick forest that bordered the river. Gravlox, intently focused on helping the wounded female clutching to his side for support, failed to notice the paladin and his dark companion shadowing the goblin's every move.

The beating of leathery wings often heralded Taurnil's arrival. No rush of air accompanied the thin red portal that rippled through the light of dawn next to Gideon. The alert paladin was on his feet in a moment, a throwing axe instantly in his strong hand. He took several steps away from the portal and pulled his arm back to throw. A scantily clad female leg slipped through the portal, slowly testing the ground, before two gloved hands appeared and widened the shimmering red crease of magic.

Gideon's arm lowered just slightly as the full form of Keturah stepped through the magical portal. The soft glow of dawn played with her red hair, causing it to shimmer, a color somewhere between the deep hues of golden wheat and the slick crimson shine of fresh blood.

Seeing the axe poised to fly at her head, Keturah quickly held up a hand. "Wait!" she called to the warrior, closing the portal behind her with a flick of her delicate wrist. "I am a friend." Keturah tried to assume the friendliest pose she could, a stance that the seasoned paladin interpreted as ill-intentioned seduction.

Gideon grinned, knowing that his target was too close to dodge and completely devoid of armor in her sheer red dress. The axe spun from his hand with expert precision. Keturah's eyes went wide with surprise. In a flurry of red she spun as the axe neared her face, catching the wooden handle as it passed her vision.

The beautiful woman plucked the flying axe out of the air and completed her spin, using her own momentum to toss the axe back at Gideon's feet. "Is that how you greet all women?" The spin maneuver had kicked some dust up onto the bottom of her elegant dress, something the woman quickly fixed. "It is no wonder that most of you brutish warrior types don't breed. Or does the tower require that all paladins be celibate?" Keturah smirked and stood straight, watching the confused expression on Gideon's face.

The warrior's muscled arm reached to the hilt of his sword, the familiar leather and steel giving him comfort. "Darius, the captain of the guard sent me!" the woman shouted, tired of defending herself and not wanting the man to waste any energy.

Gideon's hand stayed on the hilt of his sword and his gaze bore into the woman relentlessly. "Gideon, I'm not here to hurt you!" Keturah said, holding her arms out wide for the man's inspection.

The paladin took his hand from the weapon on his back and picked his throwing axe up from the ground. "Who are you and why have you come to me?" Gideon resolved not to charge the woman where she stood, partly because she knew his name and partly because she should not have been able to avoid his axe. It was a perfect throw and the ease with which she had denied it frightened the paladin greatly.

"My name is Keturah," the mysterious woman replied. She

placed a delicate hand into a seamless pocket on her flowing gown. "Darius wants me to help you find the king. Although I cannot personally join you on your quest, I have someone who might help." She withdrew her hand from the pocket and revealed a jet black scorpion that skittered around her glove.

Placing the creature on the ground, Keturah whispered to it, summoning Taurnil. The demon was somewhat dwarfed by the hulking paladin, standing between the two humans and flexing its healed wings.

For the first time in his life, Gideon thought he was about to die. The sinewy creature before him assaulted every divine sensibility the paladin had. He could smell the stink of the abyss washing the area in a foul haze.

"Begone, demon," Gideon growled under his breath, feeling the holy energy of Vrysinoch filling his body. The symbol on his back flared to life in the presence of such a foul creature.

"Do not worry, paladin," Keturah said sharply. "Taurnil lives in the abyss, yes, but he is not a denizen of that place. I created him, I control him." Taurnil turned his head just slightly to look over his shoulder at the woman, his three tongues moving eerily around his pale lips. "We have reason to believe that the goblins are behind the disappearance of the king," she continued, moving to the beast's side and placing a hand on his shoulder. "Two of them were spotted on the other side of the river and have escaped."

"So I heard," was Gideon's gruff response. "I spent the entire day yesterday talking to the village, gathering information. I also heard a rumor that your pet couldn't even handle two puny goblins, even with support from the militia." Gideon spat on the ground at Taurnil's feet, an open challenge. The beast spread his wings wide and hissed in return. Green acid flew from the creature's tongues and landed on the ground with a sizzle.

"These goblins aren't like anything we have ever encountered," Keturah answered. "One of them is a powerful shaman. Do not underestimate those two. They are heading south along the Clawflow, presumably toward Reikall. Follow them. Taurnil can scout from the air. Find out what you can, bring the king back if he still lives." Keturah didn't wait for a response before snapping her fingers and vanishing.

Taurnil and Gideon stood in the drowsy light of morning and stared at each other. The intensity of the paladin's eyes evaporated in the inky blackness of the pale demon's lightless orbs. Gideon looked away.

"The moment I sense your treachery, demon, I will not hesitate to cut you down." Gideon began walking toward the riverbank, heading south.

"I could kill you with a thought," Taurnil hissed back through his jagged maw. It was a lie, but one that Gideon had no way of knowing. Taurnil, a creature created from pure magical essence, could not use much magic himself. He had command over shadows and could manipulate light, but his arcane abilities were very limited beyond the realms of optical illusion.

"We will shadow these goblins, all the way to Reikall if we must. I will pursue from the eastern bank of the river, to protect the villages we pass." Gideon pointed toward the forest with his armored hand. "You will fly above the forest and track them. We meet up every night at dusk and every morning at dawn. You have the advantage of mobility, so I expect you to come and find me."

Taurnil was already a few feet above Gideon's head when the paladin finished speaking. He lowered his head and took off for the distant shore, wanting more than anything to find vengeance on the other side of the river.

Gideon shook his head, glad to be rid of the demonic beast for a while. His muscled body was warm in the morning sun and the gleaming steel covering his left arm reflected the summer brightly. Patches of brilliant white light danced about the man's leather boots as he walked.

The riverbank still wet with morning dew, the tall grasses rising up beyond the tall man's belted waist. Gideon crouched down low, trying to make out any signs of the goblin pair on the other side. No movement on the other riverbank betrayed the presence of enemies. Still holding his crouch, Gideon moved further south through the tall grasses, his body getting soaked by dew with every step. A large shadow darted among the tree tops on the other side, something Gideon could only hope was Taurnil.

Having no clear sign to follow other than the airborne demon, Gideon subtly made his way back from the edge of the Clawflow and took off in a jog, trying to match Taurnil's pace from a distance.

The small goblins were easy for Taurnil to spot. The demon was perched quietly in the upper boughs of a tree, waiting for the pair to move by underneath them. Green turned to brown and then to black on the leaves beneath the sinewy beast's ashen skin. The very presence of such evil tainted the living plants around him.

Gravlox came into view beneath the tree first, leading Vorst behind him. They were moving slowly, their pace diminished by the jagged gash on Vorst's hip. Taurnil looked down to the barb on the end of his leathery wing and smiled, remembering the hit that nearly impaled the goblin. The three humanoids were barely more than two miles south of Cobblestreet but it was clear that Vorst needed to rest her aching side.

Gravlox gingerly set the female goblin down against the base of the tree and took his travelling pack off. He produced some sort of food from the pack and fed it to his injured companion one piece at a time. Vorst's eyes slowly rolled back in her head as she ate and Taurnil quickly straightened his back and turned to put a thick branch between her vision and his skin. Taurnil was quick and Vorst was slightly delirious — she didn't notice the beast in the tree above her.

The goblin foreman sat down on the grass beside the female, letting go a long sigh. Vorst leaned her head to rest it on Gravlox's shoulder, a gesture that clearly unsettled the recipient. Gravlox put a tentative arm around Vorst's back and pulled her in close, trying his best to comfort the wounded goblin. Taurnil cocked his head to the side, having no way of comprehending the scene unfolding beneath him.

Keturah often placed her arms on the demon's back and shoulders much the way the two goblins did, but Taurnil did not know why. He always understood the gesture to be one of ownership and control, nothing more. Taurnil's mind raced, thinking back to the times when Keturah had touched him, wondering if there was any ulterior motive behind the woman's actions. The beast did not feel the pangs of physical attraction and was immune to all of the softer emotions that accompanied such feelings.

Inquisitively, Taurnil continued to stare down at the goblins from his high perch. The two goblins were speaking to each other in soft tones, a language that reminded Taurnil of the high-pitched wails of tormented souls in the abyss. The wounded goblin moved herself closer to her companion, nestling her head next to his. Even the emotionless beast in the tree could tell that Gravlox felt unnerved and cautious. Taurnil, sensing the trepidation underneath Gravlox's shaking hands, readied his wings for flight. He expected some sort of trick or other form of treachery aimed at himself or the male goblin. Everything felt like an elaborate trap, one that Taurnil had no way of anticipating.

The demon did not like feeling powerless.

Much to the surprise of both Taurnil and Gravlox, the wounded female goblin reached an arm up behind her companion's bald head and their lips met. The kiss lingered for what felt like an eternity to all three of them. Taurnil fully expected a dagger to flash up and rip the life from the male goblin. Why else would the wounded one have gotten so close to him if not to kill him? "Goblin, you are more a fool than I had thought, letting your guard down," Taurnil whispered past his jagged teeth. The three tongues within his maw writhed, playing out the beast's frustrated confusion.

Gravlox's hand grasped the rugged bark of the tree, supporting Vorst as their limbs became entangled. Something around the two goblins was different. The air became charged as though lightning had just struck the ground. The leaves on the ground swirled through the air, ever so slightly, dancing softly on the warm earth. Taurnil could feel the magic seeping from the goblin's hand and climbing up the tree. Leaves began to grow anew beneath the demon's feet.

It took a conscious effort for Taurnil not to lose his connection to the foul magic of the abyss, so strong was the energy washing over him through the tree branches. The emotion accompanying the pure magic was completely foreign to Taurnil, an exotic rush of heat that caused his wings to flex and his arms to tighten. He tried to conjure a wave of ethereal darkness around his feet, hoping to stem the flow of energy into his body, but no magic would obey his call. The abyss felt so far away, like a distant memory of a dream.

Miraculously, the seeping wound on Vorst's hip closed and the flesh knitted itself back together. Taurnil could only watch in bewilderment as the leaves around the pair swirled faster and faster. The beast closed his black eyes and tried to conjure forth a vivid image of his home in the maelstrom darkness of the abyss. Fleeting images of blackened evil approached the edges of his mind but Taurnil could not hold them.

Suddenly, as quickly as the warm energy had assaulted the demon, it retreated. Wave after wave of magic left the beast and coursed back through the bark and into Gravlox's hand. The goblins pulled away from each other and Vorst stood. The female goblin offered a hand to her mate and pulled him from the ground. The two of them continued to speak but Taurnil did not understand. Within a moment, Vorst had darted out of view with Gravlox fast on her heels.

Taurnil looked up at the sky, the strong summer sun stinging his soulless eyes. Acid pumped from his tongues and filled his mouth with bile, a familiar and comforting taste. Taurnil spat the glob of poison out, dissolving the nearest tree branch to toxic ash. He smiled, truly enjoying the decay that radiated from his corrupted body. The abyss called to Taurnil, filling his physical form and wrapping his mind in a cold embrace. His wings shot out, shredding the dying leaves and cutting through the branches as he thrashed. With the goblins out of sight, the abyss was alive inside him again.

Taurnil dropped to the ground with a thud, sending a cloud of dark grey ash into the air. "Yes," he bellowed, feeling the magical connection solidifying in the area of his being where a soul should have been. "These two are strong," he cackled, "but whatever magic connects them can be severed by the black claws of the abyss."

The monster clicked his sharp claws together and flexed. A wide smile covered his face as he leapt into the air and took flight.

GRAVLOX BREATHED HEAVILY, his chest rising and falling with the crunch of leaves and twigs under his naked feet. Vorst was always a few steps ahead of him, running with boundless energy. The two goblins had been moving at a frantic pace for the entire day, slowing only once to cross a small stream. Somehow the healing magic that Gravlox had called forth during their kiss had energized Vorst and brought a new lust for life into her step. Gravlox *thought* it was the result of magic, at least.

It wasn't until around midnight that their bodies started to tire and Vorst had to stop. Gravlox arrived at the creek where Vorst had stopped, a tributary of the mighty Clawflow, just a few steps behind her. Vorst was already floating on her back in the calm stream, casually splashing around with her delicate arms. Her travelling pack was resting on the mossy shore, along with the short leather pants that the female goblin always wore.

Gravlox quickly came to a halt and removed his own animal hide vest and studded skirt, tossing them to ground before jumping into the stream. The water was cool against his pale skin, making what little hair he had stand on end. Vorst swam over to him, splashing water on his face and jumping about. The stream wasn't deep, but there was plenty of water for Vorst to latch onto Gravlox's shoulders and dunk his head beneath the surface.

The taller goblin planted his strong feet on the slick pebbles of the streambed and pushed upwards, grabbing onto Vorst's legs and sending her vaulting skyward. The two goblins landed with a splash but came up quickly, locked in a kiss. A warm moment passed before Vorst pulled away.

"Um, Grav?" she said in a small voice, her eyes intently probing the surface of the water.

"Yeah, Vorst?" Gravlox was staring at her beautiful head, bald and gleaming with water. He loved when she whispered to him. Her voice sounded like the gentle hum of the stream around them, high-pitched and airy, full of life.

"When we get back to Kanebullar Mountain..." Vorst's voice trailed off but she lifted her head from the water and looked into Gravlox's eyes. "Will you live with me? We can find a new cave, a bigger one, and live together?" The smaller goblin was embarrassed as soon as she said it and pulled Gravlox in tight to avoid looking at him when he responded.

"I would love to do that, Vorst." He kissed her on the top of her head, pulling her in as tightly as possible. "Maybe we could even be married..." Gravlox could feel Vorst nodding slowly into his chest. Both of them smiled.

Marriage was a concept stolen from the human kingdoms and adapted to a goblin society that naturally devalued the family unit due to the inability for goblin pairs to reproduce. Rather than wearing wedding bands like the human corpses that goblins often looted after a raid, Lady Scrapple's progeny practiced a much more permanent symbol of union. Two goblins, after falling in love with one another, were expected to proclaim that love by cutting the pinky finger of their spouse's left hand off. The removal of the finger could never be undone or easily hidden. Everyone knew that a nine-fingered goblin was married. The pain associated with the ritual only served to solidify the bonds of love, a willing sacrifice between

109

two goblins.

After an attack on a human settlement or caravan, goblins would loot the bodies of the fallen soldiers, taking every scrap of metal they could, wedding bands included. The ease with which a human could hide his marriage from the world or have the evidence of such a bond stolen after death is what led goblins to design their own physical manifestation of marriage.

Vorst subconsciously rubbed the pinky of her left hand, running her fingertips over the knobby joint that signified her availability. "I would like that, Grav," she said, giving him another kiss.

The two goblins spent another moment together in the stream before climbing to the grass and collecting their belongings. Having no need for sleep, they simply slowed their pace to a casual walk in order for their bodies to recover, following the small stream to the south. The darkness of night was thick about the pair, muffling their footfalls and making the world disappear. They walked in silence, hand in hand, and listened to the calm sounds of the stream and forest.

After nightfall Gravlox spotted a small cave opening farther down the path that piqued his curiosity. His natural night-vision was enhanced by years of working in the dark mines of Kanebullar Mountain and allowed him a good view of the cave. The opening was a slight hole in the ground, partially covered by fallen branches and leaves. Putting a hand on Vorst's shoulder, Gravlox balanced himself and peered over the edge of the formation to get a better look.

"Looks like a cave vent, some sort of air passage to a larger chamber down below," Gravlox said, pushing the debris from the area. "Sometimes we drill chimneys like this in the ceilings of caverns so that air can move from chamber to chamber as the miners work," Gravlox explained.

"Is this a natural opening or something man-made?" Vorst got down on her belly, peering into the opening.

"It's hard to tell," Gravlox replied. He moved slowly about the hole on his hands and knees, using his weight to test the ground's stability. "Some animal probably lives down there and uses the opening to come out and hunt. Come on, Vorst, we should get going."

Gravlox reached a hand down and lifted Vorst from the ground. The female goblin jumped up and landed with a subtle thud that shifted the rocks beneath her feet. Gravlox took one step and, all of a sudden, the earth beneath their feet gave way. The small opening in the ground was instantly larger than both the small goblins combined, swallowing them in the blink of an eye.

Thinking quickly, Gravlox was able to wrap an arm around Vorst and the two slid down the falling cascade of stone together. The goblins were enveloped by the hail of small rocks and dirt and fell into a sloped chamber a dozen feet below the mossy surface of the forest floor. The slanted floor of the cavern was angled steeply, carrying the two goblins even further underground.

Gravlox was able to latch a hand around the base of a root protruding from the smooth stone but it gave way almost as quickly as he had touched it. A crumbling chunk of stony dirt hit Vorst in the shoulder, knocking her away from Gravlox. The goblins reached out to one another but there was nothing they could do. The slanted stone of the cavern acted as a natural slide, rushing the pair underground with mounting speed.

Despite the dirt in his eyes, Gravlox could make out the end of the slide in the dark cavern. The stone narrowed considerably, but with a natural partition separating him from Vorst. A similar taper existed a few feet below the falling form of Vorst. "Gravlox!" the terrified goblin called out through the sea of falling rock and dirt.

"Vorst! Take my hand!" Gravlox reached out and tried to find his falling companion but the stone partition between the two goblins was quickly approaching. He knew if he let his wrist hit the solid barrier, it would surely shatter. Gravlox closed his eyes and hoped for the best, crossing his arms over his chest as his feet went through the narrow gap in the cavern.

His head banged painfully off the stone ceiling and he shot through a nearly vertical tunnel. Stones pelted his head and chest but the sloped rock beneath him disappeared. Gravlox knew he was in free-fall.

Somewhere far beneath him, the shaman could hear the sounds of water flowing. His body slammed into a wall of solid limestone, scrambling his senses and boggling his mind. The world around the goblin spun in a dizzying haze of dark splotches that obscured his vision. Gravlox knew he was still falling but couldn't tell which direction. He was almost thankful when his bruised body finally came to a halt, face down in a very shallow pool of water.

Groggily, Gravlox managed to roll himself over. He wasn't sure if it was blood or cave water, but he coughed a stream of warm liquid out of his mouth and rubbed his eyes. A wave of sharp pain shot through his back as the battered goblin managed to bring himself to a sitting position. The cavern was huge, a large underground dome covered in slick moss and pale mushrooms.

He could see the opening in the ceiling above him, a small hole in the stone about thirty feet above his head. The sloped cavern he had first landed in was out of view, just a small pocket in the stone above the larger chamber. Following the route he had taken with his eyes, Gravlox traced out the likely path that Vorst had travelled. He knew that his beloved companion was in a different chamber but she could not have landed too far from him.

"There must be a tunnel that connects us," Gravlox mumbled as he got to his wobbly feet. The foreman drew his sword from the sheath at his hip, inspecting the weapon to ensure that it hadn't gotten damaged during his plummet. Luckily, it was intact and made a wonderful cane to support his bruised legs. Gravlox hobbled to the side of the chamber where he had fallen and tapped on the rock, hoping to hear a similar tapping from the other side to signify Vorst's presence.

Goblins, living in the dark chambers beneath Kanebullar Mountain, often communicated by tapping on the stone walls that

112

separated the various passages from one another. Deep in the mines, goblins had developed a sophisticated language of tapping and scraping that the rest of the goblin society was quick to adapt.

Are you alright? Gravlox tapped on the wall. *Can you breathe? Are you alive?* No tapping came back from the other side. *Vorst, are you alive?* Gravlox tapped faster on the wall, panic gripping him fully. He endured another excruciating moment of silence. Using the hilt of his sword, Gravlox tapped even harder on the wall, throwing what remained of his strength into every blow. *Vorst!* His sword hilt cried out on the stone. *Where are you? Are you alive?* A tear streaked down his dirty face and fell to the floor.

Gravlox, came the slow reply from the wall. The taps were faint, almost impossible to hear above the sound of the underground stream in the chamber. *I am alive.* Gravlox was so overcome with joy that he simply collapsed to the floor and cried. *Are you badly hurt?* Vorst asked, her taps coming with more strength than before.

No, Gravlox replied with his sword hilt. *Are you?* He feared what the response might be.

Nothing that won't heal, came her characteristic response. Gravlox could see her smiling on the other side of the stone, grinning from ear to ear at his worry. *Is there a stream on your side?* Gravlox searched the cavern, hoping that the stream went under the rocks and into Vorst's cavern.

Yes, he tapped out excitedly, scrambling for the edge of the water. He dunked his head in, trying to see where the water went. It was nearly impossible to tell with certainty, but Gravlox felt the water rushing as though it was moving under the stone wall and into another chamber. The opening was narrow, less than a foot in diameter, but it gave him hope. *I am going to try to swim to you,* Gravlox tapped out as he removed his pack.

He attached his sword belt to the rest of his travelling gear and then fixed a long length of rope to his ankle, the other end tightly tied to his equipment. *Be careful,* Vorst tapped on the other side of the stone, *I can hear something. I think there are footsteps coming from another cavern. They sound close, getting louder.* Gravlox didn't waste a moment.

The goblin dove down on his belly in the shallow stream, pushing himself along the cavern floor as flat as he could. Thankfully, the stream deepened where it met the stone wall and he was able to slide a hand under the ledge and pull himself down. His eyes grew wide with panic when he realized how far he would have to crawl before the stone above his head gave way to air. Gravlox rotated in the water, placing his hands above his head and clawing his way through the submerged passage.

He was wedged into the stone tightly, his face smashed against the rock above him, his back being cut by the rock beneath him. Without being able to turn his head, the goblin had no idea how far the tunnel would take him. *Hurry,* came the tapping, barely understandable to the underwater goblin. The warm water coursed past his body, moving much faster than Gravlox.

Panic gave way to sheer terror in a matter of moments. Gravlox's small lungs burned. It took every fiber of his will to keep from screaming in the narrow tunnel and filling his body with cave water. Frantically, Gravlox clawed and scraped at the stone, pulling himself along, inch by painful inch. *Hurry,* Vorst repeated. *Hurry, something is coming.*

Gravlox grit his teeth and tried to pull himself further along the tunnel but his hips were stuck. *Gravlox... Hurry.*

Eleven

"STILL NO REPORT from Darius, sir." The soldier was impeccably dressed, his fine mail armor betraying his inexperience. Herod preferred a warrior with a few dents in his shield. There was a long pause before anyone in the throne room spoke again.

"Alright. Thank you for the update." Herod stood before the throne on the raised dais, his body clad in heavy steel plates. Herod's twin longswords, Maelstrom and Regret, dangled on his hips, their sharp points hovering right above the stone. No one had seen the prince's famed weapons in years. Their very presence indicated the gravity of the situation. "What is your name, soldier?" Herod's deep voice boomed through the stone hall, echoing with a new-found air of command.

"Apollonius, my liege," replied the well kempt man, offering a rigid bow. "I live to serve the throne."

Herod smiled. His right hand moved to his left hip, slowly drawing Maelstrom from its golden sheath. "You serve the throne..." Herod muttered. The room full of soldiers stood on edge, silently awaiting the prince's action.

Prince Herod lifted the blood-red blade before him, holding it up for everyone in the room to see. With a simple thought, the sword burst into flame in his hands. The fire was not real, in the physical sense, but ethereal. Black, translucent flames licked up the red steel and sent a thick plume of ash swirling toward the ceiling.

Maelstrom swung down with the prince's arm, cutting a line of incorporeal fire through the air, and connected with the seat of the throne with a resounding thunder. The stone of the royal seat was torn asunder. A thin line of molten rock seeped from the edges of the laceration as the throne crumbled to ruins on the dais. A chorus of hushed gasps met the prince's rigid gaze as he turned back to the assembly before him.

"You say you serve the throne." Herod looked as many men in the eyes as he could, striking fear into their very souls. "I ask you now to serve your city. Talonrend needs you, not the throne. This is the hour of her greatest weakness." A priest standing off to the side of the assembly opened his mouth to speak but an upraised hand from the prince stopped him cold.

"All of you assembled in this hall, you are the city guard. I ask you now to protect your city, as you have sworn to do. Darius, your leader and my friend, has been killed. Treachery held the blade that took his life. I do not know who commands such treachery, but we will discover them, and we will kill them. Trust no one but myself, Master Brenning, and each other. Anyone approaching the castle without my consent is to be considered hostile."

Master Brenning stood near the priest to the prince's right. He was wearing the traditional armor and tabard of the royal guard, signifying him as Darius' replacement. The proud smith stood slightly taller at the mention of his name.

"You soldiers are no longer the city guard of Talonrend. I commission you now as Templars of Peace, ordered to protect the city at all costs. All those who do not wish to be a part of this order may throw down your arms and leave the castle unharmed. You will not be exiled from the city, but you may no longer serve in its guard. All those who wish to serve as guardians of the people,"

Herod lifted Maelstrom high above his head, ordering the weapon to extinguish its fire so that the sunlight streaming in from the windows glinted on its dark crimson edge, "kneel!"

Every man in the large audience hall kneeled at once, without hesitation. Every man except for one. The priest of Vrysinoch stood steadfast next to Master Brenning's kneeling form, locking eyes with the prince.

"Only a king has the power to commission such an order," the old priest spat. He turned to face the crowd of kneeling templars but none of the armed men even glanced at him.

"Our rightful king is missing, likely dead. Our guard captain is missing, likely dead as well." Herod pointed his red sword at the withered priest menacingly. "Who are you to say that a prince cannot protect his castle and his city?"

"I am a holy priest of Vrysinoch!" the man cried out. "You cannot take such actions without the approval of Vrysinoch! The tower does not approve! You are not our king!" The wrinkled old man stretched his hand out in the direction of the prince, pointing a crooked finger, a sneer plastered to his ugly face.

"I have been tormented by Vrysinoch for far too long," Herod said with solemnity as he lowered Maelstrom back to his side. "It is time for your god to truly protect you, priest." The words of damnation rolled off of Herod's tongue and left a sweet taste in his mouth. The prince slashed Maelstrom through the air in the direction of the priest who instinctively raised his hands to defend himself. Thirty feet of open air separated the two men but Maelstrom understood the prince's intent.

Ethereal tendrils of acrid black smoke shot forward from the tip of the sword, circling about each other wildly as they sped toward the priest. The black smoke materialized into six clutching hands that latched onto the priest from all directions. Herod held the sword steady, leveled at the old man's splotched forehead.

Master Brenning, the man who had made the sword, knew what was about to happen. He closed his eyes tightly and kneeled lower to the stone, making his body as small as possible. One sharp tug of Herod's wrist pulled the sword back across his body and stretched the ghastly tendrils taut. When the sword reached the end of its arc, the black hands receded to their origin, taking six bloody chunks of the priest with them and depositing the remains of the shattered priest at Herod's feet. Blood splattered Master Brenning's armor as the priest exploded in a rain of gore. The man never had the chance to scream.

"Vrysinoch is no longer your guardian," Herod called to the kneeling soldiers. "The paladins who serve the tower have not shown themselves. With the command of my brother, I doubt they will leave their tower, even when it comes to open warfare in the streets of Talonrend. You must protect each other now." A wave of his hand commanded the templars to rise and they obeyed in unison. "Apollonius!" Herod called to the soldier standing in the front row.

"Yes, sir!" the loyal man barked back.

"Go to the tower. Tell those cowards what has happened here." The eager soldier nodded. "If the priests refuse to summon the Vrysinoch Guard, kill them until one of the priests agrees." Apollonius nodded again, more solemnly. "The army is to be gathered at once, inside the walls. Every paladin, healer, warrior, and pit fighter is henceforth called to serve." Herod scanned the room and searched the men's faces for any signs of doubt. "Failure to heed that call is treason."

Satisfied that none of the murmurs were of dissent, Herod continued his rousing speech. "Send runners to each of the villages. The militia is also called to serve. Every city along the Clawflow is required to send thirty able-bodied men, with arms and armor if possible. Organize the militia outside the walls in camps." Herod turned to Master Brenning and offered the man a stiff salute. "See to it that the militia is properly equipped and well fed. I feel a war on the horizon."

The burly smith returned the salute with a grim smile.

Some minutes later, after much cheering and applauding from the gathered templars, Herod left the audience chamber and returned to his personal chambers. Master Brenning hurried along behind the inspired prince. The two men stopped in front of the brand new steel door that barred the way to Herod's personal chambers.

The heavy door was inscribed with enchanted runes, every line weaving a strong magic that protected the room beyond from unwanted visitors. Two similar doors had also been installed on the front of the castle and the drawbridge was being modified by Master Brenning's chief smiths.

Herod waved his hand in front of the steel and the runes glowed to life, unlocking with a series of metallic clicks. "Master Brenning," the prince said with a smile before stepping into his chambers, "you are a genius. This door will only admit myself, no one else?"

The hairy man nodded with excitement, strands of his thick beard flying about his face. "Your command will allow visitors to enter, but only those you name specifically. Your new armor also awaits you in your chamber," Master Brenning chimed in. "And it is always good to see my favorite swords being put to use. Maelstrom and Regret have hidden in their sheaths for far too long."

"I wish that you still made weapons of their caliber, Master Brenning." Herod thumbed the hilts of his magnificent swords with nothing but true appreciation showing on his face.

"Those two swords are my masterwork, Herod. After I crafted those weapons, I turned my focus to armor. I have only made one weapon since, but it wasn't a longsword."

Prince Herod took a hesitant step into his room, but turned back to face the smith. "Your last weapon was not a hand-and-a-half sword, honor-bound to a disgruntled paladin, was it?"

Master Brenning's deep laugh resonated through the stone halls. "Indeed, my prince." The smith's eyes took on a glossy sheen and he looked through Herod rather than at him. "Nevidal, the

119

sword is called. It simply means 'wonder', in the old language. Maelstrom and Regret may be the strongest paired weapons in the entire realm, but Nevidal is stronger still. Gideon could slay an entire army with that sword..."

Herod waited a moment before speaking, allowing the smith his moment of reverie. "Assuming that Gideon's own soul would not be destroyed in the process?" he asked.

"Yes," Master Brenning muttered, "there is that one small matter. Hopefully Gideon can learn to control the weapon before that happens. A blade like that is not something to be trifled with. In the hands of anyone else, it would reap nothing but disaster. The Blood Foundry can be a tricky forge, especially when it comes to weapons."

"Your sacred forge has never ceased to amaze me, Master Brenning. Your capabilities as a smith are only outshined by your undying loyalty." Prince Herod gave the man a rigid salute, showing him nothing but respect and friendship.

Master Brenning returned the gesture and spun on his heel to leave. As the new captain of the guard, Brenning had plenty of work to do around the castle. His smiths were almost finished installing new doors at the end of the drawbridge, enchanted plates of steel designed to keep out all forms of magical intrusion.

Brenning stood in front of the massive metal doors, staring at the parapet above. Two of his smiths were standing on the top of the stone wall, fitting an iron mount onto one of the crenellations so that a heavy ballista could be stationed there. With his mind's eye, Brenning imagined the new fortifications and defenses of Castle Talon. Ballistae lined the parapet, manned by seasoned soldiers of unflinching loyalty. The moat would be filled with large iron spikes rising up out of the water. Master Brenning imagined small catapults stationed near the castle's round towers, filled with loose sacks of caltrops that could be easily set on fire and launched onto the ground before the moat, slowing the assault of any army.

The smith's vision turned to the city itself. "All of these buildings will need to be removed," he whispered, not wanting anyone to hear. The row of houses and buildings closest to the castle were too close, Brenning thought. He could not see well past that first row and into the city proper. "Herod will not like that idea," he muttered, shaking his head. "But we need to have sight. A clear view of the enemy is the first step toward defeating the enemy, whoever that may turn out to be..."

"Sir!" a soldier behind Master Brenning called to him, interrupting the daydream. Brenning turned to see the man, a newly commissioned templar, standing on the top of the parapet with a crossbow in hand. The templar pointed and Brenning turned, drawing a short sword from his side in the process. The burly man was not a soldier by profession, but neither was he a novice to melee combat.

A man approached the drawbridge wearing a plain brown shirt with matching leather breeches, his head hung low in thought. "Fire at his feet and reload quickly," Master Brenning called to the templar. The man walking toward the castle was easily recognized by the smith as Jan. Apparently, the steward had not gotten wind of his exile from the castle. A heavy, steel tipped bolt thudded into the banded wood of the drawbridge, causing Jan to jerk back reflexively.

"Halt!" the templar called out from above. The clicking sound as the crossbow reloaded quickly followed the soldier's voice.

"What are you doing here, Jan?" Master Brenning took a step in front of the door, squaring off against the steward across the drawbridge.

"What in Vrysinoch's name is going on here?" Jan's eyes darted around the castle, examining the new fortifications and finally finding the stone cold stare of the burly smith. "I am the king's steward! Am I no longer permitted entry into the castle?" His tone was incredulous and spiteful.

"By order of the Sovereign Prince Herod, ruler of Talonrend and commander of both the Vrysinoch Guard and the Templars of

Peace, you are hereby exiled from Castle Talon and from Talonrend herself, on pain of death. You are under arrest and will be escorted outside of the city." Jan's jaw dropped and his legs began to noticeably tremble.

Have they found me out? Did Keturah turn on me? Tentatively, he took a step back. Master Brenning matched his movement and took a confident step forward onto the drawbridge, openly challenging the smaller man.

Brenning motioned with his hand and the templar fired a second bolt. Jan saw the deadly missile speeding toward his chest and reached a hand out to block it. Dark magic swirled about his wrist and formed into a solid buckler of necrotic energy that easily shattered the bolt and then dissipated. Jan turned and began to run.

"It seems you've been hiding a great many secrets, traitor!" Master Brenning yelled, taking off in pursuit of Jan. The smith's powerful legs closed the gap quickly but all it took for Jan to escape was a few lines of arcane summoning. A bright orange portal ripped through the air, crackling and popping with energy. Without a moment of hesitation, Jan leapt through the portal and began to close it behind him.

Reaching out through the portal and trying to grasp Jan's arm to pull him back, Brenning was sucked through the closing gateway with a pop. A strange tingling energy rippled through the smith's muscular back and vibrated his beard hairs. The sensation of falling gripped his chest and caused him to grit his teeth, expecting the worst. Master Brenning landed on cold stone with a heavy thud and felt the wind rush out of his lungs. He was dazed but not severely injured.

Brenning got slowly to his knees, clutching his sword close to his chest and looked around in the darkness. At first, Master Brenning thought he must have missed the portal and landed on the other side of the stone walkway leading to the drawbridge. The inky blackness of the world around him assured him that he was no longer in Talonrend.

"Jan!" he called to the darkness, anger filling his gravelly voice. Master Brenning stood and swung his sword about in a wide arc. It clanged loudly against a stone to his right. The smith reached a muscled hand to the stone and felt the edges, the turn of a wall. Putting his back to the wet, mossy stone, Master Brenning waved his sword about in frustration. "Jan!" he shouted again, hearing his own voice echo around him.

A tiny ball of brilliant white light appeared somewhere in the distance, too small for Master Brenning to identify. Slowly, the glowing orb grew in size, illuminating the room. Brenning lowered his sword and shielded his eyes from the intense light as he scanned the prison. The area was circular, made of large stone blocks covered in a thick carpet of verdant moss. Everything was damp and glistened in the bright light with little drops of water. What Brenning had thought was the edge of a stone wall was actually the opening to a small passage. Water trickled over the stone lazily to slicken the moss at his feet. Three small metal bars were set into the stone at narrow intervals, effectively blocking the opening to anything as large as a human.

The stone walls of the circular chamber extended well over triple the smith's height but did not meet a ceiling there. The top of the chamber was high overhead, another twenty or thirty feet above the top of the cylindrical prison. Master Brenning could barely make out the dark outlines of roots poking through the stone ceiling. A brown drop of insipid water fell through the humid air to the mossy carpet below.

Jan stepped forward from the ball of brilliant light, placing a gigantic shadow over the trapped smith. The former steward hovered above his captive on a black disc of swirling energy. Jan's laughter filled the room.

"Master Brenning, so nice to see you again," he cackled, sending little bolts of black magic dancing from his fingertips and sinking into the stone. "Welcome to my kingdom!"

Brenning spat on the stone and averted his eyes. Defeated, the

123

humbled smith sank to the mossy stone and rested his back against the wall.

Jan knew that he would never bring the smith to despair. He might kill the proud man, but he would never be able to break his spirit. Annoyed at the thought, Jan dispelled the magical light with a wave of his hand. "Enjoy your stay in the sewers of Reikall," he calmly said before disappearing through another portal of conjured magic.

Master Brenning closed his eyes and let his anger subside. There was nothing he could do to escape his stone prison. With a grunt of exasperation, Brenning pressed his ear to the wall to listen for anything that might give him hope.

Twelve

A SMALL GOBLIN hand grabbed the top of his bald head. He could feel it distinctly, but at the same time the touch felt like it was miles away. The pale fingers reached around his head and clenched down firmly on his scraped neck, closing with surprising strength. The hand began to pull, raking his battered body against the sharp stones, but the strong goblin hand would not relent. Slowly, his body began to move forward. Walls of solid rock closed in on his hips with every inch, adding a deep crimson to the rushing water.

Suddenly, the water disappeared. Gravlox felt only the cavern floor beneath his back as he gasped for air. Covered in cuts and bruises, the small goblin was thankful to be alive. Vorst pulled the rope behind her companion and retrieved his pack from the water.

They heard the footsteps resounding against the walls. The chamber was small, much smaller than the one Gravlox had come from, and it reeked of death. The echoing footfalls were coming from nearby but the sound was steady, neither approaching nor retreating.

We need to look, Gravlox tapped on the stone. The two goblins crawled on their hands and knees to an opening in the wall. Hesitantly, Gravlox placed a hand on Vorst's back as she peered around the corner. Almost instantly, the female goblin jerked her head back and rolled into the chamber.

Hundreds. Her fingers drilled the code into Gravlox's forearm in a silent panic. *Humans. They are marching. The tunnel extends far to the North, back toward their city.* Both goblins dared another look around the corner of the stone. Hundreds of human forms shambled through the rock tunnel. Some of them hit their heads on the ceiling above or scraped into the sides of the tunnel but none of them slowed or stopped.

Mindless, Gravlox signaled. *I don't think they will attack.* The two goblins straightened in the passageway and drew their weapons. Acting on instinct, Gravlox stabbed out with his short sword and impaled a thin human female. The tip of his weapon protruded garishly from the front of her chest but no blood spilled forth. The walking corpse turned and swung her arms out to claw at him but an arrow removed the woman's head from her shoulders with a splatter of rotted brains.

The other human forms were totally oblivious to the fight and the defeated woman crumbled to ash on the cavern floor without a sound. The legion continued its march, scattering the ashes as they went.

"They're zombies," Vorst muttered in disbelief. "Endless ranks of the dead." Both goblins shook their heads and wondered where they had come from. Vorst quickstepped through the river of corpses and retrieved her arrow from the ground, blowing the dust off the head before placing it back in her quiver.

"Should we continue on toward the necromancer that summoned this army? That is what Lady Scrapple wants. You of course are not bound by her will." Vorst playfully poked him in the stomach.

"We could march with them. If this cave system leads all the way to the city, it probably comes up inside the walls." The endless line of undead marched on, paying the goblins no heed. "Our quest is to take the city from the humans. It seems as if the alliance between necromancer and goblin has not been harmed. Yael and his troops are probably preparing the assault right now."

Vorst wrapped her sinewy arms around Gravlox's waist and held him close. "I don't want to fight anymore. Not against humans, not against anything. I just want to go home. I feel like I only found you moments ago, and now you talk of war. Is war against the humans what you really want, Gravlox?"

The naïve goblin foreman had never thought of that. Was there more to the goblin existence than bloody conquest? The goblins of Kanebullar Mountain were happy, content to live in the dark tunnels and passageways under the earth. They did not need a human city to live in, they already had a home. He returned her hug with all his strength, not willing to let her go.

A vicious tug in the center of Vorst's mind nearly toppled her. Lady Scrapple was telepathically commanding her minion, forcing her to fight. Gravlox watched in horror as her small hands took the sword away from him and leveled it against his neck.

"No…" Gravlox didn't know what to say. He had never felt the influence of the hive mind and therefore could not sympathize. "Vorst… Please," he begged, falling to his knees with the sword still resting against his neck.

Her eyes glazed over with pale fog and she pulled the sword back, gripping it tightly. Calm serenity danced about her soft features in the lightless cavern. The goblin's face betrayed no emotion. Vorst's arm swung, but her hand let go of the weapon and she collapsed to the floor. "I don't know how long I can resist it, Grav," she cried into his immediate embrace. "I'm not strong like you."

Gravlox held her tight against his chest. He had no words to comfort her. No inspirational speech came to him in a moment of clarity. The two lovers rocked back and forth on the cold cave floor and held each other for a long time as the horde of undead marched on.

TWO VERY DIFFERENT companions peered into the collapsed entrance of a cave shaft many feet above Gravlox and Vorst.

"You're sure they went down this passage?" Gideon asked, never allowing his hand to wander far from the throwing axes at his side.

"I am sure of it. I watched from a distance as the ground swallowed them. They did not expect it, nor did I," the demon hissed in response. Taurnil's acidic tongues tasted the air with urgency, guiding the lightless orbs of the vile beast down to the ground. "The female goblin went down on this side of the collapse." Taurnil spat a glob of acid onto the fallen leaves. "I can taste her in the air."

Gideon investigated the area but could not discern anything useful in the waning light. "If they are apart from each other, they should be easier to kill. The male goblin is the stronger of the two, by all accounts." The warrior brushed some leaves and broken sticks aside and tested the stability of the ground.

"I will rip his useless heart from his scrawny chest." Taurnil gnashed his broken teeth, biting the words as they came out.

"Is that what you said right before he forced you to retreat at Cobblestreet?" Gideon taunted, standing to his full height and easily towering over the demon.

Sinewy wings beat the air and dry leaves were tossed about the small clearing in a frenzy as Taurnil ascended. Without a word the beast dove for the ground, crashing into the rubble of the cavern entrance with a gracelessness bordering on reckless.

Not wasting any time, Gideon shook his head, dove feet-first into the stone chimney, and made the painful plummet down to the hard stone below. With a showy flourish, Taurnil's powerful wings brought him safely to the stone floor without a scratch or bruise.

Taurnil and Gideon stood in the lightless chamber and listened to the shuffling undead feet, unsure of their next move. "What is that noise?" Gideon asked.

"It is Reikall," Taurnil hissed in response. "The army marches through the lightless caves." Gideon closed his eyes against the darkness and pulled forth the energy within him, reawakening the strong bond with Vrysinoch that resided deep within his soul. When he opened his eyes, they glowed with white energy. Speaking the words to a simple cantrip, Gideon caused the rune on his back to flare to life. An ethereal eagle began to take form in the palm of his hand, illuminating the area.

Taurnil shielded his eyes from the piercing magical light and took a step back. The demon was visibly repulsed by the pure holy energy of Vrysinoch's paladin. Gideon smiled and tossed the small eagle into the air where it took flight, casting white light throughout the cavern.

VORST AND GRAVLOX, sitting on the stone around the corner from Gideon and Taurnil, saw the light and took cover. Gravlox scrambled to his feet, pulling Vorst behind him and the two goblins ran down the corridor in a hastened panic.

"Were you followed?" Vorst whispered once the two goblins were farther down the tunnel. Gravlox shook his head and stole a glance over his shoulder, unnerved by the sudden light.

We need to hide, he tapped on Vorst's arm. She looked around the underground complex nervously before finally spotting a cubby just large enough to conceal the two of them. Vorst and Gravlox darted into the cubby to wait, watching the glowing light from a distance.

"These men are dead." Gideon's tone was even and deadly serious. His deep voice echoed through the cavern, resounding around the mindless corpses that took no heed.

"Of course," Taurnil responded. "Hurry, I can taste the goblin scum in the air. They can't be far." Gideon didn't follow the demon.

"These men are dead," he repeated, staring at the endless river of zombies.

"Yes," the winged beast hissed, "and so are the women and children. What does it matter?" Taurnil turned to face the unmoving paladin. "Does the paladin fear these mindless undead?" he snickered.

"They are all *dead!*" he shouted so loudly that it rang in his ears. Gideon unhooked one of the throwing axes at his side and flexed, gripping the polished wood firmly. He felt the weight of the axe, the balance of its head at the end of his fingers. The luminescent eagle continued to circle around the cavern, casting magical light on Taurnil's pale skin.

Taurnil squared his shoulders to the man and flexed his wings. "What will you do, paladin? These corpses march toward Talon-rend, something you have certainly deduced by now. My master controls them. With us, you will surely be spared. Keturah is well aware that you are a formidable warrior. It would be a shame to kill you now, underground, where no one will see you fall."

Gideon raised the axe up to his chest and inspected its razor edge in the gleaming light. "These corpses," he sneered, "are families. Sons march through these caves; daughters, husbands, wives, all of them loved by someone. You destroyed that."

Taurnil's sinewy wings shot out from his body and beat the air with strength. The throwing axe cut the air where the demon had been standing and clanged against the damp stone of the wall.

Another axe was in the paladin's strong hand before Taurnil's wings could beat a second time. The demon launched a glob of acid and spun, flying to the wall and finding an easy perch. The acid sizzled into the stone not far behind the ducking warrior, who exploded from the ground in a wild rush, sending an axe whirling end over end for Taurnil's chest. A sharp claw swiped the missile from the air and sent it to the stone below.

The slanted ceiling of the underground chamber wasn't high

enough to afford Taurnil the room he needed to get out of the large paladin's reach. Gideon came on in a rush of steel, an axe in each hand. Taurnil's claws batted the axes out wide but the demon was clinging to the stone and leaving his back exposed. Drawing his wings in tight, the demon launched from the wall and collapsed on top of the paladin.

Gideon tried to pull his arms inside Taurnil's wings but wasn't quick enough. The demon wrapped the warrior in his strong embrace as they rolled on the stone floor. Taurnil used his superior position to pin Gideon's arms out wide where he dropped his axes. The beast brought his face down within inches of Gideon's mouth, snarling with his three writhing tongues. Acid dripped down onto the paladin's face, sizzling and boiling his skin.

"You cannot kill me," the demon hissed, spitting more acid with every word. The corrosive slime dug holes into the paladin's skin. The pain was excruciating. Gideon twisted and writhed, trying in vain to turn his face away from Taurnil's terrible maw.

Gideon thrashed violently and managed a weak headbutt. Taurnil barely noticed the blow. The sword on Gideon's back burned with holy fire. The magical eagle circling above the fight screeched in pain.

Vrysinoch heard that screech. The eagle dove down, tucking its wings against its sides and loosing another piercing scream. The sound cut the air and reverberated off the walls of the chamber, dazing Taurnil with its ferocity. Waves of divine magic emanated from the bird as it bit deeply into the demon's pale back.

Gideon scrambled, pushing the beast away and trying to scrape the remaining acid from his face. Taurnil whirled on the eagle, knocking it to the ground and dispelling the magic.

The two warriors stood in the cavern with just an arm's length separating them. The glow from Gideon's cantrip was gone but the cavern shined even brighter than before. Nevidal, Gideon's hand-and-a-half sword, glowed with fierce energy, bathing the walls in an eerie light. With grim determination, Gideon reached up and grasped the hilt of the mighty blade. In response, Nevidal surged with energy, flaring to life at the touch of the paladin's hand and nearly blinding the two warriors.

"I may not be able to defeat you," Gideon coughed through his scarred face, "but Vrysinoch is more powerful than both of us. You will die here."

Gideon drew his sword.

Thirteen

PRINCE HEROD STOOD tall atop the Talonrend city walls. Herod wasn't sure if a man was supposed to feel more terror looking up at the wall from the ground or looking down upon the city from the top.

"Apollonius," the Prince called to the man as he reached the top of the winding staircase that connected the top of Terror's Lament with the base. "Has there been any news of Master Brenning? I have not seen him in some time." The obedient soldier shook his head and stooped over to catch his breath.

"Now you understand why I left my armor at the bottom of the wall with the other guards." The prince laughed and walked over to Apollonius. "I have faith that my friend will return to us in due time." He patted the heavily armored soldier on the back and directed his view out over the city.

"Tell me, Apollonius, when was the last time you stood upon this wall and gazed out upon the rooftops of Talonrend?" The prince had often done just that, but with his brother, King Lucius, at his side.

"Never, my liege. Only recently did I enlist to be a guardsman. Wall duty is assigned to the most veteran soldiers in the guard. I am not old enough to have earned that honor yet." The prince had never realized how young the soldier was. The man had a bit of a beard, but nothing uncommon for an average man of twenty years.

Herod nodded and turned around to face the north. "There isn't much out here, Apollonius," the prince lamented. "We have the farms and fields to the north and west, the villages along the Clawflow to the east, and Reikall somewhere to the south. This is truly a lonely and desolate land." The purple caps of distant mountains could be seen far to the north like the tiny silhouettes of children standing in a row.

"Do not forget Kanebullar Mountain, my liege, across the river," Apollonius was quick to point out. The monolithic natural structure loomed on the horizon like a watchful overseer, poised to strike.

"And what is beyond that?" the prince asked. "In all of the histories of Talonrend, no one has ever ventured that far beyond the Clawflow. We are a young kingdom, compared to the Green City from which our ancestors came, but it surprises me that no one has ever gone out to map the rest of the world."

"Such is the fate of every frontier city," Apollonius replied. "I am sure that the leaders of the Green City looked out to the east, to where your castle stands strong today, and were filled with such trepidation." The young soldier sounded at ease with Talonrend's surroundings.

"Gather a group of volunteers for me, Apollonius. Get a patrol of five or six men together to travel to the north and another patrol to scout the east, beyond the Clawflow. I need to know what is out there if I am to be a good king." Prince Herod turned to make his way back down the winding staircase to the city.

"I will gladly lead such an expedition, sire." The soldier saluted but his eagerness was cut short as Herod grabbed him forcefully by the arm.

"No!" the prince shouted at him. "You need to stay in the city. I fear that the number of people I can trust within these walls is quickly diminishing. I need you by my side." Apollonius bowed. "You are my personal guard, remember that." The soldier bowed again much lower.

"I shall see to it that a patrol is organized at once for each area. A scribe and a cartographer shall accompany both groups." The soldier saluted and followed Herod back down to the city.

After the prince had donned his armor once more at the base of the wall he continued with Apollonius into the city proper. The two armored men walked down the wide avenues of Talonrend back to the castle without another word passing between them.

You will never be king. Herod was constantly reminded of his station in life by the nagging voice of his clawed god, Vrysinoch. The message echoed in the prince's head with every heavy crunch of his armored boot. Herod looked upon the castle, his brother's castle, and wondered what he was doing. Soldiers lined the parapet with crossbows and spears. Guards flanked the enchanted door and patrols of armored men could be seen moving beyond the moat in tight formations. *If I will never be king,* Herod responded to Vrysinoch in his head, *why do I do all of this? Why do I try to protect my brother's people? Why do I protect myself?*

Vrysinoch did not answer.

YAEL MOVED WITH his troops far to the north of Talonrend. The grassy fields and open plains provided little cover, but goblins are small. The soldier drones marched in coordinated blocks all at the behest of Lady Scrapple. The army of Kanebullar Mountain was comprised almost exclusively of these mindless drones. Each goblin soldier carried a spear, sword or mace, and had a small dagger tucked under its belt. The drones were never heavily armored, but the goblin at the head of each column carried a heavy metal shield on each arm and wore a thick helmet of shining iron plates.

Each column of drones had a captain, a goblin at the center of the group who was only partially enslaved by Lady Scrapple. The captains typically wielded javelins or throwing knives and wore light shirts of hardened animal hide. Tasked with singling out important targets for kills at range, the captains were afforded a measure more of freedom and discretion on the battlefield.

Yael was a commander in the goblin army. He, like Vorst, was almost fully autonomous. The goblins obeyed his orders but only because the Mistress of the Mountain forced them to obey. In a sense, Lady Scrapple was carrying out the will of Yael through the drones. The goblin commander often thought about that fact and what it might mean for him. With enough intelligence to understand that he was a slave, Yael frequently entertained the idea of ordering his troops to kill themselves just to see how Lady Scrapple would respond.

Yael's ranks were arrayed in the grassy field in perfectly straight lines. Each block consisted of ten rows of ten and Yael had been assigned to command three such blocks. Three hundred identical goblin soldiers stood before him on the plain. Their pale skin was beginning to take on a crimson luster as many of the goblins, being above ground for the first time in their lives, developed sunburn. The air was hot and thick about the army and smelled strongly of moist dirt and damp caves.

Engineers had dug a wide tunnel from the base of Kanebullar Mountain to the eastern bank of the Clawflow which allowed supplies to be carried half the distance to the army underground in fast carts moving along hastily assembled tracks. From the river, goblin teams waited until nightfall to transport the supply carts overland to the waiting army. Yael had ordered more construction materials, a shipment which he was still waiting to receive.

"We need hammers, nails, fasteners, metal braces; things with which to build. We can harvest all the lumber we could ever need from the forest but without tools, it is meaningless." Yael was one of the few goblins to have seen the human walls up close. The drone assistant attending to Yael nodded vigorously and the commander knew that Lady Scrapple had heard every word.

"Their walls are higher than our short arms can reach," he said to the drone with a shake of his head. "We must build siege towers, ladders, catapults, trebuchets! We must build great engines of war!" Yael had a way of working himself into to exhaustion over preparations. Even when conducting exercises within Kanebullar Mountain, the commander was relentless when it came to proper preparation. Yael assumed it was why he had been promoted to his position so early, which made him all the more angry that Lady Scrapple would not afford him the supplies he needed to build the siege engines.

With a wave of his scaly hand, Yael's troops dropped to their bellies on the field. The commander surveyed the army before him. Four other goblin commanders had been summoned to the field, each controlling three blocks of mindless soldiers. Another force of five blocks had been positioned on the eastern bank of the Clawflow as well, poised to overrun the human settlements to further add to the chaos of open warfare. Yael was smart enough to know that two thousand goblin soldiers would never be enough to take down the high walls of Talonrend, especially without proper siege equipment.

The commander ordered his soldiers to sit before returning to the comfort of his tent at the back of the army. Yael had met with the other leaders the day before but none of them seemed to share his concerns. Perhaps Yael didn't trust the hive mind enough, or perhaps his passion for preparedness had consumed him, but the goblin was thoroughly uncomfortable with the entire plan. "You hide something..." the goblin muttered as he splashed some water on his head and picked up a large parchment to use as a fan. "You would think that a proper general would tell her commanders the *entire* plan before deploying troops to the field."

Yael's joints locked into place and the parchment crumpled in his hand as Lady Scrapple invaded his body. Awkwardly overbalanced, the rigid goblin fell flat on his face in the dry dirt. Motionless, Yael remained on the floor of his tent for what felt like an eternity. He could feel the hive mind probing through his consciousness, investigating his memories, searching his being. Yael's eyes, filled with dirt and dust as they were, clouded over with a grey mist as Lady Scrapple searched every ounce of his body and mind.

A slow line of drool escaped Yael's open mouth and wet the dirt beneath his frozen face. The parchment was still clutched tightly in the goblin's right hand and the edges of the thick paper cut into the pale flesh of his side painfully. Droplets of blood began to mix with the dirt and spittle on the floor of the tent.

Suddenly, just as quickly as his creator had taken over his being, Lady Scrapple was gone. Yael gathered his wits and shook the dust from his clothes in silence. He attempted to stand, but the churning sensation in his gut knocked him back to the ground. Sitting on the hard soil, beneath a plain white canopy that served as his tent, Yael couldn't help but wonder if his entire company was being used as fodder. The possibility that his anger and questioning had turned him into fodder bothered him even more.

"If I am going to serve only as a distraction to provide cover for the actual attack," Yael said through gritted teeth, "I will die surrounded by human corpses."

Fourteen

H E COULD FEEL the muscles of his arms breaking down and knitting back together, growing stronger and threatening to rip out of his skin at any moment. Gideon's legs flexed and bulged with renewed life. His bones elongated, adding inches to his height and making his clothes seem like the garments of a child.

Loosing a primal roar at the top of his lungs, the paladin scraped his boots against the stone and charged.

Taurnil spread his arms wide and met the ferocious paladin head on, ducking his head at the last moment to avoid being rent in half by Nevidal's blinding overhand swing. The demon tried to use his natural agility to outmaneuver Gideon's hulking frame but the paladin matched him step for step with speed unnatural for his size.

Without an easy path to the side of the wildly swinging man, Taurnil had to quickly back step and use his sinewy wings to avoid the frenzy. Gideon's pursuit was inexorable. Swing after swing, Nevidal filled the damp cavern with blazing holy light. The sword was a blur, cutting the air with such speed that the retreating demon had no opportunity to parry.

If any emotion could be seen in the dark, soulless eyes of the winged Taurnil, fear would have shown itself in those lightless orbs. The demon tried to parry, tried to mount a counterattack, tried to stab out with his wings. Nevidal met every strike before it truly began.

Gritting his teeth and pressing forward, Gideon braced himself for the acid that he was sure would fly for his face. He had the evil creature back up against the wall, alternating high and low strokes to keep Taurnil's clawed feet planted firmly on the stone floor. A glob of sizzling acid broke through the glowing light of Nevidal's blade and divine magic flared to life around the paladin, encasing him in a fiery sphere of protection. The acid popped and crackled against the magical shield before falling to the ground harmlessly inert.

Fire engulfed the berserking paladin, swaying with his steps and surging forward with every lunge. Gideon could feel the intense heat of the cleansing flames but his skin did not burn. Smoke curled towards the ceiling of the cavern but its tendrils avoided the paladin's lungs as if the smoke itself were alive. The man's sweat ran off of his scalp and turned to mist in the flames at his feet.

Taurnil felt the cold stone against his back and knew he was trapped. Nevidal's brilliant light flashed before his eyes in a dazzling pattern the demon could never hope to discern. His claws flew about in front of him recklessly, trying desperately to keep the edge from his pale flesh.

Reaching within himself, Taurnil calmed his frantic mind and found his inner well of magic. The cord of ethereal servitude connecting master and slave thrummed with violent energy that begged for release. Keturah could feel the panic within her minion as keenly as the flailing demon felt the stone at his back.

Seated behind a massive oak desk in the grand study of the Artificer's Guild, the beautiful woman's eyes glazed over as the telepathic communion solidified. With whitened knuckles, Keturah's forearms bulged and her hands clenched the desk, digging lines into the polished wood.

Her sable tresses flew wildly about her face as the raw energy of her communion whirled around the study in a ghastly fog. Books flew from their shelves and pelted the walls in a maelstrom of fury as the powerful wizard pumped wave after wave of arcane strength into her puppet.

Taurnil's desperate parries began to hit their mark and Nevidal rang out violently against the demon's sharp claws. A jagged grin broke out on Taurnil's pale face. Overwhelming strength surged through the demon's body, hastening his blocks and turning the radiant weapon aside time after time.

Gideon could sense the energy flowing into his adversary. A song to Vrysinoch escaped his lips and the two mighty warriors found themselves on equal footing.

Keturah arched her back let loose a ghastly scream amplified by her two-tone ethereal voice. A bolt of lightning shot forth from the wizard, jettisoned through the incorporeal tunnel of magic, and found its way into her pet.

Flashes of purple lightning shattered the super-heated air all over the cavern, striking the stone with enough force to sunder it and send up a shower of rock and dirt. More than one of the arcane bolts collided with the divine shield surrounding the paladin's body. Gideon could feel his sacred protection waning and knew he had lost the upper hand.

With a growl that was more out of frustration than ferocity, the paladin hefted his mighty sword above his head, poising for a deadly overhand chop. Demonic claws reached high to stop the fatal blow. Nevidal surged brighter, a holy flare in the underground arena. Gideon stepped in close, exposing his left flank to the biting maw of the demon and shortening the angle of his sword to connect the hilt with the top of Taurnil's head. The winged beast bit down hard on the soft flesh above the paladin's meager armor a split-second before the heavy hilt of the hand-and-a-half sword cracked into his skull with resounding force.

Taurnil slumped against the stone and a lightning strike blasted apart the cavern floor between the dueling champions. Gideon flew backwards through the churning air and landed painfully on his back with the wet stone pressing up against his muscled flesh. Pain coursed through the man's shoulder, blurring his vision and scrambling his keen senses. Nevidal's enchanted might worked furiously to counter the necrotic poison eating the paladin's shoulder as he writhed on the blasted stone floor. Swiping frantically at the wound, Gideon grabbed onto the bleeding, wriggling tongue and ripped it free from his torn skin. The disembodied tongue had been severed by the lightning strike but it had done its work. Poison continued to pump out of the bloody tongue as it slithered aimlessly on the ground.

Gideon tried to stand but a thick gush of blood forced him back to his knees. With Nevidal still magically bound to his hands, all the paladin could hope to do was crawl inch by painful inch toward his crumpled adversary to finish the work.

Vrysinoch's restorative magic could only do so much. The vile poison sizzled within the warrior's veins and ate away at his flesh from the inside. The blood and muscle of his shoulder began to coagulate into a blackened ash of corrupted flesh.

The blazing sword flickered. Its glow faded with every pained shuffle of Gideon's weakened legs. Skin sloughed off his shoulder in fetid clumps like rotten apples falling from a dead tree. The holy magic imbued in Nevidal was still attempting to embolden the stubborn warrior, but the poison broke down tissue faster than the magic could knit it together.

Taurnil's wings twitched pathetically as they scraped against the stone. The once proud demon from the abyss lay nearly motionless. A stream of thick black blood meandered from his scalp and mouth to his ashen chest and pooled on the blasted rocks. The hard pommel of Nevidal had left a massive dent in the top of Taurnil's skull.

"You..." Gideon managed to cough past the blood in his throat. "You are dead, demon." The paladin tightened his grip on the large sword he used as a cane to pull himself along. "I will harvest..." A fit of coughing shuddered through Gideon's chest and sent more blood splattering out in front of him. "I will harvest your soul," he said with finality as he shakily stood before the fallen beast.

Gideon's heart raced at an uncontrollable pace. Adrenaline and Nevidal's enchantment combined in his body with the demon's poison in a virulent tempest of life and death. The sword hummed in his grip, eager for a kill. He knew that satisfying the blade would dispel the divine magic and allow the poison to consume him. The pain was so immense that Gideon started to smile at the thought of death.

Vrysinoch's champion loomed over the broken creature with a peaceful grin on his face. He mustered what was left of his resolve to raise his right hand up high. Nevidal gave off a faint bluish glow, barely enough light to reflect off the blood staining the ground, but the blade managed to release one last spark of energy as it swooped in for the kill.

Tears streamed down Keturah's face. The grand study of the Artificer's Guild was in ruins. Small fires smoldered in every corner. Priceless arcane tomes had been turned to powder in the fury of her spellcasting. The lightning storm had taken every ounce of magical energy the woman possessed. Her features were gaunt and emaciated. Her once lustrous hair hung limp at her shoulders. The flesh around her piercing eyes was dark and her cheeks sunk in, giving her a hollow and lifeless appearance. She used a sleeve of her beautiful gown to wipe a line of mucus from her inflamed nose and cracked lips.

With a whimper, Keturah mouthed the words to her final spell. Tendrils of oily smoke billowed up from her empty eye sockets. A gentle breeze made its way into the grand study from a shattered window set into the northern wall of the room. The soft whisper of the wind picked up the bone dry ashes of Keturah's corpse from under the folds of her elegant dress and scattered them around the room. Her dead hair snapped and blew away, but the spell was finished.

The final spark from Gideon's sword stole his vision long enough for the paladin to miss the wisp of smoke that curled around Taurnil's broken body. In the blink of an eye, the demon reverted back to his natural form. Nevidal clanged against the bloody stone with the sound of thunder and a small, jet black scorpion skittered away into the darkness unseen.

The momentum of the missed execution pulled him to the ground. His body was too weak to even gasp. Resigned to bitter agony, Gideon looked around the darkened cavern one last time. "A quiet place, but not..." his voice trailed off into a strained cough of blood.

Nevidal winked out and left the warrior in pitch black darkness.

Fifteen

"**I** HATE WALL patrol," Stratos grumbled. The soldier was a tall man, remarkably lanky and thin for his height, and he sported a thick, curly beard of brown hair. He pulled a strip of white cloth from under his tunic and used it to wipe the sweat from his forehead. His heavy metal boots clinked loudly against the polished stone of Terror's Lament as the newly recruited soldier walked.

Next to Stratos, Teysa tugged at the shining steel breastplate she wore and used a hand to keep the sun out of her eyes. She was Stratos' younger sister and bore a stark resemblance to her sibling's thin frame. The two had been inseparable from a very young age and had even joined the city guard together. After being commissioned by Herod as Templars of Peace, Stratos and Teysa tried to take an extra measure of pride in their patrolling despite the punishing heat.

The deep green talon embossed on the templar's armor burned under the hot afternoon sun. Stratos pulled the chainmail coif back from his head. Sweat poured from his sunburned skin and sizzled on the stone walkway. The two soldiers stopped their patrol and sat down with their backs to the wall.

145

"Why do we have to walk in so much armor?" Teysa groaned. Their canteen had been empty for the past two hours but their patrol lasted another three.

"I know what you mean." Stratos' rag was soaked beyond use so he tossed it over the wall. All of the templars atop the high walls of Talonrend had recently been ordered to make their patrols with a full armament. Teysa slipped one of her scalloped steel gauntlets off and let it clang to the walkway.

"I'm not used to all this heavy armor. My hands are starting to blister. My feet feel like they are on fire." She began to unlace the straps on the back of her steel greaves. "I don't understand why we have to walk so many patrols."

Three other pairs of templars were slowly making their own rounds on different sections of the walls. They looked like shining stars, reflecting brilliantly against the pale landscape of the Talonrend countryside.

Teysa removed her heavy breastplate and set her greaves and gauntlets inside her chest piece's hollow shell. "Come on, let's keep moving. I'm going to stash my armor for the rest of the patrol." She stretched a hand down to lift Stratos off the stone. The supple leather and mail the guard wore under her steel breathed the gentle wind and cooled her body. The woman had only been patrolling the wall for a few weeks and hated every minute of it.

Stratos breathed heavily under the oppressive weight of his armor. The skinny man shrugged his shoulders and tried to adjust the fit as he walked. Nothing helped keep the heat at bay. "I don't understand why we need to have swords with us too." He thumbed the pommel of the blade on his hip and wondered if he would ever need to draw it. "What do we need swords for? Nothing can get up here and we certainly can't throw them with any effect."

Teysa hefted her crossbow up on her shoulder and looked over the edge of the wall. The two templars were on the northern face of Terror's Lament. "There isn't even anything out there..." The vast openness of the grassy plain was daunting, like an endless ocean filled with the unknown.

Stratos carried a similar crossbow across his shoulders. He set the large weapon down against the stone parapet and peered out into the vastness. "What is everyone afraid of out there? What are we protecting the kingdom against?" Stratos put a hand on Teysa's shoulder and pulled her back.

"No sane person living behind these high walls should be afraid of anything. Talonrend is impenetrable. No army has ever broken through Terror's Lament and no army ever will." Teysa shook her head against the heat of the day and ran a hand through her long blonde hair. She could see the redness under Stratos' curly beard and knew he must be burning.

"It isn't the people who are afraid," she continued. Teysa drew her sword and held it to the back of her head. With one tug of the blade, she cut the majority of her hair off and tossed it to the ground outside the city. "The bloody prince is the problem. Herod is afraid of his own shadow without his brother here to protect him."

Teysa offered the sword to Stratos, indicating that he should cut his thick beard from his chin to ease the heat. With a look of terror on his face, Stratos refused the sword and backed away. "Oh no, not my beard." He held his hands in a defensive posture in front of him. "Do you know how long it took me to grow this? I'm not crazy enough to cut it off just because of a little heat!"

Teysa shrugged and sheathed the sword. She walked past Stratos, continuing her patrol with her armor in hand.

The templar hesitated a moment before catching up to Teysa. Something caught his eye, something lurking just on the fringes of his peripheral vision. "Teysa! Did you see that?" He grabbed the crossbow and leveled it on the parapet, trying to discern what he had seen.

"Oh, settle down, Stratos. Nothing is out there." The confident woman kept walking and tugging at the leather jerkin for relief.

Stratos leaned over the edge with his crossbow and looked directly down the glistening wall. "Teysa, something moved down at the base of the wall. Look at it, I can't tell." The panic in his voice brought Teysa back. She knew he wasn't kidding.

Her leather and mail armor was much more flexible than Stratos' heavy plate and allowed her the necessary movement to more clearly see the base of the wall. "I don't see anything, Stratos. You have heat stroke. Let's find some water."

Teysa's soft armor certainly afforded her mobility but it did nothing to stop the flying goblin arrow that ripped through her chest.

"Teysa, no!" Stratos screamed, pulling her to the ground. He could see the blood-soaked feathers protruding less than an inch out of the woman's body. With his other hand around her back, Stratos felt the tip of the arrow scrape against his gauntlet.

Stratos slammed the visor of his helmet down over his eyes and breathed in heavily to calm his nerves. Offering a meager prayer to Vrysinoch, Stratos stole a glance over the parapet. Two goblins crouched at the foot of the wall, hidden in the tall grasses. One of them was holding a small wooden bow and grinning from ear to ear.

Stratos dropped back to the stone and drew his sword. The other guards on the wall were too far away to hear his call. He gripped his sword tightly and stood up. Teysa was lying motionless. There wasn't much blood, but he knew she was dead.

With a grunt of rage, Stratos gripped the parapet and launched himself over the wall. The terrified goblins below shrieked in fear and one of them managed to scramble out of the way before the flailing ball of living steel landed. The unfortunate goblin holding the bow was crushed in an instant.

YAEL PACED THE grounds in front of his soldiers. He had been waiting for the two scouts to return from the walls for hours. When

Keegar, the surviving goblin from the scouting expedition, finally ran back into the camp, he was greeted with a harsh glare.

"Where is the other scout?" Yael yelled. He knew before Keegar spoke what had happened. The only reason for one goblin to return alone was the death of the second goblin. Keegar cowered before Yael. He fell to his knees before the commander and recounted the story of his scouting mission.

"The humans know that we are here. If any of the humans died, then we are no longer safe here. They will send their armies out against us. Thousands of humans will march into our camps! They will kill all of us!" Yael struck the scout and knocked him to the ground in his anger. Keegar's nose broke under the weight of the blow.

"She knew this would happen… She caused this to happen!" Yael wasn't a stupid goblin. His fears were confirmed. Lady Scrapple had full control of the scouting goblins. She wanted the human army to come out from behind their high walls. The hundreds of goblins arrayed in the field before their commander were going to be used as fodder. For his minor rebellion against the hive mind, Yael's forces had been condemned.

"Keegar!" the commander called to the bloodied goblin. "Come with me. We need to make plans." The scout fell into line behind Yael and followed him back to his tent.

"I've been thinking," Yael explained when the two were alone. "Our entire block of soldiers is going to be used as fodder."

Keegar nodded but did not quite understand. "The Lady does what is best for the mountain. We serve her."

"Of course…" Yael said. "Keegar," the commander shook his head, not knowing how to explain it all to the scout. "When you were at the wall… How did you get out of the way of the falling soldier?"

"I jumped. I saw him coming and I jumped…" Keegar spoke slowly. It was obvious that he was trying to piece things together.

"But your companion on the scouting mission, he did not have

149

the same reaction?" Yael could feel the presence of Lady Scrapple invading his mind. She was like a slow poison tearing at his consciousness, taking more and more with every passing second.

"We are far from the mountain, Keegar, farther than any of us have gone before. And we are numerous. More goblins are outside of the mountain than Lady Scrapple can control." Yael gasped from the effort. Veins on his pale skull throbbed and pounded.

Clutching the center tent pole for support, Yael managed to speak once more before he collapsed: "Don't you see, Keegar? Our distance and numbers strain her abilities! We can be *free*! She can only control... us if we let her."

Keegar stood in front of the exhausted commander and was completely lost. A line of drool escaped his mouth and landed on Yael's face. The goblin scout ducked his head and exited the tent, unsure of where he should go.

Sixteen

F OUR GOBLIN EYES stared into the darkness of the cave. Nothing inside the cave moved. The soft trickle of water accompanied the endless scuffling of undead in the underground corridor.

"What happened?" Vorst whispered. "Is he dead?" The small goblin held a sword in her hand.

"I can't tell. I think he is." Gravlox was positioned just behind Vorst, using the smaller goblin as a shield against his mounting fears.

"He just collapsed though. I didn't see the winged one strike him. Maybe he's alive." Vorst's voice seemed far away in the damp cavern. The music that so often wove itself into her high-pitched timbre was gone. That comforting quality was replaced by fear, something Gravlox wasn't accustomed to hearing.

"I've seen it happen in the mines. When one of my miners has worked for a long time, sometimes they will just fall down and die. It only happens in the ones that have been in the mine for many, many years though. I don't know how to tell how old a human is." Somehow, Gravlox found the courage to take a step towards the slumped figure.

"I'm not positive, but this one doesn't look old enough to die like that. Maybe he decided to sleep." Vorst remained with her feet planted firmly on the ground as Gravlox continued his approach.

"I still don't understand why they do that," he muttered, never taking his eyes from Gideon's back.

"We should kill him, just to make sure he is dead," Vorst whispered. The man groaned then, but didn't move.

"He killed that winged thing we fought in the forest," Gravlox said. He glanced quickly over his shoulder and gave Vorst a smile. "Maybe this one is our friend."

Vorst shook her head but she knew that Gravlox couldn't see. The man let out another groan. It was weaker than the first, more of a whimper than anything.

The goblin foreman reached a hand out toward the fallen warrior and gently touched his shoulder. Gideon attempted to roll but only managed to cough and half turn his head. A thin line of blood made its way down Gideon's face and dripped onto the cavern floor.

Immediately, Gravlox could sense the immense energy radiating from the paladin. "He is powerful," the goblin said with astonishment, "but he is nearly dead."

Vorst was kneeling beside the paladin and inspecting his wounds. Her eyes darted all around the cavern. "Where is his left arm? Humans have two arms, just like us."

The foreman hadn't even noticed the brutal wound. Gideon's left arm ended in a short stump just inches from his shoulder. The skin was black like burnt ashes. Vorst picked up the sleeve of armor and set it down next to the paladin. The man attempted another groan but wasn't successful.

"Can you heal him, Grav?" Vorst was holding his hand and looking down at the battered man with sorrow in her eyes.

"I'm not sure how I even did that..." Gravlox gripped the man's ashen shoulder and closed his eyes. Not having any clue how to connect to the well of magic within himself, Gravlox concentrated on the feeling he got from accessing magic. Before he could enter into the clairvoyant state of spellcasting, Vorst kissed him and took him there herself.

Consumed by the whirling riptides of magic within his body, Gravlox could feel the malevolent poison in the man's body. The acid was eating through blood and flesh at an alarming rate. The foreman's primal magic wove itself into the regenerative force of Gideon's enchanted sword. Vrysinoch's soft voice whispered through the cavern and echoed off the walls.

The devilish poison fought back with wicked resolve. Gideon began to cough and wheeze, hacking up a stream of thick, black, congealed blood. The concerted efforts of Gravlox and Vrysinoch began to halt the progress of the poison and knit some of the broken tissue back together.

Coughing, the paladin crawled to his knees. Nevidal was still magically bound to his hand, making it awkward for the man to position himself. The paladin couldn't see in the dark like the two goblins but their eyes betrayed their presence. With all the strength he could muster, Gideon knocked the goblins aside and turned to face them.

"My god," the paladin stammered when he realized what had been touching him. With his back against the wall of the cave, Gideon swung Nevidal out in front of him. It was a feeble attack, one easily defeated by nothing more than Vorst's outstretched hand. She grabbed the blade and meant to disarm the man but despite his weakness, the paladin did not let the weapon go. She could see the man's fingers barely wrapped about the hilt of the hand-and-a-half sword. The sheer weight of the weapon alone should have dropped it to the stone but the stubborn blade didn't even waver.

With a high-pitched accent that grated against human ears and a halting knowledge of the human language, Vorst attempted to reason with the man. "Friend. We both friend." Vorst pointed to herself and then to Gravlox and said both of their names. "Both friend."

153

The paladin backed as far as he could against the wall. He could barely make out the images of the two 'friends' in the darkness. "Goblins..." The paladin's voice came out raspy and strained.

Vorst nodded her head vigorously, mistaking the anger in Gideon's voice for plain recognition. "Goblins!" she confirmed, pointing to her chest. "Gravlox," she patted the foreman on the back. "Gravlox is shaman. He heals you. Stay still. You hurt. Gravlox is shaman, heals you."

Gideon nodded slowly. Still clutching the sword he could not drop, he awkwardly pointed to himself and said his name. To the goblins, his voice was deep and mysterious, full of darkness and potential evil.

"My sword," Gideon said, growing stronger. The holy magic was still coursing into him and regenerating his body. The only way to halt the enchantment would be to feed a soul to Nevidal. The clever paladin realized at once that the shaman's magic had at least halted the devastating tide of poison within his blood. "I have to kill someone, to end the enchantment that makes me stronger."

Vorst understood the man's words but not the concepts he espoused. Defensively, the female goblin backed away and placed a hand over Gravlox's chest.

Gideon waved his hand in front of him as best he could to calm the goblins. He had no intentions of killing either of them. "His magic, I feel it," he said. He placed his hand over his heart and glanced down at the blackened stump where his left arm used to hang. "Thank you."

A long moment passed in the darkness between the trio. "You must kill..." Vorst responded. "Who must you kill?" She positioned herself in front of her goblin lover, not knowing what would happen.

"I didn't mean you," Gideon managed a smile. He could feel his body growing steadily stronger but he knew that he was a very long way from being whole again. "If I kill your shaman, his magic will leave me and I will die. I won't risk that." He winced as he spoke but didn't hold back. "Friends," he said, holding his sword over his chest and indicated with his chin toward Gravlox.

"Find someone for to kill," Vorst chuckled. She stood and pointed toward the corridor where endless ranks of the dead were marching toward Talonrend.

"I almost forgot..." Gideon used the length of his mighty sword to lift himself off the ground. Gravlox tentatively moved toward the massive warrior who stood closer to eight feet tall than seven due to the marvelous enchantment.

The three unlikely friends stood in the corridor and watched as entire families shambled down the tunnel. Some women even held little undead babies to their bosoms as they trudged onward. Gideon waited until an older man walked past and used his long sword to herd him into the larger cavern.

The zombie appeared to be about forty. He had a ragged, half-torn beard hanging from his chin and wore a thick leather apron over a white shirt and matching pants. He was covered in dirt and grime and his feet had worn through his boots to reveal bloody toes and blisters. The man had been walking for quite some time in the damp tunnels beneath the surface.

Completely mindless, the zombie flailed about in a meager attempt to scratch and bite the tall paladin. Gideon's heavy boot crashed into the man's maggot-ridden chest and caved it in. The zombie stumbled backward and landed on his back. With one quick swipe, the zombie's head rolled away from its shoulders. The mighty paladin's remaining shoulder bulged as layer upon layer of corded muscle reconstituted itself.

Frustration overcame the man and he loosed a roar that shook the earth. A dozen more brutal cuts had the decomposing corpse scattered into piles of fetid flesh all about the cavern. "His soul was not with his body." Gideon hung his head in defeat.

Vorst grabbed at the paladin's arm. "Poison still in flesh. You end enchantment, Gideon dies, yes?" The look in the man's eyes told her that such a fate would be welcomed.

"If I cannot cure the demon's poison, ending the enchantment will kill me. If the shaman dies, the poison will kill me. If the poison is cured before I can take a soul, the enchantment will kill me." Gideon kicked his discarded armor and spat on the ground. "I am condemned. The shaman's magic prevents the corruption from taking me now, but my sword's magic will overcome my body eventually. I can last for a few more days, a week at the most, before I cannot control it any longer. You should leave me here to die..."

Using the goblin language of finger taps, Vorst translated everything the human said for Gravlox. The shaman nodded his head solemnly.

"He is right, Vorst. We should abandon him. There are always more humans to take his place. One human is no loss." Gravlox picked up the armor sleeve and rolled it in his hands. It was far too large to fit his scrawny arms but he put it in his pack nonetheless.

"This man can help us, Grav! Look at the undead in that tunnel." She forcefully turned him back to the corridor. "With a powerful warrior like this one, we can do something about that. The army here marches for the human city. Look at how many there are! They will kill everyone in that city without mercy."

"Isn't that exactly why we came here?" Gravlox was cynical. "Yael ordered us to go to the necromancer who did this and salvage the goblin alliance with these monsters! Have you forgotten that, Vorst?"

Tears welled up in her eyes. "Gravlox.... Listen to yourself. You are an outcast, exiled from our mountain home. Have you forgotten *that?*" She shook Gravlox forcefully and took a step back in disgust. "If the human kingdom falls to Lady Scrapple, what do you think she will do? Will she let us go?"

Gravlox digested the words as he looked at Gideon's ashy shoulder. "She will hunt us relentlessly..." He knew it was true. "As long as Lady Scrapple is alive, we will never be safe."

Vorst nodded. "Exactly. We must help the humans now. If they can defeat the armies at their doorstep, maybe they will help us defeat Lady Scrapple. We have to try."

"Humans will never help us. Look at us, Vorst. We are goblins. They hate us. Even this one tried to kill you while I was saving it." He had doubt stamped all over his pale face. "I don't know... Even if we can turn back the army of our kin, what will happen to us? Do we live with the humans? Will they take us in behind their walls to walk among their children?" Downtrodden, he couldn't meet Vorst's intense gaze. His mind searched desperately for answers that he knew he didn't have.

"We can figure that out *after* we kill Lady Scrapple and free the rest of the goblins," Vorst said with a renewed strength in her melodic voice. "If we save this human, he will help us after it's done." The two goblins hugged each other for what felt like an eternity to Gideon, who was still standing awkwardly in the cavern. Vorst explained to the man what their plan was and he smiled to show his support.

Using the rope to guide Gideon through the lightless tunnels, Gravlox and Vorst ran past the zombie horde. They went against the flow of undead flesh, seeking the source of the rampant corruption. Reikall was only a day's run from the cavern where Taurnil fell but Gideon could not match the fevered pace of the goblins. His towering form was not fit for the cramped tunnels and he repeatedly bashed his head against the low hanging stone.

After an hour of running, the man was too tired to go on. The stink of the animated corpses was stifling. Being not far under the surface, it didn't take long for Gravlox to find a side passage that led to the surface. Gideon had to crawl on his chest, a difficult task with only one arm and sword in his right hand, but he made it. The three rested on the surface and were glad to be out of the horrid smell.

"I think I can track the passage from above, on the surface," Gideon told Vorst after he caught his breath. He gripped the hilt of his sword tightly and called upon the divine powers bestowed upon him as a paladin. A tiny ethereal eagle materialized on the tip of his sword and took flight. The small ball of sculpted magic landed softly on the man's shoulder and he whispered a gentle incantation to it. Without hesitation, the glowing eagle took wing and glided just inches above the ground.

"It worked," he said with a voice that indicated his surprise. "The bird will show us the way. It can sense the magic that animated the undead and can track them for us. We can stay on the surface for now." Gideon's powerful enchantment still coursed through his veins and enlarged his stature. He stood nearly ten feet tall and towered above the diminutive goblins like the walls of Talonrend hovering high over a beggar slumped against the base of the stone. "Let's go."

Seventeen

THE NEWLY COMMISSIONED Templars of Peace were arrayed outside of Terror's Lament. One thousand men, fully clad in steel plate, stood perfectly still in front of the massive eastern gate to the city. They had been organized into ten centuries and every single soldier was outfitted with masterwork equipment from Master Brenning's armory. Even though the grizzled old smith was nowhere to be seen in the city, his smiths had worked tirelessly for the past few days to outfit the new military campaign.

Supporting each century of soldiers was a unit of twenty-five mounted cavalry called an alaris. The cavalry were designed for maximum effectiveness on the open plains that surrounded the walls of Talonrend. Some of the mounted soldiers carried lances but most of the warriors in each alaris wielded a heavy two-headed flail and a kite shield emblazoned with the symbol of Vrysinoch.

The Templars of Peace were supported by the common militia that was summoned from the outlying villages along the Clawflow and the city's own residents. Some of the men and women in the militia were volunteers but the majority of the force was comprised of draftees. Lacking the training required for vigorous melee combat in the open fields, the soldiers of the militia were typically taught how to fire a bow or crossbow as part of a volley. Primarily, the militia was used to man Terror's Lament, but pockets of draftees had been placed with crossbows all around the base of the wall. It was impossible to count every individual, but roughly three thousand villagers had answered the call to serve their prince. Most of the soldier's families had come as well, fearing that an attack would come from east of the Clawflow and destroy their homes. The city was packed with civilians. Even the royal audience hall had been set up as a shelter for the refugees. Fortunately, most of the families had also brought large stores of food and other essential goods with them so a siege upon the city wouldn't mean the death of the kingdom.

By the time the Templars of Peace had been outfitted with their equipment, little had remained in the royal armories for the militia to use. Farmers and other tradesmen had brought their own makeshift weapons from the villages. Everything from pitchforks to crude swords and simple brass knuckles could be seen among the commoners. The people not fortunate enough to have received a bow or crossbow were exclusively stationed as reserves, lying in wait just inside the first wall of Terror's Lament. If any section of the wall fell or if the gate itself was destroyed, the militia would be there to fill the hole and slow the encroaching army enough for an alaris or a century to be deployed to that area. Prince Herod understood that the militia behind the wall wouldn't last long if they were engaged, but that's exactly why they were stationed *behind* the wall.

The regal prince sat atop a magnificent warhorse in front of the gate. He was clad in golden armor fit for a god. The sun reflected so brightly off of his shield that even the horses in the nearest alaris turned their heads. Maelstrom and Regret were strapped to his hips and a heavy lance was suspended in a horizontal sheath just below his right stirrup. The golden shield was one that few soldiers recognized; until that morning, it had hung above the bed of King Lucius. Herod had the holy seal of Vrysinoch stripped from the metal and the whole device had been coated in solid gold. It was highly impractical, Herod knew, but he didn't intend to use it.

"Mighty soldiers of Talonrend! Defenders of civilization and peace!" Herod's voice boomed out over the army, amplified by the wall at his back. "The songs of war have brought you all here, but it is not a war we have chosen." The prince scanned the soldiers in front of him to gauge their reactions but none of them made a move. "We are engaged in a great defensive war, one that will be remembered for millennia! The high walls of Talonrend will be tested. The resolve of this army will be tested. The strength in our arms and the courage in our hearts will be tested. Talonrend will prevail!" A chorus of enthusiastic cheers rose up before him.

"We did not choose this war and we are not obligated to fight it. But keep this in mind: If you cast aside your weapons today, your families will be slaughtered tomorrow. If you grow tired of fighting and turn back, the men around you will die. We do not fight for any new lands or wealth or resources, we fight to hold onto everything we already have. A great army has amassed against us and our very lives are at stake." The soldiers pounded their weapons against the ground and sent a tremendous thunder into the air.

"The great walls of this city have never been breached!" More cheers erupted all around the soldiers but most of them were from the militia. The veteran soldiers knew the truth of the matter; the walls had never been breached because they had never been attacked. "These walls will not be breached today! They will not be breached tomorrow! They will stand for a thousand years as a testament to your courage!" Again, it was the drafted soldiers who celebrated with the most fervor.

"Some five hundred goblins have been seen in the north. A handful of goblins have been seen in the east, just past the Clawflow. They will need ten times that number if the filthy goblins expect to kill even a single citizen of Talonrend!" That was a claim the entire army could support. Vigorous cheers and salutations rang out through the city and sent adrenaline into the hearts of many.

"We do not know what else hides in the darkness of the forest, waiting to attack alongside the goblins like cowards." Images of fire breathing dragons soared through the prince's mind. "Whatever foes might show themselves on the field of battle will die on the field of battle!" Herod's warhorse reared up and kicked the air, bringing more shouts from the soldiers.Herod hefted the golden shield in both hands above his head and displayed it to the army. "As many of you know, my dear friend Master Brenning has gone missing. This shield used to belong to my brother." The soldiers were captivated by the golden relic and rendered silent by its magnificence. "Whoever has the good fortune to find Master Brenning or to bring me the head of his killer will claim this shield as their prize!" Roars broke the silence and forced Herod to give the army a minute to calm down before continuing. "My brother is dead. I accept that. His shield represents the monarchy, a prize waiting to be claimed by a hero. I have no children and have decided against producing any. Whoever claims this shield will be my heir and the heir to Talonrend!" The cheers that followed that proclamation were deafening. The army was hungry for glory and honor, things they had never had the chance to earn.

A FEW MILES to the north of the gathered army, Yael and Keegar strapped on their armor and prepared to move. The five hundred goblins formerly under Yael's direction had been completely overcome by Lady Scrapple's will. The goblin commander had proved, to himself at least, that the Mistress of the Mountain was not omnipotent. Her powers had a limit and with the distance at which the goblins had been deployed, her limits were being reached.

Yael and Keegar watched helplessly as the five hundred goblins on the plain readied themselves for the incoming war. They were only lightly armed and armored. Most of the goblins wore crude leather shirts and a few of them had small wooden bucklers attached to their forearms. To make up for their short reach against the taller humans, almost all of the goblins wielded spears or javelins.

The army began to march south in unison and used the tall grasses to hide their movements as best they could. The five blocks of drones waited at the edge of the plain with their weapons drawn. With such pale skin, the tall grasses north of Talonrend concealed the army quite well. The sun glinting off the human's armor made Terror's Lament appear on fire.

THE CITY WAS calm and peaceful. Not a single person could be seen walking down the streets or standing among the smoldering ruins. A great fire had ravaged the once vibrant city and, judging by the heat still emanating from many of the collapsed buildings, Gideon could tell that the city had died recently. The three companions had made it to Reikall as the sun began to set a day after they left the caves. It was becoming painfully obvious that Nevidal's enchantment was going to kill the powerful man. By the time he looked upon the savagery of the ruined city, he was a giant. At almost twelve feet tall, the paladin had to stoop just to get through the city's front gate.

Everywhere they went nothing but death and suffering greeted them. It was a place devoid of not only life, but lacking hope as well. Gideon's astral bird still guided the group but it moved noticeably slower, as if Vrysinoch was saddened as well. Reikall was a city built from large squares of cut marble stacked on top of one another to form intimidating and beautiful structures. The sullen atmosphere didn't fit the architecture.

"This place is huge," Gravlox remarked, looking up at a colossal building that sported four white pillars and held what was left of the roof. One of the pillars had tumbled to the ground and huge chunks of soot-stained marble blocked the road. The incorporeal eagle floated gently through the fallen pillar with ease but the goblins were not even half as tall as the debris. Without as much as a grunt, Gideon wrapped his bulging right arm around the corner of the stone and pushed with his monstrous legs. The chunk of marble pillar moved as easily as if it had been a feather.

Vorst pointed to an area behind much smaller ruined building to the left of the road. "We could go around..." she said, but they were already following the bird unhindered once again. Gideon simply looked at her with sadness and shrugged.

They continued on through the smoldering ashes of Reikall until the bird glided to a stop on the edge of a moss-covered well at the center of a market square. Merchant stalls lined the border of the clearing and the whole place stank of death. Down a wide boulevard flanked by dead trees to the east of the market, one structure dominated everything. Reikall's royal castle was a larger building than anything the group had ever seen before. Turrets and spires wearing jewelry of stained glass clawed their way above the smoke and ashes to touch the sky. Only one small section of the keep had been destroyed. A square tower near the gatehouse and drawbridge had tumbled into the castle's moat. Like Castle Talon, the land around the royal residence had been built up to give the castle an even better view. Where there had once been a gentle embankment of rolling green grass was nothing but black dirt. Not even weeds grew along the banks of the moats. Everything was dead.

The eagle chirped once and dove down the well before Gideon could get to it. "What do we do?" Vorst asked. She tapped out the question in the goblin language on Gravlox's hand so he could follow.

"I guess we go down too," Gideon said as he peered into the well.

"Will he fit?" Gravlox asked skeptically. The huge man's broad shoulders were at least six feet wide but he did only have a single arm to worry about. The paladin understood the concern before

Vorst translated the question to him. He shook his head and walked to the other side of the market, toward the castle.

The trees that had once beautified the approach to Reikall's keep were tall and slender. Although their broad leaves had fallen to the ground and withered some time before Gideon ever laid eyes upon them, he still found the sight captivating. The paladin had lived his entire youth in a poor farming village where every structure and plant served a function. His adulthood was spent in the Talonrend arena and a smoky blacksmith's shop. Even Castle Talon, for all of its impressive size, was not particularly beautiful to the eye. Standing before the long boulevard and gazing up at the marble castle, Gideon wished he had been born in Reikall.

The giant leaned against one of the dead trees and let out a long sigh. The tower where the priests of Vrysinoch lived in Talonrend was aesthetically pleasing beyond question, but to Gideon, it represented a place of oppression. He had trained there for a decade alongside the other paladins, but he was never allowed to be an individual. All aspects of a paladin's life were meant to be for the good of the whole with no concern for the self. At first, it made sense to him. When fighting as a cohesive unit there was no room for personal issues or desires. That very oppression led Gideon to leave the tower at the end of his training. Somewhere deep inside his soul, the man wanted desperately to worry about just himself.

The slender trees and the wide open road gave him that. The boulevard and the castle were works of art meant to be admired. The paladin felt that he would love to live in a place like Reikall. Gideon could hear the small goblins shuffling about nervously behind him. He sighed, turned, and left his longing behind.

"What are we going to do?" Vorst asked. She had to strain her neck to look the giant in the eyes as she spoke. Gideon wrapped his arm, still tightly grasping Nevidal, around the tall tree he had been leaning against and ripped it from the earth. Sullenly, he marched to the well and bade the goblins grab the top of withered plant. With frightening ease, the paladin gently lowered Gravlox and

Vorst to the bottom of the well where the glowing bird awaited them. The eagle was perched between two iron bars that were part of a larger grate set into the wall of the well. Without much effort, the skinny goblins slid through the bars into the passageway beyond.

The sewer channel was large enough to allow them both to stand and walk side by side. Letting loose an occasional screech, the bird continued to flap its silent wings and guide the pair along the underbelly of the city.

Vibrations from their footfalls caused chunks of rotting moss and other unidentifiable and fetid objects to fall from the crusted top of the sewer tunnels and onto the goblins as they moved. Eventually, Gravlox and Vorst came to a larger intersection of tunnels and sewers beneath the city.

The small, glowing cantrip guided the two goblins to a cramped passage that angled steeply downward. Without hesitation, Vorst jumped into the sewer tunnel and slid down the slick moss with Gravlox not far behind. Had the two goblins waited a moment between sliding, they wouldn't have collided so painfully at the bottom of the passage. Vorst's face was contorted against a set of three iron bars at the end of the slanted sewer. When her male companion slammed directly into her back, Vorst's contorted face became a clear image of pain and regret.

Master Brenning heard the clumsy creatures smack into the iron bars right next to his head. He recognized the screeching qualities in the two voices and knew that his visitors were not human. Mustering all the strength he could, Brenning got to his feet and brushed the dirt from his clothes.

"What in Vrysinoch's name?" Master Brenning jumped back a step when he noticed the incorporeal eagle casually gliding above his head. His sleep had denied him the frightful occasion of seeing the eagle enter the room.

The burly smith drew his sword and snarled. He had just enough light from the glow of the magical bird to tell that it was a pair of goblins who had found his sewer prison. "Have at me, then!" He yelled, slapping the flat of his blade against his hairy chest to summon his courage.

Within seconds, the stone around the edges of the iron bars exploded into a flurry of dirt and grime. Two tangled goblins dropped to the floor of the chamber right behind the loud iron bars. Fortunately for the goblins, the older man was too stunned from the blast to react with his sword before Gravlox and Vorst were on their feet.

"Friends," Vorst said, patting her hands in the air to calm Master Brenning. The softly glowing eagle landed on the smith's shoulder, pecked his face once with its ghostly beak, and dissipated in a burst of light that seemed to attach itself to the moss and continued to glow. Something about the peacefulness of the flitting bird eased the smith's mind and calmed his blood. He lowered the sword but did not sheath it.

"Both friends," she repeated and took another step closer. "Human with us. Work with humans." Her choppy command of the human language was unusual for a goblin and brought more questions than answers to the blacksmith.

Master Brenning's eyes kept darting back and forth from the goblin pair to the exploded sewer tunnel in the wall. It was hard to tell which surprised him more.

"Shaman," the amused female goblin stated as she patted Gravlox on the back. Brenning's face went pale in the darkness because he knew that attempting to defend himself would be fruitless. He sheathed his sword and took a confident step towards the goblins. Gravlox and Vorst had no idea what to make of the smith's outstretched hand so they simply let it hang awkwardly in the air.

After painfully slow introductions had been made, the three beings in the bottom of the sewer containment area sat down. The tunnel that Gravlox and Vorst had come down was far too narrow to allow the broad-shouldered smith to squeeze through. The walls of the circular chamber were far too smooth to attempt a climb and the smith had been trapped underground for days. He needed food and clean water. The man wasn't on the verge of death, but the sooner he was out of the dim underground, the better.

"Well," Gravlox asked. "How do we get out?"

Eighteen

T HE FIRST GOBLIN wave came from the north, just as expected. About a hundred screaming goblins came rushing from the grass line waving weapons above their heads. The century stationed on the northern flank dug their heels in and waited for the charge to meet them. An alaris was stationed to the side of the century, ready to cut a diagonal swath of death through the measly charge.

"It must be a feint," Herod said to Apollonius from atop his warhorse. "Even if all of our soldiers were stationed *inside* the walls, not a single one of those filthy goblins would breach." Apollonius shook his head and looked to the east, expecting a second charge to compliment the first.

The goblins were halfway from the grass line to Terror's Lament when the alaris met their charge. Thundering hooves blasted through the weak charge. Goblin blood and bones flew through the air as dozens of the mindless drones were killed. As soon as the alaris had passed through the charge, a hail of arrows and crossbow bolts showered down upon what remained of the first attack. None of the first one hundred goblins ever made it to the steel clad soldiers of the century positioned on the north side of Talonrend.

Silence shrouded the bloody battlefield. The alaris trotted slowly back into place at the right flank of the century and waited for a
second charge. The human army had survived the first minutes of
war without a casualty. In their eagerness, the militia stationed atop
Terror's Lament had fired nearly a dozen missiles for every target.
Had they known how many goblins would face them that day, the
soldiers would have thought twice about firing too many arrows.

Waiting for the next attack, the army was on edge. After an
hour of standing in the bright sunlight, the soldiers were losing
their focus. More and more of the militia on the walls lost the edge
that adrenaline had given them. They sat down against the parapet
and took off their roughshod helmets and hats. The sun was relentless.

Another hour of silence passed before Herod decided to act.
"The alaris stationed on the southern flank, bring them up, Apollonius." The prince turned his warhorse toward the east and trotted
out away from the wall. The eager soldier was riding a warhorse of
his own taken from the prince's personal stables. The beast reared
under his legs and took off.

In just a few minutes, twenty six mounted riders trotted up to
the prince and saluted. "Good," Herod said as he met their approach. "I want you to execute a sortie. We know the goblins are
camped out to the north. They sent a fifth of their number against
us but even they aren't stupid enough to waste so many soldiers."

"Sir, with all due respect, why not?" The leader of the alaris
wore a helmet fashioned with a large metal spike to designate his
leadership and make him easier to spot. Curiously, the man also
wore a set of throwing axes on his side like Gideon had.

"Why not?" Herod asked with venom in his voice. He had no
patience for sarcasm.

"Why must the goblins be smarter than that? They send a
bunch of goblins, wave after wave until they are all dead." The alaris captain used a mailed hand to shade his eyes from the sun.

"We can't afford to believe that, captain, even if it proves to be

170

true. I am responsible for all of the lives here today. That includes the humans and the goblins. I want the goblins to die. If they will not come to us, we must go to them." Prince Herod indicated toward the man's throwing axes with a nod.

The alaris captain smiled and handed an axe to the prince. The handle was well worn and wrapped in supple leather strips. Curiously, the blade of the weapon was unscathed and pristine. "Throwing axes are not a very common sight in my army. I've seen things like these before. Actually, I've been attacked by very similar axes by a man named Gideon. Know him?" The prince handed the axe back to its owner.

"Gideon.... Yeah, I used to know him. We worked at the same armory together. We get to make these axes after we've been there for a few years." He tossed the weapon into the air and flipped it around before catching it again in his other hand.

"You have never used that axe. Have you ever been in a life or death situation, captain?"

"Just when I come home late to my wife," the man said with a chuckle.

"Perfect." Herod managed a grin despite the captain's relaxed attitude. "Go scout the goblin position. Kill as many of them as you can but don't risk your men. Figure out where they are hiding and how many more have joined their ranks. Then come back and report to me."

"Of course, my liege," the captain said with a stiff salute before he led his men away to the north.

Prince Herod watched his well-organized cavalry kick a cloud of dust into the air as they departed. "Where are the paladins? Where is Gideon?" The prince didn't dare let anyone near him catch a word of what he was saying. As far as the army knew, the paladins had been ordered to stay within the city walls and protect the people should a breach occur. In reality, the prince hadn't seen anyone from the Tower of Wings since he openly denied Vrysinoch. The paladins, assuming they still remained within the city, were cowering inside their tower. Herod only hoped that if the holy warriors were needed to fight back the gathering enemies, they would be ready and willing to do so.

YAEL AND KEEGAR crouched on the top of a slanted, thatched roof and watched the alaris gallop past. The solitary farm house was one of the few structures on the plain between Talonrend and the villages along the Clawflow. "Lady Scrapple!" Yael screamed at the younger Keegar. He knew that even though the hive mind was ignoring his consciousness, she could still be reached. "Lady Scrapple!" he yelled again into the frightened goblin's face. "They are sending heavy cavalry to the blocks positioned in the north! Those goblins need to get into anti-cavalry formations now!" Yael shook Keegar's body forcefully and knew by the mist in his eyes that Lady Scrapple had heard him.

The goblin blocks crouched in the high grasses moved immediately. They crawled along their bellies toward the incoming alaris and fanned out in a circular pattern. Just as expected, the human riders galloped onto the prepared battlefield. It took them a moment to realize they were surrounded. The captain clenched his hand into a fist in the air which ordered the riders to halt. The well prepared goblins never gave them a chance. A hundred diminutive drones swarmed the alaris with long spears that shined in the sunlight. Before the captain could even draw his sword, a spear head lodged itself under his horse's chin and sent the beast sprawling to the ground.

Two more spears bit into the horse's flank and silenced the animal's screams in a burst of blood. The alaris captain scrambled to his feet and tried to remove the blade at his side from its scabbard but it wouldn't budge. The horse's fall had bent the blade and locked it into the sheath.

A trio of goblins rushed the captain with spears and caused him to roll to his side to avoid being skewered. His armor was strong and the one spear head that did connect with his breastplate was easily deflected. Frustrated, the captain ripped the sheathed sword from his side and threw it at the nearest goblin which caused the beast to flinch. A throwing axe followed the sheathed blade and thudded into the goblin's lightly armored chest. The other two pale-skinned creatures pressing the alaris captain didn't notice their comrade's death. They poked and prodded with their longer weapons until the captain was pinned against his fallen horse's bloody corpse.

With a steel-bladed axe in his hand, the captain slashed side to side across his body to keep the deadly spear heads from finding their mark. The poorly constructed weapons splintered within moments so the two goblins threw the wooden shafts against the captain's armor and charged. With no room to dodge in the wicked melee, the alaris captain met the rush with his arms out wide and caught each goblin under the chin. Their pale skin crinkled and writhed as the muscular soldier hoisted the attackers off their feet. Holding the goblins at arm's length nearly three feet above the ground, the captain was defenseless against the third attacker he had knocked back with his thrown sword. No grin widened on the face of the ugly creature and it didn't let out a howl of victory. A blank stare bore into the alaris captain as he struggled to keep the flailing goblins tight in his clutches.

The free goblin picked up a stone and heaved it at the soldier, knocking a small dent in the man's strong armor. A broken spear shaft followed the rock but sank into the back of the goblin in the captain's right hand. The soldier banged the heads of his captives together with such force that both the creatures fell limp in his grasp. With a shield made of goblin flesh before him, the captain ran with all his strength at the third assailant and trampled the poor beast to the ground. Heavy steel boots crushed the soft goblin flesh and sent bits of bone flying among the grasses. Disgusted, the captain tossed aside the two dead goblins like chaff and drew another axe from his side.

Another line of goblins was nearly upon him by the time he loosed the missile. More goblins than the soldier had ever seen poured over him in a heartbeat. His thick armor was well built and prevented him from being quickly stomped into human mush but the immense weight of the armor made it impossible for the man to regain his feet. For a brief moment, the captain could see the sparse strands of wispy clouds that layered the sky. Soon, however, an ugly goblin face filled his vision, biting and spitting to chew at his face. The pile of goblins grew by the second as more of the stinking creatures leapt atop the fallen captain. Finally, after what felt like hours of being slowly crushed under all of that squirming weight, the captain succumbed to suffocation and died.

Yael and Keegar watched from a distance as the entire human cavalry unit disappeared into the maw of the waiting goblin ambush. "Her will must be getting weaker, Keegar," the pale-skinned leader remarked.

"Who is getting weaker?" Keegar wondered, still not comprehending Yael's discovery.

Yael backhanded his assistant out of frustration. It was a blow he truly wanted to deliver to Lady Scrapple herself. "The Mistress of the Mountain, Keegar. She is growing weaker every day trying to control so many goblins. We are too far from the mountain for her to fully control us. We are free out here, don't you feel it?"

The confused expression that followed showed Yael that Keegar did not fully understand his newly acquired mental freedom. "What did you do before you left the mountain for this campaign?" Yael asked, trying to make him think for the first time in his life.

"Back home? I lived with the soldiers and trained with them every day." Keegar scratched his wrinkled head as his tiny goblin brain worked furiously behind his beady eyes.

"What sorts of skills did you train?" the commander asked to lead his thinking in the right direction. Yael, as a high ranking member of the military, knew well the daily training regimens of the soldiers. The mindless drones rarely ever practiced anything but group attacks with spears or swords. A few goblins, those with more autonomy, were trained for specialized tasks such as scouting or stealth infiltration.

"I ran, I guess." Keegar was unsure of himself. He had never consciously experienced mental freedom before and the sensation was hitting him like a flood. "Every day I would train with the other goblins using my sword, and then I would run. Sometimes I would get to use a bow, but I was never very good at it."

Yael nodded. "How long would you run?" The wise goblin noted the thick leg muscles and dexterous frame of his companion with appreciation. It was obvious that Keegar had done nothing but athletic training for his entire life.

"I ran for as long as I had to..." His voice trailed off and his ugly features twisted into an expression of curiosity.

"Did you ever *want* to run, Keegar?" The commander smiled and knew he had succeeded.

"I..." Jagged teeth broke through the goblin's wide grin and he jumped up and down with excitement. "I always ran because I didn't know what else to do."

"Yes, you were being trained as a scout, Keegar! You were running so that one day, you could run faster than any of the other goblins and make reports. Lady Scrapple made you learn to shoot a bow so you could defend yourself while out alone. Scouts are the most valuable part of any army and the information you carried was worth more than your life. Our mother knew that if you were sent too far away, she wouldn't be able to control you and so you had to be fast enough to make it back alive."

Keegar jumped off the farmhouse roof and landed in a perfectly balanced roll. He began to run circles around the dilapidated building. "I *want* to run now!" he shouted back to Yael with glee.

"Lady Scrapple knew that there was a possibility that she could lose control..." Yael whispered under his breath. "She knew...."

Looking over his shoulder at the dark silhouette of the massive mountain, Yael couldn't help but wonder what that meant. "If she knew, why would she send so many of us? What is so important about this human city that she would risk losing her control?" Yael climbed slowly down from the rooftop to join the elated scout in his celebration of freedom.

With the alaris thoroughly destroyed, the battlefield was quiet again. The towering walls of Talonrend reached to the bright summer sky to the west. Behind the goblin pair, Kanebullar Mountain loomed like the mighty shadow of a god poised to fly from the stars.

Nineteen

S TALE WATER TRICKLED down from somewhere above and played beautifully in the reflecting light of the magically luminescent moss. All around them, soft colors darted about like a torch tossed into a room full of gemstones. "Can the shaman get us out?" Master Brenning asked. He pointed to Gravlox and then pointed up to the dripping water overhead. "Grav… lox?" The man tried to pronounce the name the best he could but the high-pitched goblin language was far too complex for the smith to control. The foreign word came out as a bit of an embarrassing squeal that left his cheeks flushed.

Gravlox and Vorst both laughed at the attempt and tried to imitate the unusual sound. The barrel-chested smith's strained falsetto was still much deeper than any sounds the goblins knew how to make. "Gravlox," the foreman repeated, pointing to his chest and smiling. Vorst tapped a translation of Brenning's question against the stone.

The shaman didn't know what to do. He wasn't familiar enough with his innate magical abilities to command the energy much beyond short bursts like the one that had destroyed the small tunnel opening in the sewer wall. "I can try," Gravlox said, more to himself than anyone else.

Calming his mind to concentrate, Gravlox closed his eyes and placed both of his hands against the stone. He remembered the feeling of energy he commanded in the clearing against the human soldiers.. The magic within his small body swirled and made him nauseous. Gasping for breath against the swell of energy, Gravlox let it go. Tiny cracks shot forth from his hands and split the stone where he was kneeling. Tendrils of black smoke curled up from his hands. "There is too much magic," he whispered. "I can't control it."

Vorst and Master Brenning moved away from the shaman and watched him in silence as the cracks along the stone slowly spread. They weren't deep, violent fissures, just a small sign of the unpredictability of shamanistic power.

Try again, Vorst tapped against the stone floor, although she wasn't sure if Gravlox would even notice.

Gravlox put his hands against the damp floor of the sewer and sought out the unstable source of magic within his soul that connected him to everything. His pale hands trembled with energy and the air around his fingertips crackled. More black smoke curled away into the stagnant air and a profound shudder rocked Gravlox's body. He could sense the immense river of natural magic coursing just beneath the edge of his consciousness. The shaman could see the glowing river like a fire on the horizon, blurred by a distant setting sun. With a hesitant mind, Gravlox reached toward that fire and brushed it with his fingertips. The jolt was unlike anything he had ever felt before. Pure white magic shot through his body and brought him to the ground. With a violent convulsion that nearly broke his spine, Gravlox retreated his consciousness from the source of magic.

Approaching the fire more slowly, he called out to it. No words accompanied the message, just a magical sensation of peacefulness. The burning image of magic revolted against the telepathic communication and raged with blind fury. A great heat swelled up in the stone chamber, sizzling the moist water droplets and causing the moss to wilt.

Fire was surrounding Gravlox in the mysterious realm of magical connections. He had not tried to approach and manipulate the
essence but somehow it surrounded him, burning his mind and
tearing away at the walls of his sanity. A voice behind the fire
pushed out like the blast from a massive furnace and tore through
the air. "Get out!" it yelled. The disembodied voice was full of anger
and restlessness that betrayed underlying fear.

Gravlox did not waver. His magical being held firm against the
torrent of ethereal flames that continued to assault his mind. Without thinking, Gravlox stepped forward through the fiery wall and
saw a face on the other side. His features were strained, tortured
even, and Gravlox could make out thick white ropes binding the
face and holding it above the flames. Gravlox tried to reach out to
the face with calming energy but the fires lashed out at him before
he got near.

The sewer around the three beings shimmered in unseen heat.
Vorst and Master Brenning both feared that they might be blown
apart by the release of energy when Gravlox's trance subsided.

With fire licking all around and igniting the world, the face
turned to snarl and spit at Gravlox's intrusion. The shaman recognized the face at once and nearly lost his concentration. Gravlox
sent another magical wave of energy toward the burning face. The
message was delivered like a barrage with fleeting images of pain,
fear, darkness, and suffering. As if the face understood the communication perfectly, the fires subsided and died to smoldering embers. The face struggled against the white ropes, tossing and turning
in every possible direction.

Gravlox could feel his strength deteriorating and knew that his
willpower was about to break. The shaman sent one final message
flying forth from his mind, a message of urgency and a clear mental
picture of the sewer where he was trapped.

Fully exhausted and moments from his mental breaking point,
Gravlox collapsed into a heap on the floor. The stones of the sewer

were hot to the touch and steamed where his pale skin trapped water against them. Vorst rushed to his side, thankful that her beloved had survived and equally thankful that Gravlox had not destroyed the entire city.

"The magic wasn't mine," Gravlox managed to say. He rolled to his side and coughed. The air of the sewer was too hot and too stagnant to offer any relief. "Gideon, it was his. Everything I felt was coming from him. He could set the whole world on fire, but he is coming to help us." Vorst cradled him in her arms and held his head close to her chest.

"Human friend comes and rescues us," Vorst said without taking her eyes from Gravlox.

Master Brenning breathed a sigh of relief for the first time in many days. "I'm very interested in meeting this friend of yours," he muttered, but knew the goblins weren't listening.

Within a few short minutes, a thunderous sound shook the sewer and knocked moss from the walls. The shimmering magical light wavered in the air and more water started to drip down from above. A second report followed the first and a large stone fell to the ground beside Vorst. More and more hits rocked the chamber until a large shaft of natural light suddenly appeared. The three shielded their eyes against the brilliant sunlight as one more strike turned the top of the sewer system into rubble.

A massive tree was lowered into the sewer, temporarily blocking the harsh sunlight. Gravlox and Vorst, knowing the trick well, grabbed onto the tree limbs and held on tightly. Master Brenning, not knowing what to expect, shook his head and wrapped his arms around the tree next to Vorst. One great heave had all three of them sprawled out in the sunlight behind the Castle of Reikall.

Master Brenning recognized Nevidal before he made the connection between the massive man and the apprentice he had once trained. The two men didn't say much but rather nodded their appreciation to one another in a solemn moment of silence. The old smith stroked his beard as he walked around Gideon's tree-like legs and inspected the tight cords of muscle breaking out all over his body. There was no question that the paladin was nearly consumed by his sword's enchantment. Gravlox's healing magic had staved off the demonic poison well enough to stabilize the mixture of magic working within the paladin but the enchantment could not be stopped. Without the remnants of the poison slowing Nevidal's consumption, Gideon would surely be dead.

"There isn't much time," Master Brenning said while Vorst acted as a translator for Gravlox. "We need to return to Talonrend before it suffers the same fate as this once-fair city." The four companions stood behind a castle they had previously thought beautiful. From a distance, they couldn't see the charred streaks of ash around the shattered windows and the dried patches of splattered blood that dotted the stones. Reikall had undergone great terror and had not survived.

"You need food," Vorst replied. They had none with them and the city was so consumed by blight that anything they might salvage from the ruins was sure to be rotten.

"I can get food along the way, but we have to move, now," Gideon said definitively. Gravlox, Vorst, and Master Brenning climbed atop the giant's shoulders and hooked themselves into the leather straps of his armor. The metal sleeve, tucked away in Vorst's pack, had remained unchanged by Nevidal's magic, but the rest of Gideon's armament had grown with him. The paladin's braided black beard was well over the average height of a normal human and swayed calmly back and forth with every step like a great pendulum.

Speed and endurance were two things of which Gideon's enchanted body had a great deal. He bounded into the forest, leaping streams and fallen trees as though they were puddles and broken sticks. It didn't take the paladin long to spot a deer and deftly cleave it in half with his sword. A flare of holy radiance from Nevidal cooked the meat of the animal almost instantly. Able to make fantastic speed, the group could see Terror's Lament shining high against the sun before nightfall.

"The goblins will come from the east, from the river," Vorst said, pointing at the imposing shadow of Kanebullar Mountain far in the distance.

"We should return to the city at once and warn them of the incoming horde of undead!" Master Brenning shouted. He beat his fists into Gideon's back but the huge man remained silent.

"Your people will kill both of us." Vorst knew it was true. She would never be accepted into Talonrend, even to help fight a war. She pulled Gravlox down from the harness and led him by the hand in the direction of the river. "If we can just tell them that there is more to life than war and conquest..."

Gravlox stopped and brought Vorst tight against his side. "Are you alright?" he asked in the high-pitched goblin language. The concern in his voice did little to mask his fear.

"I can feel her again. In the dead city, it was like I was free. I felt like you. We are closer to her again. Lady Scrapple knows I am here. I sense her presence like a painful splinter in my back that I cannot reach. I know she is there and can see me. I'm scared, Gravlox." Vorst buried her head in his chest and fought back tears.

The two humans didn't know what to make of Vorst's sudden and emotional outburst. Until very recently, Gideon and Master Brenning had never imagined that the short, pale-skinned creatures were capable of any emotions at all, much less love and fear.

"If we don't return to the city at once, we will be branded as traitors and exiled!" Master Brenning's bearded cheeks flushed a deep red as he yelled. Few people who had known the revered smith had ever seen him so torn. Before anyone else could speak, Brenning started trudging through the open plain toward Talonrend.

"Do we just leave them here, then?" Gideon called after his former teacher. "These two goblins saved both of our lives. We have a debt to them." With one massive stride, Gideon was able to put a hand firmly on Brenning's back and turn him around. "We cannot leave them until we know that they are safe."

"The goblin army is camped out there by the river," Vorst said, pointing east. "If we return, they kill us, both of us." She stood hand in hand with Gravlox, looking Master Brenning in the eyes.

The smith ruffled a hand through his beard. "We have to prove your worth, then, to the folk of Talonrend. If you were spies," Brenning spit as though the very taste of the word disgusted him, "you wouldn't have dragged me out of that hole. I owe you that much."

"We should make ourselves useful then," Gideon said. "Master Brenning, go back to the city and tell them I rescued you. Don't mention the goblins, but we need to warn them of the reanimated corpses approaching the city." The paladin smiled and the sword in his hands flared to life. "I will stay with these two brave warriors and see if we can't go and stop this invasion before I die."

"Yes, there is also the matter of that sword..." Master Brenning thought back on how many years it had taken him to craft it. The project had nearly bankrupted his forge, but it was his life's work, whether Gideon knew it or not. "You do recall how to stop that enchantment, right?"

The humor of Brenning's jest was lost upon the giant paladin. "I have to kill someone. The abominations in the caves didn't have souls."

"And as far as I know, no offense to you two, goblins do not have souls either. At least, goblins do not have any souls that would please Nevidal." Master Brenning thought to his long hours of study in the library at the Artificer's Guild that had led up to the forging of Nevidal. He had lived in that library for what felt like a lifetime.

"You may want to try a graveyard," he said wistfully, entranced by the soft magical glow of the weapon. "Souls are said to linger there. All sorts of aspiring magic users and artificers visit graveyards at night to see if they can't capture the wandering souls and harness their energy. Most of the time, the dark energies of a captured soul will turn against the wizard and either kill him or corrupt him. Poor fellows..." The smith, despite loathing the amount of time he had spent away from his beloved forge, had truly enjoyed his time of study in the library and remembered almost everything he had read.

"If I find any souls wandering a graveyard, I will be sure to tell you." Gideon managed a half smile as he hefted the wicked blade in his strong grip.

Brenning's unruly beard jostled as he laughed. "If I remember correctly, a few of the famous necromancers throughout magical history have recorded finding flowers that bloom atop gravestones in the dead of night. The ghost flowers, as they are called, are rumored to be born out of the combined souls of everyone buried at the site. Pluck me one, will you?" Master Brenning turned to make his way back to Talonrend before Vorst furiously burst into action.

"What's wrong?" Gravlox asked with a fearful voice.

Vorst ripped through her pack and withdrew the lantern she had stolen from the necromancer the two had killed. Lifting the lantern above her body like a warrior who had just decapitated a dragon, Vorst was too excited to even speak. Gideon and Brenning stared at her in wonder, looking all around and worried that the small goblin's actions might be a prelude to danger.

"This... This, metal torch," goblins didn't use lanterns or oil lamps so Vorst had no idea what the word might be in the human language, "This has soul. Take soul!" she said, jumping up and down.

"What are you talking about?" Master Brenning said, his tone suddenly serious. "That beat up lantern has a soul locked inside?"

Mimicking the motions of the necromancer at the graveyard, Vorst tried her best to explain that the man had captured ghost flowers within the object before she had stolen it. "We try and find necromancer dust for poison, got metal torch full of glowing flowers from graveyard!"

Stunned into silence, the humans stood slack-jawed and stared at the elated goblin female until she finally threw it at Master Brenning and yelled. He caught the lantern and peered through the glass, seeing the swirling mist of captured souls up close for the first time.

"Not yet," Gideon said as he took the lantern from Master Brenning. It was awkward to hold the item with the handle of Nevidal still firmly attached to his palm. "The enchantment will end, yes, but if I am going into a war against soulless goblins, I will need my sword." He patted the throwing axes dangling from his side. The deadly projectiles looked like tiny playthings against the giant's tree-like legs. "I will keep this with me and use it when the time comes. The enchantment won't kill me just yet."

"So you think," Brenning scoffed. The burly smith shook his head, unsure of how much time Gideon had left before the holy magic consumed him. Using the rope from Vorst's pack, Gideon tied the lantern around his neck.

"Go now, warn the city, and get them ready for our two goblin guests." The giant shrugged to adjust the rope that felt like an unwanted collar of oppression. Knowing that a captured soul was lingering inside the magical metal lantern made the paladin uneasy.

Without another word, Gideon, Gravlox, and Vorst watched as the man they rescued from Reikall disappeared into the horizon toward the towering stone walls. The paladin felt a renewed vigor for battle with the lantern swinging awkwardly around his huge neck. Using his massive fingers and making sure not to let Nevidal accidentally touch anyone, Gideon hoisted the two goblins onto his back and began striding toward the Clawflow.

Yael and Keegar saw the fast approaching giant and fled back to their own lines. The hand-and-a-half sword pulsed and thrummed with every powerful step the man took, sending fear into every goblin who managed to see him. "We will need more than a cavalry defense for that behemoth," Yael whispered to himself. Images of a sprawling goblin army flitted through his head, mental communications from Lady Scrapple. "Yes, it is time," he said with more confidence. "We must strike now. If every human is as large as that one, we are doomed." Keegar's thickly muscled legs propelled him much faster ahead of Yael, who struggled to keep the scout in his sight. A foreign emotion, something between nausea and curiosity, crept up from the depths of Yael's mind and made him stop. He knew that Lady Scrapple was inside his mind and he keenly felt her presence like a tangible object resting in the back of his skull. She was suggesting that Yael go and meet the main bulk of her forces. It wasn't a command. Lady Scrapple was *asking* Yael for obedience. The pale-skinned goblin readily complied and turned his course for the river.

The sheer number of goblins arrayed on the eastern bank of the Clawflow River took Yael's breath away. The army stretched for miles to either side and seemed to extend all the way back to Kanebullar Mountain. Spear tips and arrowheads glinted in the waning sunlight as the rigid drones swayed slowly in the breeze. "Oh, Mistress..." Yael couldn't believe what he was seeing. "This is why you can't control us all... There are so many..." Lady Scrapple sent telepathic emotions of peace and silence to the commander as he surveyed the army.

This is what you were bred for, Yael. The voice was strangely soothing, coming from the back of Yael's consciousness. It felt almost like a thought, except that it wasn't in Yael's own voice. *They will listen to you, Yael. You are their commander. Start the invasion. I will move when the time is right and destroy the human walls.* Yael sucked in a deep breath and tried to steady himself. *There will be more soldiers, always more soldiers. Do not concern yourself with their safety. Victory is the only path now, Yael. Make the mountain proud.*

Lady Scrapple's departure was even more shocking than her speech. In an instant, faster than he could respond or even think, the Mistress of the Mountain was gone. It was then that Yael realized she had always been there. Her sudden disappearance left a gaping void in the outer reaches of Yael's mind. It was a chasm he did not know how to fill. "Are there any left in the mountain?" he finally managed to say after he regained his composure. None of the goblins responded. "They are mindless, totally vacant," Yael reminded himself.

"Soldiers of Kanebullar Mountain!" Yael shouted. At once, the thousands of empty goblin eyes locked onto their commander. He stood on the bank opposite the army and looked slowly from one flank to the other as he spoke. "We take the human city this night!" Yael would have continued, but he realized that inspiration was meaningless to soldiers lacking the capacity to understand it. "To me," he commanded and the response was overwhelming. Goblins splashed through the river without hesitation. The once clear current of the Clawflow turned into a muddy morass of goblin soldiers as wave after wave of the drones swam across. They assembled themselves into the blocks as quickly as they could and Yael was forced all the way back to an abandoned farm house in order to make room for the army.

Catapults, trebuchets, and all manner of siege equipment floated across the river alongside the endless army. Platoons of goblins all wearing leather vests stained with red hauled massive baskets and long lengths of animal hide that Yael had never seen before. He couldn't begin to imagine what their purpose was so the commander shrugged and continued to watch the assembly. Finally, after the goblin horde had filled in the entire area of farmland between the rickety house and the river, Yael had to order a charge. There was simply nowhere else for the drones to continue their muster.

A wicked and toothy smile broke out on the commander's pale face.

Twenty

"GOBLINS FROM THE north!" The shout rang out from the parapet and all eyes turned to see a thin line of dark creatures running toward the city. "Push north! Defend the walls!" Herod called back with fervor. The horsemen and foot soldiers inched toward the northern walls, eager to spill goblin blood. There had been a lull in the action in the quiet hours since the alaris had galloped out, never to return. Master Brenning sat tall in his saddle next to the prince. His horse was barded in silver and gold armor that glowed in the soft light of the dying day. The burly smith wore plates of steel that he had crafted himself. They fit tightly over his chest and served as a painful reminder of how young and thin he had been when he made the armor.

"It's just a feint," Master Brenning scoffed. He watched the soldiers moving away from the eastern gate and shook his head. "These goblins are much smarter than you think, my liege."

Herod turned his warhorse to face his most trusted advisor. "You presume to know much about our enemies, Master Brenning."

"I told you already, Gideon was working with two goblins. They saved me. The goblins were rogues who had left the army. You cannot afford to underestimate their cunning!" Brenning had told the prince a hundred times. No matter how much he told everyone, not a single person believed his story.

"For the last time, Brenning, I will believe you when I meet these goblins myself! Why is it so hard for you to understand that these goblins we fight today are just as stupid as they look and act? We have scouted out their location, we know they will come from the north. Our walls are well defended from every single approach. We can hold off a million of the stinking creatures if we have to. Why should we not push out to meet their attack and crush them under our feet?" Herod's horse whinnied and stamped the ground as a crudely-made goblin arrow struck near the animal's feet.

"What did I tell you?" Brenning screamed. He moved his powerful horse closer to the wall and looked up to the archers. "How many?" he called up to the lookouts.

"None, sir, I can't see a single goblin!" The lookout was leaning far over the wall and squinting against the darkness of dusk.

Herod ordered the soldiers to crowd back against the gatehouse and called for the portcullis to be raised. "Where did that arrow come from?" he barked. None of the men could see anything other than darkness on the horizon.

"The better question would be to ask why no others have followed it. The goblins test their range." Brenning didn't mean for the prince to hear his remark but he had said it louder than he thought.

"Clever bastards..." Herod muttered. "One volley, flaming arrows, light up the sky!" he shouted to the wall. Within seconds the archers sent brilliant streaks of fire soaring out over the soldiers to litter the battlefield.

"Get the men back into the city. We need to move behind the walls to hold our advantage as long as possible." Master Brenning had his horse turned in an instant and galloped for the gate. The portcullis was slowly creaking upwards on its metal chains and offered just enough room for the soldiers to start pouring through on hands and knees.

Remembering the river of undead men and women walking the dark tunnels from Reikall to Talonrend, Brenning realized the goblin plan. "They want us to cower behind our walls..." he said to himself. "We have no place left to run and nowhere to turn for help."

What the men had mistaken for empty darkness in the fields beyond the walls was actually an unimaginable sea of living creatures. The goblins were packed together so tightly that their dark leather armor had created the illusion of empty space. At the sight of the blazing flares, the goblin army charged.

High-pitched wails and screams filled the night air for miles around the city. Herod commanded two of his best runners to order the retreat of his army from the north but, in the panic, it was impossible to know which orders had effect and which died before they reached their destinations. The alaris trying to push through the gatehouse was causing so much commotion that Herod ordered the unit of horsemen to sacrifice themselves in order to slow the goblins. Untrained militia soldiers stationed behind the walls only added to the quagmire of men attempting to run to safety. Herod was still outside the gate when the first line of goblins fell upon the retreat.

"Brenning! I need you!" the prince called. The smith realized that in the tight quarters between the walls his horse was too frightened to be of any use. He dismounted the unruly beast and pushed his way out from the horde of soldiers back to Herod's side. "Close the gate!" Herod yelled, even though only half of the soldiers had made their way back to safety. With a resounding crash, the heavy steel portcullis thundered into the dirt and sealed the city.

"Rally around the prince!" Brenning waved his sword above his head to organize the remaining troops. The first line of the human defenses held well despite the confusion and panic behind them. Goblin corpses started to pile up around the gatehouse and each human that fell took at least 10 of the noisy creatures with them. The press of enemies was relentless. Pale-skinned goblins came in at every angle and with all manner of weapons.

The archers overhead rained death upon the field, firing as fast as they could into the goblin tide. Dozens of goblins died with every volley but their numbers were simply too great for it to matter. Arrows, hammers, javelins, and even rocks answered the human volley with devastating effect. The goblins were completely unorganized in their attacks but fought with such numbers that they quickly broke through the initial human defense.

Brenning leapt into the fight with reckless abandon. He wore a shield strapped onto his back and picked up a well-balanced mace to wield in his left hand. The burly man spun his way through the goblin ranks and used his short sword and mace combination to blast any foe unlucky enough to get in his path. The shield on his back rang out with hit after hit and many goblins got close enough to ding his chest plate just before they died.

YAEL'S EYES GREW wide with amazement as he watched the onslaught. He had only intended to let a few thousand goblins die in the first real attack but the beauty of the carnage mesmerized him. The commander was drunk with power. He had never felt so alive in his life. When he gave an order, the telepathic relays of Lady Scrapple's consciousness delivered the order instantaneously to the corresponding drones. Scrapple's mental connections spread throughout the entire army, a sensation that felt awkwardly comforting to Yael. The goblin matriarch was helping Yael, but not directly controlling him or watching his thoughts.

The goblin troops in red had cleared out a large area of the field and used it to light fires under their makeshift balloons. In groups of four the goblins piled into their wicker baskets and floated up into the air. Long ropes were passed along the ground through the goblin army and pulled the hot air balloons towards the towering walls. Yael couldn't help but smile as he saw nearly a hundred such balloons dotting the battlefield.

RAGE AND ADRENALINE coursed through Brenning's blood, turning him into a senseless killing machine. Countless spear heads and arrow tips ricocheted off his polished armor every minute, but still the man fought on. His sword and his looted mace were so slick with goblin blood that they nearly flew from his hands as he executed a vicious two-handed swing that blasted a tiny goblin to pieces. All around the courageous smith, the humans at the gate rallied. Cheers floated through the air to mingle with the deadly missiles flying to and from the wall.

Covered in blood and missing a hand, one of Herod's runners collapsed at the prince's feet with a message. "Goblins...in the north..." the man gasped.

"Yes, I know there are goblins in the north! What is it?" The soldiers outside the gate had formed a semi-circle around their commander with their backs to the wall and no goblin had yet tried to attack the regal man atop his warhorse.

"Sir, the goblins in the north... they have been turned back! Our cavalry overran them, they are fleeing!" the winded runner used the shield of the nearest soldier for support as he delivered his message.

"Good!" the prince bellowed. "Stay back behind the shield wall and try not to get in the way."

"Yes sir," the man nodded before falling to the ground. The battle raged on all around the sheltered prince and his remaining soldiers.

Herod looked to his last remaining runner. The man was young, maybe 20 years old, and wore a scrappy beard on his chin.

His arms were scrawny and lanky, but the soldier's legs were huge with muscle. "Get to the officers in the north," the prince bade the runner. "Have them move every alaris in sight to our aid. Tell them to leave the archers and the militia where they are, but every other man is to relieve our position immediately! Return to me as soon as you have delivered the message. Go!" Herod watched the young runner depart through the shield wall toward the north.

"My liege, on the horizon!" Herod's gut churned as he imagined a mighty dragon swooping down from the clouds to lay waste to his precious city. He turned his head in the direction of the soldier's pointing arm but saw no dragon.

"What are they?" the prince asked but the men around him could only shrug. "Illuminating volley!" he called to the archers on the wall who fired a line of flaming arrows into the sky a moment later.

"Flying machines, sir!" one of the soldiers guarding the prince shouted. "They are coming toward us, higher than the walls!"

A fresh wave of panic filled the air. Herod stood with his back against Terror's Lament and contemplated death. The balloon brigades made slow and steady progress toward Talonrend. An occasional arrow would fly from the basket of a nearing balloon but no real attack was ever mounted until the first line of balloons neared the wall.

An alaris came thundering down upon the goblin flank from the north just in time to kill the few drones that had been holding the guide ropes to the flying machines. The balloons continued to drift lazily toward the high city walls as the alaris reached the main bulk of soldiers still fighting in front of the gate.

A surge of morale propelled the soldiers at the front line into a killing frenzy. Horses shattered goblin skulls like a child stepping on insects. The relatively tiny creatures were no match for armored hooves and swinging flails that rained down upon them from impossibly high angles. Human warriors charged into the wake of the cavalry, eager to kill any survivors. After two devastating passes of the alaris, not enough of the riders were left alive to press their advantage again.

For a brief moment, the tide of goblins seemed to slow. The humans reformed their barricade around the prince and more soldiers came from the northern flank to support them. Then, with precision that only comes from a hive mind entity, the goblins began their siege.

Drone warriors fell back to get out of the way of the plethora of flying projectiles that bombarded the human position. Catapults and trebuchets sent huge boulders slamming into the thick stone walls of Talonrend at an alarming rate. Goblin archers unleashed a hailstorm of arrows accompanied by a shower of smaller rocks from soldiers wielding slings.

Ingenious goblin miners and alchemists ensured that every payload of rock that slammed into the human knights and walls was laced with high levels of rich magnesium. The jagged shards of metal coated the battlefield in what the goblins frequently called "flare stone".

Goblins in red leather vests stood up on the edges of their floating baskets and leapt toward the gatehouse. Their outfits were coated in a volatile magical substance used in the mines of Kanebullar Mountain to blast through tough deposits of ore. On impact with the ground, the magically imbued oil turned the unfortunate bombardier into a highly explosive mess of goblin gore. Fires from the exploding oil quickly spread to the chunks of magnesium littering the battlefield and turned the ground into a blazing inferno.

Steel-clad human knights were cooked alive in their armor and fell to the ground without a chance.

"Open the damned portcullis!" Herod screamed. The prince scrambled out of his saddle as his horse's mane caught fire. A sliver of shrapnel from one of the trebuchet blasts had punctured his fine armor and subsequently ignited. Herod clawed at the burning piece of metal but, with his bulky gloves, he couldn't get the stubborn debris loose. He could feel the flesh over his ribs on his left side start

194

to bubble and ooze as the fire took hold. Thinking to smother the ember, Herod clamped his gauntlet over the puncture, but the magically induced burn would not be extinguished so easily.

Reeling from the agony and screaming at the top of his lungs, Herod pushed his way toward the opening portcullis. The heavy metal bars of the gate were slow to rise amidst the tumult of war. Soldiers scrambled all around the wounded prince to make it to the safety of the walls as the fires burned. Men fell flat on their chests to shimmy their way through to the other side where more soldiers waited to try to beat the fires from their armor and skin.

A thoroughly blood-soaked hand ripped the prince from the burning ground and forcefully shoved him through the opening in the gate where a host of healthy warriors immediately attended to his many wounds. Master Brenning grinned at the prince and turned back to direct the flow of wounded soldiers through the gate. His sword and mace were long gone and the shield strapped to his back had taken so many hits that it was reduced to splintered bits of kindling and leather.

Handfuls of mindless goblin drones rushed through the portcullis on the heels of the retreating men but were cut down almost immediately by the awaiting militia. Firebombs and boulders continued to hammer the walls and great chunks of stone began to fall from the parapets. The outer wall of Terror's Lament was crumbling.

More payloads of rock and magnesium flew over the walls and through the gaps in the portcullis bars, causing more panic and spreading flames among the militia and wounded. Through the smoke of chaos, Brenning spotted a group of five goblins rushing the gatehouse in unison. Each goblin wore a backpack filled with volatile ore attached to a red leather vest. The seasoned blacksmith beat his fists against his armored chest and grabbed the nearest healthy soldier by the wrist. "What's your name, son?" he shouted into the knight's face.

"Nef," the panicked soldier replied. "My friends call me Nef." Master Brenning shook the knight violently by the arm in an effort to knock the confusion from his mind.

"Build a pair of statues for us, Herod! Nef and Brenning are about to save Talonrend!" The smith smiled wildly as he shoved Nef through the portcullis and back into the licking flames. Master Brenning stood beside the young knight and patted him on the back. Nef drew his weapon, a curved scimitar that looked more like a mantle ornament than a tool designed to take life.

"For Talonrend and King Lucius!" Brenning cried as the two poorly-armed warriors rushed through the smoke and fire toward the red vested goblins that dripped with volatile oil.

The massive portcullis slammed shut just before the explosion.

Twenty-One

"**W**HAT DO WE do?" Vorst whispered into the night. The two goblins crouched down behind the tall grasses of the plain as the massive army of their kin marched to the city walls. Gideon knelt beside them and Nevidal glowed faintly in his hand.

"We need to attack, to keep the humans from being overrun." Gideon's deep voice rustled the amber stalks like a ghost. Fires burned around the base of Terror's Lament and threatened to spread throughout the plains.

"If we attack now, we die. We must wait. There are too many goblins for us to be effective." Vorst tapped everything she said into the palm of Gravlox's hand, translating the conversation as she went. "As long as the walls don't come down, the humans can survive." The shaking tone of her voice betrayed her fear.

Gravlox gently kissed the back of Vorst's hand. "If we can find Yael, we might be able to stop the invasion before they break through the walls. It might work."

After Vorst translated the message into the human language, the three agreed on their plan. They would find the goblin field commander, kill him, and hope that the war would end. If the death of Yael didn't end the carnage, the three agreed that only Lady Scrapple's demise would bring peace.

As the blindingly bright fires continued to burn, there came a lull in the combat. The goblin balloons continued their aerial assault over Terror's Lament but the bulk of the goblin forces held back. A broken stretch of thirty yards separated the battered stone walls from the sea of pale-faced creatures swarming about as far as the eye could see.

Catapults and trebuchets continued to deliver their devastating cargo into the walls with great, thunderous reports. Thick plumes of smoke choked the air for miles around and the heat at the top of the walls was nearly unbearable. Archers covered their mouths with anything they could find and fired arrow after arrow into the tough leather of the hovering balloons. Many of the flying machines went down, but not before spreading more fire and devastation throughout the human ranks.

"We can't wait for their next move," Gideon growled, and the three companions took off toward the back of the goblin lines. The paladin's great braided beard swung furiously from side to side as the giant ran. His throwing axes, unaffected by Nevidal's divine enchantment, looked like tiny toys attached to a belt so thick it could have served as rigging for a ship.

Imbued with godlike strength and speed, the two goblins watched from a distance as their hulking giant friend crashed into the back of Lady Scrapple's army. With one foot planted firmly in the Clawflow River, Gideon swatted goblins away as if they were nothing but tiny flies buzzing about his meal.

Swords and spears alike were shattered into rubble with every pass of Nevidal, the wickedly sharp sword the size of a tree. Holy fire flew off the blade in great balls as big as boulders. The giant paladin fought with fury. He swung the mighty sword with his remaining arm as quickly as he could. A song in praise of Vrysinoch found his lips and escaped, the tune bringing a strange sense of peace to the wanton death all around him.

Not being able to run nearly as fast as the giant, Gravlox and Vorst could only watch as hundreds of their kin were lifted through the air or rent to pieces by the brutal sword. Gideon's boots snuffed the life from dozens of goblins at a time. The paladin's inexorable march was accented by the piercing screams of dying goblins and the sizzling of blood off the flames of his sword. From the wall, the surviving humans could see the great arcs of fire dancing through the smoke of the battle but had no way of discerning the man's giant form.

The two rogue goblins stopped not far from the destructive giant and scanned the army for any sign of Yael. "Look," Gravlox pointed to the lone farmhouse standing amidst the sea of their kin. With vision perfected in the lightless mines of Kanebullar Mountain, Gravlox could easily discern the form of a lone goblin standing atop the human structure. "That must be him," the shaman said with determination.

Without a moment of hesitation, the two sprinted through the mess of goblins. The mindless drones didn't even possess enough autonomy to get out of the way as Gravlox stormed through them. Lacking enough will to think for themselves, the horde of warriors let the unrecognized goblins pass without incident.

Before long, Gravlox and Vorst stood below the battered farmhouse and locked eyes with Yael. "You may be a powerful shaman," the goblin commander called out to the pair from his perch, "but I am the Mountain!" He spread his arms out wide and surveyed the sea of his minions. "This is my destiny!" he shouted with spit flying from his mouth. "Everything you see is under my command. I am Lady Scrapple's chosen! Her commander!" The goblin drones surrounding the two at the base of the building all turned at once and leveled their weapons.

"They listen to *me*, now!" Yael howled into the night. The nearest soldiers charged in at Gravlox and Vorst with flawless unison. The shaman gripped his short sword tightly in both hands and Vorst wasted no time putting her deadly bow to work. Four goblins struggled for life and clawed at the arrow shafts buried in their flesh by the time the first drone engaged Gravlox's sword.

The shaman met the charging spearhead with a sidelong swipe of his sword that pushed the thrust wide to his left. The stone and mortar of the farmhouse at his back reminded him of his days beneath the mountain. The mines were full of such rough textures and Gravlox had grown to love them. With a slash aimed for Gravlox's neck, the spearhead came whirring back in and again the shaman beat the attack with a well-timed parry.

A second goblin stood next to the spear-wielding drone and brandished a mean looking jagged mace. The warrior executed a powerful overhand chop with the crude weapon that forced Gravlox to roll to his side and into the thrusting metal of the spear. The shaman caught the longer weapon's shaft with his sword hilt just before the pointed tip would have opened his chest. He turned the spear aside with a rotation of his wrist and continued the motion into a downward swing that pinned the spear against the ground. The second goblin drone bore down on Gravlox with his mace but the shaman was quicker and able to sidestep the blow. In the same motion, Gravlox's pale foot snapped through the weapon's wooden shaft and buried the deadly point in the dirt.

Mimicking Gideon's style of combat, Gravlox threw his sword the short distance into the chest of the second goblin drone. The pale creature dropped his mace to the ground and fell down dead. The shaman scrambled to the fallen mace and snatched it from the ground as the first goblin, now clutching a large rock in his hands, leapt at Gravlox and attempted to overpower him. The spiked mace ripped through the pale creature's innards and halted his body midflight. Gravlox pounded his attacker's corpse a second time with the vicious weapon, caving in his skull with ease.

Vorst held back the tide with her bow well enough, but her quiver was nearly depleted. A bloody ring of dead goblins surrounded the two lovers like an ancient rune of death etched into the dirt. Yael made the soldiers hesitate a moment to regroup and then unleashed them in a full wave meant to overrun the two rogues.

The shaman felt his pale skin pressed against the cool stone of the farmhouse and willed his consciousness into the bricks. He could sense an energy in the building; not a source of magic, but a sensation of readiness, like the elements of the stones and mortar waiting to be used. As a mine foreman, Gravlox had witnessed gifted miners using shamanistic magic to blast through rock and extract difficult ore with ease. Closing his eyes and remembering scenes from his previous life, Gravlox willed the stone wall of the farmhouse to life.

The grey stones of the inanimate building absorbed the energy as fast as Gravlox could deliver it. As the second screaming wave of goblin drones cleared the bloody ground to the shaman and reared their weapons back for the kill, the stone wall exploded. The conical blast was directed against the oncoming creatures and, miraculously, the two rogues were spared. Chips of stone flew through the goblins ranks like daggers and large chunks of hard mortar shattered their bones.

The farmhouse trembled and rocked from the force of the explosion, lingering only a moment before the entire building collapsed to the ground. Yael roared as he went down in the heap of rubble and dust.

Gravlox, Vorst, and the enemy commander removed themselves from the debris of the farmhouse in seconds, ready to fight. Yael held a sword similar to the one in Gravlox's hand. Vorst loosed her last arrow at the commander but the shot ricocheted off a fallen section of the farmhouse's roof and went wide of its mark by inches. She dropped her bow to the ground and pulled a small dagger from her belt with a snarl.

Yael tossed his blade from hand to hand as the three goblins circled in the debris. Drone soldiers all around the fallen farmhouse made a wall of spears and other weapons that prevented any of the combatants from fleeing. Gravlox positioned himself with his back to the city; he could see the dark outline of the giant paladin wading through scores of goblins off in the distance. His great fiery sword sent marvelous gouts of light sailing over the battlefield, briefly illuminating random parts of the plain.

The goblin army looked limitless.

Vorst kept herself well to the side of the shaman but close enough that she could leap to him if the need arose.

"Look around you, Gravlox," Yael said with a sneer. "The mountain has come to fight. You cannot stop us all. Even if you kill ten thousand of us, you will die." The commander glanced over his shoulder at the destruction wrought by Gideon and his divine enchantment. His estimation of the goblin casualties seemed accurate. "Unless you have a hundred more giants with you, this city will fall. You cannot stop that."

Gravlox continued to circle in the rubble. Broken wooden beams and crumbled stone made his footing unstable. "Have you ever dreamed of greater things than being a slave?" he called out. He spoke loudly enough for the nearby drones to hear him but, if they comprehended anything he was saying, they didn't show it. "There is more to life than slavery! We can be free, *all* of us. Don't you feel it, Yael?"

The commander stopped circling for just a moment, mulling over Gravlox's statements in light of his own recent revelations. He could feel the consciousness of Lady Scrapple in the back of his mind, stirring and growing restless. Lady Scrapple took interest in the situation, but did not take control. Whether the Mistress of the Mountain chose not to overcome Yael's consciousness or her lack of dominance was merely a result of her waning power, Yael could not tell. There was an awkward level of disconnect between the pathways of his own mind and the intricate relays of the collective. Images of fire and brimstone flashed through his mind from matriarch. He saw telepathic images of Terror's Lament surrounded by fire and cheering goblins as it tumbled down.

"Yael," he heard, but the voice was somewhere in the distance, too far away for him to recognize. A thousand different scenes flashed through the commander's mind in an instant. He saw himself sitting atop a throne made from the piled bodies of dead humans. Yael saw an entire world devoid of human life where the goblin race was free to walk amongst the trees and spread throughout the entire land. The final image imparted to him was of his own short sword piercing Gravlox's heart. Yael enjoyed what he saw.

"I have more power than you could ever imagine, traitor," Yael said. He inched forward through the cluttered rubble and ordered the drones to begin closing the circle with their spear tips out in front of them. "You, Gravlox, are the enemy. You have chosen to ally with the filthy human scum, and for what?"

"For love," Vorst whispered, but no one could hear her soft plea.

"If you are so bent on helping these pathetic surface dwellers," Yael continued, "then you will die like one." The goblin commander planted a foot on a large black kettle that had been overturned in the tumult. He launched himself through the air, howling like a banshee, with his sword aimed right for the shaman's chest.

Gravlox had plenty of time to anticipate the jump and waited until the last possible second. He sidestepped the leap and tried to use his own sword to disarm the flying goblin but missed. Yael retracted his arm before he hit the ground and Gravlox's sword cut through nothing but air. Vorst slashed at the commander from his side with her dagger aimed low and was met by a deft parry that turned her blade well before its mark.

Gravlox wasted no time and attacked with his own weapon, executing a slicing chop that Yael easily ducked. The commander brought his sword up and in to his chest as he spun, deflecting another strike from Vorst's dagger before extending his arm and snapping his wrist. Gravlox had to stumble backward to avoid losing his nose. The movement was too fast for the untrained foreman to follow.

After being well trained by the Ministry of Assassinations, Vorst was well versed in combat, although she was used to killing targets that were completely unaware of her presence. With Yael spinning his body between her and Gravlox, she couldn't find an opening to go for a kill. She had to settle for smaller nicks and cuts scored on the commander's back.

Yael was pressing Gravlox with a furious attack combination. He used the tip of his sword to force Gravlox to parry again and again, each time striking just a little closer to the shaman's shoulder. After four such attacks, Gravlox blocked the swing with his hilt and Yael turned the blade sideways as he punched with his sword hand. Blood splattered from Gravlox's mouth and nose.

The commander turned just in time to use his free hand to clamp down on Vorst's wrist and turn her attack aside. Gravlox tripped over backward on the broken remnants of a table and his sword flew from his hand.

Yael seized the opportunity and slashed out with his blade against Vorst. Still locked tightly in his grip, she was forced to turn her body sideways to avoid being skewered. Vorst kicked out with her leg and slammed her foot into Yael's knee. The commander buckled but did not let go. He slashed again with his sword and drew a thin line of blood down Vorst's side. The female goblin yelped and clenched her teeth against the pain.

The ground was too uneven for Gravlox to quickly get to his feet, so he snatched Vorst's bow from the ground and pulled himself to Yael's feet. Using the bow as club, Gravlox swung the weapon hard into the back of the commander's legs. He attacked furiously, hitting him again and again until Yael finally fell to the rubble. Vorst was quick to bear down on the fallen foe with her dagger leading the way.

The tip of her blade bit into the soft, pale flesh of Yael's gut and a spurt of blood wet her hands. Yael had both of his arms in front of him, holding the blade back and using all of his strength to keep it from sinking in to the hilt.

Gravlox was on his feet. He found his sword in the wreckage and scampered back to where Yael slowly bled. His sword glimmered in the dancing firelight of the war as he lifted it above his head for the killing blow. Vorst rolled to her side, withdrawing her dagger and covering her face. Yael used one hand to clutch his wound and his other offered a meager defense that both of them knew was useless. Gravlox's sword whistled through the air with deadly precision.

With the blade just inches from the commander's face, a powerful, sinewy wing sent Gravlox flying over the ruined farmhouse. He landed painfully on a collection of fallen stones that cut into his back, but managed to keep hold of his sword. Taurnil bellowed a deep, throaty laugh that sent shivers down Gravlox's spine.

"I've already seen you die once, beast," Gravlox muttered through the pain. "How many lives do you have?" Swirling tendrils of acrid smoke wafted up from the ground and mingled with the smoke already choking the night sky. With the flickering light of Nevidal's holy magic at his back, Taurnil was truly frightening. Yael managed to sit up against a piece of rubble and clutch his side to stem the bleeding.

"Gideon!" Vorst called out but she knew the paladin was too far away to hear her. Gravlox used his innate shamanistic connection to the vast realms of magic to navigate the swirl of goblins and find Gideon on the battlefield. Like before, his magical essence raged like a towering inferno of hatred and violence. Gideon felt the magical plea for help in his soul and the fires of his hatred licked the heavens.

Twenty-Two

INSIDE THE HIGH walls of Talonrend, the city was quiet. Herod had ordered the militia and all the remaining soldiers inside the city during the respite. The prince's eyes darted nervously from building to building, expecting *something*, but he wasn't sure what. There was tension in the air hanging like a thick curtain. Soldiers stood nervously in the streets and paced back and forth. The occasional boulder smashed into the walls and shook the ground under their feet.

Archers maintained their posts on the tops of Terror's Lament but it had been hours since any goblin soldiers had come within bow range. Herod looked up at the Tower of Wings with a frown. The doors at the base of the tower were locked and the building was eerily silent. The soft glow of fire outside the city illuminated the highest reaches of the magnificent tower, making the wings dance and flicker. Another siege engine made the ground shake. Herod wondered how long the triple-layered walls would hold.

The prince gripped the soft leather handles of his swords as he paced back and forth in one of the city's marketplaces. Empty vendor stalls loomed high above him like sinister giants waiting to come to life. Even late into the night, there should always be merchants trying to turn a profit. The whorehouses that lined the busiest streets in the city had extinguished their lamps and boarded up their windows. The whole of Talonrend was prepared for war. Herod knew that if Terror's Lament fell, every single person inside the city would surely die. The roiling tide of goblins waiting just beyond his doorstep was overwhelming.

"What do we do now, sire?" someone wearing a fine set of silken clothing asked quietly in the darkness. Herod turned to see the man, one of his advisors, but he couldn't remember his name. The monarchy of Talonrend had always been counseled by a small advisory group, but Herod had rarely concerned himself with such things. After all, he was never the king. With Brenning dead, the prince was in dire need of good counsel.

"I do not know, good sir," Herod responded. The earth beneath his feet shook again as another blast ripped chunks of smooth stone from the walls. The prince paused for a moment, reflecting. "That last blast," he mused, "I felt it before I heard it, right?" he asked the advisor.

"Sometimes, when things happen far away, it takes time for their sounds to reach your ears, my liege." The advisor was old, perhaps older than sixty, and spoke with a steady voice despite the fear brought on by the war. Another shockwave vibrated the stones and dirt of the marketplace and again, a loud blast followed almost immediately.

The calm and steady voice of the advisor gave way to fear in an instant. "No, sir, I fear you are correct. That blast at the wall was *not* the origin of vibration." The man moved away, staring at the ground. Slight tremors shook through the dirt floor of the marketplace faster and faster. The soldiers standing nearby readied their weapons but did not know what to do.

Herod moved his back closer to a building and shut the visor on his helmet. Panic was spreading throughout the ranks and crept its way into the prince's resolve. A large grey moth flitted through the night air, going to and from the various merchant stalls as if inspecting some hidden wares that none of the men could see. Herod thought back to his favorite afternoons he spent leaning against the parapet of Castle Talon while ducks playfully swam in the moat. The moth, a simple creature like the ducks, would never know the cruelties of war. It might be caught unaware under the vicious blast of a goblin trebuchet, but the little grey animal would not suffer. The ducks in the moat would never be tormented by the nagging worries of a siege. The moth lifted up from a wooden railing and disappeared over a rooftop, oblivious to the horror that surrounded it.

Another tremor rippled out from the center of the marketplace. The army held its breath. Prince Herod drew Maelstrom and Regret from their sheaths and steadied the rise and fall of his chest.

Herod's advisor shrieked and leapt back into the morass of gathered soldiers as the ground of the empty marketplace sank. A gaping, cavernous hole opened up and swallowed the empty wooden stalls in an instant. Shouts of panic rose up throughout the army, indicating that many such holes had appeared all over Talon-rend. The prince peered into the oily darkness of the cave. He could hear movement but saw nothing. "What is it?" he heard an eager soldier call out.

"It's like..." Herod pondered, "shuffling feet? Thousands of shuffling feet..." He knew that if goblins were about to pour forth from the holes their charge would be accented by a host of battle cries. "Everyone at the ready!" he shouted and soldiers throughout the city unsheathed their weapons. A chorus of unhallowed screams rose up from the streets as the entire population of Reikall shambled up from the caves on dead legs.

"I WILL SEND you back to hell where you came from!" the giant's voice washed over the battlefield. It was late into the night and Gid-

eon stood just a few feet taller than Terror's Lament. The small metal lantern roped around his neck was lost in the thick tangle of his
braided beard. One monstrous arm pumped furiously through the
horde of goblins, smashing them to pulp by the dozen. The paladin
had fallen within himself to the tune of his song and the swing of
his sword. Nevidal burned with a furious light, blinding all those it
cut down in a plume of ragged smoke.

With two surreal leaps, Gideon cleared the distance from the
rear of the goblin army to the ruined farmhouse where Taurnil
stood cackling like a fiend. Using his powerful wings, Taurnil took
off into the air and narrowly avoided being stomped to powder.
Gideon smiled as he sang out to his god and the demon trembled.
Everything trembled.

Taurnil knew that he could not stand against such a towering
foe. Nevidal swept through the air like a guard tower being thrown
by Vrysinoch himself. The sword, sixty feet of enchanted steel,
whirled back and forth in front of the paladin, taunting Taurnil to
advance.

At the command of Yael, the goblin drones stopped trying to
bring down the raging behemoth and simply fled from his devastating footfalls. Tens of thousands of goblin soldiers were scattered in
pieces across the battlefield for their efforts trying to stop him. For
as many as he left dead in his wake, Gideon could not discern
where the sea of pale faced creatures ended. Yael continued to order
the retreat and save as many goblin lives as he could.

Lady Scrapple's consciousness fought to turn her siege weapons upon the giant as quickly as she could. The catapults and trebuchets loaded the largest boulders they had and fired upon Gideon.
The paladin's exposed skin took hit after hit from the boulders, forcing him to block the shots with Nevidal.

Using the boulders for a distraction, Taurnil heaved glob after
sticky glob of acid at the giant, but it only sizzled and evaporated
from the heat of Nevidal's holy fire.

DEEP IN THE catacombs under the Artificer's Guild, Jan peered into an enchanted crystal ball. The battle was going perfectly. A smile creased the man's face as he watched his undead army destroying Talonrend from the inside. Soldiers ran through the streets in total chaos as the shambling zombies clawed at them and pulled them to the ground with overwhelming numbers. Only two sections of the battle were not going as planned.

Jan rotated the crystal scrying device and spoke a short incantation. The magical fluid locked inside the clear ball swirled and reacted, taking Jan through the battlefield and outside the massive stone walls. He looked on through the mists as Gideon, missing an arm, deflected boulders with his sword. Taurnil darted around the paladin's head and spat caustic acid everywhere he could.

"Damned demon doesn't stand a chance," Jan muttered. He didn't care about Taurnil. The abyssal monster was his sister's pet, not his. Jan swiveled the crystal ball again to get a better view of the surrounding goblins. He could see Gravlox and Vorst scampering off behind the farmhouse ruins but did not recognize them. The goblin commander was coordinating a partial retreat, moving the drone soldiers out of Nevidal's fiery reach.

Taurnil stretched his claws out wide and timed a diving strike with a shower of boulders from a goblin trebuchet stationed along the western bank of the Clawflow. The winged demon collided with the paladin seconds after spinning chunks of stone struck the man squarely in the back. Razor-sharp claws tore into the vulnerable flesh surrounding Gideon's charred stump where his left arm used to be. The demon planted his hooked talons firmly in the giant's side and scythed back and forth as quickly as he could.

Jan watched the scene with growing excitement, eager to see the holy warrior fall. With a whispered arcane phrase, he opened a tiny sliver in the night sky several yards from the giant and let a controlled portion of his magic flow through the gateway. Taurnil's lean frame bulged from the surge of potent energy and the demon's strikes became faster by the second.

With a howl of pain and anger, Nevidal came rushing in for Taurnil's body, but a well-aimed catapult shot sent a spray of sharp debris into Gideon's eyes. With only one arm, the paladin was defenseless against the stinging rocks. Another large chunk exploded against the hilt of the sword and the man stumbled. Blood flowed freely from the ragged cuts on his shoulder and side.

Jan laughed as he watched the paladin start to fall. Gideon's knees hit the ground with the force of thunder and another boulder sailed just inches above his head. Taurnil's virulent tongues twisted their way from the demon's maw and latched into the paladin's skin just below his burnt stump. Deadly poison pumped into the holy warrior and a flying stone the size of a horse crashed into his legs, nearly throwing Taurnil to the ground. The missile broke apart upon impact and spinning chunks of shattered rock tore through the unfortunate goblins nearby.

"Just kill him, finally," Jan said through a sinister grin. "I want to see him suffer and die." Jan's darkly colored robes shimmered with the sound of his voice and the necromantic runes attached to the cloth pulsed with power.

Gideon was determined not to let the evil demon have his victory. Ignoring the pain in his entire body and the deadly missiles flying through the air, Gideon slammed the heavy, flaming edge of his sword through his own side. The blade didn't cut deeply but cleaved away enough of his skin to dislodge Taurnil and send the monster haphazardly careening through the air.

"No," Jan shook his head in disbelief. "He cannot prevail!" the man shouted into his crystal ball. He pumped more of his magical energy into the winged demon and willed it to recover. Disoriented from the blow, Taurnil flapped his wings and beat the air furiously. For all of his effort and the magical augmentation from Jan, Taurnil could not right himself enough to fly.

Gideon grunted and hefted Nevidal high over his head. Jan gasped in the darkness of the catacombs under the Artificer's Guild. Yael looked on with horror as the demon was torn asunder in mid air.

An explosion of blood and necrotic magic leapt from Taurnil's smoldering corpse. Jan reached with his soul through the crystal ball. His magical essence screamed through the ethereal corridors of space and ripped open the seam Jan had created. The shimmering robes of darkness he wore pulsed with malevolence to herald the arrival of the powerful necromancer on the field of combat.

With his shining black boots pointed toward the ground, Jan descended slowly through the air, laughing all the while.

A bolt of purple magic arced from his fingertips. The magical projectile sped toward Yael and mingled with the goblin commander's being. Just as quickly as it had appeared, the magical bolt shot through the stupefied creature's mouth and into his consciousness.

The entire battlefield calmed. The drone soldiers stopped moving. They continued to breathe, but their lungs were filled by shallow, raspy breaths. Yael was alive and relatively unharmed, but his capacity to think and make decisions was rendered useless. The necromancer cackled as he felt the telepathic connections between the thousands of drones and their hive mind. The battlefield was vibrantly alive; he could practically taste the life around him. Life sickened Jan.

Gideon's huge arm flexed. He was kneeling, which placed his head somewhere around thirty feet above the ground. The two goblin rogues cowered behind a piece of fallen roof that smoldered with a remnant of Nevidal's holy energy.

Everything was eerily quiet. Nothing remained of Taurnil. After his body was rent, it disintegrated as if he had never existed at all.

The paladin's masterful sword glowed in his hand; it was hungry for the blood of evil. Jan lifted a hand casually into the air and spoke the words to an ancient incantation of beckoning. The slightest trace of dismay crossed Jan's face but he immediately suppressed the emotion. Gideon remained calm, staring into the eyes of darkness.

"I will have your soul, holy warrior," Jan spoke in an even tone. His eyes were statuesque, pitiless orbs of contempt. He repeated the words of the spell, a powerful utterance that was supposed to rip the soul from his target.

The paladin remained motionless. Gideon gazed into Jan's wicked eyes and saw no mercy there, no humanity. Jan had given himself fully to the dark magic of necromancy; the undead spells had consumed him.

Gravlox held Vorst's hand tightly as he watched the scene unfold. "I can feel his power," the shaman spoke in a hushed tone. "He is death."

"Your soul, paladin," Jan shouted with a voice of command that brought fear to everyone in earshot. "Surrender your soul!"

The small metal lantern resting underneath Gideon's immense beard slowly creaked open. Small wisps of white smoke escaped from the lantern. The ghostly flower trapped within the magical device curled through the air in front of Gideon and slowly drifted toward Jan's outstretched hand. The paladin, somewhat familiar with such powerful spells, recognized a moment of opportunity.

Gideon collapsed to his side, feigning instant death, and willed his sword to extinguish itself. The night sky swallowed the battlefield without Nevidal's flames holding the darkness at bay. Gideon landed on his left side, keeping his wide open eyes locked on the necromancer. Jan pulled the soul in with bolts of lightning and blighted pulses of energy.

The captive soul within reach, Jan closed his eyes and let out a howl of glee. Gideon didn't waste the opportunity. He lashed out with speed unexpected for his gigantic size. Nevidal cut through the air and sliced the floating soul in half. The sword drank the air and pulled the shattered soul into its steel. In an instant, Gideon returned to his normal height and build.

The transformation happened so quickly that Jan assumed the man had teleported. Outraged, Jan struck the ground with his fist and released a wave of death upon everything around him. A wall of black ash emanated from the epicenter, immersing everything in sorrow and decay.

"Hold on," Gravlox shouted, grabbing Vorst by the arm. He didn't have time to think or even breathe. The shaman reached into the realms of magic and summoned a countering wave of healing. Thick green roots erupted from the broken ground and formed a cocoon surrounding Gravlox and Vorst that protected them from Jan's torrent of death. A similar case of roots rose up to protect and heal Gideon. Seconds later, when the roots receded back into the ground, Gideon flexed his powerful left arm. Taurnil's poison had left his regenerated body. Gravlox collapsed to the ground exhausted. The shaman's vision blurred and he struggled to regain his breath. The magical effort was more taxing than anything he had ever done before.

It was Gideon's turn to laugh. Jan's wave of necrotic death slaughtered thousands of unprotected goblins for nearly a mile in every direction. The magic turned their pale skin to blackened husks, as though the goblin corpses had been rotting in the fields for weeks. Yael's decomposing skeleton stood with his rusting sword tip buried in the ground. The goblin army was broken.

Twenty-Three

MAELSTROM WOVE A beautiful song of destruction through the clawing ranks of undead.

Talonrend was in disarray, with soldiers and citizens alike dying in every street. The zombies were entirely unarmed but they felt no pain and wanted only to taste warm flesh. Families barred their doors and nailed boards over their windows, but still the horde was able to kill thousands. The sheer number of animated corpses was able to collapse whole walls and tear families apart with their disease-ridden hands.

Sweat dripped from Herod's head to mingle with the blood and flesh staining his regal armor. Soldiers had leapt to the defense of the prince as soon as the undead had appeared but it took them only moments to realize that Herod was far beyond their abilities. The shambling monsters fell to pieces as the dark tendrils of Maelstrom cut them down. Brenning's masterwork creation whistled through the air with every swipe.

"My prince!" a sentry called to Herod from across a street. The templar was wearing a set of heavy mail that showed dozens of holes and bloodstains. He clutched a battered crossbow to his chest and his eyes darted around the city as he spoke. "Men on the wall report that the zombies are being contained, but there have been heavy losses!" the man yelled. A wall next to the man began to crumble into the street. Bricks and mortar fell onto the cobblestones and three undead rushed the templar. The man lifted his broken crossbow high above his head and smashed it down on the nearest zombie's rotting skull. Decrepit bones and fetid skin flew all over the man's armor. The second zombie raked its gnarled fist against the soldier's helmet and lunged in with its remaining teeth barred.

Herod jerked his sword up and shot two thick tendrils of magic from Maelstrom's blade that ripped through the zombies and cut them to ribbons. The soldier's expression as his undead assailants broke apart was enough to make the prince laugh aloud.

"Thank you..." the startled man stuttered. "Thank you, my liege."

"Have you heard any news from the gatehouse? What of Master Brenning?" Herod sprinted across the broken street to meet the soldier. "What news of the goblins?" he shouted into the man's face.

The soldier straightened and dropped his crossbow down by his side. "The goblins have pulled back. The market sector is ruined, they overran it, sir."

"I know, son, I know." Herod patted a hand on the young man's shoulder. "I was in the market when it happened. Has there been any news of Master Brenning?" he asked again.

The soldier hesitated, giving Herod all the answer he needed. "We haven't heard anything yet, sir." Both of their heads hung low.

"You've done well," the prince said, trying to repair the man's confidence. "There must be another attack coming. Spread the word to regroup at the gatehouse, inside the walls."

"Yes sir," the soldier replied.

"For Talonrend!" Herod shouted as he took off down the street.

The area around the gate was consumed by chaos. Fires still smoldered everywhere the prince looked. Bloody parts of men and zombies alike were scattered all over the cobblestone and one particularly garish bloodstain on the stone wall made the man shudder.

A hole the size of a small house had opened up almost directly in front of the gatehouse. Few soldiers remained near the site and they were all leaning against the walls clutching at various wounds. Three men in fine armor lay dead, riddled with infected cuts and bite marks.

Herod could see a face peering over the top of the wall in his direction. "What of the goblins?" the prince shouted up to him.

"It seems that we have won the night, sir," the man called back in a hoarse voice. He had been shouting commands and relaying information all night.

"I need to see it," the prince said. He made his way past the line of wounded soldiers to the nearest door that would take him inside Terror's Lament. After the long trek up the spiral staircase to the top, the prince was winded. His regal armor was made from solid steel plates emblazoned with the emblems of the city. The plates were certainly effective, but also restrictively heavy. Herod clutched at the burn on his side, a painful reminder of the moment when his armor had failed him.

"You're hurt, my liege," was the first thing Herod heard when he reached the cool air of the top.

Standing up as straight as he could manage, Herod waved off the observation. "It's nothing, trust me," he said. "Now, show me this retreat."

The soldier was a burly man, young but well-muscled, and sporting a healthy beard under his helmet's chinstrap. There was a small shield strapped to his back. The man turned to lead the prince to a tower at the corner of Terror's Lament. Herod noticed a crude goblin arrow lodged between the iron banding of the soldier's shield. The prince nodded his appreciation of the man's mettle and followed him to the tower.

A telescope was mounted next to a large ballista inside the square tower. Half a dozen archers stood inside the tower, scanning the dark horizon for any signs of attack. "There used to be some sort of light out there, but we could never tell what it was," one of the archers said.

Herod peered through the lens of the brass telescope. "Bah, it's too dark. This is useless." He moved away from the scope frustrated.

"Light up the sky for your prince, men," the guard with the shield barked. Herod put his eye back to the lens with a smile. A series of twelve flaming arrows, fired two at a time, lit up the night sky brilliantly.

Herod was breathless. He shook his head and used his thumb to wipe the lens before placing his eye against it again. "Fire another round," he said softly.

More fiery arrows arced through the air and cast light all over the battlefield. "Everything is dead..." the prince muttered in disbelief. "They are all just... dead."

"Yes, my prince," the guard responded. "We don't know what happened, but some of the goblins have retreated back across the river, and the rest of them have simply fallen over dead." He scratched his beard ponderously.

"Fire one more round," Herod said to the guard. More arrows illuminated the night as the prince gazed through the telescope. "There, a clearing, something is happening there." He pointed to the spot on the battlefield but the soldiers inside the tower couldn't see. "Gideon!" Herod shouted with excitement. He could just barely see the champion's form in the flickering light. His excitement quickly turned to dismay. "Jan," his voice dripped with malice.

The prince pounded his fist into the stone of the tower and spun. "Lift the portcullis," he commanded. Without another word, the prince ripped open the door to the spiral staircase and flew down the steps.

The steel portcullis creaked slowly up on heavy chains. Breathing heavily, Herod darted under the portcullis and shouted back to the tower for it to be closed. The prince leaned over his knees to catch his breath. He unstrapped the leather bindings of his greaves and let them drop to the ground. His breastplate and gloves followed. Herod kept his helmet seated firmly upon his head and took off again toward the clearing in the battlefield.

GIDEON ROSE FROM his crouch on the ground and stood to his normal height. He lifted his sword in his hand and smiled as he slid it into the leather sheath on his back. His hand released from the hilt for the first time in days.

Gravlox and Vorst climbed out from behind their place among the rubble to stand next to the paladin. Jan took a few hesitant steps backward, unsure of how to strike against them. Apart from his sister Keturah, he had never met another spell caster able to withstand his magic. The goblin shaman not only surprised him with his power, Gravlox inspired fear in the empty space where Jan's heart should have been.

The necromancer spread his arms out in front of him and pulled at the magical tendrils of the corpses scattered in the grass. Bones broke through the rotted skin and floated through the air to hover about Jan's body. With a flick of his wrist, the bones jolted and spun, forming a whirling barrier of pale bone around him.

Gravlox reached down and plucked a small shard of magnesium from the dirt. It was a sharp piece of metal and rock that had shattered against Gideon's back. He held the rock in his hands and beckoned to it with his natural, magical spirit. The magnesium responded, alive with energy.

Gravlox hurled the shard toward the spinning bone armor surrounding the necromancer and willed it to ignite. A spark flew from Gravlox's outstretched hand and struck the magnesium shard just as it hit the bones and burst into flame.

Jan responded quickly, jumping back and dousing the armor in a thick fog of black magic. Jan felt the heat from the explosion singe his skin but quickly dissipate. He could sense that Gravlox was only testing him. Jan thrust his hands forward, blasting the smothering fog toward the shaman and his companions.

Gideon stepped forward and the holy symbol etched into his back flared with life. He arched his neck and screeched, sending a bright splash of holy magic into the air that quickly dissolved the evil fog.

At an impasse, Gravlox and Vorst stood beside the paladin and measured Jan. His black robes shimmered in the dancing firelight that dotted the scene.

"Be gone!" Jan shouted, twirling and sending forth a purple skull from his chest. The magical cantrip cackled as it flew toward the three. Small slivers of lightning bounced around the skull, sizzling the air.

"We have to run," Vorst said, clearly panicked. She turned on her heels to retreat but Gravlox caught her arm.

"It isn't real," he growled to her, trying not to break his mental concentration.

The magical skull was followed immediately by a beam of dark energy filled with sharp fragments of bone. Gideon knocked the goblins to the ground and the beam passed harmlessly over their heads.

The paladin grabbed a throwing axe from his belt and looked to Gravlox. "Time the attack," he whispered, and Vorst tapped the message's translation. The paladin rushed over the rubble of the farmhouse, ducking and dodging bolts of necrotic magic the whole way.

Vorst scampered parallel to Gideon, making her way through the debris. Jan pumped his arms furiously, covering the area with suppressive fire. The bones continued to swirl around his black robes. Gravlox dropped to the ground and pushed his hands through the dirt and stone. He could feel the depletion of his energy but knew he had to press on. A thick pillar of jagged earth sprang up under the necromancer, threatening to impale him.

Without a moment of hesitation, Jan summoned a magical gust

of wind that lifted him above the pillar and out of harm's reach. Gideon launched his axe perfectly. The weapon spun end over end directly for Jan's head. Vorst launched herself up at the necromancer's feet at the same moment.

Jan pushed himself higher and the bone wall protected him, morphing into a rounded sphere that easily deflected the axe. Vorst landed a hit on the top of Jan's black boot and her tiny dagger bit through the soft leather easily and protruded out the bottom of Jan's boot. A fast-moving bone knocked her in the head as Jan continued to levitate higher. Vorst had to let go of her blade in order to avoid being dragged too high into the air. She tucked and hit the ground hard, but was altogether unharmed.

"Get back!" Gravlox shouted through his weariness. With his flawless vision he could see the outline of Herod charging into the fight. Like a taskmaster whipping his slave, Herod slashed with Maelstrom. The dark tendrils broke through Jan's bone wall as easily as if the barrier were made of thin paper. Jan yelped, feeling the sting of the black tendrils wrapping around his waist. Unable to understand Gravlox's warning, Gideon assumed that the black tendrils connecting Jan and the prince were some form of evil instigated by the necromancer. He snatched another axe from his belt and chopped down on the ethereal bands as hard as he could. Gideon stole a glance over his shoulder and saw Herod but did not understand.

The prince growled in frustration as Maelstrom's tendrils evaporated into dust.

Jan laughed hysterically. The magical swirl of wind carried Jan higher and higher into the smoke-filled air. "So," he bellowed, "the fearless leader has come out from his castle to play!"

Herod grasped the hilt of Maelstrom firmly, watching the necromancer ascend. He lashed out with the blade again and again, tearing chunks of Jan's bone armor from the sky. The blood-red blade pulsed with every swing, drinking in the violence and loving each drop. Jan responded to the repeated attacks by sending forth a ripple of decaying magic. The spell crashed into Herod's unarmored chest and sent him sprawling to the ground. He frantically clutched and scraped at the wound in his side. The cut he suffered earlier was starting to rot and fester. Necromantic energy coursed through his body and filled his blood with disease.

With a great sigh filled with pain and acrimony, the prince returned Maelstrom to its sheath on his hip and slowly moved his hand over his other sword's hilt. His eyes clouded over when he drew Regret. The blade, forged by Master Brenning in the renowned Blood Foundry, reflected the shimmering fires of the battlefield off its translucent edge. Regret had a deep blue hue, like a crystal with flecks of gold suspended in its matrix.

The sword was weightless. Had Herod released his fingers from the hilt, the blade would not have fallen an inch. "Brenning," the prince murmured to the sword, "if only you were here..." Herod moved the weapon slowly through the air, watching the myriad array of colors scattering over the ground. The hilt was made from the same crystalline material as the blade; the entire weapon had been crafted from the same piece of wondrous material.

When the blade moved, even slowly, it was nearly impossible to track. Gravlox watched the prince testing Regret and was mesmerized. The sword seemed to disappear when it was in motion but reappeared instantly when it was still.

"You should see this, Brenning," Herod spoke to the night. "Truly, you have outdone even your high standards." The prince locked eyes with Jan, his former servant and trusted friend, and found his strength.

He gritted his teeth and charged. Jan, still hovering high above the ruined field, rained down a shower of sulfuric fire that engulfed the entire area. Evil winds blew through the rotted corpses and tossed bones into the air. Gideon had to brace himself to keep from being blown over. Vorst held onto Gravlox tightly and the pair ducked into a crater to avoid being picked up by the storm.

If the swirling torrent of death had any effect on the stalwart prince, he did not show it. Running at a fast pace, Herod swung Regret downward as he neared the hovering necromancer. Some unseen force vaulted the prince high into the air, higher than Jan, and held him there for a breath. The deep blue sword reappeared in his hand and throbbed with energy. Blue and gold sparks flew in every direction from the blade to join the magical storm.

Gideon tried to watch the action far above his head but the violent winds made his eyes water and obscured his vision. Impossibly fast, Herod vanished with his blade and reappeared behind the necromancer. In the blink of an eye, the prince materialized a dozen times at various angles all around Jan's form. Before Gideon had the time to bring a hand up to his face to shield himself from the storm, the winds stopped. Everything stopped.

Dull black robes drifted lazily to the ground. Herod stood up in the midst of the rubble as though he had been crouching there forever. Maelstrom and Regret were both secured within their sheaths. The prince stretched his back and yawned, physically exhausted.

"It is time that we return to Talonrend, Gideon." Herod said calmly to the holy warrior who stared at him slack-jawed.

"My liege, Master Brenning said he would return to the city when the fighting first started. Where is he?" Gideon's voice trembled. The carnage all around him was a grim omen of what he would find on the other side of the high walls.

Herod shook his head. He couldn't look Gideon in the eyes or speak past the lump in his throat.

"He was a good man," Gideon said softly. He pointed to the location where Gravlox and Vorst were hiding. "Those two goblins saved his life. Actually, they saved my life as well." The paladin walked toward the crater and helped the two goblins climb out.

Horribly mispronouncing their names, Gideon attempted to introduce Gravlox and Vorst to Herod. "We both friends," Vorst said as she held Gravlox's hand and giggled. "We both friends of humans."

Herod shook his head, not knowing what to believe. He had

seen enough in the last few hours to open his mind to any possibilities.

"Gravlox is shaman," she said happily in her high pitched goblin voice. "Both friends."

Looking to Gideon for some kind of explanation, Herod could only guess the answers to his questions. "You are telling me that these two *goblins* saved your life and saved Master Brenning?"

The paladin nodded. "I'm sure we will have plenty of time to go over the details once everything is back to normal." His eyes surveyed the battlefield and the heavily damaged walls. "Well," he continued, "once everything is normal enough."

Herod thought back to the golden shield and the promise he had made to his army concerning the revered smith. *You will never be king,* Vrysinoch gently echoed in the back of his mind. *You will never sit upon your brother's throne.*

Epilogue

CROWS CAME FROM miles around. Thousands upon thousands of goblin skeletons covered the fields from Talonrend to the banks of the Clawflow. To the north of Terror's Lament, a large plot of land had been cleared and excavated and now served as a mass grave for all of the human dead. After the first plot had been filled with corpses, a pyre had been constructed to burn the rest of the bodies.

The city behind the walls was eerily quiet. A heavy shroud of death clung to the shattered houses and storefronts. Loads of stone and dirt were being carted into Talonrend to fill the gaping holes that dotted the streets.

The royal bedchamber inside Castle Talon was draped with thin wisps of silken cloth and windows had been cut in the stone walls. Servants stood beside the windows with fans, moving fresh air through the room to cool the prince. Herod's wound festered.

The prince wasn't weak and frail like a dying man should have been. His heart was strong and his stubborn spirit was stronger. Still, the disease spread through his body. His skin radiated heat like a blazing forge.

Gideon kneeled at the prince's side and prayed to Vrysinoch

for healing. He could feel the intricate web of magic connecting the world around him, but no matter where he searched, he could not find even the slightest shred of mercy.

"Sir," the paladin said softly, "the shaman, Gravlox...." Gideon pulled the sheet back slowly from the prince's side and looked at the garish burn. The necromancer's spell had ravaged the open wound. Rags were piled beneath the weeping cut to catch the putrid ooze.

"I will not have a *goblin* walking freely in my city!" Herod shouted. His voice was full of life that contradicted his body's decay.

"Herod, look at yourself! You will die if you stay like this." He hung his head in frustration. "He can heal you. The paladins have tried to save you; I have tried to save you, Gravlox... Just let him try." He beat his hands into the white sheets of the bed.

"It is only your word, Gideon, which has spared those two goblins from the end of a noose. They will rot in the dungeon for eternity before I let either of them put their filthy hands on me!" Spittle flew from the prince's mouth. His vivid animation sent a fresh wave of puss and blood out of his side to splatter the sheets.

The paladin closed his eyes and thought about the dungeon beneath Castle Talon. Although no one besides official templars were permitted to visit the underground cells, Gideon had done so unchallenged. With Herod in no condition to physically stop him, Gideon's reputation afforded him many privileges that his lack of rank otherwise denied him. *Gravlox could easily escape that cell*, Gideon thought to himself. *He has power far beyond anything I have ever seen.*

Gideon rose up from his knees slowly and shook the memory of Gravlox's cell from his head. "Then it will be your death," he said to the prince. Gideon pushed through the white silk and exited the room without so much as glancing over his shoulder.

DEEP INSIDE THE dark labyrinth of Kanebullar Mountain, Lady Scrapple's rage consumed her. Goblin servants entered her chambers timidly. More than half of them ended as a red stain on the stone walls. Her thick, root-like appendages flailed wildly, splattering anything unfortunate enough to get caught in their path.

Dozens of pulsating arms spread through the mountain, rapidly replenishing the goblin army. She was evolving and adapting, lengthening the gestation period of her spawn to create taller and more muscular underlings.

Lady Scrapple's vast consciousness flew over the miles from Kanebullar Mountain to Talonrend. She prodded, searching the emptiness of space for any shred of Vorst's mind that she could latch onto and devour. The edges of Vorst's mind appeared like bright tongues of flame in a world of darkness. Lady Scrapple could feel the goblin and pushed her mental powers to their limits. Vorst's vibrant fire fought back against the intrusion with such solidarity that the Mistress of the Mountain was forced to retreat. She seethed in her mountain lair and vowed a thousand times to kill Vorst. The matriarch managed a grim smile as she imagined tearing Vorst limb by limb and feeding her to a pack of wild dogs.

WIND HOWLED OVER the opening to a solitary cave nestled just below the snow line of an unnamed mountain north of Talonrend. The icy waters of a gentle stream trickled from an elevated lake before meandering to the plains and joining the Clawflow. A tall creature with thick fur covering his well-built torso drank from the stream before returning to his cave.

The minotaur sat just inside the cave opening, basking in the soothing heat of the fire behind him. His black, beady eyes watched with great interest as a clan of orcs steadily marched through a valley not far from his cave. They carried a great banner ahead of them, draped in furs and painted with blood.

"The Wolf Jaw clan," the minotaur growled with a raspy voice. He knew the orcs well. "The whole Wolf Jaw clan..." Several hundred of the cruel orcs, the entirety of the clan, marched south.

On a normal day, the minotaur would have pounded his fists into the cave wall to summon his own clan and slaughter the orcs. The horned beast hated everything that didn't belong to his own clan. But this was not a normal day. With a shake of his heavy head, the minotaur turned back into the cave. Oil dripped from the goblin slowly rotating on a spit above the flames. Goblin meat didn't taste particularly good, but the minotaur was hungry and nothing wandered into his cave without suffering repercussions.

There was an open scroll held to the ground with rocks sitting in front of the roasting creature. The various tribes and clans of the snowy mountains rarely welcomed visitors and never entertained emissaries. Minotaurs spoke a gruff language that was seldom written, but the runes inscribed on the scroll were clear. For what felt like the hundredth time since the goblin had wandered into his cave that morning, the minotaur read the scroll. *Gather your clan. Talonrend will fall.*

THE GOBLIN WARS

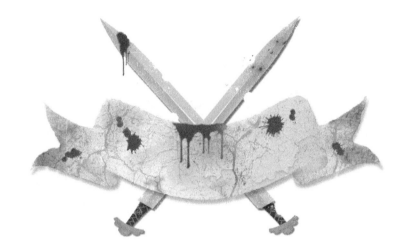

PART TWO

Death of a king

"PULL YOUR SCARF around, Seamus," an elderly woman called into the brisk night air. Wind whipped around her words and stole her breath with a cloud of fog. Seamus, a tall and hulking brute of a man, looked back at her and gave a sigh, reluctantly tightening the knitted cloth about his neck.

"Hundreds o' other folk around here for you to yell at, you old coot," Seamus retorted. The pair of chilled farmers marched near the front of the refugee column heading west, leaving Terror's Lament and the once-safe city of Talonrend far behind. "Pull your own damn scarf tighter…" Seamus mumbled to himself, far out of his mother's hearing.

"How much longer do you think it will take, Uncle Seamus?" a red-haired, freckled boy asked excitedly. The boy, affectionately called 'Squirt' by everyone in the column, had been tagging along with Seamus and his mother for miles. Most of the time, no one paid the lad much attention. All he did was eat their food and he was too young to help carry supplies.

"Do you know how far it is from Talonrend," Seamus spat as he said the name of his former home, trying to purge the awful flavor from his mouth, "to the Green City?" He reached down and ruffled the boy's hair and pushed him in the back, urging him to leave.

"How far is it, Uncle Seamus?" The boy continued to prod.

"I'm not your uncle!" Seamus cajoled, using his heavy hands to push the boy away. "Stop calling me that." In his heart, Seamus knew that every member of the column was as much the boy's family as his blood relatives. Squirt had been a street urchin living on scraps without a family. He called all the older refugees his aunt or uncle.

"How far is it to the Green City?" Squirt demanded again, undeterred. "Just tell me how far!"

"I'm not sure anyone here knows that for certain, boy," Seamus told him honestly. "But by my reckoning, if you can't see the city, we aren't there yet." The middle-aged farmer had no idea how far he and the boy would have to walk and everyone in the column just hoped they were moving in the right direction. Food was already becoming scarce and the massive column frightened away all of the game.

"Will we make it there before it snows?" Squirt asked, hopping up and down with the limitless energy afforded him by youth.

"Squirt, I hope we make it there before winter really sets in, but if I tell you the truth..." Seamus' voice trailed off. He didn't want to frighten the boy.

"Tell me!" Squirt begged, tugging on the big man's hairy arm.

Seamus let out a long sigh and looked to his mother ten paces behind him, trying in vain to keep her teeth from chattering. "We will probably have to make camp somewhere before the snows pile up and then we will have to wait it out. If we are lucky, we will find enough deer and rabbit to last us through the winter. Then, when the snows melt and the wagons can continue, we will keep moving west and make it to the Green City by summer."

Squirt's eyes grew big and he hesitated for a second before bounding back to Seamus' side. "I didn't know it would take that long," he said with a voice full of wonder and awe.

"Yes," Seamus said after he cleared his throat. "I just hope the

Green City actually exists. Some of the ancient folk say they have been there and seen it, but once a mind has reached a certain age, you just can't trust it anymore." Seamus gave a sly smirk over his shoulder to his mother and Squirt ran off to pester someone else.

Ever since Seamus was as young as Squirt, he had felt a calling somewhere deep in his mind. He had never been particularly religious, but he knew he was destined by Vrysinoch for something great. When the goblins had arrived outside Terror's Lament, Seamus had left his farm and volunteered for the militia. His particular group didn't see any action, but Seamus wasn't concerned.

When people started leaving Talonrend after the battle, Seamus knew he had to go with them. Without much consideration, he had left everything behind and set out with thousands of other refugees to discover his purpose in life.

One

I N THE DARK, damp dungeon beneath the keep of Talonrend, Gravlox and Vorst stared into the calm darkness with nothing but silence passing between them. A human jailer sat at a rickety table and fought off sleep with his head leaning against the stone. Two layers of iron bars separated Gravlox from Vorst and only one other inmate kept them company.

A second guard, dressed impeccably and striding with a tall, proud gait, descended the spiral staircase and woke the snoozing man with a wave of his bright torch. The human prisoner, a one-armed man who refused to wear any of his meager clothing, beat an old wooden bowl against the bars of his cell at the new guard.

"Wake up now," the clean cut human said with a polite but firm tone. He shook the weary jailer out of his seat and pointed him toward the staircase. "Apollonius has need of you," he stated before turning toward the cells.

"Apollonius is a coward!" the one-armed man shouted through a mouth of rotted teeth. He slammed the wooden bowl against the bars of his cell as he howled.

"How would you know, old man?" The new guard fired back with a smirk. "You've been in that cell longer than Apollonius has been alive." The guard dismissed him with a wave and sauntered to the two goblin holding cells.

With one hand, the man brushed a cobweb out of his path, careful to not let any fall on his finely pressed jacket. Gravlox noticed his other hand wandering close to the shinning pommel of his sword.

"I've heard that Talonrend lives because of you two," the guard said quietly to the goblin pair. With her hands gripping the rusted iron bars, she gazed up at the tall human and searched his face for compassion.

"We found Gideon, the paladin," Vorst responded. "He saved your city." She shook her head and moved away from the bars.

"Gideon insists that you two saved us all," the guard responded flatly. The one-armed man howled and danced about his cell wildly, throwing the wooden bowl against the walls.

"Do you believe him?" Vorst dared to ask. She sat on the floor at the back of her tiny cell and tried to push the fear out of her voice.

"I don't know what to believe..." the human finally said. His eyes left the goblins but his hand remained firmly planted on the pommel of his weapon. Pointing at Gravlox, he let a hint of a smile creep to his face. "I saw him on the field against Jan," he whispered with obvious wonder. "He is a legend."

"I try to teach Gravlox, but he only knows a few of your words," Vorst told the human quickly. The last time they were questioned, a jailer attempted to kill Gravlox because he didn't respond.

"What is he?" The guard asked, reaching a hand through the metal bars of Gravlox's cell.

"Shaman," Gravlox told the man. He pointed a pale finger to his grimy chest and tried to form a sentence. "I...shaman," he finally managed.

"A shaman," the man repeated quietly. "Is that a priest where you live?" The guard turned to Vorst and nervously scratched the palm of his hand against the pommel of his sword.

"What is priest?" Vorst inquired. "Gravlox is a shaman, power-ful shaman."

"I saw him use magic on the battlefield," the man explained and gestured with his hands. "When Jan attacked, I saw him protect you with magic. Our priests do that sometimes, by the power of Vrysinoch. Protection and healing can only come from our god."

Vorst shook her head and tried to piece together the meaning of what she heard. The gaps in her understanding of the human lan-guage made conversation difficult. "Healing and protection come from the ground," she told the man. "Shaman draw energy from the world! Everything is magic." She motioned with her hands to eve-rything around her, turning circles in the small cell.

Gravlox, standing as close to his companion as the dungeon al-lowed, reached through the iron bars and touched Vorst's cell. The man, leaning casually against the bars, could feel Gravlox's magic. The shaman summoned a small burst of energy into his fingertips and sent the magical signal hurtling through the rusted iron.

The man's eyes grew wide and he tried to take a step back, but his hand wouldn't budge from the metal. Gravlox smiled and rel-ished the moment, sending more and more magic through the cell and into the human, forcing images of the battlefield to dance through the guard's head. Gravlox showed him the moment when he summoned a great blast of magic to destroy the sewer tunnel be-neath Reikall and the man whimpered in terror.

"Stop it, Grav!" Vorst yelled at him in her native language. "Don't hurt him."

Gravlox retracted his hand from the cell bar and returned to his ragged pile of filth to sit. The one-armed man, watching the commo-tion, hurled his wooden bowl out of his cell and knocked the guard squarely on the shoulder.

With fear taking hold of the soldier, the man drew his sword and backed away, nearly tripping on the uneven stone floor. "No!" Vorst shouted at Gravlox, "Don't hurt him!"

The guard looked around the dark dungeon once and ran for

the staircase.

"I can get us out of here, Vorst," Gravlox said once the guard was gone. The one-armed man flailed about gleefully in a pile of his own filth, singing a children's song loudly to himself.

"I know you can, Grav, but where would we go? What would we do?" She hung her head and leaned against the bars. "We can't go back to the mountain."

"Wouldn't anywhere be better than this?" Gravlox said with his hands around the cell bars to emphasize his point. "I hate it here."

Vorst let out a long, high-pitched sigh. "We have to trust in the paladin," she offered after a moment. "Gideon can get us out. If we break out of here, the humans will never trust us."

Gravlox reached for her hand and held it tightly, clinging to the comfort of her grip, and considered everything they had been through together. "Is this where you want to live?" he asked Vorst.

"I..." Vorst searched her mind for the right answer. "I don't know," she finally replied. "We can't go back to the mountain. If the humans will accept us, why not stay with them?"

"Will they ever accept us?" Gravlox's voice was full of pain and longing. The one-armed man jumped from foot to foot, stomping clouds of muck and grime into the stagnant air around his cell.

"As long as we have each other, does it matter?" Vorst whispered, barely audible. She squeezed his hand and tried to settle his mind but knew that nothing she could do would bring him comfort.

"I don't want to live my life always looking over my shoulder. I did enough of that in Kanebullar Mountain. Are there any other goblins out there? Are there any more goblins like us?" Gravlox stared at the roughly cut stone walls and tried to imagine a life in the human city.

"I don't think so, Grav. The orcs in the snowy mountain ranges look similar to us, but they aren't goblins. I've never heard of any other groups of our kind."

Gravlox smirked. "The orcs and other creatures of the northern mountains would sooner eat us than live with us." The shaman walked away from the rusted bars and paced the area of his small cell. "Perhaps it would be best for us to live here with these giants."

A long silence passed between the goblins. The torch left hanging on the wall by the guard flickered and smoked, making the air heavy and hard to breathe. The one-armed man slouched down with his back against the metal bars and hummed a tuneless song while he counted his toes.

"Vorst..." Gravlox whispered, trying to find his courage. "Can you still feel her?" he asked gently. "Can you feel Lady Scrapple?"

Vorst slumped and closed her eyes. "I don't think so," she murmured without any confidence. "At least, it isn't like it was before. She doesn't control me, Gravlox, if that's what you are asking."

"YOU ARE GETTING worse, my liege," Gideon stated in an even tone. The prince was pale, almost lifeless, and looked weak in both body and soul as he struggled to stay awake. The paladin hated his daily visits to Castle Talon.

"I'm sorry," Herod breathed through spikes of pain that wracked his entire body. "I'm sorry, Gideon. What am I to do? What will become of Talonrend after my death?"

A long silence passed between them. Gideon squeezed the prince's hand but Herod was too weak to return the gesture. Two soldiers stood to either side of the prince's bed with large paper fans to keep the air circulating around the chamber. Gideon stole a glance at one of the soldiers who nodded grimly in response. "Has anyone been asking about the prince?" he questioned one of the guards.

"They did the first day, sir, but we turned them away," the man replied. He moved the fan back and forth methodically, never taking his eyes from Herod's body.

"Good. If word gets out..." Gideon's voice trailed off and he averted his eyes.

"Understood," the guard confirmed. "Apollonius is the only one who hears our reports."

"Very well," Gideon said. "The city is falling apart around us..." he whispered.

"Sir," the other guard asked Gideon tentatively. "How many people have left the city?"

Gideon turned to him and shook his head. Citizens had been fleeing by the hundreds since the battle, and none of the incentives offered by the monarchy had done anything to stem the tide.

"Over half of the city's population is on the road now," the paladin remarked with sorrow coating his once powerful voice. "From what I've heard, the villages along the Clawflow are ghost towns. The goblin retreat burned almost everything. Cobblestreet is nothing but a pile of ashes and the same is true of the other settlements between here and the mountains."

"Vrysinoch save us..." one of the guards muttered under his breath. "How will we make it through winter?"

Gideon stood and took a step back from the dying prince. "Our stores should last us through the winter, even with the last harvest being burned by the goblins and trampled by the refugees." He tried to work a bit of optimism into his voice, but the sight of Herod's frail body made such confidence impossible. "We could probably withstand a full year without another harvest, but any more than that and we will die."

Herod stirred under the white silk sheets that covered his bed. "When they come again..." he coughed and sputtered. "The siege will... end us..."

"I fear that our prince speaks the truth," Gideon said as he turned for the magical door that led to the rest of the castle. "The goblin army can sustain a siege for months, if not years. Without any assistance from the outside, we will die behind our walls long before they want for food."

"How many Templars remain in my city, Gideon?" Herod asked without turning his head or opening his eyes.

240

"All of them, my liege," Gideon responded. "Most of the militia travels west with the refugees, but the Templars have chosen to stay, down to a man. Do you have orders for them, sir?"

Herod chewed his bottom lip, thinking deeply. "If I am still alive when the goblin horde returns," he coughed into the silk sheets, "slit my throat and evacuate the city. Fight them for as long as you can from the walls, and then run. Take the Templars and try to find the refugees on the road. Protect the people and make it to the Green City."

Gideon nodded solemnly. "And if Vrysinoch takes you before the siege?"

With a cough comprised of more blood than air, Herod managed a chuckle. "Then do what you want, paladin. I have no heir, but without subjects, the monarchy dies with me in this bed. The Templars will listen to you and Apollonius, of that I have no doubt. When I am dead, you are free to choose your own path."

Gideon left the royal bedchamber with a frown. He whispered a prayer to Vrysinoch as he walked down the stone hallway to the throne room and searched the intricate web of magical energy for any hint of an answer. He could detect the ever-present power emanating from the prince's swords at his bedside, but Vrysinoch was eerily silent.

A STEADY WIND cut through the half-frozen tree limbs and scattered dead leaves all over the camp. Tongues of orange flame reached into the night sky from the center of a mass of huddled orcs. The ragged standard of the Wolf Jaw Clan flapped against the dark serenity of midnight.

"I say we kill 'em," one of the burly humanoids grunted through a mouth of jagged teeth. The other orcs nodded in agreement and smiled at one another across the fire.

"Me axe be hungry," another orc said with anticipation.

Jurnorgel, the tallest orc of the Wolf Jaw Clan, shook his head and lifted a hand to silence the eager gathering. "Fightin' now be death," he cautioned his bloodthirsty kin.

"Death be what we're lookin' for!" an orc holding a long piece of iron chain yelled up at the sky. Jurnorgel reached over the fire and clamped a hand down tightly on the orc's throat to silence him, lifting him off the ground with ease.

"Must be quiet now," Jurnorgel told them in the softest voice he could muster. He pulled the unfortunate orc over the fire with a single powerful tug and shoved the side of his face down into the hot coals. The disobedient soldier tried to scream but Jurnorgel's powerful hand around his windpipe reduced his cries to nothing more than a whimper. "Minotaurs be all around in these hills, watchin' us and waitin' on us to fight. Half Goat Clan is just over that ridge, wantin' the same blood. I say we wait, Wolf Jaw waits."

Jurnorgel stood and tossed the burned orc from his grip like a used piece of firewood and calmly rolled his own wrist across the ground to extinguish the flames on his knuckles and bracer. The burned orc writhed in pain on the ground but didn't dare to make any sound.

"How long we wait, chief?" Jurnorgel's son asked. Kraasghull ran a thick hand through his dirty and matted hair.

Jurnorgel looked each of the orcs of his band in the eye before responding. "We leave Half Goat alone," he told them with a grave voice that left no room for argument. "Orc clans come from the mountains now to kill puny humans, not Half Goats. We kill all the humans," he placed a meaty arm around his son's back, "then we kill other orcs."

Kraasghull nodded and puffed out his chest in an attempt to imitate his father's strong presence of command. "After Wolf Jaw eats the tiny human clan, we roast Half Goats over fires made from their children's bones!" The orcs smiled, restraining their war cries, and jumped from foot to foot with their weapons held high. Nothing excited the Wolf Jaw Clan more than the thought of eating Half Goat orcs.

TALONREND FELT EMPTY. The merchants had deserted Talonrend along with the refugees, sweeping up the poor and rich alike in their exodus. A few families wealthy enough to have stores of food saved in larders under their houses elected to stay behind with the city guard, but even they boarded up their windows and barred their doors.

Crows and stray dogs ran through the streets and played among the fallen buildings. Rotting remnants of the undead army and bits of fallen soldiers littered the cobblestones at Gideon's feet. With a hand never far from the hilts of his throwing axes, the tall paladin walked from Castle Talon's drawbridge toward the city streets. A pair of young soldiers stood anxiously at the foot of the bridge with spears held high, turning to watch Gideon's approach.

"How fares the prince?" one of them asked. His voice betrayed his youth and Gideon knew that he must have been freshly recruited out of the militia.

"Not well," Gideon replied without slowing his gait. "He may be dead by the morning..." he muttered without care as to who might hear.

Gideon continued down the empty streets until he reached the brilliant glass door of the Tower of Wings. Weaving a path through the unseen realms of magic, the holy warrior searched for the enchanted lock's magical signature within his mind and took comfort in the memory of the place. *Open*, he commanded the lock with a burst of holy energy that caused the symbol of Vrysinoch on his back to flair to life. He could feel heat emanating from the tower but the beautiful glass door did not respond.

No, thundered Vrysinoch's voice so forcefully that it nearly knocked Gideon to the ground. His mind was consumed by the resonating power of the word echoing off the walls of his consciousness.

Regaining his composure and locating the magical lock within his mind once again, Gideon braced himself and ordered the door to open.

A short pause filled the air with tension before the hidden voice whispered. *No,* Gideon heard inside his mind. The denial was followed by a hiss and the sound of talons scraping.

"Vrysinoch..." Gideon clenched his teeth as though the word itself brought pain. "Let me in." He slammed a heavy fist into the glass door with enough force to shatter it, but succeeded in no more than bruising his hand.

Why? came the incorporeal response.

"Vrysinoch... I am your paladin, your chosen warrior... What more can you ask of me?" Gideon begged. Sorrow dripped from his words like blood.

Souls, Gideon of Talonrend, I hunger for souls. Vrysinoch's voice hissed with magical influence. Nevidal added its call to the cacophony of scraping talons inside Gideon's mind from the sheath on his back.

"How many goblins have I slain in your name? How many men have I killed with your sword?" Gideon demanded with incredulity. "I bear your mark!" he yelled and slammed another fist against the glass door.

Goblins have no souls, Gideon, Vrysinoch cackled with an avian hiss. *It is your soul that I long to taste.*

The strong paladin hung his head in defeat and slumped his back against the beautiful glass door. "You have already taken so much..." he mouthed. Without another sound, Vrysinoch's divine presence fled his mind and left him with a profound sense of emptiness.

"Sir?" an old, familiar voice called to Gideon from behind. "I heard you pounding on the door..."

Gideon rose to his feet and turned, bearing a grin at the sight of his friend. "Asterion!" the paladin nearly shouted. He reached a hand out to greet the priest as he walked through the open glass door into the tower's foyer. "It seems I can no longer open this door on my own."

"That's what old friends are for, Gideon." Asterion waved an arm around the quiet foyer to indicate their solitude. "It seems that now, more than ever, allies are a hard commodity to find." The priest let out a long sigh and shook his wrinkled head. "Most of the others have already left."

"How many still remain, Asterion?" Gideon asked as he moved around the spectacularly decorated room. Marble and glass statues of Vrysinoch were scattered throughout the space in a circular pattern, standing guard in front of epic portraits depicting the winged god doing battle against all manner of evil creatures.

Asterion paused for a moment and scratched his head. "The Archbishop is still here, locked away in his room like a madman," he said grimly with a nod toward the ceiling. "And two of the devotees have elected to stay. I dare say that I am the only priest left in Talonrend."

"The people need you now more than ever, I would think," Gideon replied with an edge of contempt creeping into his voice. "When did everyone leave?"

"The Archbishop ordered us to lock the doors as soon as the goblin horde arrived. The paladins were told to stand down." Asterion placed a hand on Gideon's shoulder and gazed up at the painted ceiling. "After the battle, your brothers fled. Most of them went ahead of the refugees on the road to the Green City, but some of them travelled east in search of vengeance against the goblins. The priests went with them, for the most part. Some returned to the villages along the Clawflow and others simply vanished."

245

"Damn the Archbishop!" Gideon roared. "Think of the lives he could have saved! The wounded soldiers had nowhere to turn. Their prayers of healing could have spared the lives of hundreds, if not thousands." Gideon's rage boiled over and he ripped a throwing axe from his belt. The likenesses of Vrysinoch all over the room glared at him and taunted his anger. With one swing, Gideon shattered the top of the nearest statue. "The paladins could have held the field for days, even against a horde like that. The militia wouldn't have been forced to retreat inside the walls. Talonrend wouldn't have fallen into their trap."

Bits of marble flew from a carved pedestal as Gideon shattered another image of his god. "I know," Asterion spoke softly. "The Archbishop won't allow any of us to aid what he calls an illegitimate ruler. With no corpse to prove that King Lucius is dead, the Archbishop will not support Prince Herod. He would rather watch this city die than go against the laws of the monarchy."

"Suddenly I remember why I left this awful place," Gideon sneered sarcastically. "Why are you still here?"

Asterion smiled weakly and shrugged. "I have no idea," he muttered. "I guess I just didn't know where to go. I saw no point in fleeing with my tail between my legs like a beaten dog. Who knows, maybe I'll join the city guard," Asterion jested. The plain brown robe concealing his frail body shook as the old man laughed at his own joke.

"As good a reason as any," Gideon said as he moved toward the staircase ascending into the tower.

"I do not know why you have returned here, Gideon," Asterion stated solemnly. "Do not make me regret opening that door."

Gideon nodded once before climbing the stairs.

S NARLSNOUT THE GLUTTONOUS, a massive orc with a wiry white beard covering his tremendous waves of naked fat, sat upon a dais of carved stone. The crisp morning air brought crystals of frost to his labored breathing and a smile to his hideous visage. Snarlsnout watched as two simple-minded orcs used their war clubs to smash a chunk of rancid meat into a slimy pulp that the chieftain could slurp past his toothless gums.

The slaves, castrated orcs shackled to the stone dais, offered the runny meat to Snarlsnout in wooden bowls one after another until the entire liquid breakfast was devoured.

Flapping high above his head, the ragged standard of the Half Goat Clan greeted the cresting sun. Snarlsnout clutched an old horn in one of his gout-ridden hands and blew the call to assemble. Within minutes, several hundred orcs stood at attention before the stone platform with their weapons held ready.

"Today," Snarlsnout struggled to shout above the clan. "We rid ourselves of the plague!" His slurred voice echoed over the assembled orcs as it had done every morning for nearly a hundred years. "The Wolf Jaw cowards," he continued over the sounds of violent cheering, "are just beyond that ridge." Snarlsnout tried to lift an arm high enough to point but found once again that his immense weight made the mundane task impossible.

"We wait until they march," Snarlsnout commanded his clan. "Then we descend upon them with a storm of death unlike anything they have ever known!" The gouty chieftain's eloquent speech was lost on the majority of his dim-witted subjects, but still they roared to life. "Half Goats kill Wolf Jaws!" Snarlsnout whipped their furor into a blood rage. "Half Goats kill everything!"

Banners adorned with goat skulls and bloodstained furs flew through the air. Snarlsnout looked on with amusement as two brawny soldiers near the front of the assembly were consumed by excitement. It didn't take long for a brawl to leave one of them dead.

Fifty chained and castrated orc slaves rushed to the dais and lifted the chieftain into the air on their hunched and scarred shoulders. Snarlsnout used a large stick to guide his unfortunate bearers through the crowd of Half Goat orcs. Everywhere he passed, orc warriors sang the chieftain's praises and worshipped him like a god. A hearty laugh rumbled up from beneath Snarlsnout's overwhelming layers of fat that served as his prison and his home.

An hour later, the Half Goat Clan neared the Wolf Jaw orcs marching ahead of them through the frozen valley. The ground was hard beneath their feet, but the heavy snows of winter were still far away in the desolate mountains.

"Orders, chief? Attack?" Snarlsnout's most trusted general asked with a booming voice. The simple question twisted the general's face into a pained expression of profound stupidity. Stringing more than two words together to form a sentence was a task not often asked of the burly orc and it confused his head.

"Send the first wave, Gurr," Snarlsnout said after a brief moment of pondering. "Just arrows at first," the massive orc mused. "Wait until they turn around to charge. I want them to see us coming!"

Gurr stood motionless for several minutes, processing the information and weaving his uneasy mind around the words. Eventually, confusion yielded to vague understanding and Gurr smiled at his leader. "Fear!" he shouted with a pounding of his chest.

The brave general turned to the army at his heels and raised a flowing standard. The columns abruptly halted and waited for the next command. Scratching his bare chin, Gurr looked through a sack full of brightly colored banners for the one indicating the appropriate tactic.

"Arrows first, Gurr, then the charge..." Snarlsnout reminded him softly.

With mounting frustration, Gurr howled to himself and grabbed the largest banner from the bag with a meaty hand. He waved it wildly above his head with shouts of unabashed glee before tossing it to the ground and drawing his sword. The orc clan burst into action and fell into step behind the charging general.

"I'm not sure why I bother bringing the other flags," Snarlsnout coughed to himself through pained laughter. "Gurr only recognizes the one for a full charge anyway. Perhaps that is what makes him such a fine general. The Wolf Jaw Clan will never suspect *another* full charge, not after the last twenty-eight times Gurr has ordered it."

Half Goat orcs swarmed past the elevated stone dais like flies around a carcass. Snarlsnout looked on with pleasure as his subjects flooded the frosted valley laid out before him. The speedy Gurr was so far ahead of the charging horde that Snarlsnout could see his individual shape reach the rear of the Wolf Jaw column. The enemy orcs quickly turned and surrounded the lone fighter, but it was a scene the chieftain has witnessed many times before. At the end of the battle, Gurr would come limping back triumphantly with a large sack of bloody heads slung over his shoulder. Of that, Snarlsnout the Gluttonous was certain.

STEAMING BLOOD FLOWED freely from both Wolf Jaw and Half Goat orcs alike. The crisp layer of frost coating the valley floor quickly turned to slick brown slush that made the field of battle treacherously unstable.

Howls of rage echoed through the valley, Gurr's voice loudest among them. The slow-witted orc general cleaved his heavy sword in wide arcs before him, tearing chunks of blood and gore free from the bellies of those closest to him. A javelin, weighted on the back side and designed to slow and maim, ripped through the leather jerkin covering Gurr's chest. The sharp metal point exited his left shoulder with a spray of blood that would have killed a lesser being. Gurr fell to his knees.

The missile weighed twice as much the orc's sword and was covered with vicious barbs that tore Gurr's muscle as he squirmed. Grunting from the effort, he grasped the wooden shaft of the weapon in his huge right hand and yanked hard on it, shredding his shoulder in the process.

The left side of Gurr's body began to numb. Whether from blood loss or pain, Gurr didn't care. A sinister smile creased his face when the javelin fell to the ground with a thud. Numbness was good, Gurr knew. Numbness took away fear. Numbness killed enemies.

A few strides in front of Gurr, an orc slashed wildly with a scythe at a brawny, spear-wielding brute, poking and prodding the larger warrior without attempting to close the gap. Gurr's tight hand wrapped around the scythe-wielder's throat with such intensity that the orc dropped his weapon and tried to scream. He shook the lesser beast and threw him to the ground like one of his used mates and charged. Terror played out on the bigger orc's twisted face. The general's bloody fist crashed into the Half Goat emblem painted on the stunned orc's armor.

Allegiances were meaningless to Gurr. If the general had an appetite to kill, which he most certainly had, every living thing in his sight had good cause to run. The orc's ribs bent and snapped under the weight of Gurr's punch and the Half Goat soldier fell before the rage, adding another nameless body to the wake of death.

Hefting his sword above his head with one mighty hand, Gurr surveyed the field for the next closest target. Within moments, a trio of axe-wielding orcs were scattered into pieces at Gurr's feet. He wiped the spattered gore from his face with the back of his wrist, tasted the potent viscera with a smile, and rushed deeper into the sounds of chaos.

"FILTHY CUR," JURNORGEL muttered to himself as he watched his clan in battle. A defensive ring of guards had been set up around the chieftain and his most powerful ally, a half-blooded shaman without a name.

"These dogs attack the wrong clan!" he yelled through the tumult around him. His guards shifted nervously back and forth. They were outnumbered and hard pressed. "Wolves kill dogs..."

"Shall I turn back this vile tide, my lord?" the shaman asked in a quiet voice laced with a thick accent from some distant land. The half-orc was short and lean compared to his purebred associates but more feared than anyone in the clan. Orcs born with the gift of magic were rare, but every clan had at least one dedicated shaman that could heal their wounds after battle.

The shaman had appeared without warning one night shortly after a goblin emissary had rallied the clan. He spoke the guttural orc language flawlessly, but with a refined dignity so unnatural to the brutes that it made them uneasy.

"Hurt them, shaman, but do not kill them," Jurnorgel commanded. "If we are going to take the human city, we need more orcs than just one clan. Turn them back."

From their position atop a small crest near the end of the frosted valley, Jurnorgel and the shaman watched the carnage. Battle lines quickly dissolved into a wild fray and the ranks were consumed by more fist fights than actual combat.

Lowering his head and closing his hands tightly about his staff, the peculiar half-orc uttered a stream of arcane words that melted the light snow drifting into his breath. Like someone blowing out a candle, the world darkened with sudden and terrifying speed. A heavy mist descended on the orcs, deadening their sounds and making their hands clammy with humidity.

The shaman fell to his knees clutching his staff, never opening his eyes, and uttered one final word that sent a shockwave through the valley. A roiling cascade of dirt sped through the battlefield and knocked down every combatant it touched. Attempting to rise, the orcs found the mist stifling and debilitating. A thick curtain of humid fog stole their breath and felt like heavy chains weighing down their arms.

Though many tried, no screams rose up into the magical darkness. The faint sounds of metal scraping against the ground could be heard as soldiers dropped their weapons, but all of it sounded distant and barely relevant, like a voice at the edge of awareness quickly fading.

The valley was dark and still as death.

Unaffected by the spell, the shaman rose to his feet and tossed his staff playfully from one hand to the other. "Be prepared to order a retreat, great chieftain. There is no honor in killing the Half Goat Clan whilst they struggle to breathe." The half-blooded creature smirked and twirled his wooden staff high above his head. With a great sweeping motion more for show than effect, he slammed the staff into the ground. At once, all of the screams that had been suffocated by the magical mist tore through the valley in a piercing wail and were sucked into the half-orc's staff.

"There..." the shaman chuckled. "All better."

War horns sounded from both ends of the valley as the terrified orcs scrambled to their feet. Both clans rushed to their leaders for instruction, still thirsty for blood, but unsure what it would cost.

All the while the shaman laughed to himself and mindlessly twirled his staff.

Four

THE TOWER OF Wings held an eerie sense of solitude and despair despite the bright sunshine reflecting off of the glass walls. The spiral staircase, carved from brilliant marble and adorned with gold filigree, was shrouded in gloom. The tower's living magic was said to be a result of the resident's holiness, an active reflection of Talonrend's devotion to their winged god. With almost everyone gone, the air inside was stagnant and tasted of stale emptiness.

Gideon reached the landing that housed most of the tower's sleeping quarters and pushed the door open with ease. The common area that connected the individual chambers was quiet and dark. Gideon whispered the words of his favorite cantrip and summoned a magical bird to illuminate the room. A thick layer of dust covered the bookshelves and old sheets were draped over the chairs and couches.

Without giving much attention to the abandoned common room, Gideon went directly to his former living quarters and opened the locked door with a slam from his shoulder. A small cot rested vertically against the far wall and stacks of books covered the floor. The paladin dropped to his knees, scattered the books with a sweep of his hand, and drew an axe from his belt. It didn't take long for Gideon to rip up a small section of the wooden floorboards and find his hidden stash.

Everything was just as he left it. Gideon took a small package wrapped in red silk out from the cubby and left the room without repairing the damage to the floor.

Asterion, reading while reclining in a soft chair, didn't bother saying goodbye to the paladin as he exited the tower and strode toward Castle Talon.

The soldiers standing watch behind the crenellations nodded as Gideon pushed through the enchanted doors of the keep. He went quickly to a side door off of the throne room that led to the dungeon beneath the castle. The torture chamber buried within the thick walls of Terror's Lament typically housed common criminals and prisoners delivered from villages along the Clawflow. Castle Talon's own dungeon was reserved for traitors and other high profile prisoners, such as Gravlox and Vorst.

Gideon grabbed a lit torch from a wall and held it in front of him. The goblins sat in their cramped cells and stared at the metal bars with visible resignation. The one-armed prisoner was lying vertically against his cell walls with his head wedged painfully between the bottoms of two bars.

"Gravlox," Gideon whispered to the goblin quietly enough to not disturb the sleeping lunatic a few feet away. "Gravlox," he whispered again and rattled the bars. "Wake up."

The shaman lifted his head and brought his eyes up from the floor.

"Goblins don't sleep," Vorst said from another cell. "Gravlox is… resting," she decided after a pause.

"Gravlox," Gideon began again with the shaman's attentions. "I have something for you." He slipped the red cloth package through the bars and nearly dropped it when the one-armed prisoner made a groan in his sleep.

"Thank you," Gravlox managed to say with his poor

knowledge of the human language.

"What is it?" Vorst asked, pressing her face against the bars to get a better view.

Gideon pulled back the silk and placed a small metal hoop in the shaman's outstretched hand. "I wore it on my arm when I was in training at the tower." He let go of the enchanted metal and took a step back from the prison cell. "The younger paladins use them as armbands to help hone their magical abilities. For you, it might work as a circlet." Gideon couldn't help but chuckle as Vorst told Gravlox what to do. The one-armed man stirred slightly in his sleep and fell over into a pile of his own filth.

"The energy imbued into the steel amplifies a paladin's ability to navigate the world of magic. I thought it might help you control your own abilities." Gideon looked to Vorst for a translation, but it was clear from the expression on the shaman's face that he understood the purpose of the item as soon as he touched it.

"What do you feel?" Vorst asked in her high-pitched voice. She stared in wonder as the shaman placed the circlet above his ears. Gravlox flexed his arms as though he had somehow grown suddenly stronger. His eyes rolled back in his head and he clutched at a metal bar for support.

Gideon took a cautious step backward and the hilt of his sword hit the carved stone wall. "Be careful..." he murmured, but he knew Gravlox could not understand.

"Grav, you need to take it off!" Vorst shouted, awakening the other prisoner. Visible streaks of power emanated from Gravlox's fingertips as he swayed back and forth. Gripping the metal cell door hard enough to turn his knuckles white, Gravlox wrenched the bars free from the floor and ceiling and hoisted the heavy door above his head.

The iron bars clanged to the ground like thunder and the one-armed prisoner began to shout. "Someone must have heard that," Gideon growled as he peered up the dank staircase. "We need to run!"

Gravlox ripped the iron door from Vorst's cell with similar ease and the three of them bounded up the staircase. The old man yelled and howled a stream of incoherent curses and exclamations behind them.

A guard, wearing a leather jerkin denoting his position, was waiting for the three with his sword drawn at the top of the stairs. "Back off!" Gideon yelled to him without slowing his pace.

The soldier, clearly confused, lowered his sword but did not get out of the way. Gideon's fist slammed into the man's gut and doubled him over. The paladin pointed to the front entrance of Castle Talon and told the goblins to run.

The gasping soldier managed to choke out a scream before Gideon hit him squarely in the back of the head and sent him to the ground. By the time the three made it to the front entrance, the drawbridge was being raised and shouts of alarm came from every direction.

Gravlox glanced over his shoulder for advice but Gideon continued to wave him forward. They burst from the keep followed by shouts and the thrumming of several crossbows. The bolts were hastily fired and none of them landed close to the running escapees. The drawbridge was a quarter of the way up when Vorst leapt from the edge. Gravlox and Gideon followed quickly behind Vorst and landed in a pile on the stone walkway beyond the moat.

"Come on!" Gideon roared as he untangled himself. The three were on their feet and running before the soldiers could fire a second volley.

With the drawbridge raised, it didn't take long for Gideon and the two goblins to put sufficient distance between themselves and any pursuit that might follow.

"Why did you do that?" Vorst asked when they finally sat down in a cramped alleyway between two brothels.

Gravlox shook his head and looked at his hands. Gideon plucked the circlet from the shaman's head and handed it to him, motioning that he should not wear it unless he needs to.

Vorst looked up to Gideon with despair etched onto her pale face. "Grav could have gotten us out before. I felt it..." she trailed off. "I told him not to do it. Now we are escaped prisoners." She buried her head in her hands. "They will hunt us now. We have broken their trust."

Gideon couldn't find any words sufficient to ease her sorrow. They would be hunted, he knew. Any chance of getting Herod accepting the goblin pair into the city was surely destroyed. "Well?" he said, "whatever happens, I owe you two my life. I will help you as best I can, but we may need to leave the city."

Running his hands along the smooth enchanted metal of the circlet, Gravlox let his gaze fall on each of them. His face showed nothing but anger and resolution. "I will not be controlled," he spoke in his native tongue. "Not by Lady Scrapple, not by any human prince, and certainly not by a metal cage buried beneath a castle."

The expression on Vorst's face was enough to tell Gideon what the shaman was saying. Vorst placed a hand on Gravlox's shoulder and a long moment passed before anyone spoke.

"Talonrend can expect another attack," Gideon said evenly. "I do not think it will be immediate, but it is coming."

Vorst nodded and considered the short amount of time it would require for Lady Scrapple to replace her army. "We need to find a way to stop it," she decided. "Perhaps even kill Lady Scrapple."

Gravlox stood and brushed the dirt from his leather skirt. "The mountain will be in disarray, at least for now. If we move quickly, we might be able to return unseen." Vorst translated the plan for Gideon but it was obvious that she disagreed with it.

"Grav..." she muttered, ashamed of her lack of control. "I can't go back to the mountain. If I get that close to her..." Her voice trailed off and Gravlox knew she was right. Returning to Kanebullar Mountain with Vorst was a risk he wasn't willing to take.

"If I go to the mountain," Gideon suggested with a flex of his hand, sensing Vorst's apprehension, "I can kill her. Just give me a map or something and I will handle it."

Gravlox shook his head.

"Your sword," Vorst said, pointing to the hilt resting behind the paladin's head. "It doesn't work with goblins, remember? How many goblins did you kill without returning to your normal size?" It was a question Gideon didn't want to answer.

"Lady Scrapple has no soul?" he asked, trying to hide his disappointment.

"I don't know," Vorst replied. "But something must be done before her army returns." Her tone was grave and serious, but not without hope.

Gideon scoffed and gestured to Terror's Lament towering high above the city. "These walls held before, they will hold again," he said.

"The first battle was likely a test of the city's defenses," Vorst stated. "Remember the balloons? When they come again, Lady Scrapple will bring more flying machines, blasting oils from the mines, catapults and trebuchets to tear down the walls. She will not make the same mistake again, no matter how expendable the soldiers may be."

Gideon thought for a moment how he would attempt to lead an army against the heavily fortified city, but came up with nothing. "What about others?" he wondered aloud after some time. "Do the goblins have any allies that would join in the battle?"

Vorst shook her head. "There are no other goblins," she said with a pained expression. "Lady Scrapple's goblins. Us," she pointed to Gravlox tentatively, "we can't survive on our own."

"What about outsiders?" Gideon gestured toward the mountain range lowing to the north. "Other things live in the wilds besides goblins."

"Possibly," Vorst mused. "I have never heard of any such alliances existing, but that certainly does not make it impossible. There are hordes of orcs and other beasts in those mountains that would love to see this city fall."

"So what do we do?" Gravlox asked after Vorst translated the conversation for him.

Gideon rubbed his hands together and turned his gaze back upon the tower at the center of Talonrend. "We need information, that much is clear," he said without looking back to the goblins. "I might know where we can find some of our answers." He motioned for the two goblins to keep close to the walls of the nearby buildings and exited the alley in the direction of the tower. With so many refugees already on the road outside Talonrend, it didn't require much stealth for the goblins to move through the streets of Talonrend unnoticed.

A REON, ONE OF the two devotees who choose to stay in the Tower of Wings after the exodus, knelt next to Prince Herod's body and listened for the man's breath. "He is still alive," the young priest said through a mask of white silk. "Though I have no clue as to how long he will live."

Apollonius watched the devotee dab some of the sweat from Herod's brow with a rag. "What is it that ails him? Is there a cure?" he asked with desperation.

"If I knew the answer to either of those questions, wouldn't the prince be healthy by now?" Areon snapped. He rolled the prince from side to side in the bed to remove the sweat-soaked sheets and replace them with fresh linen.

"I only meant," Apollonius started with frustration, "is it some disease? An infection? Do you know anything?"

Areon let out a long sigh and stood straight to look Apollonius in the eyes. "I doubt that it is contagious," he patted his mask with a thoughtful finger, "but I would rather not take any chances. If it was an infection, he would either be dead or better by now. My best guess is magic, although none of my prayers have shown any power to heal him."

The soldier regarded Areon with a scrutinizing expression. "Have any of the other wounded shown similar ailments?"

"I would not know," Areon stated coldly as he began to leave the prince's bedchamber. "The two of us devotees who stayed long enough to see the end of the fight are students of Asterion, a battle priest. All of the real healers left with the paladins or the refugees. I'm afraid that most of the wounded were treated only by conventional methods."

Apollonius balled his fists suppressing the urge to scream at the devotee, but couldn't find any words to adequately describe how he felt. Areon looked to the prince and frowned once more before leaving.

THE LONG TRAIN of refugees moved slower every day. Cold air froze the ground and hints of snowflakes danced in Seamus' foggy breath. His scarf was pulled tightly around his mouth and nose in a poor attempt to keep his lips from cracking. The group had caught up with a small band of paladins who had stopped to bury one of their brethren. A sickness was spreading through the refugees that had many of them throwing up throughout the night and dead on their feet.

The trail, if it could be called such a thing, was covered in rocks and wild plants that tangled the wheels on their wagons and caused more than a few of the mules to fall from broken ankles.

"I thought we would at least see something by now," Seamus murmured under his scarf. "There won't be any of us left at this rate." Squirt padded alongside the older man, but was too sick to ask questions. His eyes were halfway glazed as he stared blankly at the path under his feet. Food was running low and children too young to help carry supplies were given the least of what remained.

A paladin, Corvus by name, trudged next to Seamus with a

bulging pack strapped to his shoulders. "Our histories say that it took months for the settlers from the Green City to get to Talonrend," the warrior stated with a lack of emotion as though he were identifying the color of the sky.

"Yeah, but they didn't know where they were going," Seamus retorted. He tried to sound confident but the wind and the cold stole the strength of his words.

"They were also plagued by all manner of creatures and suffered hundreds of casualties along the way," the paladin recounted.

Seamus stopped in his path and rubbed the top of his head. His legs were sore and the bottoms of his feet were plagued with blisters. "Maybe we should never 'ave left..." he lamented. Squirt collapsed behind him with a thud but no one had the strength to help him back to his feet. Maybe one of the paladins further down the trail would help the poor boy. Maybe not.

The column halted with the onset of dusk, and fires were lit to cook what remained of the mules and other animals that had perished. Corvus climbed to the top of a wagon with a bowl of hot broth and attempted to keep watch. Weariness made his eyes tired, and the glare from the cooking fires made it impossible to see more than a few feet beyond the circled wagons. Sleep quickly overcame him.

Seamus tossed and turned on the hard ground. His sheepskin blanket kept him warm but did nothing to ease his aching back. He watched as Corvus' bowl tumbled from his sleeping hands and knew that he should either rouse the paladin or keep watch himself, but Seamus couldn't find the energy to move. There were other paladins spread out among the long line of refugees. Surely, Seamus thought to himself, one of them would raise the alarm if the camp came under attack. Let the tired paladin sleep.

The fire was little more than a collection of ashes when morning broke and the refugees began to stir. Corvus moved from his perch atop a wagon and collected his frost-covered bowl from the ground. In addition to his weighty traveling pack, the man wore a large shield over his shoulders and carried a heavy mace on his belt. With a grim nod, Corvus produced a bow from his belongings and set off ahead of the column to scout and hunt.

The wagons were creaking along the frozen dirt at a comfortable pace when Corvus returned at noon with two squirrels dangling from his side. He tossed them into the back of one of the wagons and fell into step beside Seamus.

"See anything out there?" the refugee asked to pass the time. Corvus ran a hand through his patchy beard and adjusted the straps of his pack.

"We are being followed," the paladin said in a low voice so that no one else would hear. "Watched, at least, but by what I cannot tell."

"You seein' tracks?" Seamus questioned a bit too loudly, but if any of the other refugees noticed, they were either too weary or too depressed to care.

Corvus shielded his mouth with a hand and whispered, "I saw a rider. He was far to the north of us, probably several miles away, but he was there."

"Bah!" Seamus snorted and shook his head. "It was a bear, methinks, or a mountain lion come to feast on our mules. It's nothing."

"I know what I saw," the paladin mumbled. "I have never heard of any mountain lions that carry banners. The rider was flying a standard, of that I am sure."

"We've too many o' us for a lone bandit, lest he's mad in the head!" Seamus nearly bellowed, somehow finding great mirth in the situation.

"And if it is a scout serving some larger group that intends to attack?" Corvus countered. "We must be ready to defend ourselves."

"And who would it be out there, hmm?" Seamus asked. "No one's alive in these plains and no one's alive in those mountains either. You're seein' ghosts on the wind, you are." Seamus stretched his aching back and surveyed the refugees like a shepherd counting his flock. "Besides," he said more seriously, "what's wantin' to kill us won't have no trouble doin' so. How many bandits would it take to murder this whole lot of sorry farmers? Not many, I'm for thinking."

Corvus sighed and adjusted his pack again. "I'm afraid that you have made a valid point," the paladin conceded. "These farmers are not fit for combat." He took a step back to inspect the burly refugee and pretended to analyze him. "Though I have no doubt that if a tavern brawl broke out, we would have strong chance."

Seamus puffed out his chest and flexed. "Crackin' skulls with beer mugs be me best skill, I'll have you know."

Corvus managed a chuckle despite the tragic nature of their situation. "I fear that riders seldom meet with refugee bands to have a drink and a friendly brawl..." he murmured, looking to the horizon.

They camped that night on a low, boulder-strewn rise. Corvus watched a squirrel rotating slowly on a spit over the cook fire and licked his lips. Seamus passed him a jug of cider that had gone bad a week ago and the paladin sipped it reluctantly. It tasted terrible, but was warm and took some of the chill from his bones.

"Someone else will take the watch tonight," Corvus said to the farmer as he handed him back the cider. Seamus choked down a large gulp and nodded.

"We's gonna' find that rider o' yours?" he asked with a hint of excitement.

"Eat your squirrel and be ready to move an hour after nightfall," the paladin whispered. He took another sip of the hot cider and climbed to the top of a wagon to rest until dusk.

Corvus felt energized and light on his feet when he roused Seamus for the hunt.

"I got no weapon," the refugee whispered as he stood.

The paladin unstrapped his shield and handed it to the confused looking farmer. "We don't want a fight," Corvus reminded him. "We just want to know what's out there." Corvus gripped his hunting bow tightly and sent up a silent prayer to Vrysinoch.

The two men hurried out of the camp as quickly as they could and made for the north. They came to a stand of fir trees a mile or so beyond the wagons and Corvus motioned for them to get down. The paladin crawled through the underbrush, listening intently for movement, but determined the area was clear.

Seamus moved to the center of the copse and leaned against a tree to watch Corvus climb and get a vantage point. "What you seein'?" he whispered in the direction the paladin had gone.

"Shhh," came the immediate response. A moment later, Corvus dropped to the ground with a roll and began using an arrow to draw a crude map in the dirt.

"Half a mile, maybe less," he whispered, pointing to a circle he had drawn.

"How many?" Seamus asked as he tightened the straps of the shield to his wrist. The burly farmer by no means qualified as a soldier, but he knew how to use something heavy to kill a man. The shield, a huge piece of crafted steel designed to guard the entire body, was much larger and sturdier than anything Seamus was accustomed to wielding in a bar fight. The holy symbols etched into the metal glowed faintly with comforting light.

"More than one," was all that Corvus could say with certainty. "Be ready, but be quiet!" he implored.

They stalked through the night slowly, wincing with every broken twig. Seamus wrapped his scarf around his mouth and tried to steady his breathing, but adrenaline made his heart pound with a fury he could not control. An ancient feeling of purpose began to grow inside Seamus' chest, though he tried his best to ignore it. Charging into an unknown enemy camp in search of glory was an easy way to die.

"Hear that?" Corvus dared to whisper. "Dogs, or some other animal." They crept closer to a small ring of five tents that were partially concealed by pine trees.

Seamus shook his head and pointed, his eyes going wide. "Not dogs…" he murmured. "Wolves. Great. Big. Wolves." Seamus guided the paladin's sight to a low branch where several massive wolves were tied.

Corvus tried to gulp down his fear. Every instinct he had told him to run. Footsteps coming from the other side of a tent nearly made him faint. A shadowy figure, taller and wider than a man, moved toward the wolves with a hunk of meat hanging casually from his oversized fist.

"That's…" Seamus stuttered as he peered through the darkness.

"Orcs," Corvus finished for him. The paladin motioned for the two to begin their retreat and held a finger over his mouth in a desperate plea for silence. The pair didn't make it five steps before Seamus' clumsy foot snapped a twig that made one of the wolves growl in their direction. The orc, feeding the wolves one by one with chunks of meat, turned on his heels and scanned for the source of the sound.

"If he sees us, run," Corvus whispered in a barely audible breath. The orc continued to peer into the darkness, but didn't raise an alarm. One of the wolves pawed at the ground and licked the air, issuing a low growl directly at the frozen humans.

Seamus nudged the paladin and looked to the man's bow. The wolf howled and shattered the quiet of the night. It pulled fiercely on its chain and snarled; eager for a kill. The orc wasted no time unhooking the chain from the beast's harness and set it free.

Corvus loosed a single arrow in the direction of the wolf as he turned to flee. "Run!" he shouted to Seamus who was breathing heavily at his back. The two ran as quickly as they could, but were no match for the spectacular speed of the bloodthirsty wolf.

The charging orc shouted a stream of incomprehensible words and the wolf leapt through the air. Its claws clanged loudly against the paladin's shield, strapped firmly to Seamus' wrist, and the beast fell back in a momentary daze. Corvus got his bow up for a second shot and managed to sink an arrow in the side of the wolf so deeply it might have gone out the other side.

Gripping the shield with all of his strength, Seamus rushed at the wounded beast and smashed into its face with a great thud. By the time Seamus recovered from his own charge enough to peer over the edge of the shield, the orc was upon him. With fists the size of the farmer's head, he rained down blow after blow that crushed Seamus to the ground.

Corvus came in hard with his flanged mace swinging in a wide arc. The weighted steel crashed into the orc's forearm before the creature even saw it coming. Bones snapped under the skin and in an instant, the arm was rendered useless.

The wolf, drooling a sticky mess of blood from its mouth, lunged back into the fight. Seamus was able to deflect the brunt of the wolf's lunge with the shield, but the beast managed to get a claw inside his defense. He grit his teeth in pain and held back a scream as the wolf tore a sizeable chunk from the skin over his ribs. Seamus dropped to his knees and dug the bottom of the shield into the ground for support. Suddenly less courageous, he ducked his head and waited for the wolf to circle him.

The blood-rush of battle danced in the orc's eyes as he again went on the offensive. The orc swung with his only remaining arm and caught Corvus by the throat with a meaty hand. The paladin kicked and swung his mace but had no momentum and could barely reach the orc's body. With no noticeable effort, the orc lifted Corvus high off the ground and clenched his fingers.

Corvus struggled and clawed at the orc's hand but knew that he was overmatched. The creature smiled and cocked his head with obvious pleasure, slowly squeezing the life from the human's neck.

Seamus clutched at the bleeding wound on his side and waited for the wolf. Whimpering and pawing tentatively at the ground, the beast circled the entrenched shield and was met by a fearsome kick that connected cleanly with its jaw. Seamus wasted no time. Grunting away the pain, the farmer ripped the shield up from the ground and swung it in a deadly arc above his head. The wolf was too dazed from the kick to dodge. The shield edge cracked into the beast's spine and partially severed its head in a pool of grisly blood.

Dizzy from blood loss and breathing heavily, Seamus turned and saw Corvus struggling for his life in the powerful grip of the orc. The bloody shield weighed heavily on Seamus' arm. He unstrapped it and let it clang to the ground. The paladin's mace wasn't far off and the orc paid him no heed.

Seamus swung the mace down as hard he could into the orc's back but his torn chest stole the strength from his arms. The orc winced and turned, but did not fall. Corvus flailed wildly and the orc tossed him into the farmer with a flick of his wrist.

"The bow," Seamus muttered as he untangled himself from the paladin. Corvus gasped for air and vomited before he could stand.

The orc cackled and charged with his functional arm leading the way. Seamus ducked into the charge and wrapped the orc in a grapple he instantly regretted. The green-skinned creature far outmatched the physical strength of both humans combined. Vicious hits from the orc's elbow pounded into the back of Seamus' skull. Splotchy shades of grey and purple swirled through his vision and the metallic taste of blood mingled with the bile at the back of his throat. Each thunderous hit threatened to shake the teeth from his skull, but Seamus dug his heels into the dirt and pushed back.

An arrow whistled through the air and caught the orc in the forearm with enough force to rip the flesh open, spraying blood all over Seamus' face. The farmer dropped to the ground and rolled, but the world spun in his head and he couldn't make sense of direction.

A second arrow landed solidly in the orc's unarmored chest and brought him to his knees. The third arrow bit so deeply into the orc's eye that it protruded from the back of the beast's skull. Exhausted, and still fighting the effects of strangulation, Corvus could barely help the battered farmer to his feet.

The two humans limped across the ground to the copse of trees half a mile away before Corvus dared to call upon his god. He placed a hand over Seamus' torn side and spoke a prayer to Vry-sinoch that was answered with a bright flare of light. The wound wasn't completely healed, but the bleeding stopped immediately and Seamus' breathing steadied into a normal rhythm. Knowing that the farmer would live, Corvus decided against calling down a second wave of healing magic for himself. The paladin propped himself against a tree with his mace and bow resting across his legs and let the exhaustion overwhelm his senses.

Sleep came in painful fits of labored breathing, but dawn broke without any signs of an orc pursuit.

"I lived," was all that Seamus had energy to say when he awoke with the sun warming his bruised body.

"We have to..." Corvus' voice trailed off into a fit of coughing. He rubbed his sore neck and used his bow like a staff to help him stand. "We have to warn the others," the paladin managed once his coughing subsided.

"Damned orcs..." Seamus muttered. He glanced around the clearing, looking for the paladin's shield, but saw only the heavy mace partially buried under some leaves. "You left the shield?" he asked.

"And most of my arrows," Corvus confirmed with a sigh. "I didn't really have the luxury of scavenging the battlefield. I don't think orcs are very fond of shields in any case, if you're worried about them taking it."

Seamus rubbed his wrist where the shield had been strapped. The leather left two thin cuts in his skin that had already crusted with scabs. Despite being relatively safe, he felt defenseless without it. "It's just..." he started to say but didn't know the right words. He wasn't trained in combat but didn't want to appear helpless before the paladin.

"Here," Corvus said as he kicked the mace in Seamus' direction. "Take it. Just promise me that you won't let *that* fall into orc hands as well. The grimy beasts love their clubs, and a mace like that would be a prized weapon among their clan I'm sure."

Seamus nodded his appreciation and lifted the mace from the ground with subtle reverence. "I can never repay you," the grateful farmer stated but Corvus was already hobbling out of the copse in the direction of the refugee caravan.

"ASTERION!" GIDEON SHOUTED as he pounded on the glass door of the Tower. Gravlox and Vorst hid across the street from the Tower of Wings. They crouched behind an empty merchant's cart that had been abandoned in front of a shop. The door opened a moment later and Asterion smiled to see his old friend once again.

"Gideon—" he started to say but the big man pushed him aside and waved for the goblins to run to his side. Gideon placed a hand over the old priest's mouth in anticipation of a shout but Asterion only smiled when he saw the goblin pair scamper into the foyer. Gideon let the door close behind him and waited for Asterion to speak.

"Goblins!" the priest said with more astonishment than anything. Asterion turned to Gideon with his eyes wide and his mouth agape. "I had heard rumors that there were two in the city but never did I dream that I would meet them. Why have you brought them here?"

Gideon introduced the two goblins to the priest before explaining his plan. "We think the goblins might be rallying other forces to their cause," he stated. "I need to use the star room to find out what else is out there and from where the next threat may come."

Asterion shook his wrinkled head and frowned. "You could not open the door to this tower on your own, Gideon. What makes you think that Vrysinoch will allow you entry into the star room? Only a servant of Vrysinoch may use such sacred objects, you know that. Even entering the room without Vrysinoch's blessing could prove catastrophic."

A long pause passed between them but Asterion already knew what the paladin would say.

"You are a priest in good standing with Vrysinoch, are you not?" Gideon asked the man blatantly. Asterion nodded his head but averted his eyes. "You can use the star room for us. For everyone. For Talonrend."

"And if the Archbishop discovers I have allowed a paladin of ill repute and his two goblin companions into the tower, he will have me exiled. And if he finds out I let you three use the star room, he will have my head on a pike before sundown." Asterion folded his arms across his chest and put on an uncharacteristic look of defiance. "I cannot risk that," he said with finality.

"You said yourself that the Archbishop hasn't been seen in days, Asterion," Gideon pleaded. "Think about what will happen to you if the city is attacked again. We have no militia. We have no paladins! What will we do? Talonrend will be overrun and you will die in this tower alongside the Archbishop. Is that what you want?"

Asterion thought about it a long moment before sitting down and smoothing the wrinkles of his robe. "What of the prince?" he asked at length, keeping his gaze fixed on the two goblins. "Did Herod release those two or did you break them out? Do you have a royal decree stating the three of you are to be the saviors of Talonrend?" His tone was sarcastic and incredulous.

Frustration welled up within the paladin and he fought hard to keep it down. "The prince is nearly dead, old friend," he stated with more bite than he intended.

"And when he finally does pass on, the Archbishop will surely try to take over the city! If I make an enemy of him now, what kind of fool would I be when he ascends to the throne of Talonrend?" Asterion threw his hands up in the air and sighed. "I cannot risk any more than I already have, Gideon. Do not ask me to do this."

"You would condemn the city?"

"My hands are tied."

"You have already taken a great risk just by letting me into the tower, Asterion," Gideon said, forming a plan in his mind. "Clearly, your loyalties to the Archbishop are not as iron-clad as you would have me believe."

Asterion rocked back in his chair and smiled. "I'm not like you," he laughed. "I won't run off after my first disagreement with the Archbishop. I've butted heads with that man before, yes, but would I risk my life for your sake?" He shook his head after a moment of contemplation. "Such a course of action would not be prudent."

"I'm not asking you to risk your life for me," Gideon began. "I'm asking you to risk your life for Talonrend. Look around! The city is in shambles and you sit in this tower and wait for what? Vrysinoch to swoop down from the heavens and snatch you up with his talons?"

Asterion began to respond with an angry shake of his fist, but the paladin cut him off. "Take us to the star room, use its magic to search the wilderness, and then *leave* this place," Gideon implored.

"Where would I go?" Asterion asked. "How far would I have to run to live beyond the reach of the Archbishop? You know how vindictive he is, Gideon. He would hunt me relentlessly."

With a great sweep of his arm, Gideon smiled and looked at the goblins. "Your place is with us. You are a battle priest, a holy warrior trained for combat and the open road! Come north and together we can push the tide of monsters back into the mountains."

Despite his advanced age and relative passivity compared to the fiery paladin, Asterion enjoyed the idea of leaving Talonrend in search of a fight. In fact, the more Asterion thought about it, the better the whole plan seemed. A wide smile broke out on his wrinkled face and he arched an eyebrow as he looked at the goblins. "How soon do you intend to leave?" He tried to keep the excitement from his voice but it was obvious that his passions had been ensnared.

"The sooner we get to the star room and figure out exactly what we are up against, the sooner we can set foot on the open road." Gideon helped the priest up from his chair and wrapped him in a hearty embrace.

"Follow me," Asterion said eagerly as he brushed past the goblins and headed for the spiral staircase.

"What exactly is the star room?" Vorst asked as the group descended. The stairs under the tower were dark and gloomy, a stark contrast to the brightly lit room above. Images of Vrysinoch were carved into the walls, but instead of beautiful icons depicting the mercy and power of the god, the carvings displayed scenes of torment. One particularly gruesome etching showed Vrysinoch's leathery talons ripping a disfavored priest limb by limb. Vorst shuddered as she passed by the scene.

"The star room," Asterion explained, "is all that remains of the first disciples of Vrysinoch after their pilgrimage from the Green City." Asterion lifted a withered finger toward the dark ceiling and identified the names of some of the pilgrims. "After they built the temple in the cavern underneath Castle Talon, the disciples came to this place and constructed the Tower of Wings. Considerable magic was employed to raise this temple, as you might have guessed. With such an expenditure of magical energy, strange things are bound to happen."

Gideon snorted with obvious derision and shook his head. "They were mad, all of them. Fanatics who killed themselves in the name of their god." Gideon stopped a moment at the image of one of the priests being burned at the stake. "Purification, they called it." He spat on the wall and walked on.

"Yes," Asterion continued with a frown. "The first disciples lived in a constant state of communion with Vrysinoch. When Vrysinoch spoke to them, they listened. It was demanded of the disciples that they purify their bodies for the final ascent. Many chose to burn themselves. Others attempted to scrape all of their skin from their bones and claimed that it was the flesh that served as a vessel for disease and impurity."

"What happened to the disciples that didn't want to kill themselves?" Vorst asked tentatively, although she feared the answer.

Asterion stopped in front of a simple wooden door and turned to face the group, now half a dozen or more stories underground. "The disciples who didn't kill themselves in the first purification...." He placed a hand on the door and pushed it open. A gust of cold air and a cloud of dust rushed from the star room. "They built this room out of the bones of the disciples. Be warned," he cautioned sternly, "strange magic lingers here."

Gravlox could feel it as soon as the door opened. The gust of cold wind sought him out and enveloped him in a shroud none of the others could see. When he closed his eyes and tried to seek out the magic of the room, he found nothing. Something was there, in the realm of magic, but it would not let him in or show itself to him. The cold air had severed Gravlox's magical self from the physical world. He was powerless.

Do you feel it? Gravlox tapped in the goblin code on Vorst's shoulder. She shook her head and stepped as close to the room as she could without entering. Asterion walked into the star room, but Gideon stayed behind.

"No?" Gravlox asked with an expression he hoped conveyed his confusion to the paladin.

Gideon shook his head and motioned with his hands for Gravlox to stay back. He reached a pointed finger into the doorway and another chilling gust of wind came forth to meet him. The paladin pointed to the hilt of his sword and shrugged, obviously unsure of what might happen if he entered the room. Gravlox contented himself to study the macabre depictions on the staircase's walls as he waited.

The star room was constructed like a small, underground stage. A row of benches was cut into the soft mud of one wall and a platform was built across from it. No torches or magical means of illumination were present in the room, but Asterion did not have any trouble seeing every detail. The stage was built from bones with a backdrop of human skulls making up the far wall.

A faint blue glow appeared before the priest at his command. Asterion closed his eyes and spoke to the blue haze. Within in an instant, more and more of the blue glow seeped out of the wall of skulls and formed into a host of specters.

"They will show us potential futures," Asterion whispered, remembering the first time he had used the chamber and revealed his own destiny. Two of the specters fell to the ground and formed themselves into a tall square resembling Terror's Lament. Another specter pointed a ghastly finger at Asterion's chest and split apart into an army of miniature blue goblins. The scale goblin army charged into the spectral walls of Talonrend and disintegrated.

A great rumbling shook the bones of the stage and rattled some of the skulls from their resting place in the wall. A specter twice the size of the miniature walls swooped down from the top of the skulls in the shape of a dragon and breathed a cone of ethereal fire over the walls. The blue wisps forming Terror's Lament and the dragon broke apart and landed on the stage as a horde of orc warriors. Each soldier was no taller than one of Asterion's fingers, but they filled every inch of the stage.

The blue orc army marched in place for a moment and then stopped abruptly, forming into tents, huts, and other structures common to orc society. The broken and melted walls of Talonrend rose up from the bones to encompass the orc city. Another specter pulled itself free from the skull wall and split itself into hundreds of tiny goblins that walked into the city and mingled with the orc buildings.

Asterion stood from the dirt bench and waved his hand, scattering the wisps and erasing the scene. He spoke another line of arcane words and the specters assembled themselves into figures closely resembling their group. A ghostly image of Vorst stood next to the likenesses of Gravlox, Gideon, and Asterion and the four of them walked forward on spectral feet. The group stopped, looked around, and then flailed as though set on fire. The four images burned with blue flames and crumpled on the ground where a large azure dragon's foot landed on them from above. The image dissipated instantly and the specters formed into a single column, one Asterion easily recognized as the Winged Tower. The Tower trembled and blue fire danced through the spectral wisps until the structure collapsed on itself.

With a shriek that broke the silence, the blue ghosts jolted and flew into the bones. An inky blackness overcame the star room that Asterion's eyes could not penetrate. He reached a hand out and felt for the edge of the bone stage. The old priest gasped and stood, hurriedly exiting the room.

"What did you see?" Gideon asked as the priest emerged from the darkness. "Have the goblins found an ally?"

"A dragon," Asterion gasped as he considered the implications. "A great blue dragon destroyed the city."

"That is only one possible future," the priest reminded them. "In another scene, the goblins attacked again, but were repelled easily. Still another showed orcs coming out of the mountains and conquering Talonrend."

"None of those are particularly favorable," Gideon stated. "But these are only some of the potential futures. Or they could be nothing more than the imaginations of old ghosts."

The four ascended the tight spiral staircase quickly, eager to get out of the gloom and return to the sunlight. "Meet me at the gate tomorrow at dawn," Asterion said to Gideon and the goblins with a nod. "No matter what future we will find, we must travel north. If the goblins come, the walls will hold. We must seek out this dragon…"

A chilling shudder coursed through Vorst's spine as she imagined coming face to face with a dragon.

"I'll see you at dawn, Asterion," Gideon said as he led the goblins out of the towers. "With so many of the residents out on the road as refugees, it shouldn't be difficult to find an abandoned building to hide you two for the night." The goblins nodded their appreciation and stuck to the shadows as they scampered through the town.

THE SUN BROKE around the sides of Kanebullar Mountain and warmed the smooth stones of Terror's Lament. It would take several hours for the light of the sun to pass over the high walls and illuminate the town. Gravlox shielded his eyes from the sunlight as he walked through the gate with Vorst and Gideon.

Asterion stood with his back to the light and looked up at the top of the walls. "There are soldiers everywhere," he said, motioning to the guards with a hand. "How did you get them out of the city?"

"Only one soldier asked anything about them," Gideon shrugged. "I just told them the goblins were to be released and I wasn't questioned further. The soldiers are so young and untrained they don't know any better. In any case, I would like to be far away from here before they figure it out."

Black scorch marks stained the front of the outermost gatehouse. Large chunks of rubble had fallen from the walls, but Talonrend lacked the manpower necessary to start clearing the wreckage. Everywhere they looked, skeletons littered the plains in crumpled masses. Rotting goblin bones created a sea of waist-high carnage Asterion and Gideon did not look forward to traversing.

Gravlox and Vorst stared up at the silhouette of Kanebullar Mountain and shook their heads. The fallen goblin army did not bother them nearly as much as the ever present shadow of the mountain. Vorst reached out and grabbed Gravlox by the hand. "Let's get moving," she said quietly, but Gravlox had already put his feet in motion.

Gideon's boots stomped through goblin skeletons with a chorus of cracks of and crunches that made him sick to his stomach. "Master Brenning is somewhere among these bones," the paladin said solemnly. "Herod saw him leave the gate and no one has heard anything of his return." Gideon surveyed the sea of bones and wondered where his friend's corpse might lay.

"Just because he hasn't returned to Talonrend," Asterion said without much optimism, "does not mean Master Brenning is dead." The words were hollow and tasted like a lie on his tongue.

The four companions trudged north and tried to ignore the vast multitude of bones that surrounded their footsteps.

Talonrend stood a few miles behind the group when they stopped for the night to set their camp. The air was cold and filled with specks of frost that nestled in Gideon's beard before melting and dripping to the ground.

"We will start to climb tomorrow," Asterion said as he broke off a piece of bread and handed it to Vorst. The base of the mountain range was only half a day's walk away. "It will get cold up in the mountains," the old priest stated, pulling his cloak tightly about his shoulders. Gideon grunted and hooked his fingers underneath the leather straps of the harness that crossed his muscled chest.

"Do you have anything warmer than that?" Asterion asked, pointing to Gravlox's meager vest and Vorst's even slighter garb. Gravlox sat on the ground in front of the cooking fire and pulled his knees in tightly against his chest to ward off the breeze.

Gravlox and Vorst had never experienced any temperatures that would require more than a simple animal hide. Even the highest elevated chambers of Kanebullar Mountain were comfortably warm.

"We can make fire," Vorst responded after relaying the question to Gravlox.

Gideon chuckled and gazed up at the mountain range before them. "If we can bring down a bear," he laughed, "we would surely get enough hide to cover them both from head to toe."

Asterion's wasn't quite so jovial. "Until we can get them something warmer," he stated, "my magic will have to suffice." The old priest placed a wrinkled hand on Vorst's shoulder and spoke the lines to a short spell that poured light over the goblin's body.

Immediately, Gravlox sensed the origin of the power. He could feel something above him, miles above the clouds even, sending small bursts of energy down to the ground. The shaman cocked his head to the side and tried to send his own subconscious into the air to seek out the source of the magical heat. His mind soared and scoured the air but found nothing.

Placing one hand firmly on the ground, Gravlox beckoned to the energy he felt bubbling forth like magma between his fingers. Not fully aware of what the result might be, Gravlox ripped a fistful of dirt from the ground and conjured images of goblin furnaces in his mind. The dirt sprang to life in the air and rained a shower of harmless sparks down upon Vorst's scowling face but something else lingered within Gravlox's shamanistic senses.

"We might want to step back," Gideon muttered as he placed a protective hand over Asterion's chest. Vorst scrambled on all fours to a hide behind a tree stump.

Gravlox's face contorted and his fingers trembled. The shaman's mind latched onto a pool of untapped energy that quickly filled his senses and overwhelmed his control. With a boom like an anvil thrown from Terror's Lament to the cobblestone below, a searing gout of flame burst forth from the ground at Gravlox's feet and spiraled wildly into the sky. The pillar of fire spun and twirled as it laced the air with ash high above Gravlox's head.

Panicked and fearing for his life, Gravlox severed the connection between his mind and the ever-flowing energy within his body. The snaking river of animated flames curled in on itself and erupted in a hail of embers and smoldering ashes that covered the ground

281

and painfully stung the goblin's exposed flesh.

"Fire," was all that Gravlox was able to say before he collapsed to the ground with a smile plastered to his singed face.

Asterion brushed a layer of ash from his cloak and helped Vorst to her feet. "Your friend is rather... interesting," the old priest muttered to himself in disbelief.

Seven

"**T**HERE ARE ORCS following us," Corvus whispered to a group of huddled paladins just after sunrise. The men were worn down and hungry, but that didn't stop a gleam from creeping into the edges of their eyes at the prospect of battle. There were forty or more paladins scattered through the refugee train and Corvus had gathered a handful of them to help him scout.

"Did you get a look at their camp?" a grizzled old warrior asked as he rubbed the hilt of his mace.

"We saw some tents, but they had wolves with them." Corvus lowered his voice as a woman carrying a jug of water walked past the group.

The older paladin glanced at his three comrades and Corvus, licking his lips. "The ones with wolves are just outriders, scouts for the army. Their mounts are too rare to risk on raid." One of the younger paladins cleared his throat and swallowed nervously. "There's an army of the green-skinned bastards out there, I can promise you that."

Seamus walked up to the five paladins with Corvus' mace tucked securely under his belt. "What do we do now?" the gruff farmer asked with an edge of fear in his voice.

The old paladin gave Seamus a hearty pat on his shoulder. "Are you ready to fight again?" he asked. Seamus was still bruised and battered from his previous encounter with the orcs and honestly had little taste for battle left in his stomach. He nodded despite his fear.

"Then we must press our attack. They won't expect it." The veteran grinned a toothy smile and spat on the frosted grass. "We kill the outriders, the army might turn back. It's the best chance we have to put a few of them under the ground before they do the same to us."

Corvus rubbed at his sore neck, but knew he couldn't object. It was the only option they had. "I'll need more arrows," Corvus muttered under his fogging breath.

The five paladins and Seamus set out in the direction of the orc outriders without much more deliberation. It didn't take long for them to reach the copse of trees.

"I can see banners moving this way," the youngest paladin stated with a cold voice steeled by the prospect of battle. Three tall banners swayed with footsteps just beyond a low rise a hundred or so yards away.

"Do we set an ambush?" Seamus asked, trying to give his voice the battle-hardened quality he heard when the other men spoke.

The paladins smiled and stifled a laugh. "We crusade in the holy name of Vrysinoch!" the veteran haughtily replied as he took the huge shield from his back and strapped it to his wrist.

Corvus flexed his bow and counted the arrows in his quiver. "We fight as one," he explained to the farmer. "One mind, one shield, one mace. When paladins of Vrysinoch muster on the field of battle, it is as one soldier. Our cohesion will be their undoing."

Seamus let a smile flicker at the edges of his mouth before he realized that he had no place in such a tactic. "What should I do?" he questioned.

"Stay by my side," Corvus reassured him. "I only have a bow

so I'll need your strong arm at my back."

The farmer couldn't help but puff his chest out. He wanted nothing more than to be useful and find a place among the holy warriors he respected so much.

"Now," the youngest paladin bellowed into crisp air with calm and deadly look to his eyes. "We march."

The four fully outfitted paladins locked their shields together and beat their heavy maces against their steel breastplates in thunderous unison.

"Won't they hear us coming?" Seamus implored with more than a hint of fear.

Corvus stretched his shoulders and nocked an arrow loosely on his bowstring. "Yes, my friend. That is the idea! To battle!" he shouted at the top of his lungs. The four interlocked paladins took up a low, rumbling hymn that steadied the shaking in Seamus' hands and calmed his racing heart.

The orcs howled and wolves snarled not far from their view. The dark and melodious hymn increased in volume with every step, building into a deafening crescendo that swelled inside Seamus' chest like a creature ready to burst forth from his heart.

"True glory cannot be attained by stabbing your foes in the back or lying in ambush and waiting for them to fall into your trap!" Corvus lifted his bow as he shouted over the moving shield wall. "The glory of Vrysinoch is to meet your enemies face to face and send them to their graves!"

The shield wall gained speed and the first of the orcs crested the rise less than thirty paces in front of them. A dozen green-skinned warriors, brandishing axes, spears, knives, and clubs, broke into a full charge at the sight of the paladins. Six huge, snarling wolves tugged at their harnesses. Seamus could see the drool flying from their muscular jaws, but the resonating hymn gave him strength. Images of the wolf he killed lying dead at his feet flashed through his mind and the untrained farmer felt invincible.

Corvus loosed his first arrow into the chest of an unarmored orc as the wolves were set free and the shield wall crashed into the outriders. The hymn diminished into a flurry of grunts and blood-crazed yells. Flawlessly maintaining their unity, the paladins lowered into a crouch, shoved forward with their huge shields, and swung their maces in a devastating arc. Several of the orcs howled in pain, but none of them went down.

Seamus tensed as a wolf circled the shield wall. He lifted his mace to strike, but an arrow from Corvus' bow tore into the beast and laid it low before he could strike. The orcs came against the shield wall again, thrusting their spears up high and hacking with their axes like deranged lumberjacks trying to fell a giant redwood.

The paladins pushed again and staggered the orcs, pausing just long enough to swing once with their maces, and Seamus noticed a faint glow at the top of their breastplates. Corvus chanted a prayer to Vrysinoch and the steel of the four breastplates erupted with dazzling color. A pair of wolves circling the shield wall cowered at the light and shrank back with their tails between their legs. Seamus wasted no time bashing one wolf's skull to pulp as Corvus shot the other twice in rapid succession.

With another resounding, coordinated shout, the paladins surged onward and attacked again. Three growling orcs collapsed to the ground and were trampled by the steady march of eight steel boots.

Several orcs with long spears skirted the sides of the shield wall and forced the outer two paladins to turn their facing. Simultaneously jabbing high and low, an orc managed to slip under the shield wall with the tip of his spear and put a ragged puncture in the polished greave of the veteran paladin.

The man shrieked and wavered, dropping his mace to clutch at his leg, but the shield wall held. Bands of white light shot out from the wounded paladin's shield and latched onto the adjacent shields with the sound of a heavy door slamming into its frame. The old veteran hobbled backward and slipped his arm free of his shield as the other paladins relentlessly pressed onward. A thick stream of blood oozed from the hole in his leg.

Corvus and Seamus stepped around the wounded man in a protective posture and braced themselves for the rest of the wolves coming around the shield wall. Half a dozen orcs, deterred by the impregnable steel wall trampling over their fallen compatriots, followed closely on the heels of their pets.

Seamus heard the twang of a bowstring as he swung his mace down hard on the back of a lunging wolf. The arrow raced over the farmer's shoulder and grazed the cheek of a wolf before striking an orc in the forearm.

Scrambling out of the path of snapping jaws, Seamus brought the mace in sharply with a backhand that drew blood from the wolf's mouth. A spear point came in at the farmer from the side, but the orc, recently shot with an arrow, couldn't put enough strength into the blow to skewer the big man. Seamus lunged, thrashing wildly with his mace, and bashed the stunned wolf hard enough to break its neck. The orc thrust again with his spear and caught Seamus in the belly, inches below his ribcage.

The orc flashed a wicked grin and twisted the spear. An arrow shot past Seamus' arm but the orc was too close and the missile went wide. With a brilliant flash of light, Corvus beckoned to his misfired arrow and motioned with an outstretched hand for the flying shaft to return. A sizzling crack split the air and the arrow obeyed.

Seamus smashed his mace down on the wooden haft of the spear just as the redirected arrow split the orc's green head open in a shower of sticky blood.

The shield wall, perfectly intact with the wounded veteran's shield held in place by holy magic, hacked down and trampled the last orcs stupid enough to continue attacking them. Turning as one, the three interlocked paladins rushed into place and divided the remaining orcs from their snarling pets.

Three wolves, howling and dripping foam from their mighty jaws, charged at Seamus and Corvus with a flurry of raking claws and teeth too chaotic to follow. The big farmer was able to parry the first bite with his mace, but quickly found himself outmatched in both speed and power.

The wolves pounced and clawed their way on top of Seamus' chest. Their teeth bit into his skin fiercely and all that he could do was scream. Huge teeth clamped down on Seamus' forearm as he wailed and thrashed. Wolves bit at his legs and blood leaked freely from the torn wound in his gut. Seamus could sense his end rapidly approaching as each scream was weaker than the last.

At that moment, it seemed apparent Vrysinoch had a different plan for bringing about the death of Seamus the farmer.

The shield wall drove forward into the scattering orcs like a heavily loaded wagon charging down a steep hill. The last of the orc band threw their weapons at the shield wall in exasperation and fled.

Corvus, down to his last two arrows, carefully fired a shot into the fray of wolves clawing through Seamus' torso. The arrow blasted into the side of a wolf and laid it low. Two other wolves clawed and raked away at their prey. Corvus clutched his final arrow and lunged head first between the two animals. With a deafening shockwave that split the ground hundreds of feet in every direction, Corvus' holy symbol flared to life. A brilliant orb of white light grew from the paladin's back and engulfed the four creatures for a moment before exploding.

The ground shook and the sky thundered with rage. Corvus stabbed out with his arrow but, the explosion of light had blinded him. Bursts of forked lightning stretched out from the sky and blasted into the ground all around them. The other paladins shrieked and panicked, but their cries were lost in the resounding storm.

A minute passed with the tempest striking and whirling violently. Corvus tried to steady the flow of magic from his mind, but couldn't find the strength to take hold of such a torrent. The paladin thought he heard Seamus' voice crying out to him, but Corvus' mind was not where it should have been. Nothing but stinging white light filled Corvus' vision and the crash of a hundred lightning strikes blasted his ears.

A hand reached out to him through the maelstrom. Incorporeal fingers brushed against Corvus' consciousness and beckoned to him. It was one of the other paladins, of that Corvus had no doubt. His mind was thrown about wildly on the untamed currents of magic that fed the storm. Somehow, the hand that clutched at Corvus' being was steady. Without sight, the floating paladin knew he had to grasp any anchor he could.

The hand jerked and pulled at Corvus' mind, growing in power with each tug, and the lost paladin gave himself over to the other man's magical presence.

In the space of a heartbeat, the holy storm subsided. Corvus scrambled to his feet and stumbled back to the ground in his blindness.

"Calm down, man," one of the paladins called out behind him. Corvus spun and reached out to steady himself, but tripped on the broken ground and fell to his back.

"I'm blind," was all that Corvus choked out before a wave of dizziness overcame him.

"No," whispered the veteran paladin from somewhere far to Corvus' left. The sky gave a low rumble and the blind paladin had to fight to keep the holy magic from erupting again. With a steady, smooth voice, the veteran whispered, "Corvus, you have ascended."

J URNORGEL, THE PROUD leader of the Wolf Jaw Clan, paced nervously about his small, frost covered ridge. The strange half-orc shaman stood calmly off to the side, content to watch the meeting rather than to partake in it.

Ragged banners flapped noisily in the crisp breeze as the Half Goat leadership ascended the rise. Scores of enslaved orcs struggled and growled as they bore the weight of Snarlsnout the Gluttonous' stone dais slowly up the ridge. Gurr, with a banner in each hand, marched eagerly in front of the Half Goat procession.

An orcish parley was an odd thing to witness. Without any white flags, the only way to tell that two orc clans intended to meet peacefully was the absence of war cries. Even so, most diplomatic meetings between Half Goats and Wolf Jaws ended abruptly in an outburst of violence. The shaman rubbed his hand along the polished wood of his staff and kept a burst of powerful magic in the palm of his hand.

"Snarlsnout," Jurnorgel called to the approaching chieftain. "Why'd ye' attack?" the big orc questioned.

The Half Goat chieftain cleared his immense throat and the chained slaves stopped, keeping a respectful distance between the two leaders. Gurr kept on walking, oblivious to the halted procession, and soon found himself awkwardly occupying the wrong side of the parley.

"Jurnorgel," Snarlsnout rasped through rotted gums. "It has been too long since our clans have met on the battlefield!"

Jurnorgel shook his head and let his stringy hair fall over his eyes. His fists balled at his sides. "That is not our purpose!" he bellowed with a voice full of rage. Jurnorgel pointed a meaty finger to the south. "The human city awaits us! Glory! Plunder! Women!" The chieftain tried to control his aggression but the thought of pillaging a human stronghold was beyond his wildest dreams. "Orcs will know victory!" he shouted at the top of his lungs, spraying Gurr with several volleys of spit.

"I have heard the same promises, young one," Snarlsnout rebuked with a harsh bout of laughter. "Half Goat orcs need to keep their steel sharp! Long marches dull the senses." Snarlsnout's beady eyes drifted to the half-orc standing off behind the parley and the chieftain thought for a moment he recognized the strange creature.

The coupling of an orc with a human wasn't entirely uncommon, but the unfortunate human almost never survived the ordeal. Offspring of such mating was unusual and most half-orc children were killed by their stronger, full-blooded counterparts. Snarlsnout had met few such oddities in his lengthy stint as chieftain, and this particular half-orc was as odd as any.

"Use a whetstone," Jurnorgel retorted sarcastically. Visions of Talonrend's walls crumbling to dust beneath his feet filled his head. "We must focus on the greater prize!" he yelled with glazed eyes.

Gurr shuffled slowly back to Snarlsnout's stone dais and grunted. His bloody sword was strapped firmly to his back and the dim-witted orc wanted nothing more than to draw it and charge. Snarlsnout could see the bubbling aggression behind Gurr's eyes and knew he had to conclude the meeting before a brawl broke out.

"You have my word, Jurnorgel," the fat chieftain stated. "We will march behind your clan, where you can see us, and will not attack." Gurr's eyes went wide and his jaw drooped stupidly to one side.

"Chief," Gurr started, but was cut off by a low bark from Snarlsnout. The old chieftain wished he had the strength to get out of his chair and throttle the unruly orc, but he could barely lift his gouty fingers enough to point.

"Half Goats cannot be trusted!" Jurnorgel shouted in defiance.

The half-orc shaman closed his eyes and shook his head. Slowly, as though he was too disinterested to find the right words, the eloquent creature strode into the clearing between the clans. "Why not march side by side?" he wondered aloud as he met Gurr's ferocious gaze.

"The valley is certainly large enough to accommodate both clans," he pointed out with a wave of his hands. His speech, so oddly misplaced among the brutish warriors, had effect.

"Then we can see the Half Goat treachery before it is too late." Jurnorgel concluded with a toothy smile.

Snarlsnout studied the shaman's face for a long moment before speaking, trying to register where it fell in his memory. Unable to attach a name to the half-blooded visage, he belched and agreed to the proposal. "It is a good plan. Marching side by side, I don't have to worry about a Wolf Jaw knife slipping into my back." He nodded, sending a splash of ripples along his numerous chins.

Jurnorgel spat on the ground but nodded his consent as well. The half-orc bowed to both parties with a completely un-orc-like flourish and casually walked down the ridge.

"That's it?" Gurr asked more to the back of the shaman than anyone remaining at the parley.

"That's it," Snarlsnout stated with solemnity. With a chorus of grunts and deep breaths, the slaves hoisted the stone dais upon their shoulders and trudged back to the Half Goat lines with Gurr confusedly shambling along behind them.

The orc column, a great, stumbling mass of poorly organized brutes, made steady progress out of the snowy valley. Fights and murders occurred regularly between the two rival clans, but somehow, all-out battle was avoided.

"The patrol should've been 'ere by now," Jurnorgel muttered across a fire at the Wolf Jaw shaman. "Maybe they ran into trouble."

The strange half-orc pondered for a moment and lazily pushed a burning stick farther into the flames. "Perhaps the group is merely lost, chieftain," the shaman replied with a smile. "They took several wolves with them, so I doubt that any stray beast or human could have killed them."

Jurnorgel ripped a stringy bit of meat from a stick and gulped it down. He used the burnt skewer to motion all around him at the other gathered orcs. "There are hundreds of us! Thousands, now that the Half Goats are alongside," he said with a belch. "Impossible. Somethin' felled 'em, of that I'm sure."

An uneasy silence filled the air between the shaman and the Wolf Jaw chieftain. It could not be denied, the raucous gathering of green-skinned warriors was loud enough to be heard for miles. "You may be right," the half-orc admitted. "Perhaps I should go and investigate?"

The chieftain spat a bit of gristle from his mouth and tossed the empty skewer into the fire. "Take a wolf and be quick about it. Things don't feel right."

The shaman stood with a nod and snatched up his wooden staff from a nearby tree. "I shall return at once," he stated with a bow. "Try not to get killed."

"DID YOU FEEL that?" Gideon awoke with a start. The sun had just broken around the sides of Kanebullar Mountain in the east. It would be several hours or more until the sun crept high enough to extinguish the mountain's shadow.

Asterion rolled to his side and rubbed the sleep from his eyes. "What is it?" the priest asked without much concern.

"Get the goblins," Gideon commanded with a tone that set Asterion into quick motion. "I felt something. A..." he couldn't quite find the words to describe it, "disturbance, like a flash of light pierced my mind while I slept, but I know beyond a doubt that it was real."

"Describe it," Asterion urged without a hint of weariness. The old priest moved closer to Gideon, ensuring he didn't miss a single word.

"It felt like something hit the edge of a web and my mind felt the vibrations at the other end..." Gideon tried his best to put into words what he had experienced, but it was a sensation completely alien to him.

"Can you lead us in the direction of the magical jolt?" Asterion asked excitedly when Gideon finished his description.

"With certainty," the paladin replied.

Gravlox and Vorst heard the men speaking and returned to the meager camp. The goblin pair, lacking the natural need for sleep, had been patrolling and scouting for hours.

"Did you feel it too?" Gideon called at Gravlox when he came into view. Vorst tapped out the message on Gravlox's hand as she scanned the campsite for enemies.

Gravlox shook his head.

"What happened?" Vorst asked once she was sure that the area was safe. "Are you hurt?"

Gideon sighed and put his hands on his hips. "I was hoping you would have felt it too," he said to Gravlox. "Some sort of magical shockwave woke me. For a moment, I thought we were under attack." Gideon pointed away from the shadow of Kanebullar Mountain. "It came from the west."

"What does it mean?" Vorst asked the humans.

Asterion grinned and seemed to drink in the air with a breath. "There are other paladins nearby!" he exclaimed. "One of them probably tried to call out for help. We must go to their rescue!" The old priest beamed and felt more alive than he had in decades.

"We move at once," Gideon stated with finality. "We must find these paladins and help them, if indeed they are in trouble."

Gravlox feared the idea of being near more than a handful of humans, but it was evident from the speed at which Gideon and Asterion collected their belongings that there was no room for debate. The group set off toward the west with Gideon leading the way and Asterion chatting noisily at his side.

"Could it have been Lady Scrapple?" Gravlox wondered as they trekked through the foothills. "Was it an attack?"

Vorst grimaced and squeezed Gravlox's hand tighter. "I don't think Lady Scrapple can speak to humans," she responded with a hint of fear staining her melodic voice.

"What if it is a diversion? A message sent by Lady Scrapple or someone else to take us away from the north?" Images of the chamber beneath the Tower of Wings flitted through Vorst's mind. All of the threats to Talonrend had come from the north, not the west.

"I'm not sure," she said after a moment of hesitation. "It could be misdirection, but I think Asterion knows more than he let on. He wouldn't have agreed to change course so quickly if he thought it could be the wrong decision."

Her words did little to comfort the nervous goblin. "Have you felt her in your mind again?" Gravlox dared to ask.

"Not since the battle," Vorst snapped. Now that she had tasted a few weeks of true freedom, the thought of being so viciously controlled made her sick to her stomach.

"Sometimes..." Gravlox stumbled around the words, regretting that he had broached the subject at all. "I worry about you," he whispered.

Vorst's glare pierced through him like an arrow.

Gravlox wanted to apologize for questioning her, but thought it prudent to keep his mouth shut. The four companions hiked through the frosted foothills until a few hours past dusk, using magical light created by Asterion to guide them.

THE ASCENDED PALADIN sat on a large rock at the edge of a campfire. His eyes, devoid of traditional sight, picked up flares of white energy that marked the exact locations of the other magic users around him.

The intensity of the light correlated with the depth of magic present within each of the paladins that Corvus could identify. The old veteran, sitting at his side with a hand on his shoulder, flared the brightest.

"I've only read about this," the gruff man said in true wonder. "I wish I could see what you see." There was a hint of mirth underneath the paladin's words that Corvus found insulting.

"I'd rather have my vision back," he replied dryly. "I rather enjoyed being able to go for a piss without tripping on everything." Corvus rubbed a fresh bruise on his leg and remembered a particularly heavy rock he had stumbled upon. Blindness took more than a few hours to grow accustomed to.

"Once you learn to control the magic within your soul, you will be the strongest paladin alive!" the veteran marveled. "The anointed one of Vrysinoch! Chosen by our god!"

Corvus didn't appreciate the manner he was being regarded. The young paladin had planned on a life of soldiering and doing good for the people, not living as a cripple. Even if he was 'ascended', whatever that might mean, Corvus hated being treated like an experiment or a freak show.

When the paladins had returned to the refugee train, the others couldn't help but spread the word of Corvus' predicament. Corvus hated the attention and resented his brothers for it.

Seamus was the only one who seemed unbothered by it all. With his typically gruff demeanor, the farmer thrust a hot bowl of soup into Corvus' hands and plopped down noisily beside him on the log. "What ye thinkin' about?" Seamus asked as he slurped his own soup.

"I'm trying very hard not explode," Corvus said with no hint of humor or sarcasm. "The river of magic within me is beyond my control."

Seamus didn't understand the first thing about being a paladin, so he wisely held his tongue.

"If my concentration breaks for just a moment, I lose control." Corvus' hand clenched so tightly around his spoon that his knuckles turned white. "Watch," he said through gritted teeth.

The other paladins, nearly two score of them from throughout the refugee train, were gathered around a different fire barely a stone's throw away. They talked noisily, mostly about their ascended brethren, and stole curious glances at him every chance they got.

To Corvus, the paladins were nothing more than varying gradients of lights against an inky background. He let some of his control over the flow of magic slip from his grasp and another nova of mental energy pulsed out.

The paladins jerked their heads in unison and gasped. "See?" Corvus smiled when he heard Seamus burst out in laughter. "My magic is uncontrollable. It's like my mind is trapped in the intricate weave the binds the paladins together. I can't make it back to the real world."

Seamus set his bowl down and rubbed his hands together against the cold. "Any chance you could make some heat?" he jested in a poor attempt to lighten the mood.

Corvus let out a long sigh. "I would probably set you on fire or melt the skin from your fingers." The magic was far stronger than anything Corvus had ever known. He had heard rumors of paladins ascending in the past, calling forth unimaginable bursts of holy magic during battles against insurmountable odds, but he had always brushed them off as legend.

"What's it feel like?" Seamus wondered. As a poor farmer, he had never encountered a true magic user before and the idea of someone snapping their fingers and setting him ablaze was terrifying.

"The magic?" Corvus replied with a rare grin. "Imagine a river flowing just beneath your consciousness. If you can send your mind deep enough into your being, you can find that river and approach it."

Corvus still remembered the first time he had found magic within himself, and counted it among his treasured memories. He had been young, younger than most who discovered magic, and it had changed his life forever. Corvus had been an apprentice to a blacksmith who worked at the fighting pits. His days were spent sharpening swords, mending armor, and cleaning blood off the training room's floor.

When the fighters left for the night, Corvus would take a lance and jab at the mannequins, pretending to be a mighty warrior fighting a battle to save the king. One night, a few of the fighters returned to the training room, drunk from the celebration of recent victories, and tried to make the young apprentice boy their next victim.

He had tried to defend himself with a lance, but the warriors outnumbered and outweighed him severely. Offering up a prayer to his winged god, Corvus found the river of magic within him. Beams of light shot forth from the lance and engulfed to boy in white flame. Within moments, the terrified Corvus had killed the drunken fighters and burned the training room to the ground. The paladins of the Tower found him the next day and recruited him.

"What's in the river?" Seamus asked, shattering Corvus' reminiscence.

"Anything you desire," the blind paladin replied with awe. "Once you learn how to find the river, you can pull that energy up to the surface and, with the help of Vrysinoch, mold it into a spell."

"I don't have any rivers," Seamus said with mock despair. "I's born a farmer and I'll die a farmer."

Or a refugee, shivering and starving in the middle of nowhere, Corvus thought. He turned his eyes in the direction of Seamus' voice, but saw no spark of light. There was no magic about the man like there was emanating from the other holy warriors.

"There were certain priests and paladins of the Tower that believed anyone could learn the art of magic," Corvus said to take his mind from grim reality. "If those people are to be believed, one must have a certain amount of faith in Vrysinoch before the path to the river is opened. But who can say for sure?" If truth be told, my faith was nearly non-existent when I discovered magic." Corvus shrugged.

He heard footsteps coming from behind him and turned to see a small flicker of white light approaching. The magical essences of the other paladins varied slightly in size and intensity, but somehow, Corvus knew beyond a doubt who the man was when he neared.

"We're moving out," the old veteran stated. Due to his lack of reference, Corvus couldn't quite tell if the man had a brighter mark upon his vision or was standing closer than he normally would. Corvus reached out his hand awkwardly and brushed against the veteran's tunic.

The man ignored the blind paladin's groping and informed him of the plan. "We have thirty-five paladins, most of whom still have all of their gear. I think there are a hundred or so militia among the refugees and a few hundred more strong enough to fight if they need to."

"I don't like where this is heading," Corvus wasn't sure if it was the prospect of marching without regular vision or the thought of abandoning the refugee column that made him shudder.

"We split the fighting men into groups and spread them along the line," the man continued in a gruff voice. "I say we travel back east and see what's following us. If there are more orcs out in the foothills, we will have to fight them eventually. I'd rather the battle take place away from the caravan than while we sleep. It would be best if the civilians aren't in our way when the fight is on."

Corvus couldn't argue with his logic. A great battle was coming; he could feel it in his bones. The poor refugees would be cut down like wheat to a scythe if the orcs hit the column. "What if we find an entire orc clan?" he asked, trying not to let fear manifest in his voice.

"We do the same thing we will do if we find only a single orc," the veteran grumbled. "We link our shields, offer our prayers to Vrysinoch, and march for the victory of Talonrend."

"You'd best get ready," Seamus whispered. Disappointment oozed from his words.

A sharp laugh escaped Corvus mouth. "Don't think for a minute you get to stay behind," he told the farmer. "If I'm risking my neck for you, you better be risking your neck for me."

For a moment, Seamus was glad that Corvus was blind. He didn't want the paladin to see the huge smile splayed across his face.

B EADS OF SWEAT dripped off his brow and stung his eyes. The bright white cloth of the sheets made him squint. In a word, Herod was miserable. The prince's spirit raged within him, full of vim and vigor, perhaps stronger than it had ever been before. Herod's festering wound laced the room with a thick stench of death.

"How do you feel, my prince?" Apollonius asked in hushed tones. The dutiful soldier wore a thin strip of cloth over his mouth and nose just like the two guards by the door. They said it was to prevent any new sicknesses from being introduced to the room, but Herod knew better. The stench of his princely rot was too awful to bear.

Herod gave the man a long stare before answering. "I feel only slightly better than I smell," he replied loudly enough for the guards to hear. "What news do you have for me today?" Confined by weakness to his deathbed, Herod had lost any shred of patience he once had for small talk.

The soldier grimaced behind his strip of cloth and a look of pity flashed in his eyes. "The goblins have escaped, sir. They have been gone for more than a day, but I was just informed moments ago."

Herod gave a weak wave of his hand and dismissed the news as though it was a fly buzzing about his food. "If I was truly serious about their capture, I would have had them killed."

That set Apollonius back on his heels. "What..." he stammered. "Then why did you imprison them at all?"

"Half of the city has deserted. Allowing a pair of goblins to walk among them would have surely made the others leave." Herod stifled a cough that brought a bit of blood to the back of his throat. "If I killed them, I would have lost Gideon, my greatest paladin. What was I to do?"

Apollonius mulled over the possibilities and agreed with a shrug. "You knew they would escape. It was the only way to keep both the Templars and Gideon happy."

"Now you understand why I've never had a stomach for politics," Herod mused. A chortle brought a fresh wave of pain up from his chest that stole the air from his lungs. "I assume that Gideon and the goblins could not be found within the city?"

Apollonius nodded and grinned. "And thus you have released them without releasing them."

"Perhaps my brother was right for abandoning his throne. Decisions like that will drive a man insane." *Or to the bottom of an expensive bottle*, Herod thought with suppressed laughter.

"Should I send a search party?" Apollonius asked.

The prince tried to prop himself up on his elbows but the pain in his side threatened to smother his consciousness. "We need to spare everyone we can. Have any goblins been spotted?"

Apollonius leafed through a set of loosely bound parchments and quietly added up rows of numbers. "Goblins have been seen beyond the walls, your highness. Almost two dozen instances now. Some of those reports are bound to be illusions created by paranoia, but we must not ignore them all. Terror's Lament sustained significant damage during the attack and repairs are moving slowly. Should they come again, we will have to defend the inner walls."

"Good, good," Herod muttered. His eyes fluttered shut for a

moment as he spoke. "What do the goblins do out there?" he asked with mild disinterest.

"Most of the reports say they are scavenging the field or wandering around aimlessly." Apollonius organized his parchments and slid them back into the leather pouch at his side.

"Have you seen them yourself, Apollonius?"

"Not since the battle," the soldier replied.

"Then don't take it seriously," Herod coughed. Flecks of blood flew from his mouth and splattered on the fresh sheets. "Fearful men see only what they fear." Images of Vrysinoch flitted through the prince's mind. *You will never be king,* Herod recited to himself. He knew those words were true.

WHEN THEY FINALLY stopped to make camp, Gravlox's weary feet were covered in a myriad of blisters. Their camp was set at the center of a triangle of tumbled boulders that offered protection from the wind. Vorst plopped down on top of one of the rocks and rooted through Gravlox's pack for the magical circlet.

She felt the cold metal slide between her fingers and wondered what it would feel like to put it on. The three males of the group busied themselves with bedrolls and food preparation so Vorst let the small ring of metal fall gently between her ears.

Vorst expected a rush of magic to fill her mind and let her summon dazzling bolts of lightning with a snap of her fingers. At the very least, she had expected to feel different. The cool metal lacked even the decency to feel uncomfortable on her head, but rather fit so well she knew it wouldn't take long for her to get used to wearing it.

With a disappointed sigh, she tucked the magical circlet back inside Gravlox's pack and slid down the side of the rock to be with the others.

"Are you sure you can keep the watch again tonight?" Asterion asked inquisitively. "We can assign shifts." The old priest spread his bedroll out close to one of the boulders.

"We get tired," Vorst explained, "but we don't sleep. Gravlox and I will take the watch. He needs time to practice with his circlet."

When the moon was high above them, Vorst led Gravlox a few hundred feet away from their camp and handed the enchanted metal band to him with a touch of reverence. "Try it on again," she bade him.

Gravlox ran his fingers along the smooth steel and tested the integrity of the metal. To his touch, it felt like a simple band, entirely mundane, but once he let it fall down around his ears, Gravlox could feel the power it contained. His magical consciousness dove deep within his mind and found the wellspring of energy.

Latching firmly onto the source of magic, Gravlox asked, "What should I do?" Being able to freely speak his native tongue brought a smile to the shaman's face. The human language was confusing and Gravlox still didn't understand how Vorst spoke it with such ease.

"Remember when we stumbled into that clearing..." Vorst saw that he remembered and backed away as he began focusing.

Gravlox closed his eyes and brought forth an image of soldiers aiming their crossbows. He remembered the sounds the crossbows had made as their bolts fired. Gravlox's hands dug into the dirt and he felt a surge of power rising up as if the land itself offered him its spirit.

A great spike of viscous rock rose up under his palms and balled around his fists, ever-shifting gauntlets of sizzling magma. Gravlox spun to his right and slammed into tree trunk. Bark flew and bits of smoking wood exploded as his fists hammered away.

Vorst grabbed a fallen tree branch as long as she was tall and charged, using it as a spear. Gravlox saw her from the corner of his eye and rolled to his left, bringing up his hands in front of his face to block.

Vorst pivoted and planted the stick behind Gravlox as he came out of his roll. Using her momentum, the small goblin swung around the stick and landed both of her feet solidly on the side of Gravlox's face. The shaman grunted and planted a fiery hand on the ground to keep from falling.

Dried leaves and twigs caught ablaze immediately and started to fill the small area with thin wisps of smoke.

Somewhere nearby, Vorst heard a crash as a flying boulder smashed down through the tops of a dozen or more pine trees. "Gravlox!" Vorst screamed, thinking that the shaman had somehow started using his magic to hurl boulders.

Gravlox, fully immersed in the magical realm, couldn't hear her shout over the sizzle of the growing fire. The thunder of hooves finally brought Gravlox from his reverie. Three minotaurs, each more than triple the height of a goblin, bellowed their way into the clearing.

The minotaurs were clad in full battle gear with heavy sheets of plate mail that glimmered in the light of the fire. Their horns were sharpened and banded with steel and their heavy metal greaves adorned their legs and feet. Each minotaur held a single-bladed axe so large that they would have made Nevidal look like a child's toy.

Vorst shrieked and scrambled out of the way, narrowly dodging the thunderous hooves. Instinctively, she reached for the hilt of her short sword, but she realized she was unarmed. The three minotaurs focused their rage on Gravlox and bore down on him through the fledgling flames.

One of the minotaurs shouldered into a burning pine tree and barely seemed to notice. The tree groaned and splintered, scratching the minotaur's armor. It did nothing to stop the beast as it was ripped free from the ground and tossed aside. Gravlox saw them coming and knew he had nowhere to run. He slammed his fists together in front of him and loosed a high-pitched war cry, sending forth a volatile gout of flame.

Fire licked and curled around the armored minotaurs. Gravlox knew the flame wouldn't do much to slow the charge, but the smokescreen it created was blinding. He ducked and ran as fast as his short legs could carry him, trying with desperation to get to Vorst at the edge of the clearing.

The minotaurs crashed through the smoke and fire and swung their axes down hard, destroying everything in their path. Luckily, Gravlox had moved far enough away to not be caught in the assault.

The shaman's eyes darted around, but he saw no opening. The three minotaurs fanned out before him and used their bulk to fill the space between the boulders that blocked Gravlox's escape. Vorst cowered just behind one of the beasts, only a few feet away, but unable to help. Even if she had a sword, the minotaurs were so heavily armored it would have taken days for Vorst's attacks to have any effect.

One of the minotaurs ducked and slid to the side, offering a momentary gap in the line. Gravlox tensed and got ready to lunge for the opening. Right as he was about to leap, a boulder twice the size of the shaman's body flew through the gap and slammed into the rock behind Gravlox's head.

Shards of broken stone exploded all around the tight space. Boulder fragments dinged and ricocheted off the minotaur's armor and bits of stone found their way into Gravlox's exposed back. He leapt forward and punched out with a molten fist, connecting solidly with the center minotaur's steel greave. The minotaur kicked and swung its heavy axe down, narrowly missing Gravlox's head.

Another axe head flew in from the side and Gravlox was forced to fall to his stomach to avoid being killed. The center minotaur didn't hesitate and stomped his armored hoof down hard on Gravlox's back. Thinking quickly, Gravlox willed his molten fists into a solid stone shield that wrapped around his body and dissipated the force of the stomp.

The minotaurs snarled and the growing flames crackled, but Gravlox could hear Vorst's high-pitched yell above it all. She had jumped from one of the smoldering pine trees and landed on the minotaur attempting to crush Gravlox. Her small fists beat furiously into the minotaur's head and for a moment, the minotaur backed away.

Vorst took a vicious hit to her side that made her gasp for breath. She clutched at the beast's horns, but they had been sharpened for battle and cut deeply into Vorst's skin.

Gravlox rolled to his side and beckoned to the ground, molding it and shaping it with his mind. He ripped his hands free of the soil and summoned forth a great spike of stone that blasted the minotaur's lower body.

Vorst stumbled from her perch and hit the ground hard next to Gravlox. She coughed and looked into his eyes, searching for some hint of an answer. Gravlox steeled his gaze and dove deeper into the realm of magic and found a place of serenity within himself.

Using the circlet to amplify his shamanistic abilities, Gravlox whispered a prayer of sorts to the earth. The ground rumbled and shook violently. The wounded minotaur fell to his knees and the other two had to use their long axes to keep their balance.

"Run!" Gravlox shouted as he pulled Vorst to her feet. The two goblins took off through the burning trees with as much speed as they could muster. The ground rumbled again and split under their feet with a tremendous crack that shot lava high into the air. Minotaur bellows pierced the night and Gravlox could hear another boulder smash down into the trees behind him.

The earthquake hit a crescendo and Gravlox could feel his connection the ground waning. His body was being drained and Gravlox couldn't help but slow his frantic pace.

"We have to get back to the others!" Vorst yelled as she panted for breath. She tugged at Gravlox's arm but he was too exhausted to continue. With a final breath of release, Gravlox severed his mental connection to the bedrock and the earthquake subsided immediately. "They won't be far behind," Vorst reminded him. She hoped that the minotaurs had succumbed to the fire and the smoke, but knew that counting on luck would be suicide. Propping Gravlox up against her shoulder, Vorst carried him the rest of the way back to their camp.

"Gideon!" Vorst called out when they arrived at the small circle of boulders. "Asterion?" she shouted out again with a touch of panic. The battle and the earthquake were loud enough that the two sleeping humans should have awakened minutes ago.

"Gravlox!" Vorst screamed as she sat him down against a rock. "They're gone. What do we do?" Gravlox cleared the sweat from his brow and tried to rub the weariness from his eyes.

The camp was dark and the moon hid behind a layer of smoke and clouds, but Gravlox had spent almost all of his life in the underground tunnels of Kanebullar Mountain. He had gone days without seeing the light of a fire and his eyes were well accustomed to the inky blackness of night. He glanced over his shoulder and looked for signs that the two men had gone toward the sounds of battle. That's when he noticed the blood.

The rock behind Vorst was so evenly coated with blood that Gravlox hadn't realized it at first. He ran his hand along the rock and the blood was warm and slick under his fingers. There was no way for him to tell who the blood belonged to, but he was sure that it was fresh.

"Vorst, look," he whispered as he showed her the red stain on his pale fingers. They searched through the camp and it became obvious there had been a fight. A few yards behind the camp, in the direction of the mountains, Gravlox found two of Gideon's throwing axes. One of them was soaked in fresh blood but the other was buried halfway in the dirt.

"They fought back," Vorst said quietly. She kept looking back toward the fire and wondering if the minotaurs would come charging at them once more. She shuddered as she considered how big the boulder throwing minotaur must have been.

"This blood might not be theirs," Gravlox stated defiantly, "but we need to keep moving."

Vorst gathered what she could of the traveling gear and slid one of the throwing axes through her belt. "Where will we go?"

"We need to search deeper into the mountains. If the minotaurs captured him, we have to get him back."

Vorst shook her head and gulped down her fear. At least now she had a weapon.

S EAMUS, GUIDING CORVUS by the shoulder, led the paladin's expeditionary force. They marched in a line, three abreast, and sang hymns to Vrysinoch that set their pace. They weren't exactly sure where they were headed, but the foothills of the mountains were where the orcs made their homes.

A pair of young paladins flanked the group and scouted. Corvus wanted badly to join them, but even after a day of marching, he had not grown accustomed to his blindness. Seamus had fashioned him a sturdy walking stick and the ascended paladin clung to it like a drowning man who had found a floating log. One of the more scholastically minded paladins, a skilled blacksmith who had joined the Tower much later in life than the rest, had carved a powerful enchantment into the staff that allowed Corvus to summon the thing with a word.

The stiff wind carried hints of snow that melted on their metal breastplates and fogged their breath. Corvus wore a heavy woolen hood pulled low over his nose to keep the chill from his face.

The other paladins, if they spoke to Corvus at all, did so with hushed voices as though they were speaking to Vrysinoch himself. Corvus hated it. He resented their reverence and wished for the return of his eyesight. He could sense all of their movements, even the paths of the paladins walking behind him, but what good would that do against a horde of orc berserkers?

"How many orcs be in a clan?" Seamus asked.

Far more than our pitiful number, Corvus thought. "The way they breed, there could be hundreds," he decided not to soften his answer.

"We've not seen them before now, so there is no way to know for sure," the old veteran chimed in from the row behind Seamus. "We study books written about the orcs and other races, but until the goblins sieged the city, most of us had never seen anything but the occasional minotaur in the fighting pit."

"Then who wrote ye books?" the farmer wondered. "Someone must've seen himself a right number o' beasts."

The veteran let out a long sigh. He had questioned the accuracy of the Tower's teachings for years. "Most of the books came from the Green City, brought by the first settlers of Talonrend, if the histories are to be believed." Even as he spoke, he wasn't sure he believed those histories. "The old texts speak of orc settlements built like strongholds in the mountains, constantly warring against each other or anything else that stepped onto their land. The original settlers drove them out of the foothills and forced them to live deeper in the wilds of the mountains."

"Maybe they're now just fightin' among themselves?" Seamus theorized. He didn't like the idea of such powerful warriors organizing and building strongholds.

"We pray that is the case," Corvus asserted, "but we must assume the orcs are preparing an assault." He shot a hand out and pointed northeast. "There!" he shouted, urging Seamus forward but nearly losing his balance. "Do you see it?"

"What is it?" the veteran asked, straining to see. The rolling hills and fogging autumn air made it hard to distinguish scraggly pine trees from approaching orcs.

Corvus took a moment to let the shapes materialize in his mind, watching the white splotches grow and form. "The scouts are returning," he said once he was sure. Two paladin heads bobbed up over a low rise a few hundred yards away and it was apparent that they were running.

The marching paladins broke into a sprint to meet the approaching scouts. "We've seen them!" one of the scouts shouted. Seamus led Corvus by the hand over the rocky terrain as quickly as the blind paladin could manage.

"Orcs?" the big farmer asked after the scouts had caught their breath. "How many?"

"Not a clan," one of the scouts, a young paladin with brightly polished armor, replied. "Just a half-orc."

"How many half-orcs? A raiding party?" Corvus asked eagerly. He had never seen a half-orc but had read descriptions of them from the books at the Tower. Half-orcs were said to be more human in appearance and mannerism than their full-blooded orc relatives, but with the primal savagery that made them deadly and unpredictable. Living in familial clans as hunters and nomads, most orcs lacked the intellect and cunning required for successful leadership. Thus, orc clans almost never rose to a level at which they could compete with human civilization. A half-orc, possessed of both a sharp mind and an orcish body, was the perfect combination of cunning and brawn.

The young scout shook his head. "There was only one. We followed him and watched him from a distance, but never saw any others."

Turning to Seamus, the old veteran furled his brow and rubbed his chin. "You're sure the orc you killed with the wolves was a full blood?" he asked, trying to recall exactly what the orcs he had helped to slay looked like.

"His skin was green an' he was huge," Seamus retorted. "What's so special 'bout a half-orc anyway?"

Corvus cleared his throat. "Most orc clans are led by a shaman, a spiritual leader similar to our priests. While shaman do not offer prayers to a god in exchange for magical prowess, they can instead call upon the magical energies trapped within the ground to bring about destruction. Half-orcs, with partially human heritage, are often powerful shaman that possess the sharpness of mind needed to hone their magical abilities."

The scout nodded in agreement and continued with his report. "We never saw him cast, but the only thing he carried was a wooden staff. Not even a half-orc would be stupid enough to wander the foothills unarmed."

"He must be a shaman," Corvus concluded with finality. "How far away is he?"

The scout looked back the way he had come and tried to gauge the distance. "Maybe a few miles," he said. "Not much more."

Seamus noted the nervous tone of the scout's voice and caught a glint of fear in his eyes. Years of gambling in seedy taverns had made the gruff man an incredible interpreter of body language. He could tell that there was something more.

"Get on with it, lad," Seamus bade him, slapping the paladin on the shoulder for good measure.

"We saw some tracks near the half-orc's camp." The two scouts glanced nervously at each other. "It's probably nothing, but the tracks looked like hoof prints. Deep hoof prints."

"Impossible..." the old veteran murmured under his breath.

"What's impossible 'bout a deer?" Seamus blurted out with confusion.

"I reckon those prints were from something walking upright, son," the paladin chided. "The half-orc might have brought some friends from the caves." He looked around the gathering of paladins and could see the fear in their eyes as easily as he could feel it forming in tight knots in his stomach. "Have any of you boys ever seen a minotaur?"

"HOW WILL WE know where to look?" her voice was high and thin with no attempts to conceal her trepidation.

Snowflakes fell silently between them, muffling the world with a white haze. Gravlox studied the ground and looked for any sign of tracks that might reveal a path. After several agonizing minutes of searching, he found a tall pine that had recently been cut. A long, deep gash oozed sap onto the frosted ground.

"If it was Gideon's sword that left this mark, we will find a dead minotaur nearby," Gravlox reassured her. The cold night air was starting to have a serious effect on the goblins. While they tolerated the elements better than humans, Lady Scrapple had not made their bodies warm enough to endure the frost unclothed.

Gravlox found a dead branch underneath one of the pines and focused what remained of his magical energy. With the aid of Gideon's enchanted circlet, he drew forth heat from the earth and captured it within the branch. Using the paladin's throwing axe, Gravlox broke the branch in two and handed one segment to Vorst.

"Just keep touching the wood," he explained. "It should keep you warm." The enchanted walking sticks gave off subtle waves of heat that melted the snowflakes before they reached Vorst's pale shoulders.

"Thank you," she whispered and kissed him softly on the cheek. "Let's keep searching."

It didn't take much longer for Gravlox to find a blood trail leading west. The two goblins followed the line of fresh blood over two small hills and finally to a thin stream that snaked out from the snow-capped mountains. On the other side of the stream, a dead minotaur was propped up against a tree.

The beast was wearing a full set of steel armor that bore a wicked puncture wound in the breastplate. Vorst gave the corpse a kick to confirm that it was indeed dead before helping Gravlox search the area.

"More hoof prints," Gravlox said, pointing to a fresh set of tracks.

Vorst studied the tracks and found a clump of droppings nearby that confirmed her suspicions. "They had horses," she concluded. "We're already slower than them on foot, but now they must be long gone." Overwhelming sadness gripped her beautiful voice and pulled at Gravlox's heart.

Gravlox had seen many horses during the battle outside of Talonrend and the huge beasts terrified him. He knew she was right—there was no way two goblins on foot could ever catch an organized group of minotaurs on horseback.

Eleven

THE HALF-ORC, KEENLY aware of the paladin eyes watching him, twirled his staff and set out toward the northeast. A simple conjuration of mist a few hundred feet above the shaman allowed his vision to survey the area in a wide circle about him. With a bemused smile, the half-orc watched as the paladins scurried off to warn their companions.

A mile and a half from the small group of paladins, the shaman rendezvoused with a pair of minotaurs that eagerly awaited his arrival.

"Gorak!" one of them called out in guttural tones. "Our chieftain has captured two of the humans!"

The shaman sighed and rubbed his forehead with the palm of his hand. "How many times do I have to tell you?" he quipped harshly. "_Gorak_ is the orcish word for _wizard_, not my name. I grow weary of telling you such basic facts..." The half-orc let his voice trail off to hide his growing anger.

"Then what should we call you?" the other minotaur asked. While minotaurs were renowned for their prowess in battle and their innate ability to design and execute battlefield tactics, their lack of advanced language severely limited their communications with other races.

"Names are things given to subordinates by their superiors as a means of control," the shaman explained, "as I have no superior," the shaman spread his arms and exaggeratedly looked about the area, "I have no name."

The two minotaurs exchanged a confused look and the shaman knew his logic was lost. "Fine," he let out a great sigh of defeat, "call me *Undrakk*, your own word for tyrant." Undrakk grinned and mulled the name over in his mind the way a queen might savor the complexities of a fine wine. The orcish language and the runes of the minotaurs were undoubtedly related, and it was no coincidence that the word for wizard was similar to that which meant tyrant. Only a human could achieve the title of wizard, and only a human could be seen as a tyrant in the eyes of the mountain races.

"Now, what is this business about capturing a pair of humans?" he asked with mild curiosity.

"The chieftain sent us to tell you," the minotaur bellowed, "we found two of them setting up camp not far to the east. They were tired and one of them is old," he smiled and puffed his chest out with pride, "we captured them with ease."

"Take me to them at once!" Undrakk ordered sharply. He climbed atop his horse and the two minotaurs began to run ahead of him. While a horse would certainly outdistance a minotaur over the course of several hours, an athletic minotaur could run quickly enough on two legs to keep up with the pounding gallops of a horse.

NEVIDAL RESTED PEACEFULLY in its sheath, tied to the back of a horse. Blindfolded, Gideon felt the absence of his sword as painfully as though he was missing a limb. His weapon had become such a real part of his soul that Gideon could feel the coarse hair of the horse's tail as it flicked against the pommel.

Asterion groaned and spat with discomfort from the back of another horse. Their hands had been tied behind their backs, and nooses hung loosely from their necks, the other end of which was tied firmly around the waist of a minotaur. If they tried to jump, the speed of the horses would likely snap their necks. Gideon mumbled a short prayer to Vrysinoch, but heard nothing in return.

The group rode for nearly an hour, heading north into the snowy mountains. When they finally stopped, Gideon could hear a stream rushing by and felt a heavy blanket of snow settling over his shoulders. The cold was stifling and threatened to break his concentration. He couldn't understand what the minotaurs were saying, but a newcomer had joined them. He focused on the new creature's peculiar voice, lacking all of the gruff and guttural qualities of the minotaurs. Whatever new being it was, the voice bore an unmistakable air of command that reminded Gideon of a pompous human aristocrat.

After a few moments of discussion, Gideon and Asterion were picked up by the shoulders and carried into a cave where their blindfolds were removed. Pacing casually in front of them, a strange half-orc tossed his staff from hand to hand. "What are you doing in my mountains?" the half-orc demanded with perfect command of the human language.

Hearing the green-skinned creature speak his language so comfortably set Gideon back on his heels. "We..." the paladin stammered, "we were... looking for threats to Talonrend," Gideon finished with sadness in his heart.

The half-orc laughed and tossed Nevidal, still sheathed, from one hand to the other. "Where is your army, puny human? You may have slain one of my pets, no small feat I assure you, but that does not make you capable of killing us all!" The half-orc tossed his head back and loosed another wild cackle as the minotaurs tightened their grips on their weapons.

Gideon grimaced when the half-orc wrapped his thin fingers

around Nevidal's hilt. The paladin could feel those smooth fingers touching his weapon and the sensation made him sick.

"Oh?" the half-orc said inquisitively, taking a step closer. "A prized family heirloom, perhaps?" The half-orc could read Gideon's trepidation, but misunderstood its source. He jerked his hand back on the hilt, but the blade did not move.

"You cannot draw it!" Gideon growled through clenched teeth. Watching someone touch his sacred weapon was the vilest torture that Gideon could imagine.

The half-orc yanked harder on the hilt and brought Gideon to his knees with a wave of sickening nausea. Undrakk clutched Nevidal's hilt with both hands and swung the weapon in a wide arc, attempting to fling the sheath away. Much to the half-orc's dismay, the blade and sheath were like a single piece of uncut stone. With a growl of rage unfitting for a creature previously so calm and controlling, the half-orc threw the sword with all of his might against the cavern wall. Nevidal clanged against the rock and fell to the ground not far from Gideon's feet.

"What sorcery is this?" the half-orc screamed, overcome by frustration and anger. "Where did you get that blade? Where did you steal it?" Undrakk charged in at Gideon and threatened to strike him, but the stoic paladin stood his ground.

Gideon's stomach settled and he felt a wave of familiarity ease his mind. Nevidal was so close he could taste the divine magic seeping from the weapon, begging to be used. "That is my sword," Gideon explained flatly. "Only I can draw my sword." He closed his eyes as he spoke and envisioned Nevidal burning in his hands, cutting the half-orc to ribbons. The fully armored minotaurs standing around the edges of the cave could sense Gideon's calm. They licked their lips and took a slow step backward, preparing to charge into battle.

Undrakk had every confidence that if a fight broke out, he could obliterate the two captives as well as the minotaurs in the cave, but something about the human's posture and sense of calm made him hold back. Dismissing the bound prisoners with a wave of his hand, Undrakk spun on his heel and marched out of the cavern. For a moment, he thought about taking the magical sword with him as he exited, but he wanted nothing more to do with that bizarre artifact. "Kill them," the half-orc remarked casually over his shoulder in the rough minotaur language.

"WE COULD TRACK them," Vorst wondered aloud as she paced the frosted ground. "If they stop to camp or return to where they live, we would eventually catch up to them," she muttered. Her eyes followed the deep tracks in the dirt. The horse prints were smaller and more rounded compared to the deep impressions left by the minotaurs.

Vorst stood in front of the dead minotaur and stared into its lifeless eyes. Slumped against the tree as it was, the beast's torso and head rose several inches above Vorst's standing height. The minotaur's armor was made from thick plates of dull steel connected by leather straps at the joints. The helmet, painted with red streaks in the pattern of lightning, had a vertical slit bisecting it that ended in clasps at the top and bottom. Vorst flicked apart the clasps and the helmet split in two, falling to the ground on either side of the corpse.

Vorst expected to see a feral snarl frozen on the dead creature's hairy face, but instead the minotaur appeared calm in death. Its eyes stared ahead blankly and a thin layer of frost was building up on its bushy eyebrows. "I wonder if something controls them, too..." Vorst whispered as a shudder ran down her spine. She turned from the corpse and looked to Gravlox, but the shaman paid her no attention.

Gravlox felt the weight of the enchanted circlet resting firmly between his large ears. Each time he donned the magical relic, it fit more perfectly, as though it was adapting to Gravlox's body and becoming part of his magical self. *Gideon felt something out there*, the shaman remembered as he gazed toward the west.

Not wanting to break his concentration, Vorst sat down a few paces from the dead minotaur and rubbed her enchanted walking stick in her hands for warmth. During her years as an assassin in Kanebullar Mountain, she had studied human sources of magic as much as she could. What little knowledge the goblins had been able to compile regarding holy magic told her Gravlox's shamanistic abilities were entirely separated from Gideon's powers. What one of them could feel or sense, the other could not. Gravlox drew his strength from the elements of the earth and the air, the natural things that surrounded him. Gideon channeled his strength from an otherworldly being he worshiped as a god.

Gravlox focused his energy and sent his magical consciousness soaring out over the trees and foothills. He remembered what Gideon's magical presence had felt like, a towering beacon of burning rage that threatened to consume anything that wandered too close. That had been when Gideon had been under the effects of Nevidal, the strongest magical enchantment Gravlox had ever witnessed.

His mind searched and scoured the bleak emptiness of the foothills for miles around. Gravlox tried desperately to find some hint of the spark that had jolted Gideon from his sleep the day before. The shaman stretched his magical senses further than he ever had before, pushing his mind to the limit of his capabilities. Suddenly, like a candle lit in the utter darkness of a goblin mineshaft, Gravlox found something.

His mind reached and clawed, trying desperately to latch onto the magical energy he felt some ten miles away. The small fleck of golden light shimmered and danced, but did not waver. With one final burst of energy, Gravlox drove his magical senses directly into the light. His mind was forcefully and instantly repelled. So sudden was the severance of his body from his magical consciousness that it left Gravlox panting on his knees. Several errant wisps of steam rose

321

from the shaman's head and back as he struggled to fill his lungs with air.

"What did you see?" Vorst asked tentatively. Doubt filled her voice. Everything she knew about human and goblin magic told her that the two could not mix. Shamanistic magic was as different from a paladin's prayer as her body was from the minotaur corpse lying a few feet to her right.

"I think it was a paladin," Gravlox huffed breathlessly. "It reminded me of Gideon, the first time our minds met."

"What if it was another shaman?" Vorst asked as she climbed to her feet. "It could be an orc, a minotaur, or even another goblin," she stated.

"No," Gravlox stated with finality as he turned to regard her. "It was a paladin, just like Gideon." The shaman shook his weary head and cleared his mind. "We set out at once."

Twelve

"**W**HAT SHOULD WE do?" Asterion whispered. His hands were tied tightly behind his back with a thick rope his frail body could not hope to break. The four minotaurs left in the cave drew their weapons and began to approach.

Gideon called out with his mind to Nevidal, resting on the hard stone only an arm's length away. He could feel the blade, sense the magic stored within, but possessed no means to summon it to his hand. A gentle prayer to Vrysinoch broke through the paladin's lips and joined the words that Asterion was chanting a few feet away.

"Do something!" Gideon shouted when one of the minotaurs took a lazy swing at his chest with a spiked mace. He easily sidestepped the attack, but had nowhere to run. If his attackers had been human, he would have considered ramming one of them with his head and sprinting out of the cave. To head butt a minotaur would be suicide, and Gideon knew even with his hands free he would have a hard time wrestling one of the huge beasts to the ground.

Asterion summoned all of his faith and beckoned to his winged god, attempting to conjure a sphere of fire before him, but his entreating call was in vain. No searing ray of magma shot up from the cave floor. No blinding orb of light descended from the heavens to explode with a violent crash of divine power. Asterion's prayers went unanswered.

"Perhaps…" The old man said as he narrowly dodged a half-hearted swing of an axe, "this is where we die." The minotaurs marched slowly toward the two humans, swinging their weapons out wide and herding the pair into a small corner of the cave. Only meager strands of light penetrated the falling snow outside the cave entrance and the hulking warriors blocked out most of it with their massive frames. Asterion let the growing darkness wash over him and made no attempt to block the next attack.

The priest let out a pained grunt as the steel axe head cut a gash across his right shoulder. The minotaurs toyed with them and laughed, poking and prodding with their weapons without inflicting any life-threatening injuries.

Gideon's rage boiled. He bore the sacred mark of Vrysinoch! The paladin cursed his god as he ducked under a slow moving mace. His back was against the wall and his right arm brushed up against Asterion's left.

One of the minotaurs took a step forward and swung his axe down fiercely, aiming for Asterion's wrinkled head. Gideon waited until the last possible moment before shoving the old priest to the ground and deflecting the blow with his armored sleeve. The axe hit the ground with a resounding clang and Gideon stomped his foot down hard on the haft. The weapon, designed for a creature several feet taller than a human and far more muscled, was constructed entirely of steel and almost five feet in length.

Gideon planted his foot down firmly on the back of the axe head and jerked forward, startling the minotaur and making him hesitate. A heavy spiked mace struck Gideon in the back and tore several lines of flesh from his body, but Gideon's concentration was too great.

He kicked off of the axe head with one foot and planted his

other foot firmly on the weapon's handle. Confused and off balance, the minotaur howled and ducked his head, attempting to gore open Gideon's chest. Without hesitation, Gideon vaulted over the lowered head of the beast and arched his back so that his bound hands caught the minotaur under his chin. The armored minotaur stumbled backward and tried to keep his footing with Gideon throwing all of his weight forward to choke the unfortunate creature. One of the other minotaurs turned from Asterion to swing at the paladin, but the attack was clumsy and rushed. The blade only drew a thin line of blood from Gideon's forearm.

Gideon flexed his muscled body and felt the minotaur flail against his back. Thinking only of self-preservation, the gasping minotaur drew a small dagger from his belt and cut the rope from his neck, freeing Gideon's hands.

In one deft maneuver, Gideon rolled to his left and plucked Nevidal from the cave floor. He came up on one knee and smiled as the four minotaurs backed away, one of them gasping for air. Nevidal rang against its sheath as Gideon drew his sword.

His muscles tightened in anticipation for the rush of raw energy that the blade usually released. Instead of relishing the overwhelming flood of Nevidal's magical enchantment, Gideon felt nothing. The blade, still razor sharp and deadly, released no magic.

The four minotaurs squared off against Gideon, setting their hooves and readying their huge weapons. Asterion crawled on his knees to avoid the fight and none of the combatants paid the old man much attention. Gideon cleared the doubts from his mind about his dormant weapon and feinted once to his left before spinning and slashing at the minotaur to his right. Nevidal slammed into the minotaur's long axe and Gideon twisted his hands, slicing the weapon down the smooth steel of the axe and severing the fingers from the minotaur's hands. The beast howled and fell back against the wall of the cavern. Gideon straightened and looked the beasts in their hollow eyes.

The other three minotaurs wasted no time and charged in

unison. One of them held a spiked mace nearly as long as Gideon was tall, and the others swung heavy axes over their heads. In the cramped and asymmetrical cavern, the height of the minotaurs was their greatest disadvantage. One of the beasts accidentally dropped its axe after its overhand chop got lodged in the stone above.

Gideon turned and twisted, deftly parrying an axe from his left and sidestepping the spiked mace. The minotaurs were brutally strong and imposing, but their primary battle tactic relied upon shock and awe, not the practiced techniques of a trained fighter. Nevidal sent a flurry of sparks into the air with every parry and it didn't take long for Gideon to hook the blade under the spiked head of the mace and disarm one of the minotaurs. Gideon swung his sword in a wide arc, aiming to cut the disarmed minotaur in half at the waist, but the beast's armor was too thick. In the moment it took Gideon to pull his sword back and ready another strike, an armored minotaur fist crashed into his jaw like a blacksmith hammering iron.

Gideon's vision blurred and he spat two of his teeth onto the minotaur in front of him as he fell. The beast lumbered on, pushing its companions out of the way, and tried to stomp Gideon's chest to pulp. The paladin rolled and scrambled to his feet with Nevidal ready to strike again.

The unarmed minotaur lowered its head and charged with a great howl. Gideon took a step back and easily batted the minotaur aside. The beast fought on instincts fueled by frustration and rage, which left it vulnerable and exposed. Gideon brought Nevidal down as the charging creature passed him and ripped a gash deep enough in the minotaur's armor to be fatal. The hairy monstrosity growled and crumpled to the floor where it twitched, dying.

The remaining minotaurs, one with blood flowing freely from its missing fingers, scampered past Gideon and out of the cave. The paladin slashed as they fled, cutting a thin line in one of the mino-taur's heavy legplates, but he did not pursue them.

"Thank the heavens!" Asterion rejoiced, still cowering against the cavern wall. The old man was cut in several places and his shoulder likely required stitches, but he wasn't in any mortal danger.

"Thank the heavens?" Gideon questioned with derision. "I did not see Vrysinoch swoop down to save you." Gideon plucked his sheath from the ground and strapped it over his shoulder, returning Nevidal to his back with a sigh. "You should be thanking me," he said as he helped the priest to his feet.

"Yes, I suppose," Asterion responded defensively.

"The enchantment on my sword doesn't work here," Gideon explained, "and I saw you praying. What aid did Vrysinoch send? Something isn't right."

Asterion grit his teeth and frowned. No matter how deeply he concentrated, he couldn't connect himself to the divine magic that usually rested just beyond his fingertips. "Perhaps..." Asterion wondered, "we have fallen into disfavor with Vrysinoch." Asterion hated to even consider that possibility. He had devoted his entire life to service in the name of his god. Priests of Vrysinoch typically developed a stronger connection to magic as they aged – they were never cut off.

A sharp laugh filled the small cavern. "I have lived my entire life in disfavor!" Gideon nearly yelled. He spread his arms out wide and filled his nostrils with the scent of freshly spilled blood. "How much more can Vrysinoch hate me?"

It was then that Gideon realized that the cave was not just a single chamber, but extended further into the foothills. A small opening, too narrow for a minotaur to crawl through, was poorly hidden behind a clump of sticks and leaves. Gideon brushed the debris aside and peered into the darkness. The tunnel turned only a few feet in, but the feeling that something lurked on the other side was unmistakable. "We need a torch," Gideon said, grabbing one of the sticks. He handed it to Asterion and told him to light it.

"With what magic?" the priest threw his hands up in defeat. "I didn't happen to bring any flint, either."

"Try it outside the cavern," Gideon suggested, hoping that their loss of divine magic was a local event rather than a permanent result of something they had done.

Asterion pulled his cloak about his wounded shoulder and walked several paces away from the cavern. He prayed to Vrysinoch and sent his mind out in search of an answer, looking for a spark of energy that would set the stick ablaze and give them a torch. Asterion's consciousness moved incredibly slowly, but he could feel the power returning. The priest took a step back and then another, feeling the increase in his abilities with every inch.

The stick blazed to life and Asterion hurried back into the cavern. "In this cave, we are cut off from Vrysinoch, perhaps from all forms of magic," he rushed to explain. Asterion thought of Gravlox and wondered if his shamanistic abilities would also be silenced in the peculiar cave.

"Their leader, the half-orc, he must have been a magic user," Gideon surmised. "He spoke with such confidence and controlled the minotaurs so easily, yet he was not built like a warrior."

"That is why he forced his minions to attack us, instead of doing it himself," Asterion concluded. "The closer he is to the cave, the weaker he becomes. He might've known that you are a paladin and chose this location for that exact reason."

Gideon gave the minotaur corpse a spiteful kick and watched the beast's horned head slump to the side. "Even without my divine powers, I am unstoppable."

Asterion lowered his voice and placed a gentle hand on the paladin's shoulder. "Do not let pride overcome you," he chided respectfully. "Arrogance will get you killed."

Gideon let Asterion's words hang in the air without acknowledgement. He grabbed the makeshift torch from the priest and thrust it into the small tunnel. With a grunt, Gideon squeezed himself into the tunnel. There was barely enough room for the big man to crawl and he had to constantly stop to shift his sword to a different spot on his back. Asterion followed behind, his movements slowed by age rather than size.

After several minutes of twisting and turning in the cramped passageway, Gideon saw light coming from a source other than his torch. He hesitated. Asterion's words echoed in his head. If there was something alive on the other side of the passage, he would be defenseless against it. For a moment, Gideon thought to abandon the investigation and shimmy his way back out of the tunnel. Smoke drifting up from the torch blew into Gideon's face and he struggled to stifle a cough.

"What is it?" Asterion called from a few feet behind him, ruining what remained of their subtlety. Gideon held his breath and pulled himself around the next turn of the tunnel, jabbing the torch out before him. Unfortunately, Gideon had gone too far. His powerful legs propelled him around the blind turn in the tunnel and sent him falling nearly a dozen feet to the hard stone below.

Gideon shook the momentary dizziness from his head and leapt to his feet, ready to defend himself. The room, lit by Gideon's fallen torch and a smoldering collection of embers sitting in a metal brazier, was empty. Asterion poked his head tentatively around the edge of the tunnel and scanned the room.

"There's nothing here," Gideon grumbled with a hint of dissatisfaction. He had expected some sort of mysterious temple with a pulsating crystal in the center, sapping all of the magic from the air. Gideon envisioned a huddled group of robed acolytes chanting and worshipping the dark artifact that stole his magic, but the room before him was small and ultimately uncharacteristic.

A few piles of damp leaves and sticks were scattered around the cavern and the meager light made shadows dance on the walls.

Asterion dropped gracefully to his feet and brushed the dirt from his clothing. "This is merely an antechamber," the old man asserted with confidence. Gideon studied the room and looked for another connecting tunnel like the one he had just come through, but found nothing.

"This is a dead end," the paladin replied. "Whatever denies our magic here must be a natural phenomenon." He wracked his mind, searching everything he had learned at the Tower, but thought of nothing natural that could so completely cut him off from his sword.

The priest waited a moment, letting Gideon struggle to find an answer, before pointing to the shadows on the stone. "Look how they move," he whispered, hoping that Gideon would draw the same conclusion he had. A long moment of silence made it obvious that Gideon's powers of deduction were not as sharp as they should be.

"Air is moving from this chamber, through the tunnel, and out of the cave above," Asterion explained like he was teaching pupils at the Tower. "Therefore, another opening must exist. The shadows would not move and flicker unless airflow was causing the fire to shimmer."

Gideon knew that the old priest was right, but he saw no opening anywhere in the chamber. "Then find the next door," he growled with more venom in his voice than he meant.

Asterion smiled to himself and began tapping his fingers against the stone as he walked around the room. "Someone has taken great lengths to conceal whatever it is that has cut off our magic."

Softly humming the tune to a hymn, the priest walked around the perimeter of the cavern, gently tapping his fingers every few inches. At one grime-covered patch of stone near the smoldering brazier, the old man's fingers made no sound. The wrinkled skin of Asterion's hand passed effortlessly through the stone without the slightest noise.

Gideon grunted and moved to Asterion's side. "An illusion," he sneered. The powerful warrior believed that such low-handed trickery was better suited to thieves and jesters than to honorable persons. He thought back to the way the minotaurs had toyed with him, seeking to torture their captives rather than execute them. No, Gideon concluded silently, an illusion was exactly the type of magic that he should have expected.

"Can we pass?" he asked, longing for the heavy familiarity of the throwing axes that usually dangled from belt. He was nervous about wielding Nevidal. What if the magical enchantment returned *after* a battle concluded? He would be forced to kill Asterion to satisfy the blade or risk being consumed by the power.

Asterion felt out the edges of the passageway before taking a bold step through the rock. The dark tunnel was tall enough for Gideon to stand, but so narrow that if a fight began, he would never be able to swing his hand-and-a-half sword freely.

The chamber beyond the hidden tunnel was almost exactly what Gideon had hoped to find. In complete contrast to the previous cavern, the large spherical space at the end of the second passageway was decorated with beautiful tapestries and brilliant golden candelabras. The floor was covered in hundreds of tiny, fist-sized eggs that pulsed with red light. At the far end of the chamber, a pool of silky black liquid flowed from a carved stone skull into a basin on the floor. Although the liquid did not leave the basin by any visible means, the endless stream did not cause it to overflow.

"The eggs..." Asterion gasped. He reached out, nearly touching one, but thought better of it and pulled back his hand. A thick red webbing of slime stretched between the eggs, linking them and carrying their red light all over the chamber. The priest peered into one of the eggs intently and studied the moving shadows contained within the milky shell. He couldn't see much, but the pupa moved quicker, agitated, and emanated a violent aura of fear and anger.

Gideon reached out with mind, attempting to sense a source of magic within the room, but was immediately repulsed. Whatever it was that severed his connection to Nevidal reacted with such ferocity to Gideon's mind he nearly fell to his knees. In the brief moment that it took for his magical consciousness to be repelled, Gideon could feel the presence of other beings in the cavern.

"We aren't alone," he informed Asterion, trying to cover the fear in his voice. "I felt two others, maybe more, somewhere among us."

Asterion gulped and took a step back inside the tunnel. "If they wanted to hurt us, they could have already," he whispered. "Let's count our blessings and leave this place before our luck runs out." Gideon nodded and urged Asterion forward.

The two emerged from the cave system and drank in the cold night air. "What were they?" Asterion asked of the two beings Gideon had felt.

"I don't know, but they came from the pool at the end of the chamber and they felt powerful—too powerful for us to handle." Gideon shook his head and tried to clear his mind, but none of it made sense.

"Perhaps they were cloaked, made invisible with magic similar to the illusion of the stone wall." Asterion paced the ground in front of the cave opening and rubbed his arms together for warmth. He was thankful that the minotaurs hadn't taken his heavy traveling cloak when he was captured.

"No," Gideon responded. "They would have ambushed us if they were simply waiting under the protection of an invisibility spell." Gideon thought back to the brief moment he had felt their power. The memory was overwhelming. "They *were* the pool of liquid," he finally said, unsure of how to put words to what he had felt.

Asterion nodded and continued his solemn pacing.

"What does it mean?" Gideon begged after a few minutes elapsed. "What does any of it mean?"

Asterion rubbed a sheen of sweat from his brow and stopped his pacing. "Have you ever studied the properties of a phylactery?" he asked the paladin.

Gideon flexed in response. "I spent most of my abridged time at the Tower training and fighting, not reading books." More and more, Gideon was realizing how absurdly little he knew about life beyond Terror's Lament.

"A phylactery," Asterion explained softly, "is an enchanted vessel designed to contain the still-living magical essence of a powerful wizard once their human body is deceased." The old priest pondered a moment before continuing. "I have never heard of a phylactery in liquid form..." he breathed, imagining the possibilities of two powerful souls occupying the same unusual phylactery.

"Could it be a tribal shaman, someone like the half-orc who captured us?" Even as Gideon spoke, he realized the terrifying possibilities. He had witnessed the end of a human far more powerful than any half-orc.

Thirteen

G RAVLOX AND VORST trekked through the rocky foothills as quickly as their short legs could carry them. Without the need for sleep or much rest, the goblins traversed
several miles before Gravlox stopped to scout ahead with his magical senses.

"We aren't far," Gravlox said as he opened his eyes and let his
consciousness return to his physical body. The enchanted circlet
atop his head hummed with fading power.

"How many of them are out there?" Vorst asked. Gravlox had
barely spoken to her since they had turned away from Gideon's
trail. The shaman had tried to use his abilities to find the captured
humans but was unable to see even a glimmer of Gideon's magic
soul. Gideon and Asterion were either too far away or already dead.
The thought sickened Vorst.

"I can only see one," Gravlox told her, pointing a finger east. "It
is a brilliant light, brighter than Gideon..." Gravlox rubbed his
hands together and set his feet in motion once more. A throwing
axe swung back and forth at his side as he trekked, a solemn reminder of the man he had left behind.

Vorst walked a few paces behind Gravlox. Silence hung between them like the stench of death. She didn't know what they would do when they reached their destination. Gideon had thought he felt the presence of other paladins in the foothills, but Gravlox could only see one. A solitary magic user, stronger in power than Gideon, could easily destroy them.

"How do you know it is a paladin?" she dared to ask. "What if the light you see is something different? What will we do?" *What if it isn't human?* She wanted say. During her time as an assassin in Kanebullar Mountain, Vorst had studied some of the properties of magic. A powerfully enchanted artifact could give off emanations similar to a magically gifted human or goblin.

"Gideon felt a paladin as well, Vorst," Gravlox muttered as though the explanation was painfully obvious.

Vorst's anger boiled over. "Which side are the humans on?" Vorst yelled. "Humans only *killed* goblins during the battle, or did you forget that? We are escaped prisoners! They will cut us down without hesitation."

Gravlox turned and gazed into Vorst's eyes for a long moment before responding. He could see her anger, her rage, all of her emotions welling up from the fear that sat in the pit of her stomach. "If they will not listen to reason and help us find Gideon," he stated grimly, "then I will kill them."

SNARLSNOUT THE GLUTTONOUS waited impatiently for his slaves to carry him to the top of a small rise covered with scraggly pine trees. The morning air was bright and cold and carried the distinct scent of pine sap to the orc chieftain. Several miles ahead of him, Snarlsnout could see a faint black line that his scouts had discovered to be the human convoy.

"Where will they go?" he asked the gentle breeze. Snarlsnout knew the land to the west well. The Half Goat Clan controlled the lower reaches of the mountains from Talonrend to a small river they called Goat Stream. Their lands were bordered to the north by cave-dwelling minotaurs. To the south, the land opened up to a wide plain of swaying grass as far as the eye could see.

The Wolf Jaw Clan lived several miles to the north of Goat Stream. The nomadic clan of orcs, unlike the agriculturally minded Half Goats, mingled with the cave-dwelling minotaurs and other beasts that lived in the snowy mountains. Snarlsnout tried to remember any tales he had ever heard of orcs crossing Goat Stream to the west and returning. He had been chieftain of the Half Goat Clan for several generations, but still he could not recall a single detail about the lands west of the river.

Common orc legends spoke of great winged creatures strong enough to carry deer and wolves in their talons. If the superstitious rumors were to be believed, the forested region beyond Goat Stream was home to hundreds of wicked beasts that could tear an orc apart in an instant.

Snarlsnout sighed. Deep in his gut, he felt pity for the human refugee column. Even if they somehow survived a meeting with the two orc clans, they would have to march through the wild forest. According to his scouts, the human column had no escort. Snarlsnout had expected an impressive array of human soldiers to be guarding the caravan, but no such army had been seen.

"They have no idea..." the mountainous chieftain whispered. He thought of his clansmen, eager for battle and indescribably brutal. Since the scouts had spotted the human column, the scent of blood was in the air.

"Take me back to the clan," Snarlsnout ordered his slaves. The chained orcs heaved and grunted under the weight of the stone dais, struggling to carry it down the slope without tripping, but they obeyed without a word of discontent.

APOLLONIUS RAN AS quickly as his heavy armor would allow. Steel greaves pounded on the streets of Talonrend and sent a thunderous wall of sound into the air. Apollonius led a group of eight soldiers from the gatehouse on the eastern side of Talonrend through Terror's Lament. Several guards waved to them and pointed, shouting excitedly.

The nine soldiers stopped to catch their breath next to one of the guards. "Which direction?" Apollonius demanded. The young soldier pointed directly east. His face was pale and full of fear.

"Another attack?" The guard asked sheepishly. The new recruit was so untrained he had his sword buckled on the wrong side of his body.

"We can't be sure, but we must respond as though it is," Apollonius replied. "Lower the portcullis behind us and send someone to warn Herod." He looked up toward the top of Terror's Lament and shook his head. "Where are the damned archers?"

The guard gulped down his fear and looked away. "Training, sir," he muttered.

"All of them?" Apollonius could tell by the look in the man's face that not a single archer remained on the walls. "After you warn Herod," he hurriedly explained, "get the archers from their damned training!"

The young guard offered a rigid salute and broke away at a run for the palace. "The portcullis!" Apollonius shouted at the man's back. Whether his senses were dulled by fear or the loud noise of his metal boots, the guard did not turn back.

Apollonius loosed a bellow of rage and frustration and grabbed the nearest soldier in his party. "Kharon," he commanded, "shut the portcullis and get to the wall. You will be our eyes. If you see anything, call down a warning." The highly trained and experienced Templar nodded and ran to the gatehouse without a word.

Since Darius' death, Apollonius had made an effort to learn the names and skills of every soldier left under his command. Most of them were young, untrained, and nowhere close to being ready for battle, but Kharon was one of the best. The battle-hardened veteran had survived the goblin attack and Apollonius trusted him beyond the shadow of a doubt.

The remaining eight soldiers drew their weapons and exited the city at a measured pace. Several hundred feet to the east, they could see dust rising up from the field of bones, reminding Apollonius of horses running in a circle. He motioned with his hand and the seven men behind him fanned out in a semi-circle with their swords leveled before them.

Their heavy boots crunched through the tangle of goblin bones like a fully-loaded wagon rolling over loose cobblestone. With every step, Apollonius felt something other than dry bones breaking beneath his greaves. Subtle snaps of energy popped and crackled with every bone he crushed. At first, Apollonius thought the tingling sensation he felt was part of the thrilling anticipation of battle. It didn't take the commander long to realize something else was happening.

With a raised fist, Apollonius slowed the marching group to a halt. "Do you feel it?" he whispered through the slotted mouth guard of his helm.

"What is it, sir?" several of the soldiers responded. "Magic?"

Apollonius steadied his breathing and kicked some of the bones out from under his feet. They appeared normal, as far as he could tell. Pale, white and yellow shards of broken skeletons crunched loudly as he stopped on them. A distinctive pang of energy accompanied his footfall and gave him pause.

"Sir," one of the soldiers offered a handful of bones out to the commander. Apollonius took the bones in his armored fingers and rolled them around, searching for anything unusual. With a sigh, Apollonius made a tight fist and crushed the bones in his gauntlet. Underneath the dry snap that he expected, Apollonius heard a gentle buzz escape his closed hand.

All of the soldiers grabbed handfuls of bones and crushed them in their palms. It was clear they also felt the otherworldly sensation.

One of the men smashed a goblin bone and tossed it into the air directly above his head. Although there was no wind, the broken bones moved noticeably toward the growing dust cloud to the east.

Apollonius watched the soldiers throw handfuls of shattered bones into the air and all of them appeared drawn to the shadow of Kanebullar Mountain. "We need to move," Apollonius commanded.

The closer the eight men got to the swirling cloud, the quicker the bones at their feet moved. The smaller fragments skittered and jumped across the ground as if blown by a strong wind. Apollonius looked over his shoulder and was relieved to see Kharon standing atop Terror's Lament with a dozen or more archers. The soldiers took measured steps; they were nervous and visibly shaken by the magic of the bones.

After several fearful minutes of slow marching, Apollonius brought them to a halt. The towering monstrosity of whirling bones and dirt looked to be a hundred feet high. Despite none of the soldiers being magically inclined, they could all distinctly feel the power that flowed from the whirlwind. Wave after wave of malevolent energy cascaded around them like sheets of driving rain in a storm.

Without warning, a deafening bellow rose up from the depths of the tornado and burst forth. Several of the soldiers were knocked back by the force of the sound and Apollonius turned to cover his ears. The roar resonated in his metal helmet and confused his thoughts. "Turn back!" he managed to shout. Whether the other men could hear him or not above the ringing in their heads was irrelevant. A hideous screech echoed out of the magical whirlwind and the Templars broke ranks.

Hundreds of screeches joined the first and the bones of the tornado sprang to life. They joined together in unnatural ways, forming grotesque amalgamations of goblin corpses. The animated bone creatures were thrown from the tempest where they exploded into pursuit of the soldiers.

Apollonius heard the rattling footsteps of one of the creatures about to reach him. Ducking his head, the commander rolled across the ground and turned, coming up with his sword in front of him. The beast, if it could even be called such a thing, was quadrupedal, but with hundreds of skeletal arms lashing out in all directions. Apollonius steeled his resolve and met the charging equine creature with a thrust of his sword. Bones erupted and showered against his armor.

For a moment, Apollonius believed he had slain his adversary.

"GIVE ME THE damned bow!" Kharon yelled. He pushed the young archer aside and snatched the wooden crossbow from his hands with one fluid motion. The boy, barely sixteen, had just accidentally loosed a bolt into the stone parapet, missing Kharon's chest by mere inches. The fighting was still too far away, but the Templar leveled the crossbow and waited patiently.

Apollonius shook off the force of the crashing bones and turned, evaluating the plight of his comrades. Two soldiers circled and flanked a bone creature that resembled a skeletal goblin with four pairs of overly long arms. The two men timed and alternated their strikes, slowly hacking the bizarre bone creature to bits.

The horse-like monster that had shattered itself upon Apollonius' armor reformed behind the captain, striking down with its brittle hooves. Apollonius lifted his left arm above his head to deflect the blow and cut a slashing arc in front of him with his sword. The creature crashed against him like a wave breaking around an immovable rock. With another two swings of Apollonius' sword, the creature was again reduced to little more than skeletal debris.

The other monstrosities fighting amidst the Templars were equally outmatched. Reinforced steel armor proved far too thick for the flailing collections of animated bones to puncture. Within moments, the eight soldiers were free of their assailants. As they ran toward the slowly raising portcullis of Terror's Lament, Apollonius could hear the skeletal creatures reforming.

Kharon waited until the last possible second to give the signal for the archers to fire. In sloppy, untrained attempt at unison, a volley of crossbow bolts shot out from the parapet and obliterated the three creatures chasing the Templars. The fresh recruits barely had enough time to reload their weapons before the magical enemies reassembled and began their chase anew.

Apollonius and his Templars made it to the gate without losing a man. With the portcullis only a few feet above the ground, they had to drop to their bellies to make it through. The strange skeletal beasts crashed into the iron bars of Terror's Lament and shattered, sending hundreds of bone fragments all over the ground.

"Hold!" Kharon called from atop the parapets. The uneasy recruits leveled their crossbows and waited to fire. It took only seconds for the bones to reassemble into new and even more bizarre monstrosities.

"Fire!" Kharon's voice echoed from the stone walls. A devastating volley tore through the shambling skeletons and scattered them once more. An uneasy silence followed.

Apollonius and his men got to their feet with their swords drawn. Nervously, their eyes darted from each other to the broken pieces of bone at their feet. Suddenly, with a great peal of thunder, the bones launched into the air and raced away from the city as if pulled by unseen, magical strings. "What do you see?" Apollonius called to the archers.

A moment passed and a fierce wind began to howl through the metal bars of the portcullis.

"Something is coming!" Kharon called down to the Templars. "I see..." his voice broke off as he gasped for air. Apollonius couldn't tell if the soldier had been suddenly killed or merely stunned into silence. Without hesitation, the captain ripped open a door in the wall and began ascending the stone staircase as quickly as he could. Shouts of confusion rang out from above and below but with the wind, it was impossible to tell what was happening.

When Apollonius burst forth from the interior staircase, he too lost the air from his lungs. Several of the recruits cowered down behind the crenellations and others, Kharon included, stood slack-jawed with their weapons at their sides.

Perhaps a mile or more away from the city walls, thousands of goblin skeletons had joined together into one unholy beast. "Run..." was the only word that Kharon managed to whisper past the fear that clutched his throat. Even at a considerable distance, the bone creature was easy to see.

A flap of its skeletal wings sent a tower of dust and debris into the air beneath the colossal undead dragon. Wave after wave of dark magic swelled up from the ground and into the dragon. Luckily, the beast roared once and turned away from Terror's Lament. It circled through the air and beat its massive wings, flying in the direction of Kanebullar Mountain. There, atop the ancestral home of the goblin race, the great bone dragon settled down to wait.

DEEP WITHIN A cave north of Talonrend, a strange pool of black liquid shimmered and pulsed. *We have done it, brother,* a disembodied female voice whispered above the dark pool.

Yes, sister, we have, echoed an ethereal response.

The black liquid churned and bubbled, raging with energy and raw emotion. One of the eggs near the pool wriggled and cracked, hatching a coal-black scorpion shrouded in acrid smoke. *Taurnil. My child,* beckoned the sultry female voice. *Awaken your brothers and sisters.*

The scorpion clacked its claws and the chamber filled with an impenetrable inky blackness. Several hundred eggs began to crack at once.

LADY SCRAPPLE WRITHED and bellowed with uncontainable joy. Her slimy appendages thrashed against the stone walls of her chamber like never before. All throughout Kanebullar Mountain, her control began to wane. The bone dragon was a massive being, created from the gathered remains of an entire goblin army, and it took nearly all of her energy to control it. Without the magical guidance offered by the Mistress of the Mountain, the wondrous monstrosity, the ultimate goblin weapon of war, would crumble.

Fourteen

"HOLD YOUR POSITION," Corvus called with an upraised hand. A small group of paladins crouched just beneath the crest of a rolling hill and waited with their weapons drawn. The blind leader turned rapidly, sharply jerking his head back and forth.

Seamus stood next to Corvus and tried in vain to see the things the paladin described. The band of holy warriors had traveled north and then doubled back to the east, moving parallel to the refugee column, but leaving the head of the caravan exposed. Although the tracks they followed felt erratic and often misplaced, they were unmistakably minotaur.

Corvus' magical vision made his eyes dart frantically from light to light. "We are surrounded," he whispered once the men had gathered. A few scattered grunts were all the reply the trained fighters gave.

"What is it?" one of them asked as he tightened the forearm straps of his heavy shield.

"One..." Corvus struggled to put his magical vision into words, "thing approaches from the northeast." He pointed a hand in the general direction they had been traveling. Corvus could see the oddly shaped ball of energy steadily growing larger. He had tried several times to communicate with the magical consciousness, but had been violently repulsed.

"What else is out there?" Seamus asked as quietly as he could manage. Fear gripped his throat and made his voice crack.

Corvus turned to the west. "I can see many distant lights," he explained, "like dozens of magic users spread out in a field."

One of the older paladins adjusted a strap on his armor. "Magic users wouldn't spread out unless they had reason," he stated. "It sounds like a group of priests marching with an army."

"Or tribes of orcs with their shaman," Corvus corrected. "We should—"

"Goblins, sir!" one of the men scouting to the northeast shouted. The group exploded into action. Within seconds, the paladins formed two rows of interlocking shields with their swords gripped tightly at their sides. A subtle chant rose up and they began to march. The two lines moved in perfect unison—slowly, confidently, and inexorably.

Corvus stood next to Seamus and joined in the battle hymn from behind the lines. He let his mind swirl in the rumbling notes and could feel his body and soul strengthen with each verse. Vrysinoch was certainly among them.

The first row of paladins reached the crest of a sloping hill and halted at once. They planted their shields in the ground and surveyed the landscape through slots in their helmets.

"One, sir!" one of the men broke his chant just long enough to call out before taking the song up again.

"Friends!" a squeaky, high-pitched voice shouted from somewhere ahead. Corvus jerked his body in the direction of the voice out of reflex, but saw nothing—his eyes were useless. He couldn't recognize any magical presence other than the growing lights that resided within his brethren.

"Friends!" the voice called out again and Corvus knew his men were waiting for an order. If there had been a goblin army on the other side of the ridge, they would have marched down the slope and cut the beasts to ribbons with ease. Had it been orcs, the paladins would have formed a defensive circle atop the high ground and waited for a charge.

A single goblin calling out in his own language was enough to pique Corvus' curiosity. "Hold!" he barked at his men. It was a slow trek, but with help from Seamus' guiding arm, Corvus crested the hill. The whistle-like goblin voice called out a third time and Corvus spread his arms out wide as a gesture of invitation.

"If you are a friend, come forward!" he answered. The two rows of soldiers behind him stopped their chanting and waited. Corvus was impressed; he had only been with them for a short while and not a single person questioned his authority or his decision. The small troop was well trained. During battle, they were as one.

Hesitantly, Vorst crept from around the side of a small boulder and tossed Gideon's throwing axe onto the ground between her and Corvus. "Paladins..." Vorst marveled at the sight.

"How..." Corvus was so surprised by the idea of a talking goblin that he wasn't sure what to say. "How do you know what we are?" he finally asked.

Vorst took a step closer and looked up into the man's sightless eyes. "We fought with Gideon," she stated calmly, pointing to the axe, "the giant paladin. He saved our lives."

Corvus took a moment to process Vorst's words before he understood. "You must be one of the goblins Herod captured after the battle. I've heard rumors, but I didn't think they were true."

"Another goblin approaches, sir," a soldier in the front row called down. He lifted his sword to point toward Gravlox, forgetting his commander could not see.

"To the left," Seamus whispered, following the soldier's outstretched arm.

Gravlox was not as confident as Vorst that the humans wouldn't try to kill them. He strode forward with one of the axes dangling from his belt and Gideon's enchanted armlet seated between his pointy ears. Gravlox held his hands out to his side, but not as a sign of surrender. Sparks of magical fire danced between his fingertips and each step he took made the ground tremble and surge with energy.

It didn't take Corvus any effort to locate such a violent consciousness. Gravlox appeared perfectly in Corvus' vision as a raw conduit of destructive force contained within the meager body of a goblin. A thick lump of fear nestled in the man's throat and refused to leave. "There must be more..." Corvus sputtered, unable to believe such a powerful magical signature could be made by only a single creature.

"Gravlox!" Vorst scolded, but her thin voice was lost amidst the clangor of the men. The shaman strode forward to within a few feet of the first paladin line.

"An armlet," one of the soldiers called to Corvus. "He must have killed a paladin and stolen it!"

"Hold your ground," Corvus reminded the paladins. With an army marching toward them from the west, the last thing he wanted was a bloodbath due to poor diplomacy with a solitary pair of goblins.

Turning back in the direction he presumed Vorst's voice to be coming from, Corvus stretched his right arm out and invited the goblin to shake his hand. Whether Vorst understood the human custom or not, she made no attempt to return the gesture. If hostilities were going to happen, Corvus wanted the shaman to be the one to initiate them, so he let a momentary silence fill the air.

Finally, after a tense minute of inaction, Corvus spoke. "Is your friend going to kill us?" he questioned. His voice cracked as he spoke but Corvus felt no shame for his overt fear. He knew beyond a doubt that the small shaman could kill him before any of his paladins would have the chance to move. Vorst and Gravlox exchanged several sentences in the high-pitched goblin language before the bright light of the shaman's magical spirit began to dim.

Corvus watched cautiously with curiosity as Gravlox let his power recede. The magical energy, instead of going out like a candle in the wind or dispersing into the air, flowed out of the goblin like a waterfall. The power rushed out of Gravlox's body and sank into the ground as though it had been there all along. What was even more thought-provoking to the ascended paladin, was that as soon as the energy entered the soil, Corvus could no longer see or feel it.

"Gideon is lost," Vorst stated, breaking Corvus' silent contemplation.

"By lost, do you mean dead?" Corvus responded. He had never met Gideon, but after the battle, everyone in Talonrend knew the name. Especially among the paladins, Gideon was a living legend.

"I don't know," Vorst admitted, "but he was captured by minotaurs with Asterion."

"The old man?" Corvus was startled. He knew Asterion very well. The veteran priest was one of the most respected members of the Tower and had trained Corvus and the rest of the paladins in the use of divine magic.

"Yes," was all Vorst said.

"Come then, goblins. We have much to discuss." With that, Corvus and Seamus turned to walk back to the shallow valley on the other side of the ridge. The paladins followed, but each of them kept an eye on Gravlox and a hand on their weapon.

You nearly got us killed, Vorst tapped in the goblin code against Gravlox's palm. *I told you they would help us. Not every human is as evil as you think.*

Seamus and Corvus sat down on the grass with the goblin pair and attempted to lay out a plan. If Gideon and Asterion were being held hostage by a band of minotaurs, Corvus had every intention of rescuing them.

Less than half an hour into their discussion, several of the sentries watching the ridge called out an alarm. Corvus stood to call back to the sentry, but had no need. The unmistakable rumble of a distant war cry filled his ears.

"Orcs!" one of the men yelled as he fell into line with his shield.

"A whole army!" Another soldier added.

"May Vrysinoch protect us..." Corvus muttered as Seamus led him slowly by the arm back to the ridge.

The battle hymn began, but was soon drowned out by the screams of orcs and the howling of wolves.

Fifteen

T HE REFUGEES CIRCLED their hundreds of wagons, but knew that was more of a formality than a defensive maneu- ver. The militia that were scattered among the peasants climbed to the tops of the wagons with bows in their hands. Some of the stronger men, armed with makeshift clubs or rusty swords taken from their fireplace mantles, formed a meager line in front of the wagons.

"Tell the women and children to run!" one of the men shouted from atop a cloth-covered wagon. Tears ran down his face and he did nothing to hide them. The charging orcs came into view only a hundred or so yards from the wagons. "Run!" the man screamed, gripping his bow so tightly the rough wood cut his palm. The orcs held all manner of wicked weapons in their green hands, but next to all that glinting steel, the distinct glow of torches filled the night.

"They aren't here to raid and then leave..." he muttered to the nervous man crouching beside him. "They're here to kill us all."

The women were moving behind the wagons, but not quickly enough. The orcs would be upon them before they could flee and the paladins were too far away to see the battle and return. "Get out of here!" the bow-wielding man yelled as loudly as he could. His wife and two children scrambled to escape through the cluster of terrified refugees. He pulled a crude arrow from a bundle by his side and loosed it into the approaching mass of warriors. One of them went down. One... in a sea of thousands.

The men in front of the wagons started to break before the howling orcs felled a single one of them. Hundreds of refugees had answered the paladins' call to defend the wagons, but by time the orcs hit the line, less than half of the men remained. The others threw down their arms and fled with the women and children.

The guard sighed and watched his family run away through a gap in the wagons and disappear into the night. He turned back to the onslaught and loosed another arrow into the mass of battling orcs and humans below the wagon. One of the combatants fell, but he couldn't tell the race of his victim.

An orc thrashed his way through two of the defending humans and tossed a torch onto the canvas wagon. The fire immediately took to the wagon top and the vehicle's structure began to buckle. He grabbed another arrow and sent it hurtling into the orc at the foot of the wagon. The wooden arrow punched into the beast's shoulder, but didn't slow him.

Gurr looked up at the pesky archer and ripped the arrow from his shoulder with an energizing spurt of blood. The archer met his gaze and nocked another arrow. The bowstring thrummed and Gurr felt the arrow rip through his chest. The mighty orc warlord bellowed with glee and used his huge sword to chop off the shaft of the arrow. One hand after another, Gurr scaled the side of the burning wagon with half of an arrow buried in his chest.

The man loosed a third arrow before he leaped from the burning wagon. The wooden missile cut through Gurr's left leg and continued out the other side, trailing a red stream of orc blood. As he landed, the farmer-turned-archer felt the delicate bones of his ankle splinter. He knew he would never rise again.

Gurr hefted his mighty sword high above his head and smiled. The hole in his upper thigh oozed a steady stream of blood and the pain gave the maddened orc strength. With one powerful leap, Gurr vaulted from the burning wagon and landed with his sword planted firmly in the chest of the human archer. Blood flew from the man's ribcage and ragged screams filled Gurr's ears. Screams sharpened his resolve.

The Half Goat warlord forced all of his weight onto the hilt of the sword and drove the blade down into the dirt, nailing the man to the ground with the crosspiece. Every muscle in Gurr's hardened body absorbed the man's anguish like a piece of cloth tossed into a river. Gurr's arms and legs surged with so much power his skin nearly broke apart.

The orc warrior rose to his full height and placed a heavy foot on the man's unprotected throat. Gurr plucked an empty burlap sack from his leather belt and tossed it onto the man's bleeding chest. With one hand on either side of the archer's face, Gurr twisted and pulled, all the while applying the pressure of his entire body weight to the man's throat.

The archer's head came free of his spine with a sickening gout of warm blood. Gurr stuffed the trophy into his sack and ripped his sword free of the mutilated carcass. He licked the blood from his hands as he searched the burning chaos around him for another victim.

"CAN YOU SENSE it?" the old man excitedly asked. "There is magic nearby." He could feel a wave of energy not far away. The violent surge of magic felt familiar and brought a smile to his wrinkled face.

"I can," the paladin nodded. "Our brothers are fighting!" Gideon lowered his head and broke into a sprint. He felt the holy battle hymn of the paladins calling to his soul, beckoning him to add his strength to theirs.

Asterion knew he could not keep up with the athletically superior man. He stopped, latched onto the magical call with his mind, and summoned a great burst of divine light beneath his fingertips. Asterion molded the light and formed it with his hands into the rough shape of Vrysinoch's wings. When he finished, Asterion released his hold over the raw magic and the wings fluttered to life before him, as real as if they had been attached to a giant eagle.

The old priest smiled and took a step forward, walking directly between the two feathery appendages. It had been a long time since he had conjured such a spell, but Asterion was incredibly skilled and benefited from several decades of rigorous training. The wings grasped onto his shoulders and Asterion felt his muscles weave together with the sinew of his creation. He snatched his staff from the ground and leapt into the air. His wings carried him above the trees with a single beat and launched him in the direction of the fighting.

JURNORGEL TOSSED HIS head back and howled at the sky. Standing just over eight feet tall, the warlord of the Wolf Jaw Clan towered over his compatriots. The orcs nearest to him cowered and bowed down before their god-like champion.

"We kill!" Jurnorgel screamed at his clan. Wolf bones rattled against his armor and spit flew from his mouth. Behind him, a small orc lifted the clan banner high above his head and joined the howling war cries.

Jurnorgel's weapons, a straight sword and a double-headed axe, each as long as the orc was tall, rattled against his back. The massive wolf at his side howled and clawed at the chains around its neck and body. The rallying cry continued until Jurnorgel could see the first wave of Wolf Jaw orcs crash against the human warriors atop the distant ridge.

"Charge!" he screamed, leading his band of clansmen across

the rocky ground. When they had closed half of the distance to the humans, Jurnorgel drew his axe and cut the chains that bound his wolf to his side. The beast hurtled forward, much faster than any of the orcs, and dove into the fray.

"THERE," VORST POINTED at the charging mass of orcs, "that one must be their leader." Gravlox spotted the monstrously tall orc and watched him sprinting up the ridge. "Orcs have no organization or discipline," Vorst explained to the battle-ready shaman. "You must kill their leader." Unmistakable desperation filled her voice.

Gravlox nodded solemnly and closed his eyes. The magical circlet atop his head hummed and vibrated against his skin. The shaman summoned all of the magic he could and dug his hands down into the rocky soil. The ground shook and pulsed, surging with untapped potential, and Gravlox commanded it to do his will.

The paladins holding the ridge fought cohesively and held their ground against the initial assault. The human battle hymn filtered through the howling and wailing orc cries like a desperate man pleading before a crowded gallows. Chanting in rhythmic unison, the song swelled in strength until it became louder than the sounds of battle. With shields held high, the small band of paladins repelled the onslaught and weathered the furious storm of orcs.

Gravlox watched Jurnorgel approach the ridge. With a massive axe held out before him, the monstrous warlord charged. The shaman sifted through the magic at his fingertips until he located exactly the type of power he needed. The circlet cleared his mind and focused his consciousness like never before.

Fight me, Gravlox beckoned directly into the orc's mind. Jurnorgel stopped mid-sprint and nearly lost his balance. Straightening, he scanned the ridge and spotted the goblin pair, locking eyes with Gravlox. It was not the first time Jurnorgel had felt the intrusions of a magic user. The orc summoned every ounce of his formidable rage into an iron wall of mental resolve and easily sealed his violent thoughts.

Gravlox scampered to his right, farther down the ridge and away from the paladins. Jurnorgel followed him with measured footsteps and an outward calm that contradicted his inner vitality. Gravlox ripped his hands through the stony soil and wove the intricate magic of the earth into a devastating volley.

Chunks of dirt and rock the size of his head blasted against the orc's muscled chest, but the enchanted wolf bones all over his body absorbed the attack with ease. Gravlox dove his mind deeper into the wellspring of magic and latched onto a seething pocket of molten rock a mile beneath the surface. It took every ounce of energy he had, but the shaman was able to control the magma. He lifted it through the ground with blinding speed and hurled it at the orc in a single, fluid motion.

Jurnorgel's wolf bones rattled against the fiery impact, but the mighty warlord did not slow. He shielded his eyes with his massive axe and pressed onward. The powerful enchantment encased his body with a soothing, regenerative mist that fully nullified Gravlox's shamanistic magic. The liquid limestone cooled and showered a hail of small pebbles all over the ground.

The physically outmatched goblin had only a moment to prepare himself for Jurnorgel's wicked overhand chop that threatened to split him in half. Gravlox launched himself backward and narrowly avoided the beastly orc's sharp blade. The chieftain pressed on, following Gravlox with swipe after swipe of his weapon.

Scrambling at full speed through the rocky terrain, Gravlox managed to dart between a pair of small boulders and disappear into a thicket of trees. Jurnorgel bellowed into the chilly air and tossed his weapon from hand to hand as though it weighed little more than a loaf of bread.

"Run, Grav!" Vorst shouted. Gravlox cursed under his breath and pumped his legs as hard as they would go. Behind him, the shaman could hear Jurnorgel begin chopping the trees down with casual blows from his axe.

Suddenly, with a blinding explosion, a sharp blast of magic fell from the sky and encased Jurnorgel in a prism of brilliant light. Gravlox spun on his heels and summoned a small wave of magic into his hands. His eyes darted to Vorst and fear gripped his chest— but only for a moment. The female goblin shouted and her smile was undeniable. Gravlox spotted Asterion flying overhead and let the magic flickering at his fingertips dissipate back to the earth.

The terrified orc thrashed and wailed, but was unable to free himself from the opalescent chains of light that smashed into his body. Slack-jawed, Gravlox stared in disbelief as Asterion flew about the orc warlord with the speed of a nimble bird. The old priest lifted his hands toward the sky and pulled a massive, glowing beam of light toward himself. When he had gathered a boulder-sized sphere of magical radiance into his palms, Asterion let it loose with a piercing scream that sounded more avian than human. Hundreds of bright white magical shards rained devastation down upon Jurnorgel and the rest of the orc clan.

The hard pressed paladins shouted at the sight. Their hymn grew louder as the orcs fell, wave after wave, to Asterion's storm of holy missiles.

With a violent crack of power, Jurnorgel's defensive enchantments visibly broke. Gravlox sensed the dissipation of magic and wasted no time. The goblin called out to one of the flying light shards and brought it to his hand. It burned the skin of his fingers and was painful to behold, but it filled Gravlox with fresh confidence. He pulled himself on top of the nearest boulder and leaped, landing squarely on the shoulders of the dazed chieftain.

Gravlox drove the fragment of pure light down with all of the physical and magical strength he could muster. The makeshift dagger bit through the orc's skull and splattered Gravlox's face and arms with blood. Jurnorgel fell limply to the ground.

Mentally and physically drained, Asterion descended to the

ridge and joined Vorst and Gravlox. Gideon, sword in hand, crashed through the thin line of trees and joined the fight without hesitation. The empowered paladin added to the chaos of battle as he cut the fleeing remnants of the Wolf Jaw Clan down like wheat before a scythe.

In mere minutes, the battle had turned from a desperate last stand into a complete rout. Only a handful of the Wolf Jaw orcs managed to run back to their leader alive.

"We couldn't find you," Vorst explained to Gideon, ashamed of her failure.

The stoic paladin nodded as he sheathed Nevidal and extinguished the blade's inner light. His bulging muscles relaxed as he returned to his natural proportions. "We found a phylactery in a cave," he replied. "Somehow, it blocked our magic."

Asterion wiped the sleeve of his traveling robe across his forehead. He was sweating profusely and could barely catch his breath. Gideon supported the old man's weight with his shoulder. "The phylactery..." he gasped from one knee, "is made of the same malevolence that attacked the city."

Vorst translated the message to Gravlox by tapping on his palm. "It is from the mountain?" The shaman asked with her aid.

"Not goblin," Asterion managed to say. "It is Jan. Stronger than before... much stronger..." Gideon lifted the man off the ground as the priest's eyes rolled back in his head and he succumbed to the comforts of sleep.

"We must turn back," Corvus stated with finality as he approached the group. Seamus led the blind paladin by the arm to Gideon's side. "Protecting the peasants is our first responsibility. Without the people, we are no better than a group of street thugs."

"I doubt this small band of orcs is the only one in these hills," Gideon retorted gruffly. "If you left the peasants to fend for themselves, you'll have a lot of graves to dig."

Seamus looked at the bloody, green-skinned corpses that surrounded them. He knew Gideon was right.

The paladins' song died down as they collected their dead. In the initial onslaught, four of the humans had been cut down. Their bodies were placed on their shields and the survivors organized them into a line on the ridge.

"Normally, the honor of sending our dead back to Vrysinoch's wings would be reserved for Asterion, but I fear he has nothing left to give." Corvus inspected the unconscious priest with his magical sight and could barely detect a faint hint of energy in Asterion's frail body. "It will take him days, if not weeks, to recover."

Corvus walked solemnly toward the gathered paladins at the top of the ridge and began humming the first notes of a funeral dirge. The other soldiers joined in the eerie, unsettling tune and he began the high-pitched wail of the song's melody.

A shimmering white light settled over the four fallen paladins and slowly engulfed their corpses. Corvus' voice rose and fell with the sorrowful song and little white birds fluttered out of the sky to land on the bodies.

"The Valkyrie-Animus," Gideon explained to the goblins with a whisper. "They come to guide the dead to Vrysinoch's wings for their eternal flight."

Vorst pried her awestruck gaze from the magical scene and looked up to Gideon. "Why don't you sing?" she asked, hesitant to speak, lest she interrupt the beautiful dirge.

Gideon grunted. "I pity them." He scratched his braided beard and looked away from the funeral. "Spending and eternity with a petty and merciless god is nothing short of damnation. I sing during battle when Vrysinoch grants me strength, but without Nevidal in my grasp, I am alone."

"Wha—" Vorst began to question further, but Gideon turned and stalked angrily away from her.

Sixteen

FTER THE CONCLUSION of the funeral, Gideon and Corvus gathered the remaining paladins and took stock of their situation. "How far away are the refugees?" Gideon asked with doubt in his voice.

"A day's journey on foot," Corvus replied. The paladins were eager to set out and leave the stinking orc corpses to rot in the sun. "How high is the sun?" Corvus asked, tilting his useless eyes toward the sky.

"Just past midday, sir," one of the dutiful paladins replied. He tightened the straps that held his shield to his back and checked the faces of the other soldiers for support. "We could make it back by dawn," he offered eagerly.

"Perhaps," Asterion interrupted as he weakly approached the group, "I can help facilitate our travels."

"Don't even think about it," Corvus told the old man sternly. "You need to rest. You're in no condition to be using magic."

Without a word, Asterion waved off the paladin and began gathering divine energy for a powerful incantation.

"I said no!" Corvus yelled, pushing aside several paladins as he stepped in front of Asterion. To Corvus, Asterion's hands appeared in his vision as white tendrils of elastic energy ready to be woven together into a spell. They grew in brightness and Corvus brought his hands to his eyes, but nothing could block the magical light. He turned away, cursed the old man, and spat on the ground.

"You're too weak to use so much magic in a single day." Several of the other paladins nodded in agreement. Slowly, Asterion's gathered light began to wane.

"I think..." the old priest gasped for breath. "You are right..." Corvus could feel Asterion's power fading and ran to his side, catching the man under the arms before he fell. Without pause for consideration, Corvus summoned his own considerable energy and willed the magic flowing through him to bolster Asterion's weakened abilities.

"Yes..." the priest whispered. He felt the surge of energy rush through his body and his mind cleared. With practiced hands, he molded the light into a small triangle and threw it high into the air. At once, Corvus and Asterion jolted, releasing their combined energy, and the spell took flight.

A celestial bird grew from the radiant triangle and circled overhead. Exhausted and panting, Asterion dropped to his knees and struggled to keep his eyes open.

"The stubborn old man only summoned an image of Vrysinoch," Gideon muttered. With a grunt, he began searching for sticks large enough to make a stretcher. "We'll have to carry him back to your camp."

"I don't know," Corvus pondered, investigating the magical creature with his otherworldly vision. "Something isn't right. Any priest of Vrysinoch should be able to conjure such images with ease. Even a man of his age shouldn't be taxed so noticeably by such a minor summoning." As if to accentuate his point, Asterion let out a groan and crumpled to the grass as he succumbed to sleep.

"What is it?" Vorst tentatively asked. Corvus could only shake his head.

"A guide?" Seamus stared up at the gliding bird in awe. He subconsciously balled his fists and wanted desperately to be like the paladins. Having lived the life of a simple farmer, he couldn't help but feel inadequate next to the holy warriors. He didn't resent them, but in the pit of his stomach Seamus wanted to join them. Until recently, the farmer had never seen magic outside of small cantrips and illusions used during services at the temple in Cobblestreet. Witnessing the summoning of a mysterious bird and watching the paladins slay orcs with divinely-infused weapons had turned Seamus' curiosity into an emotion that skirted the boundaries of inspiration and jealousy.

Gideon hefted the priest's body onto a hastily constructed stretcher and told Seamus to help him carry it. The two men held the slumbering priest between them as the column of paladins set off to the south.

Gravlox and Vorst followed the ensemble with trepidation. "How many humans will be there?" Gravlox asked in his native language. "Will any of them try to kill us?"

Vorst shook her head and tried to imagine what it would be like to walk among hundreds of tall humans. The thought made her stomach churn in angry knots. "We will be fine," she said, trying to convince herself more than anyone.

With a sigh, Gravlox quickened his pace. "I can kill any of them..." he mused. "If they try to touch us, I will."

"No," Vorst replied flatly. "Let Gideon and the other paladins protect us. We need to earn their trust, not slaughter them." She stopped walking and forced Gravlox to turn and meet her gaze. Uneasy tension hung in the air like morning fog.

"Why?" was all that Gravlox said.

Vorst stared at him and crossed her arms. "Why?" she angrily repeated. "Why? Because I *cannot* return to the mountain. That's why." She readjusted her meager clothing and trudged past Gravlox.

In the back of her mind, Vorst let her consciousness slither back to the familiar connections of her kin. She probed across the vast distance to the network of interwoven minds that made up the goblin race. While the thoughts of Lady Scrapple were too far removed to be anything more than vague and fleeting, Vorst knew beyond a doubt the emotion they expressed: hatred.

Suddenly, the magical bird circling high above the travelling group let out a piercing screech that made several of the humans cry out in pain.

"What in Vrysinoch's name?" one of them shouted and cursed. He clutched his hands over his ears and staggered. "Have we angered it?" the man shouted.

With a rapid beating of its wings, the bird dove to the ground behind the group and loosed another painful caw.

The bird reared back on its magical legs and at once, the paladins were filled with terror.

"Run!" Gideon shouted above the clamor of confusion. "Vrysinoch be damned, run!" he screamed again, grabbing a dazed paladin by the shoulder as he sped past him with Asterion's stretcher secured under one of his muscled arms.

Most of the soldiers fell into step behind Gideon and ran for their lives. A third grating screech, accompanied by a powerful gust of wind, emanated from the bird's white beak.

"What's happening?" an older paladin yelled with fear as the wind lifted his legs from the ground. Terrified, the man continued to ferociously pump his legs.

"That old man knew what he was doing after all," Corvus said, smiling as the celestial wind lifted him from the ground. "Jump!" he yelled to the others, "and keep running!"

As the wind grew stronger, their feet were gradually lifted from the ground until they were all sprinting an arm's length above the rocks and dirt.

After only an hour or so of running with Vrysinoch's magical aid, the bird dissipated and the paladins tumbled to the ground on top of a gentle rise that afforded them an excellent view of the plains — and the smoke billowing up into the sky.

The smell of fires and burning meat hung in the air. "They're in trouble," Corvus growled, doubled over and breathing heavily from exhaustion. "We have to save them!"

"Save what?" Gideon spat, setting Asterion on the ground and rubbing the new blisters on his hands. "The refugees are dead, just like I said."

Gravlox and Vorst crested the rise with a sheen of sweat on their brows, but otherwise physically better off than the humans. "It could be a trap," Vorst thought aloud, stretching her thin legs.

"We *must* go!" Corvus implored, turning to face the rest of the paladins, but unsure of where to look.

Seamus touched the blind paladin's shoulder and directed him toward the gathering men. "Where we gon' leave the priest?" Seamus chided the over-zealous leader. "Leave 'im here to die?"

"Ugh," Corvus sighed, crestfallen. "Someone must stay behind and guard him."

Gideon inched closer to the columns of smoke on the horizon. "I'd rather kill orcs and minotaurs than sit here while others reap the glory," he said under his breath.

"We will stay," Vorst spoke up. *We have to watch the priest while they search for survivors,* she tapped in the goblin code against Gravlox's palm.

I should go with the warriors, Gravlox responded, flexing his arm to show his strength.

"An orc nearly killed you!" Vorst shouted at the shaman in the high-pitched goblin language, startling Corvus with her sudden outburst. "You need to heal the priest," she added, turning her back to end the discussion.

"I'm for stayin' too," Seamus chimed in with a smile.

"It is settled," Corvus announced to the gathered paladins. "Seamus and the goblins will stay behind to protect Asterion as we reunite with the refugee caravan." His voice rang out over the eager men as they drew their weapons and formed interlocking columns. Scattered murmurs of dissent flitted through the ranks, but most of the men trusted the unusual goblin pair to protect their comrade.

Without further debate, the paladins began singing a hymn to Vrysinoch as they marched toward the billowing smoke.

Gideon begrudgingly fell into line at the edge of the first row. He held a throwing axe in each hand and felt the cool comfort of Nevidal's scabbard against his back. The air was cold, but scents of death and smoke lingered on the wind.

"There won't be any left," the stoic man angrily spat.

"Orcs or refugees?" the paladin at Gideon's left asked between verses of the battle hymn.

"Ha," Gideon chortled. "Either. Orcs aren't likely to stay once the plunder is gone. We are only certain to find one thing."

The shield-bearing paladin shook his head and swallowed. "What's that?" he asked, but he already knew the answer.

"Corpses."

"GURR, WE MUST wait!" Snarlsnout the Gluttonous bellowed at the warlord over a bag of severed human heads. Undrakk smiled and picked at his teeth with a whittled stick.

"The Wolf Jaw Clan has already fallen to that group of paladins," the half-orc shaman stated as though he was describing the weather. "The Half Goats would surely perish at their hands as well." With a twirl of his staff, Undrakk turned away and strolled toward a nearby cook fire.

"Wolf Jaws are weak!" Gurr yelled, sending a huge glob of spit onto the face of one of Snarlsnout's slaves. "Look!" Gurr pointed at the four rows of warriors marching in the distance. "There are less than..." Struggling to come up with the largest number he knew, Gurr resorted to counting on his blood-soaked fingers. "Less than many of them!" he finally bellowed, letting his frustration out in the form of a war cry.

Some of the nearby Half Goat orcs stomped and howled with their weapons held high at the sound of their warlord's bloodthirsty cry. With his monstrous feet, Snarlsnout directed his slaves to turn his stone dais around to face his clan. "I am your chief!" he shouted above the din. "We wait!"

"How long?" Gurr shouted back for all the orcs to hear.

"The minotaur clans from the north should be joining us before the next full moon," Snarlsnout explained. His voice carried an undeniable weight of authority that soothed the ferocious Half Goats and temporarily slaked their thirst for carnage. "We wait for the minotaurs… and then we kill!" Snarlsnout let out a booming laugh that shook his enormous body to the core.

Despite the clear logic laid out before him, Gurr's rage would not dissipate. The imposing warlord ripped open the clan's bag of battle banners and quickly found the only one he recognized, the symbol for an all-out charge.

"Put it down, Gurr," Snarlsnout warned from his dais. "Those men will cut you to ribbons before your half-witted brain can even think enough to scream."

Gurr stared his chieftain in the eyes for a long moment. Undrakk wandered back toward the dais as he pulled a mouthful of roasted pig flesh from a skewer. Finally, Gurr turned back to the assembled clan and lifted the banner into the air.

"Kill!" Gurr shouted at the top of his lungs.

Exasperated, Snarlsnout lifted his gouty hands as high from his throne as he could and called out to the warriors. "If you charge, you will die," he bellowed out solemnly. The orcs nearest to the dais heard his words and some of them stopped, causing an uneasy ripple of confused emotions to reverberate through the clan.

Without waiting for any further words to be exchanged, Gurr drew his sword and took off at a sprint for the marching paladins.

"Hold, Half Goats, we must hold," Snarlsnout pled. Several of the orcs closest to Gurr followed the warlord's suicidal charge, but nearly all of the green-skinned warriors obeyed their chieftain.

"Well spoken," Undrakk mocked once he finished his meat and properly cleaned his hands. "Although you will have to find a new warlord to replace Gurr in the morning."

Snarlsnout let out a frustrated sigh that quickly devolved into a painful fit of coughing. "How many did the Wolf Jaw Clan lose?" he managed to ask after several moments of wheezing.

"Nearly half of their best warriors, by all accounts," Undrakk replied. "But worry is not suited to the regal air of a chieftain. When the minotaur clans arrive, you will have more than enough fighters to kill every living thing from here to Talonrend."

Undrakk's words did more to unsettle the leader than comfort him. "I hope you are right," Snarlsnout remarked. "I hope you are right..."

"WHAT DID I tell you?" Gideon growled as he stepped over the burned remains of a covered wagon. The stench of scorched flesh assaulted his senses and made him gag.

"They're... dead..." Corvus didn't need vision to picture the carnage before him. "Search for survivors. Salvage what you can," he commanded the paladins, "we will leave as soon as possible." The eager battle hymn quickly died as the men began searching through what was once several miles of refugees.

"Help me..." a voice drifted from underneath a toppled wagon. Gideon and one of the paladins rushed to move the wreckage from atop the struggling girl. No more than ten, she had blood streaming down her face from a garish cut across her forehead. Her left arm was bent grotesquely backward under her body and the small bones of her wrist poked through the skin of her hand. It was a wonder she was alive.

"Can you heal her?" the paladin at Gideon's side asked with a hopeful voice. Solemnly, Gideon shook his head and looked away.

"Several years ago, perhaps," he stated. His mind drifted away from the horrible scene in front of him and he thought to his years of training at the Tower. "Outside of battle, Vrysinoch does not speak to me," he said, more to himself than the dying girl.

"I can heal minor cuts and wounds, but this..." the man sputtered. He lifted the girl's head from the dirty ground and used his fingers to push the sliced skin of her forehead back into position. Despite the wound already clotting and scabbing at the edges, it still leaked hot blood over his fingers.

"We'll get you patched up," the man attempted to comfort the bloody girl. "What's your name?" he asked as he cradled her.

"Corshana," she weakly replied. The skin of her face pulled awkwardly as she spoke, sending another fresh line of blood down her cheek.

Much more violently than he intended, Gideon grabbed the paladin under the arm and ripped him away from the girl. "We can't help her," Gideon whispered into the man's face. He turned his back on the girl and took one of his throwing axes from his belt.

"What in Vrysinoch's name do you think you're doing?" the man shrieked, doing little to keep his voice from reaching the girl's ears. "We can't just kill her."

Gideon sighed and cracked his neck. "We can," he said. "And we will." Horror filled the younger man's eyes and he knew Gideon was serious. "Even if she sustained these kinds of injuries back in Talonrend and *not* on the open road, it would have taken the priests weeks to treat her. We either kill her now, or let a fever take her in the night."

The paladin started to speak but couldn't find the words to argue. Lost, he turned back to the girl and tried to keep his own tears at bay. "Corshana," he whispered as he knelt at her side. Gideon moved silently behind her with an axe in his hand. "Where did your family go, Corshana?"

Struggling to shake her head, she managed a feeble shrug.

"I'm so sorry," the paladin whispered past the lump in his throat. "Vrysinoch be with you," he muttered as Gideon's axe cleaved into her skull. Blood splattered the man's armor and clothes. He held the girl in his arms and rocked her back and forth for a long moment while Gideon rummaged through the nearest wagons for anything useful.

"There's no one here," Gideon said upon his return. He lifted the man from the ground and watched Corshana's corpse slide from his grasp.

After several more minutes of searching, Gideon returned to Corvus at the front of what was left of the column. "How many survived?" Gideon asked.

Corvus noted the obvious lack of optimism in his voice. "Several dozen," he cheerfully responded, pointing in the direction of several relatively undamaged wagons. "The survivors are being grouped there," he explained. "We need to spread out and search the area south as well. Many of the refuges likely fled when the orcs arrived and may still be hiding among the trees and boulders."

A glint of movement caught Gideon's attention and reeled him back toward the west. "We won't have time," he shouted at the blind paladin. "They're coming."

Orc battle cries drifted to their ears from a distant ridge. "Can you see them?" Corvus begged with a voice that plainly displayed his panic. "How many are there?"

Gideon wiped Corshana's blood from his axe and drew a second from his belt. "Begin the chant," he called over his shoulder as he ran for the other paladins. "Form a line!"

"CAN YOU WAKE him?" Vorst asked Gravlox from her position at Asterion's side. "He looks sick." Seamus paced nervously around the grass. He was thankful to not be with the paladins, should battle commence, but felt helpless in the presence of such foreign creatures.

"I don't know," Gravlox stated. He took the enchanted circlet from his head and felt along the sides of the smooth metal. It hummed gently in response to his touch. "When I talk to the ground, I only find anger and violence." Gravlox was uncertain of how to put his magical experiences into words.

"Grav..." Vorst's voice dropped lower, keeping it from Seamus' ears despite the language barrier. "Do you remember that time in the woods?" She crept closer to him and placed a hand delicately in his palm. Memories of their rejuvenating kiss skipped through Gravlox's mind.

"Yes," he whispered, leaning closer to her.

"You used magic in the forest," Vorst explained, playfully pulling back from his side. "Not the magic of a shaman speaking to the ground, but something else." Vorst sat with her legs folded under her for a moment and relished in the memory of their kiss. In that moment, she had never felt so alive.

"I don't remember how I did it," Gravlox admitted. "It just... happened. I'm not sure that kind of magic would help a human." He watched the gentle rise and fall of Asterion's chest and placed the circlet back between his ears.

As he steadied his breathing, Gravlox closed his eyes and sent his mind weaving down the energetic strands of the earth's magic he had grown accustomed to. He felt the emotions of the soil, malleable and eager to be manipulated. His mind grasped the stoic and eternal sentiments of the bedrock far below the surface, ready to be captured and summoned. Further into the ground, Gravlox's mind dove through a seething pocket of magma that recoiled from his touch. As the powerful circlet hummed, Gravlox backed away from the magma and searched elsewhere for the specific power that he sought.

Retreating back closer to the soil above the layers of bedrock, he found the soft magical connections that linked a system of nearby tree roots to the surrounding earth. Gravlox's consciousness mingled and swirled with the essence of the tree roots, searching for something useful. Instead of violent power waiting to be consumed and utilized, he found an altogether new magical source. It was not the regenerating and soothing force he had expected and hoped to find. Much to his excitement, Gravlox felt the waiting energy of creation pulsing between the roots of the tree.

Before he could delve further into the intricate web of creation, a distant chorus of screams and shouts shattered his reverie. "What's happening?" he asked, blinking away the grogginess in his eyes.

"More orcs," Vorst hurriedly shouted. "They're attacking the paladins."

"Should we be running?" Seamus asked with a hint of panic creeping into his voice.

"No," Gravlox declared, doing his best to make his voice sound as human as possible. Reverting back to his native language, Gravlox stated that he intended to fight if any of the orcs approached them.

"They're charging right into the paladins…" Vorst watched the tiny figures clash from atop the small rise in the land. None of the attackers seemed to notice the stationary group so far away.

THE PALADINS, KNOWING they were outnumbered at least two to one, formed a small circle of shields around Corvus that could not be outflanked. They all locked their shields magically into place and prepared to weather the assault—all except a single paladin.

Gideon strode ahead of the circular shield wall with a throwing axe gripped tightly in each hand. The remaining refugees shrieked and cowered behind whatever meager cover they could find among the wreckage.

Be with me, Vrysinoch, Gideon silently prayed as the orc charge neared. *Let me kill these foul beasts in your name!* Gideon felt a slight hint of power emanate from Nevidal at his back, but then it was gone. The holy symbol tattooed on his shoulder was as cold and lifeless as his blade. *I figured as much,* he scoffed at his god. *I am no longer your paladin. Because of the girl? She was dead before I ever found her.*

The lead orc came into sight and Gideon knew that his physical stature alone would not be enough. Gurr, the mighty Half Goat warlord, held a sword the size of a small tree above his head and howled with wild abandon. Gideon lifted an axe in his direction and beckoned to the crazed orc.

Like a steel tide crashing against an immovable cliff, the orcs slammed into the paladins. Gideon caught a screaming orc soldier squarely in the chest with his throwing axe and nearly rent the creature in two. The garish wound spat life onto Gideon's hand and made his grip slick with blood. Cursing Vrysinoch for the lack of his sword's power, he grunted and let the small weapon fall from his grasp.

A second orc thrust at Gideon with a reckless spear jab he easily parried with his mailed sleeve. The orc, overbalanced and barely competent from the start, stumbled over the butt of his long weapon into Gideon's rushing fist. A second punch shattered the orc's ugly face and sent the creature sprawling to the ground. Poorly equipped and undisciplined orcs smashed into the paladin shield wall behind Gideon, but no others attempted to fight him.

Slowly, Gideon walked over the corpse he had just made and squared off against the monstrously tall warlord. Gurr scraped his feet against his ground and crouched, staring Gideon in the eyes.

"You die, human," Gurr growled through sharpened teeth. He swung his gigantic blade lazily above his head and the bloody burlap sack on his belt fluttered in the breeze.

Gideon nodded and threw his axe as hard as he could. With measured timing, Gurr snatched the twirling axe from the air by the hilt. Never breaking eye contact with the paladin, the massive orc crushed the small weapon to splinters and let the axe's remains fall through his fingers.

For the first time in years, Gideon felt a knot of fear tie itself in his chest. He gulped and tried to shake the dizzying feeling of helplessness from his mind. Before he could set his feet and draw his remaining axes, Gurr was upon him. The mighty orc brought his sword down with unexpected speed.

Caught off guard by the creature's deft strike, Gideon barely lunged from the blade's path. He hit the ground in a roll and came up with another axe in his hand, slashing wildly in front of him. Gideon's sweeping blade hit nothing but air. Frantically, the paladin's eyes darted around in search of the hulking warrior.

Behind him, Gideon heard the unmistakable sound of a heavy sword cutting the air. With a grunt of frustration, Gideon dove forward again, but he was too late. Gurr's huge sword bit into his back directly between his shoulder blades. Luckily, the sword tip clanged against Nevidal's sheath and prevented the weapon from cleaving his back wide open.

Gideon lunged forward in pain and landed on his knees. As quickly as his torn back would allow, he pivoted on his heel and prepared to parry. Before he could properly adjust the blade of his axe, Gurr's sword crashed into the handle and shattered it. With ferocity born of desperation, Gideon leapt over the orc's sword and grappled the green-skinned foe.

Surprised by the sudden maneuver, Gurr dropped his sword and wrapped his huge arms around Gideon's slashed back. Even beneath the paladin, Gurr was far stronger. He grasped his wrists, locked his arms together, and began compressing Gideon's spine.

The paladin struggled for breath, but knew he would live. With Nevidal strapped securely to his back, the orc couldn't break his spine. Still, Gideon knew he could not defeat the warlord. "Help..." he breathlessly called out. Surrounded by the din of chaotic battle and the steady pulsing of the battle hymn, Gideon's words were lost.

He tried to push himself to his knees, but the orc had managed to wrap his legs around the paladin's waist to immobilize him. Gurr smiled calmly into Gideon's panicked eyes and clamped a meaty hand over the human's mouth. "You die, wretched scum," he whispered with a heavy orcish accent.

Gurr's hand tasted like dried blood and rotten meat against his mouth. With the skin and muscle of his upper back torn, Gideon couldn't even lift his neck to gasp at the air. His eyes fluttered shut and he let his mind wander away from his body.

FROM THE CENTER of the shield wall, Corvus used his divine sight to direct the flow of the battle hymn's inspiring energy. As the men sang, holy light enveloped them, wrapping them with a protective layer of magic. Whenever an orc managed to get a strike over one of the shields, Corvus was there with a blast of mental energy that sent the creature flying back. Before long, the song of praise drowned out the screams of the orcs entirely.

An orc launched a clumsy spear over the top of the shield circle, aimed for Corvus head, but Vrysinoch struck it down with a bolt of holy light. The shoddy projectile sizzled in the air and fell at Corvus' feet with a dull thud. Turning in slow circles behind the line, Corvus' vision showed him all of the wounds his men had taken. Weaving Vrysinoch's intricate magic into small bursts of healing, Corvus infused the paladins with regenerative light that stitched their injured flesh together.

"Help..." a soft voice resonated in Corvus' mind from the battlefield. He could feel Gideon's spirit weakening by the second. The once-brilliant orb of light that identified Gideon's presence to Corvus' blind eyes had been reduced to a small speck, a hint of its former glory.

Focusing all of his attention, Corvus drew magical strength from the ring of paladins and channeled it into a single blast of healing. With surgeon-like precision, he pushed the healing energy into Gideon's soul. Immediately, the strength of the shield wall began to wane.

An orc swung his double-bladed axe into one of the shields and where magic had once protected, wood splintered and an unfortunate paladin's arm splintered with it. Still, Corvus directed the magic of the battle hymn into Gideon's body until he could see the man rise to his feet. Another paladin failed to parry a spiked ball on the end of a chain that wrapped around the side of his mace and connected solidly with his helmet. With his magical vision, Corvus saw the paladin's skull cave in, but he also felt Gideon's soul pulse and brim with vitality.

IN ONE MOTION, Gideon flexed his legs, ripped an arm free from Gurr's pinning weight, and rose to his knees above the orc warlord. Vrysinoch's strength imbued him once more. Gideon slammed his mailed fist into the orc's chin and scrambled to his feet.

"Pull back!" he screamed at the wavering line of shields. Several orcs pushed through a gap in the wall and began overpowering the smaller humans. Without looking, Gideon knew Gurr was only a few steps behind him.

Corvus frantically gathered all of the remaining energy and formed it into a solitary ball of holy light. The ascended paladin was out of options. Orcs attacked him at the center of the shield wall and his own magical defenses would not hold forever. Unsure of the results, Corvus severed the connection of his own mind to the gathered sphere of magic in the air and let it violently unravel.

With a sound like lightning splitting stone, the orb shattered and fell back to the ground, sending a crashing wave of divine power into every living thing it touched. The paladins, immediately emboldened, scrambled back to protect their leader. The orcs fell to the ground in unison, dazed and breathless. Gurr, bellowing at the top of his lungs, found himself chained to the ground by ethereal straps of white magic.

At once, the paladins left their wounded and fled. Refugees poured from the broken wagons and ruined campsites to run with their fellow humans. Dozens of them fleet of foot enough to keep pace despite their injuries joined the frantic retreat.

"Thank you," Gideon commended Corvus as he ran alongside the man and guided his footsteps. "That beast was unlike anything I've ever fought."

"Your sword," Corvus panted, struggling to match Gideon's long stride. "Why did it remain on your back?"

"Vrysinoch does not protect me any longer," Gideon said without a trace of doubt or regret. "How did you push the orcs back like that? I've never seen anything like it."

Panting and holding onto Gideon's arm desperately, Corvus could barely keep up. "I do not know," he muttered between breaths. "And I don't know how long it will last."

SEAMUS SAW THE running paladins and refugees and rushed to wake Asterion. He shook the old man violently by the shoulder. Thankfully, the wizened man was easily roused from his exhausted slumber and slowly made it to his feet.

"Get ready to move!" Gideon shouted as he came into sight of Asterion, Seamus, and the goblins.

Without hesitation, Asterion dove his mind back into the realm of magic and began weaving together a spell.

"No!" Corvus yelled. "You're too weak!"

Asterion ignored him and continued stitching together the edges of a brilliant white circle that floated just inches from the ground.

With Gideon's help, Corvus slid to a stop next to the stooped over man and begged him to stop. "Asterion..." he panted, "you'll kill yourself. Your body can't keep using magic!"

When it became apparent Asterion had no intention of interrupting his spell, Corvus grit his teeth and tried to summon what remained of his energy to aid the old man and keep him from dying of exertion. The clangor of the running refugees and disorganized paladins was too much for Corvus to ignore. His concentration slipped and he was simply too tired to summon his last reserves.

At once, Corvus felt the magic that bound the orc assault party dissipate as keenly as if it had been a tree branch struck by lightning next to his ear. "They're coming!" he cried out, clutching his head with dizziness. "The orcs are coming!" Only a moment later, sounds of orc battle cries floated across the small expanse of plain to the huddled mass around Asterion.

"Whatever you're doing, you need to hurry up, old man!" Gideon shouted. "There won't be any of us left to save!" Instinctively, he reached for the hilt of his sword. His fingers brushed against Nevidal's cold metal. Gideon grimaced.

"I need a weapon," he growled at the paladins with his fingers twitching where his axes used to hang.

"Your sword," Vorst pointed to the weapon on his back.

Gideon looked wistfully to the sky. "I... I don't know what will happen."

"Here," one of the paladins strode next to Gideon and held out his shield. "Take the spear. Pull it out gently so you don't crack the tip."

"Huh," Gideon removed the orc spear from the man's shield and tossed it from hand to hand. It was poorly crafted, far too heavy, and sported a slight bend in the shaft near the base. "Thanks, I guess," he told the man as he turned to place himself between the cowering refugees and the screaming orcs.

"Through the portal!" Corvus' voice rose above the sounds of chaos. Gideon turned to see a white disc of blazing light spread flat on the stony ground. It was large enough for one man to pass through at a time.

"Where's it go?" Seamus asked with wonder, staring into the brilliant depths. He thought he could make out a face on the other side, beckoning him through, but it turned out to only be his reflection.

"The star room beneath the Tower of Wings," Asterion said, wearily taking a step and vanishing into the white disc. His body passed through the portal as easily as if it was water, and then he was gone.

"Everyone through the portal!" Corvus yelled. He tried to add a subtle magical component to his voice to make the words ring out farther, but even such a small cantrip proved too taxing. Several of the closest refugees approached the portal with apprehension, but when Seamus shoved one in the back and he fell through without so much as a shout of dismay, the rest of the refugees swarmed in.

"My baby..." one of the women sobbed. She clutched the infant tightly to her chest and refused to jump into the portal.

The first orcs to reach the group crashed against a disorganized assembly of paladins guarding a nearly indiscernible rise in the land. The dying screams of men and orcs alike joined the confused shouts of the remaining refugees.

"I'll take her myself," Corvus snapped at the woman angrily. Not knowing exactly where she was, Corvus attempted to rip the babe from her arms, but succeeded only in ramming the back of his fist into the mother's jaw and knocking her backward. With a sound like wind through a bellows, she fell through the portal to safety.

377

Seamus shrugged and helped the last group of refugees through the portal before jumping in after them. A thrown orc knife clipped Corvus in the arm and he knew his men would all die if they didn't get to the portal.

"Retreat!" he yelled, waving in the direction of the battle sounds. "To safety!"

Slowly, the paladins formed into a small line and marched in reverse. More than a dozen of the men had fallen atop the rise, but their shields still held firm with magic.

Gravlox felt the familiar surge of the earth as he rent it up into the sky. The ground enjoyed the release almost as much as the shaman did. When he ran his fingers through the dirt and let his mind drift into the soil, the very bedrock begged for freedom. Rocks flew in every direction as Gravlox lifted a chunk of earth the size of a modest tavern into the air. As though he were gently moving a glass vial on a shelf, Gravlox moved his hand through the air and sent the massive pile of dirt and stone hurtling in front of the paladins. Nearly a score of orcs were crushed beneath it before they could react.

"Let's go," Gravlox said to Vorst with determination. She nodded and the two sprinted toward the portal.

Taking full advantage of their momentary reprieve, Gideon guided the remaining paladins through the portal. Before he could step through, a hand shot across the shimmering disc and stopped him. "The star room..." Corvus warned him.

"I know," Gideon grunted in reply. "Better chances there than here," he scoffed as he brushed past Corvus' arm and dropped through the barrier of light.

Corvus heard the goblins speaking and knew they were about to step through. "You may die," he said quickly, listening for the sounds of orcs.

"I know." Vorst grabbed the blind man's hand, wrapped her other arm around Gravlox's waist, and jumped into the portal.

Seamus, the last to make the journey, tumbled into the star room beneath the Tower of Wings only a heartbeat before an orc spear ripped through the space where he had been standing.

Seventeen

NEARLY SIXTY HUMANS, groaning and clutching at various wounds, stumbled through the cramped star room beneath the Tower of Wings. The paladins helped the refugees to their feet and escorted them to the lobby of the tower. There was much work to do and the men were eager to begin preparing the defenses of the city.

"Only those blessed by Vrysinoch may set foot in the star room..." Gideon muttered. He helped Corvus to his feet and sought out the goblin pair. "And yet here I stand."

Vorst felt something release from the back of her consciousness. Like a wild horse breaking from a heavy yoke, her mind ran free. Truly *free*. "Gravlox!" she shouted. "I can't feel her! She's gone!" Vorst's mind ran so quickly she could barely speak. Her words came out as an elated jumble of goblin and human sounds that did little to convey her joy.

Gravlox glanced up at Vorst once, but soon let his attention drift back to the metal circlet on his head. Something was wrong — terribly wrong. Gravlox knew beyond a doubt crossing through the portal had been a mistake. Angrily, he shouldered past the jumping Vorst and left the room before his mind could be further tainted.

The shaman slumped against the intricately adorned wall outside the star room and attempted to weave his mind through the magical passageways he had grown accustomed to. He placed his hands against the ground and tried to force his mind into the earth. Only minutes ago, he had spoken to the magical essence of the earth as easily as if it was an only friend. Now, after exiting the star room, Gravlox felt as though chewing a tunnel through bedrock back to Kanebullar Mountain would be easier than conjuring a simple shamanistic spell.

Gravlox flung the enchanted circlet against the opposite wall in disgust.

"I'm free!" Vorst shouted once more, bounding from the room with a smile plastered to her face. She tugged at Gravlox's arm, searching for acknowledgement, but found none.

"I'm dead, Vorst," he finally muttered, barely audible. "My mind is dead." As if to prove his point, Gravlox ran his hands over a flagstone on the ground. Commanding the rock to lift into the air and do his bidding should have been a minimally taxing chore. Despite his most powerful mental concentration, Gravlox could not bring the stone to do as much as gently vibrate.

He got up from the wall and gave the circlet a swift kick for good measure before ascending the staircase at the end of the underground corridor.

"Don't you get it?" Vorst begged with tears welling up in her soft eyes. "I'm finally free..." All her life, Lady Scrapple's presence had been a subtle and persistent itch inside the back of her skull she could never satisfy.

Vorst couldn't help but imagine all of the wonderful new possibilities life without the threat of mental occupation would afford her. She could travel near to Kanebullar Mountain, perhaps even sneak inside, without being instantly detected and overpowered. Somehow, stepping into the star room had triggered some kind of Vrysinoch-powered defense that severed magical connections. To Vorst, Gravlox's sudden loss of ability was practically meaningless.

"I'm free," she repeated dozens of times. She could not have asked for a greater gift from the winged god of mankind.

"Are you alright?" Corvus asked Asterion once he was certain he was in front of the correct man. Asterion's magical signature within Corvus' vision was almost opaque. While it retained a particularly large shape Corvus easily recognized, it was eerily dark, unlike the shimmering white it should have been.

The old priest gave a cough and a meek nod. "How many... did we leave behind?" he asked without opening his weary eyes.

"We held off the orcs," Corvus said, but there was no happiness in his voice. "We got the refugees home safely. But there were hardly any left to save..."

Asterion's face twisted into a frown that made the wrinkles around his mouth appear far deeper than they were. "Gideon was right... we were too late."

"Damn the orcs!" Corvus let his emotions run wild. "There are more of them still alive out there! More refugees!" He slammed his fist into the bone wall of the star room and knocked several remains from their resting places. "We must go back. There are more refugees still hiding among the rubble."

"There are," Asterion whispered. "Of that, you can be certain. But they will be little more than corpses by time you reach them again."

Leaving so many people to die violent deaths at the hands of a rampaging orc clan was too much for Corvus to try and accept. "We'll take horses! The fastest horses! We can make it back to the caravan in four days!" Even as he spoke, Corvus knew the caravan was at least a week's ride from Talonrend. The refugees would likely die in less than a few hours when the orc clan fell upon them once more.

"They are with Vrysinoch now, Corvus," Asterion chided. "Pray for their souls, but keep them out of your mind."

Corvus turned from the old priest and shook his head. "It isn't fair," he told the bones that lined the walls. "We could have saved them..."

The sound of metal scraping against metal drew the attention of everyone still in the star room. In the corner farthest from the door, Gideon held Nevidal firmly in one hand and the sword's sheath in the other. With a grunt, he dropped the sheath the ground and wrapped both of hands around Nevidal's hilt.

The few remaining paladins gasped and backed away. They had heard stories and knew what drawing the blade meant.

"Gideon," Asterion said with authority that denied his exhaustion. He opened his eyes and watched him swing the weapon slowly through the air. "Think, Gideon," Asterion spoke.

Silent tension filled the room and refused to let anyone breathe. Moving lightly about the corner of the room, Gideon executed a short practice routine with the weapon as though he was preparing for a fight in the arena.

Turning back to stare Asterion directly in the eyes, Gideon tossed the blade from one hand to the other.

In an instant, a storm cloud of ire washed over Gideon's visage and he slammed Nevidal into the ground with a primal scream. He left the room, and his sword, behind without another word.

"Where will we go?" Vorst asked Corvus as he exited the star room. Asterion hobbled along at the man's side. "Is it safe?"

Corvus thought for a moment before responding. "I will speak to Herod on your behalf," he declared with a smile.

"What makes you think he will listen?" Asterion posited. "The prince has been known to be rather stubborn at times."

Corvus' mind wandered back to before he lost his vision. He had never met the prince of Talonrend, or anyone of royal blood, for that matter. He used to be a regular paladin—one of dozens. Being a natural leader, he had risen to a favored position among the other paladins on the road, but that was when there had been people to protect. Miles from Talonrend, the ascended paladin commanded significant respect and obedience. Inside Terror's Lament, Corvus was unsure of his station.

"I suppose..." he thought aloud, "that I would have very little influence over the prince's mind, even if I were to speak with him."

Asterion chuckled and let out a long sigh. "Perhaps you two could claim one of the abandoned houses near the Tower as your own? On the other side of the Clawflow, how do goblins live? Do you build houses in your society?"

Vorst shook her head. Thinking about Kanebullar Mountain filled her with both trepidation and joy. "I lived in a cave next to my shop," she explained. Vorst tried to recall memories of the mountain—the smells, the constant and familiar temperature, the calm darkness of the winding tunnels—but she could not. Scraps of memories floated to her mind like leaves sinking into a rushing stream. For a brief moment, Vorst had to consider the possibility that her memories of her home were somehow linked to Lady Scrapple's mind.

"Are you alright?" Asterion asked, staring down at her stern expression.

"Yes..." she replied. "Just..." Vorst didn't know how to begin to explain her newly acquired mental freedom and the consequences that came with it. She could barely fathom it herself. "One of the abandoned houses should be fine," she finally declared.

GIDEON, A TOWER of seething violence, stormed through the lower levels of the Tower of Wings. Smashing marble busts and priceless portraits as he went, the furious man climbed the twelve staircases that led to the highest floor. A banded wooden door met him at the top.

His fists pounded into the door relentlessly. "Archbishop!" he yelled between strikes. "Open the damned door!" There was no response.

"Archbishop!" he continued to shout until his voice was hoarse. Finally, one of the door's metal bands began to splinter and cave inwards. Gideon snatched a small marble statuette from a pillar next to the door and used it to pry open one of the planks. After a great deal of work, he had enough room to reach an arm inside and lift the locking bar from its place.

The wooden door swung open silently. Gideon hesitated. He had never before set foot inside the Archbishop's quarters. In fact, he had only seen the Archbishop a handful of times, and always from afar. He remembered the man to be portly, with thick red hair and a wispy beard that grew down to his chest.

Gideon took a slow step over the threshold and called out once more. A bird clattered against the glass wall, but all else was frighteningly still. A huge mirror stood against one of the circular walls next to a delicate tapestry showing Vrysinoch flying above the citizens of Talonrend.

"Archbishop?" Gideon called once more. A thin curtain separated a small sleeping nook from the rest of the single suite. For all the opulence of the tower, Gideon had expected lavish furnishings fit for a king. The meager trappings in the room made him uneasy. He keenly felt Nevidal's absence and instinctively reached for an axe on his belt, forgetting that they had all been lost.

Gideon grumbled and cracked his knuckles. He didn't expect a fight, but something about the man's quarters greatly unnerved him. "Archbishop?" he called once more to no avail. His hand felt the edge of the simple cloth guarding the sleeping quarters and Gideon slowly pulled it back. The stench of death stung his nostrils and made him turn away.

Rot had set in long ago. The Archbishop's body was crumpled in the corner of the sleeping area with a dagger buried to the hilt in his chest. "Murder..."

Gideon ran down the winding staircases as quickly as he could. "Asterion!" he called out, finding the old priest asleep in a high-backed chair. "Asterion!" he shook him from his slumber.

"Yes? Can't it wait?" he protested. His frail body looked worse than ever. It was obvious the creation of the portal had nearly killed him.

"I'm sorry," Gideon stammered. "The Archbishop is dead." Gideon didn't know any other way to say it.

"What?" Asterion roared, suddenly alive with uncharacteristic anger. "You *killed* the Archbishop?"

Bewildered at the accusation, Gideon took a step backward and held his hands out before him. "What? No!" he yelled, pointing to the staircase. "He was murdered!"

Asterion narrowed his eyes at Gideon. "Why didn't you just say that?" the priest chided. Breathing heavily from his sudden outburst, Asterion turned and began to slowly climb the many stairs that led to the top of the Tower of Wings.

When they reached the top, Asterion took a long moment to collect himself and slow his heart rate. "You know, I've only been in this room once before," he said. The priest inspected the broken panel of the banded door with a frown. "When the goblins were spotted outside the city, I came here to deliver the news to the Archbishop. As a battle priest, I would have been given command of the paladins. As you said before, the paladins could have held the field for days against the siege."

Gideon suppressed the anger that made his hands ball into fists. "What was his reasoning? Why stand down?"

Asterion sighed. "He warned of a trap," he said with a shrug. "The Archbishop feared moving the paladins outside the city would make them vulnerable. When I tried to reason with him, he sent me away and told me he would take command of the soldiers personally should the need arise. So we sat in the Tower throughout the entire battle." There was more guilt in Asterion's voice than anything else.

Gideon pushed the broken door open and stepped lightly into the Archbishop's quarters once more. The same bird clattered noisily against the glass wall and flew away.

"Perhaps," Asterion pondered, "the Archbishop was not in his right mind in the days prior to the siege?" He pulled the curtain away from the sleeping area and covered his mouth with a hand. "He has certainly been dead for quite some time," he remarked.

"Who would have reason to kill him?" Gideon asked. While he had always resented the theocratic leadership, he had never *seriously* considered killing the Archbishop himself.

"I heard tales the royal assistant turned out to be a conspirator in league with the goblins." Asterion slowly removed the dagger from the Archbishop's gut and inspected it. "Preventing the paladins from leaving the tower certainly helped his cause, I do believe."

Gideon mulled over the possibilities. "How could a human ever choose to help goblins?"

Asterion laughed aloud and set the dagger down on the Archbishop's bed. "Have you not done that very thing? Haven't we all?" he jested.

"You know what I meant," Gideon scowled. For all of his resentment toward Vrysinoch, the Archbishop, and almost every authority figure he had ever met, Gideon loved Talonrend and could not imagine betraying his city.

"We must tell Herod, if the prince still lives," Asterion said, tossing the dagger next to the Archbishop's corpse.

"Let me get my sword," Gideon said with a sigh. His empty scabbard made him feel like less of a man. He had carried Nevidal on his back every single day since Master Brenning had made it for him a dozen or so years before. He had still been a paladin in good standing then, before he forsook the life of religion and decided to write his own destiny.

Asterion and Gideon descended the stairs slowly. The priest's old legs were so wracked with exhaustion he was barely able to walk. With Gideon's supporting arm, they made it back into the bowels of the Tower of Wings and stood before the open door of the star room once more.

"I'm not sure why Vrysinoch has cast me out so completely," Gideon remarked. "The moment I stepped inside that room, I could feel him abandon me. Why is the star room different from the rest of the Tower, Asterion? Why have I been punished for entering?"

Asterion leaned against the stone wall and shook his head. "The star room has always been shrouded in mystery," he explained. "I was first taken here on the night of my ordination, much like the paladins are when they complete their first segment of training. We were taught to speak to the bones, and they readily responded. However, none of the priests could explain *how* the spirits of the dead have remained here. The star room is a sacred place, of that I have no doubt. I'm sorry you were forced to enter, but I knew no other way."

"Do not blame yourself, Asterion," Gideon said. "You did the right thing." With a hesitant step, Gideon crossed the threshold into the room once more. He tensed, waiting for a sensation, anything, that would indicate the presence of Vrysinoch. Besides a slight temperature drop, he felt nothing. The bones were silent.

Gideon wrapped a hand around Nevidal's hilt. He flexed and pulled, but the blade did not budge. Using both of his hands, Gideon tried to wrench the sword from the soft earth that held it, but he could not even begin to move the weapon.

Suddenly, as Gideon let his hands fall from the hilt, he felt Vrysinoch's presence rush back to him. The holy symbol tattooed on his shoulder flared brilliantly to life and Gideon's mind swam in the presence of the deity.

You are not worthy to wield my blade, Gideon of Talonrend. Vrysinoch's hissing voice flooded his consciousness and overwhelmed his senses. *You abandoned me long ago...*

Gideon grunted and fell to his knees. With all the mental fortitude he could muster, Gideon tried to force Vrysinoch from his mind. Like a twig pushing against a mountain, Vrysinoch did not leave.

Such arrogance! Vrysinoch screeched in his mind. The piercing voice was enough to make Gideon's eardrums throb and rattle with pain. *You think to command me?* Vrysinoch laughed and cawed. The god's voice, part human and part avian, rang with a hint of palpable magic that Asterion could feel from the doorway. The old priest took a step back and began reciting prayers for Gideon's safety.

"What more do you want from me?" Gideon spat. He grabbed Nevidal's hilt again and pulled himself up to his knees. "How many more souls?"

Vrysinoch's hideous laugh filled the room and shook hundreds of bones from their resting places along the walls. For a moment, Gideon feared the star room might collapse and bring the entire Tower of Wings crashing down on his head.

There is only one more soul you must harvest, Gideon of Talonrend. With a flash of light, the star room erupted with whirling souls. Ghastly blue images danced around the room before congealing into a single image. Seated on two powerful legs before Gideon was the image of a massive, skeletal dragon. The dragon pulsed with power, but did not move.

"You want me to slay a dragon..." Gideon breathed in disbelief. "It cannot be done."

The souls began to slowly fade, or so it appeared. Like liquid dripping from the floor into the air above, fragments of the ghostly image seeped away from the dragon's body. Gideon stared with wonder as the skeletal beast started melting apart. Then, with a snap, the dripping cords of oozing ghost violently straightened above the dragon's body.

Gideon studied the image, but couldn't understand. "I'm sorry," he whispered. He feared if he failed Vrysinoch one more time, it wouldn't be his sword stuck to the floor of the star room—it would be his soul.

"Marionette strings..." Asterion muttered from the doorway with an awestruck expression. As soon as the words left his lips, the image of the dragon vanished and the room became uncomfortably silent.

Gideon gave one final tug on Nevidal's hilt before exiting the room. "What does it mean?" he asked.

"I can't be sure," Asterion hesitantly replied, "but I believe you are to find a skeletal dragon and slay the one who controls it."

Gideon scoffed and made for the staircase. "Sounds easy," he called over his shoulder. "Especially without my sword."

THE DRAWBRIDGE LEADING to Castle Talon creaked beneath Gideon's weight. Men with crossbows guarded the parapet, but they were few and far between. "Does the prince still live?" Gideon called out to one of them.

"As of this morning," the man responded. Gideon could see the awe in the young soldier's eyes as he watched Gideon enter the keep. Apparently, several weeks of absence hadn't diminished his reputation among the common soldiers.

Upon entering the keep's audience chamber, the rent throne gave Gideon pause. He remembered the first time he had ever set foot in Castle Talon. Prince Herod had charged him from the throne's dais, but Gideon had easily overpowered the smaller man. A speck of dried blood still marked the spot where Nevidal's hilt had smashed Herod's face during their duel. Gideon smirked. "A king should be a better fighter," he told the broken throne.

Herod's bedchamber was frigidly cold. Silk curtains still hung in the air, but cold wind blew in from outside. "Herod," Gideon said after a guard announced his presence. "Good to see you're still alive, my prince."

One of the armed attendants in the room gathered several of the curtains together and tied them to the wall behind Herod's bed. "I'm afraid I haven't moved much since last we spoke," the dying prince responded. Herod's body had vastly deteriorated. Bed sores coated the undersides of his arms and his hair had been shaved in anticipation of it falling out.

"I bring grave news," Gideon told him. He waved the attendants out of the room and Herod nodded, sending them scurrying into the hallway.

"Are you here to tell me that Talonrend has been attacked and most of her citizens have fled?" Herod jested, coughing up a bit of phlegm in the process. "There is far little I can image that could be considered worse news."

Gideon let his head hang low. "The refugees are dead."

Thick silence filled every inch of the room. After a long moment, Herod wheezed and broke the silence, but did not speak.

"How many are left in the city?" Gideon finally asked.

Herod let another solemn moment pass before answering. "Just over a thousand Templars and guardsmen, maybe three thousand citizens, and only a few hundred skilled craftsmen and merchants. Many of the militia stayed, but they are farmers unaccustomed to life in Talonrend and away from their fields. Most of them now patrol the walls."

"How long will the stores last?"

"They'll last," Herod said with a shred of confidence. "We were stocked to support well over ten thousand for nearly a year. If you don't mind stale grains, you'll have plenty of food."

"We brought some of the refugees back." Gideon explained. "But not nearly enough."

"How many?"

"A hundred, give or take a dozen. Almost half of them are paladins from the Tower."

"Finally, some good news," Herod chuckled meekly. "Although if we are to rebuild, it is tradesmen, builders, and smiths we will need, not soldiers."

Gideon nodded. "Has there been any news from the villages along the Clawflow? Have there been any goblin or orc sightings?"

"Orc?" Herod questioned, "I've not heard of orcs coming near Talonrend for decades."

"We fought them on the road," Gideon said. "Two different clans, by my estimation."

The prince tried to speak but was beset by another bout of pained coughing. He convulsed and spat dark blood onto the sheets. One of the attendants rushed into the room and held a tankard of water to the prince's lips.

Gideon took a step backward and watched the servant work. "I should go," he stated when it became apparent that Herod's voice would not return quickly.

"Wait," he managed to gasp between wet coughs.

Gideon stopped short of the doorway and turned back to the prince.

"When I die... Apollonius...." Herod wheezed so violently his head knocked the jug of water from the attendant's hands. "Apollonius will support... you... for the throne..."

Gideon felt like he had just been hit with a smith's hammer in the center of his chest. "Herod, I..." He was at a loss for words. A thousand different thoughts rushed through his head. Behind all of them, the image of a skeletal dragon flitted through his mind.

"I forgot," Gideon quickly said to change the subject, "the Archbishop was murdered."

Herod shook his head dismissively as he pounded on his chest to get his lungs to cooperate. The news of the Archbishop's untimely demise didn't seem to faze the prince. Herod stretched out one of his hands to signal Gideon to leave.

Two other armed attendants entered the room with wet cloths and more water. The glint of metal caught Gideon's eye. On a peg

392

near the door, Herod's magisterial tabard hung loosely over his sword belt. Maelstrom and Regret, Master Brenning's most legendary creations, rested calmly under a thin layer of dust.

Gideon waited a moment before reaching a hand out and touching the leather of the sword belt. No one inside the cold room noticed his movement. Gideon let out a sigh and thought of Nevidal trapped in the floor of the star room. He let his hand fall back to his side and took a step into the hallway.

"Fine," Gideon conceded, keenly feeling the absence of his own weapons. He took a step back into the room and quickly snatched the sword belt from the wooden peg. Without any means of properly concealing his theft, Gideon strapped the swords around his waist and pulled his travelling cloak tightly around his body as he walked out of the castle.

GIDEON WAS HALFWAY through the center of Talonrend when Apollonius found him. "Gideon!" the soldier called out. "I heard you had arrived."

"What of it?" Gideon responded, holding his cloak shut in front of him. The hilts of his new swords poked up under the cloth of the cloak, but Apollonius didn't seem to notice.

"Have you spoken to the prince?" the young captain inquired. He wore his military armor complete with golden epaulettes and a short sword laden with emeralds identifying him as the captain of the guard.

"I have," Gideon responded. "He does not look well."

Apollonius took a step closer and lowered his voice, despite the two men being alone on the deserted streets. "I fear the prince will not last more than another week. When he meets Vrysinoch —"

"You will be king," Gideon cut him off. "You have the support of the military and that is all that matters." Apollonius looked bewildered. He shook his head and started to protest, but Gideon interrupted him again. "There are orcs coming from the west and a band of minotaurs is working with them. There might be more. Send couriers to the villages along the Clawflow and get the people inside the walls. When the orcs arrive, the goblins will be surely be with them."

"No," Apollonius stammered. "*You're* to be the new king!" he practically shouted.

Gideon pushed past the man in the direction of the Tower of Wings. "I have a dragon's master to kill," he said flatly, rubbing his palms over the hilts of Maelstrom and Regret.

"The bone dragon?" Apollonius wondered aloud with obvious confusion.

Gideon turned on his heel and looked the younger man in the eyes. "Where?" he demanded like a criminal asking for ransom.

"The dragon..." Apollonius' eyes grew wide. "It formed from the bones of the goblins outside the walls... We..."

A huge smile broke out on Gideon's face. Finally, after years of living an uncertain life, he knew exactly what it would take to earn the favor of Vrysinoch. "Thank you, Apollonius," Gideon said with a refreshing wave of calm. He continued in the direction of the Tower—he needed to find Gravlox and Vorst and learn everything he could about the leader of Kanebullar Mountain.

SEVERAL HUNDRED MINOTAURS descended from the foothills to join the two orc clans as they assembled on the plains three score miles west of Talonrend. Undrakk, the mysterious half-orc shaman, walked ahead of the thunderous group with all the authority and respect of a king.

Atop the rocky rise where the humans had made their magical escape, the war counsel convened. Snarlsnout sat on his stone platform like a god dedicated to gluttony. Slaves brought him mashed pieces of rancid goat meat that he noisily slurped from wooden bowls.

Next to Snarlsnout, Gurr paced nervously back and forth. The minotaurs, taller and broader of chest than even the largest of orcs, made the fierce warlord uneasy. In addition to the minotaur presence, Gurr also felt a fresh pang of defeat—something he had not experienced in a long, long time. He was hungry for human flesh and vengeance.

Kraasghull, the newly appointed leader of the Wolf Jaw Clan, sat cross-legged on the ground a few paces from the Half Goat entourage. After Jurnorgel's death, Kraasghull was unsure of how to lead the Wolf Jaw Clan. The warriors were restless and in the presence of their ancestral nemesis, Kraasghull was unable to prevent brawls and murders from tearing the two clans apart. Only the overwhelming threat of the minotaurs was able to hold the alliance together.

Undrakk stepped forward to address the gathering. "Chieftains," he began with a twirl of his magical staff. "The time has almost come." He dipped into a low bow and ushered the minotaur leader forward to introduce him. "This is Qul, the leader of the northern clans."

"*King* of the Mountains!" Qul corrected as he strode forth. The minotaur king was beyond monstrous. He stood somewhere over fourteen feet tall and weighed as much as several draft horses combined. In full battle regalia, his armored chest was as thick as Undrakk was tall. For weapons, Qul had two metal clubs strapped over his back most humans wouldn't even be able lift from the ground. Qul disdained slicing weapons such as axes and swords. When the minotaur king engaged in battle, he wanted to hear the bones of his foes snapping with every strike.

"Soon I will be king of the world!" he bellowed. A silver medallion around his neck let Qul communicate and understand most of the common languages including the human and orc tongues. It changed his speech from the gruff language of the minotaurs to a dialect the assembled orcs could certainly understand.

Snarlsnout, from his vantage point above the rest of the orcs, could not see the top of Qul's hairy head. He looked beyond the towering beast to the gathered army Qul had brought with him. Unlike orcs who charged into battle wearing very light armor so as to remain agile, minotaurs dressed for war much like a castle would prepare for heavy bombardment. They wore large plates of solid metal that covered nearly every inch of their muscled bodied.

It made sense, Snarlsnout had to admit. Orcs always relied on numbers and ferocity in battle. Like goblins, they were relatively easy to replace. A single orc female could produce more than a dozen other orcs in her lifetime and orc children were ready for the battlefield by the age of five. The advantage of the minotaurs was just the opposite. A single minotaur trained for war could slaughter orcs for hours before falling. Although Snarlsnout had little previous interaction with the mountain-dwelling clans, he knew that incubating a minotaur in the womb took nearly two years and birth frequently killed the mother. While the females of the Half Goat Clan were certainly with the army, few of them were soldiers. As Snarlsnout surveyed the gathered minotaurs, he suspected that every single adult member of the clan was dressed for battle.

"Remind me never to piss off a minotaur clan," he mumbled to no one in particular. He glanced down at Gurr and shook his head. The foolhardy orc had puffed out his chest in an attempt to look intimidating, but even Gurr knew that Qul would utterly destroy him in battle.

"We are one week's march from the high walls of Talonrend," Undrakk explained to the gathering. Qul took a step back and respectively lowered his head as Undrakk spoke. Snarlsnout noted the small gesture of obedience with a curious look.

"I have seen their walls," Kraasghull interjected. "How will we bring them down?"

A few scattered murmurs came from the orcs, but the minotaurs remained peacefully silent.

Undrakk smiled and spread his arms out wide. The sounds of wings beating the air swelled up from somewhere north of the armies and Snarlsnout looked to the sky. His rheumy eyes could barely make out the small black dots rising into the air from behind the minotaur lines.

"We will go over them," Undrakk yelled with glee. "Talonrend will be ours!"

TAURNIL CLACKED HIS oily black claws together with glee. The small scorpion stood before a pool of shimmering black liquid that flowed from a carved stone skull. His master's energy roiled with energy waiting to be unleashed.

Your brothers have joined the orcs, Keturah's voice echoed through the chamber. Taurnil could feel her joy. *It is time for you to free us.*

Taurnil skittered through the chamber of broken eggs and slowly made his way to the cave opening where the bodies of several minotaurs were still strewn about on the stone. Using Taurnil's many eyes, Jan and Keturah inspected the corpses.

That one, Keturah purred as Taurnil approached a dead minotaur that still had all of its limbs. The small scorpion reared back on its hind legs and punched its inky black stinger into the flesh of the minotaur. Putrid liquid from the cave rushed from Taurnil's tail and into the minotaur's vein.

Jan telepathically directed Taurnil to another corpse where the scorpion's tail stinger struck again. Within moments, the black liquid of the phylactery corrupted the two minotaur corpses completely and the once-dead creatures began to stir. Keturah's stolen heart slowly beat to life, but no blood flowed through her organs.

"It worked, brother," she said from the ground as her muscles awakened. Her human voice grated with the heavy vocal cords of the minotaur's neck, but they functioned nonetheless.

It took several long moments for Jan and Keturah to fully enslave the muscle structures of their new minotaur bodies. Keturah was the first to stand. With a lumbering stretch, she tested the colossal size of the beast she inhabited. "You were right to have Gideon brought here," she said awkwardly. Her thick bovine tongue slurred her words. "He delivered the finest bodies we could have hoped for."

Jan and Keturah, both occupying similar male bodies, lumbered from the cave entrance with as much grace as a drunk being tossed out of a tavern. "I could get used to this," Jan remarked, feeling his massive body with his rough hands. Despite his breath frosting the wintry air, the thick hair covering his body kept him warm. He flexed and watched with wonder as his muscles bulged all over his arms and chest.

"You better get used to it, brother," Keturah chided. She tried to adjust her brown mane into a more feminine position, but soon gave up. "I don't know if the phylactery will hold our spirits again. The magic is not permanent."

"Speaking of which," Jan remarked, "I need to test my abilities. We were in that cave for weeks, right next to the eggs. They soaked up every ounce of magical energy they could."

"Let's move," Keturah said flatly. She was eager to test her powerful legs and thundering hooves on the rocky soil. "It will take a few days to reach Talonrend."

Keturah began pumping her legs and any hint of regret she might have had washed away. Her new body was incredibly powerful. Even wearing heavy plate armor over her thighs and torso, she was faster than any human she had ever seen. Competitions of strength and physical ability were often held between pit fights in the Talonrend arena and she had seen many foot races. No human compared to her speed. Her hooves pounded against the stony soil and sent clumps of dirt and rocks flying up behind her. As her pace continued to increase, Keturah felt her chest heaving and her ribcage shifting lower against her center of mass. Before she knew it, her hands hit the ground as balled fists and she began galloping, nearly doubling her speed.

Jan ran up alongside her, matching her stride, and grinned. Before his human form had died outside Terror's Lament, Jan's only fear had been facing a trained soldier in single combat. Without the use of his powerful magical abilities, he was nothing more than an average built man with little muscle and even less tenacity. Jan knew without a doubt his minotaur body would be able to easily crush any human who stood in his way.

Eighteen

GRAVLOX PACED BACK and forth on the creaky floorboards of an abandoned home. Dust covered everything and the only window was covered with a wooden shutter. In the darkness, his goblin vision allowed him to see as clearly as if it were bright sunlight. In more ways than one, he felt like he was back in the tunnels of Kanebullar Mountain.

When he called out with his mind to the realm of magic, he achieved nothing more than a minor headache. He ran his hands along the stone walls and tried to speak to them. After one final effort, he collapsed into an old wooden chair and lifted his feet up to a small stool. The human furniture was far too large for his body, but he slouched and made the best of it.

Gravlox looked down at his clothes and let out a long sigh of despair. During all of the fighting and running and fleeing, he had dropped his traveling pack and the sword Vorst had given him. His enchanted circlet was still somewhere in the star room, and he was left with only his leather vest and studded skirt.

"I am nothing," he told the three empty chairs around the table. His stomach growled and he couldn't remember the last time he had eaten. While he required far less food than the larger humans and his body remained efficient with only minor sustenance, he still felt strong pangs of hunger that soured his mood.

With a grunt, Gravlox carried one of the wooden chairs into another room and placed it beneath a cabinet. Using the chair as a ladder, he was barely able to reach the bottom of the cabinet. After a moment of blindly groping with his hand, he found a chunk of bread stale enough to be used as a blacksmith's hammer. He brought the bread down to the table and eagerly began scraping the green and blue mold from the surface into a little pile. When he had the bread entirely cleaned, he tossed it aside and began mashing the mold into a gooey ball. It wasn't nearly as desirable as the white cave mold he often ate in the mines of Kanebullar Mountain, but it tasted good enough.

Gravlox was about to search another cabinet when he heard Vorst's voice from outside. Back in his home, Gravlox had nearly swooned every time he heard her squeaky voice. At that moment, so consumed by self-loathing and doubt, it grated against his ears and made him wince. He trudged to a door at the back of the house and yelled at her to be quiet.

In her typical manner, Vorst ignored his chastisement and continued leaping through the air and rolling through grass and flowers. Behind the abandoned house, there was a small courtyard encased by three other houses in a square pattern. The small goblin couldn't be seen, but her piercing voice surely carried through the surrounding buildings and into the streets.

Gravlox stood in the back doorway for several long moments as he contemplated his sudden return to life as an average goblin. A *weak* goblin. He shook his head and bit back a growing lump in his throat. "I want..." He couldn't finish the thought. What did he want? His power to return? Surely. But to what end? Life in a deserted human city, while he had only experienced a few short hours of it, did not hold much appeal.

The front door to the house swung open and brought Gravlox from his trance. Gideon stood in the doorway with his travelling cloak pushed back behind the hilts of two swords. The former paladin strode through the dark room with an air of confidence and determination Gravlox had never seen.

"Vorst!" he called out, waving the goblin to his side. "I've heard tales of a dragon rising from the bones of the goblins in the field," he told her with a gleam in his eyes. "I intend to kill the one who controls the dragon."

Vorst didn't bother to translate the conversation into the goblin language for Gravlox to participate. "Lady Scrapple controls a dragon?" she said with amazement. Her mind reeled and thought of the implications. If the matriarch's mind was so thoroughly consumed by reining in a dragon, was that why her telepathic link to the hive had been lost?

"I need to know everything about Lady Scrapple."

Vorst smiled, but shook her head. "No one sees her," she said softly, suddenly afraid of speaking out. "She lives in the deepest chamber of our mountain, but cannot move." Gideon's perplexed expression made her continue. "She *is* the mountain," Vorst finally said. She had never before attempted to put Lady Scrapple into words. Every goblin was born with an innate sense of what and who the Mistress of the Mountain was. After all, she was a living part of each goblin mind, until Gravlox was born and her link with Vorst was severed.

"If you're going to kill Lady Scrapple," Vorst began, "you need to find the goblins that bring food to her. They will lead you to her cave."

"So she *can* be killed," Gideon concluded with a smile.

"I think so..." Vorst thought back to all the other goblins she knew in the mountain. While she certainly cherished her newly acquired freedom, she wasn't sure the rest of the goblin race would be able to comprehend the death of their master.

"Good," Gideon said as he turned to leave. Vorst took Gravlox by the hand and chased after the man.

"We're coming with you," she stated defiantly. Before Gideon had the chance to protest, she and Gravlox began gathering what little they had and made ready to leave.

"Fine," Gideon replied. He knew there was no use arguing. "You'll need new weapons. I intend to cleave my way through Kanebullar Mountain. We'll have to fight for every inch of ground." Gideon flexed his arms and felt the fleeting warmth of the winter sun on his head. His braided beard swung back and forth as he checked the street for civilians before motioning for the two goblins to leave the abandoned house.

At the city guard's armory, the rescued paladins had gathered with the remaining Templars and militia to discuss the defense of the city. Their patrols were spread thin, but the Templars managed to find enough men to reinforce the western portion of Terror's Lament, a section of wall they had all believed safe just a day earlier. Everywhere he looked, Gideon found soldiers oiling their armor, sharpening blades, and making repairs to their gear. There was an air of easiness and camaraderie in the armory, but he could practically taste the coming war.

As it turned out, Gideon's reputation was not the only one that had spread among the military. The returned paladins had told almost everyone of the heroic exploits of the goblin pair that walked among their midst. Several of the guardsmen went up to Gravlox and offered to shake his hand, a gesture he didn't understand but returned nonetheless.

My magic is gone, Gravlox tapped against Vorst's palm as they walked. *I'm not a good fighter without it.*

I know, was all Vorst curtly responded. She walked ahead of him with her head tilted just barely higher than usual. Gravlox had never been shunned by a female before and the strange feeling hurt. A hundred thoughts raced through his mind, but he pushed them away.

Gideon led them to a storeroom at the back of the armory compound the held rations and proper traveling gear. After a moment, he had a large pack full of enough supplies to last several weeks assembled and strapped to his back. Without Nevidal encumbering his entire torso, Gideon felt he could easily fight without having to abandon the supplies.

One of the younger militiamen that had been watching Gravlox with awe stepped into the storeroom and spoke. "Gideon," he stammered, "I mean... Sir."

Gideon laughed and addressed the younger soldier. "What is it?"

"Well, it's just that..."

"Out with it!" Gideon sarcastically chided to ease the tension.

"I have something that might help them," he blurted out, awkwardly pointing to the two goblins. The guard motioned for the three to stay where they were and ran off.

A short moment later he returned, panting and clutching several items inside a blanket. "I salvaged these from the battlefield," he said with a bit of pride. Gideon knew the man intended to keep the goblin items as trophies, but it didn't matter. They could use whatever help they could get.

The man unrolled his blanket and revealed several goblin swords, a pair of goblin daggers, a crude looking mace, and several pieces of leather armor that looked to be in decent condition.

Immediately, Gravlox found a leather breastplate that fit him well and picked up one of the swords. It was heavier than he was used to, but the hilt fit nicely in his small hand and he knew it was the best weapon he was likely to find. Vorst put two of the daggers through her belt and tied a goblin sword to the inside of her leather vest.

"I can shoot," she said, miming the motion of an archer pulling a bowstring.

Gideon searched the storeroom for a bow but only found longbows designed for hunting and target practice. Vorst was far too small of stature to wield a bow made for a human male.

"I can get you a bow," Gideon reassured her. Although he didn't enjoy the notion of returning to Master Brenning's forge, he knew he would find a bow small enough for a goblin.

Gideon and the two goblins thanked the young soldier and set out into the empty streets once again. On their way to Dragon's Breath Armory, they only crossed by a handful of guards, all of which respectfully nodded and saluted Gideon.

Master Brenning's forge was a colossal building, just as Gideon remembered from his days as an apprentice. Four towering chimneys marked the corners of the forge, but only one of them puffed black smoke into the air. Gideon opened the door and let the familiar heat and smell of the place wash over him.

"Smells like the mines," Gravlox remarked quietly. It was a smell he had known all of his life, but not one he had particularly missed.

Less than a dozen smiths remained at Dragon's Breath Armory and that stark fact shook Gideon to his bones. The fall of Talonrend was something Gideon thought he could learn to accept. All kingdoms rise and all kingdoms fall. In a thousand years, the story of Talonrend would be confined to a few short pages in a history book. Looking at the three cold forges in the large room was like staring at Master Brenning's headstone. When Gideon did his apprenticeship at Dragon's Breath Armory, there were so many smiths that he would often have to wait in a long line just to get access to an anvil to pound out a piece of iron.

Gideon sighed and walked to the back corner of the first floor where most of the ranged weapons were made. Hand crossbows were not commonly crafted by the smiths of such a legendary forge, but they did occasionally make ornamental and ceremonial pieces favored by the wealthy. Gideon found a small hand crossbow hanging from a peg above one of the cold forges and took it down for inspection. The string was made of loosely wound cotton and designed exclusively for appearances. Gideon ripped the cotton string from the weapon and searched through a cabinet of tools until he found a wax and sinew string that he could cut down to fit the smaller frame.

When the alteration had been finished, Gideon tested the hand crossbow and showed Vorst how to operate it. Using a small brass crank of the left side of the weapon, she could easily pull the string back and an automatic latching mechanism would trip, locking the string into place while simultaneously lifting a bolt from a box underneath the bow and placing it in the track. With one pull of the ornate trigger, the hand crossbow fired a metal-tipped bolt forcefully enough to puncture most armor. Gideon pulled a quiver of two dozen bolts from the cabinet and fit it snugly over Vorst's shoulder.

The few smiths that remained in the building watched Gideon and the goblins carefully, but none of them said a word. As the three were about to leave, Gideon thought of returning to the Blood Foundry where Nevidal had been magically entwined with his life essence. It wasn't far from him, only several flights of stairs beneath the ground floor, but it only took a moment for Gideon to realize that returning there would be pointless. Regardless of what immensely powerful weapons Master Brenning might have left there before his untimely death, Vrysinoch would surely prevent Gideon from wielding them.

With a shake of his head and scratch of his thick beard, Gideon led the small group out of the Dragon's Breath Forge. "Get some sleep," he told Vorst and Gravlox. "We leave in the morning for Kanebullar Mountain."

"We don't sleep..." Vorst replied, but she didn't bother explaining her goblin physiology. "We will meet you one street before the gatehouse," she said.

Gideon nodded and walked off through the empty streets of Talonrend toward the guard house to find a bunk for the night.

Nineteen

QUL RECLINED ON a soft heap of cushions and pried a female orc from his naked chest. Several orc women, slaves given to him by the two clans as tribute, were scattered about the lavish tent in various states of abuse and disregard. The minotaur king moved around the tent with all the confidence and authority of a god mingling with his supplicants. He dressed in his battle gear and strapped his two metal poles across his back. His black plate armor weighed nearly four thousand pounds, but Qul had trained relentlessly for combat. During the two decades he spent as a royal guard for the previous king, he would train every morning by attaching ropes to his waist and tying the ends to a heavy log. Weighted down, he would run through the cave systems for several hours before joining the other royal guards for half a day of intense combat training.

One night, when Qul thought himself strong enough to lead the clan, he snuck into the previous king's cavern to facilitate his ascension. Instead of murdering the royal family while they slept as was customary, Qul bellowed, issuing his challenge. Once all five members of the family had been aroused, Qul gave them time to arm themselves before the slaughter began. Even against five, Qul was hardly tested. He was proclaimed king of the minotaur clan within an hour.

The morning sun glinted against the heavy plates of Qul's armor. His royal compound, a set of six tents arranged in a square with guards positioned around the border, smelled of roasting meat and freshly brewed mead.

A smaller minotaur, not that any member of the clan was larger than Qul, brought the king a large bowl of hearty stew and a barrel of mead large enough for a human to use for bathing. The minotaur king enjoyed eating in the open. The strong sun burned his cave-attuned eyes, but he could look upon his entire clan. Cook fires trailed lazy streaks of smoke into the air as the camp collectively awoke. It was a marvelous sight, and Qul relished the glory of being their leader. The minotaur clan, the only band of such creatures known to exist anywhere within a thousand miles of Talonrend, had not marched to war for centuries. Their last campaign, several decades before Qul was born, had been against a rival clan of orcs that had overstepped their bounds. The Falling Star Clan, responsible for several nighttime raids upon the minotaur livestock and food stores, had been completely and utterly annihilated. It had taken over two years of military campaigning, but the very last survivor of the Falling Stars had been hunted and eventually executed.

Qul loved the finality of war. Eradicating the previous royal family had been the most exhilarating experience of his life. In a single battle, he had single-handedly ended a family. One hereditary line had been extinguished by his hand and that fact filled Qul with violent pride. In this war with the humans of Talonrend, he promised himself and his clan that he would extinguish hundreds of family lines, if not thousands. Qul knew there would only be one battle. Minotaurs were not likely to dig in for a siege, and Qul was intent on taking the city in a single afternoon. With the help of a hundred or so winged demons, his fearless warriors would be ferried over the high walls of Talonrend where they would slaughter and pillage until nothing remained.

When he had finished his meal, Qul swept open the flap to the tent that housed his throne and maps. The royal seat, a colossal structure crafted from the bones and skulls of other humanoid races, was surrounded by several of Qul's most trusted battle advisers. The generals welcomed their king with low bows and words of praise. A map was laid out on a wooden table in front of the throne depicting Talonrend and the surrounding hills. Qul took his seat on the throne and commenced the war council with a thump of his fist.

Undrakk, the mysterious half-orc shaman, was the first to speak. "The combined armies will move slowly," he explained, leaning against his staff in the corner of the tent. "It will take four more days to reach the city walls. On the final approach, we need to wait until darkness. They know we are coming, but we might as well retain what advantage we can."

The gathered minotaurs nodded in agreement. Qul knew that his generals were not so much concurring with Undrakk's plan as they were trying to appease the powerful being.

"Is there any cover from the west or the north?" Qul asked, inspecting the map.

"There are small rises in the land here and here," Undrakk showed him with a smile. "We can move out of the foothills to these positions and gather behind the rises. Their lookouts atop the city walls will surely spot the army, but their bows shouldn't have the range to be effective."

Something about the elegant tones of Undrakk's voice mesmerized Qul. The king had never been fond of magic and those who could wield it, but he would readily sacrifice his closest allies and companions if it meant keeping Undrakk on his side. He knew the half-orc exuded confidence that was well earned. The prospect of making an enemy of the shaman terrified Qul.

"Where will the orc clans attack?" Qul asked. He thought of hundreds of wild-eyed orcs charging the high walls of the city and being cut down with ease. He would love to see the two clans torn apart by the human defenders.

"The orcs will wait a mile or so behind this point here," Undrakk stated. He pointed to a third rise marked on the map with a brown line.

"Wait?" Qul questioned. Images of massive orc casualties flittered from his head. "Orcs are not known for their patience." Despite his severe reservations, he decided not to antagonize Undrakk.

"They will this time," Undrakk replied with a slight chuckle. "Once enough minotaurs have been ferried over the walls by our winged demons, your soldiers can open the portcullises and let the orc clans storm the streets."

Another plan began to formulate inside Qul's large bovine skull. *If we never raise the portcullis, the city will be exclusively ours.* The king tried to image what a human throne would look like. His chair had been occupied by several dozen minotaur kings and was an important symbol to his clan. However, a human throne would certainly make a wonderful trophy.

Undrakk snickered as though he could read Qul's thoughts.

"Are you sure the demons can carry us?" One of Qul's generals asked with a hesitant tone. "They are small and sinewy, just skin and bones." Qul had to admit that he held the same reservations.

Undrakk faced the general and casually tossed his staff from hand to hand. "I will ensure that their wings beat hard enough and their arms can support your... stature." He turned to face the massive king and looked over Qul's armored body. "For some of the larger minotaurs," he said with a smirk, "it may take several demons. Luckily, we have plenty."

Qul let out a gruff sigh and waited for the strange half-orc to leave his tent before conferring with his generals. "The orcs will never enter the city," he said them in a low voice. The generals smiled and nodded their agreement. They had been counting on that exact plan.

"When we get to the walls, we can take them easily. That is our first objective." Qul looked each of his generals squarely in the eyes and was met by intense stares of unquenchable bloodlust. "Secure the walls and find a way down to the keep. It will be heavily defended, but it will fall. Once the keep is ours, their men will either surrender or attempt to flee. Let the demons deal with any survivors."

"And the orcs? What if they come to the walls?" one of the generals asked. An unmistakable tinge of violence painted his rumbling voice.

"We will use the human defenses against them. They have bows and ballistae and all manner of things to prevent a ground assault. Once the keep is ours, we slaughter every orc we can."

The generals looked at each other and knew that they were all in agreement. They were hungry for war and even hungrier for a place to call their home. It had been centuries since the minotaur clans had bothered to build settlements above the surface. Their race longed to dwell in the sunlight of the surface and to build great cities and monuments that would demand respect from the other humanoid civilizations. With Talonrend occupied, Qul could proclaim himself as the rightful ruler of *everything*. No clan could hope to contest him. No human kingdom would dare rise against him. Qul would build a minotaur city strong enough to rule the world.

Only one thing gave him pause. As he shifted his weight on his ancient throne, he couldn't shake the nagging sensation that Undrakk was playing him for a fool.

SEAMUS WAS LOST. He had been to Talonrend a few times, but he had never felt truly lost before. The middle-aged farmer wasn't used to stagnation. Seamus had grown up on a small farm between two of the villages that dotted the Clawflow. If he wasn't busy tending to the farm's many needs, he spent his days hunting and learning what he could of carpentry. As he aged, he found himself frequenting taverns and gambling halls after his working duties were finished.

When Talonrend called for a militia, Seamus had eagerly acquiesced. He had expected to find a life of glorious soldiering and conquest as a member of the militia. He wasn't prepared for the utter boredom of war. Seamus' group of barely-armed militiamen hadn't gotten a chance to fight during the initial conflict with the goblin army, and something deep within the pit of his stomach urged him to take to the open road when the battle ended. When he joined the refugee caravan, his head was filled with visions of the Green City and a legendary empire that spanned further than he could see. Back in Talonrend, most of the people he had known were dead and he was left with nothing to do. Still, the sensation of destiny urged him to seek out adventure.

Seamus rolled from the bunk that had been given to him at the guard house and shook a haze of sleep from his mind. Most of the city was deserted. There weren't many taverns open and gambling seemed neither prudent nor accessible. He had left everything he owned on the road.

"Hungry?" one of the younger men in the barracks asked. The bunks were directly connected to a large storehouse of food and other goods, but Seamus hadn't eaten much.

"Not much," he replied quietly. He picked up an overripe apple from a barrel and thanked the young soldier before exiting the building. It was morning and the sun hadn't yet crested the high walls of Talonrend. The streets were thick with fog and dreary shadows that danced on their own.

Seamus let out a long sigh and sat down with his back to the barracks like a penniless beggar. From the corner of his eyes, he caught a glimpse of something moving through the morning fog. Curiosity got the better of him and he stood to investigate. Before he could take a step, the shadow darted through a patch of mist and escaped down the street.

"What the..." Seamus muttered under his breath. He scanned the street, checking for anyone who might think him a fool for chasing ghosts through the mist, and found he was alone. With a shake of his head, Seamus set off after whatever it was that moved through the street.

He spotted the apparition again, and then another time, always ahead of him and always just beyond the edges of his vision. "I'm mad," he concluded, but that didn't stop his feet from moving.

After several minutes of being led down the empty streets of Talonrend, the thick fog parted and showed him an open door. Seamus gazed up at the Tower of Wings and covered his eyes against the bright rays reflected from the top. He looked back at the open door and wondered what it could mean.

"Hello?" he called, not sure what to expect. His voice echoed once before dying off. With hesitant steps, he walked into the Tower's foyer. Instantly, he felt a sensation of calm wash over his body and he knew he had been led to the Tower for a purpose.

Seamus felt a cool breeze from his back push him in the direction of the staircase and was powerless to resist. His feet plodded, one in front of the other, and carried him down several flights of stairs to the underground hallway that ended in the star room.

"Oh," he cooed almost affectionately. Eerie light emanating from somewhere he couldn't see glinted off the hilt of Gideon's sword. Without another thought, Seamus bounded into the room and wrapped his hands around the weapon. He felt the blade calling to him, begging to be released, and he was more than willing to set it free.

With a fierce tug, Seamus ripped Nevidal from the soft ground and held it before his marveling eyes. The sword shimmered with power and Seamus felt as though his life had purpose for the first time. *He* would wield the legendary blade, the chosen weapon of Vrysinoch, and *he* would become the savior of Talonrend.

Yes, my son, he heard an avian hiss flood into his brain. *Yes...*

Suddenly, Seamus' left shoulder exploded into pain. Searing, biting agony twisted his flesh and brought him to his knees. He screamed and clawed at his shoulder. He ripped his shirt and watched in horror as a brilliant white light streamed from a hideous gash that grew just beside his shoulder blade. Seamus rolled to the dirt and tried to extinguish the holy fire, but he knew his efforts were in vain. Still, he thrashed about on the ground and wept.

After several agonizing moments of the worst pain Seamus had ever experienced, the fire sputtered out. The blazing sensation of bubbling flesh faded into a much more manageable throb and Seamus climbed to his feet. Using the reflection of Nevidal's blade as a mirror, Seamus watched his burnt skin knit itself back together as a garish scar in the shape a talon clutching an emerald. He knew beyond a doubt that he had been chosen by his god.

"Thank you..." was all he managed to say before running from the star room with Gideon's sword in hand. He stopped before he left the open door of the Tower and considered hiding the weapon until he could find a place to store it. The moment he considered dropping it, a sharp pain shot through his hand and he knew he could not be separated from the sword. It was as much a part of him as the fingers extending from his palm.

Seamus turned back into the foyer and searched for anything he could use to conceal the weapon. Without hesitation, he ripped an elegant tapestry from the wall and wrapped the sword in delicate cloth. It seemed fitting that a tapestry depicting Vrysinoch would be used to hide the deity's sword.

Once the weapon was as concealed as it was ever going to be, Seamus took off at a sprint for the barracks. Not waiting or attempting any kind of stealth, he crashed through the front door of the building and bolted to the storehouse. With the sword still held firmly in his right hand, he filled a burlap sack with as much food as he could carry and sped out of the storehouse before most of the soldiers had awoken.

Seamus wasn't sure where to go. He looked for a shadow dancing in the street, but too much sunlight was reflecting off the Tower of Wings and most of the fog had burned away. Without any plan easily coming to him, he ran for the gatehouse at the eastern edge of the city.

When he reached the interior portcullis, he tossed the tapestry into an alley and approached the guards on duty as though he knew exactly what he was doing. "Taking supplies to the top?" one of the Templars asked when he spotted the sack of food in Seamus' hands.

Seamus nodded and walked briskly past the man.

One of the other guards laughed and pointed at the sword. "Easier to carry supplies if you sheath your sword, man!" he called, pointing at Seamus and getting the other guards to laugh as well.

"I..." Seamus stammered, "I don't own a sheath!" he finally replied. The other guards howled with laughter, but let him pass. With a sigh of relief, Seamus found that the entryway to the stairs of Terror's Lament was open, so he began to climb. It took him a long time to carry everything to the top, but he made it without dropping the cumbersome weapon.

The bright sunlight seared his eyes and nearly blinded him. Looking around on top of the interior wall, he saw several guards patrolling, but thankfully, none of them spotted him. Their gazes were all held away from Talonrend and Seamus was able to walk to the southeast corner of the wall without being stopped. Each corner of the interior wall was outfitted with a low roof and several small crossbows bolted to the stone parapet. Three buckets of steel bolts were arranged in one corner of the outpost and Seamus eagerly hid his food behind them.

One of the guards patrolling the wall approached from the southern section and waved. Seamus let his sword hang awkwardly at his side while he waved back and took a step out from the low-hanging roof.

"Here to patrol?" the soldier asked, stopping several paces in front of Seamus. "Where's your armor?"

The man wore a hardened leather jerkin and a matching set of steel greaves and gauntlets. He held a steel barbute under one arm and an official short sword dangled in a sheath at his belt. Seamus looked around and saw other patrolmen walking, but none of them were close enough to pay him any attention. After all, most of the guards were stationed on the outer portion of the walls and the south side was the least defended.

A swelling began in Seamus' chest when he looked at the armored guard and it would not stop. The sword in his hand thrummed with power and released a palpable aura of violence.

"You alright?" the soldier questioned. His hand drifted to the hilt of his short sword and Seamus didn't wait another moment. With furious bloodlust in his eyes, Seamus lunged. He lifted Nevidal high above his head and cut the man down in a flash of steel and unbridled rage.

Seamus stood over the bleeding corpse and let Nevidal slide from his grip. The hand-and-a-half sword clanged to the stone floor next to the dead soldier like the ringing of a funeral bell. Seamus fell to his knees. He didn't feel remorse. He felt nothing—nothing but the call of the powerful sword to kill again. Seamus didn't dare touch the hilt. He kicked the blade against the base of the parapet and set to work removing the dead man's armor.

The breastplate, splattered with warm blood and separated at the top where Nevidal had sliced it, fit snuggly over Seamus' chest. The greaves were slightly too large for Seamus to comfortably wear, but he managed. Seamus slide the steel barbute over his head and it fit him nicely. With a smile, he drew the dead man's short sword and swung it through the air.

As though driven by some unseen force of violent ire, Seamus began cutting the corpse into small sections. He hacked the arms off at the elbows and then again at the shoulder. He removed the head and sliced open the man's belly, spilling his innards over the edge of a low crenellation. Working methodically, Seamus diced the body into a dozen small pieces and dropped them over the interior side of the wall, one every few paces, where they wouldn't be likely to be found.

When his grim work was finished, Seamus carried Nevidal by the blade back to the southeast outpost and hid it behind the barrels that concealed his food. At once, the inner fervor that urged him to violence dissipated. Seamus grimaced at what he had done and began walking the south side of Terror's Lament with a slight hint of divine purpose guiding his steps. He had no idea why Vrysinoch, or perhaps the sword itself, had led him to commit murder atop Terror's Lament, but patrolling the massive walls gave him purpose.

That night as Seamus curled up between the barrels of bolts and cold stone parapet of the outpost, he dreamt of war. He saw a massive army of orcs, goblins, and all manner of wild beasts attacking the city walls. In the midst of all the chaos, Seamus saw himself. He was wielding Nevidal with both hands, cleaving through foes three at a time. Standing atop a fallen section of the walls and surrounded by corpses, Seamus was the very definition of heroic glory. Despite the cold wind that sent chills down his spine, it was the best night of sleep he had ever known.

GRAVLOX, VORST, AND Gideon marched through the field east of Talonrend as quickly as they could. Something ominous about the desecrated land still lingered and threatened to devour them with every step. Gideon's large travelling cloak billowed out behind him. A stiff breeze planted tiny flecks of frost in his braided beard. On the horizon, they could see the black dots that represented Cobblestreet, the nearest village to Talonrend and the most direct path to Kanebullar Mountain.

"I didn't believe them…" Gideon said with a voice full of awe. Far above the tiny silhouette of Cobblestreet, a massive creature took flight. "Some of the Templars spoke of a dragon made of bones, but I didn't believe them."

Gravlox searched all around him for traces of the magical world. His mind yearned for something to consume, something to use, but only the scattered bones of his kin remained.

"Why does the dragon not attack?" Gideon asked to no one in particular. "Surely, a dragon would have no trouble destroying one small frontier city."

Vorst smiled and tried to imagine Lady Scrapple exhausting every ounce of her energy to control the mythical beast. "The more goblins she controls, the weaker her mind becomes," she said. "A dragon must be incredibly hard to dominate."

"Why bother to dominate it? Turning the dragon loose might not be such a bad idea." Gideon had rarely felt fear in his entire life, but watching a bone dragon flying lazily above a mountain lair he meant to infiltrate shook him to his core.

Vorst knew by the relative lack of bones remaining on the battlefield that the skeleton was made of goblin corpses. "She made the dragon," Vorst explained. "Now, she *is* the dragon."

With Gideon's hardened physique and the natural endurance of the goblin race, the group reached Cobblestreet a few hours after nightfall. The town was nearly empty. The cobblestones that gave the village its name echoed under Gideon's boots with an eerie hollowness. Even at night, there should have been taverns roaring with drunken exuberance and brothels flashing candlelight through red tinted glass.

The three travelers reached the center of the village without seeing a single soul. A marble fountain decorated with vivid images of Vrysinoch sat lifeless between rows of empty merchant stalls. The nearby businesses were mostly boarded up and the village itself smelled of death. Gideon couldn't help but think of Reikall and all of the beautiful buildings he had seen completely desolated. Cobblestreet was a village of less than a thousand, but it still unnerved him.

Gideon leaned against the quiet fountain and gazed up at the shadow of the huge mountain. He couldn't see the dragon any longer, but he knew it was there. In that moment, Gideon knew he would end the goblin threat once and for all.

"We should camp," he told Vorst. The small goblin was busy inspecting the reliefs of Vrysinoch that adorned the base of the fountain.

"Is this your god? The human version of Lady Scrapple?" She asked, never taking her eyes from the images.

"No," Gideon stated coldly. He began walking toward the

noise of the river when something about Vorst's question struck him as odd. In the Tower of Wings, Vorst had seen hundreds of images of Vrysinoch. She knew exactly what the sacred bird looked like. Had she not realized until now that the others worshipped the deity?

Gideon shook his head and continued walking. He thought of the goblin hive mind. Was Vrysinoch the human equivalent? Was religion really any different from direct mental control? When he was a devout follower and paladin, Gideon obeyed the orders of the priests and Archbishop without question or hesitation. When the Archbishop spoke it was a mandate from Vrysinoch himself... or so Gideon had foolishly believed. He had never realized it before, but goblin society wasn't dissimilar to his own. The notion was terrifying.

Gideon found a general store one street south of the village square that looked small enough to be easily defensible. With a heavy fist and a clouded mind, he slammed on the door. When no answer came from the other side, he lowered his shoulder and pushed until he felt the locking bar on the other side splinter and fall to the ground.

Somewhere inside the pitch darkness of the store, a woman gasped.

"I'm sorry," Gideon immediately called out. He was tired and his mind was churning with theories of religion and obedience. The last thing he wanted was a fight. "Just looking for a place to sleep is all," he explained.

He heard several hushed whispered and a brief moment of arguing before he got a reply. "Is it just you?" the female voice called from somewhere to his left. The room wasn't very large and Gideon thought he could make out a huddled mass of several people.

"I have..." he stopped. How could he explain his travelling companions? "I have two friends with me," he said. "One male and one female."

After several more moments of hushed whispers and debate,

one of the shrouded figures stepped forward and opened the door to a flickering lantern.

"Come in," the woman holding the lantern beckoned. She was tall, nearly as tall as Gideon, and exuded an air of confidence that didn't match her otherwise gentle features.

Gideon took a step forward and began to speak, when Vorst, deep in conversation with Gravlox, obliviously walked through the door behind him.

The woman shrieked and drew a dagger from her belt at the sight of the goblins. To Gideon's left, a man jumped at him from the shadows with a heavy metal gauntlet covering his balled fist.

"No!" Gideon yelled, sidestepping the would-be ambusher. With one easy motion he brought his own mailed arm down on the man hard and sent him sprawling to the floorboards. The woman yelled again and stabbed at him, but Gideon predicted the obvious maneuver and deflected the blade off his armor. Or he would have, had the attack not been a well-executed feint that revealed the woman's true skill. In the blink of an eye, she had rotated her body toward Gideon and jammed her off-hand against his mailed arm. Before he could react, he felt the point of her weapon pricking the soft skin under his chin. In the midst of the flourish, the woman had somehow maintained a steady grip on her lantern and the flame had not gone out.

"We're not here to hurt you," Gideon said with gritted teeth. The clumsy man from the corner slowly lifted himself up and struggled against a wooden stool for balance. "I swear," Gideon re-iterated.

The woman looked boldly into Gideon's eyes and he saw no fear lurking behind her grimace. The dagger point twisted and drew forth a bead of blood. "What are you doing in my store?" she demanded. Her voice had a hint of the village accent that reminded Gideon of his youth.

"We just need a place to sleep for the night. We'll check some-place else," he reasoned.

"Why should I let you terrorize someone else in my village?" the woman practically snarled.

"Your village? You own the store *and* you're the mayor of Cobblestreet?" The fire in the woman's eyes didn't lessen, but she did ease up on her dagger slightly.

"Look at his swords, Melkora," the man said as he rubbed the back of his head. "He would kill you in a heartbeat."

"Is that so?" Melkora replied slyly. She took a step back and glanced down at the hilts of Maelstrom and Regret. In an instant, the color drained from her face and Melkora's heart nearly stopped beating.

Gideon pulled away from her dagger and she made no move to stop him.

"Told you," the man snickered.

Gideon knew that her reaction was more than simple fear of his obviously well-crafted blades. She recognized them. Gideon stared her down and watcher her confidence melt like a candle tossed upon a raging pyre. "How do you know these swords?" he demanded.

Melkora's eyes withered beneath Gideon's stare and she retreated further into the store. "I..." she stammered. "I worked for the prince."

Gideon had dealt with enough cheats and sweet talking swindlers in the fighting pits to know a bad liar when he saw one. "How do you know these swords?" he repeated.

Melkora backed into the store counter and knocked a book to the floor. She had nowhere left to flee. "No," she begged, dropping her dagger and putting her hands in the air.

"My sister is a thief," the man said. It was obvious from his tone that he had no idea who once owned the swords. "She probably tried to steal them."

Gideon nearly lost his composure at the thought of a village thief attempting to steal the prince's swords. Where would she sell them? Who could afford to buy them? Even the most idiotic of fences wouldn't dare to buy royal property that was so easily recognizable. "Tell me how you know the swords, Melkora."

The terrified woman hung her head in shame. "I have seen them before is all," she whispered past the growing lump in her throat. "I never tried to steal them." Her eyes peered through stray locks of golden hair that obscured her downcast face. Gideon saw a flicker of hope in those eyes and let his posture relax.

"These are Herod's swords," he explained to the obviously confused man. "I am on official business from Castle Talon and need a place to stay for the night." He pointed to Gravlox and Vorst standing behind him. "My traveling companions require lodging as well. We will be gone by dawn, I promise you."

Melkora slowly nodded her head and collected herself. "This is my brother, Torvald," she introduced. Motioning to a dark corner behind a set of shelves covered in various wares, she called to two children. "My brother's sons," she explained, wrapping them each in a gentle hug.

"Thank you for opening your store to us," Gideon replied. His statement was more a confirmation of his demands than it was a gesture of appreciation, although he was glad Melkora's demeanor had softened.

"The goblins killed my parents," Melkora said with her gaze glued to Vorst. "When their army moved through, they didn't destroy much, but they did kill anyone who tried to stop them."

"I'm sorry for your loss," Gideon muttered, "but they are different. They fought on our side during the siege and they are as loyal to Talonrend as Herod himself."

Melkora's mind refused to believe what she heard. Her store had a small apartment above it where she lived. She had watched her mother and father try to defend Cobblestreet from the horde that crossed the river. Her father was brave and had killed a handful of the goblins, but there were only so many villagers. The endless goblin swarm had swept them away as Melkora watched helplessly from a window.

"You fought at the siege?" Torvald asked with admiration. He appeared to be slightly older and stronger than Melkora, although he clearly had no idea what he was doing when it came to physical combat.

Gideon was glad the two siblings had not heard the wild tales of his exploits that circulated everywhere else. He was dead tired and had little patience for celebrity treatment. "Yes," he said. "I fought alongside the militia. We lost hundreds of excellent men that day."

Melkora set her lantern down on the counter and crossed her arms over her chest. "After seeing the army pass through Cobblestreet, I don't know how Talonrend survived."

"She has high walls," Gideon said. "And goblins are exceptionally short. Now, how about beds?"

Melkora had significant doubts about letting a pair of goblins into her home, but the fear that welled up in her chest when she saw Maelstrom and Regret on Gideon's belt had not yet dissipated. Whatever the warrior wanted from her, he could easily take it.

"Follow me," Melkora said. There was a wooden staircase in the corner of the general store that led to the upstairs apartment.

"We will keep watch," Vorst said. "Goblins do not need sleep like humans. We will watch."

Gideon remembered the last night he had spent under the protective watch of Gravlox and Vorst and been captured by a band of minotaurs. It had been a valiant fight, but he could not battle five fully armored minotaurs on his own while half asleep. He resolved to rest with his back to the door and one eye open.

Vorst could tell that her presence filled the human family with more than curiosity. They were terrified of her and Gravlox. Goblins had taken the woman's parents and destroyed her livelihood. The village she had grown up in was a lifeless husk of what it had once been.

"Come with me, Grav," Vorst ordered her companion. Gravlox readily obeyed and followed her back into the street. It didn't take long for the door to be shut behind them and blocked with a heavy piece of furniture.

"Where are we going?" Gravlox questioned. She led him to the center of Cobblestreet and then east toward the Clawflow. At the edge of the rushing river, she stopped. The water was choked with the debris left behind by the goblin campaign. A huge swath of once-grassy riverbank had been trampled into filthy mud on either side of the river. To the north, stones and makeshift planks were still in place that served as a temporary bridge.

"Do you remember this place?" Vorst asked. She took a quick step onto a rickety plank and somehow the waterlogged wood held her weight.

Gravlox scampered after her and chased her into the mud on the other side of the river. "Of course I remember it," he said. The night air was cold enough to frost his breath and make his feet shiver where the river had touched them.

Vorst followed the swath of destruction the goblin army had left behind until she found what remained of the Cobblestreet graveyard. The headstone had been trampled into the mud and several nearby trees had been felled and chopped into timber.

"Do you remember the ghost flowers?" she whispered, prying one of the headstones up from the cloying mud.

Gravlox wandered to the headstone and sat in front of it. He scraped mud out of the carved letters and traced them with his fingers. "Can you read their language as well?" he asked, indicating the strange symbols.

Vorst sat next to him on the muddy ground and sighed. "Not very well," she said. "I haven't had much practice."

The human language continued to baffle Gravlox. While he had learned several of the more common words and phrases, complex sentences still sounded like guttural barks compared to the melodious and high-pitched goblin speech. "You've never told me, Vorst," he began. "How can you speak their language?"

Vorst sighed and leaned back on her hands. "I was trained to be an assassin, Grav, you know that." Her voice was so sweet and delicate that it contrasted with her words in an ugly manner.

"But who taught you to speak?" Gravlox had been aching to ask that very question since the first time he heard her communicate with a human.

Vorst waited a long time before responding. "Before I started my training... I served Lady Scrapple as an emissary of sorts."

Since goblin society rarely required spoken diplomacy with other races, Gravlox had a difficult time understanding what it meant to act as an emissary. "What did you do?" he asked.

Vorst didn't know where to begin. When she thought back to her year and half as an official diplomat for Lady Scrapple, she realized that she had played a part in the orchestration of the war. "Lady Scrapple would invade my body and use me to communicate her plans to others." With the feeling of true freedom fresh on her mind, it was painful to imagine being so wholly dominated.

"Do you remember the man outside Talonrend that fought Gideon?" Gravlox nodded. "I met with him and another human female in the woods not far from here. That's how I knew where to look for a necromancer for your poison." She felt like she had betrayed him; her memories tasted like bitter deceit.

Gravlox could tell how much it pained Vorst to recall her past. "When Gideon kills Lady Scrapple..."

"I don't know what will happen." Vorst remembered the exact moment she felt freedom for the first time. The disconnect from the hive mind had been jarring, but it was the most wonderful sensation she had ever known. "The goblins will have no direction. They will be leaderless. Chaos will ensue and Kanebullar Mountain will not be safe. When it is done, we need to run as quickly as we can." Her voice was deadly serious and she sounded afraid.

Gravlox inched closer to her and slid his hand around her back. She shivered against his touch, but did not pull away. "We'll make it out," he whispered. There was no way Gravlox could predict the future, but his words still brought comfort to them both.

"Where will we go from there? Back to Talonrend to fight the orcs and minotaurs?" her voice was full of pain and longing.

"Maybe it will be finished by then." It wasn't much consolation. "Talonrend withstood the entire goblin army. What's a few hundred orcs? The city will still stand when we return." Gravlox knew Vorst longed for something more. She needed something permanent to give her hope and purpose.

"Gravlox... I..." Their lips met before she could whisper another word. In the cold mud of the trampled graveyard, they held each other and experienced a closeness that neither of them had ever thought possible.

In front of the lovers, the muddy headstone swayed back and forth. Gravlox felt it with his mind, but he didn't care. He was lost in the kiss. After what only felt like a single heartbeat, Vorst pulled away.

"The flowers," she gasped. The wispy tendrils of a single ghost flower slithered from the ground and slowly climbed atop the stone.

"Souls of the dead," he said. Something about the ethereal vine frightened Gravlox, but it intrigued him more than anything.

"When I die," Vorst began before Gravlox cut her off with another kiss. She pulled away from him and looked deeply into his eyes. "I'd like to become one of these flowers," she finished.

Gravlox smiled and brought her back in close to him.

MELKORA GAVE GIDEON the privacy of the apartment's only bedroom and slept against the wall in the upstairs hallway. Torvald and his children slept in a small root cellar under the general store where it was safest. She didn't quite know what to make of the man, but Melkora feared him above all else.

As a thief, Melkora had broken into Castle Talon several times. She had never stolen anything from the castle, but had eavesdropped on plenty of conversations and sold the information she gleaned to wealthy aristocrats looking for fresh gossip.

With her back against the rough wooden wall of her hallway, she barely slept. At any moment, Melkora expected Gideon to rip open the door, slaughter everyone in the building, and steal all of her possessions.

An hour or more before dawn, Melkora rose from her fitful slumber and walked silently to the small closet at the end of the hall. Cursing herself for not regularly oiling the hinges of the closet door, she pulled it open and waited for someone to hear. After a moment, she thought it safe and pulled a hidden string that unlatched a false panel in the back of the closet. Behind the secret compartment hung Melkora's only belonging worth hiding.

Roisin, the Rose of the Forest, once belonged to a wealthy merchant that had often travelled through Cobblestreet on his way between Reikall and Talonrend. Melkora couldn't remember the merchant's name, but she would never forget the look on his face when he learned that his dagger had been stolen.

The Rose of the Forest, so named for the intricate pattern of leaves and flower petals etched into its hilt, was an exquisite piece of art with a razor's edge. Melkora had never used Roisin against an opponent in battle, but had trained with it for years and had no doubts concerning its effectiveness. Using target dummies she set up in the forest, Melkora had never found a material strong enough to resist the blade.

She took Roisin from a hook in her closet and clutched it tightly to her chest. Her eyes filled with wonder as she watched an inky black liquid course through the delicately etched veins of each leaf. Melkora had watched it a thousand times, but it never ceased to amaze her.

"Going to kill me?" Gideon asked from directly behind her. He clamped a heavy hand down on her shoulder and disarmed her before she entirely knew what was going on.

"How did you—"

"I heard the closet door opening." Gideon knew he had no right spying on the woman and sneaking up on her, but he couldn't be too safe. No one could be trusted.

Melkora sighed and let her arms hang in defeat. "Give it back," she said, holding her hand out for the return of her weapon.

"For a thief, you aren't very quiet," Gideon said. His gaze fell to the dagger and as he inspected it, he could feel his consciousness drawn toward the beautiful design. It took him several concerted efforts to stop staring at the dagger. "No wonder you didn't hear me coming..." he said as he gave the weapon back. Gideon noticed the flowing black liquid within the leaves on the dagger's hilt and took a cautious step back.

"Poison?" he asked with overt derision. "A woman's weapon indeed."

Melkora shook her head and fetched a leather sheath from the closet before returning the false panel and shutting the door. "I don't know," she admitted. "I've never killed anyone." Her voice was full of shame. Gideon pitied her.

"Taking a life is nothing to be proud of," he explained with a comforting tone. When she looked confused, Gideon continued. "A thief can take a purse or a coin and claim it for herself, yes?" She nodded. "But what if you learn the man it was taken from hasn't done anything wrong and needs the money to feed his children?" Gideon thought of the hundreds of goblins he had slain and the scores of orcs he had left to rot in the foothills. Every last one of them tainted his soul. "You can't give a life back."

Melkora understood, but her apparent bravado would not be calmed. She had a yearning for dangerous adventure that lurked just behind the soft green of her eyes. It was a yearning that Gideon had seen before—a yearning that typically got young men killed.

"Where are you going?" Melkora stubbornly asked. She eyed the prince's swords and Gideon knew what she was thinking.

"You want to know how I got these swords." A flicker of recognition played across her face and gave her away. "Let's say the prince no longer needs them and leave it at that."

Melkora's jaw nearly fell from her head. "You stole them!" she shouted. Her eyes beamed with newfound respect. "And yet you lecture me on the virtues of a thief!"

Gideon couldn't help but feel sorry for the young woman. From the looks of it, she had a reputable and legal business, a sturdy home, and at least a brother and a pair of nephews. A life of crime offered little reward and demanded that she risk everything.

"I'm coming with you," Melkora said as though she were stating a simple fact of the weather. "I'll get my gear."

"You haven't heard where I'm going," Gideon reminded her.

"Try me."

"Into the heart of Kanebullar Mountain to slay the leader of the goblin race, a hive mind entity guarded by a skeletal dragon and thousands of slaves, a being older than Talonrend and more powerful than Vrysinoch." Gideon stood in the hallway with his hands on his hips as the woman collected herself. He wasn't sure if she believed him, but she had stopped in her tracks.

"Into the mountain?" she finally asked.

"Why else would I have two goblins traveling with me? They are my guides." Gideon turned and collected his heavy cloak from the bedroom before walking down the narrow staircase. The sun was just beginning to cast its glow around the side of the mountain to warm the village streets. In the town courtyard, he could hear two high-pitched goblin voices busily speaking back and forth.

"I'm still coming with you," Melkora said defiantly, although a hint of fear still played under her voice.

Gideon stood in the doorway and let his mass block the woman's path. "It will not be easy," he said.

"I can handle it."

"Are you prepared to die? Can you leave everything behind? Even if we survive, there might not be anything left when we return. The orc clans have rallied together in the west and they will likely attack Talonrend within the week." Gideon let his words hang in the air while Melkora tried to absorb what he had said.

"The way it sounds, I'm as good as dead staying here and waiting for Cobblestreet to rebuild. My only child left with the refugee caravan weeks ago. What more do I have to lose?" Melkora took a step forward and Gideon extended his hand.

"Welcome aboard," Gideon said, taking her hand and clapping her on the shoulder. She smiled from ear to ear. "The goblins can be noisy and their language will grate against your ears, but I trust them with my life. I used to carry the most powerful sword ever created but believe me when I tell you this: I've never met anyone or anything as potently destructive as Gravlox. I have no doubt he could bring the mountain crashing down on top of us."

Melkora pat the dagger at her side and stretched her arms. "I can't spend the rest of my life waiting for a miracle. Give me a moment to say goodbye to my brother. I don't own my own armor, but there are few pieces somewhere in the shop that might fit."

Gideon pulled his cloak back and showed her his sleeve of mail. "I've never been too fond of armor. Meet us at the fountain when you're ready." With that, he left the woman to her business and stepped out into the light of dawn.

"Melkora will be joining us," Gideon said to Vorst at the fountain. There wasn't another soul to be seen down any of the streets.

"We're eager to free our brothers and sisters," Vorst replied.

Gideon sat down on the edge of the empty fountain and took a roll of bread from his pack. "What's the mountain like? How is it organized?"

Vorst laughed. "It isn't organized like one of your cities with buildings and streets paved with stone. It is dark and there are thousands of tunnels. You would get lost for weeks." As she spoke, Gideon noticed a disfiguring wound on her hand that he had not seen before. Where her left pinky finger had been, the skin was bubbling and starting to form a scab as though it had been freshly cauterized.

"Was there a fight?" he asked, indicating the wound with a nod

431

of his head. "I didn't hear anything."

Vorst lifted Gravlox's left hand up to reveal a similarly garish amputation. She didn't know how to adequately explain what had happened in the graveyard, so she smiled and silently hoped that he wouldn't ask her any more questions.

Gideon could tell that the wounds, whether self-inflicted or not, were identical for a purpose. He instinctively pulled his own left hand closer to his chest. "You're both insane," he muttered under his breath, but Vorst had already turned her attention back to Gravlox.

Several moments later, Melkora emerged from her store with a pack slung over her shoulder and Roisin at her side. She wore an ill-fitting leather jerkin covered in brass studs that was obviously made for someone much larger than her. To accommodate for the large size of the jerkin, Melkora had cut a strip out of the back and tied it with heavy string like a corset. He wasn't sure if it would be useful in battle, but Gideon had to admit it was a fine choice as far as her figure was concerned.

The four unlikely companions set out at once through the forest beyond the Clawflow. Following the tracks left by the goblin army was easy, but nothing about the mountain's looming presence made anyone feel confident.

QUL LED HIS march from the very front. His heavy plate armor and massive hooves thundered with every step, just as he intended. The greatest warriors of the minotaur race marched in step behind him, and Undrakk had produced a horse from somewhere that he rode with elegance unnatural to his heritage. The half-orc was an unsettling presence among the clan, but no one would dare challenge him.

A mile to the south of the minotaur battle formation, the combined orc clans made so much noise Qul thought another battle must have been joined. One of Qul's generals, a squat minotaur carrying a wide assortment of axes over his back, called to the king and reported the arrival of two minotaurs from the north.

Qul stopped his stride and waited for his clansmen to approach as the column continued marching behind him. The general halted as well and tensed. Something about the stride of the two minotaurs was off-putting and Qul could sense it as well. Minotaurs, while typically bipedal in everyday life as well as combat, often covered great distances utilizing their ability to gallop on all fours, as any hoofed creature typically did. The two minotaurs from the north walked standing upright, but their movements weren't fluid and their balance seemed precarious at best.

"Qul!" one of them called once he was in earshot. The voice was distinctly minotaur in origin, but the king knew beyond a doubt that something more was happening. Without hesitation, he drew one of the giant metal poles from his back and his general armed himself with a double-bladed axe.

"Stop!" Qul commanded with an outstretched hand. "State your business." He noticed one of the winged demons that normally followed behind his soldiers was circling overhead and wore a menacing expression.

Keturah and Jan stopped several paces in front of the king and his generals. "We're from Talonrend," Keturah explained. "The half-orc must have told you we were coming."

Qul let some of the tension in his muscles dissipate but didn't drop his weapon. "He calls himself Undrakk. He said you would be human." One of the generals stepped in front of Qul and flipped his axe over in his hands.

"Yes, well..." Keturah said through her stolen voice in the gruff minotaur language. "There were... complications. We had to borrow these bodies from you, gracious king."

"You killed my soldiers?" Qul asked. His voice wasn't full of rage like Keturah imagined it would have been. The king showed restraint. The shorter minotaur in front of Qul foamed at the mouth like a rabid dog, but even he did not strike. Keturah noted the unquestioned obedience with a smile. It was the mark of a great king that he did not resort to violence hastily.

"The soldiers were already dead, my liege," she responded. "We are giving new purpose to their glorious bodies in death."

Qul waited a long moment before sheathing his weapon. When he did, the general in front of him followed suit immediately. "Will your demons be ready to fly us over the walls?" he asked as though they were old friends.

Keturah reflexively brought a hand to her head to tousle her long red hair, but her body's thick fingers got tangled in her mane. "The demons will be more than ready. They are strong and eager to serve."

Qul glanced up at the creature flying not far from his reach. "What of that one?" he asked. "It is different."

The once-human sorceress untangled her fingers from her mane and motioned for Taurnil to join her. "He is my guardian," she said. Keturah attempted to caress her unholy slave as she had done hundreds of times before, but Taurnil jerked away from the abrasive skin of her massive fingers. In an instant, her expression hardened from one of playful seductress to heartless master. "I have a special task for him once the battle begins," she stated flatly.

With a nod of authority, Qul turned from the possessed corpses and took his place at the front of the marching column. His battle plans were coming together as well as he could have hoped. In a few days, he would drag his throne into Castle Talon and proclaim himself king of the known world.

Twenty-One

THE TRAIL TO Kanebullar Mountain was easy to follow. The goblin army had razed almost everything in their way. A swath of destruction wide enough to be used for horse races curled through the once-vibrant forest to the base of the mountain. After their second day of travelling, Gideon and Melkora were lighting a fire behind a fallen tree to the side of the path when a large group of goblins approached.

Without hesitation, Melkora drew her dagger and made ready to lunge. Gideon clamped a hand down on her shoulder and held her still. "What are you doing?" he whispered angrily. The goblins, six of them in total, were quite a ways up the path and distracted by the many things they carried.

"They don't know we're here," Melkora responded. "We should attack before they see us!" Gravlox and Vorst had left to hunt whatever small game remained in the area and wouldn't be back until long after nightfall.

"There are six of them," Gideon said. He was beginning to worry the woman's courage might get them killed. "There will be hundreds more once we are inside."

"I need to fight," Melkora urged. There was no denying the

435

bloodlust in her eyes. She had trained with Roisin for years and was eager to test her skills against living opponents.

When the goblins neared, Gideon noticed how remarkably unusual they appeared. "Those are not normal goblins," he said. They were larger than Gravlox and Vorst and their skin looked tough like old leather, not the pale shade of grey he was used to seeing.

"How many goblins have you seen?" Melkora snidely replied. "Maybe these are from a different group. Either way, we must kill them."

Gideon nearly hit the woman to calm her down. "I killed hundreds of them outside Terror's Lament. Something isn't right. I've never seen goblins so large."

"Hundreds?" Melkora gaped. Gideon pulled her roughly to the ground as the goblins marched past their position without incident.

"They're carrying equipment," Gideon said. He remembered the goblin balloons that had assaulted Talonrend before and knew there weren't enough men to shoot them all down. It was only one group of six large goblins, but Gideon knew there would be more. Goblins were expendable. If one small group was headed toward the city, there would be hundreds more not far behind.

"You need to teach me how to fight," Melkora said. The eagerness in her voice had been replaced with overt awe. "I've never had formal training."

"Tonight," he said. "We can spar tonight."

Still crouching out of sight of the path, Gideon kicked the beginnings of his fire and scattered the sticks across the hillside. His stomach was in knots and a thousand questions plagued his mind.

Gravlox and Vorst walked back into the makeshift campsite several hours after dark with a pair of slain rabbits. Gideon pulled the crossbow bolts from the critters and set to skinning them with a small knife.

"No fire?" Gravlox asked with a heavy accent. He still hadn't learned much of the human language, but had been making a concerted effort.

"We saw a goblin patrol today," Gideon explained. He told Gravlox and Vorst of the small force that had marched toward Cobblestreet.

"You're sure they were larger than us?" Vorst questioned. She was small by goblin standards, but she had never seen or heard of any goblin that stood over four feet.

"Considerably," Gideon affirmed. He held his hand out to Melkora's chest and indicated the approximate height of the goblins. Vorst shook her head in disbelief.

"I do not know what it means," she said after a long moment of contemplation. "But it cannot be good. If Lady Scrapple has found a way to make stronger goblins, she may have found a better way over the city walls."

After Gideon had finished cleaning the rabbits, he tossed one to the goblins and stowed the other in his pack. They still had some food left from Cobblestreet, and Gideon had no intentions of alerting the goblin hive mind to their presence by lighting a fire.

"Are you ready to practice?" Gideon asked when he had finished his meager portion.

Melkora got to her feet and hastily tore Roisin from its sheath. Gideon laughed at her eagerness and tossed her a stick that had been intended for the fire.

"I have no intention of letting you poison me with that pretty dagger. Come, we need to move far from here if we want to properly spar." Gideon led the woman away from the trampled path and deep into the forest at the base of the mountain. When they were far enough from the path as to not be heard by travelling bands of goblins, Gideon ripped a branch from a nearby tree that was in the rough shape of Nevidal. He longed for the familiar weight of his blade on his back and a set of throwing axes dangling at his side.

Without warning, Melkora lunged at Gideon with her stick held directly in front of her. The forest was dark and light of the moon barely made it through the dense trees. Melkora hadn't taken the time to properly assess her surroundings. Half way through her lunge, her foot caught on a protruding tree root and sent her sprawling to the ground. Melkora landed with a thud at Gideon's feet and her stick snapped under her weight.

Gideon helped her regain her feet with an outstretched hand. "You need to be more careful," he chided. "Always look at everything around you. The battlefield is as much an opponent as the one you are trying to kill. Through careful inspection, you can turn the area to your favor."

Melkora readied herself in a low crouch. At Gideon's nod, she leapt over the root and stabbed wildly in front of her. He stepped backward with one foot and brought his mailed arm down in front of him as a shield easily knocking the stick from the woman's hand.

"Use the battlefield," Gideon continued to explain. "Look for every advantage you can take. Use the root to spring yourself higher into the air. Come at me from an angle that puts my back to a tree." He pointed out the seemingly obvious features of the dark terrain and Melkora nodded. Gideon felt bad for agreeing to take her along, but he knew there had been no use arguing. Had he turned her offer down, she would have simply followed them from a distance.

"Again," Gideon commanded. Melkora hastily obeyed. With one foot positioned on the tree root, she launched herself from the ground. Faster than Gideon had thought her capable, she kicked out with her other foot and bounced off a nearby tree trunk with her stick leading the way. Gideon's original orientation was useless to deflect the incoming strike so he turned and ducked, raising a fist above his head to deflect the stab. Again, the stick went flying form Melkora's hand.

"Where did you learn all this?" Melkora asked as she retrieved her practice weapon.

Hesitantly, Gideon responded, "I trained at the Tower of Wings to be a paladin, but most of what I know came from the fighting pits."

Melkora's face tightened at the mention of the Tower. "Do you believe that Vrysinoch will protect you?" she asked him forcefully. Twirling and spinning with more grace than she had previously demonstrated, Melkora leapt horizontally from a tree trunk and grabbed onto a low hanging branch. Using her forward momentum, she managed to land a kick against Gideon's arms that sent him staggering back and tripping on a bit of forest debris.

In a flash, Melkora was on top of Gideon with her stick at his throat and a wild grin on her face.

"You're fast," Gideon said. He accepted her hand as she helped him from the ground. "More important than your speed, you're a good learner. Growing from your mistakes is often a matter of life and death."

Before he had finished his words, Gideon pivoted on his heel and reached out with his hand. Melkora tried to dodge but was too late. His fist connected with Melkora's side but instead of knocking her down, Gideon slid his arm past her and wrapped her waist in his powerful grip. With a single motion, he hefted her above his head and tossed her across the small clearing like a farmer handling a dead calf.

"Speed will only get you so far, Melkora," he said. "You need strength as well."

The woman smiled and grabbed at her side. It was obvious that she was in pain, but got to her feet nonetheless. "That's why I have this," she replied. She drew Roisin from its sheath and slashed at the nearest tree branch. The intricate blade sheared the branch cleanly without slowing.

"Impressive," Gideon said with genuine admiration. Melkora stabbed the blade deep into the trunk of the tree with very little effort. Again, exhibiting minimal force, she pulled the dagger from the wood. Gideon couldn't begin to imagine how sharp the blade must be.

"It is curious," he said, "how a shop owner in Cobblestreet came to own such a marvelous weapon." Melkora smiled knowingly and sheathed Roisin.

"As curious as a pit fighter who carries the prince's own swords?" she questioned playfully.

Gideon looked down at the hilts of the swords and remembered watching Prince Herod challenge Jan amidst the chaos of the siege. He was eager to try the weapons against goblin hive mind.

"I've never used them," Gideon said, suddenly feeling ashamed for having stolen them.

"Why not now?" Melkora asked. She was just as eager to see the blades in action as Gideon was to try them. She didn't need to ask a second time.

With a slight flourish, Gideon drew Maelstrom from his belt and swung the blood-red sword through the air. It felt heavy in his grip, but perfectly balanced. It was only half the length of Nevidal and Gideon found that he wasn't quite sure how to position his feet to wield it. Not expecting much, Gideon swung Maelstrom down hard in front of him and a tendril of inky darkness shot forth from the blade. As if alive on its own, the tendril wrapped itself around a tree trunk and tightened. When Gideon jerked the blade backward, the tree shuddered and was cut.

It would take him several attempts, but Gideon knew he could fell the entire tree with the black tendrils if he wanted to.

Melkora marveled at the sight and pointed at Gideon's other sword. The blue crystal of Regret's blade and hilt shimmered in the dull moonlight as if luminescent from within. Regret was weightless in his hand. The sword was smaller and thicker than Maelstrom, but far more deadly.

Gideon moved the weapon slowly through the air and watched as it vanished. Whenever the blade was moving, it could not be seen. Gideon didn't know if Regret's vanishing was due to a property of the crystal from which it was forged, or if Master Brenning had somehow created the enchantment on his own. Gideon attacked the nearest tree, a large birch with few low hanging boughs, and he felt Regret's magic flow through his veins.

The blade urged him to move with magical speed. When Gideon thought of moving behind the tree, the weapon responded and teleported him to that exact location. When he imagined himself standing behind another tree farther away, he felt Regret strain and refuse to move him. The effective range was short, but in close combat, Gideon was a blur of unbelievable speed.

A rustle in the nearby woods caught his attention. Melkora froze and gripped her dagger so tightly that the carved hilt cut into her palm. Gideon held up a hand to keep her calm.

The rustling grew louder and he strained to see through the darkness. It was no use. Beyond the small clearing where he stood, everything was pitch black.

Melkora let out a steadying breath and inched forward. Small twigs broke under her step making Gideon flinch. With an explosion of high-pitched screams, three large goblins crashed into the clearing with their weapons drawn.

Gideon felt the thoughts of Regret emanating from the crystal itself. It told him where to go and where to strike. Without hesitation, Gideon allowed the blade to control his movements. He suddenly appeared directly behind the first goblin in the group and swung the vanishing blade down hard at its back. The creature screamed and fell to the forest floor as a bloody corpse.

A second goblin swung a crude mace down at Gideon's back. Without looking, he could feel the attack coming and knew exactly where to move to dodge. The blade magically jumped Gideon several feet forward and turned him around to face the two attackers.

The third goblin, nearly human height and the tallest of the three, wielded a long wooden spear with a barbed point. He jabbed at Melkora's gut but was far too slow to strike the lithe woman. She leapt up and spun her body sideways, rolled down the length of the spear, and sank her blade up to the hilt through the goblin's skull.

The last remaining goblin, a young looking creature holding a crude hand axe, came at Gideon without a hint of fear. The clumsy beast never stood a chance. In the blink of an eye, Gideon appeared behind the brute and deftly eviscerated the goblin with a single swing. The bloody creature fell limply to the ground with a weak groan.

"They know we're here," Gideon seethed with frustration. "They know we'll be coming." He grabbed Melkora by the wrist and started running back to their camp.

"How do you know?" Melkora asked. "It was just a wandering patrol."

Gideon tore through the branches that scratched at him and pulled Melkora along viciously. "What one sees, they all see," he told her.

The two humans crashed into the small campsite completely out of breath. "They found us," Gideon said between heaving breaths. "We have to run."

Gravlox and Vorst burst into action and grabbed their gear. The four companions sprinted from their campsite and started heading east away from the mountain.

"Wait," Vorst called from several paces behind Gideon. The group stopped and turned. "They will expect us to run from them. There are likely hundreds of goblins in this forest that expect us to flee the mountain."

"Fight our way to the top?" Melkora suggested. She was eager for another chance to kill, but perhaps not quite as eager as she had been the previous day.

"That would be suicide," Gideon said. "If we are spotted by another group, they will all know exactly where we are. We can't fight the entire mountain. Vorst, is there a way inside on the north slope?"

Vorst thought for a moment before answering. "There is," she said, "but it would take at least three days to get there."

At once, Gravlox, Gideon, and Vorst felt an intense blast of mental energy that knocked them to the ground. Vorst clutched at her head and tried to force the mental intrusion back from whence it came. The energy was so similar to the presence of Lady Scrapple that Vorst thought she had been completely returned to the hive mind.

"What is it?" Gideon asked, struggling to think clearly through the pain. Melkora stood next to the three in a panic.

"Something is here," Vorst spat through gritted teeth.

Far overhead, the unmistakable sound of heavy wings beating the air thundered from the mountaintop. The skeletal dragon took flight.

"Lady Scrapple's mind..." Vorst panted. "It is too powerful."

Gravlox was determined not to be taken over. He felt the mental intrusion weighing down his consciousness like a heavy iron weight chained to his skull. His thoughts were still his own, but they were sluggish and incoherent. He reached down to his side and felt the weapon dangling against his hip.

"Why can I feel it?" Gideon practically begged from his side on the dirty forest floor.

An unholy roar shattered the night sky and Melkora watched the undead dragon begin to fly west toward Cobblestreet and Talonrend. As the dragon travelled farther away, the mind numbing pain in their heads subsided to a dull throb.

"The dragon..." Gideon breathed. He knew beyond a doubt it was the dragon's mind that had brought him to his knees.

"Lady Scrapple's mind has been bound to the dragon," Vorst said with confidence. She didn't fully understand how she knew, but she had *felt* it with her very being.

"Why could I feel it?" Gideon asked a second time.

"Why could I not?" Melkora added.

"The dragon must only affect the minds of those connected to magic," Vorst said. "Perhaps my connection to Lady Scrapple is starting to return." She did nothing to hide the sadness in her voice. She had tasted so little of freedom that to return to the hive would be a fate worse than death.

Gideon slowly rose to his feet. The dragon flew far enough away from Kanebullar Mountain that he was able to think clearly once again. "We can't take any more risks," he said. "They know we're coming. Even if it takes several days to reach the north entrance, we have to get there. If we're caught by another patrol on this side of the mountain..."

"I know," Vorst said. The other two nodded in agreement. "If we move quickly, we can reach the north entrance in two days."

The bone dragon roared again in the distance and something lit up the sky. Melkora couldn't be sure. It looked like fire on the horizon that could only mean one thing—Cobblestreet was under attack.

Twenty-Two

THE GUARDS ATOP Terror's Lament gathered at the eastern wall and strained their eyes to see the growing smoke on the horizon. Cobblestreet was far from Talonrend, but the entire village burned. The smell of fire made its way on the wind to Talonrend and the Templars prepared for war.

Apollonius inspected his men from atop the parapet that watched over Castle Talon's drawbridge. Every man of fighting age left in the city had been rallied in front of the castle. The Templars, several hundred of them in gleaming armor, knelt at the front of the militia and listened to their leader.

"Our scouts have confirmed what everyone has heard by now. The rumors are true," he told the men. From atop the parapet, his booming voice made up for his lack of experience and carried the full weight of his authority. "A great skeletal dragon has come down from Kanebullar Mountain to besiege us once more."

Murmurs flew through the crowd and dozens of the untrained men audibly gasped, but none of them fled.

"Those of you who have returned from the western road know an army of orcs approaches as well. Let them come!" Apollonius drew his short sword that identified his office and held it high

445

above his head. "We have fought them before and our mighty walls still stand!" The men cheered and drew their own weapons and banged them against their armor and shields.

Below the parapet, the door to Castle Talon creaked open and the crowd went silent. Herod, supported by the arms of two young priests, shuffled out of the castle. He was too weak to call out to the men, but his presence alone inspired them.

"They will try to come over our walls again," Apollonius shouted. "We will shoot them down again!" The men roared and cheered. "We expect the dragon to arrive before nightfall. Set your bolts and arrows aflame and kill the beast!" Apollonius had no idea if metal projectiles, on fire or not, would cause the dragon any harm, but he had to tell them something. The men needed some sort of strategy to protect their hope.

"When the orcs arrive," he continued with a bit of increased confidence, "they will never climb our high walls!" That was a promise Apollonius felt he could keep. He was not a military genius by any means, but he could not imagine any land army summiting all three sections of Terror's Lament without catastrophic casualties. If they did manage to get over the walls though... It was not a possibility Apollonius was ready to entertain.

After the lieutenants had received their individual orders and dispersed to organize their men, Apollonius made his way down to the drawbridge to speak with Herod. "How are you feeling, sir?" the young officer asked.

"Have you ever felt the inside of a grave?" Herod's wound bled through his silk bandages and grotesque black ooze dripped onto the flagstones. "I've always said this place would fall to a dragon," he remarked. "I just never thought it would be during my reign."

"We'll hold, sir," Apollonius reassured him. "The walls will not be breached."

"My brother loved these walls." With the help of the priests, Herod walked over to the moat and propped himself up with one of the drawbridge chains. It was too cold for any life to be seen in the water and the edges of the moat were slick with ice.

"Is it safe for you to be out of your chambers?" Apollonius asked, more to the priests than Herod.

The prince ignored his concern and kept staring at Terror's Lament. "Lucius put everything he had into the creation of the walls. Every morning, the king would take two of the guardsmen and run atop the inner wall. The walls are eight miles long in total—how many men do we have to guard them?"

Apollonius counted the divisions in his head. "A handful over two thousand fighting men, if memory serves." He thought of the hundreds of militiamen that had left with the refugees after the first battle. Some of the soldiers had undoubtedly left for their homes in the villages along the Clawflow, but almost all of them had gone west in search of a dream. No matter where they had gone, they had surely died.

Herod stifled a cough in the back of his throat. "How many will be stationed atop the walls?"

"Half, my liege. The rest will be either held in reserve or used as needed to sally forth and destroy any siege equipment the orcs might bring." Apollonius had made his men scour the city for as many crossbows, hunting bows, bolts, and arrows they could find. Still, he was not sure there would be enough for a thousand men to fire more than two volleys. They would have to make every shot count.

"Good. Tell the men to conserve their ammunition. I don't want to waste a thousand bolts against a dragon if the crossbows won't take the beast down." Herod wrapped his cloak tightly about his shoulders to ward off the cold.

"How does one go about killing a dragon made of goblin bones?" Apollonius' question felt sarcastic and foolish, but he was desperate for an answer.

Herod pointed to the tall tower that stood at the center of Talonrend. "Let the priests and paladins handle the dragon. Their spells are better suited for such tasks than mundane crossbow bolts and burning arrows."

Apollonius wasn't sure he liked the answer Herod gave him, but it was something. "I will speak with the Tower at once, your majesty."

"Don't bother assigning any guards to the castle, Apollonius," Herod firmly ordered. "If they get over the walls, I'll be as good as dead anyway. We can't afford to spare a single man for me."

Apollonius saluted the prince and began walking toward the Tower of Wings. If truth be told, he had never considered assigning soldiers to defend the dying prince. Castle Talon employed a dozen or more of its own guards and the prince was right: they would need every last man to defend the walls.

SEAMUS SAT ON a barrel of supplies in the southeast outpost and watched smoke curl up against the winter clouds. He didn't understand what it meant, but he had heard the other soldiers, the *real* soldiers, talking about a dragon. As far as he was concerned, dragons were just as unlikely as finding the Green City. They were the beasts of legend drunken warriors would discuss over a pint of ale.

At the back of his mind, a subtle voice still guided his actions. For the first time in his life, Seamus felt worthy. He wasn't sure why he felt the way he did or what it meant, but he never wanted to lose it.

Soldiers came and went through the small outpost and gathered or delivered supplies as they were instructed. All day long, Seamus leaned against the parapet and watched the smoke grow higher and a small speck flying above the ground grow larger. By the time food had been brought to the soldiers atop the walls for lunch, there was no mistaking the shape of the bone dragon that soared toward the city. In less than an hour, it would descend upon

Talonrend and Seamus would finally get a chance to fulfill his destiny.

The bone dragon approached and Seamus grabbed Gideon's sword. He handled the weapon by the blade, careful not to cut himself and even more careful not to touch the handle. He could sense something magical about the sword and he knew when he touched it, he lost enough of his self-control to make him do terrible things.

With Nevidal in his hands, Seamus felt the ancient pull of destiny call to him once more. He felt it in his soul, a vibration deep within his aging bones that urged him to glorious deeds.

A furious gout of black flames cascaded into the base of Terror's Lament and utter chaos broke loose on the walls. Most of the soldiers were stationed on the innermost wall of the three that comprised the defenses, but some of those on the outermost portion were burned alive. The dragon, a hulking monstrosity with a wing span well over three hundred feet, hovered at the height of Talonrend's walls and continued to spew fire.

Seamus knew he had to run. It wasn't cowardice that moved his feet, but Vrysinoch's subtle murmurs within his skull. Holding onto Nevidal like a mother fleeing a burning house with her child, Seamus ran west along the wall. He sprinted as quickly as his legs could carry him.

The men guarding the walls leveled their crossbows at the mighty dragon and waited for the signal to fire. Apollonius held his own crossbow tightly in his hands and watched the dragon rear back and prepared another gout of flame. When the beast's maw was fully open, Apollonius screamed to his fellow soldiers and their bowstrings hummed in response. Five hundred bolts soaked in lamp oil sailed out from the interior wall and nearly all of them struck the dragon. Unfortunately, only a handful of the missiles actually buried themselves in the dragon's bones. Without any sinew or flesh, many of the bolts skimmed across the boney ribcage and fell down to the ground without much effect.

Apollonius smiled when the dragon released another wave of punishing black flames. He dropped to his belly behind the crenellations and waited for the blast to end. Screams echoed all along the wall from his soldiers. Some of the men set aflame leapt from the high walls to their deaths. Apollonius peeked over the parapet and saw what he had hoped for: the dragon's hot breath had ignited the oil covering the few bolts that had stuck in its bones and the beast burned. It wasn't a raging inferno, but small pockets of flame began to spread on its body.

With bated breath, Apollonius desperately prayed the dragon would somehow be hurt by the fire and retreat. Although the beast roared in what Apollonius hoped was pain, it was able to put out the small fires with only a few beats of its huge wings.

"Ballistae!" the young leader called out. Soldiers manning several large ballistae mounted along the wall aimed their shots and fired. Four of the heavy bolts, each as long as a man and topped with barbed steel, crashed into the dragon's ribs and shattered bone.

The beast wheeled through the air and backed off considerably, but only one of the ballista bolts was still lodged in its body. Apollonius had hoped to sink several of the anchored bolts into the monster from both sides and use counterweights to rip it apart. As the beast flew higher over the walls, the bolt still in its ribs pulled taut and ripped the ballista from the walls with a violent explosion of wood and broken stone.

In an instant, the man who had been operating the machine was yanked from the wall to his death.

"Reload!" Apollonius called out. It took several painfully long seconds for the cranks of each ballista to span a new bolt. As the men turned the machines, the dragon swooped down and breathed a devastating line of black fire onto the interior wall. Everywhere he looked, Apollonius saw soldiers burning alive and falling from the parapet. He knew he had to order a retreat. His only options were to surrender the wall or die in a painful blaze of black fire.

"Fire!" he called to the ballistae before most of them were ready. Several bolts tore through the air just above Apollonius' head and two of them blasted great chunks of bone out of the dragon's wings. The beast roared again and flew higher into the sky.

Apollonius knew that the men wouldn't survive long enough to fire a third time. "Retreat!" he yelled. In a flurry of motion, the men grabbed onto ropes that had been fastened to the crenellations and began rappelling down the side of the wall. Some of the soldiers close to the only door on that side of the wall scrambled down the tight staircase, but the heat in the cramped area was intolerable.

When Apollonius reached the bottom of the wall, he ordered the men to fall back to their next defensive point. All through the streets of the city, firebreaks had been created with ditches and hastily filled moats. The dragon swooped down below the walls and breathed fire out upon the roofs of houses and businesses. The wooden structures exploded with black flames.

"To the catapults!" Apollonius ordered. His men had moved several small mangonels to strategic positions through the city's eastern quarter and each of them was ready to fire a payload of jagged rocks into the air.

The dragon wheeled low and bore down upon Apollonius' position. He gave the command to fire and the catapults launched hundreds of rocks at the flying beast. The dragon recoiled and diverted its course just before unleashing more punishing flames. The houses next to Apollonius and his men were consumed by fire. Not wasting another moment, Apollonius ordered his men to retreat further into the city.

The brave young leader was out of options. He had placed his hope in the ballistae on the walls, but the men hadn't been given enough time to properly train. Most of their shots had missed and as a result, the dragon was inside the city unleashing apocalyptic havoc.

"INCOMING!" A LIEUTENANT on the western wall called out. Soldiers lifted their crossbows and pried their eyes from the destruction of the city below. Fires raged all throughout Talonrend and the men defending the eastern portion of the city had been quickly overrun.

Seemingly from everywhere at once, winged demons clutching heavily armored minotaurs rose up and assaulted the walls. "Fire at will!" the officer commanded. Crossbows all along the wall clicked, thrummed, and delivered their deadly missiles into the oncoming horde of monsters. Their shots were mostly effective, but there simply weren't enough men. Too many soldiers had been placed on the eastern wall in anticipation of the dragon.

One of the winged demons flew directly for the officer. He reloaded his crossbow as quickly as he could and lined up another shot. He pulled the trigger and sent a steel-tipped bolt into one of the beast's wings. The demon screamed and started to lose altitude.

The officer hooked the end of his crossbow around the toe of his boot and started cranking the crossbow to reload. He moved at a feverish pace, but the demon was quicker. Before its wing finally gave out, the demon surged toward the parapet and released its cargo. The minotaur fell several feet through the air and managed to grab at the stone crenellation to keep from plummeting to certain death below. The officer slammed a bolt into the track of his crossbow as quickly as he could and leaned over the edge to line up a shot at the minotaur before he could climb up the wall.

The crossbow fired and the bolt, crooked in the track, flew wildly and ricocheted off the minotaur's armored chest. With one great heave of unbelievable strength, the minotaur pulled itself over the parapet. It towered over the lieutenant like a mountain of forged steel. Its helmet was black and its horns, long ivory protrusions coming from holes in the sides of the helmet, were capped with golden spikes.

The monster pulled a giant pike from its back that sported a small axe head on one side like the ornamental halberds the guards of Castle Talon sometimes carried. With determination that barely hid his fear, the officer dropped his crossbow to the floor and drew his short sword.

The beast charged the young officer and jabbed with the point of his pike. Focusing on the deadly spear-like tip, the man brought his sword down quickly and parried the weapon away from his gut. Unfortunately, the officer had no shield and the minotaur knew exactly how to utilize his weapon. The minotaur slid the pike several feet past the man and turned it so that the axe blade acted like a hook. With a single pull, the minotaur yanked the blade toward itself and sank the bottom of the axe head into the man's back. He screamed in pain and flailed his sword but the minotaur's armor was far too thick.

The beast lowered its head and pulled again, wrenching the man forward violently. The officer's body jolted and splattered the minotaur's helmet with warm blood as it was impaled upon two sharp horns.

Shaking enthusiastically, the minotaur ripped the corpse from its horns and tossed the tattered human remains from the wall.

SEAMUS WATCHED THE officer get impaled from the safety of the southwestern outpost a quarter mile away. He saw dozens of winged demons get shot from the air, but still dozens more landed and brought raging minotaurs to the top of the wall. The defenders were hard pressed. Less than seventy minotaurs had made it to the top, but each of them could easily kill ten or more men before falling.

Nevidal was hungry in his hand. He gripped the cool metal of the wrapped hilt and waited for the perfect time to strike. He felt the insatiable desires of the blade. It wanted to drink minotaur blood. Nevidal burned with ire that energized Seamus. The poor farmer had always considered himself muscular from his life of hard work, but with the sword in his hands, he felt like a god. His muscles bulged and threatened to rip the shirt under his stolen armor. The longer he waited, the more powerful he became. Divine energy surged through his veins and his vision sharpened.

One of the minotaurs noticed him and began stalking toward the outpost. Seamus had enough time to load and fire the crossbow that rested atop a barrel of bolt to his side, but Nevidal would not allow it.

Seamus bellowed with glee and set his feet into motion. Nevidal rose high above his head and directed his path as though Seamus was the tool and the sword was the intelligent wielder. The minotaur held a bloody axe in his meaty hands and bounded toward Seamus. The two crazed combatants met with a clash of steel that thundered so loudly it drew the attention of a dozen other fighters. Nevidal slammed into the shaft of the double-headed axe and ripped it apart. The hand-and-a-half sword cleaved straight into the minotaur's heavy chest plate and sliced through flesh.

The minotaur tossed the shattered hilt of his axe aside and readjusted his grip on the wood that remained below the head. It swung fiercely downward and clipped the side of Seamus' leather helmet. Instinctively, the farmer-turned-berserker brought the hilt of his sword swinging to the side and knocked the axe head off course before it rent his skull in two. Seamus pushed forward with his left shoulder and slammed into the minotaur's bleeding chest. His weight, not even a quarter that of the beast in full armor, did nothing to move the creature.

The minotaur grunted and pushed back, nearly sending Seamus over the edge. The farmer caught himself with his left hand and steadied his feet. Nevidal twitched his bulging muscles and commanded the man to spin with the sword raised. Faster than he thought possible, Seamus deflected a blow he never saw coming.

The minotaur closed the gap between them and wrapped his huge arms around Seamus' small frame. Against any other man, the minotaur would've easily crushed the human to bloody pulp in an instant. But Seamus held Nevidal in his grip. The sword empowered him beyond his wildest dreams.

Seamus flexed his arms and legs and pushed upward. Slowly, the minotaur left its feet and began to panic. Instead of letting go of Seamus, it clamped harder and renewed its effort to break the man's spine. Seamus smiled as he felt his legs bulge with energy. Using the leverage of his shoulders locked beneath the minotaur's arms, Seamus pushed upward again and hefted the beast a foot off the stone. He took one powerful step and slammed the creature into the parapet.

The minotaur flailed and tried to release its grip, but it was too late. Straps of its heavy armor had slipped around the stone parapet and trapped it. Seamus took a step back and watched the creature scream and thrash. He lifted Nevidal above his head and leveled it at the minotaur's neck. There was a small strip of hairy flesh exposed between the beast's thick breastplate and black helmet. Seamus wanted to see the fear in the creature's eyes, but had to settle for its screams instead. He waited a moment for several of the other minotaurs to start running toward him before he beheaded the trapped beast and sent its corpse over the edge of Terror's Lament.

Three heavily armored minotaurs stood shoulder to shoulder and marched toward Seamus. He smirked and lifted Nevidal up in challenge. The minotaurs increased their pace and brandished their weapons menacingly. The death of one of their own in single combat was a rare enough event that it enraged the minotaurs beyond their typical bloodlust.

Seamus welcomed them with a taunting grin. The three beasts came upon him slashing their weapons furiously in front of them. He relinquished what control he had left to the sword and let Nevidal guide his every action. The blade dashed through the air in a blur of speed and deftly parried the three weapons.

Seamus' feet edged forward as he beat the minotaurs back with sheer ferocity. His parries hit harder than the minotaur's strikes and the three beasts were forced to step backward. Nevidal launched up under one of the minotaur's clubs and knocked it into the air. Wasting no time, Seamus dove forward and gutted the beast where it stood. The two flanking minotaurs struck at Seamus' back and sides as his sword was temporarily trapped in the innards of their comrades.

A studded club crashed into Seamus' tunic and shredded the bulging muscles of his back. He shrieked, but Nevidal had full control of his reflexes. Seamus ripped the blade from the minotaur's chest and crouched to his knees. The beast to his left swung a barbed spear that missed high over Seamus' head and clanged against the armor of the other minotaur. The failed attack gave Nevidal all the time it needed to make short work of both minotaurs. Seamus slashed out to his right and took the legs out from one of the creatures at the knees. In the same motion, Seamus completed his spin and Nevidal severed the legs of the left minotaur just above the hip. In a heap of gore, the three slain minotaurs fell silently away from Seamus.

The momentum of Seamus' circular maneuver launched Nevidal from Seamus' grasp and sent it hurtling into the base of the parapet. In an instant, Seamus' body shrank painfully back to its normal size. His muscles contracted with agonizing spasms and his bones re-knitted themselves back to their regular proportions.

Seamus felt a sense of accomplishment when the pain subsided in his joints and chest. He grabbed Nevidal by the blade and limped back to the southwestern outpost of Terror's Lament. He propped himself up against a barrel of crossbow bolts and struggled against the inviting warmth of sleep. As his eyes fluttered in the winter sunlight, Seamus experienced something he had never felt in his three decades of life: clarity.

Half a mile or more down the western length of the wall, three winged demons brought the minotaur king to the top of the wall. Qul stood more than a head taller than any other minotaur atop the wall and well over eight feet taller than any man. With his full battle armor, the minotaur king thundered with every movement. The flagstones vibrated with each of his steps and brought the nearest human warriors to their knees. Qul drew two smooth metal poles from his back and began swinging them into any piece of flesh that got in his way. When the poles accidentally connected with crenellations along the wall, the stone exploded and fell away without slowing Qul's cadence.

Seamus knew what he had to do. He watched the king cleave through a swath of human defenders like a team of harvesters bringing in the fall wheat. Seamus knew he would have to wait. He was too tired to confront such a monstrosity without a night of sleep. With Nevidal in hand, Seamus scurried from the southwestern outpost to a crenellation a quarter mile away and looped a rope around the stone.

He knew he needed to wait. Nevidal commanded him to wait. With an exhausted sigh, Seamus grabbed the rope and used what strength remained in his arms to rappel down the interior side of Terror's Lament. At the base of the wall, Seamus scampered off into an alleyway across from Castle Talon. He curled up around his stolen sword and leaned against one of the few buildings in the city that hadn't caught fire yet. There would be time to kill the minotaur king in the morning. It was what Nevidal wanted—what Nevidal *demanded*.

APOLLONIUS HAD RUN out of options. The dragon had free reign of his city and there was nothing he could do about it. Fires burned in every section of Talonrend and it would only be a matter of time until the skeletal monstrosity set its eyes upon Castle Talon. The catapults and ballistae had proven slightly effective, but the undead dragon was simply too large to be taken down.

Most of Apollonius' officers had died on the wall. He regretted stationing so many men atop Terror's Lament, but it had been his only hope. He crouched between a pair of stagnant shrubs outside an abandoned house and tracked the bone dragon through the air. The abomination flew high over the city casually tossing balls of black flame onto the rooftops and lanes. Their defense had been a resounding failure.

ASTERION PEERED AT the city from a translucent window on the second floor of the Tower of Wings. The fire created strange patterns of dancing light that reflected off the Tower in marvelous patterns. While Talonrend was completely enveloped in chaos, the Tower of Wings was peacefully quite. The opalescent walls blocked out the screams of the dying and the living alike.

The pain in Asterion's knees and hips slowed his ascent to the top of the tower. He pushed open the door to the Archbishop's quarters and wrinkled his nose against the smell. There weren't enough priests left in the city to bother with a proper funeral for the man and the body had been left to rot.

Behind a pale red curtain hanging near the Archbishop's sleeping quarters, Asterion inspected the wall for a notch he barely believed to exist. After a minute of running his fingers along the wall, one of the nails on his hand caught. A small divot, barely discernible even under careful investigation, marked the location of a hidden door.

Asterion pressed down on the divot and marveled as a hidden panel silently slid away to reveal a brilliantly lit passageway.

"Corvus!" the old man called down the stairs to the level beneath him where Corvus had been praying. After a moment, the blind paladin appeared at the doorway to the Archbishop's quarters wearing a plain white and green robe that was customary for acolytes in training.

"Yes?" he said calmly. He walked slowly to where Asterion stood and sighed. He had been waiting for the old priest's call.

"Are you ready?" Asterion asked. Despite his effort, the old man couldn't keep the excitement and awe from his voice. "The dragon has been weakened."

Corvus couldn't see the destruction of Talonrend through the walls, but he could feel it. The city burned all around the Tower of Wings and hundreds of humans had been slain. Corvus felt their souls flying through the air toward Vrysinoch's heavenly wings. He wanted to weep for them, but couldn't find the tears. He needed to keep his mind clear.

"It is time we end this. Vrysinoch has waited long enough," Corvus said with confidence. He placed a hand on Asterion's shoulder and let the old priest lead him up the hidden staircase. The top of the Tower of Wings was made into the likeness of an eagle's talon clutching a giant emerald, the symbol of the city. What few people knew was that the center of the emerald was hollow and covered in ancient runes carved by the first settles from the Green City.

"It is truly a marvelous sight," Corvus said, tracing his hands along the intricate runes.

"You can see it?" Asterion asked skeptically. He opened a pocket on his own robe and produced a scroll as old as the Tower itself.

"I can," Corvus whispered breathlessly. "It's beautiful!" He couldn't believe the images that flashed through his magical vision. He saw hundreds of runes and could feel their meanings. Instead of seeing static images carved into a gemstone, Corvus recognized the runes as living entities that moved and spoke to him.

Asterion spread the scroll out in his hands and began to read the ancient text. The words sounded like confused gibberish to Corvus, but he knew they held unbelievable power. He let his mind search out the power of the sky itself and drew it into the emerald. The two men summoned every last ounce of magical strength they could muster and channeled it into the spell on the scroll.

When Asterion completed the incantation, the small space in the center of the emerald fell silent. The Tower of Wings pulsed and released a soothing calm that bathed the city in magical silence. Men burned and screamed in the streets, but their cries turned to dust in their mouths. The sounds of battle and crossbow gears rang out from the western walls, but no one heard them. The emerald perched on top of the tower had come alive with a powerful aura of *silence*.

The great bone dragon soared above the houses and doused them in black flame. The wood cracked and glass shattered, but none of it made a sound. The world was perfectly quiet.

When sound returned to the world several long seconds later, everything was drowned out by one tremendous thunderclap that tore the sky asunder. The dull grey clouds above the city recoiled from the Tower and curled in on themselves as if a storm had suddenly roiled them. Inside the emerald, Asterion and Corvus could feel the presence of Vrysinoch speaking through the back of their mind.

I need your souls, faithful servants... the avian hiss spoke to them both. The two men nodded and shared a brief smile before the world faded into blazing light.

MELKORA, GIDEON, AND the two goblins stopped abruptly on the eastern side of Kanebullar Mountain. White light the likes of nothing they had ever seen split the sky apart. From their angle, they couldn't tell where the light had originated, but they could see into the fabric of heaven. Above the physical tear in the sky, a shimmering light danced about that marked the bottom of Vrysinoch's eternal paradise.

Gideon fell to his knees. He gazed up into heaven and saw thousands upon thousands of souls whimsically flying to and fro on the wings of astral eagles. "Vrysinoch..." he muttered. He didn't know what else to say in the presence of such an incredible sight.

"Talonrend is in trouble," Melkora said. She could feel it in her bones. "We need to hurry."

Gideon couldn't deny the truth that resonated in her words. There, on the side of Kanebullar Mountain and several miles away from his home, Gideon felt the call of Vrysinoch once more. His tattoo burned on his back and he felt Nevidal's absence as though it were a missing limb.

"I need my sword," he yelled to no one in particular. He suddenly felt foolish for leaving it behind. "I am a paladin once more!" he bellowed. Despite his newfound urgency and purpose, he couldn't help but wonder what had happened to all the souls his sword had taken in the past. Seeing the souls drifting through the sky was both a comfort and a curse. Were they the souls that Nevidal had taken trapped inside the blade? Or had they been obliterated for all eternity?

"Let's go," Melkora urged. As Gideon got to his feet, the sky changed once more. It had been late afternoon when the heavens opened, but a furious storm began to boil the sky. The broken clouds clashed into each other like huge ships tossed about in a harbor during a squall. Lightning strikes erupted from the torn sky and blasted the ground beneath. Gideon could only imagine what the scene must have been like in Talonrend.

"We aren't that far," Vorst said. The four climbed hand over foot up the steep northeastern approach to the top. Unlike the southern and western faces of Kanebullar Mountain, the northern

461

and eastern slopes were rocky and unorganized. Luckily, that also meant there were far fewer goblin patrols to avoid.

Gideon got to his feet with a broad smile on his face. He would slay in the name of his god once more.

The storm raged in the distance and at one moment Gideon thought he saw a great meteor crashing down from heaven, but he couldn't be sure. All he could do was keep his head low and continue the strenuous trek to the summit.

By nightfall, the group was nearly at the highest entrance to the tunnels of Kanebullar Mountain. "Over here," Vorst called. She pulled some rocks away from a patch of dark soil and began to dig. After a minute, she had revealed a small passageway leading down. It was barely large enough for a human to navigate on hands and knees.

"How do we know it isn't a trap?" Melkora asked. She peered into the darkness of the tunnel in vain.

"Perhaps some of my magic has returned," Gideon said. "I might be able to light the passage." He searched the mental realms of magic for anything he could onto and found what he desired. The smallest speck of energy, just enough to form into a light-giving cantrip, rested inches beyond his fingertips. Gideon called to the energy with his mind and it responded, floating over to him to be manipulated and utilized.

When he had created a small bird of light, Gideon whispered to it and released it into the dark tunnel. The bird's radiant magic illuminated the tunnel as it flew. The passageway spiraled downward at a steep angle and ended in a much larger chamber nearly twenty feet below.

With a smile, Gideon got down on his hands and started to crawl. Vorst followed closely behind with Gravlox and Melkora entering last.

The magical bird darted playfully around the narrow passage until it flittered into the larger cavern below. Gideon dropped through the tunnel opening to his feet and inspected the room.

Crudely made wooden bins of all sizes and shapes littered the ground. Each of the bins was filled with the remains of a plant-like fungus that smelled of sulfur and rotten eggs. "What is this place?" Gideon asked with a hand over his mouth.

To Vorst, the aroma was stale, but not unpleasant. She didn't know agricultural terms in the human language so she explained it as simply as she could. "Fill the boxes with dirt, put a dead goblin on top of the dirt, wait for fungus and mushrooms to grow," she said.

"And you eat that?" Gideon said with disgust.

"Why not?" Vorst led the group through the abandoned mushroom farm to a larger tunnel blocked by a roughshod wooden door. She paused for a moment and listened before opening the door a fraction of an inch and peering through. "There's no one there," she affirmed.

The door swung open and revealed the complicated network of tunnels that comprised the innards of Kanebullar Mountain. To their left, several downward sloping tunnels presented themselves. To their right, two other chambers much like the one they had come from waited in disuse.

"This one," Vorst announced as she pointed to one of the smaller tunnels to the left.

"Where will it take us?" Gideon asked. The small bird fluttered through the tunnel and around a shallow bend.

"The only way I know of to get to Lady Scrapple is through the tunnel where her food is taken. This passage will eventually lead us to one of the livestock pens farther down. From there, it shouldn't be difficult to find her." Vorst still had reservations about the death of her creator. She knew the goblins were somehow magically connected to Lady Scrapple's mind. Would Lady Scrapple's death free them all or kill them all? Vorst rubbed at the painful nub where her left pinky finger had once been. She was keenly aware that the death of the Mistress of the Mountain would be the end of the goblin race. They had no means to reproduce naturally and Lady Scrapple's budding was their sole propagation.

Vorst led the group through the passage and around several twists and turns. More than once, another tunnel would cross their path and Gideon's magical bird would temporarily illuminate it, but they never saw any goblins until they reached the livestock chamber several hundred feet deeper.

With his mind, Gideon extinguished the cantrip and waited a moment for his eyes to adjust to the near pitch black conditions. A lone torch burned on a distant wall but it was in desperate need of more fuel. The low flickering light threatened to go out at any moment. Several goblins moved about the chamber tending to their herd with water and food.

Gideon held up a hand to tell the group to stay silent. Any goblin that discovered them would instantly alert all of the others. As far as the hive knew, they had last been seen outside the mountain. Gideon intended to keep it that way. Vorst pointed to a large opening a hundred or more feet from where they crouched. Between them and next tunnel, a handful of goblins were going about their business.

Directly in front of the group was a wooden pen holding a dozen or so mammals that appeared to be a subterranean species of hornless goat. The creatures, covered in thick white hair and much shorter than their surface dwelling counterparts, bleated and paced back and forth. Vorst scooted along the ground until she had her back against one of the pen's support poles. Carefully mimicking the animal's movements, Vorst used the creature as a shield. When it moved closer to the next tunnel, she followed it until she could dive quickly behind a closer animal.

Gideon and Melkora were hesitant about fitting behind the short goats, but they got down on their bellies and shimmied along the pen as best they could. When all four of them had reached the end of the wooden enclosure, they had twenty feet left to go that was completely exposed. Less than ten feet from their position, a goblin wearing a leather vest walked from animal to animal with a bucket of grain he used to feed them. There was no way to make it to the tunnel without alerting him.

Slowly, Vorst cranked the string of her crossbow into place. With every pass of the gear, her heart stopped in her chest and she was sure one of the workers would hear her. When the string reached the latch at the back of the weapon, Vorst used her finger to slow the automatic movement of a bolt into the track from the cartridge below.

Gideon couldn't tell what her plan was, but he begged her silently not to shoot one of the goblins. They would have to kill all six goblins in the room at near instantaneous speed to ensure they would remain unseen.

Vorst flattened herself underneath one of the horizontal planks of the pen and stuck her arms and crossbow through to the other side. After several long minutes of careful aim, she pulled the trigger and launched a bolt to the other side of the chamber where it slammed into an unfortunate goat and brought the creature down.

The goblin workers scrambled into action to investigate the suddenly dead goat and the four intruders made a mad dash for the next tunnel. When they entered the pitch black tunnel, Gideon signaled for them stop and slow their breathing. They could hear the sounds of goblins working all around them. Above it all, the heavy droning of hammers striking iron added a kind of heartbeat to the dark mountain. Gideon hadn't noticed until he paused for a moment to take in his surroundings, but the air of the tunnels was unusually hot. Sweat was starting to bead up under his cloak and armor.

When they were positive the goblin workers hadn't figured out their ruse, Vorst dashed silently down the tunnel and led them through another seemingly endless maze. Halfway through the tunnel, Gideon realized if Vorst died, he would never find his way out alive. After several minutes of walking, they came to an underground stream that trickled noisily past.

Vorst stepped into the stream and waited for a moment, listening for any nearby movements. "This leads to the forges," she said, "we're close."

Gideon dipped his foot into the water and felt that it was surprisingly warm. At the wall where the stream entered the small chamber, he could see faint wisps of steam rising up and soaking the stone.

"How do we get through?" Melkora asked. Her eyes had not adjusted as well as Gideon's and she had to keep one hand against the wall to maintain her balance.

In response, Vorst mimed holding her breath and jumping into the stream. It didn't look deep enough for a human to swim through, but the water was murky and bottom was obscure.

"Where will the goblins be?" Gideon asked. He wasn't keen on swimming through an underground stream just to come out in a room full of goblins wielding hammers.

Gravlox spoke a few lines of the goblin language to Vorst. He had lived his entire life inside the mountain working in the mines that connected to the forges. His underlings were responsible for delivering regular shipments of raw materials to the smiths and he knew the layout of the area well.

"There will be many goblins," Vorst responded after listening to Gravlox. "There is a storeroom not far from the stream that connects to Lady Scrapple's chamber. There are tracks on the floor and carts. If we are careful, we might be able to hide inside a cart and wheel down the track."

Vorst's plan sounded entirely insane. Gideon and Melkora both considered turning back and searching for another route. The echoing sounds of footsteps made up their minds before they had a chance to debate.

Vorst and Gravlox dove head first into the small stream and pulled themselves under a rock ledge and out of sight. Gideon gave Melkora a shrug and slid into the warm water behind them. His sleeve of mail weighed him down, but Gideon smirked at the thought of a paladin in full plate trying to swim.

The two goblins reached the other side of the stream and emerged without drawing too much attention. Gideon swam up next to them and peeked his head out of the water just enough to get a new breath and evaluate his new surroundings. The forge room was massive. Eight blazing fires bathed the cavern in bright orange light and the smells reminded Gideon of his days spent working for Master Brenning.

When he saw Melkora's head emerging from the passage, Gideon used his hand to guide her up slowly as he had done. The large water reservoir they were in was used as a holding tank for cooling basins around the room. Small carved channels ran out in a spindle pattern away from the reservoir and carried fresh water to each of the forges where the goblin smiths could cool their metals. It had a high enough ledge around it for Gideon and Melkora raise their heads above the water without being seen.

"Where are the carts?" Melkora whispered. Under the hammering cacophony of the forges, her words were barely audible.

Vorst pointed to a section of the reservoir ledge to indicate the corresponding area of the room. "I saw two empty carts," she said quickly.

"When should we go?" Gideon questioned. He glanced over the edge of the reservoir and saw a dozen or more goblins going about their work. It would be impossible to climb out of the water without being seen by at least one of them.

Gravlox wasted no time. Pulling himself over the edge of the reservoir, he sprang from the water and ran for one of the carts. After only a split second of recognition, the goblins throughout the forge took up their hammers and charged. Throughout all of Kanebullar Mountain's vast system of tunnels and chambers, Lady Scrapple stretched her consciousness thin and ordered them all to attack the intruders.

Vorst leapt from the water on Gravlox heels and screamed for them to hurry. Gideon and Melkora weren't far behind. They had twenty or more paces to cover before reaching one of the mine carts, but a handful of goblins already blocked their path.

Gideon drew Maelstrom from its sheath, the blood-red blade glowing in the fires of the forges. With a snap of his wrist, Gideon sent thick black tendrils spiraling toward the goblin closest to him. The magical tendrils wrapped themselves around the goblin's thin waist and Gideon drew Regret before yanking the goblin in close. The beast yelped and dropped its smith's hammer to the ground as it was pulled across the forge.

Regret vanished in Gideon's hand as he brought it up to meet the goblin's wrinkled chin with an explosion of blood and gore. The blade materialized once more as it came out the back of the goblin's skull and stopped. Gideon roared and turned on the next goblin, eager to kill again. He felt Vrysinoch's power surging through his veins. It wasn't the same energy he felt when empowered by Nevidal's enchantment, but Gideon felt that his god was in the humid cavern with him.

Two goblins charged at Vorst and Gravlox with their hammers held high. Gravlox drew his heavy sword and crouched into a defense stance. Vorst jumped behind her and began cranking her hand crossbow. When the first goblin arrived, Gravlox easily parried his hammer far to the left and angled his sword downward for a quick kill. The second smith was only slightly better in combat than the first, but by the time Gravlox and parried the third hammer swing, Vorst fired her hand crossbow. The steel-tipped bolt caught the goblin just above his right eye.

There was no time for Vorst to crank another bolt into her crossbow before more goblins were upon them. In a blaze of speed, Melkora leapt into the fray with Roisin cutting a vicious arc in front of her. She felled one of the smiths in a single blow that destroyed its collar bone.

Three goblins closed in on Vorst and she was forced to pull the daggers from her belt. A hammer came in at her head from a taller goblin and Vorst struggled to get her dagger up in time. The weapons clanged off each other and then suddenly, the attacker was pulled into a dozen or more pieces by dripping black tendrils.

Vorst seized the opportunity and ran for the mining cart. With a flying leap, she bounded into the cart and yelled for the others to join her. Gravlox swung his sword up and knocked the hammer from an approaching smith. He dashed forward, shouldered the attacker down, and made a mad rush for the mining cart.

Melkora slashed the wrist from a goblin attacker and sent another hammer clattering to the floor. Despite her two quick kills, she was hard pressed. More goblins had entered the forge room and she was surrounded. Fighting desperately to keep their weapons at bay, she whipped Roisin in large circles in front of her as quickly as she could.

With a bellowing roar, Gideon jumped from a nearby anvil and landed in front of Melkora. In one motion, Maelstrom shredded four goblins and sent them to the ground. "Go!" he yelled, shoving Melkora in the direction of the cart.

Gideon stabbed with Regret and one of the goblins attempted to parry the strike with an unfinished piece of iron. The blade never slowed as it sliced the iron and bit deeply into the goblin's neck. As the last attacker fell, Gideon looked to the door at the other end of the chamber. For a moment, he thought they might be safe. No sooner did he catch his breath than another horde of goblins entered the room with weapons drawn.

"Start moving!" Gideon called to the three in the cart. Melkora flipped a switch on the side of the cart that released the brake and it started to slowly move down two narrow tracks.

Gideon watched the approaching enemies with a scrutinizing gaze. They were much larger than the smiths and resembled the goblins he had fought outside the mountain. They were nearly as tall as a human and bred for nothing but war. The four intruders had gotten lucky with the untrained smiths. Their small hammers were designed for creating, not destroying. The denizens that flooded into the forge were much different. They moved with measured footsteps and fanned out in a practiced manner. Their weapons were well-made swords and spears, and Gideon knew his armored sleeve wouldn't block everything.

No matter how much he wanted to hold his ground and put his stolen swords to the ultimate test against a hundred or more trained goblins, Gideon knew he had to run. The tattoo on his back burned and urged him forward, but he turned and leapt into the mining cart.

"We will pass through the storeroom," Vorst said as she translated for Gravlox. "There is a switch at the back of the storeroom. Left will take the cart to Lady Scrapple. Right leads toward the furnace where waste is sent for incineration."

Gideon flexed and felt his body begging for combat. His mind was sharp and his weapons were sharper. "I am ready to face her."

Twenty-Three

ASTERION'S ROBE CAUGHT fire within the emerald. His corpse crumpled next to that of Corvus, serving as the conduit for Vrysinoch's power. A violent storm raged around the Tower of Wings and consumed Talonrend in its fury. Lightning blasted through rooftops and blew chunks of Terror's Lament high into the air. Hailstones the size of wagon wheels plummeted from the sky and turned the streets to rubble. Still, through the unimaginable strength of the holy storm, Lady Scrapple's undead dragon continued to spew wave upon wave of liquid death from its boney maw.

A bolt of brilliant lightning struck the emerald and was absorbed by the magic of the Tower of Wings. Then, in rapid succession, hundreds of other lightning strikes found their way into the magical emerald until the entire stone glowed with waiting energy. The dragon swooped low past the Tower and turned over to spray a devastating gout of black flames at the base of the glass structure. When its mouth opened, the Tower unleashed a beam of condensed electricity at the beast that knocked it to the ground. The dragon's mouth smoldered and some of the smaller bones had been destroyed, but it was not defeated.

471

The creature clawed at the ground, tearing up huge chunks of the street, and took to the air once more. A soldier that had been hiding in an alleyway near where the dragon had landed rushed out and tried slice at the monster with a sword, but a swoop of the dragon's long tail sent the man flying into a building.

The storm continued to empower the Tower of Wings and send out ear-splitting blasts of electricity at the dragon. No matter how many times the beast's body was rocked by lightning, it showed no signs of dying. Apollonius watched in horror as the beast circled high above his head and crashed into the Tower of Wings. It dug its claws into the delicate glass and before long, the structure started to crack. The bone dragon opened wide its boney mouth and bit down through one of the upper floors of the Tower with a sickening crunch.

In the brutal winds of the magical storm, the Tower of Wings could not withstand the structural damage the dragon was inflicting upon it. Slowly, as if struggling to stand and shaking legs, the great glass tower tumbled to the ground and shattered.

As the emerald crashed into a large apothecary on the corner of a marketplace, it split into thousands of dazzling shards that rained down on the street. A thunderous cry from heaven came down through the clouds and washed over the ruins of the city. Vrysinoch had seen his precious temple fall.

In mocking victory, the bone dragon landed amidst the rubble of the tower and bathed the remains in black fire. The beast turned its head toward the sky and roared. It was an open challenge to Vrysinoch to descend from heaven and defend the people of Talon-rend.

Apollonius felt wet tears stream down his face. In a single afternoon, his world had been destroyed. The barracks where he lived was consumed by fire. The men he had led into battle were dead or scattered throughout the rubble like beaten dogs. He was powerless to defend the city he loved, and the one thing that had given him hope was dead on the ground underneath giant bony feet.

With a mixture of hopeless desperation and unbridled rage, Apollonius drew his sword and began to run. He was several streets away from the skeletal monstrosity, but his legs pumped furiously. He screamed as he turned a corner and came face to face with the dragon. Apollonius held his blade aloft and ran up the side of a broken building. He leapt from the rubble and brought his sword down with his eyes closed, praying that Vrysinoch would guide his strike.

Apollonius' sword, marked with a talon and emerald to designate his station, bit into the dragon's skull and sank to the hilt. The man held on for his life as the beast launched from the ground and tried to shake the weapon from its head.

The dragon twisted and turned, crying out all the while, and Apollonius tightened his grip. For a moment, the young officer thought he had destroyed the monster and saved his city. The dragon rolled in the air and sharply lost altitude. Before Apollonius could register what was happening, the beast dove head first into the top of Master Brenning's forge and Apollonius was crushed to death in an instant.

The Dragon's Breath Armory was reduced to ruins as the beast thrashed around in the rubble to right itself and take off. Although Apollonius' short sword was still lodged firmly in the top of its skull, the dragon didn't possess any vital organs capable of being injured. With a great flap of its bone wings, the beast took to the sky once more.

From the bottom of heaven, rain began to fall. It wasn't a driving rain that would have been natural to such a violent thunderstorm, but it was a gentle patter of cold, half-frozen droplets that drifted slowly down to Talonrend. Behind the icy drizzle, a shadow appeared on the floor of the sky that blocked out what little light was left in the world.

A sound much louder than the beating of the dragon's bone wings emanated from the fractured clouds and slowly, a pointed talon the size of a farmhouse broke through. Behind that yellow talon came a second foot and a tuft of brown feathers large enough to cover entire streets.

FROM A WINDOW cut into the side of the throne room of Castle Talon, Herod watched in awe as his city was torn apart. Great sections of Terror's Lament had crumbled and were lost to fire. The houses and buildings that lined the once-vibrant city streets were reduced to smoldering rubble. Anything the black fire touched turned to ash.

Herod had managed to stay positive and cling to the hope that the priests of the Tower of Wings would be able to save them. That hope had come crashing down when the iconic glass tower fell. The castle, a squat two story structure of stone and iron, rumbled with the sounds of war. Minotaurs had taken the western wall and several of the massive creatures had found their way down to the roof of Castle Talon.

The dying prince braced himself against the window and listened as thundering hooves threatened to break through the roof. It would be only a matter of time until they destroyed the drawbridge and began pounding on the castle doors. Luckily, the stained glass windows were too narrow for the bovine monsters to slip through.

As Herod watched his city burn, a castle guard on the parapet above came face to face with Qul, the minotaur king. Qul's long metal poles beat a furious rhythm against the man's body that quickly reduced him to an unrecognizable pulp. The king bellowed a blood curdling war cry and Herod heard him jump from the roof to the stone in front of the raised drawbridge. Only two guards remained inside the castle with Herod.

"Gentleman," he addressed the two stewards and the two guards. "It has been my honor to be your prince." He looked each of them in the eyes and tried to be as regal as possible despite his seeping wound. "Unfortunately, Talonrend has come to an end. Our frontier city has fallen."

No one said a word. Qul hammered on the bottom of the drawbridge with his massive poles and the wood splintered. There was only a foot or so of iron-banded wood between the furious minotaur and the human prince.

"There is a small dungeon beneath the castle and below that, the sacred shrine to Vrysinoch. It is said only members of the royal family and a select group of others are allowed to enter the shrine. Well, you've all earned my blessing. I cannot guarantee your safety if you choose to hide in the shrine, but I can guarantee your death if you stay here." Herod straightened the bottom of his royal tabard and lifted his brother's crown from a small wooden box. He placed it on his head and felt the weight of the metal and the title settling upon him.

"We will die with our king," one of the guards said defiantly. The man flexed and held his sword close to his chest.

"Yes," Herod said. "I am your king."

The drawbridge collapsed under Qul's vicious assault. The giant minotaur wasn't even winded. He immediately set to work bashing through the castle doors with his metal poles. It took him less than a minute to reduce them to splinters.

One of the two guards left at Herod's side leveled a crossbow from the back of the broken throne. Herod sat on a piece of the damaged chair and attempted to be as kingly as he knew how. He puffed out his chest and waited for his end with honor and dignity. Without his famed swords, he was defenseless. He had to admit to himself that despite having his swords, he was far too weak to fight off even the most meager assault.

The crossbow next to Herod's head fired and sent a steel-tipped bolt hurtling down the long hallway before the throne. Qul's massive body took up every inch of available space in the hall and the bolt hit him squarely in the chest where it bounced off his thick armor. The minotaur didn't notice.

The second guard raised his sword and yelled. He charged at Qul, but one swipe of the monster's heavy pole sent his sword flying from his grip. Qul's fist slammed into the man's head and splattered his brains all over a tapestry.

Against Herod's orders, the two servants left in the castle stood with their arms crossed in front of their king. They held no weapons, but they didn't back down. The guard behind the throne fired another bolt and his aim was impressively accurate. The bolt clanged when it hit Qul's steel helmet and clanged again when it fell to the floor. The guard threw his crossbow down and grabbed a decorative pike from a nearby wall. He stabbed at the slowly walking monster, fearful of getting too close, and Qul barely paid him any attention. With one meaty hand, the minotaur slapped the pike away from the soldier.

The man drew his sword and ran in low against Qul, hoping to attack his legs. As soon as he got close, Qul lifted his armored foot over the man's head and crushed him, never slowing his pace.

The two stewards stood their ground and offered solemn prayers to Vrysinoch. With a metal pole in each hand, Qul swung the weapons from both sides hard enough to cut the men in half. Their corpses fell limply to the ground at Herod's feet.

Sitting on the broken throne was awkward, but Herod truly felt like a king. He brushed a speck of blood from his tunic and rose to meet the minotaur. Even on the raised dais, Herod was several feet shorter than Qul and had to strain his neck to see the beast's black eyes under his helmet.

"I will not surrender Talonrend, foul beast," Herod said calmly. Qul made no indication that he understood.

Herod crossed his arms over his chest and waited. The towering creature stepped closer and Herod could feel the heat of its breath. With a delicate touch that contrasted his brutality, Qul returned one of his poles to his back and plucked the crown from Herod's head. The minotaur removed his helmet and inspected the crown thoroughly. It was far too small to wear in the human style, but Qul slipped it over one of his capped horns and let it hang like a piece of jewelry.

A minute later, Qul emerged from Castle Talon with Herod's bloody head impaled upon one his poles. He smashed the gearbox that released the drawbridge and slammed his pole into the center of the already demolished wood. The morbid trophy wobbled briefly, but held. He wanted any survivors to know that he was their new king.

WHEN BOTH MASSIVE feet had descended through the clouds, the rest of Vrysinoch's body appeared. All throughout the city, the battle faded and slowed. The world had not been suppressed by any magical means, but the presence of the living Vrysinoch demanded awe from humans and minotaurs alike. Even the winged demons ferrying minotaurs to the top of Terror's Lament had to pause for a moment to let their guileless minds attempt to comprehend what they were seeing.

Vrysinoch's beak, a powerful white and yellow structure resembling that of a golden eagle, opened wide enough to swallow several large catapults at once. The bird screeched and what glass remained in Talonrend instantly shattered. For miles around, the god's call echoed and caused a violent aftershock that knocked soldier's to their knees.

Lady Scrapple's bone dragon dropped low and sped toward the eastern walls of the city. Moments before, the dragon had been the largest living thing any human of Talonrend had ever seen. Vrysinoch eclipsed the sun and made the dragon look like an overgrown and unruly pet. At once, the feathered god flew after the dragon and chased it from the city.

The two powerful avian creatures flew about one another in a blur of speed that no human eye could hope to follow. Vrysinoch clawed with his talons and ripped great chunks of bones from the dragon with every swipe. In turn, the undead beast spat gouts of acrid black flames that the god was forced to dodge. As quickly as Vrysinoch was destroying the skeletal dragon, Lady Scrapple's magical consciousness latched onto fresh bones from the battlefield and used them to mend the dragon's wounds.

The moment of awe and reverence faded and the brutal fighting on the western portion of the walls resumed. Several dozen minotaurs, aided by winged demons with sharp claws, cleaved their way through swaths of human defenders. The casualties were immense on both sides, but for every minotaur that fell to a human blade, a score or more men had died.

Taurnil stood next to Jan and Keturah in the northeastern outpost of Terror's Lament and tasted the air. He could feel Gideon's presence, but it was much farther away than he had expected. "He isn't in the city," Taurnil hissed to his master.

"Can you find him?" Keturah asked with her rough minotaur voice. Her pet demon nodded and got ready to fly.

"Don't let Vrysinoch see you," she warned. Taurnil was certainly powerful, but Keturah knew he would be less than an annoying fly to a god.

Taurnil leapt from the wall and flew east, directly over Castle Talon and the city below. He kept low at first to not attract the attention of any human archer still alive, but soon realized it didn't matter. What remained of the human defenses, apart from the western wall, had been eradicated by hellish flames and heavenly lightning strikes.

When he soared over the eastern wall, Taurnil made sure to fly as low to the ground as possible. The dueling god and dragon were fighting so violently that everything within half a mile of them had been turned to rubble. The wind from Vrysinoch's monstrous wings was strong enough to blow topsoil away and reveal bedrock dozens of feet below.

Whenever Vrysinoch and the dragon clashed, the ensuing thunderclap shook the world.

Taurnil watched for a moment before taking a careful and circuitous path north toward Kanebullar Mountain and his prey. The closer he got to Gideon, the more he could taste human flesh on his three tongues.

SEVERAL HOURS AFTER Vrysinoch's arrival, the last human defending the walls fell over the side to his death. A gloating minotaur stood behind the parapet and watched the soldier plummet to his death, laughing all the while. The sun had begun to set and neither Vrysinoch nor the undead dragon had gained any advantage. Their raging battle continued and neither showed any sign of relenting.

Almost a hundred minotaurs, slightly less than half that had made the initial assault, survived. Eight winged demons carried Qul's throne to the roof of Castle Talon where the minotaur king paced back and forth. They dropped the throne and landed gently on their feet, ready to obey their new king.

"The orcs will be here soon, I believe," Qul told his assembled generals. He thought of Undrakk and shuddered. The strange half-orc brought a foul taste to his mouth that he could never purge.

"Kill them?" the nearest general asked hopefully.

"Kill them." Qul looked down from the top of the castle and watched Herod's bloody hair fluttered in the gentle evening breeze. It had been so easy to kill the human leader that Qul almost didn't believe it had happened. He reached up and touched his crown to reassure himself. Surely enough, the golden circle of gemstone still hung loosely from one his horns.

"As you instructed, the ballistae and most of the mounted crossbows were not damaged in the attack," one of the minotaur generals reported. "We should have no problems slaughtering the orcs before they breach the city."

"*My* city!" Qul bellowed at the general. He hadn't thought of a name for the spoils of his conquest, but there would be time for that later. "Where would be the easiest place to attack?" Qul asked. As much as he enjoyed intimidating his generals and showing his authority, Qul knew there were greater tasks at hand. He sat back on his throne and let his subordinates make their reports.

"The demons say there are no full breaches of the three-layered walls, but the southern section has crumbled severely and there are gaping holes in the eastern portion, both interior and exterior." The general bowed his head respectfully and took a step backward.

Qul thought for a long moment before speaking. "If there are no clear entry points, station several soldiers along each wall and save the rest on the ground." He looked to one of the nearby winged demons that stood near Jan and Keturah. "How many of you are left?" he asked the strange creature.

Jan stepped forward to answer. "Only two score, maybe a handful more," he said. While the human crossbows had been useless against the heavy plates of the minotaurs, the unarmored demons had been easy targets. Their sinewy wings were not suited well to combat and many of them had plummeted to their deaths with bolts sticking out of their limbs.

"Have them fly patrols around the walls and report to me the moment the orc clans come into sight," he ordered Jan. The possessed minotaur bowed and relayed the instructions to the demon nearest him.

"What of Undrakk?" one of the generals questioned.

Qul put on a smirk and tried to look confident. Inside, the half-orc terrified him. Qul's muscled arms and enormous body were practically useless against a skilled magic wielder. "Let him come to me," Qul decided. He desperately wanted to allow his soldiers to attack the shaman on sight, but he feared that Undrakk would still reach him and Qul would be left without a clan to lead.

"Yes, my king," the minotaur general responded. Qul waved the council away and allowed himself a moment to relax and relish in the sight of Talonrend burning. The fires were like sparkling gems in his eye and smoke was the sweetest perfume.

Twenty-Four

THE MINE CART rattled down the tracks and gained speed. Gideon shoveled some of the ore out of the bottom of the cart to make room for his legs. The goblins from the forge chased after them, but the cart was too fast. The ground sloped down and the tunnels ahead were pitch black.

"We're close to the storehouse," Vorst yelled over the noisy wheels. Melkora wrapped her arms around the side of the cart and grit her teeth against the vibrations.

Flickering light ahead indicated their imminent arrival in another chamber. Over the chattering of the metals wheels, Gideon could hear the sounds of goblins. "Get ready," he said, though he didn't have to. Melkora held Roisin tightly in her grasp and crouched below the edge of the big cart.

A dozen or more goblins were waiting for them when they arrived in the storage area. They were the large goblins, bred for combat and carrying well-made weapons and armor. Two of them stood in the center of the tracks and tried to stop the cart as it entered the room. Vorst leaned over the front and fired her crossbow, hitting one of the big goblins in the upper chest. The creature stumbled backward and fell, leaving only one goblin in their direct path. The single goblin was no match for the speeding cart and only managed to struggle for a brief moment before being dragged under the wheels to his death.

Several goblins charged at the side of the cart and Gideon whipped Maelstrom in front of them to keep them at bay. The inky black tendrils lashed out and cut deep gashes along the goblin's legs. As the cart sped by, several of the attackers attempted to throw rocks and javelin at them, but the thick metal sides of the cart deflected the missiles easily.

"The switch!" Vorst yelled in a panic. Gideon looked up and saw the tall switch silhouetted in flickering torchlight. It leaned leftward, a stark indication that the cart's path was headed toward incineration. A large goblin stood next to the switch and held onto it with all his weight.

"You've got one shot!" Gideon told Vorst. He pulled Maelstrom back behind his head and waited. There was less than fifty feet of track between the barreling mine cart and the track switch that would determine their fate.

Vorst steadied her crossbow as best she could and closed her eyes. Finding the calm place that existed between the chaos of battle and the serenity of death, she remembered shooting the majestic elk in the forest with Gravlox. Her breathing slowed and her muscles tensed. The cart rattled and she took her shot. When she opened her eyes, the goblin holding the switch fell to his knees and clutched at a small bolt protruding from his chest.

In an instant, Gideon jerked his wrist forward and summoned tendrils of dark magic from Maelstrom's tip. The grasping strands flew in front of the cart and latched onto the switch at Gideon's mental behest. With another flick of his wrist, Gideon yanked the tendrils to the side and flipped the switch from right to left. The track parts clicked into place a second before the screaming wheels passed over and took the four into the chamber of the Mistress of the Mountain.

LONG AFTER NIGHTFALL, someone grabbed Seamus' shoulder and shook him awake. He rubbed his eyes and looked up to see a score of paladins staring back at him.

"You have his sword," one of them said, pointing to Nevidal in Seamus' lap.

"Yes," he muttered wearily. "He gave it to me." Seamus hadn't bothered to concoct a believable lie regarding his theft so he thought that simple might be best. The paladin waited a moment before nodding and offering a hand to bring Seamus up from the ground.

"We lost the walls," the man said. He pointed up to the western wall and Seamus saw massive creature's prowling there that were far too large to be human. "Castle Talon has fallen as well."

"Where's the army?" Seamus asked awkwardly. He brushed his pants and armor off and held Nevidal by the blade against his shoulder.

The paladin pointed to the men standing behind him in full armor with maces and shields. "We're all that's left," he said, but there was no trace of sorrow in his voice. "A few more are certainly scattered throughout the rubble, but we are the only ones with any fight left in us." The paladins offered up a quiet cheer and gathered closer.

"I can fight," Seamus told them. He recognized their faces from the road and he could tell more than half of them knew who he was.

"Good," the man responded. He started to draw a crude map on the ground in the alley to lay out their plan. "The minotaurs have taken over the castle, but there aren't many. Only five or six have stayed there with their leader, a giant brute wearing King Lucius' crown. The flying ones, whatever they are, patrol around the castle and fly supplies over the walls."

Seamus gulped down his fear and wondered where he would fit into the plan. He wasn't trained to fight and he couldn't even remember the words to the battle hymns the paladins liked to sing. When the paladin mentioned Lucius' crown, Seamus felt his stolen sword nearly jump to life in his hands. Nevidal pulsed with hunger and commanded Seamus to slay the mighty king.

"We can form up here," the man continued, pointing to a spot on his dirt map. "We can take them. If we form a shield wall, nothing can stop us."

Seamus listened to the distant sounds of Vrysinoch and the bone dragon battling and had to question the man's courage and his sanity. If the god of Talonrend could not defeat a dragon, how could they hope to slay a minotaur that was taller than two of them combined?

When their plan had been fully laid out, the men snuck around the edge of a crumbled building south of Castle Talon and waited for a nearby patrol of flying monsters to wander off. Doing what paladins of Vrysinoch do best, the men formed into a square and began singing a battle hymn as they marched toward the minotaur king.

Four minotaur soldiers guarded the drawbridge. The wooden structure had nearly been destroyed by Qul's onslaught, but enough of it remained to be useable. In the center, Herod's head still lolled on one of Qul's metal poles. The four minotaurs drew their weapons and waited for Qul's signal to attack.

The minotaur king smiled. He admired the bravery of the paladins, but he found it hard to believe they could be so foolhardy. Qul stood from his throne on the roof of Castle Talon and yelled out the order to charge. His four trusted generals sprang into action.

The paladins pressed on with measured steps. Their formation, five across and four rows deep, was a slow moving wall of tall shields. The battle hymn rose above the din of chaos and filled them with strength. The nearest minotaur general stomped down the drawbridge and hurled an axe at the approaching humans. Before the weapon connected, he dropped down to all fours and ran. The axe whirled end over end and smashed into one of the front shields.

Splinters of wood flew into the paladin's face, but the protective magic of their hymn spared the man from serious harm.

The minotaur charged like a bull and smashed all three thousand pounds of his mass into the front line. The men braced and dug their heels into the cobblestones, but they were wholly unprepared for the sheer strength of the creature. Three paladins collapsed under the weight of the assault. Men behind the fallen soldiers struggled to help their comrades up, but the heavily armored minotaur thrashed and kicked, each hoof breaking bone as it landed. The beast's metal-capped horns speared through a metal shield and sank into the flesh of the man behind it. The paladin screamed and brought his sword down to cut the horns, but the minotaur was too quick.

With an inspiring shout, the young leader of the makeshift troop called for his men to pull back. In their very center, Seamus wrapped his hands around Nevidal's hilt and felt his body surge with power. His muscles bulged and his mind sharpened. The poor farmer felt the sensation of clarity overwhelm his consciousness and wrest control of his actions. He was Vrysinoch's tool of destruction and the city needed him.

When the paladins stepped backward, Seamus leapt from their midst with more fury than any minotaur had ever seen from a human. He swung Nevidal down in front of him and hacked wildly at the bovine monstrosity. The minotaur grunted with pain, but did not relent. Rather than retreat to preserve his body, the general reared up on his hind legs and drew a two-handed sword from his back.

Seamus had to tilt his head up to see the minotaur's helmet. With Nevidal in his hands, he felt no fear. The two swords met above Seamus' chest with a shower of sparks. The farmer pushed back and felt his empowered muscles knotting and pulsing with otherworldly energy. Slowly, the minotaur began to lose his footing and slid several inches backward.

Qul leaned over the parapet in amazement. He watched with

intense scrutiny as his general lost a direct test of brawn with a single human. "I must have that sword," he whispered. He knew beyond any doubt the sword Seamus wielded was the most powerful weapon he had ever seen.

Seamus overpowered the general and forced him to his knees. The minotaur tried to maneuver his own sword beneath Nevidal, but the blade was pressed solidly against his chest armor. He had nowhere to turn and his only option was to let his own weapon fall and hope to jump backward quicker than Seamus could strike.

As soon as the sword fell from the general's hands, Nevidal carved a deep swath of destruction through his chest that split the beast from neck to waist. The minotaur's guts spilled across the stones and the paladins cheered.

Qul bellowed with rage and leapt from the parapet. He landed on the small stone landing just before the drawbridge with a thunderous crash of hoof and rock.

"Stand down!" he ordered his three remaining generals. The minotaurs stepped back and allowed their king room to pass. Qul stood tall in front of the paladins and stared at Seamus. His deep breaths turned the air to fog and when he scraped his hooves against the stones, bits of rock broke free. He wrenched his metal pole from the drawbridge and shook Herod's lifeless head into the moat below. With both weapons tightly in his grip, Qul pointed toward Seamus and ordered him forward.

"Don't go," one of the battered paladins behind Seamus whispered. The man's voice shook and he threatened to throw down his weapons and run.

Nevidal felt the challenge and commanded Seamus' legs to stride forward. The air between Seamus and the minotaur king was thick with tension. Several winged demons circled over the paladins and waited for the order to attack. The three remaining minotaur generals fidgeted with their weapons and inched closer to the tight pack of humans.

Qul turned and motioned with his head for Seamus to follow

487

him inside. Without thinking, the farmer obeyed. He walked behind the colossal beast and entered Castle Talon. Qul had to stoop down dramatically to enter the building and could not stand fully until he reached the audience chamber in front of the ruined throne. The minotaur king turned and contemplated the courageous human for a long moment.

"You may live," Qul said slowly, his grasp of the human language facilitated by the magical amulet he had received from Undrakk. "Give me your sword." Qul held out his hand and waited.

Seamus continued to feel his arms and back bulge with strength and wondered how long his bones could endure the growth. At what point would his heart not be able to carry blood to his growing limbs? Would the magical enhancement end of its own accord?

He thought of handing the weapon over, but the mere notion of releasing Nevidal from his grasp sent a wave of pain rattling through his head. The blade did not want to be forfeited. He would not surrender.

"Take it," Seamus boldly proclaimed. "If you can."

WHEN THE HEAVY doors to Castle Talon swung shut, chaos broke out. The three generals, aided by an aerial assault of winged demons, swarmed over the paladins like flies to rotting meat.

The men locked their shields and took up a battle hymn once more. Occasional screeches and other sounds from Vrysinoch's duel against the bone dragon found their way through the city to fill the men with hope. As the fires of Talonrend raged and ethereal souls danced above the clouds high over the city, the men couldn't help but feel that they were already in hell. For most of them, the idea of death had lost its wicked sting. Their world was in ruins, and life could not possibly get any worse.

The front row of paladins stepped back into the second row to make up for their diminished numbers and waited for the three generals to crash into them. Although the force of the initial charge was enough to crush four of the paladins into the ground, their magically enhanced shields stayed locked in place. The paladins sang and pushed forward at once with a coordinated effort.

For a brief second, the three minotaurs were pushed back and the men had a chance to stab over their shields and attack. The armored beasts took the relatively weak hits without complaint. Then, like liquid fire pouring from the sky, the demons opened their jagged mouths and began spewing acid onto the paladins from above.

Their shields were useless. When they pulled them up to deflect the poison falling from the sky, the minotaurs gutted them where they stood. The acid burned and sizzled as it bore through their armor and into their skin. Several of the demons swooped low to slash at the men with their razor sharp claws. Within moments, the unified force of determined paladins had devolved into a chaotic mess of screams and death.

The three generals could not be stopped. They tore through the ranks with ease and absorbed every strike the humans could muster. The battle hymn faded and before long, there were more dead humans than living.

The last group of five paladins formed a circle and tried to protect themselves. They fought as they had been trained and waited for opportune moments before they struck. No matter how organized and perfectly timed their strikes, the human swords and maces were never strong enough to pierce the magnificent plate armor the minotaurs wore.

When the last man of the group died, only one demon had been lost. The three generals had dozens of new gashes and dings in their armor, but not a single blade had found its way to the skin. The slain demon, a small creature with pale skin and eyes like black ink, had suffered a long cut from its hips all the way to the back of one shoulder. The minotaurs noted with curiosity that no vital organs spilled out. While the creature bled, it did not come apart like they expected. Instead, when the beast shuddered and breathed its last, its skin turned to flaky ash and dissipated in a wisp of acrid smoke as though a small candle had been extinguished.

"The orcs have arrived!" a young minotaur shouted from a street south of Castle Talon. The generals turned and pushed the jubilation of their victory far from their minds. The messenger stormed up to the generals on all fours before slowing to a bipedal gait.

"Both clans?" one of the generals asked. "Where is Undrakk?"

"Yes," the minotaur hastily saluted. "They are approaching the western gate. Undrakk leads them."

The general turned to a winged demon and commanded the pale creature to carry him over the walls to the western gate. The strange being cocked its head awkwardly to the side and obeyed. With strained beats of its leathery wings, the demon lifted the heavy minotaur above the houses and fires and carried him west.

QUL COULD BARELY fathom a world in which a scrawny human would dare stand against him. Other members of his clan, fully grown minotaurs who had proven themselves in combat time and time again, were known to shake in terror before him. All but the bravest of orcs would prostrate themselves in his presence. Even the two human wizards possessing minotaur bodies had shown fear in the presence of the king.

Seamus stood several steps below the stone dais and refused to flinch. He held his sword before him and waited like a statue about to be unveiled.

"This city is mine," Qul explained, trying to make Seamus see the futility of his stubbornness. "You have no one left."

Seamus shook his head and when he did, the muscles of his back bulged and popped as they suddenly grew. He felt his heartbeat increase and he stretched, popping his back and growing several inches in the process. When Seamus opened his mouth to speak, he felt Vrysinoch breath through him from miles away.

"You will die," the god screeched above Seamus' gruff voice. "I will have your soul!"

Nevidal commanded Seamus' feet to move and they sprang to life in a blur of finely coordinated steps. Qul set his metal poles into motion before him and waited for the blade to strike. Nevidal darted under one of the swinging weapons and connected with Qul's hip. The thick metal plate gave in an inch, but did not break. In the blink of an eye, Qul's pole smashed into the sword and knocked it off course.

Seamus jumped back and narrowly avoided taking a full force hit to his ribcage. Qul moved his long arms out in wide circles and swung his weapons simultaneously across his body. With his incredible reach, Seamus knew he wouldn't be able to back far enough away. He dropped to the ground and let the metal poles pass harmlessly above his head.

From the ground, Seamus rolled over his left shoulder and came up next to the minotaur king with a horizontal slash aimed at Qul's legs. The beast turned his front leg outward and absorbed the strike with a steel greave. Qul put his poles together and swung them down like a lumberjack splitting wood. They landed on Seamus' back hard enough to split the stone floor beneath the man but somehow, Seamus survived.

Nevidal controlled Seamus' legs and rolled him to his side and down the dais stairs, revealing a spider web of cracks extending from where his chest had split the floor. Qul bellowed and laughed with glee behind his helmet. He descended the steps and pressured Seamus, slashing in front of him with both weapons in quick succession and never allowing the human to get his feet set beneath him.

Before long, Seamus felt his back touch a decorative tapestry hanging from the wall and he knew he had nowhere left to run. In a desperate attempt to buy time, Seamus turned to his right and swung Nevidal at one of the poles, parrying the minotaur's left-hand attack and accepting a hit from his right hand that was strong enough to cleave through granite. The blow knocked the wind out of him, but Seamus knew that Nevidal's magic saved his life and prevented his spine from shattering.

The temporary reprieve granted Seamus enough time to slide his blade up the metal pole and rip it across Qul's gauntlet. The metal screeched and sent a shower of sparks onto the floor. When Nevidal bit into the beast's hand, Qul pulled back and used his right pole to smash into Nevidal and turn the blade aside.

The minotaur king took several steps backward and looked at his bloody hand. His armor had failed him for the first time in his life. It had been so long since Qul had bled that he was surprised that his body still knew how. "Give me the sword," Qul beckoned, "and we can rule together. You will be my second."

Seamus leaned against the wall and felt the fabric of the tapestry against his leather armor. It was a tapestry depicting Vrysinoch looking over Talonrend with a watchful eye. As tempting as the offer was, Seamus could not surrender. The blade in his hands forbade it. The god in the sky forbade it.

"You fear me," Seamus spat.

Slowly, Qul reached up and pulled the gem-studded crown from one of his horns and cast it aside. It clattered at the base of the broken throne. Qul unsnapped three latches on this side of his helmet and let the faceplate fall from the backing. He shook his body and the other half of the helm rolled down his back and crashed to the stone. Solemnly, Qul shed his gauntlets and removed the plates from his forearms.

The minotaur king unlaced the backs of his steel greaves and let them fall from his legs. When he was only wearing his black breastplate, Qul took one of his mighty poles in both hands and leveled it in the same manner that Seamus held Nevidal.

"You are a fool," he said. "I will not be so generous again." Qul lunged from the first step of the dais and jabbed with his pole like a dexterous fencer wielding a rapier. Faster than Qul himself thought possible, he weaved the metal pole through Seamus' lightning quick reflexes and pounded the man on the shoulders and chest.

Nevidal tried to parry the rapid strikes, but Seamus felt his strength beginning to fade. The weapon thirsted for souls and required fuel that Seamus was not able provide. His thoughts slowed and his consciousness ebbed toward the blade like a moth slowly circling a deadly flame.

Seamus saw an opening and knew he had to take it. He purposely missed a parry low and let the metal pole stab into his ribs. His stolen armor ripped and the pole found its way to his skin with the wet sound of broken bones. The force of the blow knocked him backward but gave him the opportunity he needed. Seamus brought Nevidal up with all the enhanced strength he had left and the magnificent sword sheared through Qul's unarmored forearm. With a howl of pain, Qul watched his right arm fall to the ground where it twitched and squirted dark blood.

Qul took his pole in his left hand and renewed his attack. He swung the weapon high and aimed for Seamus' head. Nevidal launched skyward and met the weapon, but Seamus no longer had the fortitude to match the minotaur's strike. The sword pushed backward and Seamus knew he would lose a direct test of muscle.

His back was almost against the wall and Seamus couldn't duck for fear of exposing his head. His own sword inched closer to his body and he could smell Qul's breath mingling with his own. Seamus turned his sideways and dove to his left under Qul's bleeding stub. When he loosened his grip on Nevidal, Qul's metal pole drove it downward so hard that it cut into Seamus' own shoulder and sprayed his face with blood, but the maneuver was successful. Seamus turned on his heels and swung Nevidal as high as he could. The sword connected with the side of Qul's chest plate and split it apart.

The beast staggered back against the tapestry with a grunt. Seamus knew his strength had almost faded completely. His vision started to swirl with splotches of black and red and his lungs protested every breath they took. The exhausted farmer stumbled up the stone dais and moved behind one of the halves of the broken throne. He leaned against the chair for support and prayed to Vrysinoch that Qul would not be able to push himself from the wall.

The minotaur king had lost a significant amount of blood. The walls were stained red and the floor was slick with it. Qul used his metal pole like a cane and slowly began to move. He lifted one heavy foot in front of the other and climbed the steps of the dais like an old man stepping into his own grave.

When he reached the top, Qul tried to lift his pole and strike, but lost his footing on the bloody stones and crashed to the ground in front of the throne. Seamus raised Nevidal up to finish the beast, but Qul's body did not move. He hobbled around the throne and used his foot to weakly lift Qul's head. The minotaur king had fallen directly on Lucius' crown. One of the golden protrusions atop the circle of metal was lodged in Qul's eye. A dark, soupy mixture of blood and brain matter seeped from the wound to stain the foot of the throne.

Seamus collapsed into the side of the broken chair and let his eyes fall shut. Nevidal begged for him to rise and kill, but Seamus' mind had gone dim. There were no souls left in the castle for Nevidal to take—none but his own. He struggled to stay awake against the pull of the magical weapon and within a minute, he succumbed. Nevidal ripped the man's soul through his fingertips and into its hilt. Some of the skin around Seamus' neck and face turned to pale ash and sloughed off his bones.

With a sharp metallic clatter, Nevidal fell from his grip to the blood-soaked dais and Seamus breathed his last.

Twenty-Five

THE DESCENT INTO Lady Scrapple's chamber took far longer than Gideon expected. He steadied his breathing and calmed his mind. He wished for the feel of Nevidal in his hands. Herod's swords were incredible, but Gideon felt clumsy with them. He wasn't used to planning his strikes with both hands individually.

He smiled when the metal rails under the mine cart came to an end and they skidded to a violent stop. The chamber was large and smelled of death. Two goblins stood several paces away and paid the group no heed. They busily prepared a large tray of roasted meats and cave mushrooms as though nothing was amiss. Gideon could hear the horde of larger goblins that had followed the mine cart. He would have a minute, maybe two, to slay Lady Scrapple before they descended upon him.

Gravlox and Vorst scampered from the cart and slew the two goblins in the room without hesitation. Gideon offered Melkora his hand and pulled her from the metal box with ease.

"Thank you," she whispered. Melkora couldn't shake the feeling that she was about to die. As a thief, she had gotten herself into dangerous situations plenty of times, but her life had never seriously been at risk. She thought of Cobblestreet and her small shop. She had seen fire on the horizon shortly after the dragon flew away from Kanebullar Mountain. None of it mattered. All she had truly loved was already gone.

"I'll never see her again..." Melkora accidentally muttered under her breath. In the still cavern, her words echoed with embarrassment and grief.

"Who?" Gideon asked tentatively. He strode to the chamber's only exit with Maelstrom and Regret in his hands.

"My daughter," Melkora began, but abruptly stopped. "Forget I said anything."

Gideon didn't have time to pity the woman. "The child you sent with the refugees?" he asked unsympathetically. Melkora nodded. "She is dead."

Melkora nodded again and brushed a solitary tear from her face. She held Roisin so tightly that her knuckles turned white. "Let's go," she said defiantly.

Gravlox and Vorst joined the two humans at the exit of the feeding chamber. In front of them, they heard the rumblings of Lady Scrapple's massive maw. The sounds of running goblins echoed through the passageway behind them. "What lies beyond?" Gideon asked. He couldn't see a thing through the darkness of the tunnel.

"I have no idea," Vorst said.

The four of them, Gideon and Melkora in front, walked down the tunnel until they reached the heart of the mountain.

The air was hot and sticky with lingering moisture. The walls were rough and bore thousands of tool marks. Covering it all was the stench of stale blood and centuries of decay. Gideon stood at the edge of the feeding tunnel and stared into the deep chamber in front of him. Twenty or more feet below, the creator of the goblin race peered up at the human intruders with a mixture of curiosity and unbridled madness.

Her eyes shone like flecks of pure evil amid the sea of her pale flesh that filled the cavern from wall to wall. Her mouth, a circular structure the size of a tavern door and filled with thousands of teeth, opened and closed rapidly beneath her beady eyes. Lady Scrapple rose up slightly in her chamber and produced a hissing sound like steam pushed through a furnace.

Instinctively, Gideon stepped back and waited for an attack. He wasn't sure how Lady Scrapple would come at him, but he knew she would. He thought of leaping from the edge and landing with Regret held underneath him. Such a large, fleshy target would be impossible to miss. But with her extreme size, would the sword cause enough trauma to be effective? Would he be able to cut enough of her away before she swallowed him whole?

A subtle rumbling started in the chamber far below Gideon's feet. It grew and grew until it shook the feeding tunnel and knocked bits of stone from the ceiling. "What's happening?" Gideon shouted.

"The mountain is coming down on top of us!" Melkora shouted. A huge chunk of rock dislodged from the ceiling and crashed into her back, knocking her to the ground to be pelted again.

"Run!" Gideon yelled. He didn't wait for the others to respond before jumping off the ledge. Gideon soared through the air with his legs folded beneath him and Regret pointing downward below his feet. The chamber began to crumble all around him.

Gideon landed with a wet thud and drove Regret through Lady Scrapple's gelatinous body to the hilt. For a dozen feet in all directions, Gideon was surrounded by the goblin matron's flesh. He slashed with Regret and the skin responded by spurting thick blood onto his arms and face. The sword cut a path of destruction through her body several feet wide.

A particularly violent tremor shook the chamber and a dislodged chunk of stone fell from the ceiling and hit Gideon in the chest. He flew backward and rolled from the top of Lady Scrapple's body to a small clearing of ground. To his right, Gideon watched in horror as a protrusion came to life and ripped through the stone tunnel to reveal a thick tentacle covered in milky bulbs containing unborn goblins.

Gideon hacked at the tentacle madly, but before he could land more than two cuts, Lady Scrapple ripped another tentacle free from the stone and brought them both high above her gaping mouth. The two tentacles slammed down hard enough to crack the stone underneath Gideon's feet. He rolled to his side and the wind from the tentacle hitting the ground where he had just stood was enough to jostle his braided beard. Gideon spun and made to strike with Regret, but Lady Scrapple was quicker. By the time he turned, the tentacle had already lifted from the ground for a second pulverizing attack.

The holy tattoo on Gideon's back burned with energy. He drew Maelstrom from his hip and set to work dodging the falling tentacles and attacking Lady Scrapple's body from a distance. With every lash, Maelstrom tore chunks of bloody flesh from the huge body and hurled them all over the cavern. When Lady Scrapple's tentacles smashed down, Gideon was forced to twist and turn his body at odd angles to avoid being crushed in a single blow. Above him, the cavern still trembled and the ceiling broke apart.

Gideon thought he saw Gravlox looking down from the crumbling feeding tunnel, but he couldn't afford to let his gaze linger. He slashed again with Maelstrom and latched the blade's shadowy tendril around one of Lady Scrapple's flailing tentacles. With unnatural strength, the goblin matron ripped her tentacle upwards and jerked Gideon from his feet. She flung her arm violently sideways and Gideon, holding the sword tightly, was slammed into the cavern wall twice before he was able to break Maelstrom's magical connection.

His back blazed with pain and he rolled to his side to try and suck air into his deflated lungs. His vision blurred and he barely saw a tentacle headed straight for him. Rolling feebly over, Gideon only avoided half of the tremendous blow. Lady Scrapple's huge arm crashed down across his lower legs and he knew in an instant that they were both broken. His right ankle was twisted underneath his shin and his left femur protruded grotesquely from the skin above his knee.

"Vrysinoch..." Gideon humbly prayed. "Let me rest..." His blood spilled over the cavern floor in jolting waves of agony. He let his eyes shut and waited for a tentacle to crush the last bit of life from his chest.

Lady Scrapple did not waste the opportunity. With both tentacles held together like a giant club, she smashed them down upon Gideon's head and chest and crushed him several inches into the stone.

No, Vrysinoch's avian hiss echoed through Gideon's corpse. It wasn't a voice of sadness, but one of defiance. Gideon's soul drifted above his disfigured body as Lady Scrapple tore his remains to oozing tatters.

I will join you now, Vrysinoch, Gideon's ghost whispered as it ascended above the goblin monstrosity. *You have my soul, as you have always wanted.*

No! Vrysinoch yelled through his incorporeal consciousness. The god raged with fury and Gideon felt his physical body begin to reform. His ghost watched as Vrysinoch's energy surged into the room and latched onto every remnant of Gideon's human body that it could find. His legs were magically lifted from the floor and his bones straightened and retreated back into the skin. His head inflated and drifted back to the rest of his body, reattaching itself with a quiet pop. Lady Scrapple thrashed her tentacles at the reassembling body hovering several feet above the floor, but Vrysinoch's magic turned Gideon's skin to molten lava. She shrieked and pulled her arms back, suddenly afraid for the first time in her entire existence.

You are my champion, Gideon of Talonrend, Vrysinoch whispered into Gideon's reformed body. *I may fall, but you will live.* Gideon's body floated above the stone for another second before the magic ended and dropped him to the ground.

Gideon was naked. His armor, clothing, and weapons were still scattered about the chamber as a result of his dismemberment. Gideon flexed his arms and his upper body ignited with holy fire. The

499

flames raged all around him, but their warmth brought him strength. Gideon crouched and flexed his legs. When the muscles tightened, his lower half turned to forged steel. One foot after the other, Gideon pounded his way toward Lady Scrapple. She slashed at him and tried to crush him again, but she might as well have been a maggot trying to topple Terror's Lament.

When he reached her body, Lady Scrapple arched backward and oriented her circular maw forward in an effort to swallow Gideon whole. Her tentacles slammed into Gideon's back over and over.

The paladin smiled. With Vrysinoch guiding his steps, he lifted a foot over the edge of Lady Scrapple's mouth and pulled himself inside.

VRYSINOCH DOVE UNDERNEATH a blast of dark flames and scraped against the ground. With a flurry of feathers, the god sprang back into the air and snapped at the bone dragon, ripping the undead beast's tail off and scattering hundreds of bones to the ground.

As it had done hundreds of times before, the dragon recoiled and sent out of a wave of telepathic magic that brought the bones back to its body and in second later, it was restored as if Vrysinoch had never touched it. The dragon spiraled high above the clouds and bid Vrysinoch to chase it.

Vrysinoch sped toward the back of the bone dragon and reached his mighty talons forth, latching onto the dragon's underside. Vrysinoch began digging through the center of the dragon and raining bones down upon the city far below. The dragon curled down on itself and unleashed a torrent of black fire over Vrysinoch's back. The bird reared in pain and had to push off. Vrysinoch's entire body had been burned by the magical fire several times over and the skin beneath the feathers boiled and bled. Rebuilding Gideon's body had taken too much energy—Vrysinoch had nothing left to fight the dragon.

You must kill the source, Gideon of Talonrend. Vrysinoch projected his vast consciousness over the plains and into the heart of Kanebullar Mountain. He found Gideon's soul and attached his own mind to it. *Kill her, my champion, and end this war...*

The dragon dove after Vrysinoch and bit into the larger creature's side. Vrysinoch tried to pry himself free from the dragon's mouth, but his will to fight had all but disappeared, as had his strength. The dragon beat its powerful wings and soared higher into the air. It carried Vrysinoch hundreds of feet above the clouds until Kanebullar Mountain and Talonrend were nothing more than small dots on a distant landscape.

With a ferocious bite, the dragon tore one of Vrysinoch's burned wings from his body and spat it out. The deity's body plummeted. The dragon pursued, descending directly behind the fallen god and roasting Vrysinoch with magical fire.

My champion... I will live... through you... Vrysinoch sent a final message to Gideon's soul before crashing into the ground with a violent explosion of blood, bones, and holy light.

YES, GIDEON MENTALLY responded. His flaming body burned and destroyed Lady Scrapple from the inside. Her mouth was much larger than the paladin needed to stand fully upright. He strode deeper into the matron's innards, making a path with his flaming hands and solid steel legs. The beast writhed around him and convulsed desperately. Gideon drove a flaming hand into the bloody flesh above him and ripped open the roof of Lady Scrapple's mouth. Blood poured from the wound and sizzled into steam when it touched his holy fire.

Another step forward brought Gideon directly under Lady Scrapple's hideous eyes. He reached up and relished the feeling of his fiery fingers working their way through the back of her head. When his hand hit something hard, he clutched it and let it burn for a moment before ripping it toward him. He brought the obsidian eye up to his own eyes and looked into it with a calmness that only comes from impending victory. With a roar, Gideon dove into Lady Scrapple's immense gullet and set her entire body ablaze.

Lady Scrapple's skin bubbled and the blisters exploded, peeling her skin away and reducing her to an ashen husk until Gideon could see the cavern around him once more. The goblin matron's body liquefied in the heat and left Gideon standing amidst several stone pillars that had served as her skeleton of sorts. Gideon looked to the feeding tunnel for any sign of his companions, but found none.

In that moment, gazing up at the crumbling stone ceiling, Gideon felt Vrysinoch die. His soul, magically entwined with the god's, witnessed the fatal impact of Vrysinoch's body upon the hard ground. Gideon's magical tattoo flared once before falling still. The fires surrounding his body went out with a puff of oily smoke. His legs returned to flesh and bone and at once, the exhaustion of his battle overcame him.

Gideon's mind fell into unconsciousness and his body collapsed against a stone pillar.

Twenty-Six

BATTLE-HARDENED GOBLINS FLOODED the feeding tunnel shortly after Lady Scrapple's chamber began to collapse. Melkora shrieked as she watched Gideon dive from the tunnel to the goblin matron's huge body below. Before she could leap from the ledge to help him, a boulder shook loose above her head and blocked her path.

Gravlox and Vorst turned to face the oncoming horde. In the small tunnel, they stood shoulder to shoulder with little room next to them. The close quarters bottle-necked the attackers and gave the pair comfort. Behind them, Melkora gasped for breath—she wasn't used to the chaos of combat and panic threatened to destroy her.

The first big goblin, standing a full head taller than Gravlox, charged through the tunnel with a long spear aimed for Vorst's chest. The goblin jabbed with the spear, deftly executing several feints in the process, and nicked Vorst's forearm. She took a step back and Gravlox lunged, skewering in the goblin in a single stroke. Before they could catch their breath, another goblin was upon them.

"Get behind me!" Gravlox yelled. He pushed Vorst back and stepped in front of her with his sword. She took aim above Gravlox's shoulder and fired her small crossbow. The nearest goblin tumbled down with a bolt stuck in his chest and Gravlox darted forward to finish it.

The two bulky corpses slowed the other goblins behind them and gave Vorst enough time to reload. Her crossbow clicked and another big goblin hit the ground with a groan and a thud. Gravlox leapt from his crouch and sliced the back of the goblin's neck as it tried to rise. Two more goblins scrambled over the growing collection of corpses with swords in their hands.

Vorst spanned her crossbow and fired, taking one of them down, but not before the other goblin attacked Gravlox. He ducked out of the blade's path, rolled across the top of a dead goblin, and came up swinging. The larger goblin anticipated the maneuver and soundly parried Gravlox's strike. Gravlox sidestepped and let his blade swoop down, moving with the parry to get behind the larger goblin.

"You're too far out!" Vorst shouted at him, trying to line up another crossbow shot. Gravlox pushed the bigger goblin in the back and knocked him over a corpse. The attacker tried to get to his feet, but Gravlox brought his sword down across his back and ripped him open with a shower of blood. More goblins kept coming down the tunnel and from the sounds they made, there were thousands. Only the tightness of the feeding tunnel prevented them from swarming the trio and easily killing them.

Vorst fired another shot over Gravlox's head that struck the skull of an approaching goblin and killed it instantly. "Get back," Vorst urged Gravlox. He shambled over the mounting corpses and made his way back to Vorst slowly. One of the goblins several paces from Gravlox held a bow and pulled the string taught.

"No!" Vorst yelled, trying to pull Gravlox down to the ground. Fortunately, the goblin archer was poorly trained at the arrow only grazed Gravlox's hip. A small line of blood trickled from the wound, but it was largely superficial. Vorst began cranking the crossbow once more and aimed at the archer.

A second bow-wielding goblin appeared next to the first and a handful of other goblins slid around the archers to make a wall of crude shields. Vorst fired, aiming high to try to send her bolt above the shield wall, but the small missile clattered into the top of the tunnel harmlessly.

The shield wall advanced slowly and with purpose. The goblins measured their steps and made sure not to trip on their fallen kin. At once, with the flawless coordination granted by a shared consciousness, the shield wall broke apart and two arrows sailed down the tunnel. As quickly as the shield-bearing goblins had split, they reformed again and continued walking.

The two wooden arrows hurtled down the small tunnel with alarming accuracy. Vorst grabbed the closest corpse and attempted to use it as a shield, but an arrow blasted through the dead goblin's chest. The arrowhead protruded far enough out of the corpse's back to hit Vorst in the top of her chest and knock her down.

Gravlox dove to the ground to avoid the arrow, but pain flared in his wrist that told him he was hit. He crawled back to Melkora's feet with an arrow stuck all the way through his wrist. Vorst threw the corpse from her chest and held her wound to stem the bleeding. There was nowhere for them to run.

Melkora, seeing the two goblins severely wounded, steeled her resolve as best she could and stepped in front of them. She thought of her daughter and let her grief turn into rage. Rather than wait for the three goblins with shields to descend upon her, Melkora rushed at them. The center goblin attempted to block her strike and Roisin cleaved through the wooden shield as though it was thin as silk.

The center goblin slumped to the ground. Roisin had mercilessly torn its throat from its neck. Melkora spun and slashed at the goblin on her left. She cleaved the beast's shield arm from its chest and carved through its side with ease. The goblin to her right jumped on her back and smashed her spine with a studded wooden club. Melkora screamed and thrashed, stabbing blindly behind her with Roisin.

505

The goblin took several hits from the sharp dagger, but none of them were deep enough to be immediately fatal. Melkora grabbed at the goblin's arm latched across the front of her body. The pale-skinned creature was too strong. She took another hit to the back of her head that brought spots to her vision. Melkora brought Roisin slowly in front of her and tried to steady her hand. Careful not to prick her own skin and die to her dagger's poison, she stabbed into the goblin's arm and began to saw. Carefully, taking hit after hit to the back of her neck and head, she carved her way through the arm and shook the goblin away. The creature twisted as it fell and Melkora jumped on top of it. She drove Roisin cleanly through the beast's head just above its upper jaw. It died with a squeal.

More goblins closed in. An arrow cut the air next to Melkora's head, ricocheted off the top of the tunnel, and bit into Vorst's upper thigh. She howled in agony and grabbed at the wound, forgetting about her crossbow. Melkora jumped to her feet as quickly as her spinning vision would allow. She slashed in front of her to ward off the attacker, but only managed to cut part of the goblin's spear away.

The creature pressed on and swung its broken spear rapidly. Melkora parried the attack and tried to counter. Roisin moved slowly in her grasp and her perception was dulled by throbbing pain. The goblin hit her with the broken spear across the arms and Roisin flew from her grasp.

Melkora collapsed to her knees and searched for her weapon among the corpses. A trickle of blood dripped over her brow and into her eyes. She brushed her forehead with the back of her hand and lost her balance, tumbling beside a dead goblin. After a frantic moment of searching, she latched onto the hilt of her dagger and turned over, ready to strike. The goblin attacker, almost directly over her, dropped its broken spear to the ground. It stared blankly at the tunnel wall as though confused.

Melkora didn't waste the chance to kill the goblin. She crawled to her feet and drove Roisin through the goblin's back with a spray of blood and gore. When she pulled her arm back, the creature dropped to the ground with a thud. Dead bodies clogged the tunnel. Melkora ran back to Gravlox and Vorst and waited. After a minute without an attack, she knew something was wrong.

"Don't go..." Vorst whispered, clutching her bleeding chest. Melkora didn't listen. Despite her own injuries, she couldn't sit in the end of the tunnel and wait to die. She crept forward over the mound of corpses and inched her way closer to the two archer goblins as quietly as possible. The pair had dropped their bows by their sides and stood next to each other with blank expressions. One of them swayed slightly from leg to leg, but the other simply stared at a spot on the wall as though in a trance.

Melkora held her blade up and threatened to stab one of the archers. The goblin didn't respond. She held Roisin to the creature's pale neck and waited. Still, the goblin watched the wall and made no acknowledgement of Melkora's presence.

When she ripped the blade across the goblin's throat, blood spilled from the wound and creature yelped, but otherwise remained inattentive as it died. Melkora ran back to Gravlox and Vorst with a smile on her face.

"She's dead!" she exclaimed. "Gideon must have done it! The goblins aren't moving!" She could hardly contain her glee. The back of her head still throbbed uncontrollably, but elation helped to dull the pain.

All throughout the feeding tunnel, goblin warriors milled aimlessly about as they experienced consciousness for the first time in their lives. Most of them dropped their weapons and others had trouble standing on their own. Their minds were freed and for most, it was too much for them to comprehend.

"We should move," Melkora said. The goblins didn't appear overtly violent, but she couldn't afford to take any chances. Another skirmish would likely bring her death. "Help me clear the rocks," she said.

Gravlox was too injured to help. Six inches of wooden arrow stuck out of either side of his wrist. He felt with his fingers to see if the bones were broken and luckily, they felt intact. Vorst and Melkora use their hands to shovel fallen rocks out of their path until one large boulder remained. There wasn't enough room in the tunnel to see over the top of the rock, so they pushed it and hoped Gideon wasn't underneath them. After a minute or more of pressing their weight against the boulder, it gave way and tumbled to the chamber below with a resounding crack.

"Gideon!" Melkora called. She spotted the man covered in blood and slumped against a pointed stone pillar. The entire chamber was a disorganized mess of destroyed goblin flesh and dark red blood. The tremors had caused a land slide of sorts and a buildup of loose stones beneath the feeding tunnel served as a relatively safe ramp to the bottom. Melkora made her way down to the floor and rushed to Gideon's side.

"Wake up!" she yelled at him. Gideon didn't respond. She placed a hand on his chest and listened to his breathing. His breaths were slow and uneven. She could barely feel his heartbeat underneath his naked chest. Gideon's entire body was covered in bruises and cuts that were just starting to clot on their own. His skin, normally a deep shade of swarthy olive, had turned to a pale sheen of grey splotched with patches of black and crimson. Melkora gathered up his clothes, armor, and swords and used what strength she had left to prop his head and back up in a sitting position.

Vorst helped Gravlox carefully descend the rock slide. The arrow in his wrist helped block the bleeding, but his hand tingled from a loss of sensation.

"How do we get out?" Melkora asked. Vorst scanned the area and spotted a small tunnel running downward at the southern end of the chamber.

"That might lead us out, I don't know," Vorst said.

"We don't have time to guess," Melkora responded. "Help me carry him." She fitted Gideon's pants over his body as best she could and raised Gideon from the ground with her shoulder. Gravlox took Gideon's gear with his good arm and Vorst tried to help support the man's weight. She was far too short to be helpful though and soon gave up altogether.

Melkora grit her teeth and urged all the adrenaline in her body to help her lift. Slowly, she brought Gideon off the ground and took a few steps forward. His feet dragged on the stone like a corpse, but Melkora bore him to the southern tunnel without complaint.

HALF A DAY later, Melkora emerged from a small ventilation shaft at the eastern base of Kanebullar Mountain. The sun had set and the moon shone brightly through the sparse foliage. She collapsed into the leaves and rolled Gideon to his back next to her. Gravlox and Vorst sat down behind the two humans and tried to fight off hopelessness.

Fires burned in the distance. The sky was choked with smoke and a light haze of ash fell from the sky. Melkora found a bright star glimmering behind the smoke and oriented herself toward Cobblestreet. She knew her village had been destroyed. The dragon had burned everything in its path toward Talonrend.

"How do we help him?" Melkora asked. Her voice was thin and ragged. Her lungs burned from the effort of carrying the larger man on her shoulder. A series of lumps had formed on the back of her skull that throbbed in pain with every beat of her heart.

Vorst looked to Gravlox and knew his shamanistic powers had not returned. The two goblins exchanged several lines in their high-pitched language and Gravlox shook his head.

"We can't help him..." Vorst muttered.

Melkora knew enough about wild herbs and rudimentary medicine to make a poultice for cuts and scrapes, but Gideon's wounds were far beyond her abilities. His body was wasting away in front of her and his spirit refused to be roused.

She rested her head against the leaves and closed her eyes to the world. She wanted desperately to sleep, but her desire to guard Gideon was too powerful. She offered up a meager prayer to Vrysinoch for guidance and waited.

Vorst draped Gideon's travelling cloak over his body and removed the leather straps from his mail armor. She wove the straps around the arrow in Gravlox's wrist to stabilize it and apply pressure. Her own wound on her chest had clotted well and proved to be less serious than her initial estimation. The skin was painful to the touch, but she was not in mortal danger.

Melkora had closed her eyes for less than ten minutes when a dreadful sound brought her suddenly back to alertness. Wings beat the air somewhere overhead.

"The dragon?" Melkora fearfully whispered. Vorst stood and listened.

"No," the goblin said. "Smaller."

Taurnil descended from the smoke and landed at Gideon's feet with a twisted smile. His three tongues darted around the edges of his mouth like a hungry wolf about to feast.

Melkora couldn't find the energy to voice her horror. The winged demon reminded her of stories her grandmother would tell her as a little girl of beasts who would steal naughty children and devour them. The woman's nightmares were far less terrifying than the unholy beast that stalked toward her.

"He's mine..." Taurnil's jagged teeth and darting tongues slurred his words into a sinister hiss.

Every fiber of Melkora's body told her to run. She was battered and exhausted. Somehow, her feet inched forward and she drew Roisin from its sheath.

Fight for me, a gruff voice echoed in her head and startled her. Melkora knew the voice. She didn't recognize it perfectly, but she knew it.

Fight for me... the voice beckoned once more like a whisper carried on a gentle breeze. It was Gideon's voice. It had somehow changed, but she knew the familiarity of the voice without a doubt.

Fight for your god! Gideon urged her mind. Without thinking, Melkora launched herself toward the winged demon with reckless abandon. She swung her dagger in a blaze of steel and claws that rang in her ears like the sweetest music. In that moment, Gideon's thoughts came to her as flawlessly as if they were her own. Beneath his flowing commands that directed her strikes, Melkora felt a hint of something divine.

Roisin darted through Taurnil's flailing claws and pricked his pale flesh over and over. With every touch, the blade pumped magical poison into the creature's body, eating its tissue from the inside. Taurnil retreated and leapt into the air, spitting his own vile toxins as he flew. The flow of energy through Melkora's mind and body showed her the path of the acidic liquid before it even began and she easily dodged the attack.

Taurnil beat his wings hard and hovered a dozen or more feet above Melkora. He hissed and spat his poison again.

Melkora sidestepped and stared the demon in his black eyes. "You will die," the woman spat. Her voice was foreign to her ears and sounded more like Gideon's than her own.

Kill him, the voice in her head urged. Melkora launched herself from the ground and feathery wings sprouted from her shoulder blades to carry her higher. Taurnil growled and dove to meet her, but Melkora was faster. Her wings carried her straight under the pale beast and she drove Roisin upwards with divine strength and righteous fury. The dagger tore through the meat of Taurnil's leg and carved through bone.

Taurnil pulled away and clutched at his tattered leg. Melkora reached to strike again, but her wings dissipated. In an instant, she fell to the ground on her stomach and the hilt of her dagger knocked the wind from her lungs. The winged beast shrieked again and turned in the air to flee. Taurnil held his ruined leg together as he flew above the trees back to his master.

"He will die, Gideon," Melkora coughed as she struggled for breath. She kissed the crosspiece of her dagger and fell asleep on the cold ground.

Twenty-Seven

UNDRAKK WAITED IMPATIENTLY before the western portcullis of Terror's Lament. A winged demon carried one of the minotaur generals down over the walls and dropped the heavy beast down in front of Undrakk.

"Why is the gate not opened?" the shaman asked casually. He tossed his polished staff from hand to hand and looked anywhere except at the minotaur. Two frenzied orc clans waited at his back.

"King Qul asks that you wait here for him," the minotaur said with authority. The general puffed out his chest and tried to appear intimidating.

"Does he?" Undrakk laughed heartily. "And why is that?" He planted his staff in the ground it stood on its own accord without the touch of Undrakk's hand.

The general hesitated. "Yes…" he said without much bravado. "He wants you to wait." The minotaur stood nearly twice the height of the half-orc, but shook nervously in his heavy armor.

Undrakk's smile was unsettling. "Go and tell the good king I expect the city to be opened within the hour."

The minotaur shifted from foot to foot and slowly nodded. He waved his winged demon escort back to his side and left Undrakk as quickly as he could. When the general landed on the inside of Terror's Lament, he strode up to the castle doors and took a tentative step inside.

"My liege?" he called out. The stench of blood tickled his nose and gave him pause. "Qul?"

No response greeted him. The general walked several more paces into the castle and saw Qul face down in a pool of blood. He rushed to the king's side and lifted him from the steps with a gasp. Qul was dead. The general ripped the crown from Qul's eye and threw it against the wall in disgust.

He kicked the human's sword off the dais and lifted Seamus' corpse with one arm. He threw the body against the wall with the other dead humans and took stock of the room's carnage. Most of the throne room was coated in blood. The dais was practically soaked in it.

With Qul dead, the minotaur clan had no king. By minotaur custom, whoever committed regicide became the new monarch. The general picked up the discarded human crown and brushed some of Qul's blood from a jeweled tine. He picked up one of Qul's metal poles and prepared to exit the castle and proclaim himself the king.

Before his hand pushed open the door, it was blasted apart by a violent burst of magic. Undrakk stood in the doorway with his staff pointed at the general's chest. He opened his mouth to speak and the shaman struck him in the chest with a brilliant bolt of lightning.

A second bolt of lightning shot forth from Undrakk's staff and coursed through the general's armor. The heat from the blast roasted the minotaur's flesh and cooked him inside his breastplate. A third blast knocked the minotaur several feet backward and killed the beast.

Undrakk glided his way to the dead general and plucked the crown of Talonrend from his head with the end of his staff. He brushed the gore from the crown and set it gently between his ears.

The half-orc sauntered out of the castle with an air of palpable confidence. The nearby minotaurs saw Undrakk's crown and none of them were brave or stupid enough to challenge him. The winged demons bowed before Undrakk and the minotaurs followed suit.

"Qul is dead!" Undrakk shouted above the chaotic din. He turned to one of the demons and commanded it to rise. "Raise the portcullis," he told the pale creature. It readily obeyed.

Undrakk pointed to another pair of demons that had been scavenging among the dead paladins. "Get the two possessed minotaurs from the walls. Bring them to me," he ordered.

Facing the rest of the assembled minotaurs and demons, Undrakk magically enhanced his voice to echo throughout the entire city. "I am your king now!" he bellowed.

BY MIDNIGHT, THE two orc clans had entered the city en masse. Snarlsnout the Gluttonous sat on his chair next to Undrakk in front of the drawbridge and drank in the smell of the city's destruction.

"Your warriors will patrol the walls and guard my city," Undrakk told the chieftain. Kraasghul stood patiently to the left of the half-orc king and waited for his orders.

"The Wolf Jaw Clan will go to the villages along the river," Undrakk instructed. "Clear the villages and burn them. Kill everyone you find."

Krassghul nodded with a smile. Killing humans would suit his clan well. Behind the assembled leaders, Jan and Keturah stood tall. They were content to serve as Undrakk's advisors. The two were still getting used to life as minotaurs, but it was a life they knew they would enjoy. The view from the front of Castle Talon was intoxicating.

Winged demons patrolled the skies above and their leathery wings cast fleeting shadows over the streets.

"The dragon and the giant bird are dead," Taurnil said as he landed next to Keturah. She wrapped her arm around him and purred into his shoulder. "Gideon lives," he spat.

"What?" Keturah exclaimed aghast. "How?" Her eyes caught sight of the garish wound on Taurnil's leg and all of her newfound security vanished.

"A woman," Taurnil replied, "with the power of a god..."

DAWN FOUND GIDEON and Melkora sprawled across the ground. Bits of morning frost laced Gideon's beard and crusted Melkora's eyes. As the sun warmed Gideon's body, his skin began to change. The bruises under his flesh receded and the black splotches covering his body faded into deep shades of brown and amber.

The tissue around his wounds cracked and peeled apart, but it was not unwelcome. Brown and white feathers wove themselves between the layers of Gideon's skin and slowly pushed themselves through his body. Gideon's mind stirred. He rubbed the weariness from his eyes and sat up.

His vision was sharper than he could fathom. He saw a tiny vole scurrying under a fallen branch several hundred yards away. The sight of the creature excited Gideon's stomach in a way he could not describe. He stood from the ground and stretched his back. His spine cracked and groaned from the movement.

Great feathered wings unfolded from Gideon's back and one of them brushed across Melkora's legs. He felt the sensation of touch in his feathers and a flood of emotion rushed through his being. Gideon looked down at his body and saw small feathers growing from his skin like the petals of a flower. He wasn't transforming into a bird, but rather merging with the physical image of Vrysinoch.

He stretched his hands out before him and smiled as his fingers curled over themselves into bright yellow talons. *Vrysinoch*, he whispered silently in his head.

The god's response shook him to his core.

We are one.

THE GOBLIN WARS

PART THREE:

Rebirth of a God

Prologue

"IN THE NINTH year after the death of the Most Pure, a dragon shall be born and a brother shall return home to roost." An old priest ran his fingers over a weathered page before closing his book. His deep blue robe caught on an errantly leaning candle as he returned the tome to a shelf in his study. The tall bronze candelabra, adorned with sapphires and rings of silver, tumbled to the ground and scattered wax over the floorboards. The priest stamped out the lingering flames with a muttered curse.

Zerren, chief acolyte to the High Priest, lit another set of tapers in the corner of the room. "Why are we reading the Brother's Prophecy?" he asked with disinterest. Zerren was young and full of life. The musty library of the High Priest was the last place where he wanted to spend a beautiful afternoon. He had attempted to open the chamber's only window to allow the ocean breeze entry, but had been promptly denied.

The High Priest turned and pointed a crooked finger at Zerren's chest. "Do you recall who the siblings of the prophecy are?" he questioned. "Have you forgotten the scriptures?"

Zerren scoffed. He knew the scriptures, even the obscure passages like the Brother's Prophecy, word for word. His entire life had been devoted to academic pursuits and he was eager to replace the aging High Priest and ascend to a place of real power within the city. "There has not been a Most Pure born in Azuria for," Zerren trailed off as he tried to recall the year from the annals of history, but even his vast knowledge did not stretch that far.

"It has been seven hundred years, Zerren," the High Priest told him. "Until Hestia was born."

"Hestia? The magistrate's daughter?" The acolyte couldn't believe what he was hearing. "You've lost your mind, old man," Zerren scolded before he could remember to use a more respectful title. "Besides, no one knows if Hestia has died. Missing and dead are two different things."

"Very true," the High Priest smiled. "But you have not answered my question. Who are the brother and sister from the prophecy?"

Zerren gulped. "Druaka, of course," he sputtered, making the god's holy sign hastily over his chest. "And... Vry—" he stopped. To speak the brother's name was punishable by death, even for a well-respected priest. A bead of cold sweat ran down his forehead and dropped into his eye.

The High Priest blew a thick layer of dust from a heavy book bound in green leather and stamped with a talon clutching an emerald. "Vrysinoch," he stated with certainty, "shall return."

THAT NIGHT, ZERREN donned a plain, roughspun travelling cloak and left the tranquility of Druaka's temple. Azuria, the city in which he had spent his entire life, was a sprawling metropolis that had long since outgrown its walls. As the High Priest's assistant, Zerren was recognizable enough to warrant a disguise everywhere he went, lest he be constantly bothered for blessings and the like. Even in the slums, his present destination, almost everyone would know his face. So it was that Zerren pulled the cowl of his cloak low to cover his eyes and walked with an unappealing limp. He was, however, forbidden from removing the golden necklace that signified his position within Druaka's temple, and despite his other indiscretions, the chain was something he always respected.

By the time Zerren reached the ramshackle hovel where his younger brother lived, his brow was covered in sweat and his feet throbbed. It was not the first time he had made the several mile journey from the city's center to the southern outskirts, but the long trip still aggravated him.

He reached up through the folds of his cloak and knocked on a door so consumed by rot that pieces of it fell to the ground when touched. After a brief moment, a man opened the door and ushered Zerren inside.

"You're new?" Zerren questioned, not recognizing the door guard. The man, so young he was practically a boy, nodded and shut the door behind them.

"Only been here a few days," he responded.

Zerren untied his cloak and handed it to the man, showing him his golden chain of office as well. Without hesitation, the young guard graciously took Zerren's cloak and placed it on a peg. "Your brother is below in the study," he said after hanging up the garment.

"Take me to him," Zerren bade politely. He was impressed by the boy's nonchalant manner when interacting with one of Azuria's highest officials. Most people either groveled in subservience or bombarded Zerren with requests for favors upon seeing him out of the temple.

The boy pushed aside a small heap of refuse and led Zerren further into the shanty. In the rear of the building, the two came to a bookcase poorly concealing a downward spiraling staircase.

"Tell me," Zerren said, making conversation as they descended the two hundred wooden stairs into the bowels of the slums, "what is my brother up to these days? It has been several weeks since my last visit and I have not heard from him."

"I have not seen Master Valkoinen in several days," he said. "He spends most of his time in the study." They reached the end of the massive spiral staircase and the boy led Zerren through a maze of torch-lit corridors lined with dozens of heavy doors. His brother's underground compound, a labyrinth over a hundred feet below the slums, sprawled for miles in each direction with an untold number of secret passages and routes to the surface.

Zerren's eyes were well adjusted to the dim light of the tunnels by the time they reached the elaborate door to Valkoinen's study. "Thank you," Zerren said to the young boy. He placed a small silver coin in the boy's hand and told him to wait outside the door. Despite Zerren's numerous trips to see his brother, he would never be able to navigate the complex tunnels unaided.

The door, a massive stone portal intricately carved with all manner of artwork, swung open silently on well-oiled hinges as Zerren entered the study. With a start, Valkoinen looked up from a book on his large wooden desk. "Brother," he said from behind an alabaster mask devoid of emotion. "I was not expecting you."

"You make the recruits call you Master Valkoinen?" Zerren joked. "So pretentious. You'll always be Little Val to me."

Valkoinen motioned with a white-clad hand for Zerren to take a seat. As Master of the Alabaster Order, Valkoinen wore stark white robes that shimmered in the torch light and an alabaster mask so brilliant Zerren thought it produced light on its own. Once members were initiated into the Order and given their robes, they never wore anything else. It had been over a decade since Zerren had seen his brother's face, or even the flesh of his brother's hand.

"What were you reading?" Zerren asked from the other side of the desk. The study, more like a grand library, was packed with thousands of books and scrolls from all of known history.

Valkoinen stared at Zerren for a long time before answering. "The Brother's Prophecy," he stated. With a white-gloved hand, he pushed the book across the cluttered desk. "Do you know it?"

Zerren shook his head. "The High Priest read me that very same passage earlier today," he said. "He thinks Druaka's brother shall return soon."

Valkoinen took another long moment of silence to ponder before moving. If the Alabaster Order was known for anything, it was not their speed. The mysterious group of unorthodox wizards would spend weeks preparing simple statements to be delivered to a magistrate and writing a letter could take them months.

"I believe the High Priest is correct," Valkoinen finally said. "We exist in a strange moment."

"What do you mean?" Zerren asked.

"The Void is unstable," Valkoinen continued. His bone-white mask possessed only two small, horizontal slots at eye level, and muffled his voice.

"By Druaka's eyes, brother, will you give me an answer?" Zerren pushed the book back across the desk. "I have no patience for your riddles."

"I have lost eighteen voidcallers to the abyss." Valkoinen tilted his head downward slightly, showing as much emotion as the alabaster mask would allow. "They were trained callers performing routine tasks. They should not have been lost. The Void is unstable."

Zerren had witnessed the power of a voidcaller on several occasions. The white-clad wizards performed their art with the *opposite* of arcane or divine magic. Where a priest called on the favor of Druaka in order to control the elements, a voidcaller manipulated the *absence* of magic. To know that so many had recently died was terrifying.

"How many voidcallers do you have left?" Zerren asked cautiously.

Valkoinen folded his hands in his lap and concentrated. "The Alabaster Order sits on the precipice of annihilation. We have several promising initiates, but only a handful of fully trained voidcallers. I sent three of the five oblivion mages into the Void to search for our lost brethren, but I fear they too may be lost to us."

Zerren hung his head in despair. "No wonder I didn't see anyone on my way down. No one is left." Although the priests of Druaka outwardly denied any involvement with the Alabaster Order, and many of the common folk refused to believe it was more than a myth or fairy tale, the city relied on the organization for an alarming amount of tasks.

"I may be the last Master of the Alabaster Order, although I fear that is not the case." Zerren dreaded the day his brother would be replaced. When a new Master ascended, the old was never seen again. "I believe a Fated One will arrive with your prophesied god," he said gravely.

Zerren scoured his memory, but he did not know the term. "I've never heard you speak of a Fated One before," he said.

Valkoinen lowered his gaze and waited several minutes before speaking. "A Fated One has only been spoken of by the old Masters, never seen," he explained. "When a Fated One arrives, the world will change forever."

"Is that good or bad for us?" Zerren wondered lightly. "And for Azuria?" His brother did not find any mirth in his statement. Zerren cleared his throat awkwardly. "What will this Fated One do? Take over the Alabaster Order?"

The man behind the mask shook his head. "A Fated One has the power to do anything. Take over the Order, destroy Azuria, end the world," he said solemnly.

Zerren shuddered. He wasn't sure if he believed all of the Alabaster Order's mysticism and prophecies, but he trusted his brother's honesty. "What will you do if Druaka's brother returns to Azuria?" Zerren asked. "Regardless of the existence of a Fated One alongside him."

Valkoinen sat motionless in his chair for more than hour before he spoke. All the while, Zerren waited silently and respectfully. "If that day comes," the Master spoke slowly, "I will meet him at the gates of the city. Perhaps I will ask for forgiveness." He waited another long hour in silent contemplation. "Or perhaps not."

One

"WHERE WILL WE go?" Melkora asked. The stench of charred wood assaulted her senses and reminded her of the life she had left behind — the life that had been stolen from her. Only a little ways ahead, Gideon stretched and rubbed at the scarred markings of yesterday's wounds. His flesh appeared normal, perhaps a shade darker, but lacked the feathers and wings she had seen the previous day.

"We need to see Talonrend..." Gideon's voice trailed off into hopelessness. A thick layer of ash mingled with a blanket of snowflakes that turned the world grey. "Or what's left of it," Gideon finished after a moment.

"Cobblestreet is gone," Melkora said. Although she couldn't see the village, she knew it was true. The town was the only thing other than fields and the Clawflow River between Kanebullar Mountain and Talonrend. The dragon had to fly directly over it to reach the city.

"There may be survivors," Gideon replied, though he knew there wouldn't be anything — or anyone — left. What hadn't been ruined by the goblin army marching through was surely destroyed by the flames.

528

Gravlox and Vorst emerged from the forest with several dead rabbits riddled with crossbow bolts. "You're awake," Vorst remarked, not attempting to hide her surprise. Although Gideon never stopped breathing, she had feared for the man's life.

"You make it sound like I wouldn't ever awaken." Gideon turned back to their small clearing on the side of the mountain and sat in front of a meager collection of stones and firewood.

"I don't understand sleeping," Vorst explained, "but I know it shouldn't last more than one night." She plucked her bolts from the rabbits and began preparing the meat to be eaten.

Gideon spotted Herod's swords resting in the grass and wondered if the prince was still alive. He pushed the grim thought from his mind and focused on the emptiness in his stomach.

"Do you mind...?" Gideon could hardly believe what he saying. He could hardly believe what his body was *feeling. Craving.* Before he could consider it, he held his hand out and pointed toward a rabbit next to Vorst. With a quizzical glance, she tossed the dead animal to him and went back to skinning the others.

Gideon's stomach rumbled at the sight of the fresh kill. He sniffed the corpse and his mouth watered. When he looked back to the two rabbits Vorst was preparing to roast, his gut churned and revolted.

"Oh no," Melkora muttered, turning her head as Gideon bit into the uncooked animal like a beast.

Blood flowed down Gideon's chin as he tore the critter apart. His teeth cracked through the rabbit's bones and he licked the marrow with a smile. "Sorry," he muttered between bites, "I'm hungry."

Gideon finished the entire rabbit in a single moment and knew that his appetite wasn't sated. "I need to hunt," he said. He stood and wondered how to make Vrysinoch's wings grow from his back as they had the day before.

What do I do? Gideon whispered in his head. He waited for a response, anything, but heard only his own confusion. Not knowing what else to do, he crouched next to the fire and jumped into the air. For a split second, he felt the skin of his shoulders tighten and beg to be released, but then he crashed painfully into the ground.

Melkora couldn't keep from laughing. "Perhaps we are not meant to fly," she called.

Gideon slowly got to his feet and brushed dirt from his clothes. "It isn't like using magic," he tried to explain. The feeling of Vrysinoch entwined with his soul felt similar to the well of magical energy he had known before, but it wasn't familiar enough to be easily harnessed. "I don't know how to become a bird," he said, "but I know somehow that I can."

"That thing that attacked yesterday," Melkora asked. "What was it? I've never seen such a hideous creature."

Gideon paced around the small fire with his hands on the hilts of Herod's swords. "Taurnil," he spat. "A demon I thought I had killed."

Melkora drew Roisin from its sheath and twirled it in her fingers. "I hit him. In a day or two, he will die," she said confidently.

"I hope you are right, Melkora," Gideon responded. He knew Taurnil was likely stronger than any mundane poison, but he didn't want to ruin the memory of her accomplishment.

Gideon drew Maelstrom and stalked into the forest to hunt for game. With his heightened senses, every woodland critter within half a mile smelled like a meal. It wouldn't take him long to find a nest of squirrels or rabbits and catch them with Maelstrom's black tendrils. He only hoped that the sword's magical fire wouldn't roast the food before he could eat it.

UNDRAKK SURVEYED HIS city and drank in Talonrend's distinctly ruinous smell. Several fires still burned in the streets and bands of orcs were busy rounding up the last few humans left alive. Any survivors captured were bound hand and foot and taken to the top of Terror's Lament. Undrakk had made a sport of throwing them from the parapets and blasting them with magic before they hit the ground. He occasionally let his aim falter, but the pitiful humans died all the same.

At the front of the castle, orcs and minotaurs worked side by side to repair the drawbridge and turn Castle Talon's entryway into something more resembling an orc's fortress than a human citadel. They added rows of sharpened wooden spears to the exterior and had begun enlarging the doors to allow the tall minotaurs to approach the broken throne with ease.

Qul's chair, a massive seat large enough for half a dozen orcs to use at the same time, had been positioned left of the drawbridge and served as Jan and Keturah's shared seat as rulers of the minotaur clan. To the right, Snarlsnout's dais sat on the stone and gave the Half Goat chieftain a permanent view of the city's transformation.

Between the two savage thrones, Herod's rotting head stood in the breeze. His hair, once vibrantly brown and full of youth, had withered and scattered to the wind like dried leaves.

"Chieftain," a young orc called from inside the castle. Undrakk slowly turned to address the subordinate with a smile.

"Yes?" he casually prompted. The orc genuflected and averted his eyes from Undrakk's intense gaze.

"My liege," he sputtered, obviously terrified of being so close to the most powerful being he had ever seen. "We've found a chamber beneath the keep."

"And?" Undrakk turned back to his observation of the city. He had no time for the petty storehouses and irrelevant prisons that were bound to be discovered eventually.

"There is an old man down there," the orc continued.

"Prisoners do little to excite me," Undrakk said, paying the orc little attention. He twirled his staff from hand to hand and began sauntering down the drawbridge.

"It is a temple!" the soldier called after Undrakk. When the lofty shaman still did not seem interested, the orc got his feet and yelled. "We tried to kill him, but he is protected by something powerful!"

Undrakk stopped and let out a frustrated sigh as though every word the underling spoke added another stone to his already encumbered shoulders. "Fine," he muttered, turning on his heels with a flourish. Undrakk snatched the crude spear from the soldier's grip as he passed him and tossed the weapon into the moat below. "If you can't kill an old man, you don't need a spear." The orc gawked.

"Make yourself useful and help one of the repair crews along the wall!" Undrakk commanded.

The young orc hastily saluted and scrambled from the drawbridge with as much haste as he could safely muster.

In a side passage near the throne room, Undrakk found a crudely carved tunnel entrance he had somehow previously overlooked. With a frown, he stepped into the dark opening and conjured a faint ball of light to the end of his staff.

The tunnel wound downward at a severe angle for several hundred feet. The air cooled and tasted stale, with a distinct humidity that reminded Undrakk of the mountain caves he had fought so hard to leave. Although he had been born underground in accordance with orc custom, he was an outcast. After his birth, the once-great Iron Gate Clan had exiled Undrakk's family. They considered half breeds to be dangerous and potential traitors to the other orcs. So it was that Undrakk spent his early years clinging to his human father's side and running from cave to cave like an animal.

Undrakk reached the end of the maze-like tunnel and spat a sour taste out of his mouth. He had not considered his exile from the clan in decades and the thought of his former kin brought unwanted memories to his mind.

The underground temple was magnificent, even to Undrakk's critical eyes. Folded wings of carved stone overlapped to form an arched entrance and the tallest statue Undrakk had ever seen loomed against the far wall. In the middle of the chamber, a shriveled excuse of a man clutched a leather-bound book like a mother protecting an infant from a raging storm.

"You are?" Undrakk inquired lazily, startling the man with his unerring command of the human language.

The old priest stiffened and tried his best to puff out what little remained of his upper body. "I am Sifir, a high priest! You may not enter!" the man shouted, pulling his book closer to his chest. "You may not enter!" he screamed again.

Undrakk laughed. He admired the old man's tenacity, but stepped into the temple without hindrance. "Why not?" he asked, holding his staff high and gazing up at the marvelous stone work surrounding him.

The priest was so infuriated he could hardly form coherent words. "You..." he stammered with a mouth full of rage, "heathen!" he shrieked. "Blasphemer!"

Undrakk raised a curious eyebrow and took several more steps into the heart of the temple with his arms spread wide. When no divine retribution struck him down, he let his arms fall and lowered his voice to a sinister growl. "Your god is dead, old man. I watched him die."

Bewilderment spread across the priest's face like the shadow of death. "You do not know what you saw," he said, but his voice was weak. "The winged gods still live."

Undrakk continued his stroll through the small temple as though enjoying the delicate scents of a spring garden. He reached the stone bowl at the statue's feet when a thought occurred to him. He turned and regarded the old man. "You are the priest of the winged *gods*?" he asked.

"They will smite you, foul beast!" the man heckled, this time pointing a crooked finger at Undrakk's chest.

"*They?*" he repeated quizzically. "Of whom do you speak, old man?"

Sifir's rage boiled over into an uncontrolled fit of spittle and flailing limbs. Undrakk easily sidestepped the charging man and wrapped an arm around his chest to keep him from falling to the floor.

"Calm down, priest," Undrakk chided. He righted the man and spun him around to look at his face. "Who are the winged gods?" he asked again.

"Vrysinoch and Druaka!" Sifir raged. "The eagle and the raven! Brother and sister!" The priest's wild eyes flared with a hint of magic before turning bone white and rolling limply upward.

Undrakk pulled the man in close, catching him before he hit the ground and listening for breath. He wondered if the exertion of his screams had been fatal. When he heard the telltale signs of life from Sifir's lips, he let the man fall from his arms with a thud.

The book Sifir had been clutching slid from the priest's grasp and Undrakk picked it up gently. The symbol of Vrysinoch, a talon with an emerald, was embossed on the green leather cover. "Petty holy symbols mean nothing..." Undrakk scoffed at the highly recognizable art. His human father had taught him the basics of Talonrend's religion and the half-orc resented it all. While Undrakk had certainly witnessed incredible magical feats performed by Vrysinoch's followers, his own power flowed from the earth itself and was stronger than any divine magic he had seen.

On the reverse of the front cover, Undrakk was surprised to see a symbol he did not recognize. Faintly embossed on blue leather that felt hundreds of years older than the rest of the artifact was an image of a raven sitting atop a skull. A few lines of unrecognizable text circled the design and though they were old, Undrakk could sense their power. He brushed his fingertips over the inscription and a cold wave of nausea crept up his arm and settled into his stomach. With a sneer, Undrakk closed the book and tossed it to the ground next to the unconscious man.

Back in the keep of Castle Talon, Undrakk found an orc busily moving stones for the ongoing repairs and pulled him aside. In a low whisper, the shaman instructed the terrified orc to retrieve the strange holy book from the underground temple and take it to his chamber. Undrakk had no intention of risking the bizarre priest's wrath by absconding with such a book himself. "An old human priest lives down there," Undrakk explained. "Take him some meat and let him be." The orc nodded, but clearly didn't understand the instructions.

"Take him to the wall?" the soldier asked.

"What did I say?" Undrakk hissed. His icy stare bored into the soldier, making the orc wither. "Don't hurt him." Undrakk reiterated. "Give him food, take the book, and return. Understood?"

The orc nodded again and headed for the tunnel. Undrakk wasn't sure if what the other soldier had said about the man being resistant to death was true, but he liked the ancient priest. The babbling human was amusing and might prove useful.

VORST TOSSED FROM side to side on the hard ground. Her body was bruised and weary, but her mind was restless. Something had changed when Lady Scrapple died. Vorst's mind had been released from the connections of the hive when she had entered the magical room beneath the Tower of Wings, and something more profound happened when Gideon slaughtered her creator.

Vorst rose to her feet and brushed the leaves from her legs. Deep in the pit of her gut, she felt a pull toward Kanebullar Mountain that she had never experienced before. It was like a rope had been tied around her innards and was being slowly drawn into the depths of the mountain by a giant crank. Vorst stole a glance over her shoulder at Gravlox meditating beneath a tree. She felt sorry for him. She knew Gravlox desperately wanted to regain his shamanistic powers, but she didn't know how to help him.

When she was sure that Gravlox would not notice her departure, she scurried away from the clearing and began to climb back up the western slope of Kanebullar Mountain. An hour or more later, as the sun was just cresting around the side of the mountain, sweat beaded down Vorst's forehead from the difficult climb and she stopped beneath a small pine tree to rest her feet.

After another hour of climbing the jagged exterior of the frosted mountain, Vorst found herself face to face with one of the larger, battle-ready goblins. The pale creature towered over her and breathed heavily, but made no overt movements.

"Hello?" Vorst said tentatively in the high-pitched goblin language. The tall goblin turned its head slightly to the side and did not respond.

"Do you understand me?" Vorst prompted a second time. She noticed the sword in the goblin's hand and lifted her own arms into the air as a gesture of peace. "What's your name?" she asked.

"Name?" the goblin finally responded. His voice was raw and shaky, like he had never spoken before.

"What do they call you?" Vorst explained slowly. "My name is Vorst."

"Name?" the goblin repeated.

Vorst sighed. She knew that the creature was struggling to understand its newly acquired mental freedom and had been a mindless slave under Lady Scrapple. If the goblin race was to survive, they needed to discover the meaning of their freedom and learn to embrace it.

"What did you do before..." she wasn't sure what reaction mentioning the death of Lady Scrapple would produce, so she avoided the name altogether. "What did you do ten days ago?" she questioned.

The creature lifted his sword and swung it lazily through the air at an imaginary enemy. When he finished the slow gesture, he looked to Vorst for approval.

"All you've ever done is fight," she concluded with a grimace. The pale goblin looked crestfallen at her sadness. "Are there more of you?" she asked, pointing behind the goblin.

After a moment of processing, the goblin mimicked Vorst's gesture and pointed behind him with a grin.

"How many goblins have left the mountain?" Vorst wasn't

worried about the clumsy creatures wandering around the forest and potentially getting lost, but she knew that if the farms and food stores were not properly maintained, the entire race would die before spring. She needed to organize them and get them to continue their lives as best they could.

The goblin licked his pale lips in concentration and finally held four fingers.

Vorst took the goblin by the arm and turned him back toward the mountain. "Go find the others and return to the caves. Keep fighting as you did before. Tell the others to continue doing whatever they did ten days ago. Don't let the others leave Kanebullar Mountain." She looked the tall goblin directly in his eyes as she spoke and tried to put a hint of command behind her voice.

The goblin, accustomed to a lifetime of unquestioned servitude, welcomed her direct order and understood it much clearer than he did her questions. With a nod, the creature began climbing back up the mountain with a distinct purpose that he had lacked minutes before.

"What will come of us?" Vorst mused aloud, unintentionally grouping herself with the thousands of goblins she had abandoned those months before. Questions about her future swirled through her mind and overwhelmed her thoughts. When she had first left the mountain, a life with Gravlox in the forest had felt within reach. After she had met Gideon and became embroiled in the war, Vorst had entertained thoughts of living in Talonrend alongside humanity. She looked back to the horizon and saw the remnants of the city's fire drifting through the clouds. They would have to retake the city if she could ever settle there with Gravlox—assuming he would join her.

With her feet planted firmly in the dirt of Kanebullar Mountain, Vorst couldn't envision living anywhere else. She knew that Gravlox was right when he said the humans would never accept them. Even if they were granted protection by the human prince, the two of them would never be truly safe. Vorst gazed at the peak of

Kanebullar Mountain hundreds of feet above her. The longing in her chest magnified, but it was not alone. An equally strong force pulled her back down the mountain to the goblin meditating beneath a tree and languishing in turmoil, trying in vain to access his shamanistic abilities. Vorst had given a finger to be with him and that wasn't a promise she was about to break.

"I will follow him," she resolved, frost lacing her breath. "We will find somewhere to live *together*." Determined, Vorst trudged back down the mountain to find her nine-fingered husband and make him another promise.

GIDEON RETURNED FROM his journey into the woods with blood around his mouth and animal bones in his stomach. Melkora gazed up at him with mock horror as he approached. "How much did you eat?" she asked.

The big man chuckled softly under his breath, but inwardly couldn't come to terms with what he had done. "An entire den of rabbits," he muttered. Gravlox and Vorst sat at the edge of the small clearing with their backs to Kanebullar Mountain.

"If you're finished, we should be going," Melkora said. "Although I'm not quite sure what's left of the world." Much of the smoke from the burning villages had dissipated, but the stench of death clung to everything.

"I also ate two squirrels and a small brown rodent I didn't recognize." Gideon didn't know why he told Melkora the details of his grisly feast, but saying the words brought him a small measure of comfort.

"So," Melkora began, "how much... bird... are you?" She blushed and turned away. Nothing about Gideon frightened her, but not knowing exactly what he was rattled her nerves more than anything she had ever felt.

Gideon took several steps toward her in what he considered to be a comforting gesture. "I'm not sure," he said. "It feels as though Vrysinoch is caged within my body, and my ribs are barely able to contain him bursting out again." He flexed and tried desperately to call forth the avian wings he had used before, but nothing happened. "Something happened to Vrysinoch—something terrible. That much I know. I think," he struggled to put into words what he barely understood, "That Vrysinoch is taking refuge within me."

"Does he speak to you?" Melkora asked. She had never been particularly religious, despite faithfully attending services at the Cobblestreet temple, but she respected and revered the power of paladins and priests. The idea of directly communicating with Vrysinoch was exotically intoxicating.

Gideon laughed openly at her question. "I used to be a paladin of the Tower," he explained. "Since I left, Vrysinoch has done nothing but torment and taunt me."

Melkora tightened her knife belt around her waist and looked around the small clearing in hopes of gathering possessions before realizing she had none. "Why you?" she asked bluntly. "Why did Vrysinoch pick you?"

Gideon stroked his braided beard and thought for a long time. He was the last person he thought Vrysinoch would favor. Asterion and Corvus both had far greater faith than him. Even Apollonius, the young commander of the guard, would be better suited to divine power.

"Maybe they're all dead," Gideon thought aloud.

"Who?"

"Everyone." Gideon didn't realize the grim implication of the notion until he had already spoken it. "If I am the one Vrysinoch has chosen, there must not have been any other choices," he said after a moment of contemplation.

Before Gideon could ponder the macabre idea further, Gravlox and Vorst joined him with their weapons and gear ready or travel.

"Where will we go?" Vorst asked. The pitch of her voice was

painful to human ears, but Gideon welcomed her familiar timbre.

"We must return to Talonrend. If the city survived, there will be much work to do." In the pit of his gut, Gideon knew there wouldn't likely be much left. "I need to see Asterion. He is the oldest priest of Vrysinoch and perhaps he can shed some light on my current condition."

They reached the edge of the Clawflow River by midday and finally saw the destruction wrought by the bone dragon. Everything was burned. Where a once-vibrant village had stood just weeks before, only the broken shells of houses and businesses littered the streets like bones rising up from the earth. The black fire of the bone dragon had turned everything but the stoutest timbers to ash.

Without hesitation, Melkora ran into the river and swam to the other side. "Help me find them," she called over her shoulder, desperation evident in her voice. Gideon and the two goblins followed closely behind her, but none of them expected to find her family alive.

The fountain in the town square was one of the few structures relatively undamaged left in Cobblestreet. The fountain's low, stone foundation was turned black from fire, but the village icon was otherwise intact. "Wait," Gideon whispered, holding Melkora back by the shoulder. "We need to be careful."

The four companions ran from the fountain to a burned storehouse that had enough standing beams to provide meager cover. They crouched low behind a badly damaged table and Gideon held a finger to his lips.

"I hear something," he whispered. His heightened, bird-like hearing had trouble identifying exactly what he heard, but he was filled with the overwhelming sensation that the noise wasn't friendly.

"Torvald?" Melkora asked longingly. She strained to hear even the faintest sound that her brother might still be alive, but her ears detected nothing.

After a moment of listening, Gideon could tell that the voices he heard were neither human nor goblin. "Orcs," he muttered with disgust.

Melkora's eyes welled up with tears. She jumped and tried to run toward the invaders, but Gideon held her back with a strong hand. "Patience," he growled. "We don't know how many are out there."

"We have to save my brother!" Melkora nearly yelled with rage.

Gideon stepped in front of her and blocked her path. He looked to Gravlox and Vorst. "We move together," he said calmly. "The orcs aren't far, maybe four or five streets west, but if there are too many, we *cannot* fight them."

Melkora flashed a violent grimace and gnashed her teeth. Gideon clamped a hand down over her mouth before she could scream at him. "We must be quiet," he reminded her. He adjusted the swords at his sides and took comfort in their presence. "If we can save your brother, we will."

Gravlox looked crestfallen. He drew his sword and held it weakly before him. "I can't fight," he said to the others in the human language. "I'm not strong." He tried again to calm his tumultuous mind and find any scrap of magic he could, but concentrating so deeply only made his head throb with disappointment.

Vorst held his hand, but had no words to console him.

They ran to another ruined building, a collection of burnt wood vaguely resembling an apothecary, and Melkora brushed a line of tears from her face. "There was a wine cellar," she managed past the lump in her throat. "Torvald would've hid there. He would've been safe from the fire."

As one, they ran to another building and all four of them could hear the orcs' voices. They were close and the green-skinned creatures were loud. "What are they saying?" Melkora asked the goblin pair with a wild look in her eyes.

Vorst shook her head. "I'm not an orc," she responded. "Our languages are similar, but not the same. I don't know."

Gideon crept to the edge of the building and crouched low behind a splintered beam. "There," he pointed to a building farther along the street that still had a solitary wall standing. "The orcs are on the other side of that house. We can get close without being seen." He looked to Melkora and lowered his voice to a grave whisper. "Be quiet," he urged her. "We can still surprise them, but we have to wait." Melkora nodded and drew Roisin from her belt. She gripped the dagger so tightly Gideon thought her knuckles might break, but she didn't say a word.

From the other side of a charred wooden wall, the four companions listened to a myriad of orc voices. Gideon wasn't sure, but he thought he heard at least a dozen different orcs speaking. The creatures made no efforts toward subtlety, and they sounded happy, perhaps victorious.

Vorst stole a glance around the edge of the ruined wall, and her eyes went wide. *Too many,* she tapped on Gravlox's hand with the goblin code.

In the center of the burned street, thirty warriors of the Wolf Jaw Clan searched the ruins for survivors. Gideon heard another group, likely larger than the first, still out of sight on the outskirts of Cobblestreet. He pulled Melkora down next to him.

"We can't fight them all," he whispered urgently. Melkora grimaced and tried to contain her rage.

"Your wings," she bit angrily. "You could kill them all."

Gideon knew she was probably right. The strength he had felt during his transformation had been beyond incredible. For the brief time he had experienced the presence of Vrysinoch, Gideon had known true power. Against a god, cities were like pebbles, and mere creatures such as orcs and humans were less than dust.

With enemies all around, Gideon felt helpless. "I don't know how..." he muttered in defeat. No matter how hard he tried, how diligently he concentrated, he could do little more than make the hairs on his shoulder blades itch. He hung his head and prayed, but no answer came to him.

Gideon was too lost to his own inner turmoil to catch Melkora before she leapt beyond his grasp.

"Torvald!" the maddened woman screamed. With Roisin in hand, she charged from the ruined house and startled the nearest orc. She reached above her head and ran Roisin's razor edge along the orc's throat. At once, the rest of the search party turned on her and readied their weapons.

Vorst jumped from the rubble and pulled Gravlox along behind her. After a few paces, she dropped to her knee and slid to the rear of a burnt wagon across from Melkora. "Just like the tunnel," Vorst said.

Gravlox nodded. The ruins of Cobblestreet were not nearly as constricting as the lightless passages under Kanebullar Mountain, but the concept was the same. "They will come toward us," Gravlox responded. He strengthened his grip on his sword. "Wound them, and I will make sure they die."

Vorst counted her remaining bolts and loaded one into the crossbow strapped to her wrist. She had less than a dozen missiles, but it was better than none.

Three tall orcs with crude spears ran at Melkora from the other end of the street. They bellowed at the top of their lungs and closed the gap within seconds. The lead orc, a towering brute with a massive arm span, thrust his spear at Melkora's chest without breaking his stride.

The agile woman ducked under the spear and rolled into her oncoming attacker with grace, easily tripping him. With a yelp, the orc hit the street on his stomach, and Melkora wasted no time plunging her dagger into his back and ripping open his spine.

The second pair of orcs took the opportunity to pounce on Melkora. The woman rolled and turned, but didn't have enough room to get fully to her feet. She used the crosspiece of her dagger to deflect an incoming strike and slid to her left.

Vorst saw the opening and fired. At such a short distance, it was impossible to miss. Her bolt sank into the orc's chest and knocked him backward, giving Melkora enough time to stand and parry a strike from the third attacker.

The remaining orc lunged again, but before his spear got close, an inky black tendril wrapped around his chest and yanked him back. Gideon pulled the creature from behind and used Regret to end its life.

"Go!" Gideon shouted. A score of orcs ran their direction and were only a few buildings away. Vorst spanned her crossbow as quickly as she could and fired another bolt, striking an orc in the side of the collarbone and dropping him to the ground.

Melkora and Gideon took off together in the opposite direction, and the two goblins followed closely behind. Vorst furiously re-loaded her crossbow and set another bolt while she ran. The four rounded a corner and Vorst turned back. Quickly kneeling, she took aim, and killed another orc with a shot to the upper chest.

Before they could move again, another orc crashed through a burnt wall behind them. The creature held no weapon, but caught Gideon with a vicious punch to the back of his head that sent him sprawling. In an instant, Gravlox swung wildly and sliced a brutal gash in the back of the orc's leg. The creature kicked at Gravlox's arm and nearly knocked away the goblin's sword.

The green-skinned beast was strong, but thoroughly outnum-bered. Melkora feinted low with her dagger, and when the orc made to block, she sank Roisin to the hilt in its chest.

"We have to keep moving," Melkora said as she ripped Roisin from the orc's flesh. She flicked the blade and slid it back into the sheath on her side.

Without hesitation, they ran again. The burnt roads of Cob-blestreet flew beneath their feet, but the taller and more muscular orcs were faster. After a moment of wildly sprinting through the remains of the village, Gideon turned a corner with nowhere left to go. A large watermill on the edge of the Clawflow had toppled down in all directions and blocked the streets with charred debris.

The group turned to face the orc soldiers and readied their

weapons. *Vrysinoch,* Gideon begged silently. *We need you. Grant me your wings!*

Vorst steadied her crossbow and waited for the orcs to appear. Gravlox crouched low next to his wife. "I have no magic!" he yelled for what felt like the hundredth time since entering the room beneath the Tower of Wings.

"Try," Vorst urged. The orcs came into view and began marching down the street, organized into formation by a short, scar-covered orc carrying a banner.

"I will kill their leader," Gideon said confidently. "Perhaps they will run." He held Maelstrom in his right hand, and when he commanded, the weapon burst into flames.

"There is nothing," Gravlox whispered. He tried again to send his mind spiraling into the stone and soil beneath his feet, but although his consciousness moved, it found no wellspring of limitless energy as it had before.

"You must try!" Vorst shrieked. The orcs closed on them. She fired. Her bolt struck an orc in the thigh, but the big creature did not falter.

Gideon lashed out with Maelstrom's inky black tendrils as Melkora dove into the fray. The two humans fought side by side and easily carved a hole through the orc ranks, but there were too many. A spear point found its way through the swirling chaos of the battle and struck Melkora in the ribs. The woman screamed, threw Roisin at her grinning assailant, and fell to the ground with a whimper.

Gravlox let his sword drop from his grasp. He willed his mind to calm and closed his eyes. With his palms flat on the stone beneath him, he pushed his consciousness away from his physical body and into the realm where magic used to exist. No molten stone bubbled miles beneath the surface, waiting for him to summon and shape it. No hidden boulders or slabs of limestone called to his mind and made themselves known. Gravlox compelled his magical consciousness toward the Clawflow River, just a building's width behind him, but he found nothing. In the world of magic, there was only darkness.

Vorst fired until she was out of bolts and then plucked Gravlox's sword from the ground. She kissed the base of her missing finger, touched it to Gravlox's head, and charged the nearest orc.

Amidst the sheer darkness of Gravlox's mind, something flickered. The former shaman whirled his mind in the direction of the flicker, but just as it had appeared, it had also immediately vanished. He searched and searched with his mind, but it was not a flicker of light he had seen; it was a flicker of darkness. In the constant, unwavering eternity of the darkest night Gravlox had ever known, his mind witnessed a speck of something darker than the deepest black.

It had been small, smaller than a diamond pulled from a vein of ore, but it gave Gravlox hope. He pushed his mind to the exact location in blank space where he had seen the flicker and reached. His magical consciousness did not possess hands in the physical sense, not exactly, but he reached through the darkness and touched something.

Trembling, Gravlox opened his eyes and witnessed the chaos of battle all around him. Gideon flailed his magical sword like a whip, barely keeping a score of orcs at bay while Melkora clutched her torn side at his feet.

Gravlox opened his hand and peered into the lightless gem he suddenly held. As a mine foreman, he could easily identify every single bit of ore or gemstone native to the region, but the stone he held was like nothing he had ever seen. It was so dark it practically drank in the light around it and dulled the colors of the world.

The gem wavered and gleamed, reflecting pure darkness into the morning air, and Gravlox felt its magical pull. He looked back to the battle and watched Vorst deflect a series of well-timed jabs. She was more than a capable fighter, but she was hard pressed and losing ground. Anger welled up in the bottom of Gravlox's body and seethed through his bones.

Sensing the black gem's magic, Gravlox forced his hatred and despair into the object—and the gem greedily drank it like a goblin dying of thirst.

Without fully understanding why, Gravlox let the stone take every drop of emotion he had. When there was nothing left to give, he hurled it toward a pair of orcs flanking Vorst and about to run her through with their spears.

At once, the battle ceased. Gideon lashed Maelstrom's tentacles in front of him, aiming for an orc's muscled arm, but hit the street where the creature had stood and sent a burst of dirt into the air. Vorst swung her sword in an attempt to parry a spear in front of her chest, and when the blade connected with nothing, her momentum tumbled her to the ground.

Gideon gasped and spun around, searching the area for orcs. He struck out again with Maelstrom where the orc had been standing and realized that the beasts had not become invisible, but that they were simply gone. The weapons they had held, their meager clothing, all of it was gone. Even their foul stench had seemingly evaporated.

Vorst got to her feet and held her sword before her in a defensive posture. She turned back to Gravlox with bewilderment, but he did not know what to say.

Emotionally, Gravlox was completely drained, but he did not feel physically fatigued as he often did after using magic. "I don't know what I did," he said with confusion. "I found a gem..." He tried to find words to describe the object he had somehow pulled from the blank world without magic, but even his memory of the event would not come easily to his mind.

"We must find Torvald," Melkora gasped. Blood poured freely from her garish wound.

Gideon immediately dropped to his knees to help Melkora. "We have to stop the bleeding first," he said. He put pressure on the gash with his hands, but there was nothing to clamp down. Blood seeped through his fingers unhindered.

"I'm going to cauterize the wound," he said solemnly. Melkora nodded and bit down on the hem of her shirt. "This will hurt immensely," he whispered.

Gideon took Maelstrom in his hand and willed it to life. The blade erupted in magical fire, sizzling and popping the air. At his core, Gideon truly felt sorry for the woman. She was a thief, not a trained soldier. She had likely never been wounded in combat before. Her mind could not comprehend the unimaginable pain.

He pressed the flat of the flaming sword into Melkora's torn ribs, and the woman howled. He held the flaming sword tightly to her body, searing the flesh and closing the wound with an ugly blister. Tears rolled down Melkora's face and her howls turned into pathetic sobs that reminded Gideon of all the mortally wounded men he had watched die in the Talonrend arena.

After a moment, the wound was cauterized and Melkora succumbed to her pain. "She's lucky she passed out," Gideon said. "We need to make a bandage or the wound will get infected and she will die."

Vorst scampered into the nearby ruins in search of enough unblemished cloth to wrap the woman's side.

Three

UNDRAKK SAT WITH his back against the stone wall of his keep and summoned a small sphere of fire in front of him to warm his hands. Nevidal, the mysterious sword that had baffled him in the cave west of Talonrend, sat unsheathed on the dais in the center of the throne room. Despite the shaman's best efforts, Undrakk could not determine what set the hand-and-a-half sword apart from any regular blade.

The castle was relatively quiet, considering the general noise of the orc clans inhabiting the city, and Undrakk had the throne room to himself. "I need a name for my castle," he mused aloud to the empty halls. The human tapestries and decorations had all been torn down and burned, replaced with painted animal hides and hunting trophies.

Undrakk got to his feet and pulled his magical orb of warmth behind him. The fiery sphere cast flickering shadows over the stone that reminded him of his cave-dwelling childhood. At the front of the keep, Undrakk noted the exceptionally fast progress the minotaur and orc stone masons had made. Nearly a third of the foyer had been heightened and enlarged to allow the taller species to move freely. Through several unfinished gaps in the ceiling, Undrakk saw the newly fashioned parapet. With several more weeks of labor, the castle would be transformed into a true orc fortress.

"Thousand Spears?" Undrakk said. The word echoed through the chamber. "No," he continued. "I do not like the sound of that."

Undrakk pulled his magical ball of heat along as he paced the stone in front of the dais. "Iron Gate?" he scoffed. The name of his former clan brought a bitter taste to his mouth. "I would rather jump from the walls."

He spat on the ground and continued his frustrated pacing. "I need a name that projects confidence. A name that reminds humanity of their defeat..."

A flicker of light from his sphere caught Nevidal's edge at just the right angle to flash in his eyes. Undrakk snatched the sword from the ground and held it tightly in his hand. He remembered the last time he had gripped the hilt and had been unable to draw it from a simple sheath. Carefully, he inspected the sword's craftsmanship. It was better than standard orc weaponry by far, but the sword was not exceptional. The taper of the hilt was slightly irregular and the balance point was almost an inch too far forward, making the sword terrible for thrusting.

Undrakk commanded the magical ball of fire to move from behind him to a position between him and the dais. He held Nevidal aloft and swung, slicing the fiery sphere in half. Undrakk frowned. Nothing magical happened when the blade connected with the fire. Had the sword held magical properties, it should have at least shimmered or tingled as it connected with the magical fire in such a slow and deliberate manner.

The shaman summoned a burst of physical strength to his limbs and swung Nevidal downward with blazing speed. The sword connected with the stone of the dais and shattered, leaving the hilt and a foot of rough steel in Undrakk's hand. He smiled, kicked the broken pieces of the sword off the dais, and strode to the castle's entrance. It didn't take him long to locate a few leather straps in the building supplies piled on the drawbridge. Undrakk made a loop in one of the straps and tied the other end around Nevidal's broken hilt.

Without the aid of his magical abilities, Undrakk tossed the loop over one of the crenellations on the parapet thirty feet above him and let the hilt hang over the doorway. "Broken Sword," he said with a smile. "My city shall be named Broken Sword and my castle..." he mulled over several names before finally settling on a rhythmic moniker.

"I shall rule Broken Sword from Half-Orc Keep!" he announced. A group of reveling orcs eating around a bonfire several hundred feet away took slight notice of Undrakk's proclamation, but soon returned to their festivities.

"Half-Orc Keep," he rolled the words around his mouth and savored their taste. "I like the sound of that." Undrakk looked back at the dangling hilt once more, extinguished his magical light, and walked across the drawbridge to join his fellow orcs at their fire.

MELKORA'S RIBS ACHED like a smith was pounding a hammer into them with all his might. Every breath was more painful than the last. She groaned and clutched at her side, thankful for the crude bandage wrapped around her body. Only a small line of blood trickled from beneath the layers of cloth, a welcome relief from the torrent the orc spear had caused... a day ago? Melkora had no idea how long she had been out.

"Gideon," she called weakly. Every breath she took renewed the brutal pain and strengthened it a hundred times over.

"You're awake," Gideon said, kneeling at her side. "How are you feeling?"

Melkora tried to glare at him, but the pain made her head swim and she closed her eyes. "What happened?" she asked through gritted teeth.

"I don't know," Gideon responded. "The orcs vanished." He could barely believe it, but he knew what he had seen.

Suddenly, painful memories of her brother flashed through Melkora's mind. "Torvald!" she yelled, sending another nauseating wave of pain through her body. "We must find him!"

Gideon placed a calming hand on her shoulder and shook his head. "Gravlox and Vorst found him and the children..."

"No..."

"I'm sorry," Gideon muttered. He had no words to console her. In the past, he might have offered a prayer to Vrysinoch for the safe passage of their souls, but after everything that had happened, it didn't feel right to pray.

"Did they die with honor?" Melkora asked between violent sobs.

"With weapons in their hands, all of them," Gideon lied. In truth, Torvald and his children had died in their cellar before the orcs ever sacked the village ruins. Their twisted and charred bodies had made a pitiful sight to behold.

"They fought..." Melkora said with a hint of reassurance. "They fought."

"Dead orcs were scattered around their bodies," Gideon said weakly. "They fought bravely."

"Take me to them," Melkora said, painfully sucking in air and trying to sit herself up. After two attempts, she slumped back to the ground in defeat.

"We buried their bodies this morning," Gideon said truthfully. "I did not want to wake you." Instead of taking the three bodies to the Cobblestreet cemetery across the Clawflow, Gideon had buried them in the rubble of the town square in shallow graves.

"We need to get out of here," Gideon said. "The orcs could be back at any moment."

Melkora flashed a subtle smile. She was alive, and despite the deaths of Torvald and his children, she was thankful for her life. "How long have I been out?" she asked. The fear of orcs pressed heavily on her wounded chest.

"Only two days," Gideon said. "I used my sword to cauterize the wound. I'm not a surgeon, but I believe you will heal."

"Help me stand," she said defiantly. The pain in her side was unrelenting, but with Gideon's help, Melkora got to her feet. She opened her eyes and steadied her breathing, taking in the sights of destruction all around her.

Further up the street, Gravlox and Vorst were readying a pile of salvaged possessions for travel. "Where will we go?" Vorst asked when the two humans approached.

Gideon let out a long sigh and adjusted Melkora's weight on his shoulder. "Talonrend," he said with confidence. "I must know what happened." Although he didn't believe much would be left of the city, he clung to the hope that enough people survived to start rebuilding. Images of slaughtered refugees flashed through his mind, and what little hope he had started to erode. Almost all of the people who had stayed behind in Talonrend were members of the militia and the city guard. The Templars of Peace were exclusively male, and all of the other paladins that had been rescued were also male. If the city survived, would there be enough women left to re-populate? Gideon looked around at the ruins of Cobblestreet with newfound despair.

"Perhaps the other villages survived," Melkora said, sensing Gideon's turmoil. "We are not the last humans left east of the Green City."

Vorst looked up at the human pair and laughed. "There are thousands of goblins left in the tunnels," she said, faintly rekindling her repressed urge to return to Kanebullar Mountain. "Talonrend is large enough for both races..."

Gideon scoffed. "Let's get moving," he said, hoisting a small pack of supplies over his right shoulder and supporting Melkora with his left. "We can reach Talonrend in two days."

"And if we meet another band of orcs before we reach the city?" Melkora asked. She hated to ponder the grim reality of their situation, but the pain in her side left little room for more pleasant thoughts.

Gideon looked to Gravlox with a halfhearted smile. "Either Gravlox banishes them as he did before, or we fight." The four companions trudged along the ruined village streets heading west, moving slowly, but with purpose.

THEY REACHED THE outskirts of Talonrend in two days. "The bones are gone," Gideon said, remembering the vast field of skeletons he had seen after the battle against the goblins. Not a single bone remained in the vast fields of frost-tipped grass east of Talonrend.

"Look," Vorst said, pointing to a lone figure patrolling the top of Terror's Lament.

Gideon strained his eyes to see the silhouette, but he was too far away to tell if the figure was human, orc, or minotaur. Beside him, Melkora stooped over on a long stick she used as a cane. "Get me inside," she said meekly. Despite her relatively quick recovery, her side still ached with pain that sent razors through her chest every time she took a breath. "I need to see a healer," she stated.

"We have to wait until night," Gideon said solemnly. "There's no cover to hide us from here to the wall. If that's an orc," he pointed to the patrolling figure, "then we will have to think of something else."

Melkora let out a pained sigh. She wrapped her arms around her body and shivered. "If it snows tonight?" she asked, never taking her eyes from the ground.

Gideon drew Maelstrom and ignited the blade. "It isn't much, but magical fire heats the same as regular fire," he stated. They didn't have any flint or kindling to make a traditional fire, so Gideon had resorted to Maelstrom's magic to cook their meals each night.

Vorst shielded her eyes from the afternoon sun and tried to make out the race of the patrolman walking steadily back and forth. "Gravlox and I could probably get close enough to see," she said after a moment.

Gideon mulled over the idea. The goblins were small enough to scamper through the tall grasses unnoticed; large swaths of land had been scorched by fire and left bare. It would not be an easy run.

"What if they see us?" Gravlox asked. If only his powers would return, it wouldn't matter if the guard saw him. He could push a tide of earth up from under his feet and rise to the top of the wall in an instant.

"I doubt orcs would bother to leave the city for two goblins," Vorst replied.

"Move at dusk," Gideon said. He had to admit, the plan sounded better than anything he could think of. "If Talonrend still stands in the hands of men, get a priest and come back as quickly as you can. Hopefully, they will recognize you, or at least know enough not to shoot you."

Gideon smiled and looked back at the top of the wall. His gut sank when he realized what was missing. "The Tower of Wings..." he muttered. He should have been able to see the shining emerald atop the Tower from miles away. What little hope he had crumbled into despair and nestled in the pit of his stomach like a virulent disease.

He slumped down and thought of all the paladins he had rescued from the refugee caravan. "They're all dead," he said to himself.

"What's that?" Melkora said, pointing to a small lump on the horizon near the eastern gate. Gideon lifted his eyes and felt a strong pull in his mind. He stood, his feet seemingly moving of their own accord, and immediately knew what it was.

No, Gideon silently prayed. *No!*

He ran. In that moment, he didn't care if the guard atop Terror's Lament saw him or not. His legs pumped, and he ran harder than he ever had before. Gravlox and Vorst shouted for him, but their voices never penetrated the wall of anger in Gideon's mind. He crossed the two miles from the edge of the field to Vrysinoch's corpse faster than he thought possible.

With tears streaming down his face, Gideon collapsed. Vrysinoch's body, a broken and decaying bird longer than Terror's Lament was tall, rested in a small impact crater among a dragon's shattered skeleton.

Gideon remembered the day he had been accepted as a paladin in the Tower of Wings. The ceremony took place in the lowest level, the Star Room, with all of the priests gathered. In that dark and sacred chamber, Gideon had knelt, naked, with his shield and mace, praying that Vrysinoch would guide his life, steel his resolve, and strengthen his body. When his prayers were spoken, Gideon had sworn his oath to Vrysinoch and was blessed with an answer.

One of the priests, an older man with a dark red beard, made the tattoo on Gideon's shoulder and forever marked him as a servant of Vrysinoch. When a paladin was accepted by the winged god, the tattoo brought no pain and flared to life with magical light as it had on Gideon's back. When a paladin was rejected during the ceremony, the tattoo brought lifelong pain and faded quickly into a grotesque scar.

Gideon had only witnessed one paladin's rejection in the Star Room. The man had been a good fighter, but his heart was impure. The priests had not known it at the time, but the other paladins-in-training had been well aware of the man's fondness for brothels and dice. When the tattoo began, the rejected paladin writhed in pain. His back was torn apart by the needle, and wave after wave of blood had soaked into the Star Room floor. When the ceremony was complete, the disgraced man had fallen prostrate and wept. The priests and paladins had prayed for the man's forgiveness, but ultimately, the disgraced paladin was exiled from the Tower of Wings.

Gideon remembered the utter despair he had felt for the paladin upon seeing his denial. When he gazed upon the ruin of Vrysinoch's corpse, Gideon felt that despair first hand. *Vrysinoch,* he prayed between wails of sorrow, *why?*

He unbuckled Herod's sword belt and let Maelstrom and Regret fall to the ground. Unable to stand, Gideon crawled to giant bird's head and ran his fingers through Vrysinoch's feathers.

It was dark by the time Melkora and the goblins made it to Gideon's side. "It was an orc atop the wall," Melkora said flatly. If he heard her, Gideon did not care. He sat on the ground next to Vrysinoch's head and cried.

"The orcs have not dispatched anyone from the city," Melkora continued, ignoring Gideon's state, "but they might. We should move."

Ultimately, Melkora's logic was useless. When the sun had set behind Talonrend's high walls, Gideon was still groveling at the head of Vrysinoch's corpse. Gravlox and Vorst guarded the area from either side, waiting for the orcs to send a group of soldiers out to kill them, but none ever came.

THROUGH THE SWIRLING depths of death and sorrow, Gideon's mind tumbled. Outwardly, his sleep appeared calm and almost peaceful, but inwardly, he struggled to keep his sanity. When Vrysinoch had embedded his consciousness deep within the layers of Gideon's mind, the god had acted out of pure desperation. After the great bird's death, Vrysinoch needed a vessel to contain his mental aspect and Gideon had been an obvious choice. But the intangible transformation was taxing. Vrysinoch struggled to process his own thoughts beneath the layers of attentions given to Gideon's mind.

When Vrysinoch, through mortal eyes, gazed upon the corpse of his own physical form, something snapped in his mind. One of the tenuous strands linking Gideon's mind to Vrysinoch's violently shattered.

In his dream, Gideon slowly descended the narrow steps far beneath Castle Talon as he had done when he first met Prince Herod. Instead of mud and stone forming the walls of the complex cave system, stark white bones surrounded him. Gideon knew they were the bones of Talonrend—the people, the priests, the paladins, everyone. When at long last Gideon reached the ancient temple beneath the castle, it was in ruins.

Fires burned out of control in every corner of the small chamber, and the ornate stone statues had toppled to the floor. In the center of it all, Gideon saw a rather peculiar creature. A half-orc, stood calmly amidst the destruction. When Gideon entered, the half-orc turned slightly to regard him.

"You," Gideon spoke slowly. He recognized the creature from the cave where he had been held prisoner. "I will kill you," Gideon stated with confidence.

The half-orc cocked his head to the left and displayed a wide smile full of jagged teeth. On the ground beneath the rubble of the statues, something pulsed. It flickered, reminding Gideon of a torch being carried round a corner, then blazed to life with brilliant white light.

Vrysinoch's holy symbol, a talon clutching an emerald, filled the chamber with radiant beams and the half-orc shrieked in pain. Gideon fell to his knees, and although the light was merciless, he did not have to squint or shield his face.

"Take me back..." a whisper echoed against the walls of the underground as if a multitude of people murmured at once. "Take me back..." the voices repeated, building in strength and speaking again and again.

"To where?" Gideon asked. He couldn't see anyone else in the room other than the cowering half-orc, but he could *feel* a presence with him.

"Home," the voices answered in sharp unison. "Take me

home."

Gideon shook his head. "Where?" he begged, scouring his memory for anything that might help him understand the cryptic message.

"To the Green City, Gideon," he heard from all around him. "I will show you the way!"

WITH A START, Gideon awoke. The sun was rising, just cresting the sides of Kanebullar Mountain, and winter fog smothered the fields outside Talonrend.

"We must go," Gideon said to no one in particular. He looked around the small crater where he had slept and found Melkora curled up several feet away. She had her clothing wrapped tightly around her body and shivered.

"Melkora," Gideon called in a muffled whisper.

"They're here?" the woman said, her voice full of panic. She bolted upright, quickly grasping her wounded ribs and stifling a scream of pain.

"No," Gideon said, trying to calm her. "But we must move." He got to his feet, found Maelstrom and Regret on the ground not far from him, and helped Melkora to stand. They were too close to Terror's Lament to see anyone patrolling the top, so it was impossible to know if they were being watched.

"What's wrong?" Gravlox called, hurrying back to the group with Vorst at his side. "Orcs?"

"Not yet," Gideon replied. He wrapped his arm around Melkora's waist and helped her balance with her walking stick. Once she had her bearings and had shaken the grogginess from her head, she was strong enough to stand and move without Gideon's support.

"Where are we going?" Vorst asked. She kept her eyes trained on the top of the wall as she spoke.

For the first time in several days, Gideon smiled. Deep within his mind, he knew where he needed to go, and direction alone was enough to bring him joy. "If we can, we need to find Apollonius and the paladins. There must be survivors," he said. "We gather the paladins and head west as the refugees did. We can move faster than the civilians, hunt at night, and reach the Green City in a season, two at the most."

Melkora clutched at the pain in her ribs and shuddered at the thought of such an epic journey. "What do we do once we get there?" Melkora asked.

"If the settlers of Talonrend truly did come from the Green City, they will answer our call for help. They will raise an army. We will return to liberate Talonrend!" Gideon couldn't help but feel like a beloved general addressing his troops. Visions flashed through his mind of vast fields shimmering with the glint of steel armor.

"How will we find it?" Melkora scoffed with derision. "Did you happen upon a map while you slept?"

Gideon's smile broadened. He tapped a finger against the side of his head. "Yes," he laughed, "I did."

Four

"HOW DO WE enter the city?" Gravlox asked. The four companions crouched against the base of Terror's Lament, out of view from the sentries above.

"I know a passageway," Melkora replied. "I doubt the orcs have discovered it."

Gideon chortled. "There are no hidden tunnels or secret hallways leading through the walls."

"You," Melkora pointed, "are not a thief. Cities and castles alike are rife with secrets. If you know where to look, anything can be found."

Gideon had to smile. He thought of his former life before he left his shield and mace in the Tower of Wings. He had been so obsessed with honor, he would never have associated with a rogue such as Melkora. In fact, he would have arrested her himself. Though with Vrysinoch's bones scattered in front of Talonrend and a city controlled by orcs, honor didn't feel very important.

"Show me this passageway, thief," Gideon said, only half joking.

Melkora led the others a mile or more north of the eastern gate. At the base of the wall, several of the stones were almost indiscernibly lighter than the rest of the structure. Melkora positioned herself directly in front of the center stone and then turned around, walking three quick paces with measured steps. The pain in her side flared, but she grit her teeth and ignored it as best she could. She put her feet together, then carefully slid her left leg out until it caught on the edge of something hard buried just beneath the soil.

"Here it is," she said, motioning for the others to follow. She pushed her toes under the small loop in the soil and then tried to use her walking stick to lift the trapdoor. "Gideon," she said, embarrassed at her lack of strength. "Lift the door."

Gideon said nothing as he felt for the edge of the trapdoor and lifted it open. He felt sorry for Melkora, but he was still confident that she would recover her strength. To his surprise, a small staircase had been dug into the ground that angled under Terror's Lament.

Gideon had to admit he was impressed. Without knowing of the trapdoor's existence, he would have never guessed it was there. The passage beneath was tight and dark, but only went in a single direction.

"If Herod knew this existed..." Gideon muttered.

"He probably does," Melkora said from the front of the group. "It leads to the dungeon."

Gideon didn't understand. The only dungeon he knew of was the one beneath Castle Talon where Gravlox and Vorst had been held prisoner. There was a small jail attached to the side of the city guard barracks, but even that was several miles away in the center of the city. "There is no dungeon on this side of Talonrend," Gideon said.

"Clearly, you do not know everything there is to know about the city," Melkora playfully jabbed.

After several minutes of walking, Melkora came to a wooden door barred with a lock. "Can you give me some light?" she asked, pointing to Maelstrom.

Gideon drew the sword and brought it slowly to life, keeping the flames as low as could. In the dim firelight, Melkora produced a thin pick from the inside of her shirt and slid it into the door's lock. With deft fingers, Melkora had the lock open in an instant.

The wooden door swung open slowly to reveal a dark dungeon cell. Gideon recoiled in disgust. "How many people have died down here?" he wondered. The stench was horrifying.

"Hundreds," Melkora responded solemnly. "This is the king's private dungeon. People were tortured and killed here more often than you think."

"It isn't that bad," Vorst said, scampering on ahead.

The group emerged at the back of a dark cell and Gideon let Maelstrom burn brighter to illuminate the dungeon. Skeletons hung from shackles set in the ceiling, and a particularly putrid pile of refuse crawled with maggots and roaches.

"How many times have you been in here?" Gideon asked. He couldn't bear the thought of traversing the dungeon on a regular basis just to enter the city.

"I was more of a spy than a thief," Melkora admitted. "Actually, I wasn't a great thief. But it doesn't take much skill to listen to a man being tortured and learn useful information."

"Who would pay for such information?" Gideon asked. His foot landed in what he thought to be a dark patch of soil, but turned out to be rotting human remains. He gagged and jumped forward, kicking to get the gore off his boot.

"Aristocrats," Melkora answered as though it should have been obvious. "Aristocrats love gossip and have coins to spare." She stopped at the end of the cell and waited for a moment to let the pain in her ribs subside before picking another lock.

"If Herod knew about the passageway, why didn't he do something about it?" Gideon asked. He imagined a handful of paladins waiting with their weapons drawn for thieves and criminals to open the door, only to be killed. It would have been a flawless ambush Herod could have used to catch a score of criminals.

"The moment one door closes, thieves will find another two to take its place." Melkora opened the cell door and stood, leaning heavily on her stick. It was obvious from her facial expression that her pain was nearing its limit.

"Better to allow the tunnel he's aware of than to force criminals to find other ways into the city," Gideon mused.

Gideon had to look away when they passed a bloody, vertical table holding the corpse of a man missing both of his feet. They couldn't reach the dungeon's exit quickly enough.

"One more door to go," Melkora said between gasps. They had travelled far, and her torn ribs ached with every movement. "Give me a moment to catch my breath."

"This place makes me sick," Gideon spat. He hated the idea of waiting in the dungeon any longer than he had to, but he used the time to listen through the door for orcs. A groan drifted through the putrid air to Gideon's ears. He turned, willed Maelstrom to flare brighter, and saw the silhouette of a man chained to a chair.

With his sword ready, Gideon slowly approached the cell. The man whimpered again, and Maelstrom's light reflected off the hundreds of spikes covering the torture chair. "Melkora," Gideon called, "open this cell."

The prisoner's body was shredded. It was a wonder he had not died from blood loss or dehydration. The chair's many spikes had torn through the man's skin all over his body and blood pooled by his feet.

"To what end?" Melkora asked. She remained slouched against the wall with her hand clamped to her ribs.

"We must..." Gideon stopped. Why did he care so much what happened to the prisoner? He couldn't help the man, much less save his life. "Nevermind..."

Quietly, Gideon begged Vrysinoch for forgiveness and brought Maelstrom behind his head. When he snapped the sword forward, inky black tendrils shot between the bars of the cell and wrapped around the man's neck with precision. Gideon sighed and yanked the sword back, deftly breaking the prisoner's spine and ending his torture.

"He might have deserved his fate," Melkora said callously. "No matter how much someone offered to pay me, I never came here to rescue a prisoner." She shook her head and turned back to the lock to open it.

"You're a thief, not a murderer," Gideon replied. "You must have some sympathy."

Melkora shook her head. "What I have is *loyalty*. The people in this dungeon never did anything for me, why should I help them? They would only slow me down anyways. You killed that man out of mercy. Mercy makes you weak."

"He saw us," Gideon lied. The man had never opened his eyes and would likely have been dead within the day. "I was removing a witness."

Melkora started to argue, but knew it wasn't worth the argument. Gideon didn't know why he felt the urge to help the poor man, but he knew killing him *had* been an act of mercy, and it brought a shred of comfort to his mind.

Vorst and Gravlox both gasped when Melkora pushed open the dungeon door on the interior of Terror's Lament. Everything had changed. The two humans stood slack-jawed and speechless.

On the eastern side of the city, almost everything was destroyed. Huge swaths of destruction had been carved through the houses and businesses, and some fires still burned in the rubble. The destruction of Cobblestreet had been thorough and overwhelming, but Talonrend was the pinnacle of safety and security. To see the city in such disarray was horrifying.

Gideon took several steps into the street and had to turn away. In the center of all the destruction, the Tower of Wings had toppled, and the beautiful structure was strewn about the city in piles of debris. The radiant emerald that had adorned the top of the tower since long before Gideon was born was shattered. The morning sunlight played off the jagged fragments and cast eerie green shadows against the wall that shimmered and danced. On top of everything, the oppressive smell of smoke choked the air.

Since most of the eastern quarter of the city had been utterly devastated by dragon's fire, Gideon could see the four miles to Castle Talon... or what was once Castle Talon. It was easy to see the orcish modifications taking place around the castle. Even early in the morning, orc crews worked to turn the beautiful human city into one of their strongholds. Wooden spikes had been attached to nearly everything in sight, and barbaric banners flew over the undamaged buildings.

"The uncouth swine don't even know how to use a kitchen," Gideon spat, pointing to a large group of orcs roasting a goat over a fire in the center of a street. "They probably sleep in ditches and—"

"Gideon!" Melkora whispered harshly. "Be quiet! You'll give us away."

The brooding man could only shake his head and bite his tongue. His city was dead, and maggots had infested the corpse.

A loud commotion from the southern side of the city pulled the group's attention to the top of the interior wall. Several minotaurs held a man in a roughspun robe by his shoulders. Gideon couldn't make out the details of his face at such a distance, but he appeared badly bloodied.

"What are they..." Vorst began to ask before Melkora shushed her with a hand.

To the raucous cheers of the gathered orcs below, the minotaurs shoved the beaten man over the edge. From his posture and relatively civilized garb, Gideon recognized the half-orc from his dream standing above the crowd on a heap of rubble. Once the flailing human was only several body lengths from the ground, the half-orc fired a blast of purple lightning from his staff and incinerated him.

"Monsters," Vorst said plainly. Gideon turned and regarded her. He found it curious for a goblin to pass moral judgment on minotaurs and orcs, especially when it came to killing humans. However, he had to remind himself, Gravlox and Vorst were far from typical goblins.

"I've seen enough," Gideon said quietly. He walked back to the dungeon entrance and shook his head.

"Wait," Melkora said. "We shouldn't leave yet." She gestured with her left hand at the buildings and used her right to cradle her ribs. "We should at least scavenge the nearby ruins for supplies. There aren't enough orcs to closely monitor the entire city, and I doubt they venture this far from the castle. There has to be something useful we can find."

Gideon nodded and felt a deep pull from Vrysinoch's consciousness within his mind. He wanted desperately to leave, to march west and put Talonrend far behind him, but he knew Melkora needed more rest. "We leave at dawn tomorrow," he said.

He pulled open the hidden dungeon door on the side of the wall and took a deep breath before passing through it.

"We will return before sunrise," Vorst stated. Her nearly limitless endurance would allow her to efficiently scavenge all through the night, and her tiny stature ensured her stealth. Without any debate, she took Gravlox by the hand and bounded west through the rubble.

After a moment, Melkora hobbled through the dungeon door and sat on the filthy ground with a groan. "Will the pain ever end?" she lamented.

"It has only been a few days," Gideon said. "I'm shocked you're walking. Under normal circumstances, you would be resting in a bed for weeks after such a nasty wound."

"What's normal?" she joked.

"I have no idea," Gideon responded. "I haven't lived a normal life since," Gideon's gaze moved upward, searching for an answer. "Well, since I was a kid." Gideon held Maelstrom at his side and illuminated the blade to a gentle flicker, like the light of a single candle.

"Where did you grow up?" Melkora asked. She realized that she knew practically nothing about the man who repeatedly saved her life, and posing such a simple question made her instantly blush with embarrassment.

"About a mile from here," Gideon sighed, reluctant to recall his past. "In a house near the north side of the city, by the fighting pit." Talonrend was somewhat small, only about four miles on each side, and the northern section of town had been primarily inhabited by tradesmen and skilled laborers before the orcs settled in.

"I never understood the pit," Melkora said.

Gideon laughed. He couldn't remember the names or faces of all those he had killed to the sounds of cheering. "I don't understand it either, but they paid in gold and silver."

"You fought?" Melkora said aghast. "I thought you worked for the prince." Suddenly, she felt Gideon's past harbored a host of dark secrets that she would rather not learn.

"A man can do both," Gideon cryptically replied.

Melkora wasn't sure what to say. In her mind, Gideon took on a bloodthirsty quality that somehow tainted him as a person, despite her own life of larceny and conniving. "Which profession do you prefer?" she asked after a few minutes of silence.

Gideon laughed again. "I never died in the pit," he said happily, "but I sometimes think I will die in service to the throne." He stretched his back and found a corner not far from Melkora in which to rest his head. "What about you? What was your life before all of this?"

In the dim light of Maelstrom's magic, Melkora longed for a bed and the comfort of civilization. It was only morning, but her wound sapped all the energy from her body and made her eyelids flutter. "My parents owned the store in Cobblestreet before I inherited it," she said. "I lived there all my life."

"And your husband?" Gideon asked.

She held up her hand, but didn't open her eyes to know if Gideon saw. "I've never been married," she said with a hint of remorse.

"You mentioned a child before."

Melkora let out a long sigh and tried to keep tears from welling up in her eyes.

"I'm sorry," Gideon whispered. Her silence was telling.

"No," Melkora forgave him, "don't be. It is a simple question with a simple answer." She cleared her throat and gathered what she could of her emotions. "I was in love once, but he died before our hands could be tied, although he did give me a daughter."

"What was she like?" Gideon asked. As a paladin, he had taken a sacred vow of chastity which he had never broken. The ideas of love and family were intriguing to him. In fact, the more Gideon pondered the thought of lifelong companionship and fathering children, the more he was reminded that he had forsaken his vows when he left the Tower of Wings.

"She was a beautiful girl," Melkora said cheerfully. "She had her father's dark hair, but she had my eyes. Corshana..."

Gideon's heart caught in his throat. Melkora continued to speak, explaining Corshana's multitude of personality traits, but he heard none of them. All he could think about was the wounded refugee girl he had killed on the road. *Mercy,* he pleaded with his conscience, *I gave her mercy...*

SEVERAL HOURS AFTER midnight, Gravlox and Vorst roused the humans from their tenuous slumber. They had gathered a motley array of provisions centered mostly around food and clothing. Vorst had managed to find an entire side of salted beef that she dragged behind her in a burlap sack.

"How long will the journey take?" Melkora asked. She quickly brushed the sleep from her eyes and stood. After a few deep breaths, the pain in her side dulled to a low throb she could mostly ignore.

When Gideon contemplated the long trek, he saw the path before them as a bird might see it, drifting through the clouds. In his heart, he knew how to lead them to the Green City. His only uncertainties arose from the vast distance they would need to cover: a thousand miles by his rough estimation.

"If we stop every night to camp and hunt, it will take two seasons, maybe three," he said. Gideon hoped the downfall of Talonrend meant fewer bands of orcs would give them trouble on the road.

"And if the snowfall is too high?" Melkora asked with veiled skepticism.

"We make planks from wood that let us walk òn top of it," Gideon cheerfully responded. His fervor for their task would not be diminished by impediments such as snow. "Or I will use Maelstrom to melt the snow and give us a path," he continued.

"And if the Green City doesn't exist? If it really is just a legend and we find nothing? How long will we search?" Melkora didn't feel as pessimistic as her words sounded, but she couldn't shake the notion that they were walking to their deaths.

Images of sprawling streets and wide boulevards watched over by towering minarets flashed in the back of Gideon's head. *Take me home*, Vrysinoch bade him softly.

"The Green City exists," Gideon stated with finality. "And Vrysinoch will lead us to it."

ERREN HUNCHED OVER an ancient scroll like a cat devouring the final morsels of a mouse. In the high-backed chair next to him, the High Priest sat and gently snored. Zerren pulled a candle closer and pressed the scroll flat to get a better look at the faded words.

"This is the only surviving copy?" he asked, not knowing that the old man was asleep.

The High Priest awoke with an obnoxious snort and cleared his eyes. "What's that?" he asked. "Have you found it?"

Zerren shook his head. "Is there another copy of this scroll?" he asked again. "The ink is too faded to be of any use." He had been in the study searching for answers long enough to burn through two taper candles. His eyes hurt and his back screamed from hunching so long.

"Here," the High Priest fumbled in his blue robe and pulled out a circle of brass with a lens fixed inside it. He held it over the paper and it magnified the words underneath, making them clearer, but still barely legible.

Zerren was fascinated with the tool. "Magic?" he asked in wonder.

The High Priest laughed. "The smith who made it called it a monocle. It makes small things bigger." He couldn't help but laugh. Although he was certain he was the only person in all of Azuria to own such a device, it really was a simple invention at its core.

Zerren waved his fingers underneath the monocle, and his eyes grew wide. With a start, he pulled his hand out from the monocle and inspected it, making sure it had not grown.

Laughing so hard he thought he would choke, the High Priest nearly fell from his chair. "It only makes things appear larger," he explained. "It doesn't actually change them."

With a frown, Zerren went back to the scroll. "I'm not sure what this faded word is," he said slowly, "but I think it says when Vry—" he caught himself before saying the full name, "when the brother returns, the plane of the world will," Zerren rubbed his temples, trying to coax the right word to the surface. "Collapse?" He sat back in his chair and stretched, trying to understand the cryptic passage.

The High Priest grinned. "That is exactly what it says," he whispered.

Zerren slammed his fist into the table. "You knew what it said all along?" he shouted at the old man. He had wasted an entire hour trying to determine the text of the scroll, and it seemed he had been tricked.

"The word too faded to read is 'man'," he said, tapping on the scroll with a crooked finger. "When the Vrysinoch *man* returns, the plane of the world will collapse and be made one with the Void."

"What does it mean?" Zerren scratched his head and tried to remember anything from his education that might help him understand.

"No one can be sure," the High Priest mused, "but I imagine that Vrysinoch must have an avatar, a chosen warrior to carry his physical form."

"You mean a Champion?" Zerren clarified, but the old man shook his head.

"Druaka's Champion is simply the best fighter in Azuria. I do not doubt that Ohra has Druaka's favor, but she is not an avatar. She is only a Champion."

Zerren scoffed. "I would like to see this avatar you speak of fight against Ohra in the pit!" he exclaimed. "No one can defeat a Champion!"

"An avatar is the living embodiment of a god, you fool," the High Priest replied. "A real avatar would destroy Ohra with a single spoken word."

Zerren swallowed hard. "Does Druaka have an avatar?" he asked sheepishly, feeling like a child under a priest's tutelage again.

The High Priest adjusted his robes and rested his head against the back of his chair. "I do not know," he said. "Perhaps there is one, but then again, perhaps not."

"How can our plane collapse into the void?" Zerren asked after reading the passage again with the monocle's aid. In response, the High Priest only snored.

With a sigh, Zerren rolled up the scroll and returned it to a case hanging on the wall of the study. His mind reeled with implications as he descended the spiral staircase that led from the library to the street. His brother had spoken of the void's recent instability... "But what in Druaka's name does it mean?" he cursed as he emerged from the tower. He pulled the hood of his robe up over head and shielded his eyes from the bright sunlight. It would be dark in several hours, and he could safely return to Valkoinen's underground lair. If anyone understood the collapse of the void, it would be the leader of the Alabaster Order.

LEAVING TALONREND BEHIND was difficult, but the divine calling Gideon felt within his soul was more painful to ignore. To Gravlox and Vorst, the journey was nothing but an adventure. With

Vorst's knowledge of edible plants and Gideon's ability to hunt, the group never feared starvation as the refugees had before them. Without a permanent home to call their own, travelling hundreds of miles away from Talonrend and Kanebullar mountain did not bring tears to either goblins' eyes.

Melkora looked longingly back at the high walls of Talonrend. She had grown up and lived in Cobblestreet, but Talonrend also felt like her home. Terror's Lament had been a true symbol of safety and security. If ever there was an invasion, she could run to the high walls for protection.

Melkora's thoughts drifted back to her parents and their store. *The army will come and defend the village,* they had said, urging her to stay in Cobblestreet. Then they had died in the streets, vainly defending their store from an endless wave of goblin invaders.

The four of them stood on a low rise a mile or more west of Talonrend. The refugee path would be easy enough to follow, littered with broken items and the occasional corpse. Melkora leaned against her stick and tried to steel her mind against the sorrow she felt. "Will we ever return?" she asked the wind.

Gideon placed a hand on her shoulder and turned her around. "We will find the Green City," he whispered. "Vrysinoch will show us the way."

VRYSINOCH DID SHOW them the way. Over hills and through forests, the four companions trekked. The way was mostly clear, with large swaths of flat plains that passed easily beneath their feet. They stopped at rivers and streams, gathering water where they could and prayed for rain or melted snow when they couldn't. All the while, Vrysinoch led them. Every day they awoke physically refreshed and energized by the god's presence among them.

Gideon marched with brutal purpose. Every footfall brought

him closer to the Green City and strengthened his indefatigable resolve. With his mind so entranced, Gideon rarely spoke during the
day.

At night when they made camp, Gideon tended to Melkora's
wound. After several weeks, she was walking without the use of a
cane, greatly quickening their pace. The two humans grew closer,
telling stories of life in Talonrend and Cobblestreet as they roasted
meat above their campfires. Gideon enjoyed recounting the stories
of his childhood as an apprentice blacksmith and Melkora was easily captivated by them.

When the two humans slept, Gravlox and Vorst would wander
off slightly, always in search of the same thing. Since his passage
through the Star Room beneath the Tower of Wings, Gravlox
searched for his shamanistic magic. Every night, Gravlox calmed his
mind, focused on the familiar pathways in his mind which led to
the powers of the earth, and found nothing. Vorst stayed by his side
vigilantly, never letting her own frustrations boil over, and watched
her husband struggle. Every morning, Gravlox returned to the humans with the same result: failure.

After a month of travel, the snow began to fall in heavy sheets.
Gideon held Maelstrom aloft and willed it to burn, radiating heat in
comforting waves that kept the four from freezing. When the snow
became too deep to easily traverse, they fashioned snowshoes out of
wood and bark, always marching onward.

SEVERAL MONTHS LATER when the snows melted, Gideon began to smell salt in the air. He wasn't sure what it meant, but the
strange scent made him quicken his pace.

As the four rounded a slight bend in a creek as it emerged from
a small patch of woods, they spied a farmhouse standing tall above
acres and acres of young wheat fields. "Have we made it?" Melkora

asked breathlessly. Her ribs still carried a twinge of discomfort, but it wasn't anything she would call pain.

Gravlox and Vorst stood next to her, their thick-skinned goblin feet bare in the moist spring dirt. Vorst carried a haunch of roasted wolf meat in her pack, but its savory scent was overpowered by the salt. A blue sliver along the horizon shimmered with light, but they could see no city.

"I believe we have," Gideon said softly. He attempted to communicate with Vrysinoch, but like the hundreds of times he had tried during their journey, the god was silent.

"Shall we head to the farmhouse and ask for directions?" Melkora joked. Throughout the several months they had trekked, Gideon's knowledge of the path never faltered.

After a moment of taking in the sight, Gideon nodded. "The Green City is nearby," he said, "but I thought we would be able to see it." In his mind, the Green City was massive and unbelievable—larger than Talonrend and more beautiful than Reikall.

Gideon turned to Gravlox and Vorst. "Are there any goblins in this part of the world?" he asked. They hadn't seen any humanoid races on their journey, but that fact meant nothing. The four of them had spent several nights huddled in the darkness with the sounds of orcs all around them. Luckily enough, they had managed to move undetected.

Gravlox shrugged his shoulders. Spending almost every night with two humans had taught him much of their expressions and language. "How would we know?" he said.

With a laugh, the four of them hiked along a small ridge on the southern side of the wheat fields that led to the farmhouse. About a hundred feet from the structure, Gravlox stopped in his tracks. "Someone approaches," he said, holding up a hand and quieting the others. He crouched low and drew his sword.

"Where?" Gideon whispered. He spun around and took Maelstrom from his side, but saw nothing.

"There," Gravlox pointed to the house, but only he could see it.

What is it? Vorst tapped silently into his shoulder.

Gravlox didn't know how to describe the ripple in the air he had seen. "Gideon, send your whip directly at the farmhouse, fifty feet," he commanded.

Without hesitation, Gideon brought Maelstrom to life and sent a cascade of oily tendrils directly at the spot. The air shimmered and popped as the tendrils collided with *something*, but Gideon still could not see.

Gravlox whirled around and pointed again. "There!" he yelled, pointing down the slope of the ridge, and Gideon fired Maelstrom's tendrils again.

Gideon's aim was true. He struck the spot exactly, and the sword's black protrusions collided with something solid.

Suddenly, out of the vacant air only a few feet in front of the group, a man appeared. He was dressed in white with a pearly mask that covered his features. "Silence!" the man spoke. His voice reverberated through the air and blasted with magical force.

Gravlox and Gideon both tried to strike out at the man, but found their limbs heavy and unresponsive.

"You can see me," the man spoke directly at Gravlox.

The goblin ground his teeth in frustration and remained silent.

"You saw me," the man repeated through his mask.

Gravlox tighten his grip, extending his sword in the process. "I saw you," he confirmed.

The white mask hid the man's emotions, but his voice betrayed his excitement. "Then you are a Fated One," he said.

Gravlox stood still and tried to comprehend the man's words, but they made no sense to him. "Take off your mask," he ordered. He wanted to see the man's eyes to determine if he was merely insane, or if he believed what he spoke.

The man stood motionless for several agonizing minutes. Finally, he spoke. "Nothing lies behind my mask except the Void," he said.

"Enough of your nonsense!" Gideon yelled in frustration. He

held Maelstrom in his hand, fire licking the air. He had little patience for riddles. The more the man in white spoke, the more Gideon's ire grew. "You'll take off your mask and speak plainly, or I'll kill you where you stand," he threatened.

The man in white looked to Gideon as though he just noticed him for the first time. "You will not," he stated. His voice carried a trace of magic that gave his words power beyond their meaning.

Unfazed, Gideon lashed Maelstrom's tendrils at the man with all his strength, but the man was no longer there.

"By the house," Gravlox said, pointing again at the man in white. He was standing in front of the farmhouse door like a statue.

Gideon growled in frustration and put his sword away. He knew he wouldn't be able to catch the teleporting man, whether he could see him or not. Fighting an invisible target felt like potential suicide, even if he was somehow imbued with the strength of Vrysinoch.

"The Green City is not far," Gideon said. "I can feel it. We should move."

Gravlox pondered a moment before he spoke. "I want to talk to him," he said, pointing again at the farmhouse door. After a second, the figure faded from view again.

"Nothing but riddles and lies," Gideon spat. "Why bother?"

"If he wanted to kill us, I fear he would have," Melkora added. "Why not let them speak?"

Gideon guffawed, but he could not deny her logic. "Fine," he said. "But I still want to kill him."

The four companions wearily headed for the farmhouse. Gravlox reached up and grasped the stout piece of wood that served as a handle and pushed, searching for the man inside. The door swung open freely and revealed a well-kept dwelling. A small fire crackled in the corner beneath a cookpot and nothing seemed out of place.

In the center of the room, the man in white sat at a large table with his gloved hands folded neatly in front of him. Gideon scowled and moved to the side of the man, never taking his eyes from him.

Tentatively, Gravlox climbed into the chair on his side of the table and stood to see over the table. Behind him, Melkora and Vorst both kept their hands close to their weapons.

"You know who I am?" Gravlox asked, not waiting for the stranger to speak.

The man in white did not move, and his mask showed nothing. Not a fleck of skin could be seen anywhere on his body, making him impossible to read. "I do not," he said slowly. "I have read histories that speak of goblins and seen drawings of them, but I have never seen one myself. I can only assume you are either a member of the goblin race or else a very hideous and stunted orc."

Vorst balled her fists at the insult, but Gravlox ignored it. "We are goblins," he said, indicated his wife with a hand. "From Kanebullar Mountain, east of Talonrend."

At the mention of the city, the man reacted. It was impossible to tell if his movement indicated positive or negative emotion, but at least he reacted. "I have heard of Talonrend," he said plainly, revealing nothing, "how fares the Green City?"

"Enough of your riddles!" Gideon yelled. He reached for the man's mask and tried to rip it from his face, but his fingers stopped just short of touching it.

The man in white turned to regard Gideon, but said nothing, and looked back to Gravlox.

"We came here in search of the Green City," Gravlox said, not knowing exactly what the man meant. "We came from Talonrend."

The man in white unfolded his hands and let them rest in his lap beneath the table. After a moment, he spoke. "Talonrend *is* the Green City," he explained. "When the followers of the eagle-god, the Emerald Order as they called themselves, abandoned Azuria roughly one thousand years ago, they went east to found their new city: Talonrend. They took their giant emerald with them to serve as a beacon and cast a green glow over their buildings. Therefore Talonrend, *not* Azuria, is the Green City."

"Lies," Gideon murmured to himself, but when he begged Vrysinoch for clarification, he found no answer.

"We have been taught that the settlers of Talonrend left the Green City in search of a new home. When they reached the Clawflow River, they built Talonrend," Melkora said. The man in white listened, but never took his gaze from Gravlox.

"I am not surprised that your priests changed history to suit their needs," the strange man continued, "but I assure you, there is nothing green about Azuria. In fact, you'll find green to be the color of traitors and prisoners, not an eagle-god."

"What are you saying?" Gideon asked, regaining some of his composure.

"Do you really know nothing?" the man in white responded.

Gravlox laughed. "Yes," he answered. He liked the man's dry straightforwardness. "Teach us."

The man brought his hands back on top of the table and relaxed slightly, easing his shoulders into the chair. "A long time ago," he began, "more than a thousand years in the past, Azuria had two gods. The first was Druaka, the raven: the god of death and longevity, patience and deception. Druaka is the caretaker of souls, guiding the slain of every race into the next world. Alongside the raven was his brother. The eagle-god presided over the domains of life and birth, impulsivity and warfare. These two gods lived together in the same city.

"One year, the followers of the eagle claimed to have a Most Pure, a daughter born with the blessing of one of the gods, a being that would most certainly rule the city. But the followers of Druaka, the Alabaster Order," he pointed to his own white robes to indicate his affiliation, "did not believe the daughter to be Most Pure. One night, a mage from the Alabaster Order snuck into the eagle's temple and ran a knife through the child's skull. The next morning, war broke out in the street. Azuria fell into chaos.

"After a decade of brutal fighting, Druaka won, the eagle was banished, and the Emerald Order was cast out. All of the eagle's followers left Azuria behind. Many people went with them, even non-believers, in search of a better life. Their new city would be called, Talonrend after their god, and be purged of all references to Druaka." The man leaned forward and stared at Gravlox with empty, hollow eye sockets. "You see, Talonrend *is* the Green City."

"All of our histories…" Gideon muttered.

For once, the man turned to regard Gideon with the blank stare given by his mask. "Lies," he said plainly, using Gideon's word against him. The paladin had no response.

"Can you take us to Azuria?" Melkora asked.

The man in white turned to her and bowed his head slightly. "Of course," he responded. "I live in Azuria and know it well. The city is not far." He shifted his attention back to Gravlox and fixed the goblin with an intense, eyeless stare. "Fated One," he addressed him with reverence. "If you have nowhere to stay, the halls of Alabaster Order are always open to you."

"Gravlox is a shaman," Vorst said. "Not an invisible mage you like you."

At that, the man shifted backward in his chair. His posture conveyed befuddlement, but his mask betrayed nothing. "A shaman?" he asked quizzically.

"Not any longer," Gravlox said sullenly. "I haven't been able to use magic in months."

The man relaxed slightly, but still appeared startled. "Oh? I have only known orcs to be shaman. When a human magic user learns to commune with nature to find power, we call them a druid. No druid has ever been counted in the ranks of the Alabaster Order."

Melkora shifted her weight impatiently from foot to foot. While the history of Talonrend, if any of it was true, certainly fascinated her, the man's mysticism and cryptic language annoyed her. "Take us to the city…" her voice trailed off as she realized she had never heard the man give his name.

"Valkoinen," he added for her politely. "Nineteenth Master of the Alabaster Order." In one motion, he stood and gave a slight bow.

"Take us to the city, Valkoinen," Melkora reiterated. She rubbed her arms as though they were covered in something foul and couldn't bear the look of the unnerving white mask trained on her. She averted her eyes and stepped back, opening the door behind her.

Without so much as the gentle sound of his robe brushing the wooden floor, the man in white silently led them from the farmhouse.

The group had to walk a mile along a well-paved stone road that led north before they could see their destination. When they rounded a large bend that hugged tightly to a salt-crusted cliff, the city of Azuria opened up before their eyes.

Even from a distance, Azuria was awe inspiring. Magnificent towers spiraled into the sky, and pennants of blue and white fluttered joyfully in the breeze. The gatehouse itself was larger than Castle Talon. In the center, the raised portcullis was wide enough to permit an entire alaris of horsemen to pass abreast. To the sides of the entryway, two huge round towers stood watch, adorned with intricate statues of ravens sitting atop piles of skulls.

Wherever he set his eyes, magnificence struck Gideon with full force. He had dreamt of the Green City during the long journey from Talonrend. His mind had conjured up images of marble columns and granite statues lining wide boulevards. Everything he had imagined paled in comparison to what he saw.

"The Green City," Gideon said proudly, standing before the gatehouse like a child seeing the king's throne for the first time. Valkoinen heard the exclamation, but chose not to correct Gideon's misunderstanding of the city's name.

In the center of the massive metropolis stood a tower, similar to the one that had crowned Talonrend for hundreds of years. Azuria's central pinnacle was easily twice the height of the Tower of Wings and adorned in royal blue instead of Vrysinoch's sacred green.

As the four companions stared in amazement at the marvelous city, they failed to notice a crowd that had formed in front of them. "Orc!" an old woman spat, clinging her shawl about her hunched shoulders despite the warm ocean air. Several others took up the call, and one of them threw a stone from the road in Gravlox's direction.

Gideon drew Maelstrom from his side with angry grunt. Before he could strike the woman down, Valkoinen appeared between them and the growing mob as if he simply walked out of the wind. In their stupor, none of them had noticed Valkoinen's disappearance.

"Silence!" he commanded with magical authority. At once, the crowd hushed. Rocks fell from their hands and the people stood slack-jawed. Behind Valkoinen, a dozen others dressed in all white stepped out of the air and echoed the man's word. Gravlox could not tell if the others were real men or mere illusions, but he felt magical strength emanating from them in waves.

"These two are not orcs," Valkoinen said. Again, the others behind him echoed his words perfectly. "They are goblins, and they are here under the protection of the Alabaster Order." The crowd that had loudly jeered just minutes before stood in heavy silence. "Disperse!" Valkoinen and the others commanded. As if they were puppets on strings, the people in the mob turned and went about their business without complaint.

"Is that wise?" Gideon asked, sneering at the man's open use of magic. When Valkoinen turned, the other men in white vanished where they had stood.

"Few people in Azuria believe the Alabaster Order still exists," he said with a hint of laughter. "If they remember what just happened, they will remember it with fear."

"They will tell others!" Vorst exclaimed. She dreaded the idea of being hunted once again by humans. With every ounce of her life, she longed for Azuria to accept her and Gravlox without incident.

"Of course they will!" Valkoinen responded. "The Alabaster Order thrives on the usefulness of rumors." He lowered his voice ever so slightly. "Fear is only a tool. In the right hands, it can bend anyone, even a city, without them ever knowing. I cannot say how everyone in Azuria will respond to seeing a goblin for the first time, but I assure you, they won't dare raise a hand against you."

"Don't believe everything he says," Gideon grunted, shouldering past the man as he headed into the heart of Azuria with Melkora on his heels.

"WHAT IS IT?" The High Priest asked from a large oak chair. His head was buried in a book, and several candles flickered nearby.

Zerren watched a murky representation of the events at the gatehouse through a magically enchanted piece of stained glass. Normally, the decorative window showed the front of the city without motion, a picture placed on the glass for art's sake. However, when Zerren activated the window's magic, the scene slowly came to life and played out on the glass.

"Goblins?" Zerren remarked. The blurry images in the glass were certainly short, but he had no way of confirming their race.

The High Priest sat up and looked at the window himself. After a moment, he rose from his chair and slowly circled the table until he came to a particular bookshelf on the south side of the library.

"That tome there," he said, pointing out a leather book on the top shelf.

Zerren pulled a small step ladder to the bookshelf and used it to fetch the heavy volume. It was one he had seen before, but rarely studied. When he had set it on the table for the High Priest, the old man flipped casually through the musty pages.

"Here," he said, pointing a crooked finger at one of the book's numerous illustrations. "Is that what you see? I'm afraid my eyes are no good when it comes to details in the stained glass."

Zerren studied the picture for several moments before comparing it to the image in the glass. The book showed a short creature with a huge nose, massive ears, and boney joints like a poorly formed mannequin. It was similar enough to the magical image for Zerren to confirm his suspicion.

"Yes," he said. "Although the nose is not so large…"

The High Priest laughed and returned to his seat. "Perhaps you should meet these goblins and then fix the drawing," he suggested.

Zerren wasn't sure if the old man was being sincere or attempting a joke, so he nodded and closed the tome. "The city will be agitated," he continued. "And not only by the presence of our new guests. My brother was with them…"

"Oh?"

Zerren sighed. "For a secret organization, they aren't very good at hiding."

"Anyone who still denies the Alabaster Order is a senile fool," the High Priest scoffed. The old man held little love for the Order, but he was smart enough to utilize them when he needed their skills.

"Do you think—" Zerren mused, still watching the humans move through the city.

"That Vrysinoch has returned?" the High Priest finished for him.

Zerren started to shush the man and scold him for using the forbidden name, but quickly remembered his place. "Well?" he asked. "I don't see any giant bird circling the spires of Azuria."

"There are two humans, yes?" the High Priest asked.

Zerren nodded.

"Keep your eye on them," he said gravely, suddenly taking a very serious tone. "A Champion of Vrysinoch could be a powerful enemy against the followers of Druaka," he continued. The High Priest leaned forward in his chair and furrowed his brow. "If one of them is the eagle-god made flesh, we are surely doomed."

586

GIDEON WALKED THROUGH the city and took in the new sights and smells. The air was crisp, tangy with salt, and full of life. Toward the center of Azuria, Gideon found a huge marketplace that would've made the largest businesses in Talonrend pale in comparison. He glanced once at Melkora to see if she was still following him before he headed into the bustle of the market.

Everything was radically new. Potent fish larger than anything alive in the Clawflow River were displayed on wooden shelves next to equally foreign fruits and vegetables. The Azurians even dressed differently. Where men and women of Talonrend favored function over everything, the people Gideon saw in the market wore long silks and flashy vests embellished with white stones. Gideon looked down at his own leather garments and wondered how out of place he must seem.

Toward the southeastern corner of the vast market, the glint of metal caught Gideon's eye. He shoved through the crowd and approached a stall selling shields, armor, and a vast array of weaponry. Despite the selection and several customers milling about, everything appeared to be rather poorly built.

"Ah, one of the newcomers!" the merchant said cheerfully, following Gideon's gaze to one of the hatchets on the table. He picked it up by the head and presented the hilt for Gideon to grasp. "See anything you like?"

Gideon took the weapon and could immediately tell it was never built for combat. He shook the axe, and the head wiggled from side to side. "This isn't fit to split wood, much less to carry into battle," Gideon said. He set the axe down and felt the edge of a metal shield. Although it was brightly painted, it was far too flimsy to be of any use.

The merchant flashed a toothy smile and laughed heartily. "Of course not, good sir," he explained. "These are replicas!" he knocked his fist into the side of a jousting helmet and it made a shrill ring.

"Of what?" Gideon asked plainly. "Why bother making a replica of a sword and a shield? Sticks are adequate for practice."

With a point of his finger, the merchant indicated a small boy at the edge of the market playing with one of the swords by himself. "Children do not want to slay monsters with sticks," he happily said. "If you're looking for combat weaponry, my brother's armory sells the best weapons in Azuria!" he pointed to the north and Gideon saw the telltale image of an anvil painted on a wooden shield above a door.

"War is terrible," Gideon solemnly stated. "I do not understand why children would want to imitate it," he let his mind drift back to his own childhood and his dreams of becoming a renowned blacksmith. He had never aspired to make weapons and armor, the tools of destruction, but had set his heart on functional pieces like farming implements and ornate lanterns. He let out a long sigh and thought of his friend and mentor who had raised him at the forge.

"You like this sword, yes?" the merchant eagerly said, plucking a replica from a rack and handing it to Gideon.

He hadn't realized it, but Gideon had been intensely staring at a particular sword while he was lost in thought—the same sword that had drawn him to the stall in the first place. Hesitantly, Gideon reached for the weapon and took hold of it. "What is this?" he asked with wonder.

"A replica of the Champion's sword," the merchant beamed. "Just like the one used in the arena."

To his bewilderment, Gideon knew the sword well, for it was an exact copy of Nevidal: longer than a side sword but shorter than a two-handed sword and completely lacking ornamentation. "This weapon is built for function," Gideon said in a trance-like stupor.

"Magnificent, isn't she?"

"She?" Gideon looked up, fearful about letting the sword out of his grasp. Thankfully, the hilt fell easily away from his fingers and did not pull his soul along with it.

"Dalviné," the merchant said proudly, swinging the sword harmlessly behind the stall's wooden counter. "Champion Ohra fights with her. Have you seen the arena?" the man asked, but Gideon was too lost in thought to hear the question.

"The arena?" the man repeated, waving his hand in front of Gideon's face.

"What?" he said, finally letting his eyes leave the replica blade.

"South of the city," the man pointed behind him with his thumb, "along the coastline. You can't miss it."

Gideon nodded, not quite sure what the merchant was describing. "Thanks," he said. With a huge smile and an enthusiastic handshake, the merchant let Gideon leave his stall and return to the chaos of the busy marketplace.

"WHAT DO YOU think?" Zerren asked from a high window overlooking Azuria's bustling market. To his left, Valkoinen stood at a similar window and watched with great interest as the newcomers explored the city.

After a long moment, Valkoinen turned to regard his brother. His lifeless mask showed nothing. "I do not know." His voice was calm and level, as stark as the robe he wore.

"I think if one of them is a god, it would be obvious, don't you?" Zerren asked somewhat impatiently.

"I do not know," Valkoinen repeated. He moved his lightless gaze back to the window.

Zerren let out a long sigh. He was typically patient with his brother—more patient than any man should be—but the priest had very little tolerance for cryptic half-answers. "When you spoke with them, did they seem *magical* at all?" Zerren asked with heavy sarcasm.

Valkoinen did not move from the window. "No," he stated, completely unphased by his brother's frustration. "But the goblin male, Gravlox, saw through the void," he continued. "I approached them folded in Void, completely invisible to even the most highly trained of my apprentices, and he spotted me a hundred yards away."

Suddenly very interested, Zerren stepped away from the window and moved to a different wall of the library tower to get a better view of the goblin pair. "Could a goblin possibly be the brother from the prophecy?" he asked from his new perch.

Again, Valkoinen waited a long moment before responding. "I do not know," he said at last.

Zerren hit his fist into the stone wall of the tower. "What *do* you know?" he nearly screamed. "No one has ever ventured into the forest west of Azuria in a thousand years, and when four strangers arrive claiming to come from a city most people have never even heard of, you spend hours with them and learn *nothing*."

Valkoinen turned back to his brother and bored into him with blank holes where his eyes should have been. Zerren blanched under the oppressive weight of the stare and had to look away.

"I learned many things," the man in white said after a minute. "Things you could never begin to comprehend."

PEOPLE POINTED AT Gravlox and Vorst. Some of the nearby children screamed when they saw the goblin pair. More than anything, the citizens of Azuria asked questions. Vorst tried to answer them, but quickly became frustrated and pushed through the crowd in search of Gideon and Melkora.

When they were finally free of the swarm, Gravlox climbed up the edge of a sparkling marble fountain to take in the sights and sounds of the new city.

"What are you thinking?" Vorst asked quietly in her native language.

Gravlox spun in circles and looked at everything. The strong sun felt good against his skin, but something in his mind felt askew. The man in white had been an anomaly. Somehow, Gravlox had seen him when the others could not, and that fact rattled his mind.

"Where did the man in white go?" Gravlox asked. He searched the nearby streets within his view, but could not find him again.

"I do not like him," Vorst replied sullenly. "Without you, he could have killed us all."

Gravlox knew she was right. He wondered if the invisible man was stalking Gideon and Melkora for that very purpose. "Did you believe the things he said?" he asked, sitting down on the side of the fountain.

Vorst shook her head. "I have no reason not to, but he might benefit by lying to us," she said. "I'm sure we will see him again." She took hold of the edge of the fountain and pulled herself up next to Gravlox. To a human, the fountain was roughly waist high, but to the goblins, it was an obstacle that required some strength and determination to overcome.

"I can find him," Gravlox stated with certainty. He looked at the buildings and signs lining Azuria's avenues and felt a slight tug on his magical consciousness. Valkoinen's presence felt like a very old memory that only came back in strained flashes.

Vorst didn't know if finding the man in white was a good idea or not, but she trusted Gravlox to protect her. "Should we find Gideon and Melkora first?"

"They're in the—" Gravlox jumped up on the fountain and pointed, suddenly bursting with confidence. "I can feel them!" he shouted, drawing the attention of more onlookers. "Vorst, I can *feel* their magic!"

Vorst stood next to him and grasped his hand. "Show me," she said, but she didn't need to. Gravlox sank his mind into the long-lost well of magic resting at the edge of his consciousness and latched onto a shimmering wave of energy. When he clenched his fist, the magic leapt into existence as a blazing sphere of heat around his closed fingers.

"Gravlox..." Vorst gasped.

Without hesitation, Gravlox launched the ball of energy into the air where it exploded and rained ash down harmlessly into the fountain. He reached deeper beneath the ground and probed the dirt and rock with his mind. Thousands of feet beneath the surface, Gravlox felt the raging magic of molten rock. He beckoned to the fiery pool with his mind, and it obeyed.

"Gravlox!" Vorst yelled, shaking his shoulders violently. In his blind reverie, Gravlox lost his balance and tumbled into the fountain's water.

"I've got it!" Gravlox screamed when he surfaced. He smiled from ear to ear. "I'm a shaman once more," he bellowed, his high-pitched voice cracking. All around him, the water of the fountain steamed and bubbled, threatening to erupt with the heat Gravlox had brought with him.

"Stop!" Vorst shouted at him. By then, another crowd had gathered, and the humans who didn't look terrified wore violent and angry expressions.

Gravlox let the power subside from his body and return to the earth. He pulled himself out of the fountain and shook the water from his ears. "Vorst," he muttered in disbelief, "I'm a shaman."

"Look at what you did!" Vorst pointed to the edge of the fountain where Gravlox had been standing. The beautiful marble had turned to black slag.

"We need to find the others," Gravlox said, ignoring the damage to the fountain. He pulled Vorst down to the street with him and bounded through the crowd to the marketplace.

"HOW DID IT happen?" Gideon asked. The four companions sat at an old wooden table inside a noisy inn by the harbor. The smell of salt water mingled with the stench of vomit and sour ale, leaving an unpalatable tinge in the air. After Gravlox had found Gideon and Melkora in the market, they had explored Azuria as a group until sundown.

"I think the man in white did it somehow," Gravlox responded in his slow command of the human language. A plate of smoked meat sat in front of the group, and each of them had a tankard of fresh ale, although several empty mugs had already accumulated in front of Gideon.

The barkeep, a barrel-chested man who reminded Gideon of a clumsy and crass version of Master Brenning, lumbered to their table and collected the empty mugs. "You got a drinking problem?" he bluntly spat at Gideon. Despite the fact that the man had offered them food, drinks, and two rooms for free, knowing that the outsiders' presence would bring more patrons, he looked downright disgusted whenever he brought more beer.

"Is that an insult or an actual question?" Gideon asked with genuine curiosity. He had certainly consumed a fair amount of ale, but still maintained his balance, unlike several other patrons.

"Bah!" the barkeep growled. His lazy eye drifted, and when he turned back to the bar, he slammed his leg into the table. With a hail of incomprehensible curses, the man hit the ground and smashed the tankards beneath his bulk. For a second, Gideon contemplated not helping the man up, but he reached out his hand anyway.

"I have a question for you," Gideon said when the barkeep was standing.

"The name's Doran," the barkeep informed them. "Now what's your question?"

"Are there any old parts of Azuria?" he asked. Remembering what Valkoinen had told them, Gideon wanted to find some relic of the time before the civil war when Vrysinoch was openly praised. Perhaps then he could fulfill the god's request and take him home.

"The whole city is old," the man replied with disinterest.

Gideon caught him by the arm before he could skulk back to the bar. "Yes, I understand, but are there any parts older than the rest? Disused ruins? An old temple long forgotten?"

Something in his question piqued the barkeep's interest. The man turned, staring at Gideon with one eye while the other wandered on its own. "You're chasing trouble," he said after a moment.

"We can handle ourselves," Gideon assured him, patting the hilts of his swords.

The barkeep let out a sigh. "The sewers are older than anything, seeing as you have to build those before you build the rest of a city," he said with a tone that implied Gideon should have known it. "But the oldest buildings are farther up the coast. Go north, and you're bound to find them." He leaned in close as if he was about to divulge the most important secret he had ever known. "We call it the Old Hill," he whispered.

"How do we get there?"

The man laughed, breaking his serious demeanor for a second. "What's older than the walls and the roads?" he asked with a strange grin.

"The sewers?" Gideon prayed that the man knew of another route to the ruins and breathed a sigh of relief when the barkeep shook his head.

"You have to build a graveyard before you build the sewers. Graveyards have crypts. Crypts can lead to all sorts of old places." With a dramatic wave of his hands, the barkeep returned to his post.

"That man is insane," Melkora said evenly. "I don't believe a word he just said."

"It might be the only thing worth pursuing," Gideon said. He could not deem his journey a success or a failure until he figured out what Vrysinoch wanted him to do. "I need to take Vrysinoch *home*," he murmured. "There has to be a temple or tower or somewhere I can go."

594

"What about Talonrend?" Melkora replied. "Was that not the ultimate goal? To raise an army and return to Talonrend to free it from the orcs and minotaurs?"

Gideon shook his head at the memory and downed another tankard of warm ale. "Why?" he said. There was no hope in his voice. "Talonrend is dead. Azuria is as good a place as any." He pointed to Gravlox and Vorst with the slight beginnings of a smile. "The people don't seem to mind a pair of goblins running around either."

Melkora crossed her arms and didn't say anything.

Gideon leaned forward with his fist on the table. "Once we explore the ruins, I'll know what to do."

Melkora wasn't convinced. "You don't know for sure," she mumbled.

"I got us this far," he looked into Melkora's eyes and saw tears starting to well in them. "I will get us home."

A ZURIA'S HARBOR WAS bustling with activity well before dawn. Melkora thanked Doran the barkeep for his hospitality while the three others watched ships sailing from the wharf in the early morning light.

"Where are they going?" Gravlox asked, watching a giant, double-masted galley leave the port.

"Other lands, I assume," was all Gideon could offer in response. The dozens of ships docked in Azuria's harbor sported a plethora of foreign flags and colors. The men and women working aboard the ships were just as unique and exotic. They spoke in bizarre languages, and several of the men, captains by the look of their fancy clothing, sported large beards dyed with bright colors.

"I feel like we have lived our entire lives without knowing anything." Melkora said as she joined the others. "My aunt used to tell Torvald and me stories about the Green City. I always thought they were legends passed down from one generation to the next without a single seed of truth."

Gideon couldn't help but laugh. "The only other city I ever knew of was Reikall. Who could guess how many other kingdoms lie across the sea?" He pointed to a nearby caravel's figurehead with

596

wonder. The small ship sported a huge wooden lady with her arms stretched wide and intricate designs etched into her skin. "If the women look like that," Gideon said with a smile, "I'd like to go wherever that ship is headed."

Melkora punched him lightly on the shoulder. "We should be going," she said. The sun rose fully above the horizon and brought with it a strong breeze filled with the scents of salt and fish.

"We should have enough food left for a few days," Gravlox said. He still carried a decent amount of meat in his traveling pack along with a few skins of water.

"According to the barkeep, the Old Hill is only a few miles from here. We will be back before dusk." Melkora set off quickly for the northern part of the city. In her heart, she still wanted nothing less than to raise an army and liberate Talonrend. Searching ancient ruins for *something* felt like a potentially dangerous waste of their time.

"THE OLD HILL?" Valkoinen asked, suddenly materializing directly behind the four companions. They stood just outside the city with Azuria's high spires looming at their backs.

Gideon jumped when he heard the man's voice and turned on him, starting to draw Maelstrom from his side. "Here with more of your riddles?" he questioned.

The man in white regarded Gideon silently with an emotionless alabaster mask. "I can take you to the Old Hill," he said calmly. "It is not far."

"Thank you," Melkora replied.

"Do not thank me," Valkoinen stated, moving to the front of the group without making a sound. "The Old Hill is filled with the remnants of spirits. Most of them do not take kindly to strangers trespassing in their midst."

"You seem confident," Melkora said, taking note of the man's unwavering tone.

In a blink, Valkoinen appeared directly behind her. "The Void offers many methods of escape," he whispered.

Before Melkora could ask if he could transport her as well, Valkoinen flicked the edge of his robe into the back of her legs. When the cloth and skin connected, he stepped through the Void and brought them both several paces forward.

Melkora gasped for breath and fell to her knees.

"Walking through the Void is taxing," Valkoinen explained slowly. "But if something happens, I will bring us all back to Azuria safely."

"I feel like I was just punched in the gut by a minotaur," Melkora breathlessly replied. She got to her feet and straightened her hair. "Why doesn't it affect you?" she asked.

Valkoinen started walking away from the city without offering a response.

AFTER WALKING SEVERAL miles over broken and craggy land that used to be a dirt road, Valkoinen led the group to the edge of a deep well. The sun was high in the sky, and the smell of the ocean had been replaced with a stale, lingering scent of waste.

"The sewers," Valkoinen stated flatly. Without hesitation, he took a step downward on a staircase so worn it was nearly indecipherable from the walls of the well.

Down and down they walked, descending hundreds of feet into unknown darkness. As they walked, the white of Valkoinen's robe and mask grew brighter, eventually compensating for the eerie gloom. At the bottom of the well, several hundred feet below the surface, Valkoinen led them into a rat-infested tunnel covered with slick grime.

"How much farther?" Melkora asked, trudging through the slime with disgust.

Valkoinen did not respond. Instead, his robes flared brighter, and he continued down the sewer tunnels like a living torch.

After several turns and a sludge-filled climb over a broken gate, Melkora shrieked. Ahead, perhaps a hundred feet in front of them, something shimmered in the darkness.

"A spirit," Valkoinen said evenly, never slowing his pace. "We are almost there."

As they passed the glowing ball of energy, it changed and swirled. In one moment, it was a floating skull colored red like blood. In the next, the skull dissipated and became a dripping black candle of dim light. All the while, Melkora couldn't shake the feeling that the spirit was watching her somehow.

Around another bend in the cryptic tunnels, more spirits appeared. They took on all sorts of shapes and colors, some brilliant and other barely visible, but always hovering in the air and keeping their silent vigil. After an hour or more spent following Valkoinen's blazing white robes, they arrived at a ladder.

"That won't support my weight," Gideon said with a chuckle. Behind him, several spirits hung in the air, constantly forming and breaking apart again.

Melkora shot him a sly grin. "I'm not sure this ladder will support any of us," she added. The dangling rope ladder was beset with rot, and the planks were all but disintegrated.

Valkoinen stretched a gloved hand out and brushed one of the wooden steps which fell to pieces under his gentle touch. "I can walk us to the top," the man in white said. "Although it may make you sick."

Without warning, the ground beneath the five companions began to rumble. The stones lining the sewer floor shook and trembled until they burst upward on a wave of putrid water.

"Run!" Melkora screamed, but Gravlox grabbed her by the wrist and kept her from moving. With his other hand, he commanded the unclean water to push them onward, rising quickly past the rotting rope ladder. As the five of them shot through the musty air, nearby spirits turned and slowed their constant transformations as if fixated by the scene.

When they neared the top of the sewer, Gravlox moved some of the stones from the edges of their makeshift platform to a small square just above their heads. When they reached the vertical limit of their rapid ascent, Gravlox urged the water to push them harder, punching through the roof like a spear.

The magical flow of water launched the group from the sewer system and tossed them unceremoniously onto a patch of dirt and gravel several feet from the top of the rope ladder. Miraculously, Valkoinen had kept his composure through it all, and his stark white robe did not show a single speck of the filth that covered the others.

"I don't want to walk through your Void," Gravlox said triumphantly. "There is always another way."

Valkoinen bowed to the shaman, but did not speak.

"Thanks," Gideon spat out a mouthful of fetid water as he got to his feet. "I guess that worked."

Before them, the ruins of a small settlement stood like a grave marker in an abandoned forest. Several haphazard piles of old debris marked the locations of houses and stores along a dirt rut that at one time must have been a road. At the end of the lonely street, a towering cathedral kept watch. All of the stained glass windows had been destroyed centuries ago, but the stone skeleton of the building still remained tall.

"How long were we in the tunnels?" Melkora asked, looking at the gloomy sky. It had been close to high noon when they had entered the sewers just hours before.

"This is as light and as dark as the Old Hill ever is," Valkoinen said mysteriously. "It is simply the way of the place."

Take me home... Vrysinoch echoed through Gideon's mind. The god's intangible will pulled Gideon toward the towering cathedral with a call he could not deny.

"There!" he yelled gruffly, pointing to the ruins. Without waiting for the others, he took off.

"Gideon, wait!" Melkora called after him, but he did not slow his pace. As was his custom, Valkoinen remained silent and walked behind them with measured steps.

The ancient cathedral was massive, roughly the size of Castle Talon, but in a terrible state of disrepair. Decorative tiles that once covered the floor with beautiful patterns were cracked, missing, or under so much dust and filth they couldn't be seen.

"Where are you going?" Valkoinen asked when he reached them at the cathedral's entrance.

Gideon could not think of an answer.

"Do you know this place?" Valkoinen inquired with obvious curiosity. Although his robes and mask hid any body language he might display, even such a stoic man couldn't remove all the emotion from his voice.

Gideon trudged forward with divine purpose and cleared his mind to let Vrysinoch guide him. His heavy footsteps echoed loudly in the open foyer. Broken statues lined the crumbling walls, their talon-bearing feet grim reminders of Vrysinoch's loss.

At the center of the large chamber beyond the entryway, an unbroken statue still remained.

"Is this what you came to see?" Valkoinen asked softly. "To speak the eagle-god's name is against the law, and some say gazing upon the statue's visage brings death."

"I've seen this before," Gideon whispered, solemnly touching the base of the stone colossus before him. Massive stone wings stretched out to encircle the companions, and Vrysinoch's grim face stared at them from thirty feet above the ground.

Melkora couldn't rip her eyes from the statue. It was more glorious than anything she had seen in her life. "Where did you see this?" she asked breathlessly. "In a vision? A dream?"

Gideon shook his head. "Beneath Castle Talon," he began, but quickly lost his focus. Gideon searched the ground at Vrysinoch's feet and pushed aside the accumulated debris. "There should be a bowl here," he stated.

"For what?" Valkoinen asked. Curiously, the man in white remained rather far behind Gideon and outside the reach of the statue's wings. "I have never seen a bowl at the statue's feet."

In the back of his mind, Gideon knew the statue had to be an exact copy of the one in the caves underneath Castle Talon. Without the bowl, the statue was incomplete. "We must find the bowl and return it." His tone left no room for debate.

At once, Gideon began searching the ruins with the others right behind him. A staircase stood the statue's left that led into what remained of the cathedral's upper floors. Taking the worn steps two at a time, Gideon ascended the spiral staircase to the second floor. All around him, human-sized statues stood in various states of ruin. Their faces were marred, their features obscured, and most of them were missing at least one limb.

"What is this place?" Gideon muttered with contempt. To think of an abandoned statue of Vrysinoch existing in Talonrend was beyond blasphemy.

"I suggest you go no further," Valkoinen said behind him. A hint of magical command played across his voice.

At the end of the statue-lined hall stood a wooden door banded with iron. Gideon whirled on the man in white and growled. Vrysinoch's anger boiled deep within him. "What is behind that door?" he grunted.

Valkoinen met his gaze with a blank mask of white. "The way of the past," he said cryptically, further prodding Vrysinoch's ire.

Gideon raised his hand to strike at the man, but Valkoinen walked through the Void and appeared in a different part of the hall before he had the chance.

Take me, Vrysinoch whispered. The god's voice felt like a gentle gasp from a dying child. Vrysinoch was becoming weak.

Gideon had to tread cautiously as he approached the doorway.

The floor beneath him had rotted away and left gaping holes. A layer of dust clung to the wooden door, but it was not enough to have built up over centuries. "Someone has been here," he said. "Only a year ago, maybe less."

He reached out a hand and took hold of an iron ring on the side of the door.

"We should return to Azuria," Valkoinen said with a tinge of urgency.

"Someone is coming!" Gravlox shouted. He could feel a presence approaching through the gloom at a rapid pace. Something magical was pursuing them, and Gravlox knew beyond a doubt that it was malevolent.

"You've led us into a trap!" Gideon screamed. As much as he wanted to draw his sword and slaughter Valkoinen where he stood, Vrysinoch's command was stronger. He had to open the door and satisfy Vrysinoch's call.

"Hurry!" Melkora urged him. Valkoinen stood motionless by her side.

Gideon ripped the door open and stepped into the room beyond.

Apart from a small square of clear space just past the door, the room was filled with skulls. Each of them bore the mark of Vrysinoch, a talon clutching an emerald, carved into their forehead.

"Traitors to Azuria," Valkoinen said.

Vrysinoch wailed inside Gideon's mind and brought him to his knees.

"Even so long after the war, the eagle-god's supporters are occasionally discovered inside the city." Valkoinen did not move as he spoke, but his eyeless mask seemed to darken a shade.

"We need to run," Gravlox shouted again. He and Vorst crouched near the top of the staircase and waited for whatever it was stalking them.

In a frenzy, Gideon dove through the piles of skulls and searched for the missing piece of Vrysinoch's statue. His fingertips brushed against a stone rim, and Vrysinoch shuddered within his mind. He had found it.

Victoriously, Gideon pulled the bowl from the bottom of the skulls and charged out of the room. He leapt over a gaping hole in the rotten floor, not caring much for his footing, and crashed down hard on the floorboards. His weight and momentum were more than enough to send him falling through the floor. To Gideon, it did not matter. The only thing occupying his mind was the restoration of Vrysinoch's most glorious likeness.

He landed on the floor below, directly in front of the stone statue, and shook off the impact without a wince. Behind him, voices filled the cathedral. They were strange voices, unfamiliar and dripping with violence, but human.

Gideon cleared the remaining debris from the foot of Vrysinoch and knelt with the bowl clutched in his hands.

My son, Vrysinoch hissed with growing power.

"You must stop!" Valkoinen boomed, instantly standing directly in front of Gideon. His voice carried enough magical command to break the mind of a lesser man.

Gideon's mouth opened and issued forth an avian screech loud enough to shatter what little glass remained in the building. For the first time since he had become the nineteenth Master of the Alabaster Order, Valkoinen tasted fear. He tried to back away, but his back pressed against the giant statue. Behind Gideon, Valkoinen saw the approaching men. They were soldiers of the city guard. If it came to blows, which it certainly looked like it would, Valkoinen would have no trouble dispatching the entire squadron with a wave of his hand, but he could not risk his political standing within the city by executing a dozen guardsmen.

Melkora and the two goblins rushed down the staircase and ran for the statue. Reverently, Gideon placed the bowl on the ground at Vrysinoch's feet.

"We must flee!" Valkoinen yelled. He threw out the sleeves of his robe and they brushed against Melkora's outstretched hand. Behind the woman, Gravlox grabbed her belt and held Vorst's hand tightly as they ran.

With the chain of connection completed, Valkoinen ripped open a sliver of the world and stepped into the Void.

Seven

A T THE FOOT of Vrysinoch's statue, Gideon's mind cleaved asunder. The part of his consciousness that had housed Vrysinoch for several months finally broke off. The torrent of chaos unleashed within Gideon's thoughts was unbearable.

For the split second he managed to keep hold of his sanity and his awareness, he felt both liberated and destroyed. Vrysinoch had chosen him to be a sacred vessel, and in that moment, his mission was complete. The driving purpose that had carefully laid every step along Gideon's path was lost. In that brief moment between heartbeats, he felt truly human and alive once more.

And then the chaos…

The pure trauma caused by such a violent mental fracture took hold of Gideon's mind and shattered it. He crumpled forward and fell into the sacred bowl like a burnt offering.

Within moments, soldiers of the city guard descended upon Gideon's body with orders for his arrest.

MELKORA GASPED AND vomited the contents of her stomach onto the floor. She was kneeling with hard stone beneath her, but everything was dark. A second later, Valkoinen's brilliant robe filled the area with magical light. "Where am I?" she panted. Her head swam and her gut felt like she had spent a long night drinking in a tavern.

"Gravlox did not come through," Valkoinen said harshly. He looked around the subterranean chamber frantically, but only Melkora and Vorst remained.

Vorst shook the nausea from her body and struggled to regain her feet. "What?" she muttered, barely comprehending Valkoinen's words.

"Where did he go?" Melkora yelled. She stood in front of Valkoinen and tried to look him in the eyes, but his face held nothing beyond his white mask. "Where are Gideon and Gravlox?" she demanded. "Where are we?"

Valkoinen silenced her with a gloved hand on her shoulder. "My apologies," he began slowly. "You are in my home, the very center of the Alabaster Order. Gideon did not enter the Void. He is likely being arrested as we speak and will be returned to Azuria by tomorrow."

"And Gravlox?" Vorst cut in. She remembered holding his hand as she ran and feeling his touch. He had been with her, but then suddenly he wasn't. Gravlox had vanished as surely as they all had.

"He entered the Void." Valkoinen shook his head, truly out of answers. "But did not exit." He did not know how to explain the goblin's disappearance in any other manner. Entering the Void was remarkably similar to opening a door and stepping through it — although the door is a magical tear in reality, and the room on the other side is a vacant realm where the very essence of *nothing* exists.

"How do we get him back?" Vorst demanded. Whatever squeamishness remained in her body from the disorienting journey was quickly drowned by fear and anger.

Valkoinen regarded her silently, his mask unchanging.

"Answer me!" Vorst shouted at him. She stood on her toes and tried to push out her chest, but only reached Valkoinen's belt.

"I have no answers for you," he finally said. "The Void is unstable. When I walk through, I always find doors leading exactly where I want them to lead. Others are not so fortunate." He let out a sigh, a grave display of emotion in light of his stoic nature, and pointed toward a door. "You are all free to stay here as long as you wish. You'll find plenty of rooms and food."

"You can't just leave him in the Void," Melkora shouted. She reached up to put a hand on Valkoinen's shoulder and turn him around, but some unseen force stopped her like a wall.

The man in white turned his head ever so slightly, just enough to indicate that he was addressing the others in the room, and spoke. "I will enter the Void myself and search for him, but I cannot do it now. Time functions," he paused, searching for the right words, "differently in the Void. It would be best to wait until after Gideon's trial to attempt such a task."

Before Vorst or Melkora could question him further, Valkoinen vanished, taking the room's only light source with him.

"What do we do?" Vorst pleaded in defeat. Her anger played out in the form of choking sobs that stole her breath.

"We wait," Melkora said, crouching to wrap Vorst in an embrace. "Once Gideon has returned, we will find Gravlox. We will save him."

Vorst rubbed the stump of her missing finger and tried in vain to hold back her tears.

GIDEON GROANED AND opened his eyes, but even the meager light of a nearby torch made him wince and turn away. After a moment of silent agony, he gathered enough of his wits to begin comprehending his situation.

He was moving. His back was pressed flat against a wooden slat that felt like the bottom of a cart. Wheels squeaked along on either side of his ears, and their racket brought a fresh wave of dizziness to Gideon's head.

He tried to move his arms, but they were bound to his sides. Carefully rotating his wrists toward his body, he felt for the hilts of his weapons, but they were predictably missing. *I am alive,* he thought with a hint of relief.

As am I, Gideon of Talonrend, a voice chimed through the darkness in reply. Gideon opened his eyes again and tried to locate the voice's origin, but the nearby torch light was still too strong. Without full command over his senses, Gideon couldn't tell if the voice he had heard was in his head, his imagination, or from one of the soldiers guarding him.

"Where am I?" Gideon whispered, not wanting to draw much attention to himself.

The weight on his chest shifted and Gideon could tell it was a person sitting on him and not some inanimate object. "Keep it down, outsider," the man said. His voice was stern, but not threatening.

Mustering all of his willpower at once, Gideon opened his right eye and looked at the man sitting on his chest. The soldier was short, but stocky and muscled like a bull. He also held a small crossbow pointed directly at Gideon's head. Under normal conditions, Gideon had no doubt he could overpower the guard, even from beneath him, but the past day had been far from normal.

"Am I going to die?" Gideon asked. He wasn't sure why the question came to his mind, but he couldn't grasp enough other words to ask anything else.

The soldier grunted and readjusted his weight. "We all die," he said with a bit of a chuckle.

Gideon opened one eye again and looked at the man as best he could. "Will I die sooner than most?"

The guard's chuckle died and man's expression turned sour. "I reckon so," he said grimly.

Gideon let his head fall back against the bottom of the cart and tried to gather more of his faculties together. His mind was jumbled, and his memories of the events on the Old Hill were out of order, if not entirely missing. "What are the charges against me?" Gideon asked the soldier after a few moments.

"Ha," the man snorted. "Treason and conspiracy against the throne of Azuria would be the lesser charges," he explained as though he was speaking to a child. "But attempting to restore the graven *idol* will get you condemned before anything else."

Attempting? Gideon thought. Memories flashed through his head like fireflies flickering in the trees. He saw a glimpse of one moment, then another, and then entire scenes, but they came so quickly it was difficult to make any sense of them.

Suddenly, Gideon remembered he had not been alone in the ruined cathedral. "How many wagons are there?" he asked quietly, not wanting to directly question the soldier about his companions.

"Just two," the man replied. He leaned down and Gideon could smell his warm breath. "We didn't get your friends, if that's what you're asking," he said.

A fresh burst of relief filled Gideon's chest and for a moment, the splitting pain in his head subsided. *They are alive,* he thought with a smile.

Gideon relaxed as much as he could and let his mind drift away into sleep. Knowing the others had made an escape was enough consolation for him to find peace.

SWIRLING DARKNESS ENVELOPED Gravlox's world. The last thing he remembered, Vorst had touched his hand, and they had touched Valkoinen's fluttering robe. After that, everything turned black.

Magic surrounded him. He could feel the energy wrapping around his body like a current of warm air. When he moved, the magic moved with him. The world as Gravlox was capable of perceiving it was crafted purely of raw magic.

When he stood, he expected to feel nauseous or lightheaded. On the contrary, the strange world empowered him. His mind was clear and his muscles felt stronger than ever. Gravlox opened his eyes and drank in the darkness eagerly. He jumped from foot to foot, only giving a cursory thought to what might be underneath his feet, and reveled in his strength.

Gravlox's eyes were naturally better adjusted to complete darkness than a human's, but he could barely see his own hands in front of him. He reached within his mind to latch onto the well of magic he knew should be there, but stopped. Magic *was* there within him, but it was also waiting just beyond his fingertips. Without quite knowing what he was doing, Gravlox swirled a handful of loose magic into his palm and began to mold it.

In a few seconds, Gravlox had gathered enough magic to form a tangible crystal. He reached to the object with his mind and willed it to ignite. The shimmering fragment of magic burst into magical, heatless light and illuminated the world.

The sight before him was breathtaking.

Gravlox stood in an underground chamber similar to the tunnels beneath Kanebullar Mountain, but far more grand. The rock above his head was hundreds of feet away, and the chamber extended farther than he could see. Little rivulets of coalesced magic snaked through the rock floor like tiny, iridescent streams. Gravlox bent down to investigate the rock and was delighted by what he found. Working its way along beside the flow of magic, the experienced foreman was able to identify several veins of precious metals.

He scampered along over the magical streams, following the ore deposits almost frantically. In all of his days as the leader of a mine, Gravlox had never seen such abundance. He chased one particular vein of brightly shining copper until it ended in a pool of still water. Beneath the surface, perhaps only a few feet down, hundreds of rubies glittered in the light.

Mesmerized, Gravlox knelt beside the pool and touched the water with his fingertips. The liquid was pleasantly warm and smelled vaguely like the blasting powder used in the Kanebullar mines.

Gravlox reached through the water and tried to lift a handful of rubies from the bottom of the pool, but they were just out of his reach. He stretched further, pushing his entire arm into the pool up to his shoulder, but still his fingers did not touch the precious gemstones.

Frustrated, Gravlox sat back on his heels and shook some of the water from his arm. With a new idea in mind, he began gathering pockets of nearby magic into his hands. When he had a sphere larger than his head, he set to forming it into a large claw long enough to fetch the rubies.

Once the magical device was formed, Gravlox stood and aimed the claw directly over the pool. With a satisfied smile, he plunged the claw into the liquid. At first, the magical claw began to sizzle. Something in the water reacted with the claw of pure magic violently. Despite the rising steam, Gravlox did not want to abandon his pursuit. He sank the claw further into the water, and it began to bubble and boil, obscuring his sight of the rubies below.

When the claw touched the bottom of the strange pool, the chemical reaction reached its apex and erupted.

If anyone else had been in that particular area of the Void, they would have felt the explosion from miles away. The blast ripped through the ground and blew a giant crater where the pool of rubies had been. Boulders the size of horses flew out in all directions and smashed into millions of pieces against the splintering rock floor.

Gravlox's body was instantly obliterated.

A DAY HAD passed by the time Gideon's cart wheeled through the gates of Azuria. Melkora and Vorst stood near the back of a small crowd that had formed to watch the spectacle. Next to them, Doran the barkeep wore a sour expression.

"You're lucky you didn't go with that idiot to the Old Hill," Doran said with an ugly smirk.

Melkora thought it best not to correct the barkeep. "You could have told him visiting the Old Hill was against the law," she replied bitterly. Despite Doran's overt air of hospitality, Melkora couldn't help but think the man had set them up. The only thing that didn't fit was how the barkeep stood to benefit from their arrest.

Doran spat on the ground. "The fool should've known better than to stir up the past," he said. "The magistrates might take it easy on him, but judging by the way he's tied up, I doubt it." The cart wheeled past them into the city, and Melkora gripped Roisin's hilt until her knuckles turned white. Gideon was bound hand and foot in thick metal chains. Three menacing soldiers rode in the cart with him, one sitting on the man's chest to pin him down. Behind the cart, several more guards marched in line followed by another wagon.

"If anything happens to Gideon," Melkora said quietly so only Doran could hear, "I'll slit your throat." She didn't wait for the barkeep to respond before following Gideon's cart through the crowd with Vorst on her heels.

"WHAT HAPPENED?" ZERREN asked his brother. He peered out the window of Azuria's central tower and watched Gideon's prison cart below. Behind him, Valkoinen stood motionless in front of a tall bookcase.

"Gideon restored the statue at the Old Hill," he replied flatly.

Zerren whirled on him in anger. "You let him?" he growled. "How could you? That statue is an abomination! He spits in the face of Druaka!"

Valkoinen took the verbal assault with typical stoicism. "It is not my place to change his actions," he said after a moment.

"You could have prevented such blasphemy!" Zerren bellowed.

In an instant, Valkoinen appeared directly in front of his brother. "Do not presume to know what could or could not have been done!" Valkoinen said with such force the windows shook.

Zerren lost his composure and fell backward into the wall. Deep in his core, the priest feared the Alabaster Order intensely. All the power granted him by Druaka would likely fail if Zerren and Valkoinen ever fought.

"Something must be done," the priest muttered as he pulled himself up. All of his bravado had faded under Valkoinen's withering, eyeless stare.

The man in white didn't care for Zerren's trifling. The politics of the old civil war between Vrysinoch and Druaka interested him from an historical standpoint, but Valkoinen did not want to place himself in the center of it.

"Haven't you already done enough?" Valkoinen asked, assuming his brother had orchestrated the arrest.

Zerren shook his head. "You knew I could not stand idly by and let these outsiders profane our sacred places," he replied.

"*Our* places?" Valkoinen asked with intrigue. "As I recall, the Old Hill was abandoned by Druaka long ago."

"Just because we could not destroy that wretched statue does not mean Druaka has abandoned the Old Hill," Zerren said.

If Valkoinen could smile through his mask, he would have. "And yet the statue stands," he said. "A constant reminder and abomination."

Zerren scoffed and turned back to the window. The prison cart had reached the magisterial building several blocks from the tower. Gideon, appearing groggy and barely standing on his own power, was led by the guards into the bowels of the building.

"There will be a trial," Zerren said, more to himself than his brother.

Valkoinen did not respond.

"If what you say about the statue's restoration is true, he will be sentenced to death." Zerren walked away from the window and had to step around his unmoving brother.

"It would be wise to advise the magistrates against such action, Zerren," Valkoinen said.

"You do not think Druaka's champion could defeat such a man?" the priest asked.

After several long moments of silence, Valkoinen spoke. "I do not know, but it would be a glorious fight."

"Then why should I tell the magistrates not to sentence Gideon to death in the pit?" Zerren asked. The priest very much enjoyed watching Ohra cut down criminals and blasphemers in the arena. If Gideon had indeed attempted to restore the statue at the Old Hill, he deserved to be killed by Druaka's right hand.

Valkoinen's eyeless stare bored into his brother. "The power those two wield could tear the city apart. The destruction would take years to repair."

Zerren smiled. "Everything can be rebuilt," he said confidently. "I know exactly how I will advise the magistrates."

TALONREND HAD TRANSFORMED over the winter, and Undrakk's city of Broken Sword was nearly complete. The strange half-orc had been busy. Where stained glass and ornamented archways had once stood, sharpened wooden spears and roughly hewn stone loomed. Most of the doorways that hadn't been completely destroyed had been enlarged to allow the taller species to enter.

As he had done almost every day for several months, Undrakk stood in front of Half-Orc Keep and surveyed his kingdom with delight. Only a few of the human buildings had been allowed to remain. A huge forge not far from the castle still stood and belched thick smoke into the air as the orc and minotaur smiths plied their trade inside. Along the interior side of Terror Lament, many stone buildings had been permitted to stand and were used as storehouses, and in some cases, they were transformed into holding pens for wolves.

Everywhere Undrakk cast his gaze he saw victory. According to the latest reports, the remaining humans in the region had been pushed out to the farthest villages along the Clawflow. It would only be a matter of weeks until the orc clans burned those villages as well and sent the pathetic humans scurrying into the river to drown.

In the center of the city, almost every remnant of human life had been eradicated. A great orc tent covered in tanned hides, and painted banners rose up almost as tall as the tower that once stood in its place. Over a thousand orcs could easily fit inside and did so every night to drink their mead and eat.

Undrakk made his way down to the tent with his staff in hand. When he pulled back one of the flaps, an aroma wholly unique to orc culture greeted his nostrils. Sweat, blood, alcohol, and roasted horse mingled to form a thick haze of oil that hung in the air. Undrakk loved it. The smell of conquest was more intoxicating than any drink he could ever taste.

The half-orc shaman took his customary seat at the eastern edge of the tent on a raised platform. Beside him, the leaders of each orc clan ate their meat in peace. Undrakk couldn't help but feel accomplished. A year ago, the two orcs would have killed each other with their bare hands before they would consider sitting at the same table. Their truce alone was worthy of legend in Undrakk's eyes.

"What's next, Undrakk?" one of his generals asked with a mouth full of roasted horse. "Where is our next conquest?"

The half-orc raised a large mug of mead to his lips and took a gulp. "We need to populate," he told the Half Goat leader who had replaced Gurr. "Broken Sword is a large city with high walls and we do not fill it yet. Our first priority must be our numbers."

The orc flashed a toothy grin and ripped another chunk of meat from the bone he was holding. "I will give you more orcs!" he bellowed, spitting food all around him. The general stood and slapped Undrakk's shoulder. "I will give you more orcs tonight!" In front of the raised platform that held the city's leadership, a plethora of orc women sat on animal hide cushions for that very purpose.

To Undrakk's right, Jan and Keturah sat side by side in their stolen minotaur bodies. "Has there been any report from Kanebullar Mountain?" the shaman asked. Keturah rose from her chair and knelt in front of Undrakk out of respect. Despite her physical strength and substantial magical abilities, she feared Undrakk greatly.

"Nothing yet, sir," she reported. Several of her underlings had been dispatched to the mountain several weeks ago in order to assess the uneasy truce between orcs, minotaurs, and goblins.

"Let me know the moment they return," Undrakk said casually. "How is your companion?" he asked.

Keturah's gruff voice caught in her throat. "He lives," she replied. "Although the poison is still in his body."

"The stasis I placed him in will not endure forever," Undrakk explained. "If a cure is not found in the next season, he will likely expire." The winged demons had been an enormous asset to Undrakk not only in the taking of Talonrend, but in the following months as well. They did not eat, they quarreled less than the orc clans, and they could travel great distances without complaint. Although the demons had no overt hierarchy other Keturah as their queen, Taurnil was something of a leader to the others. His death would bring instability.

"I should return to him, my king," Keturah said solemnly. Undrakk let her leave with a nod of his head.

The night air was cool and refreshing against Keturah's hide when she exited the great tent. Since taking the body of a minotaur, she had found little need for clothes, even in the dead of winter.

The demons stayed in the various guardhouses atop the wall and often slept in tightly packed spaces like newborn pigs huddling for warmth. If the creatures weren't so terrifying, Keturah would probably have found the sight adorable.

At the base of the wall about a mile from the tent, Keturah approached a group of demons. "Take me to the top," she ordered them. Three of the demons nodded in obedience and flew to Keturah's shoulders. They sank their sharp claws into her hide and began to beat their wings.

Keturah loved the feeling of flight, despite the pain caused by the punctures in her flesh. Every time she ascended to the top of the wall in such a manner, she wondered if she would survive plummeting to the bottom. Her life was in the demons' clutches and if they wanted, they could carry her far above the city and drop her. She pushed the nagging thoughts far from her mind and landed gently on the top of the wall.

"Thank you," she told the three demons who served as her ferry. They bowed in response and waited at the top of the wall for her trip back to the ground.

Keturah walked swiftly to the southeast outpost to find Taurnil. The demon was laid out across the tops of several barrels in the corner with his side against the stone crenelations. He was breathing, but he hadn't opened his eyes in weeks.

She brushed her fingertips lightly against Taurnil's skin. Where he had once been a beautiful shade of pale, grey ash, his skin had turned to charcoal and burnt stone. The leg where he had been stabbed had been amputated in an attempt to stop the poison, but it was not enough. Without Undrakk's magical stasis, he would surely have died within days of receiving his wound.

"Taurnil..." she whispered. She ran her minotaur fingers over his face and the demon shuddered, but it was likely just the wind causing him to move.

Insidious poison coursed relentlessly underneath his black, flaking skin. What hurt Keturah most was her helplessness. There was nothing she could do to save her beloved creation and although she could likely transfer Taurnil's consciousness into another body, it would not be the same. Taurnil had been her first and most perfect spawn. He was stronger, faster, and more sinister than any of her other demons.

Before the poison had corrupted Taurnil's mind and stolen his consciousness, he was able to give Keturah a description of the woman who had stabbed him. "I will find her, my love," she told the sleeping demon. "I will find her, and I will kill her. I will send her soul to the dark abyss where she will balance on the precipice of oblivion for eternity." She made her solemn vow of revenge, and she meant every word.

Eight

GIDEON'S HOLDING CELL beneath Azuria's governmental building was not quite dilapidated, but it certainly lacked any semblance of comfort. The iron bars reminded him of the dungeon Herod had thrown Gravlox and Vorst into beneath Castle Talon. Gideon smirked at the thought. Just like the goblins, he could easily escape the prison cell if he needed to. The bars didn't quite connect to the ceiling and water had eroded several spots on the floor into large divots that offered plenty of leverage points. With Vrysinoch's divine strength filling his muscles, even a well-built prison could not contain Gideon.

As much as the idea of escape entertained him, Gideon knew he could not. Breaking out of the cell was only a temporary solution. It would not grant him freedom or respite. He longed to know what became of the others after he lost consciousness at the foot of Vrysinoch's statue, but it was not worth a lifetime of being branded a criminal. In the back of his head, Gideon knew Talonrend was lost. If what Valkoinen said about the exile of Vrysinoch's followers was true, Azuria would never send an army to help him retake the city, and an army was exactly what he needed. There were simply too many orcs and minotaurs for a small band of adventurers to handle on their own.

Gideon needed Azuria; as much as he needed food and water, he needed a place to live and call his home. He knew it the day they had set out to find the fabled Green City. If he wanted to live a *normal* life in an established society, it would have to be in Azuria.

What would become of Gravlox and Vorst? he thought, pacing his cell like a hungry dog. *Would Azuria accept them?* Until his arrest, Gideon believed Azuria was accepting enough to allow them to live. Since the city was not built in the shadow of Kanebullar Mountain, the people of Azuria did not have tragic stories of trade caravans ransacked by goblin hordes or villages beset by marauding orcs. Compared to Talonrend, Azuria was incredibly secure and peaceful.

The people treated Gravlox and Vorst as oddities to be inspected and gossiped over, not hostile enemies composed of pure evil to be slaughtered on sight. That gave Gideon hope. Perhaps Azuria would be the place where he could start a new life and make a new name for himself...

He smirked. Gideon realized he had not thought about such things in a very, very long time. In the months he had spent trekking through leagues of forests and plains, the thought of a permanent home had rarely crossed his mind. His mission had consumed every ounce of his attention and without that divine mandate, he felt lost. His feet sloshed through the muddy floor of his cell and provided a rhythmic pulse to carry his thoughts for hours.

Gideon was still in such a state of profound thought when a guard came to visit him two days after his arrest. The man, tall and proud like a soldier who had never seen real war, strode into the dungeon with a torch held above his head.

"Outsider," he called, banging the hilt of his sword against the bars to bring Gideon out of his thoughts.

"Yes?" Gideon replied, looking the man squarely in the eyes.

"You—" the man faltered under the weight of Gideon's gaze. "You need to give an official statement," he stammered, awkwardly shifting his weight from foot to foot.

"Why?" Gideon stepped forward. The man nearly sank into the floor.

"They… they…" Gideon hit his fist into the metal bar in front of him and the guard jumped. "They want to know your side of what happened!" he finally yelled all at once.

Gideon laughed. He didn't remember enough of what happened to be of any use during a legal proceeding. "What is it they say I've done?" he asked, backing away from the terrified guard.

The man stared intently at the floor under his feet. "The statue," he muttered after a moment.

"Tell them I confess to every charge against me," Gideon happily proclaimed. His memory was useless, and he knew his testimony would be valued even less, so confessing felt like the only option he had.

"What?" the man gasped, finally meeting Gideon's eyes with a ghastly expression.

"I confess," Gideon repeated.

"They'll put you to death!" the man pleaded. Instead of fear, his voice was full of pity like a man trying to explain to a young child why a lame horse had to be killed.

Gideon's smile grew. From the guard's eyes, he knew he must have looked absolutely insane in the flickering torchlight. "Tell me," he coaxed with a quiet whisper. "Does your law allow for trial by combat?"

The man nodded his head vigorously as he seemed to regain a bit of composure. "You'll fight in the pit," he said with a hint of interest beneath his overt shock.

"Good," Gideon said, turning from the guard to resume his pacing. "Tell them I confess to everything, and I would appreciate a trial by combat as soon as one can be arranged."

With another nod, the man hurried out of the dungeon and left Gideon to his silent, lightless thoughts.

MELKORA AND VORST sat patiently in Valkoinen's underground lair and waited for the strange man to speak. His speech had slowed since Gravlox's disappearance, and his apparent enthusiasm had all but faded away. Vorst couldn't help but tap her foot mindlessly against the stone floor and had to stop herself several times as they waited for Valkoinen.

Finally, the man's voice broke the silence. "Time is not the same in the Void," he explained. "Whatever is meant to happen in the Void has already happened."

Melkora was frustrated with the strange man's riddles and cryptic answers, but she knew berating him would do no good. Without any other options presenting themselves, Melkora was forced to sit and wait for Valkoinen's slow responses.

Finally, he spoke again. "We must wait to enter the Void until Gideon has been returned to you," he said evenly, never betraying a single ounce of emotion. "There is a chance Gideon's actions and Gravlox's disappearance are connected. The Void is a very confusing place, and any information, even a scrap, could be the difference between life and death."

"How will we find him?" Vorst asked. Her eyes were red with tears.

Without eyes, Valkoinen had to turn his white mask slightly to address her. "We go into the Void and search," he said after only a brief pause. "But the Void is a terrible place full of temptation and destruction."

"What sort of temptation?" Melkora asked. At her heart, she was a simple woman with few needs, but she met those needs through larceny. Anything with the gleam of value held temptation in her eyes.

Valkoinen waited for a moment before speaking. "The Void holds all manner of deception," he said. "Although it is the same plane of existence, we all perceive it in different manners."

Melkora didn't know what to think. A plane of temptation tailored to her specific desires sounded utterly terrifying. She knew what her heart longed for, and it wasn't something she looked forward to seeing.

"What is in the Void..." she said, fighting back images of Corshana, "is it real?"

"It will be real to you," Valkoinen replied. "But anything that happens to you will be very real on the physical plane," he added.

"We have no choice," Melkora said with a deep, pain-filled sigh. No matter how much she tried to steel her nerves, she knew the sight of her dead daughter would be too much for her to handle.

Melkora had to change the subject to retain her composure. "What will happen to Gideon? What are the penalties for his crimes?" she said, pushing the memory of her daughter to the back of her mind.

"My brother has great influence with the magistrates," Valkoinen said with relative speed. Something about the question seemed to bring him a sliver of energy. "I have spoken with him previously, although he does not share my view of your friend."

"What exactly is that view?" Melkora asked. As far as she could tell, Valkoinen was on their side.

Although his facial features were entirely hidden by his mask, Valkoinen *almost* appeared to smile. "My brother is rather bloodthirsty, as many priests of Druaka can be. He wishes to see Gideon fight for his life to prove his innocence."

Had her mind not been filled with such tragic and fatalistic thoughts, Melkora would have laughed. "Gideon fought in the arena in Talonrend for a living," she explained. "He is the strongest man I have ever met and a better fighter than anyone in this city."

"Oh?" Valkoinen said quizzically. "Would you wager his life on those words?"

Melkora barely considered the question before nodding. "Yes," she emphatically replied. "No one can stand against him."

"Interesting." Valkoinen tilted his mask down, and Melkora wondered what his face looked like beneath it. "I had planned on using some of my political influence to arrange the trial somewhat in Gideon's favor, but perhaps I do not need to."

Melkora wasn't sure what to make of the man in white. "Thank you," she replied after a moment of consideration, "but it would be best not to meddle in Azuria's affairs any more than we already have."

Valkoinen nodded. "So be it. I look forward to his trial."

AN OLD MAN with ragged clothes that hung loosely from his bones led Gideon from his cell to the upper floor of the government building where the magistrates had assembled. Although the old jailor had clasped Gideon's wrists in manacles, it felt like more of a formality than a security measure.

"I confess to everything," Gideon had told the man the moment he appeared at the bottom of the stairs.

"Yes, I've heard," the man replied as though he honestly didn't care. Once the chains had been more or less secured, the man opened the cell door with a large brass key and showed Gideon to the staircase.

"Have you heard anything of my companions?" Gideon asked, trying not to sound overly concerned.

The jailor laughed and Gideon didn't know if that was a good or bad reaction. "The tiny orcs?" he chuckled. "Such a curiosity! Back in my day..." Gideon stopped paying attention. The old man was obviously far too interested in his own anecdotes to answer a simple question. He reminded Gideon of some of the older priests living in the Tower of Wings before Talonrend's fall. When a mind reached a certain age, it tended to wander uncontrollably.

All the way through several floors of the building, the jailor chattered on about some wild story of his youth. Apparently, he had lived in a farming village south of Azuria and had survived several orc raids, although the green-skinned beasts had not been seen in several decades.

The man took the narrow stairs slowly, ascending them one at a time. Before they had reached their destination, the jailor was out of breath and had to stop to recover. He wheezed with every rattling breath and coughed up several gobs of phlegm.

"Are you alright?" Gideon asked the man. As best he could in shackles, Gideon used his shoulder to help keep the jailor standing as he coughed.

"Quite," he coughed more, barely containing his spittle. "Quite alright," he finally managed.

"Don't die on me," Gideon muttered, which the jailor found to be mind-numbingly hilarious. Unfortunately, his laughter brought on another violent bout of hacking that threatened to dislodge the man's lungs.

"Please," Gideon whispered under his breath, "I could never explain a dead body." Being accused of heresy was one thing, but Gideon doubted he could work his way out of a murder charge. It would be easy enough to kill such a feeble old man, and perhaps—a dark thought flashed through Gideon's mind—perhaps that was exactly what the magistrates wanted.

"Up you go," Gideon said cheerfully. He used his shoulders and forearms to lift the jailor from the wall and keep him moving forward. "They'll never believe me if you die on the stairs to the courtroom," he said with a more serious tone.

They reached the top of the long staircase and stood before a heavy door banded with thick iron. On the other side, Gideon could hear voices rapidly murmuring. "Go on, boy," the old jailor bade him. "Be respectful, and the magistrates might not kill you," he said.

Gideon couldn't tell if the man was serious or not, so he thought it best not to take chances. "Thank you," he told the man with a slight bow. The jailor smiled and turned to make the slow journey back down the staircase.

Unsure what to do next, Gideon stood at the door and waited. The chains around his wrist weren't incredibly tight, but they were uncomfortable nonetheless. As he scratched the skin beneath the old metal, he tried again to remember what had happened in the ruined cathedral. Bits and pieces of the scene flashed through his mind, but he couldn't discern between what might be real and what might be a fabrication of his thoughts.

Somewhere in the depth of his memory, Gideon felt a sense of accomplishment he believed to be a direct message from Vrysinoch. His mission, whatever he had actually done by restoring the old statue, had been for a purpose. Gideon couldn't help but smile.

The wooden door to his left creaked open on old hinges, breaking his tenuous reverie. Flakes of red rust fell to the floor, and a hideous squeal sounded through the small space. A young man with brawny shoulders and a stern expression poked his head into the staircase and looked around.

"I'm ready to confess," Gideon said with confidence.

The man glanced past Gideon's shoulder and appeared almost disappointed. "The jailor is alive and well, I assure you," he told the official. The man's expression soured further, and Gideon knew his guess had been correct.

The magisterial hall was starkly different from the musty staircase behind the iron-bound door. Three men, old and with faces like carved stone, wore ornate azure robes and sat behind a massive desk of dark wood. All around, images of Azuria's god glared down at him. It was the first time Gideon had seen such vivid images of Druaka up close. The raven, supposedly Vrysinoch's sister,

627

was thoroughly hideous. The onyx bird sat on a human skull, judging Gideon with beady, bulging eyes.

To his right, a small elevated gallery looked on with fervid interest. Gideon scanned their faces and spotted an alabaster mask in the back of the crowd. It looked exactly like Valkoinen's attire, but Gideon had no way of knowing exactly who wore the robes.

"Sit!" one of the magistrates commanded. Gideon saw a weak looking wooden chair against the wall and brought it forward. He wasn't sure if the chair would hold his weight or not, but sat down nonetheless.

The magistrate seated in the center held a large stack of parchment and rifled through them with purpose. When he found what he was looking for, he flattened the crinkled sheet with a hand and cleared his throat.

"This report is filled with some very grave accusations," he said slowly. The magistrate's voice was full of years and heavy like broken rocks.

"I confess," Gideon said without hesitation. He heard several gasps filter down from the gallery.

"To what?" the magistrate responded, looking up from his papers and meeting Gideon's eyes.

With a nod, Gideon indicated the report. "Whatever it says, I did it. I went to the Old Hill and restored the statue," he explained.

The magistrate nodded slowly and set his parchment back on the side of the large desk. "Do you know the penalty for such a crime?" he asked.

The only thing Gideon knew for sure about Azuria's legal system was the arena. "I demand trial by combat," he stated evenly, bringing another round of gasps from the audience.

"Combat?" the magistrate on the left asked with his brows raised. "The penalty for your crimes is typically met at the end of a rope, not in the arena."

"Perhaps there is some—" the central magistrate started to speak, but Gideon cut him off.

"Let Vrysinoch decide my fate in the pit," he said, bringing an immediate roar from the crowd.

The magistrate on the right banged a gavel into the desk to quiet the gallery before proceeding. His once calm demeanor had faded into snarling anger. "You profane our sacred hall!" he shouted. The other magistrates nodded in agreement. "You are a blasphemer and a heretic!" He pointed a finger at Gideon's chest as he spoke, spittle flying from his mouth.

Gideon smiled. "Is death the punishment for heresy?" he asked.

"Hang him!" someone from the gallery shouted. Gideon looked up and tried to find the owner of the voice in the crowd, but almost everyone was shouting again. As he expected, the man in white sat stoically in the back row without saying a word.

When the room was quiet again, the central magistrate stood. "For speaking *that* name, you will be put to death," he said with a sneer. "Azuria does not tolerate heretics!"

"So it will be trial by combat?" Gideon requested once more.

The magistrate shook his head. "*This*," he barked, slamming his fist into the table, "is your trial! You will face death in the arena before all of Azuria. The people must watch your demise!"

Memories of a roaring crowd and a dead minotaur flooded Gideon's mind and brought adrenaline to his veins. He flexed his legs and remembered the terrible wound that had nearly killed him. "Who will fight me?" he asked, staring at the magistrate.

"We keep a healthy stock of fighters for just such an occasion," the man responded with an arrogant sneer. He smoothed the front of his robe and reigned in his overt aggression. After conferring with his colleagues for a moment, he turned back to Gideon. "A week from today, you will face five of Azuria's strongest fighters in the arena."

Gideon shook his head. "I'm a busy man," he said. "Make it ten fighters, and let's do it tomorrow."

The gallery gasped in response, but it was obvious they loved the idea. The magistrate smiled almost as much as Gideon did. "Fine," he stated. "You will fight against ten of our men tomorrow at dawn." With a wave of his hand, the guard to Gideon's left escorted him back through the iron-banded door to the small dungeon beneath the building.

This city will know Vrysinoch's might, he thought to himself. Gideon saw a drop of sweat glisten on the nervous guard's brow.

Nine

THE SAME OLD man who had led Gideon from his cell to the court visited the dungeon later that night. He hobbled over to the small prison and offered a plate of food through the bars. "I couldn't find much, but you need to eat," he said solemnly.

Gideon took the plate and laughed. The man had brought him two hunks of cheese, a piece of hard bread, and a dead rat that looked to be a few days old. "Thank you," he said with a grin. As Vrysinoch's power slowly returned to him, his stomach yearned for food more befitting an eagle.

To the old man's horror, Gideon ripped into the dead rat and finished the rodent in a few quick bites. "Why did you bring me food?" he asked after he cleaned the last bit of blood from his chin.

The jailor took a few steps away from the cell and coughed into his arm. "You're different than the others who have come through here," he replied. "Everyone else either cries for hours on end or hurts themselves on the bars in their rage. I've worked in this jail for half a lifetime, and I know when someone has something planned." He pointed a crooked finger at Gideon's chest and shook it like a parent scolding their child.

631

"Oh?" Gideon feigned shock. "You discovered my plan?"

The man grinned from ear to ear. "An escape? One of your friends bribing a magistrate? Whatever your plan is, I intend to watch it unfold."

Gideon had to admit his confidence was rather suspicious. "Why don't you try to stop me?" he asked.

The man shook his head. "You don't live to be nearly a hundred years old by attempting to thwart prison escapes," he explained. "And by the look of you, I wouldn't live very long by trying to stop you."

"You make a fine point," Gideon said with a chuckle. "Do you want to know my plan?"

The man took a few steps forward and leaned in close to the cell bars.

"I will kill ten men in the arena tomorrow morning and earn my freedom," he whispered.

"Ha!" the man laughed in his face. "I've seen those fights," he said, "no one lives."

Gideon lifted a piece of sharp yellow cheese to his mouth and took a bite. "You've never seen *me* fight," he assured him. "Ten men is nothing." He felt Vrysinoch's energy surge through his body and knew without a doubt he would be successful. Although he never considered himself to be a bloodthirsty man, he looked forward to the next day's carnage.

After the old man left, Gideon finished his meager food and slept better than he had in months. When a patrol of guardsmen arrived at dawn to fetch him, he was ready and waiting.

They shackled his hands and feet to a heavy chain fixed about his waist and led him to a small cart on the street. As before, they made him lie down and one of the guards sat on his chest to keep him from moving. "Will I get my weapons?" Gideon asked. With Maelstrom and Regret in his hands, he had no doubt he could kill scores of men, if not hundreds.

The guard laughed and shook his head. "Jik, the arena master, will have a few pieces of equipment ready for you, but you only get your swords back if you win," he said.

"What about my opponents?" Gideon asked casually. Even with old, battered equipment, it would not matter much what his enemies carried.

"Most of the pit fighters are either criminals sentenced to do battle or lunatics who volunteer their lives in the name of gold coins. The criminals won't have much more than you, but the prize fighters who have won a few contests can afford finer weapons and armor." Gideon was surprise at how much information the guard willingly gave him. His eagerness to answer questions was likely a testament to how little a chance he thought Gideon had.

The cart moved through the city with a grueling pace. After several miles of uncomfortably slow progress, they arrived outside the arena. Gideon craned his neck to see the structure, but could only glimpse its top from his position.

The ground sloped downward and the cart descended into the bowels of the arena. After several more twists and turns, the guards formed a semicircle of loaded crossbows around Gideon and allowed him to stand. A man he presumed to be Jik came and removed Gideon's shackles with an iron key.

"This way," he said, waving off the guards dismissively. "We don't want to be late."

The two men continued through a series of confusing tunnels that smelled like dead rodents. Torches sputtered on the walls and filled the ceiling with thick smoke. Gideon ran a hand through his beard and calmed his nerves as he remembered the words to a battle hymn he learned in the Tower of Wings.

When they reached their destination, the arena's storage room, Jik threw his arms wide as though he was displaying a grand collection of fine art. In reality, the equipment he offered was only slightly better than worthless. The swords were pitted, dinged, and covered in rust. A chainmail shirt hanging from a hook in the wall was so stiff with dried blood and lack of use it could stand on its own. Gideon lifted a flanged mace from a table and laughed when the head of the weapon fell off and left him holding only the handle.

"What do you recommend?" he wondered, almost jokingly.

"What weapons do you prefer?" Jik asked, moving to a rack in the corner beneath a torch.

Gideon casually browsed through more of the ramshackle collection, but he knew nothing would even be worth a single swing. "I typically fight with a pair of enchanted swords," he explained. "One throws tendrils of fire and the other is fast as lightning."

Jik raised his eyebrows and regarded Gideon with a curious stare. "I'm afraid you won't find any of that here," he said after a moment. "But there should at least be a helmet that will fit your bald head."

Gideon inspected the armor at one of the tables and sighed. "This helmet still has blood on the inside," he said, holding it to the light for Jik to see.

"An unfortunate byproduct of arena fighting," the man jested.

"I will be fine with just my hands and my skin this time, Jik," Gideon said as he gave the man a brotherly slap on the back.

"If you lay down to die, they will not show mercy," the arena master responded. "They will torture you for the sake of the crowd."

Gideon nodded. Talonrend had employed a similar tactic for those sentenced to fight who had sought a quick and easy death. "Trust me," Gideon told him, "I will fight."

With a resigned sigh, Jik led Gideon through another short tunnel to a set of massive double doors. In their center, a black raven perched atop a skull and Gideon assumed it to be Druaka, Azuria's god. He winced at the sight and prayed to Vrysinoch for strength.

Yes, my son, the eagle responded with a hiss. *We will fight gloriously!*

Gideon stood in front of the doors and waited. He heard the roar of the crowd on the other side and knew the arena must be larger than the one in Talonrend.

"You're ready?" Jik asked with mild concern.

Gideon flexed again and felt a rush of magic overwhelm his muscles. His skin prickled and thousands of brown feathers burst forth all over his arms, chest, and legs. He stretched his hands out wide and his fingers transformed into bright yellow talons sharp as razors.

"My god..." Jik whispered, but his exclamation was not one of worship. The man shrank back against the wall and screamed at what he saw.

Gideon turned his head sharply and watched the arena master for a second before issuing forth an avian screech that nearly ruptured Jik's eardrums. "I was born for this," he said evenly, escalating Jik's panic further.

Yes, Gideon of Talonrend, you were, Vrysinoch mentally agreed. *You have set me free and restored my power. Now you will teach Azuria the true meaning of fear. You will make them bow before their true god!*

The doors of the arena opened and the crowd roared with primal bloodlust. When Gideon stepped into the sunlight of the sandy floor, they fell silent at once.

SIFIR, THE PRIEST who lived beneath what was now called Half-Orc Keep, sat with his legs crossed on the stone floor and ate a small portion of meat. At the temple's entrance, a group of four orcs watch. Sifir noticed the spears they carried and shuddered. The orcs had fed him every few days, just enough food to keep him alive, and they had always done so without lingering.

"When you finish, Undrakk wants you," one of them said roughly. The orc's command of the human language startled Sifir—

he had never heard any except the half-orc speak his tongue. The orc was also unusually perceptive, reading Sifir's perspective and pointing to a silver medallion hanging about his chest. "The minotaur amulet lets me speak to you," he explained.

Not knowing exactly what to say or do, Sifir returned to his food with a nod. The meat was properly cooked and well-seasoned, a welcomed change from the rotten specimens he was used to receiving.

"Where are you taking me?" Sifir asked quietly. Despite his attempt to prolong the meal, he finished the savory meat quickly. His stomach longed for another portion and growled when he stood.

"To Undrakk," the orc responded.

Sifir shrugged and stepped into line behind the orcs. His old bones moved slowly, but he was invigorated by the prospect of seeing daylight for the first time in over fifty years.

The trek back to the surface took several hours to complete. Every fifty yards or so, Sifir had to stop and rest for fear of passing out. "If I had more to eat, perhaps I would have more strength," he told the orc in charge, but the green-skinned beast only stared.

At the top of the passageway, Sifir gasped. The interior of Castle Talon was nothing like he remembered. All of the tapestries, paintings, and other works of art had been removed and presumably smashed. In their place, weapons and armor hung on display like a museum.

The ceiling had been very notably raised in the entryway and much of the effort to make the building minotaur accessible was still underway. In the center of the large room that previously housed the king's throne, there was nothing but an old bloodstain and a few broken chunks of the old throne. Such a sight made Sifir's heart drop.

"I will take you to Undrakk," the strange orc said, grasping Sifir's shoulder. After exchanging a few lines of their own language, the other orcs left and the priest was led to the side chamber which previously served as the royal bedroom. The heavy doors had been replaced by a flap of animal hide more befitting a tent.

The orc at Sifir's side stopped and pounded his spear butt into the ground to announce their arrival. After a brief moment, Undrakk pulled back the flap and ushered them inside.

"I trust you were not harmed?" Undrakk asked, never taking his eyes from the orc. When Sifir nodded, the orc who had brought him visibly relaxed. With a wave of Undrakk's hand, the orc bowed, removed his amulet, and hung it on a peg before retreating back into the castle.

"Thank you for the food," Sifir said awkwardly. "It has been several days since I have eaten."

Undrakk frowned and took a seat in the minimally appointed room. Instead of the large royal bed, a mat of straw and fur covered the floor. Several painted maps were strewn about, and when Undrakk motioned for Sifir to sit, the old man had to move some of them out of his way. "Would you like more food?" the half-orc asked.

Sifir didn't know if Undrakk was sincere or not, but the hunger in his gut would not let him turn down food. "Yes," he said eagerly, nodding his head.

Undrakk moved to a wooden chest in the corner of the room and produced a chunk of salted meat large enough to feed Sifir for weeks. He handed it to the man and returned to his seat on the floor.

"Eat all you can," Undrakk said dismissively. "There are more deer in the fields outside Broken Sword than you can count."

Although the haunch was cold, Sifir bit into it ferociously.

"I read your strange book," Undrakk said, tossing the leather bound holy book at Sifir's feet. The priest had not been conscious when it was stolen, but he had assumed it to be in Undrakk's possession. "Here," the half-orc continued, offering Sifir the handle of a knife, "cut your meat with this and save your teeth."

Sifir hesitated at first, but he took the knife and was grateful for it. Time had long ago removed all but a precious few of the priest's teeth, and he needed the blade's help badly.

Undrakk folded his hands in front of him and let out a long sigh. "Why have I never heard the name Druaka before?" he asked after a moment.

"Only I know the true history of humanity," Sifir explained with a mouth full of venison. "I am a High Priest! The secrets are passed down from one High Priest to the next, always preserving the record, but never disseminating it."

Undrakk mulled over the words. "Why should I believe you?" he asked quizzically.

The priest laughed. "Why should you *not* believe me?" he said. "But then again, why should I tell the truth?"

The half-orc wasn't sure if the human was trying to make a joke or simply stating a fact, but he didn't particularly care. The history of Talonrend was fascinating, even for a green-skinned creature like himself who had been raised as an orc. "I'm curious about the civil war mentioned in your book," he said, reclining on a pile of furs.

Sifir knew he had nothing to lose. What ill could possibly befall Talonrend that would be worse than being conquered by beasts? The city was lost, turned into an orc fortress, and telling Vrysinoch's secrets to *anyone* felt good. "In a city many miles from here, there were two gods," he began. Sifir leaned against his own stack of furs and set his food to the side. There would be time for that later.

"The two gods held dominion over opposite things. Vrysinoch, the eagle, is the deity of impulsivity, vigor, life, passion, and war: all the things that stir a man's blood and excite his temper. On the other hand, Druaka is the god of subtlety and deception, calculated decisions and planning. When the world was born, Vrysinoch and Druaka walked the earth and ruled together, each with their specific roles. The eagle guided birth and creation on their destined paths, and the raven ushered souls to the afterlife.

"But who were those souls?" Sifir asked rhetorically, leaning forward with excitement. "The four races had to originate somewhere. Vrysinoch created mankind," he pointed to his own chest with swelling pride, "and mankind needed a helper. So Vrysinoch created a smaller race to help the humans, and thus the goblins were born."

Undrakk wasn't sure what he believed, but the tale fascinated him, so he prompted Sifir to continue.

"Druaka did not want to be alone on the earth without a race to worship her," he went on. "So she took one of humankind's most useful creatures, cattle, and distorted it. The minotaurs were her children. When Druaka saw the relationship between humans and goblins, she created the orcs to be the servants of the minotaurs."

Undrakk scoffed. "Orcs have never served minotaurs, old man," he spat.

"Not in recent memory," Sifir corrected. "The problem with both races of servants was the population. Humans and minotaurs took too long to reproduce while orcs and goblins bred like wild rats."

"Watch yourself, priest," Undrakk chided, although he had to admit the truth of Sifir's analogy.

"After centuries of living together, the four races fought a brutal war which resulted in their separation. The orcs, goblins, and minotaurs fled to the wilds and left their gods behind. The humans, as they often do, distorted history and claimed both gods for their own. They lived for thousands of years in fear of their long lost brethren. And then came the bloody civil war," he paused for a moment. "Humanity split itself between devotees of Vrysinoch and Druaka and killed each with impunity until the eagle was defeated." Sifir took another slice of venison and brought it to his mouth.

"What do you mean by defeated?" Undrakk asked.

"Vrysinoch was banished back to the sky, and his followers were exiled," the priest answered. "They left their hometown and travelled east for two years, eventually settling two cities: Talon-

639

rend and Reikall. All of their histories were amended to remove Druaka, and they were not permitted to carry any maps on their journey." Sifir held up the leather bound book with a smile. "This is the only accurate history of the humans that made the trip from Azuria to the Green City of Talonrend."

Undrakk shook his head. "I read the entire book and saw nothing about the four races living together," he said. The more he thought about being a servant to minotaurs, the more he resented speaking to the priest at all.

Sifir tapped the side of his head with a finger. "Not everything in history is written," he said slyly.

"I saw Vrysinoch die," Undrakk said violently. "A bone dragon tore your eagle to shreds just outside the city. What does your history book say about that?"

Sifir waved him off. "The only one strong enough to kill Vrysinoch is his sister, Druaka—the god of death. What you saw was only an image of the god, a fragment of Vrysinoch's mind brought into our world, not the entire deity."

"Interesting," Undrakk muttered. "Although I grow weary of your tales. The past means nothing." He looked at the old man's leathery skin and tried to guess his age. "You are the last human remaining in the world," he said. "When you die, your race will be buried at your side."

Sifir smiled and tapped his book. "Azuria still stands!" he beamed. "Almost all of the other races went east with Vrysinoch's followers. Only a handful of orcs, goblins, and minotaurs stayed in the west. As long as a plague or famine has not eradicated them, Azuria still stands. Your victory in Talonrend means little, half-orc."

Undrakk thought of killing the insolent priest where he sat, but remembered his soldiers' warning. According to them, the man could not be killed by their weapons. With a sneer, Undrakk rose from his furs and stalked from the room. He didn't care what became of Sifir. If the orcs or minotaurs killed him, so be it. If not, the man was too old to be a threat.

MELKORA SAT NEXT to Valkoinen and Vorst in the front row of Azuria's massive arena. Word of Gideon's confession had spread like wildfire through the city, and there wasn't an empty seat in the entire stands. All around Valkoinen, the citizens stared at his white robes and whispered to each other. For once, the eyes of the city were drawn away from Vorst and fixed on one of their own.

"It is time they see the Alabaster Order in broad daylight," Valkoinen had said, insisting on accompanying Melkora and Vorst to the arena.

"When will it begin?" Melkora asked under her breath. She knew Gideon was an incredible fighter, but she couldn't suppress the fluttering in her stomach.

Valkoinen pointed to the eastern gate where ten well-armored men walked forth onto the sand in a semicircle. "Those men are not equipped like average pit fighters sentenced to die. The magistrates must have arranged for better provisions." He turned his mask slightly to the side, and Melkora felt as though he peered into the depths of her soul. "This will not be an easy fight."

GIDEON STARED AT the onlooker nearest to him. His enhanced, bird-like vision was impeccable. He could make out every flaw and imperfection in the man's face. His nose was slightly crooked, his hair was matted with dirt, and most of all, the man twitched with palpable nervousness. As Gideon surveyed the others near him, he found their fear to be the one thing they all had in common.

Across the vast arena floor, his opponents stood in shining mail .with sturdy weapons in their hands. Gideon looked each of them over and studied their posture. He could tell most of them were un-trained, but three of the group showed poise and bore scars from previous victories. Unsurprisingly, the three veterans held large shields in their off hands and carried themselves with measured confidence.

A trumpet blasted from somewhere near the top of the arena, and the ten men began to stride forward. Gideon met their pace and rushed toward the center of the arena. He wanted all of Azuria to witness Vrysinoch's countenance and tremble in terror.

When the men neared Gideon, the eager, untrained fighters broke into a sprint. Most of them held long pikes or halberds and yelled wildly, despite the eerie silence of the thousands around them.

Gideon met the first young soldier head on. Thrusting straight forward with his spear, the man tried to run Gideon through with a single strike. It was the last mistake the unfortunate soldier ever made.

With inhuman speed and accuracy, Gideon leapt into the air at the last possible moment and landed on the spear's shaft, crushing it into the sand. In shock, the soldier let go of the weapon and stumbled to the ground. Gideon used his foot to launch the spear to his hands where he twirled it around and skewered the soldier straight through.

The crowd broke their silence and roared. They were there to see blood, and Gideon was intent on staining the sand red with it.

The next two men were cut down before they even had a chance to attempt a strike with their polearms. Gideon maneuvered his spear flawlessly and knocked one halberd wide and the other high. While the men tried to get their long weapons back into posi-tion, Gideon tore their stomachs apart in rapid succession.

Four more soldiers charged at Gideon while the three veterans calmly took their time and never broke formation. Gideon reared the spear back, causing one of the charging men to raise his small buckler in defense, but Gideon's throw easily shattered the shield and the arm holding it. The man wasn't dead, but he would bleed out soon enough.

The other three untrained soldiers slowed and tried to coordinate their assault, but Gideon took to the air. He jumped and feathered wings burst forth from his back, carrying him above the arena floor. The crowd gasped and shrieked, but still most of them cheered for even more carnage.

With several beats of his mighty wings, Gideon dove back to the sand like a streak of lightning. He stretched his talons out wide and caught two soldiers with his claws, ripping the skin from their faces. The third man tried to hit him with his mace as he passed, but nothing could match Gideon's speed.

High into the air he flew, still clutching handfuls of gore between his yellow talons as the men screamed in pain on the ground below. Somewhere over the eastern side of the arena, Gideon dropped the bloody clumps of skin into the audience and circled back to finish off the last untrained soldier.

He dove down with incredible speed and, to his credit, the remaining man held his ground for several seconds longer than Gideon expected. Just before Gideon collided with the man's shield, the soldier's courage broke and he tried to run. Unfortunately for him, Gideon's knee caught him in the side of the ribs and blew the air, as well as a good portion of blood, from his chest. Bones exploded in every direction as Gideon drove him into the ground. When his momentum finally subsided, there was a massive rut in the sand stained red with gore.

Gideon stood and brushed a bone fragment from his shoulder. A bit of flesh clung to his shoulder, and he plucked it off with a blood-soaked talon. To the horror of the crowd, he dropped the morsel into his mouth and savored the fresh, metallic taste of warm blood.

The three veterans formed a triangle of shields in front of Gideon, but he could see them shaking under their armor. No amount of training could have prepared them for such a violent, unimaginable opponent.

Gideon stalked toward them and loosed a piercing, disorienting screech. He wrapped his talons around the edge of the closest shield and ripped it back, pulling the man's arm off in the process and sending a fresh torrent of gore onto the sand. He tossed the shield to the sand and pressed forward.

The two remaining soldiers tried to strike with their swords, one going high and the other low, but Gideon batted their weapons away like toys. He grabbed the soldier to his right, a young man with muscles like corded wood, and clamped a talon around his head. He tried to struggle, tried desperately to escape, but was no match for Gideon's divine strength.

All the man could do was watch with horror as Gideon's beak-like mouth tore through his neck and ended his life.

The last man, a grizzled veteran of at least thirty years, dropped his sword to the sand and fell to his knees. Gideon towered over him and breathed deeply, relishing the scent of blood and fear mixed with sand and the ocean breeze. "Get up," he commanded.

The man slowly ambled to his feet and unstrapped his shield. The metal fell to the ground with a dull thud. "I submit," the veteran muttered through his trembling throat.

"I know," Gideon replied. He stared at the soldier and let his divine strength fade. Slowly, Vrysinoch's brown feathers receded back under Gideon's skin, and his appearance returned to normal.

"Please," the man pleaded with tears in his eyes. "I have a family..." Despite his fear, the man stood as Gideon had commanded.

"Vrysinoch sends his regards."

Gideon stepped forward and punched the man hard in the stomach, doubling him over. He slammed his knee up and caught the man's chin, shattering several of his teeth and knocking him backward where he fell with a groan. In an instant, Gideon jumped on top of the poor fighter and began pummeling him, raining blow after blow upon his face.

The veteran's consciousness lasted through the first dozen punches, but faded into darkness when his jaw broke in a fourth place. His head lolled to the side, and blood seeped from his open mouth, but he still drew breath. Gideon wrapped his hands around the man's neck and looked up to the crowd. They had gone silent again, watching in fixated horror as Gideon slaughtered nearly a dozen men in the space of a few minutes. With a grin, Gideon broke the veteran's neck and stood, discarding the body like a broken piece of armor.

Gideon roared.

He gazed around the bloodstained ground and bathed in the utter completeness of his victory. It had been years since he had stepped onto a sandy arena floor, and he had missed it. Although he had killed scores of orcs on the road and hundreds of goblins in the field east of Talonrend, none of them brought the satisfaction that came with ending a human life. Gideon was Vrysinoch's tool, dispensing violent retribution with hideous efficiency.

Suddenly, a murmur spread through the crowd like wildfire. An iron gate began to move in the side of the arena wall. The gate was emblazoned with images of Druaka and before long, the crowd's murmur evolved into a chant.

"Ohra! Ohra! Ohra!" they yelled in unison. When the gate finished its ascent, the champion of Azuria stood in the shadows like a gargoyle keeping watch for demons. She held nothing in her hands, but Gideon saw the hilt of a sword protruding above her shoulder. *His* sword. Somehow, Ohra had an exact copy of Nevidal strapped to her back.

On her torso, the champion had little in the way of armor. She wore black leather gloves, a chainmail shirt fit tightly around her chest, and a studded leather skirt similar to the one Gravlox wore. Her hair was like jagged shards of ice atop her head, bone white and fiercely cut. As she entered the brilliant light of the arena, Gideon noticed a huge raven perched atop her shoulder. The creature squawked and cawed. Its beady eyes bored into him without a trace of fear.

I need you once more, Gideon prayed, but he knew it was too late. Vrysinoch had left him. When he flexed, no feathers appeared. He picked up one of the dead soldier's swords and tested it in his hand. The blade was well built, but poorly balanced and chipped from use. Compared to Maelstrom and Regret, it was nothing. If Ohra's sword truly was a copy of Nevidal, Gideon's piece of iron would be worthless.

"Heretic," Ohra addressed him. Her voice carried a hint of restraint under a thick layer of confidence. She knew Gideon was dangerous, but she had no doubt she would be victorious.

"Champion," Gideon responded. "Ever since I arrived in Azuria, I have wanted to see you fight."

"Druaka has sent me here to kill you, heretic," Ohra stated. She walked into the center of the arena and casually looked through the discarded weapons as though choosing a piece of food in the market.

Gideon pointed to the host of slaughtered bodies. "Do you truly believe you can defeat me?" he asked.

Ohra picked up a spear and broke the shaft over her knee with ease, cutting the weapon down to a more manageable size for her smaller frame.

"You fought impressively," Ohra conceded. "But no one can stand against the might of Druaka. You will fall like many before you have fallen. Your blood will stain this sand until the next rain… and then you will be forgotten."

"Your sword," Gideon indicated with a nod. The hilt stuck over her shoulder just as Nevidal had on Gideon's own back for years.

"Dalviné," Ohra said with a smile. "The right hand of the raven." As if on command, the black bird on her shoulder squawked.

"Draw it," Gideon commanded her. He wanted to know if the street merchant he had met on his first day in Azuria had spoken the truth or not.

Ohra shook her head and waved a finger like a mother scolding an insolent child. "Not yet," she said with a devilish grin. "Trust me, you do not want to face Dalviné."

"You're afraid," Gideon stated with growing confidence. Ohra looked surprised. "You're afraid to face only a single opponent with such a sword. What if I trip and kill myself on some discarded weapon? Or worse yet, what if I escape?"

Ohra took a fearful step backward. Gideon's knowledge of Dalviné clearly unnerved her.

"You'll have to kill someone in the crowd," he continued. "Or sacrifice yourself to Druaka's mercy."

"Enough of your ramblings, heretic," Ohra spat. She kicked an errant piece of bone out of her way and set her feet, drawing a huge roar from the crowd. She held her broken spear high above her head like a dagger, the sharp end pointing down and ready to strike.

Gideon admired her. The woman had just seen him slaughter ten men without taking so much as a scratch, and yet her confidence was not shaken. He remembered his own days of fighting in Talonrend's arena. He had been confident, but never foolhardy.

He brought his own sword up to his chest in salute, and the crowd went wild. The collective yell of so many gathered was deafening. Gideon cleared his head and let the energy of the crowd push a fresh wave of adrenaline through his veins.

In an instant, the two champions clashed together with a flurry of blows. Gideon moved his sword high, constantly parrying downward stabs and turning Ohra's spear wide. The woman was incredibly agile though, and Gideon's legs quickly became easy targets for Ohra's fierce kicks.

Without enough time to formulate an elaborate plan, Gideon spun toward Ohra and ducked under an overhand stab. As he spun, he slide his left foot between Ohra's legs and turned his hips, slamming his shoulder into her chin and sending her staggering backward. Against an untrained opponent, the fight would have ended with a single strike. A normal man's jaw would have shattered with such a hit.

But Ohra was anything but ordinary. She took the blow in stride, turning her own body away from the hit and lashing out with her heel as she retreated, catching Gideon's gut with a brutal kick.

Both fighters stepped away and reset their feet. Gideon knew he was stronger than Ohra, but she held every other advantage. Her smaller stature and quick legs made her a blur of motion that Gideon's size could do nothing to overcome. He needed to force a direct test of strength, but if Ohra was half as smart as she was lithe, it would never happen.

They met again in the center of the arena and this time, Ohra kept her body further back, lashing with her spear head in front of her. Again, Gideon deflected her blows, but he saw no opportunity to strike. Every time Ohra's hand went forward, her feet turned away from the attack and her torso moved just out of reach. Even Gideon's longer arms could not make up for her speed.

Ohra lunged to Gideon's right, bringing her broken spear above his head, and spun backward with a flourish. At first, Gideon saw an opportunity to strike the woman's exposed abdomen, but by the time he swung, her spear caught him in the back of the neck and knocked him forward. Suddenly overbalanced, Gideon fell forward and had to toss his sword to the side lest he risk falling on it.

He crashed to the ground at Ohra's feet and she wasted no time pouncing on him. She rained a brutal shower of fists down on Gideon's face and torso, crushing through his meager attempt to block. All the while, the raven clung to her shoulder like a beady-eyed statue.

With a roar of determination, Gideon took a punch to the side of his head and threw a fist of his own, connecting solidly with

Ohra's ribs. The woman did not relent. She continued her brutal assault unfettered, and Gideon knew he would be killed. Striking as hard as he could from his back, Gideon focused on the bottom of Ohra's ribcage and punished the area with his right fist. After several hits, Gideon's vision blurred with warm blood, but Ohra's bones gave way and cracked.

Gideon's face suffered more and more abuse, turning red and black with bloody bruises. He spat a mouthful of his teeth into the sand and pressed onward with his own violent punches. More of Ohra's ribs shattered on the left side of her body, and her punches slowed, growing weaker every second. Gideon grit his teeth and saw an opportunity. He straightened his fingers into a point and jammed them between Ohra's dislodged ribs with all his remaining might. Blood poured over his hand and he twisted it in deeper.

Ohra screamed in pain and tried to roll off of Gideon, but he dug his hand further into her chest. The crowd screamed in horror as Gideon ripped a mass of bloody innards out of Ohra's chest and threw them into the sand. Her eyes lolled back in her head. She slumped to her side, clutching at the grievous wound with both hands.

Gideon shoved her fully off his body and tried to stand, but his face was a mess, and his mental faculties had all but fled. He crawled away slowly like a dying deer making its last effort to escape the jaws of a hungry wolf.

Ohra groaned and Gideon turned his head to see her. His eyes were bloody and swollen nearly beyond use, but he forced one of them open far enough to watch her movements. *If she gets up, I'm dead,* he thought to himself with a grimace.

The black raven from Ohra's shoulder squawked and took flight, circling around the woman like a vulture. Gideon could feel wave after wave of magic emanating from the bird. He dreaded what might happen. Then, to massive cheers from the audience, the bird vanished. Much to Gideon's dismay, he could still sense the bird's magical presence. Ohra had drawn it into her body.

The champion slowly rose from the ground, clutching her garish wound and holding her guts together. She regained her feet,
said something Gideon could not comprehend, and released her
grip on her torn ribs. When her bloody hands moved from her side,
a flash of light knit her body back together in an instant.

I'm coming, Vrysinoch's voice echoed in Gideon's head. By the
startled look on Ohra's face, he knew she had heard the words as
well.

Gideon collapsed back to the ground from pain and exhaustion.
The sand stung his bloodied face and upper torso, reminding him of
all the wounds he had taken before in Talonrend's arena. Then, in
the distance, he heard a rumbling like rolling thunder. The noise
grew louder until the crowd hushed and a shadow appeared over
them.

In the sky, a winged figure circled. Gideon knew beyond a
doubt it was his god.

He laughed. His body convulsed and pushed warm globs of
blood from his battered mouth, but still he laughed. Ohra backed
away and reached for the hilt of her sword.

Azuria's champion drew Dalviné from the sheath on her back
and got into a low crouch. Unlike all the other times she had drawn
the magical sword in the arena, the crowd remained eerily silent.
The winged figure grew larger and larger as it descended, and Gideon's laughs escalated with every second.

Finally, Gideon was able to make out the winged figure, and
his heart was lifted. The stone statue of Vrysinoch he had restored
in the ruined cathedral, three stories or more of carved marble and
granite, had come alive and to his rescue. When the massive statue
landed, it blasted a crater in the arena floor and sent sand flying in
all directions.

The statue looked at Ohra with cold, marble eyes. She could
feel Vrysinoch's wrath washing over her and she trembled. Had she
not already drawn her soul-stealing sword, Ohra would have

turned and fled in a heartbeat. But with Dalviné in her hand, fleeing meant death as certainly as fighting a god.

She steadied her breathing as best she could, set her feet in a familiar stance, and leveled her sword at the statue's chest.

Vrysinoch towered over her. He took a step and the ground shook from his weight. Slowly, the statue opened its mouth and spoke. "My sister's pet," he addressed her with a grating voice that bore the weight of mountains. "I will spare you, but not without recompense."

Ohra glowered and tried to maintain her resolve, but her hands shook with fear. "Druaka will smite you, foul beast," she said as bravely as she could.

Vrysinoch chortled. "Insolent pet," he replied. "You are dust."

The statue beat its heavy, stone wings and jumped through the air. Ohra was fast and nearly leapt out of the way, but Vrysinoch's marble talon caught her legs and ground her lower half to bloody pulp. Without hesitation, Vrysinoch brought his second talon down upon Ohra's head, instantly severing it from her body.

The crowd gasped and started to panic. Their champion was dead and with fear and terror spreading, they fled the arena. The scramble to escape was nothing short of chaos. Parents left their children behind, stronger men crushed the weaker ones into the steps, and scores of people died before they ever made it to the streets.

Vrysinoch turned back to Gideon and knelt down on massive stone legs. His wings spread wide enough to cast Gideon entirely in their shade. "Rise, Gideon of Talonrend," the statue commanded.

Gideon felt a tinge of magic begin to stitch his wounds together, but he knew Vrysinoch would not heal him completely. "I will suffer for my arrogance," he whispered as he stood. His face still bled openly and throbbed with agony, but he knew he would live.

Vrysinoch cast his gaze around the carnage of the guardsmen who had tried to kill Gideon and breathed a sigh from his stony mouth. "Your... *transgressions*... must be punished. You will suffer greatly, Gideon of Talonrend." The statue slipped one of his talons through the strap of Ohra's sheath, picked Dalviné up from the sand, and hung the weapon from his huge forearm.

Despite his menacing words, Vrysinoch held out his claws and Gideon happily sank into them. "I have one more task for you," the statue said gravely. "And then your soul belongs to me."

Vrysinoch beat his marble wings and took to the sky with Gideon hanging limply in his talons. Together they soared above the chaos of the arena and flew east, away from Azuria's panicked mob and high walls.

MELKORA, VORST, AND Valkoinen were lucky to be near the arena floor when chaos broke out. Those in the upper levels of the audience pushed each other down and trampled scores of their brethren to death in a mad panic to flee. As soon as Gideon was safely in Vrysinoch's stone arms, Melkora knew they had to run.

"The magistrates have seen us," Valkoinen said slowly. He nodded toward a covered pavilion high on the northern section of the arena, and Melkora saw three men in blue robes staring at them with violent expressions plastered to their faces. "We are enemies of Azuria now."

"Can you get us out of here?" Melkora practically begged. The magistrates began to move in their direction.

Valkoinen paused for a moment and then turned to the frightened woman. "I dare not risk travelling through the Void," he said with a hint of exasperated haste. "Whatever magic brought that statue to life is powerful and still lingers here." He could feel waves of intense power radiating from the center of the arena. Although he was not sure if it would interfere with his abilities, it was not worth the risk.

"We must run," Valkoinen stated evenly. His voice betrayed more urgency than Melkora had ever heard from him, but it was still unnerving to hear such emotionless words during a time of emergency.

The three of them scrambled over broken bodies and discarded waste as quickly as they could. Exiting the arena wasn't particularly difficult, but the chaos on the street outside was immense. People screamed and ran in all directions. Thankfully, none of the panicked citizens gave Melkora, Vorst, and Valkoinen more than a passing glance.

"Follow closely," Valkoinen commanded. He moved through the swarm of people like a ship breaking apart flotsam in a stormy ocean. Melkora and Vorst ran in his wake, their hands on their weapons just in case.

The arena's location at the edge of the city made fleeing Azuria a quick endeavor. Valkoinen passed through an unmanned gate and led the others back to the farmhouse where they had first met. "We can never return," he said with certainty.

A shadow passed over them, and they looked skyward, watching the stone statue of Vrysinoch descending with Gideon's limp body in its arms. The massive eagle landed with a resounding crash and placed Gideon unceremoniously on the grass. The man was still brutally battered, but his injuries did not appear life-threatening.

"Vrysinoch," Melkora gasped, bending into a low bow. "Thank you for saving him."

The statue gazed at her with bright marble eyes. "His purpose in this world is not yet complete," he said. "Talonrend must be restored."

Melkora brightened at the prospect of retaking Talonrend with the statue by their side. "Yes, my lord," she said respectfully.

The statue turned to Valkoinen menacingly. "You have denied me for too long, Valkoinen," Vrysinoch uttered with a stony talon outstretched in accusation.

Valkoinen tipped his mask slightly. "The Alabaster Order is prepared to help you retake Talonrend," he promised.

"The Alabaster Order is weak!" Vrysinoch responded. His voice resonated with power and shook the farmhouse violently. "Your resolve is worthless. If you were truly concerned with the Green City's fate, you would have left this wretched cesspit of heresy long ago. You only venture forth now because you have nowhere left to turn."

Valkoinen bowed his head further and remained silent.

"I will return in two days," Vrysinoch said to them. "Rally as many of my followers as you can and I will lead you to Talonrend. I will lead you to victory."

Vrysinoch leapt into the sky and beat his massive wings. The gust of wind he produced was enough to knock Melkora and Vorst off their feet with ease. Only Valkoinen, ever stoic and silent, remained unmoved by the god's departure.

"HERESY!" ZERREN SHOUTED with a thin layer of foam forming around the edges of his lips. He looked out from Azuria's central tower with disgust. Fires billowed into the crystal blue sky and choked the air with ash. Somewhere in the panic caused by Vrysinoch's living statue, the mob had devolved into something resembling a riot.

"Do not worry," the High Priest said from an intricately carved chair. He smoothed the front of his azure robes and pushed a leather-bound book away from him. "The heretics will be punished, Zerren. They *will* be punished."

"How?" Zerren demanded with equal parts fury and exasperation. "Ohra is dead, old man. Druaka's champion fell with barely a fight..." He wrenched his gaze away from the city's chaos, but looking at the lethargic old priest did nothing to lift his spirits.

The withered High Priest regarded Zerren with a scrutinizing look. "You have no faith," he said with disappointment.

Zerren slammed his fist into the desk. "Where is Druaka?" he yelled. "Why did she let Ohra die? Where was *our* god when that damned statue appeared?"

The High Priest began to open his mouth to further berate Zerren, but a low rumble shook the room and silenced both of them.

Zerren whirled back to the window and scanned the sky. The High Priest rose from his chair and hobbled across the room to join his younger counterpart. The rumbling grew into an unmistakably rhythmic pattern, and both men knew what was coming. From the distance, a black figure emerged from the smoke and ash with stone wings and a fierce marble countenance full of ire.

"It has returned," the High Priest whispered. Vrysinoch's statue swooped down close to the Azuria's open market and snatched an unfortunate soul from the cobblestone like an eagle hunting fish in a stream.

To Zerren's horror, the statue climbed high into the air toward the center of the city. "We should run," the young priest uttered. Vrysinoch gained speed and flew directly at them.

"Get down!" Zerren yelled. He pulled the priest to the side as Vrysinoch threw the hapless Azurian citizen at the tower. The man crashed through the window, shattering it in a hail of glass, and slammed into the High Priest's desk where he died with a pain-filled scream.

"My god," Zerren gasped. The tower shook violently, and the High Priest lost his balance against the wall. "The statue must have hit the tower," he said, roughly pulling the High Priest to his feet. "We need to run before it comes down on top of us!"

Vrysinoch screeched, shaking the tower again. Books fell from their shelves in the study. Glass windows throughout the entire building shattered. From the top of the tower, the statue reached a stone claw through the study's window and groped for the priests.

The marble talons carved huge paths of destruction through the wooden floor with every swipe.

"Run!" Zerren shouted. He grabbed a fistful of the High Priest's robe and dragged him toward the stairs. The old man struggled to keep up, but the thrashing claws coming through the window spurred him onward.

The two priests made it to the spiral staircase leading down throughout the tower as another massive tremor shook the building. Mortar between the stones in the walls shook and crumbled under the statue's force. Zerren knew he would not have enough time to escape the tower before it came down on top of them.

Screams of terror made their way up from the streets to Zerren's ears. He could only imagine what terror the citizens of Azuria were enduring on the ground below. Vrysinoch's statue tore huge chunks of the tower away and tossed piles of rubble larger than the city fountain to the streets without regard for the people below.

Zerren and the High Priest scrambled down the deteriorating staircase as quickly as they could. The two men shielded their faces from the falling debris, but they only made it slightly more than a single story down before a giant section of the roof gave way and nearly crushed them.

In the chaos of the moment, the High Priest stumbled and reached for the wall to catch himself, but the tower shook, and he fell against the fallen stone with a crack. Zerren rushed to his side and rolled the man over. Blood poured from the old man's forehead. Zerren tried to lift him onto his shoulders, but despite the aged priest's thin form, he did not have enough strength. Zerren began the words to a divine incantation, but was cut short by another wave of falling stones. He ducked backward, pushed aside a splinter of wood with his forearm, and left the High Priest for dead.

Zerren knew another way out of the tower. There was a staircase some of the more *indiscreet* priests used to smuggle concubines in and out of the building. The young man felt the tower sway as he darted back in the direction of the study. Several steps before the study door he stopped, counting the steps quickly. At the fourth stair, Zerren used the toe of his boot to push a hidden latch underneath the stair's lip. An unseen gear clicked into place, unlocking the stair with a soft pop.

With one hand above his head to keep the falling rubble from hitting his eyes, Zerren ripped the stair away and turned to align his body with the tight, vertical ladder. He squeezed into the space and cursed as the stones crushed against his back. *The girls must be small to make it up this ladder without being skinned,* he thought.

Luckily, the shaft holding the ladder was sturdy and held against Vrysinoch's onslaught. Zerren made it to the bottom of the tower with a collection of gashes, scrapes, and bruises, but he escaped with his life.

From the street, he watched the destruction in horror. Vrysinoch's marble statue circled the building slowly, clawing its way along and wrenching huge chunks of the walls away like a sculptor with a chisel. Zerren knew he was powerless to stop it.

Azuria was in uproar. The scene at the arena had caused a panic, and the eagle-god's wild fury had turned that panic into anarchy. Zerren did not know where to go. He was alive, but everything he had known was destroyed in front of his eyes. Desperately, he clung to the hope that Druaka would arrive and swoop from the heavens with inky black wings to kill the statue, but no sign of the raven ever appeared.

When the tower was finally reduced to total ruin, Zerren still stood with his back to a storefront and looked on. The statue lifted into the air and circled several times above the fallen tower, then turned west and flew off, presumably to demolish another of Druaka's sacred structures. Zerren wasn't sure where to go. A terrified citizen ran past and shoved off of Zerren's shoulder in haste.

"Is this what is to become of Azuria?" the priest muttered to himself as he watched the citizen flee down the road. He turned his gaze back to the ruined tower. "Have we lost so easily?"

Zerren threw his hands to the sky and was overcome with despair. "Druaka!" he called. He screamed into the heavens and tore his blue robe from his chest, repeating his god's name until his throat bled and he collapsed from exertion.

There the man slept, wearing only his simple undergarments and golden chain of office, shivering in the night breeze like an abandoned child.

WHEN THE SUN arose, Zerren shielded his eyes and groaned. His neck was stiff, and his back ached with every inch he moved. After a long moment spent in agony, he gathered enough of his strength to finally stand and relieve himself against the corner of a nearby building. Zerren collected his torn robe from the ground and breathed the ash-filled air. The tower, the very center and heart of Azuria, was utterly destroyed.

Only one aspect of the desolate scene gave him a shred of hope—people were scattered around the streets, and their voices filtered through the dust and smoke. Zerren saw a group of children wandering near the stones of the fallen tower and slowly made his way to them.

"What happened?" he shouted to them, shielding his eyes against the bright sunlight.

One of the children scampered up to him with a bit of rubble in her hands.

"Where is the monster?" Zerren asked. His eyes searched the horizon, but the morning sun blinded him and obscured the sky.

The girl shook her head. "It left," she said. A wave of relief coursed through Zerren's mind.

"Where did it go?" the priest asked. He desperately wanted the girl to recount a story of the statue's death, but in the pit of his stomach, he knew he would not be so lucky.

The girl spun and pointed east toward Azuria's large gate. "It flew over the walls," she said. Something about her jovial, innocent voice made Zerren laugh. She stood in the midst of ruins and understood nothing. Zerren wished he could leave his knowledge behind and live in childlike ignorance and bliss once again.

"Where is it now?" he asked.

The girl kept pointing east. "It waits on the other side of the wall," she replied almost excitedly. "My brother saw it sleeping out there."

"Sleeping?" Zerren said aloud to no one in particular. The notion gave him hope. *Perhaps it has returned to stone...* He waved the children away and draped his torn robe over his shoulders in a poor attempt at modesty. *Azuria must rise from these ashes. A new champion will come forth and the followers of the eagle will finally be put to rest.*

ONCE THE INITIAL panic of Vrysinoch's return had subsided, Azuria prepared for war. The magistrates called the city guard and a bloodthirsty mob of Druaka's supporters formed, eager for civil war.

On the other side of the city walls, several hundred of Vrysinoch's supporters had joined the remaining members of the Alabaster Order.

"We must leave soon," Melkora said with mixed emotions. She stood on a grassy knoll far from Azuria's walls, but the distance did nothing to lessen the tension in the air. Their group had grown overnight from a handful of Alabaster Order members to hundreds, perhaps a thousand, of worried citizens eager to leave Azuria behind. Many of them had brought worldly possessions along as well. The entire sight filled Melkora with dread. She thought of her daughter and Talonrend's refugee train. Tears filled her eyes.

Behind her, Vorst sat on the grass and longed to find her husband. Gravlox had been missing for several days, and Valkoinen did not seem eager to take her into the Void to find him.

"IT IS TIME," a gentle voice whispered through the darkness. Melkora's eyes shot open and her hand reflexively went to Roisin's hilt. Standing above her, Valkoinen gazed down at her body like a specter in his stark white robes. Melkora had been given a small section of the tiny farmhouse floor on which to sleep. The boards creaked and her body ached with every movement.

Valkoinen whirled away, leaving without another word. Melkora got to her feet and tightened the straps of her leather jerkin. Her hands shook uncontrollably as she manipulated the supple leather against her skin. With the exception of her brief skirmish with the orcs who had been scouting Cobblestreet for survivors, Melkora had never even witnessed a real battle. Her stomach swirled with wave after wave of fear-bound nausea that left a pungent taste in the back of her mouth.

After a few moments of struggle, Melkora calmed her nerves long enough to properly don her armor and step through the farmhouse door into the crisp air. Those who had joined their cause and left Azuria numbered in the hundreds, but almost none of them were trained soldiers. Some distance in front of her, the top of Azuria's walls gleamed with a mixture of pre-dawn light and torches.

Melkora caught sight of a white robe in the corner of her vision and moved to intercept the person. "Valkoinen?" she asked, unable to tell the Alabaster Order members apart. The white-clad person stopped and shook their mask to say no.

"Have you seen Vorst?" Melkora asked as she approached. The person said nothing. Nervous and frustrated by the person's silence, Melkora clenched her fists and tried not to let her mixed emotions show. "You mean you haven't seen the only goblin in the entire camp? The only goblin for hundreds of miles around?" she snapped.

The white robes and mask gave her no answer. Melkora let out an aggravated sigh and started to turn away when another member of the Alabaster Order suddenly approached her from behind as though walking out of the air itself.

"The initiate does not speak yet," Valkoinen clarified, startling Melkora with his sudden words. With a wave of his cloth-covered hand, Valkoinen sent the initiate away.

"Why not?" Melkora asked, letting the anger and nervousness mostly fade from her voice.

"When an initiate first comes back from the Void," he began slowly, "they bring nothing with them—not even their voice."

Melkora took a step back and tried to process the information. "What do you mean?" she asked.

Valkoinen spoke after a moment of silent contemplation. "The Void takes everything and hesitates to give it back." He extended his arms and spread his robe wide across his chest. "Touch me," he said, his voice serious.

Hesitantly, Melkora reached out a hand and brushed the front of Valkoinen's clothing. Without warning, Valkoinen stepped forward and his robe collapsed under the gentle touch of the woman's fingertips. There was nothing beneath the white cloth.

Melkora gasped and pulled her hand back violently, clutching it to her chest as though she had been stung or burned. "What are you?" she muttered breathlessly.

"When I returned from my first jaunt into the Void, I left everything behind." He lifted the bottom of his white mask to show Melkora the empty space where his face should have been. "It took two years to find my voice and bring it back to this plane. Perhaps someday I shall find my body again, but I do not expect to. I exist as a form with a voice—nothing else."

"By Vrysinoch's wings…"

661

"Do not pity me," Valkoinen interrupted, speaking much faster than he usually did. "Every member of the Alabaster Order makes the same sacrifice. We forfeit our physical aspects in order to become one with the Void and bring even a sliver of that plane into the material world."

Melkora was not sure if she understood his words or not, but she nodded regardless. "I do not pity you, Valkoinen," she whispered. "I pity Gravlox. He has been there for so long. Will he lose his body as well?"

A long silence passed between the two as the sun crept higher into the morning sky. "I do not know," Valkoinen finally spoke. "I do not believe he is still alive."

Before Melkora could fully comprehend the gravity of Valkoinen's words, a shout snapped her attention back toward Azuria and the impending battle. She heard the telltale sound of metal crashing against metal and the scream of someone dying. "We need to run!" she yelled at Valkoinen. "We've waited long enough! The city will kill us!"

Valkoinen nodded his mask in agreement. "We must protect the people," he implored. "We cannot retake the Green City if only a handful survive." He pointed to a small rise in the land to his right where several dozen refugees were preparing to fight with bows and crossbows. "Vorst is there. Join her," he commanded. "The Alabaster Order will defend the front line. We must only hold long enough allow the people to escape. Azuria will not send her soldiers into the wilderness to chase us."

Melkora nodded and took off at a sprint for the archers. She wasn't sure what use she would be with a bow, but she was determined to live through the day no matter what was asked of her.

Ten

"RUN THESE HEATHEN beasts into the wilds where they belong!" Zerren shouted from the top of Azuria's largest gatehouse. Below him, hundreds of men cheered in reply, and the heavy portcullis separating them from Vrysinoch's faithful began to rise. Although Azuria's standing army was rather small, thousands of Druaka's followers had turned into an angry mob hungry for blood. Zerren had always been charismatic, and turning the mob into a makeshift militia had been easy.

Instead of his customary blue robe, Zerren left his chest bare and wore only a simple pair of linen trousers. His golden chain of office still swung loosely around his neck—a heavy reminder of Druaka's brutal defeat.

Zerren turned and looked eastward at the huddled mass of deserters who had sided against Azuria in her time of need. He spat. "Valkoinen..." he muttered with a voice full of disgust.

"Zerren!" Valkoinen harshly whispered, appearing directly behind his brother with an almost inaudible pop.

The priest whirled and pointed a finger at Valkoinen's chest. "You!" he bellowed. "Traitor! Why have you forsaken Druaka? Why did you turn your back on Azuria? On me!" He let his rage overtake his actions and swung at Valkoinen, connecting with nothing but air.

Instantly, Valkoinen shifted a foot to his left and reappeared. "I forsake nothing, brother," he said calmly.

Zerren recovered from his overbalanced and clumsy attack with a snarl, but did not lash out a second time. "What do you call it then?" He spread his arms out wide to encompass the destruction Vrysinoch's statue had wrought upon the city.

"It is not our war, brother," Valkoinen said. "Azuria does not need this bloodshed."

Zerren scoffed. He grabbed the chain around his neck fiercely and yelled. "I cannot stand for such heresy! You've cast your lot with the wrong god, Valkoinen. Now you must be punished!"

Valkoinen shook his mask slowly, a gesture born more of disappointment than denial. "There doesn't need to be any further conflict," he explained. He turned back to the eastern horizon and lifted a hand toward the fleeing refugees. "We will leave in peace."

Seeing Valkoinen's back as a weakness, Zerren rushed at his brother. He swung again, trying to knock the man from the gatehouse parapet, but hit only air for the second time. Faster than the priest could perceive, Valkoinen appeared directly behind him and used Zerren's momentum to force him halfway over the ledge.

Zerren yelped and tried to pull himself back, but Valkoinen held him fast with an iron grip. Commanding a physical presence beneath his robes was incredibly difficult, but Valkoinen had spent years mastering the technique. The edge of the stone parapet dug into Zerren's exposed stomach hard enough to draw a thin line of blood. "I will kill you!" The priest growled with what little air remained in his lungs.

Valkoinen laughed. "You are in no position to make such threats," he whispered, leaning down to Zerren's ear. He bent the helpless man further over the ledge, holding Zerren by the back of his head and forcing him to look at the ground.

"Druaka!" the priest wheezed.

With his alabaster mask close enough to touch Zerren's face, Valkoinen flicked the chain from his brother's neck and watched it plummet to the ground. "Druaka does not hear you," he uttered.

In a flash, Valkoinen ripped his brother away from the ledge and threw him to the base of the parapet. "Do not make me regret allowing you to live."

Before Zerren could recover his breath enough to speak, Valkoinen stepped through the Void and vanished.

The rattled priest turned back to the mob beneath him and composed himself. The portcullis was fully raised, and the men eagerly awaited Zerren's command. Although he was not a general and had never had much to do with the military, Zerren was well-respected — Azuria had turned to him to lead her sons in this holy war.

Zerren thought of his brother's cryptic threats and shook his head. "Push them into the wilds! Kill all who do not fight!" he shouted. Almost instantly, the command filtered through the crowd and the hastily assembled militia flooded through the gate.

"Such a shame," Zerren spat, grinding his knuckles into the parapet. "We could have been kings! We could have built a dynasty together!" With such a formidable alliance as the Alabaster Order backed by Druaka's church, Azuria surely would have fallen into Zerren's grasp. In that moment, with the sound of the men passing underneath him, Zerren saw his dreams of political power slipping through his fingers. Druaka's defeat in the arena meant the magistrates' hold over the city had solidified, and there was nothing Zerren could do to prevent it. Pushing out the rebels would help recover his reputation, but he feared that nothing would ever restore it.

IT TOOK A long time for the mob to move under the gatehouse. The area was large enough for twenty men to pass through at once, but their homemade arms and armor made progress painfully slow. On the other side of the gate, Zerren knew there would not be much of a battle. The soon-to-be-refugees wanted nothing more than to flee the city and given another day to organize, they would likely leave of their own accord.

With a tinge of disgrace, Zerren descended to the ground to search for his golden chain of office. The meager light did not help him much, but he plucked the precious necklace from the tall grass before long. Still awkwardly bare-chested, Zerren held the chain in his hands and watched the mob run past him.

"Where are you, Druaka?" he prayed. Perhaps it was a trick of the wind, but a faint whisper found its way to Zerren's ear.

"I'm listening!" he cried, turning frantically about and searching for the origin of the reply. "Druaka!"

I am here... Zerren heard, although he saw nothing.

"Wait—" he gasped, trying to latch onto the sound as though it was a leaf fluttering in the breeze. Suddenly, the metal between his fingers began to glow and burn his flesh. Zerren yelped and tried to jump away from the golden chain, but some unseen force kept it in his hands.

The fire grew and Zerren shouted in distress, drawing the attention of a score of nearby men. They approached the flailing priest to offer their help, but as soon as they neared him, Zerren's arms burst into violent flame.

"Someone get a bucket of water!" one of them called. The man, a veteran of the city guard and one of the only real soldiers in the group, ran and tackled Zerren to the ground. He rolled on top of the priest to try and smother the flames, but it only took seconds for the heat to start turning his armor bright red.

Several of the others threw their cloaks across Zerren's unmoving body, but nothing could quench the magical fire.

"What's happening?" a young man with a shoddy pike asked, his voice shaking with fear.

"I don't know," the first said. He lifted a hand to his brow to shield his eyes from the brilliant light. "He just," the man stammered, not believing what he had seen. "He just burst into flames."

After a moment, the flames began to die down to embers, revealing nothing but a smoldering heap of ash where Zerren had once been. "What should we—" one of the men asked, but he was cut off by a violent screech before he could finish.

From the ashes, a ghostly blue hand emerged, followed quickly by the rest of Zerren's now incorporeal form. His body, if it could be so called, was naked and covered in strange, shifting symbols and etched images of ravens. When he fully emerged from the ground and stood, the once average sized man towered above the others.

Zerren whirled his fiery visage from one man to the next, his eyes burning with divine intensity. "Druaka has made me a champion," he told them at once. His voice shook with raw, uncontrollable power. "Ohra!" he called to the ground.

Some of the men took a few hesitant steps backward.

"Ohra!" Zerren shouted again.

"She's dead," one of the men stammered, but his voice cracked with fear and obscured his words.

Zerren bent low and placed a hand on the ground. "Ohra!" he called a third time. At his command, another shimmering, blue hand reached forth from the ground and took hold of his own. With a mighty pull, Zerren brought Ohra's fiery ghost up from the ground to stand by his side, Dalviné sheathed in her hand.

The woman's appearance dissolved the fear all around them. Some of them whooped like they did in the arena. "Lead us!" they shouted, suddenly filled with inspiration.

Ohra stepped forward and drew her ghostly sword from its scabbard of fire on her back. She looked to Zerren and nodded. "We kill them all!" Her war cry washed over the nearby men like a tidal wave of magical energy they could not resist.

The two apparitions charged eastward, the crowd following closely on their heels. When they reached the bulk of the panicked refugees, several skirmishes had already broken out, and dozens of refugees and civilians were already dead.

Zerren motioned for Ohra to follow him to a small rise not far from an abandoned farmhouse where they could properly observe the battle unfolding and select where to strike. "Do you see my brother?" the priest growled. Try as he might, he could not identify Valkoinen among the chaos.

"There!" Ohra lifted a translucent hand. She pointed to a small clump of men closing in on a figure wearing a white robe and mask. As they watched, the man blinked out of existence temporarily, re-appearing a split second later behind a man with a dagger in his hand.

"It is not him," Zerren said with confidence. The white-robed figure struck the man's back with his dagger, killing him quickly, and vanished again. Before long, a handful of the mob had been re-duced to a bloody ring of corpses surrounding the solitary member of the Alabaster Order.

"How do you know?" Ohra asked. She searched for other flashes of white among the chaos.

Zerren scoffed. "My brother is too good for such mundane kill-ing. He will use magic, not a sword or dagger."

"He does not wield Druaka's magic," Ohra spat. In her days as an arena fighter, she had fought several self-proclaimed mages — and she had never lost. "His magic is an affront to our god," she continued. "I've been killing heretics like him for years."

"Go," Zerren told her. "Find Valkoinen and kill him." With a determined nod, the ghostly woman lowered her sword and ran into the fray.

"I do not want to be the one who faces him," Zerren whispered. Deep in his gut, he knew his brother was stronger than anyone else he had ever met. The grim memory of Gideon slaughtering men like wheat before a scythe flashed unwelcome through his head, and Zerren had to correct himself. "Perhaps there is one stronger," he caught himself saying, despite the hopelessness the words brought.

Give me power, he prayed, shoving the unwanted thoughts as far from his mind as possible. *Make me your instrument and I will send a river of heretics into your insatiable maw!*

For perhaps the first time in his life, Zerren could truly *feel* Druaka's presence at his side. The ghostly priest smiled, letting a sinister laugh escape his lips like a madman. "Yes," he hissed, setting his feet in motion toward the nearest group of combatants. "We kill them all!"

Zerren fell upon a small group of fleeing refugees with blazing speed. The former citizens of Azuria were far from soldiers, and they shrieked in disorganized panic. To Zerren's left, Ohra moved her ghostly sword in a vicious arc that severed one man in half at the waist. The priest dug his incorporeal hands through the air and latched onto something solid in the realm of magic. With a powerful turn of his wrist, he brought the congealed magic into the material plane and flung it at the nearest refugees where it exploded into fire.

Zerren couldn't keep himself from laughing. Killing infidels was Druaka's sacred work—and Zerren, for once, was incredibly good at it. Everywhere he looked, refugees screamed and rolled through the grass in a pathetic effort to extinguish the magical fire eating away their flesh. Before most of them could crawl more than a pace, Ohra leapt amongst the flames with her blade swinging fiercely.

"There!" Zerren yelled. He saw a white robe flash just beyond a small rise in the land and reached out magically to the robe's wearer. The mere fact that his mental probe was not immediately repulsed told him the Alabaster Order member was not his brother.

Ohra turned and followed Zerren's pointing finger to the spot, cutting a refugee's back open wide as she ran. On the other side of the rise, the heretics had formed a makeshift defense. A handful of strong men formed a meager wall of shoddy spears and farm implements in front of three white robes.

Zerren summoned another ball of fire to his fingertips and hurled it forward, but the missile blinked out of existence before it reached the men. Barely a pace ahead of him, Ohra charged with her sword held high and crashed through the refugees. To their credit, the men in white mounted a respectable defense. Wherever Ohra's blade was about to slice through flesh, the Alabaster Order blinked the weapon temporarily into the Void, letting it reappear harmlessly on the opposite side of a body. But the three robed men were only acolytes. Their skillful defense faltered within moments.

Ohra swung her sword from left to right in front of her, an attack that would've gutted a farmer, but the top half of her blade ceased to exist. Predicting the Void-based defense, Ohra stopped Dalviné just short of the man's left hip. When the acolytes' concentration failed and they released her blade back to the physical world, it materialized inside the poor farmer. Ohra laughed and wrenched the blade free in a shower of gore.

The cowardly refugees broke rank and started to run. Zerren shifted his attention to his brother's white-clad henchmen and brought fire to both of his hands. He reached forward and flames spewed from his hands hot enough to forge armor. Courageously, the acolytes held their ground against the torrent of fire and used their magic to transport the fire back into the Void before it touched them. Zerren began walking forward, pushing his stream of fire closer and closer, and the acolytes could not hold.

Zerren did not know if the acolytes died when their robes burned to ash and scattered in the wind, but he did not care. They were gone. Behind him, Azuria's soldiers had reached the back of the refugees and had begun their slaughter. Screams filled the air in every direction—some of victory and jubilation, more of death and agony.

"READY," VORST WHISPERED with her squeaky goblin accent. Melkora crouched with her knees pressed painfully into the rocky soil and waited. On either side of them, several dozen men and women held small hunting bows and waited for the command to shoot.

"Why couldn't they just let us leave?" Melkora whispered to herself. She watched helplessly as an entire family of refugees was run down by spears and swords. The mob wasn't particularly well-armed, but the refugees had nothing.

Vorst let out a deep breath and closed her eyes to steady her nerves. She rested her small crossbow against the soil and waited patiently. As she hoped, the men lowered their guard as they advanced toward the hidden line of archers. When they were almost over the rise, Vorst loosed her bolt into the lead man's skull, instantly killing him. "Now!" she screamed.

The refugees yelled and sent a brutal volley of arrows and bolts hurtling into their attackers, cutting their number by half in an instant. "Fall back!" Melkora commanded. She tossed her bow aside and drew Roisin from her side. The archers scrambled back to a secondary position, but Melkora charged forward. With the advantages of surprise and sheer ferocity bolstering her strength, she whirled and leapt through the remaining men like a dancer slashing through silk. Most of the wounds she managed to inflict were superficial, but Roisin's poison made even the most cursory scratch fatal in less than a minute.

Vorst directed the amateur archers to their second position where most of their ammunition waited. As a group, they reloaded and prepared for a second volley, but they were too late—Melkora skittered back to them in an instant with a wake of dead and dying soldiers at her back.

"There will be more," Melkora said evenly. "We must be ready."

Suddenly, a burst of flame crashed into their small earthworks, roasting two of the archers caught in the blast. As the smoke cleared, Zerren and Ohra appeared amidst the dead only a few paces away.

"Valkoinen!" Melkora shouted in desperation. "We have to run!"

Across the grassy, smoke-filled battlefield, Valkoinen's voice boomed like thunder. "Enough!" he commanded, suddenly appearing between Melkora and the two ghostly figures about to destroy her. His white robes shined motionless like a beacon of peace surrounded by chaos. He turned, regarding his brother with an emotionless mask of stoic alabaster, and pointed. "You will let these people leave," he continued.

Valkoinen's voice was so loud it caused Melkora to yelp in pain. Nearby men grabbed their ears and fell to their knees like cowering dogs before a wrathful owner.

To his left, Valkoinen extended a hand and somehow, Melkora knew it was meant for her. Quietly, she rose from the ground and slipped her fingers over Valkoinen's glove.

"We are ghosts," Zerren said with an unexpected burst of confidence. "You cannot kill us, brother. You can only delay the inevitable."

"You are right," Valkoinen responded, letting his voice fall slightly in volume. "I cannot kill you here."

Melkora's heart sank in her chest. Her bloodstained hand throbbed, but she knew Roisin's poison was useless against them.

"Be strong," Valkoinen whispered so only Melkora could hear. "Find Gravlox. Do not falter."

Another violent crack of thunder rolled forth from Valkoinen's white mask that tore the ground beneath him asunder. Melkora grit her teeth and held onto his hand as hard as she could, but when the thunder ceased, she was alone.

"Hello?" she called tentatively into a strange place oddly reminiscent of an underground cavern lit by crackling flames. A sinking feeling in the pit of her stomach confirmed her fears—she was alone in the Void.

Eleven

"**W**HAT YOU FAIL to remember, brother, is that while I cannot kill you on the grass outside Azuria, I can remove you from existence here in the Void." Valkoinen stepped forward and pulled his mask from his face, letting the stiff breeze caress his skin for the first time in years.

The two brothers stood on a small stone platform somewhere high above Azuria. Zerren steadied himself and pushed down a wave of nausea. "You're no better than me here, Little Val," he taunted with a sinister grin. "We're both mortals once more."

Valkoinen pushed the hood of his robe off his head and ran a hand through his shaggy blonde hair. He smiled and when he spoke, his voice sounded human and full of vitality, exactly as it had been before he had become the Master of the Alabaster Order. "You speak the truth," he said, almost jovially. "And when you die in the Void, Druaka cannot find your spirit. Even Vrysinoch cannot travel here. The Void is beyond the realms of gods and men." Despite the circumstances, Zerren still flinched at the mention of Vrysinoch's name.

"When you die here," Valkoinen continued unabated, "you simply cease to be."

Zerren was unshaken. The priest gazed at his brother with hatred — never in all his life had he felt such vile emotion stir within his mind. The platform on which he stood, a mere image of reality lost somewhere in the endless Void, was only slightly larger than a small house. It wouldn't take much to sprint across the stone and knock Valkoinen over the edge to his death.

"You betrayed us all," Zerren replied, slowing placing one foot in front of the other to lessen the distance between them. He hoped Valkoinen would not notice his subtlety. "Why do you support these newcomers and their forsaken eagle-god? What do you gain? What does Azuria gain?"

For once, Valkoinen's slow response was due to his own mental deliberations and not the inherent difficulties of speaking without a physical body. "Perhaps it is time for a change," he said at last. "Azuria was never meant to live without both of her gods. Vrysinoch's return might set our city on a new path, one that leads toward unity and prosperity, not tepid hopelessness."

"Hopelessness?" Zerren scoffed. "Don't be absurd. Druaka's reign has been peaceful for hundreds of years. Azuria's harbor bustles with trade, the farmers haven't had a drought in over a decade, and there hasn't even been a war since before we were born!" He pointed an accusing finger at his brother's chest. "*You* brought this chaos upon Azuria! *Your* carelessness awakened the statue and killed Druaka's champion! *You*, Valkoinen, are the corruption which must be incised from the city."

Valkoinen knew his brother would try to kill him, but Zerren's wild charge still took him by surprise. In an instant, Valkoinen crashed to the ground with his back against the cold stone, Zerren straddling his torso. While neither man was a trained fighter, the priest was simply taller and stronger than Valkoinen had ever been.

Punch after punch slammed into Valkoinen's face. He tried to arch his back and turn from the blows, but Zerren had him pinned. The priest pulled his fist back for another mighty strike. Valkoinen attempted to lift his right arm over his face in defense, but blood from his forehead obscured his vision and Zerren's fist crashed into his jaw like thunder. Valkoinen groaned and spat several of his teeth onto the stone platform.

"Brother," Valkoinen whispered through his broken mouth.

Zerren, panting and clutching his bloody hand, leaned backward. "What?" he snarled. Slowly, Zerren got to his feet and started pushing Valkoinen over the edge of the platform.

"Brother," the bloody man repeated. His face oozed blood from a myriad of cuts, and the few teeth left in his mouth were jagged and pointing in painfully unnatural directions.

Zerren used his feet to slide his brother closer to the edge.

Valkoinen's upper chest hung freely into the chasm of the Void, and his head lolled weakly from side to side.

Inexplicably, Valkoinen began to laugh. "Brother!" he called again, spitting up a glob of blood as he spoke.

Zerren growled in frustration and pushed his brother further over the stone. "You crazy bastard," he yelled. "Just die!"

Valkoinen lifted a hand as he laughed. "You don't understand, brother," he said weakly.

"I'm done with your tricks and riddles," Zerren snarled. "You're dead."

"Oh?" Valkoinen questioned with far more mirth than anyone in his situation should have had. "Have you ever been in the Void before, dear brother?" he asked.

Zerren pushed him again until the only thing keeping Valkoinen aloft was Zerren's body weight on his pelvis.

Valkoinen smiled. "If you kill me, how will you return to the material plane? How will you escape?"

The priest's eyes went wide. "Lies," he muttered. "You cannot fool me any longer, Val. We aren't children any more. I can see through your lies."

Valkoinen squirmed and pushed against the edge of the platform to move his body further over the edge. "When I brought you here, you were already dead—a ghost driven by Druaka's rage.

675

Now, your body and soul are together once more in a place where Druaka cannot find you, and you do not possess the power or knowledge to escape."

With a howl of anger directed more at himself than anyone else, Zerren shoved his brother from the ledge.

Valkoinen's laughs echoed for a long moment after he crashed into the ground and died.

MELKORA HAD SEARCHED for hours through the dimly lit underground world of the Void. "What am I supposed to do?" she cried in exasperation. She sank to the ground and rubbed the bottoms of her feet with weary hands. The cave structure, if it even was such a thing, was seemingly limitless. Everywhere she looked, Melkora saw the same thing: an endless stone ceiling parallel to an endless stone floor, all lit by some unseen crackling flames.

Searching her mind in desperation, she tried to recall every scrap of information Valkoinen had told her of the Void, but none of it made sense. "Where do I find him?" she yelled. Her voice echoed for several moments before dying unanswered.

"Gravlox!" she called. Her voice was hoarse.

She wasn't sure if eating was necessary in the Void, but her stomach begged for food and there wasn't a morsel in sight. Defeated, Melkora kicked off her boots and collapsed like a beaten dog.

As the hours crawled by, Melkora wept until she had no tears left. When sleep finally found her on the rough stone floor, it brought no respite.

WITHOUT THEIR LEADERS spurring them onward, the crazed mob soon found the thrill of killing unarmed citizens losing its luster. Vorst fired a bolt into the back of a retreating man and let her adrenaline fade. The air smelled of death, blood, and all the horrors of war. It made her sick.

Deep within her mind, Vorst felt the pull of Kanebullar Mountain calling her eastward. "This is not my fight," she caught herself saying aloud before she fully understood the meaning of her words. With a shake of her head, she pushed her longing far from her thoughts and discounted it as remnant of hopelessness. When she glanced at the corpses surrounding her, she couldn't help but think of Kanebullar Mountain as her only option.

"Where is she —" a man's voice suddenly startled Vorst from behind. She whirled and reached for a bolt, but was glad to see Gideon standing several paces away with a sword strapped to his back.

"Gideon!" she yelled as she bounded toward him. "How are you walking? You should be," she didn't want to say 'dead', but no other word came to her mind.

"I know," Gideon responded solemnly. He searched the carnage of the small rise like a wolf hunting rabbits. "Ohra?" he asked, not taking his eyes from the bodies.

Vorst shook her head. "She was here," she explained. "But she was only a ghost. When Valkoinen and Melkora vanished, the two ghosts did as well."

Gideon mulled over her words. "Away? To where?" he asked.

"I do not know," Vorst replied sullenly. "They vanished."

Gideon clutched his side and cringed. A huge bruise had spread over his ribs, and his left wrist still felt broken, but he was not one to sit idly when people needed his help. "We need to reorganize," he stated. "We can't save the people if they run in fear."

"Do you think they will attack again?" Vorst asked. The refugees were in terrible disarray. Another round of fighting would shatter them.

With a sigh, Gideon turned his head back to the survivors. "We can't take any chances," he said. "Unless Vrysinoch returns."

Gideon and Vorst pushed through the back of the refugees, urging them forward and helping the wounded regain their feet. After an hour of desperate reorganization, the meager troop had assembled roughly two miles from Azuria's gates. Tired, terrified, and some with wounds they would not survive, the refugees looked eastward in search of hope.

At their head, the four remaining members of the Alabaster Order stood next to Gideon and Vorst without saying a word. Their white robes flapped noisily in the stiff morning breeze.

"Your master is in the Void?" Gideon asked. The nearest man nodded his white mask. "And it does not matter if we move from here? Valkoinen can find us?" Gideon questioned further. He hated the idea of leaving Azuria behind without Valkoinen, Melkora, and Gravlox safely returned, but he saw no other option.

Again, the man in white silently nodded.

With a heavy sigh, Gideon set his feet in motion eastward. The men and women at his back followed his lead without question, and a deep, intrinsic knowledge of the path once again became clear in Gideon's mind. "Vrysinoch will guide us home," Gideon said to no one in particular. Talonrend, overrun with orcs and minotaurs as it was, still felt more like home than Azuria.

Twelve

"**W**OMAN," A VOICE called hesitantly through the darkness. It sounded strained and distant, like someone trying to whisper from too far away. "Woman," it beckoned again. The voice was barely audible.

After several agonizing moments of silence, the voice spoke again with increasing urgency. "Woman! You should not be here."

Melkora's eyes snapped open. Her heart raced. "Where—" all at once, Melkora remembered what had happened outside Azuria. Her heart sank, and nausea crept up the back of her throat. "The Void," she stated.

"Leave!" the disembodied voice begged.

"Hello?" Melkora replied. She tried to see through the inky black surrounding her, but could only make out dim patches of flickering light dancing at the edges of her vision. "Valkoinen?"

After a long moment of silence, the voice returned with vigor. "You know him? Please! He can find us!"

"He came with me," she stopped, trying to remember if she had seen Valkoinen since she had entered the Void. "I don't know," she stammered. "He took me—brought me—here. I don't think he came with me, but I don't know."

Another long silence passed in darkness. "Someone is here," the voice finally said. "Someone strong. It must be Valkoinen."

"Where are you?" Melkora asked. She turned and reached out her hand, but touched nothing.

"Everywhere," came the reply. "But I've lost my body."

Melkora shook her head. "I need to find my friend," she said, changing the subject to hopefully avoid any further riddles.

A few minutes of silence passed. "There are ways to bring people back from the Void," the voice explained. "It will be very difficult." The voice escalated to a powerful, urgent command. "You must not die in the Void if you wish to return to the material world. Injuries received here have dire consequences."

"Injuries? What *is* this place? I haven't seen *anything* yet that could hurt me."

"Step forward," the voice told her in a reassuring manner. "Come out of the tent and see for yourself."

Melkora kept her arms in front of her and began moving. After a few paces, her fingers brushed against a thick curtain of roughspun cloth that made her jump. Groping through the darkness, she found the edge of the curtain and pulled it slowly aside, letting her eyes adjust to the painfully bright light on the other side.

Somehow, Melkora found her head poking out of covered wagon. The smell of blood hung heavily in the air and made her cringe. In front of her, a tall orc casually picked through the pockets of a human corpse.

"The refugee train," Melkora whispered, realizing exactly where she was. "Corshana!" she yelled. The orc jerked its green head in her direction, and Melkora stifled a gasp of surprise.

Can you see me? Am I real? she thought with a sudden, debilitating rush of fear. As if in response, the orc tilted its head ever so slightly, rose to its feet, and snatched a barbed club from the ground still covered in blood.

Melkora didn't know what to do. "Hello?" she hesitantly called.

The orc snarled. Slowly, with measured steps uncharacteristically calm for an orc, the beast approached her. When he was only a few feet in front of the wagon, Melkora's resolve broke, and she ran. Her feet hit the ground in a flurry of panic, kicking dirt behind her like a charging horse.

To Melkora's immediate dismay, the orc seemed to finally recognize her for what she was and leapt after her, bellowing a guttural war cry.

Melkora ran. She had left her boots in the strange, cave-like part of the Void she had first entered, and she deeply regretted it. Broken sticks and sharp stones attacked her feet with every step, but she couldn't slow her pace—the orc was nearly upon her.

Luckily, Melkora's smaller body gave her an advantage once she entered the trees south of the refugee caravan. There wasn't enough foliage to call it a forest, but the scraggly pines and maples slowed the charging orc enough for her to build some distance.

Blood flowed from dozens of cuts on her feet as Melkora entered a small clearing. She turned, ripping Roisin from its sheath. She squared her shoulders and used the split second of calm before the orc was upon her to steady her breathing.

The orc screamed and lunged through several branches with its club held high. Trying to use her small stature to her advantage, Melkora fell to her knees and stabbed upward. The violent motion sent a jolt of pain through the old wound in her side. The orc staggered, caught fully in the chest by Melkora's blade, but the small weapon did nothing to slow the beast's momentum.

In a heap of flailing limbs, the two combatants crashed into the ground. The orc's immense weight crushed the air from Melkora's lungs and nearly shattered her ribcage. She slammed violently into the ground, turning her vision into a swirling morass of grey mixed with various shades of blood. Before she could think enough to draw breath, the orc was pummeling her with its heavy fists.

It will die, Melkora tried to inwardly tell herself. Roisin's insidious poison was certainly potent enough to end the orc's life. Another vicious strike bashed the thoughts from her head.

Hit after hit fell upon Melkora's bloody face until her consciousness expired.

"WHERE WERE YOU during the battle?" Gideon asked with a heavy heart. Behind him, several hundred refugees walked solemnly along like lost livestock. In the chaos outside Azuria, most of them had abandoned the belongings they couldn't easily carry, and the entire group severely lacked food and water. To his left, Vorst never took her eyes from her own feet.

With footsteps heavy enough to split stone, Vrysinoch's marble statue led the small caravan ceaselessly. "Where were you?" Gideon repeated. He raised his voice to be sure it reached the eagle-god's ears.

Vrysinoch did not slow when he replied. "I was watching for my sister," he stated.

"That isn't good enough," Gideon spat. He rubbed a sore area on the side of his neck which had not fully healed. He knew Vrysinoch had not entirely healed him, and it wasn't due to any lack of power on the god's part—Gideon's remaining wounds were personal, cutting far deeper than Ohra's blade ever could. With a smirk, Gideon reached behind his back and touched the familiar hilt. It was strange to have Nevidal returned to him, but there were certain things Gideon did not want to question.

Vrysinoch's voice boomed over the rolling hills and shook leaves from the nearby trees. "When my sister appears, you will all die!" he shouted without turning back. Gideon shielded himself from the intensity of the voice, but it did no good. His teeth chattered in his head.

"You will not protect us?" Gideon shouted back. "I should have figured as much from such a fickle god." He remembered all the times he had felt abandoned by Vrysinoch — the memories made his stomach churn and filled his mouth with a sour taste. His relationship with the eagle-god had never been more than tenuous, but even Gideon found it difficult to believe that Vrysinoch would leave hundreds of his followers to die horrible deaths.

Vrysinoch heaved a stony sigh that sent nearby birds flittering into the air. "Perhaps," the statue began slowly, "I will not be able to protect you all," he said. "Have you considered such a possibility?"

Gideon shook his head, but he knew the statue paid him no head. While he had always assumed Vrysinoch's inconsistent support was a result of his own lacking faith, he had never entertained the notion that Vrysinoch was not omnipotent. The idea made him shudder.

"The priests," Gideon started abruptly, seeking clarification.

"Priests know nothing," Vrysinoch said before Gideon could finish his line of thought. "When I led the first refugees from Azuria to the Green City, the priests destroyed their history books. They wiped my sister's name from their teachings."

Gideon sneered. "Save your sermon for the others. A history lesson won't protect us when the time comes."

Like a mountain rumbling under a landslide, Vrysinoch turned and regarded Gideon with stony, lifeless eyes. "Arrogant fool," the statue whispered in disgust. "Why should I risk my immortal soul to save you and your kind? Why is your species worthy of survival?"

For the first time in a very long while, Gideon was speechless. Several venomous retorts urged his mouth to speak, but he couldn't find the will to voice them. *You created humanity!* he practically yelled within the confines of his mind.

Vrysinoch was quick to respond. *I have created more than just your ungrateful flesh and blood,* the god magically hissed through Gideon's skull. *Do not assume your race is meant to survive.*

Gideon stopped walking and let the rest of the refugees catch up to him. When he felt thoroughly lost in the middle of the pack, he began moving once more. A few of the men recognized him from the arena and knew who he was, but Gideon let their questions and praise fall away until they lost interest.

Several hours after nightfall, the group stopped to sleep and made their camp. They groaned and grumbled, picking meekly at the last of the food they carried. Toward the east, Gideon could see Vrysinoch's silhouette towering above the low hills and blocking out the stars.

When the refugees awoke in the morning, animals roasted on spits above magical fires. "You give us food," Gideon said quietly to himself, "yet you do not think humanity is worthy of your protection." Despite his pride telling him to hunt and forage for his meals, Gideon bit into a nearby haunch of oily meat that fell apart in his mouth.

"Praise Vrysinoch! Food!" a woman cried from another fire. Gideon turned his back in her direction, took another bite, and threw the rest of his breakfast into the flames.

MELKORA GASPED AND spat a warm glob of blood onto the leaves beside her face. She was alive. Painfully, she tried to open her eyes, but they had swollen shut. She kept as still as she could manage and listened, hoping against all odds to *not* hear any orcs coming her way. Thankfully, the Void was deathly still.

After a long while, Melkora found the strength to begin investigating her surroundings. She groped through leaves, dirt, and pools of her own blood until she found the base of a nearby tree. With all the strength she could muster, Melkora pulled herself to the tree's trunk and got her shoulders off the ground. When she was finally in a seated position, she brought her left hand to her face to pull the swollen skin away from one of her eyes in order to see.

The sunlight was piercing, but the gruesome sight in front of her brought a smile to her battered lips. The orc, one of the largest beings Melkora had ever seen, was dead. Blood covered the beast's unmoving chest. Melkora knew most of it was hers.

When she tried to stand, a dizzying wave of sickness forced her back to the ground where she retched violently. With every heave, she could feel at least a handful of broken ribs tearing through the inside of her chest. She thought first of her garish spear wound at the hands of an orc some months ago, but then her mind recalled the horrendous evisceration Ohra had experienced on the sand of Azuria's arena.

It could always be worse, she told herself.

Suddenly, a distant voice reached her ears on a gentle breeze. She couldn't be sure, but Melkora thought it came from the destroyed caravan. With a great effort, she got to her feet and used the tree for support. Her ribs hurt more than she could describe, sending burning waves of pain through her entire body, but her skull was far worse. It was a wonder the orc hadn't crushed her eye sockets through the back of her brain.

With one hand clutched to her side and the other gingerly keeping her swollen skin from entirely blocking her vision, Melkora started to hobble toward the noise. "If it is another orc," she mumbled to herself, "let him kill me quickly."

It took her several minutes just to reach the next tree and collapse in agony against it, but she made progress. The voice, or voices, grew somewhat louder, but Melkora couldn't be certain it wasn't just her broken mind playing tricks on her. She had heard such stories before—elderly people hearing the voices of long lost loved ones as they took their last breath—but she had never believed them.

As she reached the next tree and grew closer to the commotion, her heart fluttered. "Corshana!" she tried to gasp, but her shattered chest would not let her speak. In the deepest reaches of her soul, she recognized her daughter's voice. It was distant and shaking, but it was there.

Melkora fought against the pain in her body as hard as she could, shambling haphazardly through the brush of the sparse forest, until she finally came into view of the wagons. *Gideon?* Her mind struggled to comprehend the scene before her.

Gideon stood before the front of a wagon and cleaned blood from one of his axes. Beside him, another man dressed as a paladin shook his head. The two men each spoke once before turning quickly to leave, but Melkora's mind could not fully grasp their words.

When she found enough strength left in her limbs to crawl into the small clearing, Melkora wished she hadn't. Lying gruesomely against a partially burned wagon, Corshana's corpse stared blankly back at her. Her head had been gashed open and a myriad of other wounds covered her body. *But her voice!* Melkora wanted to shriek. *I heard her voice! She was alive!*

Melkora took her hand from her eye and let her vision turn to black once more. She fell to the ground at her dead daughter's feet, too weak to even wail in anguish. *She was alive!* her mind screamed over and over. *Gideon! The axe!* Her mind rushed so quickly she could barely decipher her own thoughts.

After a panic-filled moment of hysteria, Melkora's mind settled on one grave thought before her consciousness faded: *Gideon killed my daughter.*

Thirteen

"I HEARD YOU lost someone in the Void," a woman's voice hesitantly asked from behind a stark white mask. Vorst jolted from her ceaseless trudging and shook the surprise off her face. It had been weeks since anyone had spoken to her. Melkora was gone. Gravlox was gone. Without friends or kin, Vorst had fallen to the rear of the small column like a lost child. She had sought out Gideon once, but the brooding man had barely noticed her. He seemed intent on walking silently in the shadow of the statue until they reached Talonrend.

Vorst cleared her throat. "My husband," she said eagerly in her native language, forgetting to use the human tongue.

The woman in white stopped and tilted her mask to the side.

"My husband!" Vorst clarified, using words the human could presumably understand. The thought of Gravlox being gone forever filled her already troubled mind with despair.

After a moment, the woman spoke again. "I'm sorry," she said. "I did not know. I was told," she hesitated, searching for the right words, "I was told there was a woman who vanished with my master."

"Melkora," Vorst stated. "Yes. She is gone."

Another white-robed figure suddenly appeared to the left of the first. With a similarly effeminate voice, the second mysterious human spoke. "We might be able to find her," she said. Despite her hopeful words, her tone remained tepid.

"Who are you?" Vorst asked. "Why do you want to help?"

The woman on the right shook her mask in response. "I do not know my name," she said after a minute or more of silence. "When I first entered the Void, I was not able to find my name, so I returned without it."

"My name is Valge," the other woman interjected. "We are oblivion mages, second only to Master Valkoinen within the Alabaster Order. We might be able to find your friend."

"Not my husband?" Vorst questioned. "Can you find Gravlox?" She felt selfish asking for his safety and not Melkora's, but she could not deny her own desires.

"We have a distinct connection to the Void," Valge continued unfettered. "We can sense the existence of a human woman somewhere, but I'm afraid we do not know of your husband."

"Is he dead?" Vorst muttered. She turned and tried to continue walking, but her feet would not move. As much as she dreaded the woman's answer, she had to hear it.

After a long pause, the mage without a name finally replied. "We do not know for sure," she began slowly, "but we do not believe he is alive." Her words flowed slowly from her mask, as if they themselves were burdened by their grim message.

Vorst let out a weary sigh and rubbed the scar where her little finger used to be.

"We will search for him, along with our lost brethren and your friend," Valge was quick to add.

"How?" Vorst asked. Reluctantly, she picked up her feet and continued to follow the other refugees.

The two mages fell into step beside her. "If she has not died in the Void, she must only be found and returned," one of the women said. Having looked away from the identical mages, Vorst did not know which woman was which. "But we need to know where to begin our search," she continued.

"Valkoinen did not need to take her," Vorst said. She conjured the memory in her mind as she had done a hundred times before.

The two mages thought for a long moment, all the while moving silently at Vorst's side. "We were still inside the city when the battle occurred," one of them stated. "But you are right. Our Master's actions do not make sense."

The second mage lifted her head in what Vorst presumed was excitement. "Perhaps he sent her somewhere, knowing he would never return to show her the way in a more traditional manner."

"He sent her to look for Gravlox!" Vorst joyfully clung to the conclusion. Her strong emotional display starkly contrasted the two women in stoic masks, making Vorst immediately feel uncomposed.

"You might be correct," a mage calmly replied. "What is the most personal thing you know about Melkora?"

Vorst was taken aback by the blunt question. "Umm," she faltered, not knowing how to respond.

"The Void is different to everyone," one of the mages haltingly clarified. Vorst was not sure why the members of the Alabaster Order took so long to speak, but it was apparent that whatever energy fueled the two oblivion mages was waning. "It will be personal to Melkora," the woman finished after a painfully long pause.

Vorst searched her mind for everything she knew about the woman. Sadly, she had to admit to herself that she had not gleaned very much over the months they had travelled together. "She had a family," Vorst said. She remembered the burned corpses they had discovered in Cobblestreet and shook her head. "They are all dead."

The three females walked in heavy silence for several hours before the refugee column halted for the night. Vorst knew there would be plenty of magical food in the morning, but she preferred to scavenge edible tubers and berries from the sparse plains. The earthy, wild flavors reminded her of home, of Kanebullar Mountain. When Vorst gazed intently toward the east, she thought she could just barely see the outline of the great mountain in the distance, but she knew they were still months from Talonrend. Still, Vorst could not shake the image of Kanebullar Mountain from her mind's eye.

When the sun rose in the morning, Vorst realized she had been sitting in the same spot against a tree for hours. Without anything to do but walk and no need for sleep, she was restless at night. Searching for food occupied some of her time, but the lonely hours still tormented her every single night.

With a stretch, Vorst turned back toward the refugee caravan. Fires twirled smoke into the bright morning air, carrying the scent of roasted meat everywhere it went. To her surprise, Vorst saw Gideon standing not far away, conversing with the two women of the Alabaster Order.

One of the mages, Vorst could not tell which, noticed the goblin's arrival and signaled to her with a gloved hand. "We have a plan," she said steadily.

"We can find them?" Vorst responded eagerly, suddenly finding a hopeful spring in her step.

Gideon's expression was enough to answer her question. "Perhaps we can rescue Melkora," the woman in white whispered.

Vorst tried to swallow the ever-present pain in her chest, but it would not budge. "What can I do to help?" she asked meekly. She felt helpless.

"When we reach Talonrend," Gideon began, speaking on the mages' behalf, "you need to take them to Cobblestreet. Find the ruins where her family died." His voice trailed off as if his mind was fixated on something and refused to move.

"I remember where it is," Vorst said. "But what good will it do?"

"If we find where she is in the Void, we might be able to tether her back to this world," the mage interjected.

"I don't understand," Vorst muttered. "What does that mean?"

The woman in white shook her head. Vorst could only guess

what her expression might be behind the alabaster mask. "We can do it," she said. "Trust us."

The second mage looked slightly apprehensive, her mask and robes betraying just enough emotion to tell Vorst they were not entirely confident.

"If we find Melkora," Vorst began hesitantly, "can we look for Gravlox?" She tried to focus on the mages and maintain her composure, but tears streaked her face.

The women took several minutes to respond. "We were in the Void when the fighting outside Azuria began," one of them said. "Gravlox had already entered."

"You would have seen him?" Vorst concluded.

"No," the woman said. Vorst tried to tell the two mages apart by their voices, but she found herself constantly confusing them in her head. "But we would have felt his presence. We would have known he was there," the woman continued.

"He must have escaped on his own!" Vorst shouted. Her mind refused to accept the possibility of Gravlox's death.

The woman shook her head. Although her mask did not change, everyone could hear the anguish behind it. "No one escapes the Void on their own," she said gravely. "No one."

U NDRAKK WALKED THE western top of Terror's Lament with a broad smile. A heavy, brown cloak was draped over his back to keep the chill fall wind from getting to his skin. "I have ruled Broken Sword for almost a year, Sifir," he said to the old priest following closely behind him. Undrakk let his fingers drag casually along the dented parapet, remembering vividly the fight that had won him a kingdom. He came to a section of unrepaired stone where the entire parapet had been blasted from the top of the wall by Qul's metal poles. "You should have seen him fight!" Undrakk mused, talking more to himself than the priest.

"I'm sure it was magnificent, my liege," Sifir obediently replied.

"Qul was a sight to behold. A slow witted creature, surely, but strong as, well," he laughed to himself. "Strong as a minotaur king!"

"Indeed, sire," Sifir said.

Undrakk shook his head. The politics of being a tyrant were tiresome at best. He let out a long sigh. "The praise I receive is nothing but vain pandering," he drifted off into his own thoughts as he moved past another section of wall devastated by Qul's metal poles.

"What's that, my king?"

"Those who fear me tell me only what they believe I wish to

692

hear," he explained, gazing toward the setting sun. "Those who do not fear me perceive me as an equal, and anyone who would be my equal is already dead." He thought of Jan and Keturah, the strange human siblings living in minotaur bodies. "There are but two left who still give me sound advice." While the siblings rarely criticized his ideas, they were slower than all the others to offer him praise.

"What's that you say, my lord?" Sifir offered weakly.

Undrakk whirled on the priest with terrifying fury in his eyes. The man visibly recoiled, falling to his back in the process. Undrakk knew yelling at the man would do no good. The half-orc composed himself and turned back toward the horizon with a wave of his hand. "Do you have the latest scouting report?" he asked impatiently. He couldn't help but smile at his own genius. The clans had protested when he had sent them scouting so far away from the city, but they had found the small human force with relative ease.

The old priest looked aghast for a moment, then hastily flipped through a massive ledger he had been carrying. "A runner returned yesterday morning," he said when he found the correct page. "One of the Wolf Jaw orcs said they saw the human procession make camp less than ten miles from the remains of the previous caravan."

"Their numbers?"

"The same as the last report. Two hundred and fifty-six humans, a single goblin, and—"

"One giant statue of an eagle leading them all," Undrakk finished with a hint of bitterness. No one knew exactly what the huge marble creature was, but it filled Undrakk with trepidation. The half-orc did not like what he did not understand.

"Yes, your majesty," Sifir dutifully confirmed. "Shall I alter the instructions for the next scouting party?"

Undrakk dismissed the idea with a shake of his head. "They will be here within fifty days. We need to continue preparing. Has the Wolf Jaw Clan finished their ballistae?" he asked.

Sifir, still sitting on the stone where he had fallen, sifted through another section of papers. "I believe the final testing shall be done by tonight, your highness."

"Good," Undrakk mused with a sinister grin. "We have had months to prepare," he continued, blatant arrogance lacing his unusual accent. "Even with that monstrous statue, they cannot hope to succeed against us! Several thousand orcs obey my every command!"

"They will perish, sire, of that I have no doubt," Sifir chimed.

Undrakk seethed with violent ire. He hated having Sifir as a servant, but not a single one of the orcs understood simple mathematics enough to handle the scouting reports, and the runic language of the minotaurs was too cumbersome to be dealt with efficiently. In a moment Undrakk considered to have been one of extreme weakness, he had offered the strange human priest a deal: in exchange for the man's unending service, Undrakk would not have the subterranean temple to Vrysinoch sealed or destroyed. The man was eager to fulfill his end of the bargain. Perhaps too eager.

The half-orc slammed his staff into the ground and tried to let his anger dissipate, but the man's overly joyous attitude made his blood boil. He snarled at Sifir, rushing in on the old priest like a cat trapping a mouse against a corner. Sifir gave a soft whimper of surprise and tried to scoot away, but there was nowhere left to go. His back hung precariously over the side of Terror's Lament where Qul's pole had blasted away the parapet.

"You sicken me, old man," Undrakk growled. Sifir could taste his breath.

With an effortless push, the king of Broken Sword sent Sifir hurtling over the edge. The priest let out a terrible scream before hitting the ground sixty feet below with a flourish of robes, scrolls, and loose papers.

Undrakk sighed. He had pushed Sifir from the wall several times before. It never changed anything. The orcs who had first found the strange priest were right—the man could not be injured. Despite Sifir's survival, Undrakk managed a smile. He knew the fall brought the human a measure of unbelievable horror, and that was reward enough.

After a moment of lying nearly motionless on the hard ground, Sifir hobbled to his feet, collected his papers, and shuffled off in the direction of the castle. Undrakk let out another sigh. With a twirl of his staff, he looked back to the west. "Why do you come?" he asked the far off humans. "What do you hope to gain? No one will remember your names. No one will remember your deaths. Broken Sword is mine." He amplified his final word with a bit of magic, secretly hoping the statue so many miles away would hear it and tremble.

GIDEON RUBBED HIS weary feet, looking at his leather boots with disappointment. There were holes in the sole of one and the side of the other had nearly disintegrated. Sadly, there was not a single cobbler among the refugees who could repair them. Perhaps if he had several weeks to acquire, prepare, and tan appropriate leather, he would be able to make a new pair himself, but the task would have to wait. When he thought about it, Gideon realized he had never heard any of the commoners seriously complain of blisters or any of the other woes bound to appear when travelling for so long by foot. He wondered if Vrysinoch's magical food had anything to do with their striking health as he bit into the last morsel of his breakfast.

Vorst had brought him the plump rabbit the day before, as she had done for several weeks, a common result of her nightly hunting trips. When only bones remained of the rabbit and even those had been separated from their savory marrow, Gideon wrestled on his shoddy boots and stood. The day was noticeably cooler than the last; windy, cloudless, and brilliant. In contrast, the plains between Talonrend and Azuria were a seemingly limitless expanse of the same shades of dappled brown and green. Perhaps it was because he had walked the path once before, but Gideon found his monotonous surroundings nearly unbearable.

He tied one of his only possessions, a moth-eaten blanket he had traded two squirrels for, around his waist and set his feet in motion toward the east. A half mile or so ahead of him, Vrysinoch's inexorable statue thundered onward.

After an hour, Vorst appeared at Gideon's side. "Is it ready?" he asked hopefully.

"Yes," she replied. "If they follow the same pattern, the orcs should hit my trap sometime late tonight."

Gideon smiled. "You're sure they don't know you've been watching them?"

Vorst nodded her head vigorously. "Orcs are clumsy. They don't cover their tracks or watch their own backs. They've never seen me."

"Perfect," Gideon responded. "We will camp closer to the woods. When you hear the trap go off, signal me, just like we planned."

Vorst grinned from ear to ear. She had not fought in months, and while she had never considered herself a warrior, the promise of carnage held more than enough appeal to get her blood pumping.

By the time dusk had started to settle in, they were among the toppled wagons and burnt corpses of Talonrend's ill-fated refugee caravan. Vrysinoch halted the group an hour after sunset, perhaps a mile into the scattered field of debris.

Gideon climbed atop an overturned wagon to wait for Vorst's signal. Luckily, the moon was so bright he could see for miles. It was the perfect night to ambush their orcish observers. He heard nothing for several hours, but then suddenly an orcish scream filled with fear and anguish broke through the night like a siren.

Gideon leapt from the wagon top and broke into a sprint toward the woods where he had heard the scream. Vorst had not given her signal—maybe something was wrong, or perhaps the trap was sprung just a moment too soon.

As he ran through the sparse tree line, batting branches from his face and vaulting gnarled roots to keep from tripping, Gideon found a familiar battle hymn creeping onto his lips. The holy symbol tattooed on his shoulder began to grow warm, but with a selfish grunt, he knocked the lyrics from his mind as easily as if they were a branch in his path. He felt the weight of Nevidal slapping against his back with every stride. It was the only strength he needed.

It did not take Gideon long to find the source of the orcish scream. Perhaps half a mile from the toppled wagon, the wounded beast clutched at a massive wound on the side of its face. Vorst had created a tripwire from vines that sent a heavy log smashing into the orc's head. The trap was meant to kill the creature in a single blow, as were several other such traps nearby, to keep the ambush manageably quiet. If the human refugees heard the orcs, the ensuing panic would be nothing short of chaos.

Gideon slammed against a tree to halt his momentum. Twenty feet to his right, Vorst sat atop a branch with her small crossbow aimed at the nearest enemy. Between them, the scouting party, eight uninjured orcs and one nearly dead beast, readied their weapons. They had seen Gideon, but he did not care.

He wanted them to see him.

With a cold, calculated step forward, Gideon unsheathed his sword. "Nevidal," he whispered confidently. Even in his mind, he refused to refer to the weapon as 'Dalviné' as Ohra had. Immediately, his muscles bulged, begging for carnage. He felt his back tighten like a coiled viper. His mind sharpened, and every breath he took filled him with so much energy he feared he would burst.

With a smirk and more self-control than he had ever exerted in battle, Gideon waited for the orcs to come to him. The trees were too densely situated for the tall orcs to come at him all at once in their typical style. Instead, in a rare show of what appeared to be intelligence, a single orc raised its hand. When it did, the others cowed before it.

697

"I will fight your leader," Gideon beckoned, but he knew they would not understand his words. He pointed Nevidal's tip at the orc with its hand raised, issuing the challenge in a language every creature should be able to understand.

Eagerly, the orc seemed to accept. The others parted around the orc, forming into a semicircle of crossed spears. The orc wasn't particularly large by its species' standards, but it possessed bulging muscles like corded wood. Its chest was thicker than most of the nearby trees, and its legs were wider than Gideon's waist. The orc wore simple cloth boots tied to its ankles, a roughspun loincloth, and a necklace of animal teeth that seemed to indicate rank, as none of the others had any similar ornamentation.

For a moment, Gideon's confidence faltered. He recognized the object the orc held as a weapon. Between its meaty, green hands, the creature carried a blacksmith's anvil which had been banded to a massive length of iron-reinforced tree trunk. Gideon figured the entire assembly weighed close to three hundred pounds, if not more, but the orc lifted the weapon above its head with one hand.

Gideon imitated the gesture, lifting Nevidal momentarily over his head, and wondered if he was participating in some sort of orcish salute. Whatever the gesture entailed, it felt strange to show an orc even a scrap of respect. "You killed thousands of innocent women and children," Gideon growled, suddenly feeling more primal than his silent, green-skinned foe. "You have no honor!"

The orc cocked its head to the side slightly, almost with a pondering expression, and took a step forward. Gideon did not hesitate. With a great leap, he stabbed forward from his center with both hands on Nevidal's hilt. Deftly, the orc dropped its strange weapon in a sweeping motion in front of him, easily knocking Gideon's sword aside. When the two hundred pound anvil head hit the ground, it shook the forest floor like a small earthquake.

Gideon saw an opportunity with the orc's weapon low and struck again, bringing Nevidal up toward the sky as quickly as he could. In a flash, the orc reversed its hands and pushed the haft of its weapon forward, pivoting about the anvil head, and trapping Gideon's blade at an awkward angle against his own wrist.

With a grunt, Gideon tried to push back against the orc to free himself, but even Nevidal's magical strength was not enough. The orc leaned harder on its weapon, slowly twisting Gideon's wrist further and further back. The bones and tendons of his wrist screamed in agony, but Gideon could not drop the sword to free himself.

Desperately, Gideon dropped to his knees and tried to roll under the orc's weapon. The maneuver worked, but the orc's weight crushed downward as Gideon moved, snapping his right wrist like a bundle of dry twigs. He yelped in pain as he regained his feet at the orc's side. Using his left hand to stabilize his broken wrist, he swung again, but there was no power behind his strike. The orc easily swatted Gideon's sword to the side.

Behind him, the other orcs cheered, howling for carnage as their leader stalked toward Gideon. Try as he might, Nevidal's magic would not let him transfer the sword to his uninjured arm—not before it ended a life.

Gideon only had one idea left. He backed away from the brawny orc until he felt the hands of another green-skinned beast on his shoulders, pushing him back into the circle. Grimacing from the pain, Gideon spun on his heel as quickly as he could, using Nevidal more like a whip at the end of his broken wrist. The orc behind him never saw the blade until it had slashed more than halfway through its hips.

In an instant, Gideon let his right hand fall from Nevidal's hilt. The weapon's magic dissipated, returning his muscles to their natural state. The dead orc teetered on its feet for a second, just long enough for Gideon to wrap the fingers of his left hand around the hilt and wrench it free in a torrent of blood.

The orcs screamed in fury. Gideon had broken the rules of their duel, and every one of them sought vengeance. Gideon was too close to fight them all. He quickly knocked a spear aside, kicked another orc above the ankle, and darted toward Vorst. Her crossbow thrummed and a small bolt sailed over Gideon's head, striking an orc squarely in the chest.

"Run!" Gideon shouted breathlessly. "To the next trap!"

Vorst darted between the trees, leading Gideon with her steps. In turn, they vaulted a tightly set vine between two trees, but the orc on their heels did not see it. When the beast tripped on the vine, Gideon whirled, decapitating the creature in a single blow.

Together, Gideon and Vorst charged deeper into the woods. Gideon vaulted a rotting tree trunk which Vorst had to climb and splashed down into a gentle stream. Hoping she was concealed, Vorst crouched behind the log to reload her crossbow while Gideon continued several paces forward to the other side of the stream. Two orcs followed closely, their weapons held high.

When the orcs jumped over the log, Vorst fired her crossbow, dropping one of them into the stream. Gideon charged at the second orc, swinging Nevidal furiously in his left hand. He wasn't nearly as delicate or calculating without the use of his sword arm, but he was still faster than the orc's spear. Gideon feigned once low, then re-coiled and thrusted Nevidal into the orc's gut, impaling it where it stood.

To his left, Vorst was on the back of the fallen orc, straddling its shoulders. The bolt had hit the creature in the spine, wounding it grievously, but not killing it. With more cruelty than Gideon had ever thought possible from such a typically gentle goblin, Vorst held the orc's head in the mud of the small stream until it stopped kicking.

Gideon bent over at the waist and tried to catch his breath. In his mind, he recounted each orc they had killed. "There should be three more," he gasped. His wrist felt like it was on fire. Every breath he took stoked the flames of pain like bellows feeding a furnace.

"They're going back to Talonrend," Vorst concluded, flicking a glob of mud from her hand.

"We have to stop them," Gideon growled. He didn't have time

to consider why the other orcs had fled. All he knew was they needed to die.

Vorst nodded. With a flick of her wrist, she ripped her bolt from the dead orc's back, and the two of them took off through the woods once more.

It wasn't difficult to track the three remaining orcs. When they ran, their huge feet sounded like thunder and left tracks so large and clear a novice hunter could easily follow them, even in the moonlight.

After only a few minutes of running, the orc leader and his two companions had to stop. His absurd weapon was simply too heavy for him to carry while sprinting.

Gideon and Vorst found the three orcs just outside the edge of the forest, doubled over in a clearing that smelled like death. They were surrounded by a dozen or more human corpses from Talonrend's refugee caravan. Most of the bodies had been picked clean by scavengers, but enough rotting meat still clung to the bones to make Gideon gag. Behind the three orcs, he recognized the overturned, partially burned wagon which sported a corpse at its base. The young girl's skull, stark white in the radiant moonlight, had a brutal axe wound Gideon had mercifully delivered.

All five of them were certainly out of breath, but still Gideon rushed the orc leader with little hesitation. An orc stepped forward to intercept the charge, swinging a spiked club for Gideon's legs. With a flourish, Gideon jumped over the attack, executing an abbreviated chop with his sword to disarm the orc. When he landed, the loose, rocky soil beneath his feet gave way and he slid, crashing into the orc leader's body.

Gideon dropped Nevidal to the ground. He scrambled, kicking and punching wildly, and eventually clawed his way on top of the exhausted orc leader. The beast was no doubt stronger than him, but the orc had no endurance. Gideon's reckless charge had taken the orc completely by surprise.

Gideon brought his hand back to throw a punch, but in the tumult, he had forgotten about the third orc. Before he could fully twist out of the way, the orc's spear caught him in his left bicep and lodged there. Just a moment too late, one of Vorst's bolts shredded the third orc's neck, killing it instantly. When the beast fell, its spear broke, leaving a foot of splintered wood in Gideon's arm.

The orc leader wasted no time. The muscled creature thrashed and kicked viciously, throwing Gideon to the ground. With both of his arms severely injured, Gideon could not fight. He rolled away, clumsily regained his feet, and tried to rip the spear tip from his arm, but his broken wrist was not strong enough.

Gideon knew he needed to run. He turned away from the orc, but fell to the ground almost immediately. His body hurt too much for him to stand.

Vorst was out of bolts. She snatched the first orc's club from the ground and ran forward, swinging it wildly as the orc leader attempted to rise. Luckily, the creature was too dazed to notice her. The spiked club obliterated the orc's jaw, sending him back to the ground, motionless.

When she turned back to the first orc, a wave of relief washed over her. The beast had chosen to run. "Get up," Vorst said, moving to Gideon's side. The man was nearly unconscious. "One of them escaped. There might be more orcs nearby—we must get back!"

Vorst helped as much as she could, but Gideon was tall, and she only came up to his waist. Swaying like a tree about to be felled, Gideon managed to stand after a long time.

"Your sword," Vorst said, pointing to Nevidal lying next to the orc leader's corpse.

For a moment, Gideon considered leaving the sword, as bending down to pick it up required more strength than he had left. "Take it," Gideon finally muttered. He shrugged the sheath from his back so Vorst could collect the weapon. When she bent to lift the sword into the sheath, she noticed tracks she had not seen before in the moonlight.

"Gideon, look," she said, pointing to the human footprints.

702

Gideon did not have enough energy to fully open his eyes. "What is it?" he asked, balancing himself against a broken wagon wheel.

"Human feet," she responded. Behind them, Vorst saw the unmistakable sign of an orcish pursuer.

"The tracks look too fresh to have been from the refugees. Someone was here recently." She followed the tracks to the trees where they continued further. "Wait here," she called over her shoulder.

"Certainly," Gideon muttered with a weak smile, falling down beside the wagon wheel as sleep overtook him.

Vorst scampered quickly back to the dead orcs, retrieved her bolt, reloaded her crossbow, and pursued the tracks a little ways into the trees. They ended at another orc's corpse. The hilt of a dagger protruded from the beast's bloody chest—a hilt Vorst quickly recognized.

THE SUN ROSE steadily in the sky, bathing a host of magical fires in warm light. At the edge of the woods, Vorst and Gideon emerged like wounded animals struggling for life. On her waist, Vorst carried Roisin and the spiked club she had stolen from an orc.

Vorst struggled to help Gideon walk, but the two eventually made it to a small fire with some type of fowl roasting on a spit above the flames.

"Sit here," the small goblin ordered. Silently, Gideon nodded. His right wrist had swollen badly. Luckily, the bones had not pierced his skin, so there was no risk of infection. Unluckily, the spearhead lodged in his left bicep produced a steady stream of blood that would not stop. Vorst had attempted to tourniquet the wound with leather scavenged from the dead orcs' clothing, but it hadn't helped much.

Vorst darted off in the direction of Vrysinoch, where she knew the two oblivion mages would be camped. Oddly enough, the strange women did not require sustenance in the form of food and drink, but they still grew physically tired and required sleep. No matter how much she tried to understand the bizarre notion of sleep, Vorst could not comprehend it.

When she found them, the two mages were motionless on the ground, their white masks facing directly toward the sky. They didn't look real. Their robes appeared more like artifacts meant for a museum than things which held human bodies. But then, Vorst conceded to herself, did they actually contain human bodies?

"Hello?" the small goblin said with her squeaky voice. The two robes did not respond. "Valge?" She prodded one of the robes gently with her foot. The white material collapsed beneath her touch as though nothing more than the wind was behind the fabric.

Suddenly, as if startled, the woman jolted from the ground. "What is it?" she asked with a hint of panic lacing her voice.

Vorst took a step back, drawing Roisin from her belt as the second woman rose from the ground. "I found Melkora's dagger! She was here!" Vorst practically screamed. "Find her!" She thrust Roisin out in the palm of her hand like a trophy.

The two mages exchanged an unreadable look behind their alabaster masks. "Vorst," one of them said slowly. "You hold nothing."

Vorst didn't understand. "What?" she stammered, stepping closer so the women could see the dagger more clearly. "I found it in a dead orc's body. Look!"

Again, the two women appeared puzzled. "Did anyone else see the dagger?" one of the mages asked after a moment of contemplation.

Vorst nodded vigorously. "Gideon recognized it as well," she explained.

"Did Melkora possess the item when she entered the Void?" the woman on the right asked.

"I'm sure of it," Vorst stated, her tone leaving no room for debate.

After a long silence, the woman on the left finally spoke. "Is the dagger magical or enchanted in any way?"

"Yes!" Vorst yelled before the mage could finish her sentence. "It is poisoned."

The mage nodded, causing a feeling of confidence to well in Vorst's chest. "The dagger is stuck between the Void and the material plane," the mage explained. "That is why we cannot see it. I am surprised you and Gideon have glimpsed it as well. Was Melkora magical herself? A priestess or sorceress?" she asked slowly, her voice clearly pained by the effort of speaking so frequently.

"A thief," Vorst said with a shake of her head.

"We may be able to tether her back to reality," the mage stated.

"Find one of the acolytes," the other woman began. "We will need rope, white cloth, and lots of space."

Vorst nodded again. She couldn't keep a huge smile from spreading across her face. She pointed toward Gideon's fire by the tree line. "I'll meet you there," she stammered half in goblin and half in human. Her words came too quickly for her mind to sort them out. She tucked Roisin back into her waist and sprinted toward the refugees, eager to locate an acolyte of the Alabaster Order.

Twenty minutes later, as the refugees were starting to move eastwardly again with Vrysinoch leading them, Vorst ran to Gideon's fire with a leather-bound chest in her arms and an acolyte in white robes trailing behind her. She was happy to see the two mages already in the clearing. One of them was busy tending to Gideon's wounds, a broken spear tip at her feet, and the other slowly paced a large circle in the dirt as if marking a boundary.

"We're ready!" Vorst announced breathlessly. She ran to the woman pacing and offered her the acolyte's trunk.

"Very well," the woman said after a moment. The mage placed the trunk on the ground outside the circle and opened, drawing forth a strip of white linen. Gently, she handed the cloth to Vorst. "Wrap this around the dagger so we can all see it," she said with a friendly tone. Vorst took the cloth and did as she was instructed. "Now," the woman continued, "help Valge with Gideon's wounds. There is still much preparation to be done."

With a sigh, Vorst tucked Roisin back in her belt. She wanted the tethering, whatever that meant, to begin immediately, but it was apparent the mages would not speed up their process for any reason.

THE REFUGEES WERE gone by the time Valge announced they were ready. The sky had started to darken and Vorst's stomach rumbled noisily. Behind her, Gideon sat upon a rotting log still holding his left arm tightly to his chest. It would be several weeks before he would be able to fight again — but it would probably only be several days before he *needed* to fight again. The refugees were sure to reach Talonrend within the month. If the orcs were scouting their position as thoroughly as Gideon thought they were, skirmishes were bound to happen before they reached the walls.

"Stay back," Valge said to Vorst, although the goblin was already standing outside the tethering circle. In the center of the clearing, the mages had created an intricate pattern of rope that looked more like an animal trap than any sort of magical device.

"What will happen?" Gideon grunted. Despite his brief involvement with Valkoinen, the most learned sorcerer he had ever met, he still did not trust magic he did not understand. When he was a fully-fledged paladin, he knew exactly where he drew his power. Gideon did not consider himself an expert on Gravlox's shamanistic abilities, but he understood the power of the earth and the magic it contained. However, when he considered the Alabaster Order, he was at a loss.

Valge turned, her eyeless mask boring into him like eerie, cloudless moonlight. "If she still lives in the Void, I will attempt to bring her back." The plan's explanation felt obvious, but hearing the mage speak the words made it seem real.

The other mage, sitting calmly at the edge of the circle with a bundle of white cloth in her hands, spoke slowly. "If your friend returns," she began, "Melkora will most certainly be different."

"Like you?" Vorst asked, feeling her eagerness fade into fear.

"No," the woman without a name explained. "In order to become like us, you must take magic into the Void," she paused for a long moment, struggling to find the energy to speak more. "And then you must die there," she finally said.

Valge continued where the other oblivion mage left off. "Tethering a non-magical entity is quite different than the rituals we willing subject ourselves to as acolytes."

"Is it easier or harder?" Vorst asked. She thought of the possibility of Gravlox's death and had to look away.

Valge stared directly at her. "I do not know," she stated emotionlessly. "People are subject to any number of unknown horrors in the Void," she continued, addressing Gideon as well. "If Melkora comes back, she may no longer possess the will to live."

"Or she may be a raving lunatic," the other mage added without a trace of humor in her voice.

"Will she have her body?" Vorst asked, feeling almost guilty for broaching the subject. The empty robe in the mage's hands made her nervous. Once again, she had to force thoughts of her husband far from her mind.

"I believe so," Valge replied hesitantly. "I have never seen a non-magical object, alive or otherwise, return from the Void without their body, but it does not mean it is impossible."

"And the rope?" Vorst indicated. "Is it some sort of symbol? Part of your ritual?" She did not know how such magical designs functioned, but she had seen Gideon's tattoo enough to know they were important.

Behind her white mask, Valge stifled the beginnings of laughter. "We need no such trivialities," she said quickly. "People almost always come back running. The rope is there to trip them."

Vorst could not tell if the woman was actually trying to make a joke or not, but she nodded and took a seat next to Gideon to witness the tethering.

Valge moved to the side of the rope circle with a swift sense of purpose Vorst had not seen before.

After a small running start, she was gone.

MORE THAN ANYTHING, Melkora regretted leaving her boots behind. She missed the familiar feel of Roisin's hilt, but she had learned to live without it. Sadly, she could not simply cast her blisters from her mind.

After witnessing her daughter's death and nearly dying herself at the hands of an orc, she had wandered north. Nothing in particular had drawn her in that direction, or any other direction for that matter. For months which felt like eternity, she had wandered.

In the rocky outcropping she had begun to call home, Melkora lifted a sharp stone and carved another line on the huge boulder serving as the western wall of her makeshift camp. "...Twenty three, twenty four, twenty five, twenty six," she counted the groups of lines aloud, each set representing a month spent in the Void. She knew time did not pass in the Void as it did in the material world: her nails had not grown, her hair was unchanged, and even her stomach seemed content to exist outside of time, for she had not eaten or relieved herself in twenty six months.

"Damned blisters," she cursed, wondering why her feet seemed to be the only things ravaged by the wasteland where she existed.

To the west, the sun was setting. In the Void, no crickets or other insects buzzed to welcome the night and no wolves howled at the iridescent moon. Nothing was alive. Melkora's eyes drifted to her daughter's ragged corpse, which she had dragged from its position beside the ruined wagon, and the woman cried.

For better or worse, the corpse had also remained unaffected by time. Corshana's head, matted with blood and sporting a fatal gash, still held thick locks of untamed hair. Her body appeared so recently alive that Melkora had occasionally forgotten she was dead. "Gideon killed my daughter," she said, repeating the mantra as she had done for years. The hope of revenge was the only thing encouraging her not to take her own life and join her daughter on Vrysinoch's wings.

With a sigh, the woman gave a loving pat to her daughter's bloody shoulder before entering her makeshift tent for another night of restless sleep. Her home, a term Melkora only hesitantly used to describe her dwelling, was nothing more than canvas stolen from a toppled wagon stretched between two large boulders. Nightfall did not bring a breeze, rain, or even a gentle reduction of temperature that would have made sleep easier. Instead, the only difference between the night and day in the Void was the seemingly unimportant position of the sun.

Lying on her back and staring into nothing, Melkora wondered why she slept. Her physical body seemed to benefit from the act, if only to temporarily relieve her blisters, but her mind did not. She did not feel mentally tired, nor could she feel mentally refreshed. "Perhaps it is only a habit," she conceded to herself, managing a flicker of a smile. As her eyes closed for the night, she thought of Gravlox and Vorst, how the goblins needed no sleep, and she pitied them. For her, sleep was welcomed. Sleep was perhaps the only thing that convinced her she was still alive.

But Melkora did not sleep until sunrise as she had done for twenty six months. Instead, she awoke with a jolt only a few hours after she had drifted off.

"Woman," a slow voice echoed around her. It sounded vague

and distant, yet oddly comforting. "Woman," the word beckoned to her once more. Melkora sat up and rubbed her eyes, but she could see nothing. "Woman!" the voice grew louder, more urgent. "You should not be here."

"Where—" she began, but she knew it would be of no use. Asking a disembodied voice where it was felt pointless. It was simply another trick of her surroundings. "The Void," she scoffed, lying back down and closing her eyes.

"Leave!" the voice commanded after a pause. It was stronger, like it was coming from just outside her tent.

"Hello?" Melkora responded cautiously. Something about the voice sounded strangely familiar. Was it her long awaited rescuer? Had the Alabaster Order finally come to save her? "Valkoinen?" she called out, hopeful for the first time in over two years. But before she spoke his name, she knew it was not him. The familiar and reassuring quality of the voice was that it was distinctly feminine, Melkora realized.

"You know him? Please! He can find us!" the voice called back, dashing Melkora's hopes in an instant.

Melkora grit her teeth in frustration. "He came with me," she said, sitting up once more. "I don't know," she admitted. "He took me—brought me—here. I don't think he came with me, but I don't know."

Another long silence passed in darkness and Melkora beat her fist into the wagon cover she used as a bed. "Someone is here," the voice finally said. "Someone strong. It must be Valkoinen."

Melkora was at her wits end. "Where are you?" she screamed, clawing at the darkness all around her.

"Everywhere," the voice said after a moment. "But I've lost my body."

Melkora thought of Gravlox—had he lost his body as well? Was he alive? "I need to find my friend," she said after a moment, hoping the owner of the voice might know where Gravlox was.

"There are ways to bring people back from the Void," the voice said with an optimistic tone. "It will be very difficult." Suddenly, the voice escalated to a powerful, urgent command. "You must not die in the Void if you wish to return to the material world. Injuries received here have dire consequences."

Melkora took another step forward. She wanted to run out of her tent screaming, but something held her back. Something made her cautious. She decided to try to test the voice, to see if she could learn something from it. "Injuries? What *is* this place? I haven't seen *anything* yet that could hurt me," she lied. Not only were her blisters horribly painful, but she still remembered her near-fatal encounter with a monstrous orc.

The voice did not take her bait. "Step forward," the voice told her sarcastically. "Come out of the tent and see for yourself."

Melkora scoffed. She would not be taunted so easily.

But then she heard footsteps. Great, thundering footsteps like a sprinting minotaur approached her small encampment. With a grunt of determination, Melkora threw aside the entrance of her tent and leapt into the small clearing before her.

Much to her surprise, a massive, lumbering orc charged directly for her, only a dozen paces away. Melkora ran. She had no weapon. She had no plan. Inwardly, she cursed herself. Two years she could have spent preparing!

From the corner of her eye, Melkora saw a hint of white cloth flutter in the moonlight. Before she could react, the ghost-like figure slammed into her and tackled her to the ground.

Melkora kicked and tried to claw her way to freedom, but her legs were trapped. Something wrapped its way around her ankles like a snake, holding her in place.

"Melkora!" someone shouted from a direction she could not identify. Melkora thrashed, kicking furiously to save her life, but she could not free herself.

"Melkora! Stop!" another voice, a man's voice commanded her. "You're safe," it shouted, but she could not believe what she heard.

She twisted at the waist, her eyes full of fury, and saw Vorst yelling at her from only a few paces away. Behind the short goblin, Melkora gazed upon a seated man with a great, braided beard and a bald head. As her initial panic faded, Melkora found a familiar emotion welling up inside her chest: hatred.

"Gideon killed my daughter," Melkora said flatly. Vorst stopped yelling, confusion washing over her face like a tidal wave.

"Gideon killed my daughter," Melkora repeated. Slowly, taking her time to do it correctly, she untangled herself from the rope around her feet. When she stood, the two beings in white robes around her shrank backward.

"Gideon killed my daughter," she said again. Gideon's face betrayed his fear. He was injured, that much Melkora could easily see, and he knew he could not defend himself. With careful steps, Melkora began to stalk toward him. For once, the pain in her feet did not bother her.

"Gideon killed my daughter."

Sixteen

GIDEON TRIED TO backpedal as quickly as his injuries would allow, but both of his arms were tightly bound in cloth and instead of fleeing to safety, he tripped almost as soon as he stood. In an instant, Melkora was upon him, snarling like an angry beast.

"Stop!" Gideon yelled.

With a burst of magical speed, Valge stepped once more through the Void, caught Melkora by her throat, and ripped her violently across the rope circle. Once more entangled, the two women crashed to the ground in a heap of flailing arms and legs. Without a physical body, Valge was more a flying sheet than a person, but their struggle appeared real.

"He killed her!" Melkora continued to scream.

"It was not real!" Valge commanded, adding magical power to her voice. To her side, the flames of Gideon's dwindling fire sputtered and went out. Beneath her, Melkora froze. It was as if Valge's sudden strength of voice destroyed all the energy in the area.

Ever so slowly, Valge got to her feet, but remained directly above Melkora. "What you saw was not real," the woman in white stated. "You need to stop." Valge relaxed her posture slightly, but

714

she did not move to allow Melkora to rise.

"No," Gideon said weakly from the side of the circle. With Vorst's help, he had returned to a seated position atop a log. The bandage on his upper arm had torn free and oozed blood down to his fingers.

"In time, your mind will recover," Valge said more softly, ignoring Gideon altogether.

"You will learn to accept your fortune," the other mage added. "After all, you did not lose your body to the Void."

"No," Gideon said again, drawing their attention. He looked directly at Melkora with eyes full of sorrow. "Whatever you saw was real. I killed your daughter."

"What?" Vorst gasped, looking at Gideon with shock.

In an instant, Melkora burst into tears. She was too tired to express the fury that lurked just beneath her eyes, so she did the only thing her body had strength left to do.

Gideon stood, braced himself for a moment on the log, and walked to Melkora. "You should hear it from me," he said gently.

Melkora shrieked through her sobs. If she was speaking actual words, Gideon could not understand them.

"I found your daughter after the refugees had been attacked," he began. "She was badly injured. Her arm was broken through the skin. I asked what her name was. She told me."

Melkora could not bring herself to look Gideon in the eyes. With her face buried in the dirt, she tried to rein in her sobs enough to speak. "I watched you kill her," she wept.

Gideon nodded. "I did. I killed her. She probably could have recovered from her injuries eventually, but there was not time. Even with all the healers of Talonrend, it would have taken weeks, and her survival would not have been certain. I did what was best for the people." For a moment, Gideon thought of reaching out a hand to comfort the hysterical woman, but consolation was not a skill he possessed. With a heavy sigh, he stood and turned away.

"You killed her!" Melkora continued to yell at Gideon's back.

"You could have saved her, but you killed her," she trailed off into violent sobbing.

Gideon hung his head. He didn't know the right words to say, so he simply told her the truth. "Yes," he began, still facing away from Melkora. "I killed your daughter. I knelt behind her on the grass, took one of my axes, and split her skull open. She died. I left her."

Melkora's crying regained its full force. The woman erupted in a fresh wave of agonizing tears, kicking uselessly at the ground until her last bit of strength faded.

When Gideon was standing safely behind the other mage, Valge moved to allow Melkora room to get up, but the woman remained sobbing in the dirt.

Hesitantly, Vorst crept up to her. She felt bad for asking about her husband with Melkora in such a state, but a solitary question burned through her mind like wildfire.

"Did you," she paused, fearing the answer. "Did you see Gravlox? Was he in the Void with you?"

Melkora continued to sob. "I failed," she muttered. "Valkoinen sent me to find him, but I couldn't."

"What?" Valge interjected, suddenly interested.

Vorst had expected Melkora's answer, but hearing it spoken still crushed her spirit. She sank to the ground, sat on the dirt, and did not know what to do.

Valge stared intently at Melkora through her alabaster mask. "Valkoinen *sent* you to find the goblin?" the woman asked forcefully.

Melkora nodded.

"When I found you, you were somewhere in the hillside. The landscape was similar to here," Valge said. "If your daughter was there, it was *your* iteration of the Void. Valkoinen would have known better."

Slowly, Melkora rose to a sitting position. She rubbed some of the dirt from her cheeks and cleared the tears from her eyes.

"Valkoinen sent me to a cave. There was nothing there. I searched for Gravlox, but I found nothing," she explained.

Valge and the other oblivion mage exchanged a brief look. "That must be where Gravlox is," she said. "But how did you escape into your own plane?"

"I," Melkora began, but could not remember. In her mind, she had lived in the Void for more than two years. The few hours she spent in the cave were a distant memory to her. "I think it just happened," she finally said.

"What does it mean?" Vorst asked, clinging to any shred of hope she could.

After several minutes of silence, Valge finally spoke. "When powerful mages enter the Void, the fabric of the world can become unstable. Perhaps that is what happened."

"Can you find him?" Vorst begged. She searched Valge's mask for an answer, but the unmoving alabaster showed nothing.

"The instability sometimes causes unusual phenomena on the material plane. Perhaps there is now a cave where the barrier between the physical world and the Void is torn, but it could take hundreds of years to find," the woman explained.

Gideon stepped forward. "I know of a cave where my own magic did not work," he added. "Maybe that is the place."

Slowly, Valge nodded. It was clear that so much action in such a short amount of time had nearly depleted her energy. "It is worth trying," she said after a long moment.

Vorst did not understand how any of it made sense. "The cave was like that *before* Gravlox went into the Void," she reminded him.

"It does not matter," Melkora said with a halfhearted laugh. "How long was I gone?" she asked.

"Several months, no more," Gideon told her.

"I wasn't speaking to you," she snapped. Every fiber of her body wanted to hurt Gideon, to make him pay for killing her daughter, and she fought to keep her emotions under control. "I made a mark every thirty days I spent in the Void," she scoffed.

"There were twenty seven marks when you finally rescued me. Time means nothing in the Void."

Valge nodded. "*When* you experienced the phenomenon means nothing," she told Gideon. "The important thing is that it happened."

"Can you find the cave again?" Vorst asked, trying not to get her hopes up once more.

Gideon nodded. "It isn't far from here. A week's journey at the most."

Vorst began to gather their supplies frantically. "We need to hurry!" she yelled. "We can find him!"

Valge shook her head. "We can leave tomorrow. I must rest."

"We will move much faster than Vrysinoch and the civilians," Gideon said confidently. "We can meet back with them before they reach Talonrend."

UNDRAKK SAT A huge wooden table with a pile of steaming meat in front of him and a goblet of wine in his left hand. At the other seats, the most respected members of Broken Sword busily feasted. Snarlsnout's massive stone dais had been temporarily moved into the hall for the occasion, although the gluttonous orc chieftain preferred to dine on a bucket of rancid goat parts rather than enjoy the venison and duck the others ate. In the northern corner of the room, near the broken throne, stood the only human in the city, clutching a handful of scrolls.

At the end of the long table, thirty or more orc females sat on lush blankets of fur, waiting for the feast to conclude so the real entertainment could begin, but Undrakk had hardly noticed them. He swirled red wine in a glass, held it briefly to his nose, and took another sip. By all accounts the wine was incredible, but Undrakk had far more pressing matters weighing on his mind. To the king, the wine, meat, and women were dangerous distractions.

At Undrakk's right hand, Keturah busily gnawed on a juicy deer haunch. Oils from the meat dripped through the coarse hair on her minotaur hands. Undrakk remembered sitting at Qul's feasts several times and watching the minotaur king eat. Unlike Keturah, Qul had never paused between bites to clean the drippings from his arms.

Undrakk waited for the other orcs and minotaurs to have their fill before he stood to address them. "Chieftains," he began, standing to command silence from the group at once. "Another battle is nearly upon us." Some of the orcs grunted in approval. For most of them, going several days without bloodshed was unacceptable. "The human pack will be within sight of our walls in less than ten days!"

Cheers rose up from all ends of the table. "We'll grind their bones into mortar and make rope from their skin!" one of the blood-thirsty minotaur leaders shouted.

Undrakk raised his hand to silence them once more. "We are strong and hold every advantage," he assured them. "But still they march toward us. The humans know how strong we are, they must!" he shouted, clenching his right hand in a fist. Entranced by his charisma, the room hung on every word Undrakk spoke. "Now is the time we need to remain vigilant! We must continue to prepare."

Undrakk turned his gaze on Jan, the new unofficial king of the minotaur clan. "I want half the filthy humans dead in the first minute," he stated with violent ire dancing behind his eyes.

The once-human minotaur necromancer nodded and gave an abbreviated snort. "Our charge will likely kill them all, my king. For that, I apologize." He turned toward the orcs with his arms spread wide. "There won't be any left for the rest of you!" he shouted, sending the room into a joyous uproar again.

When they quieted, Undrakk continued his speech. "I have every confidence in you, Jan," he told the minotaur. "Do not fail."

Turning back to the others, he beckoned toward Sifir with a wave of his hand. "As you may have heard," he began, taking one of the scrolls the human held. "Our latest scouting party did not return in full. The group was ambushed! Killed to a single orc!" Although everyone in the room was well aware of the slaughtered scouts, they gasped and grumbled as though they had just found out.

"Vengeance!" one of the orcs shouted with a mouthful of meat.

"Indeed," Undrakk replied confidently. "We will have vengeance. But until then, we must be alert! We cannot fall victim to their traps and trickery again." Undrakk turned to the orc he had placed in charge of organizing the patrols atop Terror's Lament. "Until the humans arrive, double the night patrol, and set sentries on the walls every fifty paces during the day," he instructed. The orc nodded obediently.

"The rest of you," Undrakk continued. "Tell your kin to be ready. Every orc and minotaur of Broken Sword is never to be seen without a weapon! We must be ready to fight when we least expect it! Tomorrow morning at dawn we will sound the war horn. Assemble your tribes and muster to your stations. Am I understood?" The orcs cheered again, pounding their huge fists on the table in anticipation.

The half-orc looked to one of the most respected warriors of the Wolf Jaw Clan next. "Your scouts continue to patrol the Clawflow River?" Undrakk asked.

The orc stood, his wolf-bone tunic rattling as he moved. Atop his head he wore a grey wolf pelt and a string of human ears dangled from his neck. "Aye," the burly orc answered. "Not a human left." He gave his necklace of ears a gentle tap.

"Have any more goblins wandered close to the river?" Undrakk inquired.

"Not after we strung up the last few," the orc said with a vicious smile.

"Perfect," Undrakk told him. "Nevertheless, double your patrols. We can't afford surprises."

The orc grinned and bowed low before taking his seat once more. After a few more rousing words of inspiration, Undrakk let his subordinates finish their feast like the carnal beasts they truly were. When all of the orcs had either left the hall to go to their own concubines or had claimed one of the females already present, Undrakk turned to Keturah with a worried look. "Come with me," he bade her, standing from his seat.

Keturah hesitantly rose from her chair and followed Undrakk out of the hall. In front of Half-Orc Keep, Undrakk leaned against one of the heavy chains supporting the drawbridge. He looked back at the castle, pride swelling in his chest. "Do you believe in what we are doing, Keturah?" he asked after a long moment.

The woman-turned-minotaur let out a long sigh. She stood over a foot taller than Undrakk, but she still felt small next to him. "I do, my king," she replied confidently. She hoped her voice did not betray her nervousness, but she feared the half-orc could read her like an open scroll. Undrakk's seemingly limitless power terrified her more than she wanted to admit.

"I believe in your commitment," Undrakk said. "But why do you choose to help us, the uncivilized beasts of the wild?" he asked, letting the hint of a smile play across his face.

Keturah stifled a laugh which came out more like a snort from her bovine snout. She pointed to her chest with her meaty hand. "Where else would I go?" she responded. "Besides, you orcs are not as uncivilized as you think."

Undrakk was still not perfectly convinced Keturah wouldn't turn against him to join the humans when they arrived, but he was confident Broken Sword would still prevail. "How do you feel living beside the very orcs who slaughtered your race and pillaged your city?" Undrakk pressed.

Keturah smiled, putting on the perfect air of obedience. "Jan is my only kin," she responded quickly. "The race of my brethren is irrelevant. What matters is that we both live. It was a human who killed my brother. It was a human I fought when I died."

"I see," Undrakk began, but Keturah cut him off.

"I have lived for months as a minotaur in Broken Sword," she continued unfettered. "The orcs treat me as a queen. The other minotaurs at least respect me as their equal. Sometimes I miss my human hair, or the feel of a silk dress tailored to every curve of my body, but Broken Sword is my home." Her large, bovine eyes bored into Undrakk with fire the half-orc had never seen before. "I will defend this city with my life," she finished, stamping her hoof into the drawbridge.

Undrakk mulled the woman's words over in his mind for a long while before nodding and changing the subject. "How has your," he didn't quite know the word to describe the relationship between Keturah and the demon Taurnil, so he settled on the first one which came to his mind, "*friend* been progressing with his healing?"

Keturah reached into a pocket on her roughly-sewn leather shirt. After a moment of gentle caressing, she lifted a jet-black scorpion up in the palm of her hand. "Taurnil heals faster when he takes his smallest form," she explained, moving her hand closer to Undrakk so the king could see the sleeping arachnid for himself.

The king crinkled his nose at the acrid stench the creature gave off. "I am truly grateful he survived," Undrakk said in quiet amazement. "Would it be possible for me to see him whole?" he asked. "The other demons see him as their leader. I want to see him fly so I know he will be ready to fight when the time comes."

Slowly, Keturah set Taurnil down on the wooden drawbridge and took a step away. With her hand outstretched, she whispered a word, sending black tendrils of inky smoke to envelop the sleeping scorpion. After a moment, Taurnil appeared within the smoke in his demonic form, but he was nowhere near the proud beast he once was.

Undrakk gasped. "It is a miracle he lives," he muttered.

Where the creature's legs and torso had once been pale as ash, his body was covered in a web of shadows. Near the original wound on his upper leg, the skin had turned black as night. From there, the disfigurement branched out along his body like streaks of lightning. Taurnil was clearly still recovering, but Undrakk had to admit to himself that the creature's new appearance was even more intimidating than its last.

"Can you fly?" Undrakk asked hesitantly. "We will need you soon."

The demon sneered.

"Show him, my pet," Keturah bade gently.

Taurnil nodded, turned toward the side of the drawbridge, and leapt into the air. He did not fly gracefully at all, but the demon did manage to keep himself aloft. After a single pass above Half-Orc Keep, Taurnil unceremoniously collapsed into the drawbridge where he instantly reverted to his scorpion form. Without wasting a second, Keturah snatched the creature from the ground and returned him to her pocket.

"He will be ready," Keturah said confidently, although her voice shook ever so slightly. "He will be ready."

Seventeen

"THIS IS THE cave," Gideon stated. They had only walked for five days, making the trip significantly shorter than Gideon had expected. With her husband's fate potentially hanging in the balance, Vorst had been a tyrant with their pace.

When she saw the cave for herself, Vorst rushed to the stony opening, but did not go inside. Behind them, the two oblivion mages followed slowly. Much to Vorst's discontent, they had brought an unused white robe and mask with them and had insisted it be cut down to a goblin's height.

Melkora had insisted on staying with the refugees. Gideon thought it was a foolish idea, especially if an orc scouting party decided to attack the column, but he had been in no position to argue for her to stay. He was glad she was nowhere near him, he admitted. She was dangerous, and Gideon did not enjoy constantly looking over his shoulder for a dagger. Deep in his gut, he entertained the notion of putting her out of her misery. He shook his head. He would do whatever it took to keep himself safe, even from a friend, but he was not a cold-blooded murderer. Not yet.

With a heavy sigh, Gideon made his way to the cave entrance to stand beside Vorst. "Gravlox," he called into the darkness, not knowing what, if anything, he should expect in return. Nothing answered him.

"Gravlox!" Vorst yelled, her voice shaking. After a few moments of unsettling silence, Vorst ran into the cave shouting her husband's name.

"That might not be how this works," Valge said once she entered the cave as well. The entire chamber wasn't very deep, perhaps less than twenty feet from front to back, but Gideon knew exactly where the magically hidden wall was located.

"Follow me," the man said grimly. His voice betrayed his uneasiness. Gideon led Vorst and the mages on his hands and knees through a small tunnel until he reached the antechamber. Everything was just as it had been when he had investigated the strange place with Asterion. "We forgot to bring a torch," Gideon muttered more to himself than anyone else. In the corner of the room, a small metal brazier still held a few remnants of a magical fire—just enough to cast eerie shadows on the walls.

"A dead end?" Vorst questioned softly. Her voice echoed off the close walls in strange patterns that made her voice unrecognizable.

Gideon found the illusory wall with ease and pointed the way.

"Wait!" Valge yelled, suddenly stricken with fear. "There is something here," she said, bringing her voice down to a subtle whisper.

"Gravlox," Vorst said under her breath with a smile.

"We cannot go with you," Valge continued. "You were right. The barrier between the Void and the material world is very thin here." She put a hand protectively over the other mage's chest, and the two women moved slowly away from the false wall.

"We do we do?" Vorst asked hesitantly. "We *cannot* turn back."

Valge held out the small white robe she had prepared like an offering before a temple altar. "Take it," she said as Vorst plucked it from her hands. "You'll know when you know." Without another word, the two mages climbed back through the passage and toward the outside.

"Take me to the next room," Vorst commanded with determination.

Gideon did as he was told. On the other side of the hidden tunnel, the scene had changed, but not by much. The phylactery, if that was what it truly was, still stood as a pool of liquid at the far end of the chamber, although it was still. At their feet, the hundreds of eggs which had covered the floor had been cracked and destroyed. Still, the soft glow of red light filled the chamber enough to allow Gideon to see, but the light did not pulse and shimmer with life as it had before.

"This is it," Gideon whispered. He feared speaking too loudly might ruin the reverence of the room.

With the white robe in hand, Vorst began to move about the room. "Grav?" she softly called. "Gravlox? Are you here?"

Something tingled against the edge of Vorst's hand, startling her at first, then washing her mind with a beautiful sense of calm.

"Gravlox," she whispered once more. "You *are* here."

As gently as she could, Vorst unfolded the small white robe in her arms. Tears flowed freely down her cheeks. Out of respect, Gideon stepped back through the narrow passage and made his way to join the oblivion mages.

"Grav," Vorst couldn't keep her voice from cracking and fading into nothing. She felt his touch once more. It began at her amputated finger, the sign of their eternal bond, and blazed through her body like fire. All at once, she felt more alive than she had ever been, and concurrently felt as though her life had ended. Gravlox would never be the same.

"I love you," she whispered past the immovable lump in her throat. With a solemn hand, Vorst unfurled the robe entirely and lifted it above the space adjacent to her left shoulder. The robe shimmered, quivering almost, and then Gravlox's hollow form took hold of it.

Although he had no physical body and was completely draped

726

in white, Vorst knew it was him. His outline was exactly as she re-membered it. With trembling hands, Vorst placed the alabaster mask where Gravlox's face should have been. When she let go, the mask did not fall to the ground. It stayed in place as easily as if it *was* Gravlox's face. From her travelling pack, Vorst produced a pair of small white gloves with nine finger spaces and slipped them over Gravlox's invisible hands.

"You're back," she said after a long moment. She went to hug her husband, but the robe collapsed against her touch. Hesitantly, she held out the palm of her hand. "Can you touch me?" she asked in her native language, her voice barely audible.

Softly at first, then growing in strength and confidence, Gravlox used his gloved hand to tap a message to his wife. *I knew you would come back for me,* he said. *Thank you.*

"I never stopped searching for you," Vorst replied as quickly as she could. She was afraid to ask her next question. "How long have you been here?" she asked, staring at his unmoving mask.

Gravlox hesitated for a moment, reminding Vorst of Valkoinen's choppy speech patterns. *I did not count,* he tapped gently against her palm. *A thousand lifetimes, maybe more. It does not matter. You are here.*

Vorst could not find any more words. She sank to her knees and wept, her tears a combination of sorrow and uncontrollable joy.

THE SUN WAS low in the sky when Vorst emerged from the cave several hours later. Her eyes were still wet with tears, and her chest hurt from her sobbing, but she could not hide the happiness plastered to her face.

"You found him?" Valge asked at once, turning from the other mage back toward the cave. Gideon also rose to his feet to welcome Gravlox's return.

When the goblin shaman finally emerged from the cave mouth, the two oblivion mages immediately fell to their knees in supplication.

"Gravlox," Gideon began, but soon trailed off. His mind was lost for words.

"We brought him back," Vorst said cheerfully.

Like a ghost hovering above the land, Gravlox glided in the direction of the two mages. At once, they gasped and tried to retreat on their knees, never taking their eyes from the leaf-strewn ground.

"They are friends," Vorst told her husband. "They are like you, like Valkoinen."

Slowly, one of the mages raised her mask from the ground to speak. Vorst and Gideon could both sense the abject terror in her voice when she spoke. "No," she gasped. "He is not like us, not like Valkoinen. He is the Fated One."

Eighteen

"THEY'RE HERE," UNDRAKK muttered. After a moment, he shook his head and let the spell enhancing his vision dissipate. Behind him, Sifir paced nervously with a rusty dagger clutched in his hands. In addition to his usual tattered robe, Sifir had somehow procured a leather arming cap and wore it as though he was going to war. Undrakk considered the sight quite comical.

The king signaled to a minotaur standing watch in the guard tower to his left. The beast nodded and lifted a brass horn to his lips. With a huge breath, the minotaur played a low note that rumbled off the sides of Terror's Lament like thunder. In the city below, thousands of warriors prepared for battle.

"Raise the portcullis!" Undrakk yelled. His commanded was repeated several times by orcs stationed below before the sounds of creaking iron reached the shaman's ears. On the ground, the orcs and minotaurs cheered.

"It is barely past dawn," Undrakk said to his human servant. The old man nodded obediently. "By noon," Undrakk continued, "I want everything in place. It will take the humans at least a day to reach us. I want the soldiers to have plenty of time to rest before the

729

combat commences."

"Yes, my liege," Sifir replied. He turned for the stairs at once. For an ancient man, Undrakk had to admit he moved rather quickly, as if the oncoming carnage gave him energy.

The king of Broken Sword turned back to the west and recast his far-sight spell. A little ways closer than the edge of the horizon, he saw the marble statue of an eagle leading a meager troop of ragged humans in his direction. At the statue's feet, three strange figures in white robes accompanied by a burly man and lithe woman looked to be the only ones of the entire group fit for warfare.

Undrakk moved his vision farther through the humans, searching for weapons and armor, but found nothing. Most of the refugees carried packs on their shoulders, but they were laden with cooking supplies, food, and other necessities of travel. None of them were soldiers. Undrakk could see it in their eyes—none of them were killers.

"This will be a bloodbath," he muttered to himself. "Another glorious bloodbath."

"WHAT'S THE PLAN?" Gideon asked. He wasn't sure who would answer him, but almost hoped Vrysinoch's statue would hear his question and tell them all what to do. He sat in the shadow of the winged god, surrounded by Vorst, Gravlox, Melkora, and the two oblivion mages, every one of them trying to come up with ideas.

"We can't take them head on," Melkora offered, her eyes never meeting Gideon's. "There must be thousands of orcs in there."

"And minotaurs," Vorst added quietly.

"And demons," Gideon finished. "Perhaps if *Vrysinoch*," he raised his voice just enough to ensure the statue heard him, "would help us, we would have a chance."

Slowly, the statue turned and took a step closer to their make-

730

shift war council. "You are an arrogant fool, Gideon of Talonrend," the statue rebuked with a voice like falling boulders.

Gideon scoffed. "Arrogance is bringing less than three hundred people to storm a fortified city," he looked up at Vrysinoch, his eyes filled with ire. "Or is that foolishness? I'm afraid I cannot tell the difference."

It was the statue's turn to scoff. "My sister will appear," Vrysinoch stated gravely. "And when the giant raven descends, I will finally kill her. When she is dead, Talonrend will be free."

Gideon balled his fists, trying in vain to dissipate some of his anger. "And what?" he yelled. "The five of us will just kill a few thousand orcs and other beasts while you fight a giant bird?"

Vrysinoch leaned down low. When he bent at the waist, it sounded like a landslide toppling a mountain. "You have your task, arrogant and foolish Gideon. Everyone must play their part."

"I don't take orders from you any longer," Gideon spat back. Suddenly, the holy tattoo on his back began to burn, but he refused to let the pain show on his face.

"Then you will die. The city will be lost," Vrysinoch replied, turning quickly away from the man.

"What must he do?" Melkora asked for him. Some part of her still wanted to strangle the life from Gideon's throat for killing her daughter, but she knew she relied on him — perhaps they all did.

Vrysinoch breathed a stony sigh, glancing sidelong at Gideon over his shoulder. "You must kill the half-orc," the god explained in a low tone.

"You cannot kill him yourself?" Gideon retorted incredulously.

"Orcs and minotaurs belong to the raven. If I kill him," Vrysinoch explained slowly. "His soul will become the property of my sister. I cannot allow that to happen."

Gideon mulled over the words, but he did not fully understand them. "Why does it make any difference who kills him?" he asked after a moment.

Vrysinoch let his head fall in disgust. "I had not thought it possible, but perhaps you are more foolish than you are arrogant. Your sword, Gideon of Talonrend," Vrysinoch's words trailed off into an indecipherable curse.

For once, Gideon did feel truly foolish. Subconsciously, he tried to reach his right hand behind his back to feel Nevidal's sheath. The pain in his slowly mending wrist stopped him quickly. "Right," he muttered, too embarrassed to lift his voice.

"THERE IS SOMETHING I must do," Vorst whispered. The chilly night wind made her shiver. She stepped a few inches closer to her husband to try and share some of his body heat, but his white robes radiated nothing.

Whatever it is, I will go with you, Gravlox tapped into her palm.

"No," Vorst shook her head. Deep within her body, she felt Kanebullar Mountain's irresistible call. "I must do this alone. I made a promise to return to Kanebullar Mountain. Perhaps if I could bring them back with me," she started, trying to convince herself more than Gravlox. She knew what she had to do, but why would the other goblins listen to her? Would there even be any still left alive after so long?

Gravlox reached for her hand once more. *Bringing them might be our only hope,* he tapped.

Vorst brushed a tear from the bottom of her eye. "You will forgive me for leaving you?" she pleaded.

Of course, Gravlox told her at once. *I waited more than a thousand years in the Void for you. I can wait another few days for your return.*

Vorst nodded, but she dared not to speak lest she cry. *I love you,* she tapped into Gravlox's glove. He started to reply, but Vorst closed his hand and smiled. *Tell me when I return,* she tapped. She couldn't see his face, but she imagined Gravlox smiling beneath his mask. The thought brought her happiness, and with it came hope for the future.

When she turned from her husband, the fleeting sense of confidence she had floundered. In the darkness, she could not see Terror's Lament, though she knew it was only a few short miles ahead of her. Beyond the city, she would have to cover nearly twenty miles to reach Kanebullar Mountain—and she would have to do it quickly. The pre-battle tension hanging in the air was so thick she could practically taste it.

Before she could change her mind, Vorst darted into the darkness, never looking back.

WHEN DAWN BROKE over the hazy silhouette of Kanebullar Mountain, Gideon, Gravlox, and the two oblivion mages stood over a crudely drawn map. Melkora was somewhere among the refugees, Gideon assumed, but he still kept an eye out for her just in case.

Towering above them, Vrysinoch's marble statue stood like a glorious sentinel in the morning light.

"We've been staring at this map for an hour," Valge muttered behind her alabaster mask. "You said it yourself, Talonrend is impossible to infiltrate. We don't have the numbers for an open battle. We don't even have the element of surprise." The woman's voice faltered as she spoke, the strain of saying so much at once obviously taking its toll on her stamina.

"There must be a way," Gideon replied, although he didn't believe it himself. Toward the east, a war horn sounded, making everyone look in the direction of Talonrend. At the base of the walls, a small dust cloud started to form.

"They're coming," Gideon said. "They will try to draw us under the walls so their archers can fire from above. We must hold our ground."

The nameless mage spread her arms wide. "Hold? Who will hold this ground?" she questioned with a voice full of doubt.

Gideon looked behind her at the nearest group of refugees. Perhaps thirty of them looked strong enough to fight, but only twenty of the men had brought any weapons with them. The other ten held makeshift slings filled with rocks in their shaking hands. Gideon looked back to the growing dust cloud and dropped his head low to the ground to listen to the distant rumble. "They're probably mounted," he said after a moment. "They'll be here in minutes. We should have spent the night digging graves, not scrounging for soldiers in a refugee camp."

With a rumble, Vrysinoch spread his wings. Behind the statue, screams began to filter into the sky as the refugees realized what was about to happen. Women cowered with their children, foolhardy men arrogantly readied for battle, and some of the smarter ones started to run.

Slowly, almost appearing to smile, Vrysinoch turned to Gideon and spoke. "Start a hymn," the god commanded. "You must not die here."

For once, Gideon listened. He hated the bitter taste the words left on his mouth, but he sang with all his might. Valge and the other mage joined the hymn as well, although they did not know the lyrics. With trembling voices, they hummed a tune they hoped matched what Gideon sang.

Even Vrysinoch faltered for a moment when he finally saw what approached them from the city. Beneath an ever-growing cloud of dust, a herd of armored minotaurs stampeded toward them. They pounded the ground on all fours, and each beast had a ballista mounted to its back with an orc ready to fire it.

"Come, sons of Talonrend," Vrysinoch bade the open air. Less than two hundred yards separated the statue from the oncoming horde. Beams of green light burst forth from the ground a hundred yards from Vrysinoch's outstretched talon. In an instant, the light receded, leaving behind the ghosts of several hundred paladins. The summoned men wasted no time. As one, they linked their shields, set their feet to take the charge, and joined Gideon's hymn as though they had been singing it all along.

Vrysinoch turned once more to Gideon and the mages. "Go," he told them. "Move north, then east. Stay alive. You must kill the half-orc with your sword. Druaka must not be allowed to have his soul."

Gideon nodded and began to run. Gravlox and the two mages followed quickly on his heels.

When the orcs saw the ghostly paladins before them, they let fire a devastating hail of ballista bolts. Despite having no real bodies, the paladins were not immune to injury. More than half of them fell after the first volley. Luckily, the orcs had anticipated having more distance before they engaged, so they did not have enough time to reload before the real battle began.

The two lines collided with unbelievable fury. The minotaurs pushed forward, crashing through ghostly shields and bodies with their horns, and the orcs riding their backs leapt into the chaos with their own weapons.

It did not take long for Vrysinoch's statue to join the fray. The massive eagle stormed through the line of paladins with an ear-splitting screech. The god's immense, stone wings slammed into a tightly formed group of orcs about to flank the paladin line. Orcish blood flew through the air like rain.

The minotaurs, over one hundred strong, continued to crush their ghostly opponents. Hard-pressed, the paladins fought with bravery, steadily felling the beasts with their magical swords, but every minotaur took a handful of paladins with it to the dirt. The towering creatures were simply too strong for the paladins to resist. After only a few moments, the paladins' hymn was drowned out by their own screams. What remained of their coordinated battle line began to crumble under the sheer ferocity of the assault.

Vrysinoch batted an orc away with a swipe of his marble claw that sent the creature hurtling through the air. All around him, orcs jabbed at his wings and back with spears, but their weapons broke against hard stone. With the ghosts falling behind him, Vrysinoch realized the statue he possessed would not endure forever. Some of the minotaurs turned their attention to him, slamming their immense weight into his legs like a demolition crew bringing down a city wall.

"Run!" Vrysinoch yelled with magically enhanced authority to the refugees behind the paladins. At once, the meager band of humans broke into a mad dash. Vrysinoch used a stony claw to point them southeast, closer to Talonrend, but away from the carnage.

"Shit," Melkora muttered under her breath. She stood amidst the refugees, side by side with a family of merchants clutching kitchen knives and shovels. When Vrysinoch's command reached her ears, she ran. "Follow me!" she shouted behind her, but she knew most of the people could not hear her over the din of battle.

At first, none of the orcs or minotaurs seemed to see the several hundred humans fleeing for their lives. For a fleeting moment, Melkora thought they might escape with their lives.

The first orcs to notice them abandoned their futile task of destroying Vrysinoch and turned, chasing the refugees like wolves. "Go!" Melkora screamed at her fellow humans. She grabbed a strong looking man by the shoulder and planted her feet. "We need to slow them down," she told him fiercely.

"Me?" the man nervously replied. Although they had run less than a quarter of a mile, the man was visibly winded. He glanced back once at his fleeing family, sighed, and tightened his grip on his sword. The weapon, if it could be called such a thing, looked more like a ceremonial piece stolen from the mantel of an officer than a tool crafted to kill.

Somehow, to Melkora's disbelief, a handful of other men stopped to join her resistance. None of them were soldiers, but they were hearty. They might slow the orcs down. Maybe they would manage to kill one.

The screaming refugees flooded past the makeshift warband

without giving them a second glance. Melkora took Roisin from her belt, unwrapped the white cloth which had been placed around it, and set her aching feet into a fighting stance.

"Shoulder to shoulder," she called out. After only a moment of hesitation, the men did as they were commanded. Before she could issue any further orders, the first of the orcs were upon them.

Four green-skinned creatures, all wielding heavy spears, thundered into Melkora's line. The first human died before he knew what was happening. The lead orc swatted the man's shovel away, stepped forward, and impaled the poor lad where he stood. Next to him, the others attempted to gang up on the beast, but their improvised weapons were useless.

The orc laughed.

With a sinister grin, he kicked the dead man in the chest, let his spear fall to the ground, and began pummeling the nearest human with his fists. Melkora wanted to rush to the refugees' aid as they struggled in vain to fight the flailing orc, but there was nothing she could do. One of the beasts charged at her with his own spear aimed right for her abdomen.

Melkora feigned terror, shrieking and holding her hands up in surrender, and waited for the orc to strike. When the spear tip was just in reach of her clothes, she deftly sidestepped the weapon. Her elbow cracked into the orc's face and sent him reeling. Melkora wasted no time pouncing on him and sinking Roisin in the orc's neck. When she turned back to the others, she saw the line had crumbled to a brawl.

The man she had first conscripted fought nobly with his rusty sword. In the very short time it took Melkora to get to her feet and return to the fighting, the man deftly parried two attacks from his opponent, and then was run through by the orc's spear. While the two fought, the orc failed to notice Melkora creeping up behind him. Roisin ripped through his lower back in a single strike.

Melkora knew the others were doomed. Even though a score of men had joined her cause, they had no armor, no training, and no proper weapons. Before she could even take a moment to identify her next target, less than half the men remained alive.

To her left, a group of three refugees had corralled an orc, keeping him at bay with an odd assortment of cutlery. As quietly as she could, Melkora snuck up behind the beast and waited for her moment. With a growl, the orc lunged forward, skewering a man holding a butcher's cleaver. An instant later, Melkora lashed out with her dagger. It was a solid hit, but not instantly fatal. The orc surged onward, bringing down two other humans before he finally fell.

The fourth orc, a tall creature with bits of bone braided into his hair, wielded a spear in each hand. Melkora waited, judging the orc's movements and searching for an opening. One of the men bravely dashed forward, attempting to dodge the spears by going low, and was eviscerated before he got a chance to attack.

Only a handful of humans remained. "He's too quick," Melkora admitted. She needed a new tactic. Waiting for the orc to display a moment of carelessness would only get her killed. Instead, she waited for the orc to tire.

One at a time, Melkora watched as the humans fell. When the last man died, the orc was breathing heavily, and his spears moved in slow circles. Melkora grit her teeth and rolled forward. She knew the orc would try to strike at her exposed back, but she also knew she would be faster. When she came up from her roll, Roisin struck the orc's groin and sank to the hilt. The creature screamed, tried to leap away from her, and collapsed to the ground in a howling mess.

Melkora, still in a tense crouch, looked toward the west in horror. Nearly half the minotaurs and orcs fighting Vrysinoch had broken away to chase the human refugees. Melkora could not fight them all.

Without any other option presenting itself in her mind, Melkora fell to her chest as innocuously as she could. She tucked Roisin into her belt, slid partially under the orc she had just killed, and waited for her enemies to pass her.

Nineteen

"**H**OW DO WE get in?" Gideon asked. Valge and the unnamed oblivion mage stood exhausted to his left. Despite their lack of physical bodies, their stamina was pathetic. They had run for only a short while, just long enough to get past the orcs and minotaurs unseen.

Gravlox reached a gloved hand up to Gideon's chest and tugged on his shirt. The small, white-clad goblin pointed to himself, then pointed both hands at Terror's Lament, still looming roughly half a mile in front of them.

Gideon took a step backward to give Gravlox space. "Be careful," he muttered, though he knew his words were an empty comfort.

With his palms pointed toward the ground, Gravlox began to tremble — but nothing happened.

"Your old magic is still in the Void," Valge said breathlessly. "You cannot do what you did before."

Gravlox turned to the woman with what Gideon guessed was a puzzled expression. "What should he do?" the paladin asked on Gravlox's behalf.

Valge shook her head, her eyeless mask boring into the ground.

"It takes years to learn Void magic," she told them. "I can try to remove the wall myself, but it is a difficult task. If only Valkoinen were here," her voice trailed off in an indiscernible groan.

"Remove the wall?" Gideon gawked. "You can do that?" He had witnessed unbelievable feats of magic in his life, but causing a section of reinforced stone wall to vanish was something he did not think possible.

"The Void is not full of magic in the sense you think it is," the unnamed mage explained. "The Void is the *absence* of magic. It is much better suited for removal than creation or destruction."

Gideon shook his head. To him, magic was a gift from Vrysinoch — at least when the fickle god felt like being generous. "If the Void has no magic, how is it so powerful?" he scoffed, adding a bit more arrogance to his voice than he intended.

"No," the mage chided. "The Void contains what is left behind when magic is used," she explained slowly. "It is the opposite of magic, the reaction to it."

Gideon consigned himself to never understanding the strange complexities of the Alabaster Order. He let out a sigh, ushered Valge toward the wall with an open hand, and waited for her to make the wall vanish.

Valge and the unnamed mage both stepped forward. They each raised a hand toward the distant wall and began to chant in a language Gideon did not recognize. Beside him, Gideon could sense Gravlox's apprehension. The goblin held himself carefully, not wanting to interfere, but intensely interested in how the two women operated.

After a moment, the air at the edge of their fingertips shimmered. Gravlox could sense the power they wielded, but it was nothing like the shamanistic energy he had commanded before. To his magical sense, it felt like the mages' power had no source. The energy they manipulated had no beginning and no end.

Imitating the women, Gravlox held out his hand and beckoned to the soil at his feet. He knew there was power held within the ground, tremendous power, but he could not find it. The magic of the world was silent.

The shimmering air in front of the two mages grew in intensity, distorting the light until the section of Terror's Lament they faced appeared twisted, almost melting. The wall began to fade before their eyes. After a few seconds, a hole large enough to drive several wagons through suddenly existed where the stone of Terror's Lament had been.

Gideon gasped. "Such power!" he said breathlessly. It was only then that he realized his mistake. "No!" he screamed, but orcs were already pouring from the new opening. "The wall is three layers thick! You have to remove all three to enter the city!" he shouted.

The two mages were doubled over from exhaustion. What little stamina they had after fleeing the minotaurs was entirely spent. Even if they were far enough away to outrun the orcs, the women would not be able to keep up. The orcs would run them down like wild hogs before they made it back to Vrysinoch's statue.

"Can you remove them?" Gideon asked. The orcs were closing quickly. By his estimation, several hundred of the creatures had been waiting inside Terror's Lament when the section of wall vanished, and every one of them was fully armed and armored.

Valge shook her head behind her mask, but Gideon paid her no attention. With trembling legs, she stepped next to him and placed a gloved hand on his shoulder. "This is the end," she whispered, barely strong enough to speak. Beside her, the unnamed mage struggled to stand.

"No," Gideon muttered in response. "It cannot be." His slowly healing wrist throbbed as he drew Nevidal from the sheath on his back. Thankfully, the enchantment binding his soul to the sword quickly made the pain in his body fade.

Gideon's muscles stretched and protested against his skin, yearning for carnage and threatening to rip his flesh apart. "Get back," he said, waving his hand behind him. The two mages struggled to move, but Gideon did not have time to help them. Before he could even set his feet properly, the inexorable tide of steel and fury was upon him.

Gravlox did not know what to do. He wanted to save the two mages, but he was only half their height—carrying them would be impossible. He felt like a coward, but he ran. He wasn't sure if his small stature made him inconspicuous or if the orcs were too focused on Gideon to notice him, but when he turned around only fifty yards from the fighting, he saw not a single orc had pursued him.

From a small patch of unremarkable grass, Gravlox watched the slaughter. The orcs closed around Gideon like a vise, surrounding him instantly and slashing wildly with their weapons. In their savage bloodlust, the orcs didn't even bother to attack the two mages. Instead, they let their fury carry them over the stumbling women, trampling them to death in a few quick moments.

In the middle of the fray, Gideon cleaved through orcs like a madman. Faster than Gravlox had ever seen anyone fight, the desperate man slashed Nevidal from side to side, cutting huge arcs in front of him. He whirled about with every strike, deflecting attacks from his sides and back, all the while growing stronger and stronger as Nevidal's enchantment flooded his body with magic.

A ring of green-skinned corpses piled up at Gideon's feet. Blood flew through the air with every swing of his sword, but Gideon could not fight them all at once. For every orc he slew, two more attacked him from angles he could not defend. Orcs thrust their spears into his back, ripping his clothing to tatters and shredding the flesh beneath. From his sides, they came at him with clubs and axes. Their weapons pounded his shoulders, shattered his ribs, and spilled his blood onto the ground.

There was only so much punishment Nevidal's enchantment could mitigate. Gideon's magically enhanced pain tolerance had a limit, which he soon found. From behind and slightly to his left, a warhammer smashed into his collarbone with a resounding crack. Pain lanced through his upper body like fire. Grimacing, Gideon felt his sword's enchantment failing. He turned upon the orc, slashing Nevidal in a horizontal arc, and ripped the beast apart at the waist, but it was not enough. Before he could think, another weapon sliced down his right leg and made him cry out in pain.

Gideon roared. Being so close to death brought a violence to his mind he had never known, but primal fury would not keep him alive — he needed a plan, a way out, *something.*

And then he saw his chance. In front of him, almost upon him, was an orc dressed differently than the others. It was not the shaman he sought to destroy, but it was one of their leaders, of that Gideon was certain. Remembering the duel he had with the strange anvil-wielding orc in the woods, Gideon planted his feet and pointed Nevidal at what he presumed was a chieftain.

Some of the orcs recognized the gesture and halted their surge, but several of them continued to attack. Gideon cut the hands off an orc to his left, whirled right to slash the throat of another attacker, and quickly returned his gaze to the orc in front of him. Thankfully, the orc bellowed something to his cohorts, immediately calming the chaotic battle.

Gideon took the moment of reprieve to gather his wits and let more of Nevidal's energy try to heal his multitude of wounds. Although his injuries did not hurt nearly as much as they should have, he knew had at least a dozen broken bones. His collarbone felt disconnected, his ribs were more like splintered logs than bones, and his body was covered with more of his own blood than was on the inside. Without Nevidal's magic sustaining him, he would have died before the chieftain ever took notice.

I only have to kill the half-orc, he tried to console himself internally. Perhaps if he could appeal to whatever honor the orcs respected in combat by fighting their leaders one at a time, the half-orc would come out to meet him. It was a risky guess, but Gideon thought it was a much better plan than cleaving his way through two hundred orcs to get to the city.

Forming a circle as the orcs had done in the woods the week be-

743

fore, the chieftain beckoned Gideon forward. The man had to step over a waist-high pile of green corpses to get to an open part of the battlefield, but the orcs around him did not impede his movement, and Gideon found himself standing in front of the leader with a strained grin on his face.

The chieftain, a predictably huge beast with half of a goat painted onto his bare chest, held two short swords out at his sides. Gideon found his fighting style peculiar for an orc, but he also found the entire ritual of a duel contradictory to everything he knew about orcs.

He didn't know if he should bow or do something else to show his respect, so Gideon waited for the orc to make the first move. All the while, Gideon constantly scanned the top of Terror's Lament for any sign of the half-orc looking on, hoping to catch the leader's attention. Many figures ran from place to place on the wall, but several had gathered in one place presumably to watch the fight. Gideon could only hope the half-orc was one of them.

VRYSINOCH THRASHED OUT with his stone wings, killing the last minotaur he faced. Between himself and Talonrend, Vrysinoch saw the orcs and minotaurs descend upon the fleeing refugees. A score or more of their corpses already littered the ground, but the bulk of them had run eastward until their legs gave out.

With a resounding clap of thunder, Vrysinoch leapt from the ground. He flew toward the refugees, staying roughly thirty feet off the ground. "Sister," he hissed. His voice rolled out like a landslide, covering the ground with its power. "I've brought you an offering."

744

MELKORA TILTED HER head to hear. Vrysinoch had followed the humans, orcs, and minotaurs closer to Talonrend, but he did not descend. The screams of the refugees pierced through the air as they were killed. Still, Vrysinoch gently hovered above them.

"Save them!" Melkora growled. Though the fighting, if such a slaughter could be called combat, was more than a hundred yards away, Melkora kept her voice down. Her hasty camouflage had worked, and she had no intention of giving it up if she did not need to.

"Fight, Vrysinoch!" she growled again past bared teeth. She had seen Vrysinoch fight! The god was unstoppable! "Why won't you help them?" she angrily spat.

Soon, the screams of the humans died down. All she could hear were the victory cries of the orcs, and the deep, grating voices of the minotaurs. After a few moments of revelry, the beasts retreated back toward Talonrend, leaving a field of unbelievable carnage in their wake. Slowly, Melkora lifted her head entirely from the ground. She did not know what she wanted or expected to see, but what she saw was as far from comforting as it could have been. Not a single human remained. Every refugee, the men, the unarmed women, and the children, had been ruthlessly slaughtered.

Melkora began to understand Gideon's intense frustration with Vrysinoch. "You are not my god," she cursed, looking away from the flying statue in disgust.

THE CHIEFTAIN CHARGED at Gideon with his swords held high, but it was not a reckless maneuver. Gideon knew the orc was skilled.

Nevidal erupted in sparks when it collided with the orc's swords. Gideon tried to push forward, but the orc was stronger. Instead, Gideon turned away to his left, letting the orc's swords swing harmlessly short of his back. The chieftain snarled. Gideon roared back, taunting the chieftain, and tried to buy as much time as he could with his posturing. The longer he waited, the more strength Vrysinoch's enchantment poured into his body.

The chieftain attacked again, this time bringing his swords in at opposite angles, hoping to cut Gideon in half at the hips. In a flash, Gideon brought Nevidal down to block the sword on his right and lashed out with his left hand, catching the orc's wrist. He twisted, slowly rotating the creature's arm into a grotesque position, all the while blocking the orc's sword on his right with Nevidal's blade. Despite being weaker than the orc, Gideon forced the chieftain to drop his sword and retreat, lest he break his wrist.

Gideon wasted no time kicking the sword away. The chieftain's expression betrayed nothing. He gripped his remaining sword in both hands and swung a mighty overhead chop toward Gideon's face. Bending at the knees into a low crouch, Gideon raised Nevidal horizontally above his head to block.

The strike from above did not come. Instead, the chieftain kept his blade aloft and kicked, knocking the man backward with ease. Gideon scrambled through the dirt like an injured animal. He could not let go of his sword, and the large weapon made him clumsy. As he tried to get out of the orc's range, the chieftain brought his sword down with blazing speed and slashed open Gideon's back.

He had already lost more blood than any normal human would be able to sustain — there wasn't enough left in his back to bleed. His skin flapped open as he climbed back to his feet. Without Nevidal's magic, he would have been dead several times over. When he stood, the chieftain stared awkwardly at him, not comprehending how Gideon had survived such a brutal wound.

Around the tightly packed circle, the other orcs still cheered. They howled for carnage, and from their perspective, the chieftain was winning. Gideon let more of Nevidal's magic fill his body as he faced his opponent over several feet of bloodstained dirt. As he stared at the chieftain, he realized he was now taller than the orc. As he absorbed more and more magic, every part of his body grew. If the chieftain was intimidated by his increasing stature, the orc did not show it.

They clashed again, the orc going low and Gideon moving to block with his blade, his strength now greater than the orc's. Gideon shoved forward with all his magical strength. He felt the cuts on his legs and the gaping wound on his back tearing further with every breath, but he did not stop.

The orc shrank back under Gideon's raw power. When the chieftain moved one of his feet to reposition himself, Gideon pulled back, instantly overbalancing the orc. The chieftain lost his footing, and Nevidal soared upward, opening the orc from groin to chin as he fell.

Nevidal begged for release. Gideon could feel the blade's energy threatening to destroy him. Every ounce of his body thrummed with violent magic he could not contain. He knew he could let the sword fall from his hands. He had slain more than enough orcs to sate Nevidal's appetite for souls, but letting go of the hilt meant certain death.

Desperate to find the half-orc, Gideon whirled toward the other orcs gathered around him. He pointed his sword at each of them in turn, hoping his ever-growing height would intimidate them into calling forth their leader.

"YOUR SACRIFICE IS ready, sister," Vrysinoch hissed into the cool air. He saw a jet-black raven which he hadn't noticed before slowly circling the human corpses. It was a good sign, but not enough. "Come, sister, lead the souls to the afterworld. Come and face me."

Several more ravens appeared, flying toward the corpses from somewhere off in the north. Some of the birds landed in order to feast upon the corpses.

Vrysinoch tucked his stony wings behind his back and dove toward the corpses, scaring most of the ravens away. Predictably, only a handful of the birds remained, and none of them had landed. "Druaka!" Vrysinoch thundered into the sky. He turned in wide circles, waiting for a sign of his sister's return.

More ravens started to fly to the corpses from every direction. Before long, several hundred ravens circled above Vrysinoch's head, and none of them could be frightened away.

"Yes, sister," Vrysinoch hissed. "Come and feast."

The world darkened. At first, Vrysinoch thought a storm cloud must have welled up in the sky. Then the darkness descended. A huge flock, probably over one million individual birds, blocked out the sun. For a split second, everything was black. Vrysinoch used his massive wings to shield his head, anticipating an onslaught of ravens, but no attack came. When he lowered his defense, the world was bright again. Everything was quieter, but the flock of ravens had vanished.

Druaka stood atop the pile of human corpses. Her shiny black feathers glistened in the sunlight. Her hooked beak and pointed talons looked sharp enough to cut through solid stone.

Vrysinoch shuddered.

Twenty

UNDRAKK PEERED FROM the top of Terror's Lament with casual curiosity. Using magic, he watched a tall human with a long, braided beard fight a Half Goat warlord amidst a seemingly innumerable sea of orc soldiers. Everything was going according to plan. The human convoy had been easily slaughtered, his casualties had been few, and the bulk of his forces still remained safely behind the walls in reserve.

The presence of the seemingly unharmed eagle statue still bothered Undrakk, but he figured it was an issue that could wait. When not a single human remained in front of his city, he would devise a method for disposing of the strange statue. With a contented sigh, Undrakk turned his vision back to the duel.

"Impressive," he mused. He tried to count the orc corpses behind the human, all slain by a single man, but soon lost focus. The Half Goat chieftain, one of his strongest fighters, would surely destroy the miserable human.

"Flawless," Undrakk smiled. The Half Goat orc ripped open the human's back with a devastating blow. The sheer ferocity of the wound made the shaman wince, but he loved every second of the fight.

But then the human rose. Undrakk could not believe what he saw. Utterly perplexed, he dismissed the magic field in front of him which enhanced his vision, shook his head to clear his mind, and recast the spell. Sure enough, the human stood on his own two feet, still with his sword in hand.

The human was covered in more blood than Undrakk had ever seen on a single creature, but his grievous wounds did not slow him. Undrakk watched more intently as the duel commenced again. A low, rumbling growl emanated from Undrakk's throat when the chieftain fell. His grip on the parapet tightened, the rough stone cutting into the palms of his hand.

Suddenly, Undrakk remembered who Gideon was. A hint of bile crept up the back of his throat. "He should be dead," the half-orc spat. "I'll have to kill him myself."

"Do be careful, my lord," Sifir chimed in behind him.

Undrakk shook his head. He had spent months listening to the strange priest, yet he still did not understand the man's loyalties. Undrakk knew the old man was conscious of his own self-preservation, but why he so willingly helped the orcs, he would never understand.

"Indeed," Undrakk absentmindedly replied. He tossed his staff from hand to hand, nervously pacing as he contemplated his next action.

After a brief moment of thought, Undrakk knew exactly what he had to do. He held his staff aloft, prepared the words to a spell within his mind, but then reconsidered. One last time, he wanted to try to kill Sifir. With more annoyance than anything else, he quickly shoved Sifir from the walls. As the man had always done, he screamed until he hit the ground, then got back to his feet as though nothing had happened.

Undrakk shook his head. "So be it," he conceded. He lifted his staff back above his head, whispered the words of a spell, and vanished.

When the shaman reappeared in the center of the throng of

orcs, everything was dark. At first, a thousand thoughts raced through Undrakk's head. He groped the air, hoping desperately he had not teleported too far and imprisoned himself in the soil. To his relief, his hand grasped the shoulder of an orc, and he knew he was on the ground as he had intended.

As suddenly as the darkness had swallowed the world, it vanished. Undrakk stood in the midst of his soldiers. For a moment, he thought he could feel the source of the sudden magical darkness, but it was a fleeting sensation. Several paces in front of him, Gideon leaned heavily on his sword amidst a ring of corpses, bringing Undrakk's mind back to his task.

A flicker of recognition danced across the human's face. "You," he said in the human tongue, a language Undrakk understood clearly. "I've come to take back my city."

Undrakk watched with subtle curiosity as the man appeared to grow in stature before him. "*Your* city?" the half-orc mused. "I thought the rulers of human cities wore crowns upon their heads."

Gideon grimaced, practically growling his frustrations.

"Then again," the half-orc continued with his peculiar manner, "perhaps it would be best to let the strongest fighter rule the others, much like the orcs do. After all," Undrakk brought his voice low to a sinister whisper. "Your leader did not put up much of a fight."

Gideon had heard enough. Nevidal's enchantment threatened to rip him apart from the inside. He needed to kill the half-orc before he lost the opportunity.

"Die!" Gideon roared, his voice so powerful it pushed the closest orcs back on their heels. He ran forward, lifting Nevidal to his eye level, and swung for the half-orc's chest.

Undrakk smiled. Such an overt attack was easy to counter. Lifting his staff, Undrakk released the energy of a spell which turned the twisted length of wood into tempered steel. He sidestepped, all the while keeping one arm tucked behind his back, and deflected Gideon's swipe with ease.

Gideon stumbled through his overbalanced attack, just barely keeping his feet under him. He knew his magically enhanced body could crush the half-orc in a pure test of strength, but Undrakk was far too devious to let Gideon get close. *Vrysinoch,* he silently prayed. *I need you.*

No answer came. Sucking in air like a man about to drown, Gideon stepped forward with his right foot and brought Nevidal in an arc across his chest. Again, Undrakk swatted the sword aside as though it were no more than a wooden toy.

Lunging in a low crouch, Gideon tried to close the distance between the half-orc and himself before Undrakk could react. The shaman cackled, spritely jumping backward without a scratch.

"You *must* be able to do better than *that,*" Undrakk taunted. Casually, he twirled his metal staff from one hand to the other. "I watched you fight from the wall!" he exclaimed. "You were brilliant. But this," he tsked like a mother scolding an insubordinate child, "this is embarrassing."

Gideon knew the half-orc was right. Despite his magical fortitude, he was too tired, and the spry shaman was simply too fast. With one last burst of speed, Gideon stabbed at Undrakk's left side, then quickly snapped his sword back, stepped forward, and lunged right. He felt Nevidal catch against something, but alas, it was only the half-orc's shirt that he shredded.

"Better," Undrakk sneered. "But not good enough." He smoothed the corner of his torn sleeve, his confident smirk turning to a vicious grin. "My turn," he stated.

With both hands on his staff, Undrakk summoned a small ball of blue magic in front of him. Spinning rapidly, the orb condensed all the water from the air and froze it into a solid projectile the size of a ballista bolt.

Gideon tensed, anticipating the missile, but was not nearly quick enough to dodge it. As he leapt to his left, the frozen bolt slammed into his chest and threw him to the ground. The huge man tried to get to his feet before the next attack came, but Undrakk's magic was relentless. Bolt after bolt of every natural element Gideon could imagine pummeled his body with unbelievable speed. Ice punctured his ribs, a jet of water hit his throat, crushing his windpipe, and a blast of flame with the intensity of a dozen furnaces charred his skin to black.

Wheezing, yet somehow alive, Gideon painfully lumbered to his knees. Made taller by magic, he looked Undrakk in the eyes and knew he had been defeated. *I failed,* he muttered in the dark recesses of his mind. He did not know if Vrysinoch could hear him, but it did not matter. He had failed.

Undrakk wore an expression of disappointment. "Humans," he scoffed, spitting on the ground at Gideon's knees. "Such a waste of flesh."

Casually, as if the act interrupted some other, vastly important task, Undrakk used the end of his staff to knock Gideon's sword from his hand, and the man fell face down in the dirt.

"Get back to the city," Undrakk commanded the orcs without waiting another moment. "They may have something else planned. We must be ready." At once, his soldiers began hurrying toward the wall.

Undrakk caught one of the passing orcs by the shoulder. "Bring me Sifir," he ordered. The orc nodded. "Be quick about it."

Several minutes later, the orc returned with Sifir cradled in his arms. "Faster to carry him," the orc grunted as he propped the man up. Undrakk sent the orc back to Broken Sword with a wave of his hand.

"Who was this man?" Undrakk demanded of the priest. He pointed to the corpse with the end of his metal staff.

After a moment, Sifir shook his head. "Some paladin or other, I suppose," Sifir began. "His tattoo marks him as one of Vrysinoch's warriors, though I do not believe it did him any good."

Undrakk grabbed the priest by his shoulders and pulled down the top of the man's robe. "You do not possess the same marking," he said, allowing the priest to cover himself back up. "Why not?"

Sifir smiled. He turned away from the dead man to face Undrakk. "I have never been a priest or paladin of *Vrysinoch*," he said.

Undrakk was perplexed. "You lived in the temple of Vrysinoch, did you not?"

The old man nodded. "Orcs live in caves in the mountains, yet they do not worship the stone that makes their walls."

"You follow Druaka?" Undrakk inquired with a quizzical expression. Somehow, he got the creeping suspicion that he had been tricked, though he could not fathom what possible gain the old man sought to achieve.

Sifir flashed a toothless grin. "I worship *nothing*."

VRYSINOCH, THREE FULL stories of eagle-shaped marble, stood across a gruesome field of human corpses from a jet-black raven.

Druaka's head, at the same level as Vrysinoch's, constantly twitched from side to side as if the giant bird tasted something unusual in the air. "It is time we settled our disputes," the raven squawked. Her voice sounded hesitant, almost strained.

"I have not seen you in several hundred years, sister," Vrysinoch replied. "When was the last time you walked the earth?" In contrast, Vrysinoch's voice was a thundering landslide of depth that shook the ground.

"Always!" Druaka squawked. "Always!"

Vrysinoch slowly began walking toward her. "Your riddles are meaningless, sister," he said. "Time has ravaged your mind, but do not worry, it will all come to an end soon."

"Always!" the raven repeated.

At once, Vrysinoch launched himself several feet into the air and slammed down in front of his sister, throwing his stone wings hard in front of him. Druaka screeched, taking the brunt of Vrysinoch's wings on her feathered chest.

She fell back, flapping wildly, and took to the air. Vrysinoch flew after her and together, the two gods soared into the clouds. Although he was made of solid stone, Vrysinoch was faster—he had always been faster.

Somewhere above the clouds, Vrysinoch's heavy talons latched into the soft skin of Druaka's grey feet. He ripped her down, twisting his body on top of hers, and tore at her throat with his stone beak. Druaka cawed in pain, thrashing her own wings against the statue, but her efforts were in vain.

As he had always been, Vrysinoch was far stronger than her. Tumbling back toward the ground, Druaka fought to keep her neck and chest from Vrysinoch's snapping beak. The eagle's talons had a grip of actual stone. Though she leaned back as far as her spine would allow, she could not escape.

Vrysinoch was too consumed by his assault to give any thought to his position as the two birds plummeted toward the ground. Entwined, they slammed into the ground, sending up a wave of dirt so large it crashed into Terror's Lament half a mile away.

At the bottom of a crater a hundred yards deep, Vrysinoch and Druaka were motionless. The statue's wings were crumbled and broken, the rest of his body cracked from the force of the impact.

The raven's body was torn and bleeding, but she had landed on top of Vrysinoch and therefore fared much better.

Druaka let out a muffled squawk as her eyes fluttered open. Every inch of her body throbbed in pain. When she tried to stand, her broken legs could not support her weight, and she fell backward into the shattered bedrock.

Not far in front of her, Vrysinoch also tried to stand. The statue Vrysinoch inhabited was so badly cracked it was nearly unrecognizable as carved stone. With a deep shudder, Vrysinoch lifted his upper body from the ground, slowly backpedalling across the crater.

"You'll die here," Druaka whispered. The bottom half of her beak hung from her jaw like a an errant splinter of wood.

Despite his condition, Vrysinoch managed a pained laugh. "I

have already died, sister," he said, his voice nowhere near as powerful as it was just minutes ago.

Druaka's mind was too rattled to comprehend her brother's words. "You will die," she softly repeated.

Vrysinoch shook his head. As he moved, bits of stone fell from his visage and scattered among the debris of the crater. "This body is only a vessel," he explained. Though the statue did not possess lungs, his words came slowly as though he struggled to breathe. "This slab of carved marble holds my consciousness, but in the end, it is useless."

Slowly, Druaka began to grasp his meaning. "Your champion is dead, brother," she squawked. "You have nowhere left to run."

Again, Vrysinoch tried to laugh. His body shook from the effort, and half of his face crumbled to the ground. "I still have one servant left, sister, but you have none. Your champion has been dead for months." He tried to move his head to look toward his sister, but his broken stone body would not respond to his commands. "You turned your own priest into a ghost—a vain effort. Where is he now?"

Druaka scoffed. When she spoke, blood poured from her mouth and neck. "My city still stands," she reminded him. "Your precious Green City is mine as well. You lost, brother." With one final effort, she tried to position herself to fly, but could not stand or beat her wings.

Both defeated, the two gods had no choice but to remain in the bottom of the crater they had created until their physical forms expired.

Twenty-One

STANDING UNNOTICED OUTSIDE a ring of jubilant orcs, Gravlox watched Gideon fight. The short goblin could not see through the crowd or above them, but Gideon's magically enhanced height was easy to follow. When the tall man went down and did not rise again, Gravlox knew he was dead.

For a moment, Gravlox considered following Vorst back to Kanebullar Mountain, where he assumed she had gone. Suddenly, a voice pulled his attention back to the battle. "You," it said in the goblin language, almost perfectly matching his own high-pitched voice.

Gravlox turned. The orcs in front of him had parted to reveal a host of corpses and their leader, a peculiarly dressed half-orc with a metal staff. In the center of the orcs, Gideon's ragged corpse lay motionless, Nevidal just inches from his bloody fingertips.

With a slight nod of recognition, Gravlox stepped forward. Surprisingly, he did not fear the half-orc as he thought he should.

"What are you?" Undrakk continued. "My scouts reported seeing a goblin with the accompanying the humans," he said. "Are you that goblin?" His voice was strange, almost entertained, as though the entire scene of bloody warfare around him was only a momentary distraction.

Gravlox shook his head. Without a voice, he did not know what to do. If he ran, he felt he would be chased and killed.

"But you do understand me?" Undrakk asked, still using the goblin language.

Again, Gravlox nodded.

Undrakk closed his eyes and tried to search for any trace of magic about Gravlox, but when he looked, he found nothing. In fact, Gravlox was so profoundly non-magical, Undrakk felt as though his own powers were weakening just by being near the strange goblin.

With a wave of his hand, Undrakk ushered the surrounding orcs back and walked up to Gravlox. He gently lifted his staff toward Gravlox's chest, poking ever so slightly. The white robes offered no resistance to his touch.

"What are you?" the half-orc repeated. He prodded Gravlox again, but the robes fluttered as if they were only filled by the wind.

Silently, Gravlox shuffled several paces backward. He clenched his fists. More than anything, Gravlox wanted to scream, to summon great bursts of magic to his hands, and to kill the half-orc where he stood. When he tried to yell, his mouth did not move. No sound issued forth.

"It does not matter," Undrakk said after studying Gravlox for a moment. "Whatever you are, you will die, just like your friends."

The half-orc's staff began to glow red, and Gravlox could feel magic being gathered around the end of it. *A shaman!* Gravlox screamed in his mind, instantly feeling the conduit of energy between the staff and the ground.

Undrakk leapt backward in shock, his face betraying his confusion. "You speak!" he shouted, holding his ears as though they were suddenly injured.

You hear me? Gravlox said within his consciousness. He wasn't sure how, but when he focused on the magic swirling about the half-orc's staff, his thoughts seemed to be transmitted as easily as if he still had a voice.

"Yes, I—" Undrakk stuttered. His usual composure was destroyed. Try as he might, he could not hide his surprise.

Stop what you are doing, Gravlox mentally commanded. *Take your clans back to the hills. Leave this city.*

A familiar smirk returned to Undrakk's face. He pointed toward the south, directing Gravlox's gaze to the field of human corpses being slowly devoured by carrion feeders. "You have lost," Undrakk said with a sickly-sweet voice. "What does a goblin want with a city? You would be the only one to live in it."

Gravlox didn't know what to say. Unsure how to turn off his telepathic connection, his inner dissonance seeped into Undrakk's mind.

"See?" the half-orc continued. "Broken Sword is not your home. It never will be. This city belongs to me now."

You deserve to die, Gravlox seethed, finally settling his thoughts into a cohesive pattern.

"Oh? According to which moral code?" Undrakk asked. "A goblin will avenge the deaths of humans?" His confident smile broadened. "How quaint."

In that moment, Gravlox knew he had no answer. He was not human. In appearance, he was closer to the orcs than the humans who had become his friends. His eyes drifted back to Gideon's lifeless body. *Perhaps they are all dead,* he thought, but Undrakk heard his words as well.

"They are," the half-orc confirmed. "Your human friends are dead." Undrakk walked slowly around Gravlox as though he was inspecting a precious work of art.

What will I do?

"Go back to your mountain," Undrakk told him. His voice sounded like a concerned parent, not a cruel, warmongering leader of orcs. "I will give you an escort. No orc or minotaur will hurt you. Go back to Kanebullar Mountain. Be among your kind. We have no qualms with your race—we will not bother you."

Gravlox let Undrakk's words swim through his mind for a long time. The offer was enticing. What other choice did he have? Even if he could kill every orc and minotaur in the city, what would be the point? He was not mankind's avenger. *I owe them nothing,* he thought with venom, remembering the time he spent in Castle Talon's dungeon even after he helped rescue their city.

"You owe humanity nothing," Undrakk whispered. "Live out the rest of your days in peace." The half-orc turned west and pointed toward Kanebullar Mountain. "You are free to leave," he said with a genuine smile.

Slowly, Gravlox nodded. His white-clothed feet barely made a sound as he moved. When he looked past Undrakk, the half-orc let the magic fade from his staff, and Gravlox's mental connection to him was severed.

I'm coming for you, Vorst, he wanted to yell. There was nothing left for him in Talonrend.

"UGH," MELKORA COUGHED, pushing a dead orc from her torso. Some of the creature's thick blood had oozed onto her skin, and it smelled terrible. She couldn't get the blood off of her quickly enough.

She didn't know how long she had waited, but the sun had fallen behind her, casting an eerie, red glow over the battlefield. Thankfully, the orcs and minotaurs had gone back into the city hours ago. Melkora hoped they wouldn't come out in the night to scavenge the battlefield or bury their dead. In the fields surrounding Talonrend, there were not enough trees to provide adequate cover. She wanted to find somewhere hide for the night, but no options clearly presented themselves.

Melkora stood slowly, keeping a wary eye for any movements. After a minute of tense waiting, she started to move. She wasn't sure where she would go, but she needed to find water or shelter at the very least.

"We lost," she whispered. Crouching to avoid detection, she darted from corpse to corpse through what used to be the Azurian refugees. She desperately wanted one of them to make a noise, anything that might indicate someone had survived, but only silence greeted her.

She considered turning back toward the west, but what would she do? "I'll need food," she told herself, although the sight of so many corpses did wonders to suppress her growing appetite.

After a few moments of aimlessly wandering, Melkora found a dead minotaur that caught her interest. The beast was covered in thick plates of metal armor that glinted in the waning light. Melkora kneeled next to the creature and slipped Roisin from her belt.

With a grunt, she rolled the minotaur onto its back and began cutting away its armor. After she had finished, she cast the heavy armor aside and began working her dagger into the creature's tough hide. It wasn't easy work and she didn't really know what she was doing, but after a few hours, she had the monster's hide removed from its upper body.

"Just leather," she told herself. The minotaur's stench was overwhelming.

She ran Roisin's edge horizontally along the inside of the hide to clean the blood and sinew from it as best she knew how. The hide, even though it was only from the top half of the minotaur's body, covered Melkora well. She searched the nearby corpses, gathering various swords, daggers, and even household knives to use as tent stakes.

The desperation of her situation fully washed over her when she looked at the meager tent of minotaur hide she had built. It wasn't large enough for her to entirely conceal herself as she slept, but it was enough to keep her warm without a fire.

GRAVLOX RAN HARDER than he ever had before. His energy, usually close to limitless, faded faster than he expected. Less than a mile from the orcs he had left, his body began to slow. Along with his physical fatigue came an overwhelming sense of nausea. He wasn't sure if he was capable of vomiting, but he could not keep the feeling under control.

When he stopped running, even his mind slowed to a halt. Every thought he attempted to make felt like it hit a solid wall of stone. Even his emotions had to be forcibly wrenched into his conscious mind.

But Gravlox would not be deterred. He had one thing left to live for in the world, and he would not be stopped by the mere fact that he was missing a body. Mentally, he tried to grit his teeth in frustration, but it was impossible. *I don't have teeth,* he managed to growl at his own mind. *I have nothing.*

Gravlox collapsed to the ground. When his knees hit the rocky soil, he felt nothing. Somehow, he had form, but not sensation. *Why am I so tired!* he silently raged. None of it made sense.

I am nothing, he told himself after several long minutes of agonizing solitude. As his body somehow recovered its stamina, his thoughts came quicker. After ten more minutes, he felt relatively normal, though whatever semblance of a stomach he possessed still roiled with nausea.

He rose from the ground slowly, taking measured steps to preserve what little energy he had. He walked for hours around the base of Terror's Lament. When the day's sunlight finally faded, he had made little progress. Defeated, he sat back on the ground to recover his energy.

There must be another way, he thought. He remembered Valkoinen moving with great speed through the air when they had first met. Gravlox wasn't sure where to begin, but he had to try.

He tried to conjure the emotion he had felt when he had latched onto the half-orc's stream of magic. Something had been there, something real, and he knew he could manipulate it. When he closed his eyes, if that was what he was even doing, the world went black. The darkness felt different than merely covering the world with a thin layer of skin. The black he perceived with his eyes shut was darker than black should be.

It was the Void.

Hesitantly, Gravlox reached forward with his mind, hoping to latch onto a stream of magic, but he felt nothing beneath his grasp. But to his mind, *nothing* had a strange meaning. The *nothing* was real—intangible, but it certainly existed. Gravlox retracted his mind for a brief moment, collected his restless thoughts into a focused effort, and plunged his consciousness deep into the Void.

To his surprise, the Void reacted. The very essence of blank nothingness recoiled from his touch like a wounded animal. *You are mine*, Gravlox told the Void. *You belong to me now. I am your master.*

Somewhere within his thoughts, Gravlox felt the Void itself submit. He felt it as easily as he had felt his own hands and feet—when he had possessed a physical body. Somehow, the Void had *become* his body. His limbs, torso, head, everything about him, was molded from the emptiness of the Void.

Take me forward, Gravlox commanded. He waited, but nothing happened. Not letting his concentration slip, he reached back into the Void with his mind and grasped it. When he brought it toward him, it obeyed, forming into a crystal of flickering darkness. Gravlox knew beyond a doubt he could bring the crystal into the material plane, but it did not help him find Vorst, so he let it fall from his fingers.

He reached forward again, this time sending his mind as far as it would stretch, and locked his mental grasp around the Void with all of his strength. Instead of pulling the Void toward him, he pulled himself forward, using the Void as an anchor.

In an instant he felt winded, but not nearly as much as had after running. Hopeful, Gravlox opened his eyes to peer into the material plane through his alabaster mask.

He recognized the scene before him. Green terraces full of crops were carved into the side of the mountain just as he remembered. To his right, a pen of animals noisily snored in a sliver of moonlight. Above him, a stocky goblin peered down from a terrace, but the creature did not seem alarmed. After a moment, the farmer went back to harvesting a plot of mushrooms.

I've done it! Gravlox thought to himself with overwhelming joy. *But I'm on the wrong side of Kanebullar Mountain.*

As quickly as he could, he dove his mind back into the Void and searched for another handhold closer to where he thought Vorst might be. Something blinked into the darkness. He wasn't sure if it had always been there and he had just noticed the movement, but it was there nonetheless. Curiously, Gravlox planted his mind next to the place where he seen the flicker and launched himself forward.

When he opened his eyes to see, he stood in a barren field next to Vorst, her face a mixture of shock and happiness. *I found you,* Gravlox said, using the Void to project his thoughts into her mind.

"You did," she said aloud. "What happened?"

Gravlox shook his head. *Everyone is dead,* he told her.

Vorst nodded. "Was Gideon able to kill their leader?" she asked. She didn't seem at all surprised to hear of the orc's victory.

No, Gravlox replied. *But I can kill the half-orc, if I must.*

Vorst looked confused. "What do you mean?"

Why would we go back?

Vorst started to speak, but she had no answer. "I," she began. "I don't know."

We can return to Kanebullar Mountain. The half-orc said he would not attack the mountain.

"Do you trust him?" Vorst asked. "Part human or not, he is still mostly an orc."

Gravlox wanted to laugh, but he wasn't sure how to transfer his mirth to Vorst's mind. *The half-orc has no reason to attack the goblins. He has his city, he does not need a mountain as well,* Gravlox reasoned.

Vorst pondered his words for a moment, but finally nodded. "You will live with me in the mountain?" She turned her eyes from his mask, choosing to speak more to the memory of his appearance than his white robes.

Always, Gravlox said immediately. *I would rather die than live without you.*

Hand in gloved hand, the two goblins continued eastward through the night, stopping only occasionally for Gravlox to rest.

Twenty-Two

THE VICTORY CELEBRATION consumed Broken Sword. Everywhere Undrakk turned his gaze, fires burned and orcs drunkenly cheered. "Quite impressive," Keturah said from his side as the two looked on from the top of Half-Orc Keep. Beneath them, Undrakk had hung a second hilt over the castle's entryway, identical to the first.

"We suffered fewer than two hundred casualties," Undrakk said with a smile. "It was hardly a battle."

"True," Keturah conceded. "But you still won."

"*We* won," Undrakk added. "Though I did not need the aid of your demons, the minotaurs played a vital role."

"Certainly," she replied.

From inside Half-Orc Keep, they could hear Snarlsnout's bellowing laughter. "I do not understand how an orc so large is even alive," Undrakk laughed, letting down his guard for the first time in months, if not years.

Keturah turned to him and placed a meaty hand on the half-orc's shoulder. "You should join the chieftains in your hall," she said. "Their leader should not be absent at this celebration."

Undrakk nodded. He understood the need for morale, and the

battle was over. "For one night, I believe I would like to be an orc."

Keturah snorted. "What does that mean?"

With a broad smile, Undrakk headed for the stairs leading down from the parapet. "I want to get drunk!" he called over his shoulder. "I want to gorge myself on roasted meat in the presence of my generals! I want to be an orc!"

WHEN DAWN BROKE, Melkora's eyes snapped open. She was tired, but couldn't afford to be groggy. Motionless, she waited, listening for sounds of her enemies, but she was alone.

She allowed herself a modicum of relaxation and instantly felt the dizzying pain of dehydration. "There won't be any *magical provisions* this morning," she sighed sarcastically.

Still tucked under her makeshift tent, she turned to watch the top of Terror's Lament. No scouts patrolled the wall. No orcs or minotaurs had started scavenging the battlefield either. Quickly, she pulled up her flap of hide, wrapped it around the discarded weapons she used for stakes, and hurried south in search of water.

GRAVLOX AND VORST reached Cobblestreet by mid-afternoon, two days after the battle at Talonrend. The short journey had been painfully slow. Gravlox could only walk a few hundred yards before he needed to stop and recover his energy. He had tried twice to step through the Void while holding Vorst, as he remembered Valkoinen doing, but he could not replicate it.

"This place looks worse than before," Vorst said. A light rain had begun to fall around them, dampening their bodies and spirits alike. Since they had last seen the burnt village, what few buildings had still been standing had fallen.

We should keep moving, Gravlox projected into her mind. The sooner they reached the mountain, the sooner they could put the memory of the last few months behind them.

Vorst nodded and continued walking. When they neared the center of town, they caught the scent of lingering smoke, and they heard orc voices loudly shouting back and forth. Out of habit, Vorst raised a hand to her lips, motioning for Gravlox to be silent.

What would I say? he telepathically jested.

The two goblins crouched behind a pile of rotting timbers. Ahead of them, a rowdy band of a dozen orcs sat around a large fire in the town square. Crude banners of wolf hides hung from long poles in the corner, and although each member of the band had a weapon nearby, it was clear they did not expect to use them.

"Scouts," Vorst whispered. She motioned toward another collapsed building, leading them subtly around the camp.

They aren't looking for us, Gravlox said. *We can cross the river upstream without being noticed.*

Moving from one heap of ruins to the next, they made their way slowly to the Clawflow River. The water was cold, but the river was shallow enough for even a short goblin to wade through without much difficulty.

Gravlox watched Vorst run across with a twinge of guilt. When she was safely standing on the opposite shore, Gravlox wrapped his consciousness around a section of the Void on the other side, took a single step forward, and appeared next to his wife.

"We should hurry," Vorst said, never taking her eyes from the mountain. The closer she became to her home, the more she felt the mountain's pull within her.

Something caught Vorst's eye when she turned back toward Kanebullar Mountain. On the Clawflow's eastern shore, directly across the river from the orc camp, a handful of large, wooden beams had been driven into the ground.

"What are those?" Vorst asked, pointing to the structures. In an instant, Gravlox teleported away.

When he reappeared a few seconds later, Vorst could almost see the animosity on his white mask. "What is it?" she asked, though she feared the answer.

Goblins, he growled. *Tied to stakes and burned*. His voice dripped with unrestrained hatred. Any feeling of neutrality he had held toward the orcs suddenly vanished. *So long as the orcs live, we will never be safe*.

Vorst brushed a slick sheen of rain from her forehead. "There is nothing we can do," she said, though her heart yearned for revenge. She probably hadn't known the dead goblins, but it made no difference. She felt connected to them on a very personal, very real level.

Wait for me, Gravlox commanded. He didn't mean for his voice to be filled with such venom when he spoke to his wife, but he could not control his emotion.

Gravlox sank his mind into the Void. He found a place in the midst of the orc camp, latched onto it, and pulled himself through the darkness. When he appeared, the orcs shouted in fear.

Clad only in white, the goblin stood motionless in the middle of the camp, but he had not accounted for the orcs' fire when he selected his destination. He was too close to it, the flames threatening to climb up his robes and devour him.

While the orcs stood in stupefied wonder, staring at the strange figure suddenly in their presence, Gravlox searched through the Void for the power of the fire beside him. The fire was not magical, but it still possessed a presence Gravlox could manipulate.

When he grasped the fire and tried to move it away from his body with his mind, the flames died. *I took them*, Gravlox gasped. The fire had not been extinguished, not in a traditional sense as he had first expected, but somehow contained *within* him.

Gravlox opened his eyes. He tried to move the fire from his body to the nearest orc in front of him, but when his concentration in the Void wavered, the flames ceased to exist altogether. Though he could not explain it, he felt magically emboldened by the fire he had consumed. *Consumed,* he repeated to himself. It was a fitting description.

One of the orcs to his right began to approach him with a sword. Gravlox dove back into the Void, found the heat within the orc's body, and wrenched it toward his own mind. When he peered back into the physical plane, the orc was frozen solid. The beast's body teetered forward once, then rocked back, and crashed into the ground where it shattered like glass.

At once, the orcs ran at him from every direction. Gravlox set his mind into motion as quickly as he could. From one place to another, he darted around the town square, only staying in one location long enough to use the Void to shatter his foes one at a time.

When only a single orc remained, the green-skinned creature tried to flee. Gravlox appeared motionless in front of the orc, his finger pointing menacingly at the beast's chest. The orc turned again to run, but Gravlox was there before the orc could take a single step.

This one must suffer, Gravlox thought. He clenched the orc's mind with his own, searching the creature for elements to manipulate. *Better suited for removal,* he remembered. In that moment, the mage's description of the powers of the Void felt rather fitting. He understood what the woman had meant. He could not create energy or bend the elements of the earth to his will, but he could consume *anything.*

The orc froze. Gravlox had sealed off the creature's thoughts, separating them from his body and rendering the orc paralyzed.

First, he used the Void to pinpoint the orc's finger bones. Ever so slowly, he ripped them from the orc's flesh, pulling the bloody digits into his own body where they ceased to exist. Next, Gravlox wrapped his mind around the orc's eyes.

Gravlox knew the orc experienced all manner of horrific pain. Unable to scream or even move, the orc's meager thoughts drifted into Gravlox's mind, and he bathed in the torment. With one final tug, Gravlox consumed the orc's heart and let the creature fall to the ground.

When he stood alone in Cobblestreet's center, Gravlox realized the full extent of the devastation he had wrought. Pools of blood, gore, and melting ice were all that remained of the orc band. He had killed them all, and he had enjoyed it. Undrakk's words crept through his mind like a thief. *We have no qualms with your race*, the half-orc had told him.

What have I done? Their short-lived truce was as broken as the bodies shattered before him.

Pulling himself through the Void, Gravlox appeared next to the burnt goblin corpses by the river. *They have been here for weeks*, he thought, examining the remains. *Maybe even months*.

In a flash, he pulled himself back across the Clawflow to the blood-stained streets. When he took the time to look, he saw the extent of the orc encampment. They had tents set up, stored food on wooden racks, and even had a small pen of piglets in front of a nearby pile of ruins. *How long had they lived here?* he wondered. Gravlox suddenly felt as though killing the orcs had been an act of murder, not warfare.

With a thought, he used the Void to remove the gate of the pig-pen, then brought himself back to Vorst. *I killed them*, he said at once.

Vorst only nodded her head. "We must get to the mountain," she said, her voice full of single-minded determination.

Gravlox was glad his wife didn't seem to mind the slaughter he had committed. *We will be there soon*, he told her. The rain had slowed, and Gravlox noticed none of it had stained his robe. Not a speck of blood marred the brilliantly white fabric.

Moonlight guided them as they reached a small opening in the side of Kanebullar Mountain. Rocks were piled around the outside of the tunnel entrance, and moss had grown on some of them. "Nothing has gone in or out in a long time," Vorst said. Her finger-tips brushed against the stone. She could feel the goblins inside, waiting for a leader, waiting for a purpose.

Vorst began throwing the rocks aside, but Gravlox made them vanish before she could finish. *Go*, Gravlox said, sensing her urgency. Vorst bounded down the tunnel without a word.

When they emerged in the heart of Kanebullar Mountain, Vorst couldn't put into words what she felt. The mountain was alive with goblins! They hurried through the tunnels, carting loads of minerals or finished products, and their voices echoed off the walls in a disorienting cacophony.

Gravlox stepped forward and some of the nearby goblins stop to stare at him. He wasn't sure, but it felt like they *recognized* him, despite his lack of features. He was sure they didn't know who he was, but they could tell he belonged there—he was a goblin.

Vorst walked to the center of the chamber, a large area designed to link dozens of other caverns as an interchange. When she spoke, the goblins around her listened. "There is a war," she began loudly, commanding their attention.

Something made her freeze. "No," she muttered, interrupting her speech, but the other goblins did not seem to notice. They stood as they had, fixated, waiting for her next words. In her mind, Vorst felt something changing. "Lady Scrapple is dead!" she yelled at nothing in particular.

Her mind burned with terrible pain. She felt as though Lady Scrapple's old mental connections had suddenly burst forth into her brain. "She is dead!" Vorst screamed.

Then she realized what had happened. When she spoke, her words travelled through more than the air around her. Every syllable she spoke echoed within the goblins' minds just as Lady Scrapple's thoughts had once echoed within her own.

She could control them—she could control them all.

"There is a war," Vorst continued, freshly emboldened. "And we must fight!" As she expected, the goblins were silent. After all, she had not commanded them to move or respond.

Vorst whirled toward her husband with a smile. "You want revenge?" she asked.

Gravlox wasn't sure how to respond. *We can live here*, he answered hesitantly. *There is no need to fight.* Deep down, he had to admit the prospect of avenging Talonrend was enticing, but what was the point?

"We will take Talonrend from them!" Vorst explained. In her heart, she knew it was her life's purpose. "It is time our race stepped out of the shadows!" She turned back toward the gathered goblins with her arms spread wide. "Prepare for war!"

When she released her hold over the goblins, they instantly cheered. Their own thoughts flooded back into their minds, and they leapt for joy. "Prepare the army!" she shouted. At once, Kanebullar Mountain erupted in activity, exactly as she had expected. "I gave an order," Vorst mused under her breath. "I am their queen."

Twenty-Three

D AWN BROKE AROUND the side of Kanebullar Mountain, bathing thousands upon thousands of goblins in gentle light. Gravlox and Vorst had spent the entire night helping their kin prepare. Most of the goblins had weapons, but it would not matter. Their numbers alone were staggering.

How many balloon teams have assembled? Gravlox asked.

With a thought, Vorst commanded the goblin in charge of her balloons to give her a report.

"Seventeen balloons," she replied after a moment. "One more than we had hoped."

Vorst's generals had assembled around them with detailed reports of their troops. She let them have their autonomy. They were bred for war, trained from birth in the ways of tactics, battle, and leadership. All Vorst need do was search their minds to confirm their loyalty—she trusted the generals to lead her soldiers as best they could.

When do we leave? Gravlox asked. He felt there was still much to do, but Vorst possessed a drive he dared not question.

"Now!" Vorst yelled over the terraces. As one, twenty thousand goblins turned their heads to view their queen.

There could be no denying how impressive the sight of the goblin army was to behold. More goblins had assaulted Talonrend the year before, thousands and thousands more, but their numbers still made Gravlox's chest swell with pride. When the soldiers began to move, their footsteps thundered from Kanebullar Mountain, filling the valleys and plains below.

As they had done before, the goblin army waited until they crossed the Clawflow River to assemble into uniform ranks. At the head of them all, Vorst stood with her crossbow in hand and a short sword strapped to her side.

When they could finally see Talonrend's walls towering high above the fields, the sun had fallen once again. *We did not bring much food*, Gravlox told his wife. *We left too soon. We should have waited.*

Vorst laughed. "We won't need supplies," she cackled. "We aren't stopping! We will take the city before dawn!" Her voice roused the army into a raucous state of cheering.

They will hear us, Gravlox warned.

"Let them," Vorst replied. "They have a few thousand orcs—we have twenty thousand goblins. They cannot stop us!"

If I learned anything from travelling with Gideon and his strange god, it is that arrogance is more dangerous than any orc, Gravlox cautioned. A knot of fear worked its way into his stomach and settled there.

Vorst didn't intend for her words to be filled with so much blind ambition, but the drive for conquest was so strong within her she felt she would die if the army paused for even a moment. "They will fall," she concluded. "The city will be ours."

WAR HORNS SOUNDED from every corner of Broken Sword. Undrakk climbed a staircase on the eastern side of Terror's Lament with a sour expression on his face. At the top, several minotaurs stood ready, heavy ballistae in their arms. Behind him, the sky was alive with demons. Keturah and Jan stood on a nearby rooftop. The building wasn't nearly as tall as Terror's Lament, but they would still be able to relay commands to the demons in the air and the minotaurs on the ground. Between the three layers of wall, Undrakk had half of his orcs waiting for a command.

Undrakk quickly conjured an area of far-sight and peered into the ranks of the goblin horde. "They outnumber us three to one," he said, but his voice was full of confidence. "It appears we will celebrate another slaughter very soon."

The minotaurs beside him grunted their approval.

At the front of the goblin army, Undrakk saw the strange, white-clad creature he had spoken with earlier. "I offered you a truce," the half-orc said emotionlessly. "We would have left you alone."

Undrakk turned toward the minotaurs and let his far-sight spell dissipate. "Pass the word along," he said. "Save the white goblin for me."

The minotaur nodded.

"I do not suspect he is a fighter, but perhaps a shaman or a mage. Kill them all, but spare that one." Undrakk looked back at the mass of goblins on the horizon one final time, the moon and stars his only visual aid. "That one must die last. He must watch his brethren suffer."

HIGH ABOVE THE walls, Taurnil circled like a giant carrion bird about to dive down for a kill. His skin was strangely dark, a constant reminder of his poisoning, but his muscles were strong, and his wings punished the air with every beat. He was ready for revenge.

While most of the winged demons faced the goblin army to the east, Taurnil had his eyes glued to the west. The woman who had poisoned him was out there—he could feel it, and Keturah had sensed her with magic. Somehow, she had lived through the first battle, but he would make sure she didn't survive another.

Taurnil silently landed on the western wall of Terror's Lament. He paced back and forth, smelling for the scent of human scum, and took off once more.

He set himself down among the myriad of refugee corpses and hissed, scaring off the scavenging birds. His three venomous tongues licked the air, savoring the sweet taste of death that clung to his every breath. Underneath the cloying flavor of rotten human flesh, he found the woman's scent. Her fear was palpable. His muscles tightened, and he leapt into the air once more, flying only a handful of feet above the ground. His eye searched for any sign of life among so much carnage.

Then he saw her. She had fled perhaps two miles from the city, but he had found her nonetheless. Taurnil dropped back to the ground in a low crouch, using the terrain to cloak his movements. The woman hid beneath a covering of some sort, perhaps even asleep for the night, and she showed no movement as he prowled closer.

Like a cat hunting a mouse, Taurnil crept through the open field until he was nearly upon her makeshift tent. The scent of her body flooded his mind with memories, pushing his seething anger to its limits.

With a flurry of claws, he vaulted from his crouch, landing directly on top of the tent. He sank his talons deep into the hide, shredding everything until his claws felt the dirt below. Taurnil hissed, spitting a stream of deadly acid as he ripped back the hide covering, but the woman was not there.

From behind him, Melkora lunged out of the earth like a geyser. She crashed into Taurnil's back and stabbed, but his wings flew out from his body, knocking her blade aside with ease.

Taurnil jumped forward, turned, and set his feet into the dirt with his wings spread wide. Up close, he could nearly drink Melkora's terror. She had nowhere to run, nowhere to hide, and no one to save her. This time, she would die.

Melkora rushed forward wildly, thrusting Roisin in front of her. Taurnil stepped forward to meet her, deflected her dagger with a claw, and used his left hand to slice into her chest. Without a shield or proper armor, Melkora could not attack and defend herself at the same time. They clashed again, and Melkora could not get her dagger past the demon's flashing talons.

Keeping her weapon safely at bay with one arm, Taurnil pushed the woman to the ground. A broad smile crept onto his face. He spat a putrid line of acid onto her chest where it burned and sizzled, bringing a series of shrieks from the woman's mouth.

Melkora pushed herself back on her elbows, scrambling to her feet as quickly as she could. Her body ached. Blood seeped from a series of cuts in her torso and the demon's acid was nothing short of agonizing. *I only need to hit him once,* she thought to herself. *But he survived it before…*

With a grunt, Melkora dove at Taurnil's legs, hoping to slash the creature's pale thighs before he could react. Taurnil laughed as he bashed her to the ground with his claws. Face down in the dirt, she whimpered, and the demon bellowed with amusement.

Taurnil moved behind her. Careful not to get too close to her dagger hand, he crouched on top of her back, using his weight to pin Melkora beneath him. He wrapped his claws around the woman's shoulders, gripping them tightly to immobilize her, and let his insidious poison run freely from his tongues.

Melkora screamed as she burned.

VORST SANK INTO the depths of her mind, attaching her will to the consciousness of all the goblins under her command. "Kill them all," she whispered. Every goblin heard the command as clearly as if it had been spoken only to them.

How will you get through the walls? Gravlox asked, still uneasy. In the darkness, he could just barely make out figures atop Terror's Lament, no doubt equipped with all manner of weapons to rain death on them from above.

Vorst motioned to the teams working several yards to her left. They lit fires beneath their balloons, piling into the baskets and waiting for the order to ascend. "We only need a single goblin to open a portcullis," she said.

A goblin will lift an iron portcullis? Gravlox implored. He wanted to yell, to tell his wife to turn back, to save their brethren from such a horrible death, but he knew her drive would not be quelled.

"Each team has enough blasting powder to take down three portcullises," Vorst snapped. She issued a mental command, and the balloons let go of their moorings, drifting into the night sky.

A suicide mission, Gravlox stated. *You send them to their deaths.*

"For the good of our race, I send them to fulfill their purpose," Vorst replied. A hint of fanaticism laced her high-pitched voice.

Gravlox shook his head. He could not stand idly by as his kin were about to be massacred. He stalked toward the walls, his white robes flowing behind him. As he moved, he attempted to calm the storm within his mind. He needed to focus.

Above him, the balloon brigades were met by a host of flying demons with claws like razors. Goblin archers from the baskets fired upon the demons with flaming arrows, shredding their ranks with each volley, but the brigades soon began to plummet back to the ground.

The battle in the sky raged, but Gravlox ignored it all. He stood several hundred yards in front of the walls—a single speck of white amidst a writhing sea of darkness. He remembered the oblivion mages removing a section of stone from the western side of Terror's Lament.

Though there was nothing inherently magical about the wall, Gravlox was able to find its position within the Void rather easily.

779

He locked his mind onto the wall, but he did not know how to make it disappear. Cleaving his mind in two, Gravlox sought another position deep within the Void, somewhere he might be able to take the wall and leave it. He wasn't sure how far his mind has travelled, but he knew it would be enough. He commanded his consciousness to entwine itself with the farthest reaches of the Void, grasped the wall with the rest of his mind, and then moved the two points together with a thought.

When he opened his eyes, the wall was gone, but he had not created a small opening as the oblivion mages had done before. The entire eastern wall, all three layers, of Terror's Lament had vanished. Even some of the buildings behind the structure had vanished, leaving gaping holes in the edge of the city.

At once, Vorst gave the order to charge. The goblin army surged forward. As they ran across the plain, no arrows or bolts rained down on them from above. The archers who had been stationed on the walls were gone.

Gravlox stood still in the center of the chaos, letting the army wash around him as though he was the only boulder in a flooded river. His mind reeled. He had not expected to be so successful, and the effort left him completely drained. Though his incorporeal body needed no oxygen to survive, he gasped at the air, struggling to breath. Every scrap of his being resonated with pain.

"FILL THE GAP!" Undrakk yelled, ordering orcs into the massive area that used to contain the eastern portion of Terror's Lament. As far as he could tell, the four mile stretch he had stood upon moments before was simply gone.

The orcs scrambled, but their numbers were too few. They would never be able to defend the entire city without the wall. "Move them right," the half-orc ordered. At his side, a war horn sounded a series of low notes, and the warriors began to fill the southeastern portion of the city as best they could.

Undrakk turned to Jan and Keturah behind him. "We will be outflanked," he said solemnly. As surely as the wall before him, his bravado had disappeared. "Take your clan to the center of the line. Funnel their forces into the corner. Some of them will move around you, but it will take time. We must spread them as thinly as possible."

The two minotaurs nodded and took off, leading several hundred of their clansmen to the center of the missing wall.

As the battle raged, Undrakk waited to join the fray. From the rooftop of a forge built into the southeastern corner of the walls, he directed his orcs with broad magical commands. To the north, Jan and Keturah kept the tide of goblins from overwhelming Undrakk's desperate position. Each minotaur took a dozen goblins to the grave before it died, but their numbers were quickly diminishing. They would not hold for more than an hour.

Directly beneath him, the Half Goat and Wolf Jaw clans fought wonderfully. Undrakk marveled at their unison. Each clan, once bitter enemies, obeyed his mental commands without hesitation, changing their positions, shifting their lines, and always supporting each other. Luckily, Undrakk's plan had paid off. The goblin army bottlenecked toward the corner of the city where their sheer numbers meant little.

Then he saw the goblin in white.

Undrakk used magic to leap over the battlefield, soaring above orcs and goblins alike to land softly in front of his prey. At once, the magical connection between their minds opened, and Undrakk could hear the goblin's thoughts.

"You have betrayed our compact," the half-orc accused.

I never agreed to anything, Gravlox replied, though his strained voice was full of sorrow.

"Your kind will die here," Undrakk said. "None of you will survive."

781

Gravlox smirked, but his mask showed nothing. *You can no longer hide behind your walls,* he said, his voice gaining confidence.

As he had done before, Undrakk searched Gravlox for any signs of magical power. He knew the goblin was responsible for removing the wall, but he could not discern how it had been done.

Gravlox could feel Undrakk's mental probe swirling about his mind. *You will not find what you seek,* he said, sounding far more cryptic than he intended.

"You use magic," Undrakk stated, pointing behind him to the missing wall. "That much is clear. But I cannot find the source of your power."

I was once a shaman like you, Gravlox told him. *Now, I have no power. I have been cut off from the magic under the earth.*

As if to taunt him, Undrakk summoned a small flicker of flame to the top of his staff. "But you have *something,*" he said. "No one can make a wall vanish with only a thought. Tell me how you did it, and I will let you live."

Gravlox saw the magical fire like a beacon within his darkened consciousness. He gripped the flame with his mind, found a place within the Void several hundred feet away, and brought the two points together.

At once, Undrakk's flame extinguished. When the half-orc tried to recast the cantrip, he could not. In that particular space, he felt a profound absence of magic he did not fully understand. "Impressive," he said after a moment. "From where do you draw your power?" Undrakk took a cautious step back. He should have felt Gravlox's magical efforts easily. No one, human, orc, goblin, or minotaur, had ever been able to hide their abilities from him.

Gravlox waited a long moment before responding, gathering as much energy as he could. *I have no magic,* he said. As he spoke, he subtly wove his mind into the shamanistic connections between Undrakk and the world around him.

Undrakk had no response. The white-clad goblin truly baffled him. "You will not end this battle?" Undrakk asked. "Despite your aggression, my offer still stands: leave Broken Sword to me. Go back to your mountain and live in peace. We do not need this bloodshed."

Gravlox shook his head. *I do not lead them,* he said, subconsciously summoning an image of Vorst to his mind.

"Oh?" Undrakk mused, raising his eyebrows.

Instantly, Gravlox knew he had erred. He had given Undrakk a clear picture of Vorst and all the emotion he felt for her. He had given Undrakk something to hunt.

"Perhaps she can be... *persuaded,*" the half-orc whispered. He vanished with a magical flourish, but Gravlox could feel his presence, and leapt through the Void after him.

Undrakk raced through the battlefield with magical speed. He knew Gravlox was following him, but he could never anticipate the goblin's movements or sense exactly where he would appear.

When he finally found Vorst, she was standing near the front of the army, not far from the main line of battle, and she was surrounded by a small ring of what Undrakk assumed to be her generals. Gravlox stepped out of the Void directly in front of the half-orc.

"I'm giving you one final chance, goblin," Undrakk snarled. He summoned a small globe of lightning to his left hand and prepared to hurl at the goblin queen. About his staff, he tried to conjure another ball of magic, but nothing appeared. He tossed the metal pole to the ground.

Gravlox projected into the shaman's mind as loudly as he could. *I am giving you one final chance!* he screamed. Vorst was so lost in the mental connections of her soldiers that she had not noticed the two new arrivals, but she heard Gravlox's voice as clearly as if they were the only creatures in the city.

"Kill him," Vorst quickly commanded. Her voice came from everywhere at once, spoken in unison by every single goblin.

Undrakk loosed a stream of lightning toward Vorst and her generals, then quickly summoned a gout of flame to follow it.

Gravlox dove his mind through the Void, immediately latching onto the two bursts of magic and teleporting them away. Wherever they landed in the material plane, Gravlox did not care. He would destroy the entire world if it kept Vorst safe.

Wasting no time, Undrakk called upon the earth beneath his feet. He infused his power into the ground, ripping open conduits of magic far under the bedrock, and pulling an enormous amount of energy to the surface. The ground ruptured violently, making the nearby goblins and orcs scramble away in fear.

When the spell finished, Undrakk stood on the shoulders of a giant made of massive boulders and huge chunks of obsidian, all held together by magical chains of brilliant lava. The abomination roared and smashed a nearby building with a fist, sending a wave of rubble cascading over the city.

Run, Gravlox yelled. Vorst and her generals turned to flee. As they ran, the stone giant hurled huge boulders after them, each one trailing a jet of molten rock behind it.

Gravlox moved his mind as fast as he knew how. Latching onto each boulder as it soared, he ripped them through the Void to crash down in other parts of the city. He didn't have time to choose where the missiles emerged into the material plane, but he didn't care.

After the giant's initial salvo, Undrakk began summoning his own magic as well. A heavy, choking mist spread out from the half-orc's body in a sphere, obscuring his image and somehow blocking Gravlox's ability to sense him in the realm of magic.

Gravlox caught a huge spear of ice as it shot out of Undrakk's magic cloud and sent it somewhere else in the city. To his horror, the stone giant began lumbering after Vorst. Gravlox pulled himself through the Void to appear in front of the beast, but it did not seem to notice him. Thinking to teleport the entire monstrosity into the Void, Gravlox tried to latch onto the creature with his mind. He focused all the energy he had left, but it was not enough. Removing the wall had consumed almost everything he possessed.

Gravlox needed something large enough to stop Undrakk's beast.

The Void was eager to provide for him. When he sank his mind into the Void's depths, he found his own monster lurking there, a shadow of himself amplified to unimaginable proportions.

Gravlox sank his mind further into the creature, wrapping his consciousness around it and willing it to the material plane. He opened his eyes, and there stood before him a copy of himself, though it was half a dozen stories tall and made of shimmering black plates of pure Void. Despite the creature's incredible mass, Gravlox found that he couldn't quite focus on it. When he looked directly where the thing stood, he saw nothing but the empty wastelands of the Void. If he looked slightly to the side and used the edges of his vision to spy the creature, he saw it without issue.

At once, Gravlox commanded the Void golem to defend his wife and then succumbed to the overwhelming weariness flooding his mind and body.

Vorst sprinted through the ranks of her army. As she ran, the goblins around her parted to let her pass, and immediately filled the gaps she left, trying in vain to slow Undrakk's stone creation.

Gravlox's Void golem was right on Undrakk's heels. The two monstrosities crashed into the ground near the back of the goblin army, instantly killing several hundred unfortunate soldiers as they fell. Undrakk was thrown from his creation. The half-orc rose slowly, the bulk of his power drained, but his swirling armor of mist had protected his body from harm.

The two beasts fought on the ground, swinging their mighty fists into each other wildly like drunkards in a tavern brawl. Chunks of stone and sheets of jet-black Void flew in all directions.

Undrakk's golem kicked out, throwing the Void monster off its chest, and scrambled to regain its footing. When the Void monster stood, it blended in almost perfectly with the night sky. Fires had broken out everywhere in the city from Undrakk's errant lightning bolts and his monster's flowing lava, but the light did not reflect off the Void in any discernible pattern.

They met again with a flurry of blows, their fists connecting like thunder, shaking the ground and sending tremors through the city. The Void creature punched forward, hitting the rock monster in the center of its chest, and began channeling the power of the Void out of its fingertips.

The rock golem brought its hands together above its head and smashed them down on the Void creature's head, turning huge sections of its shimmering black face to splinters. The Void golem held on inside the rock creature's stony chest, pumping more and more of the Void into the material plane.

After only a moment, the rock creature could not contain the chaos within its body. The silent emptiness of the Void collapsed on itself, pulling everything within a dozen yards to one miniscule point several feet above the ground.

With a quiet sizzle, both creatures vanished, leaving behind only a small, black gemstone that thudded into the dirt.

Undrakk could feel the raw power emanating from the stone. Though it was smaller than his fingernail, it held enough energy to end everything—to end the world. Undrakk knew he could harvest that energy. He could feed off it, consume it, and become more powerful than he had ever thought possible.

Across the fissured ground only a handful of feet away, Vorst stood with a handful of her goblin generals. At once, they fired their small crossbows, but Undrakk was too quick. He twisted his body through the air and summoned a burst of magic to his fingertips, making the earth rise up beneath him in pinpoint spurts to knock the bolts off course as he ran.

Vorst drew her short sword and sprinted. Her generals charged as well, running forward at full speed and throwing their bodies toward Undrakk. The half-orc blasted each of them away in turn, but his constant use of magic had drained him.

The goblin queen's fingertips brushed against the stone just seconds before Undrakk reached it.

In that moment, time stood still. Vorst's mental connections to her kin spread wildly over the entire planet, linking her at once to every goblin alive. She felt the presence of goblin tribes she had never known existed. There were hundreds of other colonies, hundreds of mountains filled with goblins, each with their own queen, but Vorst could control them all.

She looked at the half-orc spread beneath her, frozen in time, his green-skinned arm outstretched. Her grip on her sword tightened. When she closed the fingers of her left hand around the Void gem, her body was filled with strength. Vorst saw the ebb and flow of time splayed out in front of her, a tangible thing she could manipulate, a tool for her to utilize.

Vorst took another step forward. She stood directly over Undrakk, her sword in hand. She said nothing as she cut his head from his body.

Twenty-Four

KETURAH FELT EVERYTHING around her grind to a halt. For a fraction of a second, nothing moved. Her body froze. The two goblins in front of her, one leaping through the air and the other crouched low, were suspended in time as if Keturah looked upon a painting hung on a wall.

When time resumed, her goblin attackers had changed. Before, she had cut them down with impunity, using her incredible size and strength to slaughter the diminutive creatures at will. Now, the goblins moved in perfect concert with one another, as though they were the greatest duelists to ever hold weapons. Every action they took was impeccably timed, meticulously planned, and flawlessly executed.

Keturah blocked a slash from her right with her armored hand, but it was merely a feint. The goblin let his sword hit Keturah's gauntlet, released the hilt, and dove under the minotaur's legs, emerging behind her. Keturah whirled around to face the creature, but she could not fight them off from every angle.

In a moment, she was riddled with stab wounds. All around her, the other minotaurs started to fall. Their roars filled the sky, and their blood spilled across the ground.

The last thing she saw was a dirty goblin dagger moving down to slit her throat.

TAURNIL DOVE THROUGH the sky with his talons spread wide. To his left, a handful of other demons circled one of the few remaining goblin balloons. Their archers fired arrows and threw small, exploding bags of rocks at them, but Taurnil evaded the missiles with ease. He slammed into the bottom of one of the baskets and hung there, his claws digging through the woven material easily. As he pulled himself up, the goblins stabbed their swords over the edge of the basket, tearing angry red lines in his flesh.

The demon pulled himself over the edge and into the basket. Four goblins lunged at him. He slapped the first goblin's sword away with his claws and kicked the creature sharply, sending him tumbling over the edge to his death. A second goblin threw a bag of rocks at him that exploded when it hit his skin, blinding him for a moment and shredding his shoulder. Disoriented, he batted away one strike, but was hit in the leg by a second. When the smoke cleared, he deflected another sword and ran his claws through the goblin's throat.

Then the world stopped, and Taurnil felt his master die.

When time began to flow once more, Taurnil's rage consumed him. Keturah was dead, but his existence was not tied to her soul as it had once been. Taurnil thrashed out with his claws at the nearest goblin, but the small creature deftly parried his attack with the cross guard of her sword.

Taurnil recoiled in surprise. He swung again, this time attacking with both hands at once, ignoring the fourth and final goblin in the gondola. No goblin should have had the skill to block his assault. Somehow, the goblin easily dove under his attack and sank her sword into Taurnil's left ankle. The demon grunted with pain.

He reeled back to spit acid on her, but the fourth goblin was immediately upon him. The two short creatures pressed him with coordinated attacks, forcing him into the side of the basket, and he was powerless to stop them. Their weapons travelled faster than he thought possible for goblins, and half of their movements turned out to be mere distractions that left him confused and blocking in the wrong direction.

Taurnil had to retreat. He hopped over the short edge of the basket and tried to fly away, but one of the goblins caught his right wing with an iron grip. Before he could think to rip himself away, the goblin's sword stabbed through the meat of his right wing, effectively pinning him to the side of the gondola.

One of the goblins leapt from the basket onto Taurnil's shoulders. The demon hissed and spat, but the goblin's stoic expression did not change. Taurnil thrashed his claws over his head, slicing the goblin viciously and spilling the creature's blood down over his own head.

A sword crashed into Taurnil's skull. His vision blurred, suddenly full of dark splotches that blended with the night sky, and his arms refused to move. The sword hit him again, and he felt his muscles go limp. With one final effort, Taurnil tried to rip himself free of the basket, but he was not strong enough.

Leaning over Taurnil's head, the other goblin sawed a sword back and forth until his left wing fell to the ground below. The goblin straddling Taurnil's shoulders quickly succumbed to the acid boring through his skin, but his work was complete. The demon was powerless to stop the remaining goblin from skewering his skull.

A HANDFUL OF goblin balloons still floated through the sky when the last demon died. Beneath them, Vorst walked back into Talonrend with a singular purpose. Gravlox, the only goblin she could not directly access and control, lay somewhere in the midst of all the chaos. As she moved, her mind processed the actions of every member of her vast army, and she coordinated the entire battle effortlessly.

Using snippets of other goblins' vision, Vorst found her husband quickly. She wrapped him in her arms, whispering softly to him, and scooped his white robes from the ground. He was alive and still there. She was sure of it, even though he had no weight. When she moved, his robes still fluttered as though there was a body beneath them.

At first, Vorst wasn't sure where she would go, but it soon became clear to her. One foot after another, she processed toward the castle several miles away, a score of goblins moving mindlessly in a defensive circle around her.

Vorst reached the drawbridge an hour later. The goblins accompanying her quickly broke away and began dismantling the orcish banners adorning the castle. Inside the keep, a long table stretched across the audience chamber in front of a broken throne. Vorst cleared a small space from the table and set her unconscious husband down, giving him one final look before returning to the drawbridge.

"No one enters," Vorst commanded to the goblins waiting in front of the castle.

They nodded and formed a semicircle around the doorway with their weapons drawn. "Yes, my queen," one of the soldiers responded.

Vorst was caught by surprise. She knew she was their queen, but hearing it spoken aloud gave her pause. The title felt... *perfect*. With a smile, she turned from the goblins to finish her army's gruesome work and end the orcish occupation of Talonrend forever.

Before she could get very far, a flicker of movement caught her eye. She had marched with such singular purpose that she had not noticed a dozen orcs standing only thirty yards north of the castle's drawbridge. The orcs were quiet, as if waiting in ambush, but they did not rush to attack her when their eyes met.

Vorst turned back to the score of goblins guarding the castle entrance. "Did you see them?" she asked, pointing to the orcs.

One of the goblins nodded timidly.

"Why did you not tell me?" Vorst demanded. She had never considered herself to be quick to anger, but she struggled to fight the violent emotion building within her. The goblin's omission felt no different than disobedience.

"You did not ask, my queen," the goblin said softly.

Vorst stretched her consciousness into the mind of the goblin, searching for any scrap of treason, but she knew she would not find it. The goblin was merely an extension of her will, a being which possessed a semblance of autonomy, but at its core, the underling was only a carefully crafted tool.

"Tell me when you notice things," Vorst commanded.

At once, the twenty goblins began speaking over one another, telling her every scrap of information they saw. Vorst growled with frustration.

"Tell me only what is important," she clarified. *It will take a long time to get the hang of this,* she conceded to herself. Subconsciously, she realized she had never taken her vision from the orcs still standing by the castle. But the vision was different than it should have been. It was from the wrong perspective.

Vorst stifled a laugh. Responding solely to her emotion, one of the goblins had twisted its head to watch the orcs, constantly projecting its own vision into Vorst's consciousness as her own attention had been pulled elsewhere. "You're more perceptive than I thought," she said. "Now, we have orcs to kill."

The goblins moved from the entryway and formed a line two deep, slowly advancing upon the orcs' position.

"Wait," Vorst ordered them. The goblins stopped. In the moments since she had touched the Void and absorbed its power, she had let her consciousness filter through every goblin in the army, perfectly synchronizing their thoughts and coordinating their attacks. As their queen, she needed to see them fight without that benefit. "Fight on your own." She withdrew her presence from their minds, letting them assume the entirety of their autonomy once more, and watched.

Vorst could see their relative disorganization immediately. The goblins were well trained, but nothing could compare to the mental strength the presence of her mind had given them.

When the skirmish began, Vorst could tell there was something different about the orcs. She knew the green-skinned creatures were physically strong, but the orcs in front of her were incredibly muscled, with knotted torsos thicker than trees. Even more unusual, the orcs did not wield any conventional weapons. They wore no armor, only simple loincloths around their waists, and leather straps around their forearms.

The orcs bashed their goblin attackers into the ground with brutal efficiency. Their fists crushed through goblin skulls with every swing of their corded arms. Before the fight had truly begun, half of Vorst's soldiers were dead on the ground. They had struck grievous wounds on a handful of the orcs, but none of them had fallen.

Seeking to shift the melee back in her favor, Vorst let her boundless mind wash back over her subjects. The goblins' flawlessly coordinated movements surprised the orcs, killing two of them in mere seconds, but there were not enough goblins to finish the fight.

Vorst took a tentative step backward as the last of her small troop died. The unfortunate goblin had been torn asunder by a single downward punch.

Six orcs remained. They advanced a single step, but did not charge. Their ranks parted, and Vorst saw an orc so large in size he must have rivaled Lady Scrapple in weight. The creature sat upon a stone dais adorned with images of goats which had been left on the ground, a coiled whip resting in his right hand. Layer upon layer of grotesque green fat spilled over every inch of the dais, as if the orc was just a giant droplet of skin which had melted upon a chair.

Vorst used her mental connections to search for the nearest goblins. There was a group advancing through the city, but they were still almost two miles away. "Hurry," Vorst telepathically implored them. She knew they would not reach her soon enough.

The orc on the dais raised a thick finger to point at Vorst. He uttered a few lines in the orcish language that Vorst did not understand.

"Leave," she said. The goblin queen lowered her voice to what she thought resembled the deep notes of the orcs and hoped their languages were similar enough to at least convey the simple message. With her arms held calmly at her sides, she repeated the word several times.

The orc's facial expression did not change.

Vorst knew she couldn't fight them. Trying to be as non-confrontational as possible, Vorst lifted the short sword from her belt and placed it gently on the ground.

The orc chieftain cracked his whip, sending his soldiers forward in a line. Vorst had to come up with something fast. She still felt a lingering sense of magic from touching the Void, and the sensation gave her a scrap of hope.

Vorst sprinted back through the castle doors to the throne room. She heard heavy orc footsteps behind her. The orcs were not trying to run her down, but instead they moved like hunters, filling the entryway and blocking her escape route.

The goblin queen paid them no attention. She ran to Gravlox's silent form, driving her mind toward him as though he was one of her underlings which she could easily control. At the same moment, she held onto every ounce of the Void she could feel, hoping the two would form a bridge between their beings.

I need you, Vorst mentally yelled.

Somewhere in the darkness of the Void, Gravlox responded. *Let me in,* he whispered, his voice distant and rumbling. Vorst wasn't sure what he meant.

The orcs moved closer.

Vorst took a breath to steady herself and lowered her mental guard. She gasped when Gravlox's robes lost their shape.

Suddenly, Vorst could hear her husband's voice within her own head as clearly as she heard her own. *The orcs,* Gravlox began, turning her attention back to toward the castle's entrance.

Can you kill them? Vorst asked, unsure of where she should direct her inner dialogue.

She could feel Gravlox smile within her. *We can kill them together,* he replied. His confidence was infectious.

Vorst reached her hand out toward the group of orcs, and Gravlox wrapped invisible tendrils of pure Void around their bodies. The orcs stiffened, suddenly unable to move.

Teach me, Vorst whispered. She felt everything Gravlox did with her own mind, but she did not know how to command the Void herself.

Gravlox began to constrict the orcs. They struggled for breath and fought in vain against the invisible tendrils, but Gravlox did not kill them or let them go.

Find another point in the Void, Gravlox explained, shifting the Void tentacles to her consciousness. *When you have a second point, pull the two points together,* he continued.

Vorst's grasp on the Void was tenuous at best. The orcs slowly regained a fraction of their mobility as she struggled to maintain control. Eventually, she latched her mind onto a section of Void somewhere behind the castle to the west. When she pulled the orcs forward through the Void, their torsos ripped apart in a shower of blood.

Don't pull them toward you! Gravlox playfully scolded her. The body they shared was drenched in sour-smelling blood. Bits of broken orc were scattered throughout the audience chamber like discarded food scraps.

Vorst emerged from the castle several moments later. She had taken Gravlox's mask and placed it over her face, but left the rest of her body clothed in goblin garb. Her appearance was strange, but not as strange as she felt. Somehow, Gravlox resided *within* her physical body, but his boundless mind was far from contained within her skull.

To her left, the massive orc chieftain still sat on his dais. He looked startled to see a goblin emerge victorious from the castle, but his expression quickly turned to one of fear.

The chieftain raised his whip to strike. Before he uncoiled the leather, Gravlox jolted the weapon several feet through the Void where it fell onto the ground.

To the top of the wall? Vorst asked.

To the top of the wall, Gravlox repeated.

In the blink of an eye, Snarlsnout found himself several hundred feet above the city, wailing at the top of his lungs. All he could do was watch the cold stone wall fly past him as he fell.

Twenty-Five

S IFIR'S LEGS ACHED. He looked back at the walls of Talon-rend with a heavy sigh. "Two thousand years," he said. "For two thousand years I have kept your stories alive, tirelessly waiting for either of you to be worthy of entrance into the Void—to truly become immortal."

Taking care not to lose his footing on the dislodged stones, Sifir began to slowly descend the sloped side of the crater where the two gods had fallen.

Dawn had broken by the time he reached the bottom several hours later. There wasn't much room between the two giant birds, and Sifir had to push broken bits of marble out of his way to stand.

"I've waited a long, long time for this day," he said with a broad smile. Sifir tossed his cap aside and removed his stained robe, revealing a withered body covered in tattoos depicting both gods.

"Humanity had its chance," he told Vrysinoch's corpse. "Your creation has failed." He turned to Druaka. Seeing her torn and ragged body brought him a measure of happiness, but it was quickly overwhelmed by apathy. "The minotaurs had their chance as well," he said. "The Void is eternal. Gods are not."

Sifir climbed to the top of Druaka's body. With a grin, he

pushed his fingers around the sides of one of her eyes, roughly scooping it out into his hand.

He set the grotesque eye in the center of the crater with an unceremonious thud. Then, using a sharp bit of stone, he chiseled one of Vrysinoch's black eyes from the statue, placing it beside Druaka's.

Sifir could feel their presence. The gods were not dead, but they were both so weak they were only partially aware of what was happening to them. When he touched their eyes, he felt them react, begging to be released once again. "You are trapped," he whispered. "And you shall be trapped forever."

Drawing upon the massive amount of stone Gravlox had unwittingly placed in the Void, Sifir brought it back, using it to fill in the crater, leaving only enough room for his work. When he was finished, he stood in a cramped cavern three hundred feet below the surface. Several feet above his head, solid stone filled the crater as bedrock once had.

"I will have plenty of time to carve a third statue," Sifir spoke to Vrysinoch's eye. He felt the god's hatred radiating from the object, but it did not matter. Sifir was the gatekeeper of the Void, the first Fated One, and he was more powerful than both gods. "This time, your statue will not be standing triumphantly for all the world to see. No, I will make you a new image. You will be bent and disfigured, crushed by the weight of your failure, and trapped underground for the rest of time."

SEVERAL DAYS LATER, Druaka had gathered enough strength to finally bring a whisper to the otherwise silent cavern. "You cannot escape this tomb either, Void priest," she croaked.

Sifir did not turn from his carving to acknowledge her. "The goddess of patience and planning," he scoffed. "You are no better than your brother."

"You will die here," she whispered, her avian voice barely audible.

Sifir's laughs echoed in the tiny chamber. "You truly know nothing of the Void," he remarked. "Though my physical body is old and will wither, there are plenty of others to take from the Void." He thought of Valkoinen, the owner of the last human body he had stolen. "The Void is full of things foolish humans have left behind."

Epilogue

HOW MUCH HAVE you eaten? Gravlox mentally asked his wife. He had tried to remove his consciousness from her body, but in the end had given up. He didn't feel *trapped* within her, and the closeness they shared brought them both a significant measure of happiness.

You know how much, Vorst joked. A timid goblin brought her another tray of roasted meat and set it down before her. In the weeks after her army had captured Talonrend, her appetite had escalated to absurd levels. They both knew what was happening, but neither of them were eager to bring it to light.

Several hours later, after a goblin finished giving Vorst an update on the supply train being brought from Kanebullar Mountain, Gravlox decided to broach the subject of Vorst's transformation. *What have we become?* Gravlox asked her softly.

Images of all those they had killed flashed through their shared consciousness. Whether directly or indirectly, thousands had perished as a result of their actions.

Vorst took a long moment to consider her thoughts before letting Gravlox hear them. *We cannot change what we have done,* she replied.

That was not my question, Gravlox was quick to point out.

Sitting in the throne room of a keep built by human hands felt wrong to Vorst, but at the same time she knew it was where she was meant to be—where she knew she had always been destined to be.

It was all part of her plan, Vorst conceded, fully realizing exactly what she had been born to do.

She placed her hands on the smooth stone floor beneath her, feeling the warmth of the earth radiating through her body. *Go to the Void,* Vorst told her husband. *Bring me mass.* She knew why she had been eating so much, but she wanted to hasten the transformation. *Bring me as much as you can.*

His powers amplified by Vorst's boundless consciousness, Gravlox spiraled his mind through the emptiness of the Void, wrapping his thoughts around every bit of organic material he could find. There were hundreds of corpses scattered through the Void like leaves blown from a dying tree. Some of them were the orcs and minotaurs he had placed there, while others were humans from the Alabaster Order who had either died in the Void or left their bodies behind.

He brought every last one with him when his mind emerged from the Void minutes later. Vorst took their substance, consumed it, and made it part of her own growing mass. Soon, her arms were too heavy for the floor to support, and she broke through the stone.

An hour later, Vorst was large enough to fill the entire audience chamber of the castle. Her arms and legs had grown out from her in a circular pattern. From two of her limbs buried beneath the stone, she felt hundreds of tiny buds beginning to form, like small fibers growing from a seed.

"We will create the next generation," Vorst realized aloud. "We will grow and populate this city, becoming stronger than we ever were in the mountain. This was her plan!" Even the modifications the orcs had made to the castle suited her new size as though it had all been meticulously anticipated. Vorst's excitement bubbled over into Gravlox's mind, consuming him with visions of grandeur.

Our race will thrive! he added, echoing her sentiment.

Filled with trepidation, a small goblin approached her from the drawbridge. She watched his movements through his own eyes, but did not directly take control of his actions.

When the goblin spoke, Vorst knew her position as queen was unshakeable. "Lady Vorst," her servant began...

About The Author

Born and raised in Cincinnati, Ohio, Stuart Thaman graduated from Hillsdale College with degrees in politics and German, and has since sworn off life in the cold north. Now comfortably settled in Kentucky, he lives with his lovely wife, a rambunctious Boston terrier named Yoda, and two cats who probably hate him. When not writing, he enjoys smoking cigars, acquiring bruises in mosh pits, and preparing for the end of the world.

Interested in contact?
Please direct all emails to stuartthaman@gmail.com

Want to stay current with all the latest news?
Check out www.stuartthamanbooks.com

Made in the USA
Las Vegas, NV
19 April 2023

70787798R10444